A MUST-HAVE MURDER

A British Murder Mystery

THE DEVONSHIRE MYSTERIES
BOOK V

MICHAEL CAMPLING

Shadowstone
Books

Published by Shadowstone Books
ISBN: 978-1-915507-08-2

Mortals are easily tempted to pinch the life out of their neighbor's buzzing glory, and think that such killing is no murder.

— GEORGE ELIOT

GET THE SERIES PREQUEL FOR FREE

WHEN YOU JOIN THE AWKWARD SQUAD - THE HOME OF PICKY READERS

Visit: michaelcampling.com / freebooks

PROLOGUE

What on earth is she wearing this time? Kneeling on the scaffolding, Shaun tore his gaze away from the woman on the other side of the glass. Instead, he focused on the window frame, the slide of his brush, the bead of white gloss paint forming along the edge of the bristles. Each coat must be even and smooth with no streaks or dribbles. If he spattered so much as a tiny droplet of paint on the windowpane, it would have to be cleaned up thoroughly or this customer would notice. She noticed everything.

Eyes like a hawk, Shaun thought. And what eyes they were: dark as night but bright as diamonds. She saw right through you, knew what you were thinking. Well, she knew what any red-blooded man was thinking, and she didn't seem to mind one bit.

Shaun paused to reload his brush, and his attention strayed once more into the room beyond the glass. The woman stood sideways on to him, but she never so much as glanced at the window, not when she was filming, or whatever it was she did every day. It looked like something to do with YouTube or one of the other social media sites.

Whichever one it was, it obviously paid well. The house was a beauty: an old, thatched farmhouse in the small town of Chagford.

She'd told him that the house was over four hundred years old, a listed building, and he could believe that. The thick walls were made of cob, a mixture of mud and straw that needed careful treatment and the correct kind of paint, and the window frames were made from hardwood, each one divided into small panes, which made them fiddly to paint. Still, this was the kind of job Shaun was good at. He was a craftsman, specialising in period properties, and he had enough work to keep him busy. Whether it was enough to keep the wolf from his door was another matter.

Money: it couldn't buy you happiness, but it had given this woman a beautiful house in an amazing location, with farmland all around and a walled garden at the back. Plus, she had a fancy Tesla parked on the weedless gravel drive, and she could afford to have a woman come to the house every day to run errands and keep the house tidy.

I'm in the wrong job, Shaun thought for the fiftieth time. He worked almost every hour God sent, and all he had to show for it was an old Renault van, a dodgy knee and a mortgage that was never far from his thoughts.

But there was no point in comparing himself to her. No one would pay to watch him trying on different outfits, and that's pretty much all she did: pose in a bewildering assortment of clothes. Admittedly, she looked very nice, but it didn't seem like a proper job. She wasn't a model, as such, and she wasn't a singer or a comedian, so what was the point of it all?

There'd been days when she'd spent ages in front of the camera while she put on her makeup or messed about with her hair, and once, she'd had a session of opening parcels, squealing with delight and holding up all kinds of things: scarves, handbags, clothes, even jewellery. At one point she'd unwrapped a black lacy bra and dangled it from her fingertips, and Shaun hadn't known where to put himself. At the time, he'd been sanding down the paintwork by hand, trying not to make too much noise, and he might've drawn attention if he'd suddenly moved away, so he'd stayed put and tried not to look.

But today's event was all about the dress. It was deep lilac and tight in all the right places, hugging her curves, and it was something special; any fool could see that. Shaun went back to his painting, but he couldn't help catching sight of her from the corner of his eye. She was striking dramatic poses, one after the other, tossing her hair, cocking her hip, and Shaun found himself watching.

Just for a second, he thought. And why not? It was like having a front seat at a fashion show. Shaun smiled at the thought. Glamour and glitz weren't for him. The last time he'd worn a suit and tie was for his wedding, and that had been 23 years ago. So if he gazed at this beautiful woman for a moment, what did it matter? There was no harm in it.

But what was this? She was reaching behind her neck as if fumbling for the fastening of her dress. No. She wasn't going to take it off, was she?

Shaun felt his cheeks colouring. He should look away. Admiring her figure had been one thing, but this was another.

He looked down, dipping his brush back in the paint, wiping off the excess. *Keep your eyes on the job*, he told himself. *Show some self-control.*

But it didn't work.

Shaun tilted his head upward, just enough to peer through his lashes. She was shimmying out of the dress, the fabric crumpling to the floor, and she stood proudly, showing off her underwear, her hands on her hips. She was talking all the while, but her gaze never left the camera on its tripod in front of her.

Bloody hell! She looked like a film star; her bronzed skin perfect, her figure literally blowing his mind, wiping it clean. He couldn't think, couldn't tear his eyes from her.

Then she turned and her gaze locked on his.

"Sorry," Shaun said, unsure whether she could hear him or not. "Sorry, I didn't mean to…"

She looked stern, shaking her head in disapproval.

"I'll move along a bit." Shaun hooked his thumb toward the

next window, but her stern expression remained. She watched as he gathered his paint and brushes, but as Shaun shuffled along the scaffolding, he thought he heard her laughing. Yes. Her cackling laughter was loud enough to carry through the closed window. She was laughing at him, ridiculing him, enjoying his discomfort.

As if I don't feel bad enough already, Shaun thought. *There's no need for her to laugh at me. No need at all.* But still her mocking laughter found its way to his ears, and a certainty sprung up in Shaun's mind. The woman's scorn and contempt would be recorded for all the world to see. She'd be telling all her fans and followers what had happened, describing every detail. Strangers from across the globe would be taking pleasure in his embarrassment. *Dirty old man*, they'd call him. *Peeping Tom. Pervert.*

It hadn't been like that, but they wouldn't know, wouldn't care. They'd be too busy jeering, laughing at his expense.

Thank God it was Friday. He'd have the weekend to forget about the whole thing, and a few pints at the pub would help.

He tried to think about the weekend while he started work on the next window, but his mind wouldn't settle. He kept coming back to the moment she'd seen him, the scorn in her eyes, the disgust curling her lip.

It wasn't fair, and deep in his gut, Shaun's humiliation hardened, turned to something darker, something worse. "It's not right," he muttered under his breath. "She ought to know better." But that was the problem with these rich types, wasn't it? They had no idea how to treat others. They looked down from on high, and to them, the likes of Shaun were no better than bugs crawling in the dirt. It was enough to make your blood boil.

Some people need taking down a peg or two, Shaun decided. *And I know who should be first in the firing line.*

That woman. That stupid bloody woman. That bitch.

MONDAY

CHAPTER 1

Alan ran through the forest, his thigh muscles cramping, sweat slicking his back, his chest, his scalp. The crisp air of early spring did nothing to cool him, and his breath rasped in his throat, every exhalation a low moan of pain. But he couldn't stop to get his breath back, couldn't slow down.

Ahead, a shadowy figure raced into the distance, sometimes vanishing in the shadows, sometimes hidden by a curve in the trail. He was getting away, and Alan couldn't allow that. He had to catch him.

Alan threw back his head and gasped for air, pouring everything he had into a headlong dash. Arms pumping, feet pounding the dirt, he urged his tortured body onward. *I can do it*, he thought. *I'm gaining on him.*

The trail was rougher here, the path littered with loose stones and fragments from broken branches. Alan scanned the ground as he ran, but the dappled shadows made it hard to see, and the sweat from his brow stung the corners of his eyes. He blinked, lifted a hand to wipe his eyes, and that was all it took.

In mid-step his left foot caught on something, and he almost fell, but he spread his arms and twisted his body, keeping his balance. His momentum carried him forward, but his next stride was clumsy, and his right foot hit the ground at an awkward angle. A jab of pain jolted through his calf. He ran on, but each time his right foot met the trail, the pain in his calf intensified as if the muscles were being torn apart.

"Oh hell!" Alan had no choice but to stagger to a halt, wincing with every step. He pressed his hand against the nearest tree trunk, and took the weight from his right leg, staring down at it, half expecting to see signs of some terrible injury.

Footsteps on the trail grew closer, slowing as they approached, and Alan looked up to see the man he'd tried so hard to catch. This was it: the moment he'd been dreading. He'd failed, and now he'd pay the price.

"Are you all right?" Dan asked. "Did you fall?"

"No," Alan said. "I slipped a bit, that's all. I'll be all right in a minute."

Dan studied him for a second. "You don't look all right. Why don't you sit down?"

"I don't want to sit down. I don't need to sit down. I'm fine, so there's no need to make a fuss. I was doing really well. I was catching up with you."

"That's great, but you look as if you're avoiding putting weight on that leg, and that's not a good sign. Where's the injury? Is it your ankle or your knee? Or is it groin strain?"

"None of the above, and I *can* put my weight on it. You see?" Alan pushed himself off from the tree and took a step, but though he clamped his jaws shut, a grunt of pain escaped from his lips.

"For goodness' sake, stop," Dan said. "Stop for a minute and tell me what the problem is."

"All right. It's my leg. I caught my foot on something, probably a stupid bramble, and when I tried to keep going, my calf muscle hurt like hell."

"Did it feel as though anything gave way or popped?"

"No, nothing so horrendous. It's just very tight and a bit tender."

Dan nodded. "You've strained one of the muscles in your calf.

8

When you almost fell, you made a sudden change in your stride and put too much load on your calf. I expect you've torn a few muscle fibres. Are you getting a sharp pain when you try to push off from that leg?"

"Yes, that sounds about right. Is it serious, do you think?"

"Not necessarily. It's not an uncommon injury for runners. I've done it myself. It takes a while to heal, but unless it gets worse, you shouldn't need to see a doctor."

"Small mercies." Alan took a tentative step. "I think I can walk on it, so I should be okay to drive, but it's a long way back to the car."

"If it helps, you can lean on me."

"No thanks. I'll manage. Let's go."

Alan started walking, hobbling along the trail, Dan at his side.

"It's a shame," Dan said. "You were doing well. You set off at a good pace, and you covered the first K in record time."

"How far have we come?"

Dan consulted his watch. "2.8 K."

"Is that all?" Alan moaned.

"It's more than halfway."

"I know, but I thought we were getting near the end. I was shattered."

"You've got to learn to pace yourself," Dan said. "You shouldn't try to beat me. I've been running for years."

Alan didn't reply. This was the part he hated the most. The actual running was hard, but he was slowly getting fitter, even losing a little of the flab around his middle. But afterward there was always the post-run lecture: an in-depth analysis of all his flaws and physical weaknesses. There was only one way he could make it stop, and that was to match Dan's speed and give him a run for his money. That would shut him up.

"It's all about finding the right rhythm," Dan was saying. "Cadence and stride length are so important."

"Yes, you've said as much before," Alan replied. "But let's talk about something else. How's business? Any potential clients?"

Dan's enthusiasm seemed to vanish in an instant. "No. Not so much as a lost cat."

"It's early days, but things will pick up. It takes time."

"I hope so," Dan said. "When I wasn't looking for clients, cases fell in my lap, but now that I need something to investigate, nothing's happening."

Alan stopped suddenly, raising his hand. "Hang on."

"What is it? Have you had an idea?"

"No. Sorry, but I need a breather. My leg's killing me."

"Right."

The two men stood in silence, Alan taking deep breaths while Dan stared into the middle distance. After a few seconds, Alan said, "How are your online adverts going?"

"Not bad. I get a few clicks to my website, but no one has filled out the form. I may have made it too complicated."

"That wouldn't surprise me. Any emails or calls?"

"Crank calls and spam. I'm beginning to think—" Dan broke off abruptly and unfastened the pocket on his armband phone holder, the phone vibrating in his hand as he retrieved it.

Dan accepted the call and held the phone to his ear. "Dan Corrigan. How can I help?"

A pause, and then Dan said, "Yes, that's certainly something I can handle."

Dan listened, his smile becoming broader, his tone more confident. "Of course, confidentiality is our watchword."

Alan noted that *our*, but he knew better than to interrupt.

"I'll look forward to it," Dan was saying. "This afternoon at two o'clock. I'll see you then. Thank you for calling."

Dan ended the call and replaced his phone, humming under his breath.

"Well?" Alan asked. "Who was it? A new client?"

"Yes, at least, she could be. A woman called Zadie Barrington. I'm seeing her later."

"At two o'clock. I heard. Where are you meeting her?"

"At her home. She lives in Chagford, so it shouldn't take long to get there."

"About half an hour on a good day," Alan said. "Is your car okay? I saw you'd brought it back from the garage."

Dan waggled his hand in the air. "They made it run a bit better, but you know what mechanics are like. There was a lot of head shaking and dire warnings about things seizing up."

"I could drive you to Chagford."

"Thanks, but there's no need, unless you really want to come along."

Alan ran his hand over his jaw. He hadn't shaved that morning, and after his exertions he must look a complete mess. "I'd like to help, but it's almost twelve already, and I'd need to shower and get changed. Plus, I haven't had lunch yet, and anyway, it'll take me ages to get back to the car."

"In that case, I'll have to do *this*." In one movement, Dan stepped close and wrapped his arm around Alan's shoulders. "Lean on me and let me take your weight. We'll be back at the car in no time."

"I suppose I haven't got much choice," Alan grumbled, and they set off, their progress hardly elegant but so much faster than before.

"So what's the case?" Alan asked. "An unfaithful partner? A missing heirloom?"

"No, it's much more serious than that. Ms Barrington's house has been broken into. The police are treating it as a burglary, but she's not convinced."

"Interesting. What's her story?"

"My potential client believes she has a stalker, and she's worried," Dan said. "On the phone she was trying to keep it together, but I could hear the fear in her voice. She's frightened, and that tells me something else."

"She hasn't told you the whole story," Alan suggested.

"Exactly. Before it's even begun, I have an idea that there's more to this case than meets the eye."

CHAPTER 2

With Alan's help, it didn't take Dan long to find Zadie Barrington's home. The Old Manse was a fine house, sitting at the edge of the town surrounded by acres of rolling grassland.

Dan parked his Toyota RAV4 on the driveway, tucking it in beside a bright red Tesla and a metallic silver SUV, the distinctive MG logo on its boot. Both cars looked brand new, and both were electric vehicles.

"Things are looking up," Alan said. "Your new client obviously isn't short of money."

"*Potential* client," Dan replied. "And let's not jump to conclusions before we've even begun. Ms Barrington might be penniless for all we know. Besides, I haven't landed the job yet."

"You will."

"We'll see." Dan smoothed down his hair and straightened his shirt. Satisfied, he glanced at Alan and saw that he'd produced a pocket notebook and pen. "Are you going to use that?"

"Yes, I thought I'd take notes. Why not?"

"It seems a bit old school, that's all. A laptop or a tablet would've been better."

"Ah, but the notebook matches the client's expectations," Alan said. "A computer would've felt too formal, but pen and paper are more familiar and friendly. I'll jot down a few lines, and she'll know I'm really listening to her, and that's always reassuring."

Dan looked doubtfully at Alan's notebook. It was small and had a plain blue cover with an elastic strap, not unlike a Moleskine, and it looked new. Maybe Alan was right. It did convey an impression of reliability.

"Anyway, we agreed," Alan went on. "If I'm going to help you with your investigations, I have to do it in my own way."

Dan hesitated. "You do know I can't pay you, don't you? Not yet, anyway."

"That's understood. I'm here because I want to be."

"Okay. If you're ready, we'd better get started."

They exited the car and made for the front door, Alan still limping but looking like a man determined not to show his discomfort.

"The thatched roof has been replaced recently," Dan said. "And the house has been freshly painted."

"That's right," someone said, and Dan turned to see a man in overalls watching them from the corner of the house. The man had been partially concealed by a pot-grown conifer, but he stepped forward as if to get a better look at them. He was middle-aged, his skin deeply tanned and wrinkled from exposure to the sun. His overalls were clean but frayed around the edges, and they'd been patched at the knees with squares of mismatched fabric. He was tall and broad shouldered, but his small cotton cap, worn at a rakish angle, gave him an oddly comical appearance.

"Hello," Dan said. "I didn't see you there for a second. We're here to see Ms Barrington."

"She's in, right enough," the man said. "But she won't hear the knocker. You've got to press that little button by the door. It's one of those doorbells with a camera."

Dan saw the way the man's nose wrinkled when he mentioned the camera, and pegged him as a dyed-in-the-wool tradesman, resentful of being watched while he worked. He certainly wasn't the friendly type, but Dan introduced himself and Alan with a smile, adding, "And you are?"

The man clamped his lips shut, but after a moment's consideration, he said, "Shaun Brown. Painter and decorator. I'm working on the windows at the back."

"Nice to meet you, Shaun," Alan said, "but we have an appointment, so we'll let you get on."

Shaun nodded, then he turned away and slipped out of sight.

Alan started scribbling in his notebook.

"Good idea," Dan said. "We'll need to talk to him later. He could be a valuable witness."

"Actually, I was wondering how much he charges. My house could do with freshening up."

"Don't let Jay hear you say that," Dan replied, and Alan chuckled quietly.

Jay Markham had sewn up the market for painting and decorating in Dan and Alan's home village of Embervale, and he took any intrusion on his territory as a personal insult. But whereas Jay had turned his back on his chequered past and become a friend, there was something about Shaun that Dan didn't like. It wasn't just that the man had been taciturn; his eyes had held a cold hint of hostility, as if he resented their presence. And the way he'd watched them from behind the shrub had been downright shifty.

Filing his thoughts away, Dan adopted an expression of professional detachment and pressed the doorbell.

An unfamiliar voice came from the doorbell's tiny speaker. The woman's tone was curt, her words edged with an Eastern European accent: "Hello, yes?"

"I'm Dan Corrigan. Ms Barrington is expecting me."

A few seconds later, the door was opened by a woman who studied Dan and Alan as if severely displeased. Dressed smartly in a plain blouse and black skirt, the woman introduced herself as Natalya, Zadie's PA.

"You must come in," Natalya said. "Follow me."

Inside, Dan's eyebrows rose as he took in the state of the house.

Bare floorboards creaked beneath his feet, the wood coated with a fine layer of dust and grit. The ceiling was cracked, a brown stain showing where water had leaked from above, and on the walls, paint flaked from crumbling plaster.

"Definitely a doer-upper," Alan said quietly as they followed Natalya along the hallway. "Quite a task."

Natalya turned suddenly, gesturing to the steep staircase. "You must come upstairs."

"Is Ms Barrington unwell?" Dan asked and received an incredulous stare in reply.

"I wondered why we're going to meet upstairs," Dan explained. "It seems unusual."

"Zadie is in her studio. Upstairs is much better, it has been…" Natalya gestured impatiently at the uncarpeted staircase.

"Renovated?" Alan suggested, and Natalya nodded gratefully.

"Yes. Renovated. Exactly." Natalya sighed and her expression softened. "Forgive me, gentlemen. It has been a hard day, but please, come up, and everything will be explained. Do not stand on the fifth stair. It isn't safe. The man was supposed to fix it, but…" she shrugged.

"We'll mind our step," Alan said with a smile.

Natalya gazed at him. "You're making a joke."

"Sort of," Alan admitted. "Sorry."

"No need to apologise. Follow me."

Dan and Alan did as they were told, making their way up the stairs in silence. The fifth tread was badly split, and Dan stepped over it with exaggerated care. When he reached the landing, Dan said, "I see what you mean about that step. It can be hard to find good tradespeople. We met your decorator outside. How are you finding him? Is he reliable?"

Natalya grunted in disapproval. "Very slow, I think. He drinks tea instead of working. I tell him this, but he doesn't listen." Natalya drew a long breath, flaring her nostrils, then she added, "You should know that Zadie does not like to be kept waiting. She has a livestream at four, and we must fix her hair and make-up before then. She cannot be late. Do you understand?"

"Yes. We'll be as quick as we can," Dan replied. "We also have a schedule to keep."

"Okay," Natalya intoned. "Follow me."

Natalya led them along a landing and halted by a stripped pine door. "One second," she said and slipped inside, closing the door.

Dan heard a raised voice, then Natalya reappeared, looking chastened. She opened the door wide and said, "Zadie will see you now. Please, come in."

"Thanks." Dan armed himself with a smile and strode into the room, momentarily taken aback at the change in decor. The room was much larger than he'd expected, but it held relatively little in the way of furniture. A narrow desk was accompanied by a small, round-topped stool made from the same pale wood. Beside the desk, several metal stands held lights and large circles of reflective material, and one tripod was fitted with a small camera surrounded by a ring light.

White bookshelves lined one wall, each shelf filled with colour-coordinated hardbacks, and in the corner, an old wooden filing cabinet was crowned with a pale blue Anglepoise lamp and a typewriter in a matching colour.

The ceiling was dotted with inset LED lights, and since the walls were pure white, the overall effect was of dazzling illumination and open space.

But there was no sign of Zadie Barrington.

Before Dan could ask, Natalya lowered her voice and said, "She likes to make an entrance."

Sure enough, a door at the back of the room opened and a tall woman in a striking lilac dress swept into the room, her head held high. Despite her dignified expression, Zadie was clearly very beautiful, and all eyes were on her as she strode to meet Dan and Alan, her hand extended. She shook each of their hands in turn, holding on for longer than was necessary, her intense gaze lingering on their faces.

"Hello," Dan started to say, but Zadie held up a hand to stop him.

"Wait. I'm getting a vibe. It's very strong." She nodded as if deep in thought, then she pointed at Alan. "You. I'm glad you're here. I'll be safe with you."

"Oh, erm, I'm only here to assist Dan," Alan said, but Zadie shook her head.

"Not as far as I'm concerned. You're vital." She turned her attention to Dan. "And you. You'll be good at this. I can tell."

"I'll do my best," Dan replied. "But forgive my manners. We haven't even introduced ourselves."

"Yes, you have. You've already told me everything I need to know." Zadie smiled, and Dan found himself disarmed by her sincerity. Even so, he couldn't allow himself to be swept up by her charm. Zadie might become a paying client, and he had to remain objective.

Alan had no such qualms, and he was standing taller, a broad grin on his features.

"I'm Alan, and I must say, what an amazing setup you have here." He gestured to the typewriter. "Is that an Olivetti Lettera 32? I have the same one at home."

"Of course, you do," Zadie said. "Did you know that Cormac McCarthy had exactly the same model? It was sold at auction some time ago, and it fetched over £200,000."

"I didn't know that. How fascinating. I bought mine at a junk shop. I paid about twenty quid for it."

Zadie laid her hand on Alan's arm. "That typewriter called out to you, didn't it? We don't like to admit it, but objects have power. They can be totemic, representing so much more than they are."

"I think I understand what you mean," Alan said. "Does your machine have an exciting history? Is it valuable?"

Before Zadie could answer, Natalya said, "I bought it on eBay. It was very cheap."

Zadie glared at her. "It's worth is so much more than mere monetary value can describe."

"Whatever you say," Natalya replied. "You wanted something to match the lamp, and that's all I could find."

"You'd better go," Zadie snapped. "Go on. Quickly." Zadie pressed her fingertips to her temples. "Oh God! I've got a headache, and it's no wonder with all your negativity flooding the room, Nat. I just can't bear to have you around for a moment longer."

Natalya smiled sweetly. "Fine. Does that mean you don't want me to help with your hair and make-up?"

"Don't be silly. You know I can't manage without you. I just need a break from you for five minutes. Please, go and make yourself useful. Keep an eye on that decorator. Make sure he's not dawdling."

"Fine." Natalya marched from the room, leaving a stunned silence in her wake.

"Would you prefer it if we left as well?" Dan said. "If you're not feeling well, we could reschedule."

Zadie waved his words away. "That's very sweet of you, but I'll be all right. I'm sorry for that little outburst, really I am, but I'm very sensitive, you know? And Nat's wonderful most of the time. She's an excellent PA, and I know I'll have to apologise to her later, but sometimes I can feel the resentment coming off her and it drives me up the wall. I just had to take a break from her, especially with everything else that's been going on."

"Tell me about that," Dan said. "What made you call me? You mentioned that you might have a stalker."

"Take all the time you need," Alan put in. "Sit down if you like. Maybe I could fetch you a glass of water or something."

"Thank you, Alan. If you go through to my dressing room, you'll find a small fridge. There should be a reusable bottle in there, and it should be full. Nat always prepares it for me. I have to drink specially filtered water."

"No problem." Alan bustled from the room, his limp all but forgotten, and Zadie wandered over to the stool and sat down.

"I'm sorry I can't offer you a seat," she said. "I have to keep this room clear for my work. I can't do a thing if I'm surrounded by clutter."

"What is your work?" Dan asked.

Zadie arched a carefully shaped eyebrow. "Don't you know?"

"No, I'm afraid not."

"Well, well." Zadie looked around the room as if expecting someone else to share her surprise.

Alan returned bearing a red metal bottle, its side emblazoned with Zadie's initials in an elegant Gothic typeface, the letters enclosed within a swirling infinity symbol. Handing the bottle to Zadie, he said, "You've had your bottle personalised. What a good idea."

Zadie took the bottle with a smile. "The manufacturer made it for me, and they had it shipped all the way from the States. Along with a nice fee, of course."

"Product placement?" Dan asked.

"I'm a brand ambassador, but there's more to it than that. Essentially, I'm an entrepreneur."

Dan nodded wisely. "That's a world I'm familiar with. Before I came to Devon, I worked with several start-ups. I assume from all the gear that you make video content of some kind, but what is it that you do, exactly?"

"I'm an influencer, Dan. Lifestyle, diet, mindfulness, fashion. I talk about it all and people listen. They care. They want better lives for themselves. They want to *be* better, and I do what I can to help them."

"That must be very competitive," Alan said. "So many people try to make a name for themselves online, don't they?"

"It's been an uphill struggle, but I'm not just a pretty face. I've built up my business piece by piece. It's taken discipline and determination, but I have a secret weapon." Zadie smiled. "It may surprise you to learn that I have a head for figures. I know my way around a balance sheet, and I know a decent profit margin when I see it."

"You've obviously done very well," Alan replied. "But I was

wondering if any of your competitors might be jealous of your success. Envy might've prompted someone to track you down and break in."

Zadie looked thoughtful. "I doubt it. There's plenty of room for everyone, and my success doesn't hold anyone back. Quite the contrary. A rising tide lifts all boats."

"Even so, you're very much in the public eye, and that carries its own risks," Dan said. "Do you have a large following?"

Zadie batted her lashes at him. "Huge."

"You must've been subjected to some stupid comments online," Alan suggested. "The internet can bring out the worst in people."

"No, not at all. Why would you think that, Alan?"

"Fame is a two-edged sword," Alan replied. "When you stick your head above the parapet, there's usually someone ready to take a potshot at you. I've had some experience of it myself. I'm a writer."

"Me too, but I've had only the best of feedback." Zadie bestowed a warm smile on Alan. "My little book about clean eating was in all the bestseller charts, here and in the States. The reviewer for *The New York Times* said some lovely things about it. I was over the moon."

"I can imagine," Alan said. "I can't say I've ever reached those heights myself, but it must've been very encouraging."

"It was. I'm working on my next book already. My agent is very excited. There's a bidding war, apparently."

Dan looked at Zadie with fresh eyes. For someone who claimed to have a stalker, she seemed rather blasé about the disadvantages of fame. As an online celebrity, she must've been the target for any number of trolls. Was she seriously expecting them to believe that she'd escaped unscathed?

She's glossing over the sordid details, Dan decided. *But that won't do*. Leaning forward as if to exchange a confidence, Dan said, "Zadie, we'd like to help, but we can't do that unless you're open with us."

"Dan, that goes without saying. I'm all about openness."

"That's good to know, but if there have been any times when you felt threatened online, or even if there was something you found upsetting, this would be a good time to tell us about it."

Zadie looked pensive for a second, but then she shook her head. "Really, there's been nothing. My followers are like my family. I've been very blessed."

"Indeed," Dan said. "We may need to revisit that question later, but let's move on. When we spoke earlier, you mentioned a break-in. What happened?"

"It was on Sunday night or the early hours of Monday. I'd been out, having a meal with a few friends, and it went on a bit longer than I expected. I came home at about two in the morning." Zadie winced in a show of regret. "I don't usually stay out so late, for obvious reasons, but we were having a good time celebrating Melody's birthday, and we'd all had a few glasses of sauvignon blanc. You know how it is."

"Where was this?"

"Doddy."

"Pardon?" Dan said. "I didn't quite catch that."

"It's what people call Doddiscombsleigh," Alan explained. "It's a small village not far from the Teign Valley. There's a nice pub: The Nobody Inn."

Zadie rewarded Alan with a smile. "That's right. That's where we went for dinner."

"Good choice. It's half an hour's drive from here, give or take," Alan said. "How did you get there?"

"Nat drove me. She wanted to take the MG, as usual, but I said we had to go in the Tesla. Nat's insured to drive both cars, and it was supposed to be a fun trip, not a work outing. Sometimes, you need to travel in style, don't you?"

"I'll take your word for it," Alan replied. "Did your PA accompany you to the party?"

"No. Nat drove me to the pub, then I left her to her own devices. I called her when I was ready to go home."

"What time did you arrive at the pub?" Dan asked.

"Just after seven, I think. I was the first to arrive, but it wasn't long before Naomi joined me. Philippa and Connor came soon afterward. Melody was the last to turn up."

"Philippa and Connor, are they a couple?" Dan said.

Zadie shook her head, an inscrutable smile on her lips. "Definitely not."

Dan made a mental note to find out more about Connor and Philippa's relationship. For the moment, it was best to concentrate on the facts.

"So there were five of you for dinner?"

When Zadie nodded, he added, "What time was it when you left the pub?"

"Quite late. We'd only planned to stay for a bite to eat and a couple of drinks, but we were all in a good mood and no one wanted the evening to end, so we stayed until closing time. After that, Melody invited us all back to her place. She said it was the least she could do. She's such a sweetie."

"I expect you'd treated her to dinner," Dan suggested. "She wanted to return the favour."

"Yes, I did buy her dinner as it happens, but… never mind."

"Please, go on," Dan said. "The more detail you can give, the better."

Zadie looked put out. "Well, I don't want to sound mean, but I'd juggled my schedule to be there on time, and we had to wait ages before Melody showed her face. We were all starving by the time she turned up. She was having a bad hair day, apparently, but she was very apologetic. I think that's why she invited us back to her place; she wanted to make up for keeping us waiting."

"Did you all go to Melody's house?" Dan asked.

"Yes, and Melody was the perfect host. Honestly, Melody's house may be small, but she's made it an oasis of calm. She has exquisite taste. She made us feel right at home, and the time flew by."

"You said you were back home by two," Dan said, "so you stayed at Melody's house until, what, 1:30?"

"That sounds about right, but I was a bit tipsy at that stage. You could check with Natalya; she came to fetch me."

"Maybe later," Dan replied. "What did you find when you got home?"

"We came in the front door, and that was locked as usual, but when I went through to the kitchen, I realised some things had been moved."

"Go on," Dan prompted. "Please, try to recall as much detail as you can."

"I'll do my best." Zadie took a breath as if preparing to make an announcement. "The first thing I saw was a glass on the draining board, as if it had been washed up. We never leave things out to dry like that. We always dry them and put them away. But there it was, sitting there."

"What about the decorator, Shaun? Might he have been in for a drink?"

"He wasn't here. He doesn't work at the weekend."

"I should've thought of that," Dan said. "Anyway, what happened next?"

"Well, as soon as I saw that glass I was on high alert. I noticed that one of the drawers in the dresser hadn't been closed properly, and the hand towel was missing from its rail by the kitchen sink."

"That could be significant," Dan said. "What happened next?"

"I went straight to the back door to see whether it was locked. It was, but only with the latch, and I knew that wasn't right. There are two bolts, and I always use them at night or when I'm going out, but they hadn't been pushed across."

"Interesting," Alan said. "Who locked up before you left?"

"Nat. She's very security conscious. She said the bolts were fastened when we left, and I believe her."

"So somebody could've left by the back door," Dan suggested. "But how could they have got in?"

"I found a window open upstairs. Nat thinks they were all closed when we left, but they're very old, and I think someone could've poked something through and opened the catch. With the scaffolding all over the back of the house, it wouldn't have been hard to climb up."

Dan nodded. "That all sounds perfectly plausible. Did you catch anything on CCTV? I saw you have a camera on your front door."

"No. It's just a doorbell. The camera only works when you push the button. It shows who's there on an app, but it doesn't record anything."

"Do you have any other cameras?"

Zadie shook her head firmly. "I don't like them. When I lived in London, there were cameras everywhere. I came here to get away from all that."

"Surely, you spend a lot of time in front of a camera," Alan put in.

"That's different. In my studio, I'm in control. I decide what gets shown and what doesn't. When the camera goes off, I have my privacy. That's very important to me."

"I understand," Dan said. "Was anything taken?"

"Not as far as I can tell. My MacBook Pro was in my desk drawer, thank goodness. That machine is my life. I don't know what I would've done if it had been taken."

You'd have bought another one, Dan thought and immediately felt guilty for being less than sympathetic. It was beginning to sound as though Zadie had got off very lightly, but even so, her home had been violated and that could be very distressing. Making his tone gentle, he said, "Was anything else moved or disturbed?"

"Some of the clothes in my dressing room. They'd been rearranged. The hangers were in the wrong order."

"I don't like the sound of that," Alan said.

"Oh, I know it might sound silly, but I make my living with those outfits, and I know which ones I've worn for filming and which ones I haven't. Some of them will get a second outing, and I have a few special ones too. Fan favourites." She indicated her dress. "I only got this one on Friday, but my numbers went through the roof. I'll definitely wear it again."

"That's not what I meant. It's the moving of the clothes that bothers me. It makes me wonder about the man's motive. Some people have a fetish about these things."

"We don't know it was a man," Dan said. "But you're right, Alan, it could be significant." To Zadie, he added, "Did you find the missing hand towel?"

"No. It could be in the laundry, I suppose."

"Perhaps you could check," Dan suggested. "The intruder might've used it to wipe away any fingerprints, but it might contain trace evidence, maybe even DNA."

"I'll ask Nat to look for it."

"Good. The glass might be useful, too. I hope you haven't touched it."

"I don't think so," Zadie replied. "But can you do all these wonderful things? Can you check for fingerprints and DNA?"

"No," Dan said. "That's best left to the police. Earlier, you said you'd reported all this. What did the police say?"

"Not much. They didn't take me seriously. They said someone would come and see me, but no one's turned up. They didn't even seem bothered when I told them about the note?"

Dan stared at her. "What note?"

"It was in this room, sitting on my desk," Zadie said. "That's why I was so relieved that nobody had touched my computer. There was a sheet of lined paper — like a page torn out of a notebook—and someone had written a message. A horrible thing to do. It scared me out of my wits."

Dan's mouth was dry. "What did it say?"

"Just a few words. It said, *I'll see you soon*."

CHAPTER 3

D I Timothy Spiller stood with his hands behind his back and waited. Sitting at her desk, Detective Chief Inspector Caroline Montague was concentrating on a sheaf of papers, the look on her face saying she was not to be hurried.

Turning the page, she said, "Be with you in a minute."

"No rush," Spiller replied. "Mind if I take a seat?"

Without looking up, Montague gestured to a chair and Spiller sat down, readying himself. It wasn't often that he was called in to the DCI's office, and it was almost never good news.

But when Montague set her papers down and sat back, she favoured him with a kind smile. "Tim, I've been meaning to ask, how's your wife?"

"Oh, she's doing all right, thanks. We're managing."

"It was a stroke, wasn't it?"

Spiller nodded. "Out of the blue. The doctors still aren't sure what caused it. Sheila's always been fit and healthy."

"That'll help with her recovery. Is she still in hospital?"

"No, she came home yesterday. She's up and about, but she's not quite back to herself. Not yet."

"It can be difficult," Montague said. "My father had a stroke, so I understand what you're going through, and if you need to take some time, you mustn't think twice. We can manage without you. Family comes first."

"Thanks, but for the time being, I'm better off here. Sheila can't stand me getting under her feet. She's very… determined."

"I remember. We've met a couple of times. She's a trouper, that's for sure. One of a kind. How long have you been married?"

"Almost thirty years."

"That's great." Montague watched him for a moment as if sizing him up. "Have you thought about retirement, Tim?"

Spiller shook his head. "I've got a few good years in me."

"Absolutely, but you'll also have a decent pension by now, and you'd be able to spend more time with your wife."

"Thanks, but I'd rather be working. It's best all round."

"Okay. I thought you might say that, so here's what I'm proposing. We'll reduce your workload for a while, make life a bit easier." Spiller started to protest, but Montague's expression made him think better of it.

"It's already done, isn't it?" Spiller said.

"More or less. I wanted to talk to you first, but I've had a word with the other teams, and we can shift things around a bit, share the load."

"I've got two cases coming to court soon."

"And you'll see them through. But as for your ongoing investigations, I've asked Jill Clements and her team to manage the arson case and to follow up on the pharmacy break-ins."

"But that hardly leaves me anything."

Montague smiled. "It leaves you plenty, so if anything new comes in, anything major, it won't be landing on your desk."

Spiller tried to hold his tongue. He should thank the DCI politely but without enthusiasm, and then he should leave with his dignity intact. But he couldn't do it. "So what am I supposed to do, guv? Sit around like a spare part while everybody else does all the real work?"

"Not at all. Something's come up, and I need someone experienced to handle it, someone with a bit of gravitas."

"I see. A rubber-stamp job."

"Not necessarily. It's quite high profile. Have you ever heard of Zadie Barrington?"

"Yes. She was on *Bake Off*." Spiller registered the look of surprise on Montague's face and added, "Sheila never misses it, so I watch a bit now and then. Anyway, I saw Zadie once or twice. She wasn't a bad baker although she had some very strange ideas. She made a meringue out of chickpea water, but the judges didn't like it. Needless to say, she didn't win."

"You sound like quite the expert."

"Not really, but Sheila's a keen cook, so she always tells me where the contestants are going wrong." Spiller smiled sadly. Sheila wouldn't be baking for a while, and it would be no good if he tried to help her; she wouldn't stand for it.

"Right," Montague said. "Well, as your good wife might well know, Ms Barrington has written a bestselling cookery book, among other things, and she has a high profile on social media. She's what they call an influencer. A lifestyle guru."

"Let me guess. She's been arrested for having class A drugs in her designer handbag."

"Quite the contrary. She's the one who called us. Ms Barrington claims she's the victim of stalking."

"I didn't know she was on our patch."

"She lives in Chagford, and she's had a break-in. She reported it, but no one's been out to her yet, and she's spitting feathers."

Spiller said nothing. Here it was: the deafening sound of the other shoe falling to the floor.

Sure enough, Montague added, "We'd like you to follow it up."

"You're sending me to a break-in?" Spiller said. "Surely, a couple of uniforms would be more than enough."

"Ordinarily, yes, but this case is rapidly turning into a headache." Montague paused. "Are you on Twitter, Tim?"

"No. I avoid all that kind of thing like the plague."

"I would if I could, but social media is part of modern policing,

Tim, whether you and I like it or not. We need to be fully aware of it, and we need to understand how it works."

"I suppose so. I'll gen up on it. It looks like I'll have time."

"Good. When you get to grips with it, you'll understand what it means when I tell you that Zadie's tweets about us and our lack of action have been retweeted thousands of times, and that's just today. Tomorrow it might be worse."

"Or it might all die down," Spiller said. "That's how it goes with these media feeding frenzies, isn't it? There's a day or two of hysteria, and then it's all over and the herd moves on."

"That's not a chance I'm prepared to take. I want you to go out there as soon as you can and take one of the DCs with you."

"Two officers, just to calm down a celeb? I'm more than capable of handling it on my own. "

"I know that, Tim, but I want Ms Barrington to see we're taking her concerns seriously."

Spiller was temporarily rendered speechless.

"This might turn out to be a storm in a teacup," Montague went on, "but until we have evidence to the contrary, we'll treat it as a serious threat to a member of the public. So I want you to assess the risk and take further action as necessary, carrying out your duty to the best of your ability."

"Understood, ma'am," Spiller said smartly. This conversation was only going one way, so he may as well accept it. You had to pick your battles. "I'll get on it straight away."

"Excellent. I'll make sure you have everything you need. You could give her a call today, let her know we're on the case."

"No problem. I'll make an appointment. I might be able to swing by today."

"Even better." Montague smiled. "Thanks, Tim. I knew I could rely on you. You'd better make a start."

"Yes, ma'am." Spiller stood and made for the door.

"Give my best wishes to Sheila," Montague called after him.

"Will do."

As he walked back through the CID office, Spiller attracted a few curious stares. Did everyone else already know he'd been relegated to patting the hand of a hysterical celebrity? Did they have him down as a man on his way out, a spent force?

I'll show them, Spiller thought. *By the time I'm done, Zadie Barrington will be singing our praises.* He could carry out a charm offensive as well as the next man, and as for taking another officer, there was only one choice.

Spiller made his stride more purposeful as he spied his intended target. DC Collins was hunched over his desk, tapping away on his computer's keyboard, but he looked up as Spiller approached, and he eyed his boss warily.

The lad can spot bad news in the offing when he sees it, Spiller thought. *I'll make a detective of him yet.*

CHAPTER 4

Peter Armitage walked quickly along the sea front, his hands in his coat pockets and his shoulders hunched. *I'll be out of here soon*, he thought. *I'll be glad to see the back of this stinking town.*

All he needed was a little time to get back to his flat to grab his things, then he'd be gone. He'd booked a seat on the train, and once it pulled out from the station, no one would be able to find him. He'd been careful. He'd used someone else's credit card to buy the ticket, and he'd tossed his phone into the sea. He'd buy another phone later, when he got settled. Another town, another burner, another fake ID, and then he'd be all right. He'd be safe.

The streets of Teignmouth were quiet this early in the season, but above the ever-present cries of seagulls, he heard gruff voices. Peter glanced over his shoulder, but there was only a pair of teenage lads chatting and laughing as they munched on whatever hot snack nestled in the greasy paper bags they held up to their mouths.

The scent of meat and warm pastry reached Peter's nostrils, and his stomach cramped. *Pasties*, he thought. *Hot Cornish pasties*. What he wouldn't give for just one bite. He hadn't eaten since breakfast, and that meagre meal had consisted of a slice of stale bread and a scraping of jam.

Still, he could get something at home, and he'd be there soon. He turned the corner into Diamonds Avenue.

He was almost home. A hundred strides and he'd be there.

He scanned the parked cars. They all looked empty, but there was a black van that seemed out of place. It looked too new, too shiny to be on this street, but that might not mean anything.

It's just a van, Peter told himself. *It's empty*. But as he drew nearer, the van's door opened, and a man stepped out.

Peter stopped in his tracks. *Bloody hell!* They'd sent Ryan, and that could only mean one thing.

Peter had seen Ryan before, but only from across the back room of the pub. From a distance he was bad enough, but close up, he struck fear into Peter's heart. The man was built like a brick wall, his muscles scarcely constrained by his black jacket, and his mean features might've been carved from granite. His shaven head and dark goatee completed the picture.

Ryan stood perfectly still, his right fist cradled in his left palm as he faced Peter, waiting.

To hell with that.

Peter turned on his heel, but the two teenage lads had followed him, and they stood on the pavement not more than a few paces away, their eyes fixed on him, their laughter replaced by hard-faced scorn.

"Hang on, guys," Peter said. He raised his hands, his fingers spread wide, but the flinty-eyed youths threw their food to the ground and stalked toward him, their arms hanging loose at their sides.

"Go on," one of them said, his voice low. "Run. See how far you get."

Peter shook his head. "There's no need to be like that. I'm not going to run away."

"Get in the van, then," the other lad said. "Quick."

"No, I don't want to do that." Turning back to Ryan, Peter

added, "We can sort this out. We can talk here." As if to contradict him, Peter's voice cracked and failed him. His mouth and throat were dry, and he forced himself to swallow spit. "Listen, I've held up my end of the deal. I've done plenty of work, good work, but now I want out. I told all this to Harry, and he said—"

"Harry," Ryan sneered. "What are you talking about, you muppet? Harry's not the boss. He couldn't run a tap." Ryan chuckled darkly at his own joke, but not for long, then his stony mask was back. "We were expecting something from you, but you didn't deliver. That's not right."

"No, it's okay," Peter blurted. "The last batch is ready. You can have them, but only after I'm gone. I'll send you a message, tell you where they are. I swear."

Ryan shook his head very slowly. "That's not how it works, pal. That's not how we do business."

"Yeah, I know, but like I said, I want out. I can't do this anymore. I'm leaving."

"You don't get to go anywhere unless we say so. You work for us and no one else, understand?"

Peter nodded miserably. "I get it. I do. You don't want me working for the competition, but that's fine. I'm going to give up. No more passports, no more cards. I'm not going to make another thing, not for anyone."

"Oh no, pal. You're too young to retire." Ryan gave a nod and someone grabbed Peter from behind. The teenage lads hadn't made a sound as they'd approached, but they had Peter now, their hands locked onto his arms.

They lifted Peter as if he were as insubstantial as a rag doll. He tried to resist, tried to get his feet back onto the ground, but his shoes slipped uselessly against the tarmac.

Ryan slid open the van's side door and waited.

The youths set Peter down in front of Ryan, then they let go of him and stepped back, their job done. Ryan moved fast. Before Peter could react, Ryan grabbed him, pulling him close, their faces millimetres apart.

Peter recoiled from the stench of stale cigarette smoke on the man's breath, but he couldn't get away. "Please," Peter began. "This isn't… it's not…"

Ryan bared his teeth, and when he spoke, his voice was a guttural whisper, each word uttered slowly. "Get. In. The. Van."

Peter lowered his gaze. He couldn't bear to see the violence in the man's eyes.

"All right," he murmured. "I'll get in. You don't need to do anything."

"We'll see about that." Ryan pushed Peter toward the van, and the dark interior that waited to swallow him whole.

TUESDAY

CHAPTER 5

D an woke slowly, drifting from a deep and restful sleep. The sound of footsteps on the stairs made him open his eyes, and as he sat up, his bedroom door opened and Sam stepped inside, smiling. She was wearing one of his shirts and carrying two mugs.

"Morning, sleepyhead," she said softly, and Dan smiled. He probably looked like a lovestruck teenager, but he really didn't care.

"Morning. You've been down already? I didn't even hear you get up."

"You were fast asleep. I didn't have the heart to wake you."

Sam passed him a mug and Dan took it gratefully. "Thanks. Tea. That's nice."

Climbing into bed beside him, Sam said, "I know you like coffee in the mornings, but I thought this would make a change."

"Sure. Great." Dan took a sip and made appreciative noises. Tea was never going to hit the spot like a good cup of coffee, but Sam had made it for him, and that made all the difference.

Watching him carefully as if to gauge his reaction, Sam said, "It's English breakfast."

"It's a good cup of tea, but I only have ordinary Yorkshire Tea. Alan made me buy it. I don't have any English Breakfast."

"You've got it now. I brought it with me and put it in your cupboard. I brought some proper milk too. I made yours with oat milk, but I can't face that stuff in the mornings." Sam hesitated. "You don't mind, do you?"

"No, of course not." Dan took a long drink of tea, avoiding eye contact for a second or two. Lately, Sam had been bringing more and more things into his house, and that was all fine, it really was. He wanted Sam to feel at home, to treat the place as her own, but they'd never discussed it. It had just happened gradually. And that, too, was fine.

"Oh, and I left a raw steak in your fridge last night," Sam said. "That's okay, isn't it?"

Dan tried very hard not to blink, but he didn't quite succeed.

"Okay. Well, you know I don't expect you to give up meat, just because I—"

Sam's laughter cut him short. "Your face! As if I'd do that to you." She leaned over and kissed him on the forehead. "Honestly, Dan, you're a sweetheart, but you're far too easy to wind up."

"So it would seem."

"Aw, there's no need to look so put out. I was only pulling your leg."

"I know. It's okay."

"So," Sam said brightly, "you're going Chagford again today?"

Dan smiled to himself. *Going Chagford*. At one time, the Devonian habit of omitting certain prepositions had irked him no end, but in Sam's soft accent the little idiosyncrasies were rather charming.

"What are you grinning at?" Sam asked. "You'd better not be laughing at me."

"I can smile, can't I? For some reason, I'm happy. I can't think why. Unless it's something to do with… never mind."

"What?"

Dan looked Sam in the eye. "I might be feeling this way because

37

it turns out that I'm the luckiest man alive."

Sam nudged him with her elbow. "Quite right. As it goes, I'm feeling pretty good myself."

They shared a smile.

"What's she like?" Sam asked. "Zadie B, I mean."

"You asked me that last night, and I told you. She's very sharp, but she struck me as a bit eccentric. Mind you, she probably wasn't at her best. She's worried and with good reason. Someone broke into her house and left a threatening note. That's enough to upset anyone."

Dan thought of the note: a sheet torn from a notebook, block capitals in black biro, neat and expressionless. He'd taken a photo of it with his phone, but no matter how much he'd stared at it, the stark message had given nothing away.

"Yeah, but what's she *really* like? As a person."

"It's hard to say. I haven't really got to know her yet."

"You spent long enough watching videos of her prancing about," Sam said. "I thought you were never coming to bed last night. I was getting jealous."

"That was background research. I need to know what she does for a living, and besides, I was looking for trolls or patterns in the comments; anything that might suggest someone was developing an obsession."

"Did you find anything?"

"No, not really. She told me herself that she only gets positive comments, and she was right. But I can't help wondering how that can be. Someone must be policing her social media accounts, carefully controlling which comments are published. It's probably her assistant, Natalya; she's a force to be reckoned with."

"Natalya, eh? You didn't mention her yesterday. Why's that? Is she some kind of glamorous Russian type, all cheekbones and pouty lips?"

"No. Natalya is Zadie's PA. She's from Ukraine." Dan paused. "Actually, she's... problematic."

"What's that supposed to mean?"

"I told you about the note Zadie found. Well, Natalya told me that she went home to Moretonhampstead while Zadie and her friends were having a meal in Doddiscombsleigh, but she could've gone back to Zadie's house and left the note then."

"Why would she do that?" Sam asked. "Don't they get on?"

Dan recalled the way Zadie and Natalya had spoken to each other the day before. Neither of them would win prizes for tact or diplomacy. They'd been openly dismissive of each other, but if anything, that suggested an openness between them.

"I would say they have a feisty relationship," Dan said. "Natalya is very forthright, a bit severe, even. If she had a problem with Zadie, she wouldn't creep in and leave an anonymous note, she'd say something to Zadie's face."

"Quite right. Good for her. The thing is, do you trust her?"

Dan thought about it but not for long. "Yes, I do."

"There you go then. Problem solved. It's easy, this investigation lark, isn't it? How much is she paying you to sit in bed drinking tea?

"It's not quite that simple, but I'm charging a reasonable rate. I came up with a figure, and Zadie didn't hesitate."

"How much?"

"I'm not going to tell you that, Sam, so don't keep asking, please. It's between Zadie and me."

Sam pouted. "Spoilsport."

"I'll tell you one thing though. For all her fancy clothes and makeup, Zadie can't hold a candle to you."

"Get away."

"No, I mean it. You're much more beautiful."

Sam shook her head, but she smiled modestly. "You can turn on the charm when you want to, Dan Corrigan." She leaned close to him, lowering her voice. "And do you know what I'm going to do now?"

Sam's hair hung down, framing her face. She was so close now that the scent of her shampoo filled Dan's nostrils, and his heart beat a little faster. "No," he murmured. "I have no idea."

"So it'll be a surprise when I do something nice for you." She grinned and pushed him away, laughing. "I'm going to go downstairs and make some breakfast."

Dan tried to protest, but Sam was already jumping out of bed and rifling through her discarded clothes.

"How about a couple of fried eggs?" Sam went on. "And some toast."

"I haven't got any eggs," Dan started to say, but Sam sent him a knowing smile.

"You brought eggs with you?"

"Yep. And a loaf of bread. It's not sourdough, and it hasn't got olives or anything weird in it, but it's a nice crusty loaf. I bought it from the farmers' market in Bovey."

"I'm sure the bread's fine, but I don't really eat—"

"You'll like these eggs," Sam interrupted. "They're from Marjorie's hens, and those birds live like royalty. They must be the happiest birds in Devon, and when they stop laying, she keeps them as pets, so you've really got nothing to worry about. Besides, they're the best eggs you'll ever eat."

"Well, at least there'll be no food miles."

"You'll try them, then?"

Dan hesitated. He wasn't a strict vegan. He ate fish from time to time, and he'd learned not to ask too many questions about the homemade cakes at the village fair. Besides, this was a test, an exercise in give and take, and he didn't want to fail.

"Yes, thank you," he said. "Eggs would be lovely."

"Good." Sam stood, her clothes in her hand. "I'll have a quick shower, then I'll go and get started."

"Okay, I'll join you in a minute. I mean, I'll join you for breakfast, not in the, er, shower."

"That's a shame." Sam smiled salaciously then flounced from the room.

Dan stared in silence at the bedroom door. Had Sam meant her parting words as an invitation, or was she toying with him? There was only one way to find out, so Dan climbed out of bed.

CHAPTER 6

"I'm almost ready," Peter muttered to the empty front room of his one-bedroom flat. A sudden wave of pain radiated from his ribcage, and he touched the place gingerly. Did he have a cracked rib? If it needed medical attention it would have to wait. There were other problems to take care of first; problems he'd have to deal with once and for all.

It wouldn't be long now.

Peter drew a deep breath, steadying his nerves. He had a few final things to collect, and then he really would be ready. But before he could begin, a shadow fell across the window. His basement flat was reached by a set of concrete steps that led down from the pavement. The small window restricted his view, but there was someone on the steps now. Peter watched the pair of black boots as they stomped past the window, then a man's legs clad in blue jeans.

Damn. It was Ryan, and he was early.

Ryan hammered on the door, hard enough to rattle the latch.

Peter hurried across the room and stood to one side of the door. He'd left the baseball bat ready, and he picked it up, adjusting his grip on the handle as he leaned back against the wall. It was time.

"Hang on," Peter called out, making his voice deliberately thin and unsteady. "I'm just getting dressed."

The sound of a muffled curse came from beyond the door. Good. Ryan was angry now and becoming suspicious. If he thought his quarry was playing for time or trying to escape, he wouldn't hesitate.

The handle turned and the door burst inward, hitting the wall with a crash. Ryan appeared in the doorway, rushing in, but Peter was ready for him. He swung the bat with all his might, aiming high, putting his shoulders into it. The wooden bat connected with Ryan's head, and he went down hard, his body hitting the floor with a dull thud. At the same time, Peter's swing came to an end, the baseball bat hitting the doorframe with an impact that jarred through his arms.

Peter staggered back, staring at Ryan's inert form on the floor. He felt no pity. The day before, Ryan had punched him in the ribs, the kidneys, the stomach, smiling all the while. *Savage bastard*, Peter thought. *It serves him right*. But this was no time to gloat. Ryan was out cold, but how long would that last?

Peter wasn't about to hang around and find out. Taking hold of Ryan's legs, he dragged him further into the room and pushed the door closed. Bending over, he rifled through Ryan's pockets, taking his wallet, keys and a cigarette lighter. He stowed these in his pockets, then he fished out his own driving licence and stuffed it into Ryan's pocket.

Peter hurried over to the kitchen area: a sink and a small counter set against the rear wall along with a battered electric stove. His only saucepan was already full of cooking oil and sitting on the largest ring. Beside it, a stack of old pizza boxes teetered dangerously. Peter nudged the greasy boxes until they were touching the side of the saucepan, then he turned the heat up full. As the ring began to glow, he walked away, stepping over Ryan's unconscious body.

A small holdall was already packed with a few essentials and a couple of changes of clothes. Peter grabbed his bag by the handles and let himself out into the narrow walkway between his door and a brick wall.

Peter locked the door behind him. Three steps took him to the drain where a concrete gulley was supposed to take away the rainwater from the gutters. In practice, the water collected in a stinking puddle that drained only in the driest weather.

He couldn't see below the puddle's scum-streaked surface, but Peter knew there was a cast iron grid across the drain's useless mouth. He held the key over the place and let it fall. It disappeared with barely a splash, and Peter headed for the steps that led up to the street.

It was too bad about Ryan, but it couldn't be helped. Peter needed to disappear, and that was never going to be easy, especially given the company he'd been keeping. The only way was to sow confusion in his wake, letting the trail go cold while he got away. Besides, Ryan wouldn't be much missed; he was little better than a rabid animal, an attack dog who dealt out misery and suffering without remorse.

As for the flat, Peter wouldn't be sorry if the whole place burned to the ground. The floors above were all empty, and his dingy basement flat had been dismal from day one, with damp on the walls and mould on the ceiling. Fire was the best thing for it. There was nothing he'd wanted from the place. Nothing.

Except…

"Bloody hell!" Peter whispered. How could he have been so stupid? *The passports.* They were his only bargaining chip, his last hope of escaping alive if the gang ever found him, and he'd left them behind.

He'd meant to lift them from their hiding place earlier, but he'd been jittery, his mind running rings around him, and he'd been sick with nerves, his body rebelling against what he'd planned to do. He'd thrown up three times, thinking each time had to be the last, and the nausea had left him almost delirious, running on adrenaline and his need to escape. And then Ryan had turned up early, and that had been the last straw.

What am I going to do?

Peter stared at the limpid puddle of stagnant water. By now, his key would've sunk into whatever god-forsaken gunge lay at the very bottom of the drain. Even if he rolled his sleeve up to the shoulder, he wouldn't be able to find the damned key. He could have a go at breaking the door down, but he didn't have the strength, and anyway, he didn't have time; he'd already dithered for too long.

He had to cut and run, hoping that the fire would destroy every trace of his existence. Every trace. It was a damned shame, but that's the way it had to be.

Peter turned his back on the flat for good. He crept up the steps until his head reached street level, then he peeked out to check the road.

The black van was a few metres away, and it didn't look as though there was anyone in the cab. Of course, they'd only sent one man to fetch him. He was never going to be any trouble.

Peter felt in his pocket. He had Ryan's keys, and the van was there for the taking. He'd get clear, then he'd dump it somewhere in a nearby town, or maybe in Exeter. If he was careful where he left it, the van might escape attention for days or even weeks. Meanwhile, he could go anywhere, at least, anywhere he could reach on public transport. He had some cash and credit cards in his bag, plus he had Ryan's wallet, complete with cards and a good-sized wad of cash. A few separate bus rides would throw anyone off his trail.

It was as good a plan as any, and Peter headed for the street. A minute later, he was driving away, relief flooding through his veins. He turned on the radio and recognised a song from back in the day. From somewhere, he found his voice and started singing along, loud and out of tune. Yeah. This was good. Very good. For the first time in a long time, he was free.

CHAPTER 7

I t was midmorning by the time Dan and Alan arrived at The Old Manse, Dan driving his old Toyota. There was no sign of Shaun the surly decorator, but there were two extra cars in the drive, a black Audi saloon and a Mazda hatchback which Dan noticed was almost exactly the same shade of red as Zadie's Tesla.

"Our client has company," Alan said. "This could be interesting."

"Hopefully, she took my advice and had someone over to stay with her last night, but we'll find out soon enough." Dan rang the doorbell, and as they waited for it to be answered, he spotted Alan looking at him in an odd way.

"What's up?" Dan asked.

"Nothing. It's just that you were humming to yourself, that's all. I think the tune might've been 'Walking on Sunshine', although it was hard to tell."

"Really? I didn't notice."

"Well, I did, and you're not one of nature's hummers. Why are you in such high spirits?"

Dan's only reply was an enigmatic smile.

Alan nodded wisely. "Ah. I take it things are going well with Sam."

"You could say that. You could say they're going very well."

"That's good," Alan said. "I'm glad to hear it."

The two men stood in awkward silence, and Dan was glad when Natalya answered the door and invited them in.

"Zadie is in her lounge," Natalya said. "I'll take you up."

"The lounge is upstairs?" Alan asked as they followed Natalya through the chaotic hallway.

"One of them," Natalya answered over her shoulder. "The other one is downstairs, but it is not good. There is a bad smell."

"It's probably condensation," Alan said. "These old houses are prone to it unless they're treated properly. You need special paint and plaster."

Natalya paused on the landing. "This is what Shaun says, also. You know about these things?"

"Only from my own experience. I have an old cottage. It's nothing like as grand as this one, but the principles are the same."

"Perhaps we could discuss the plasterwork later," Dan said. "I'm keen to talk to Zadie."

"Of course," Natalya said. "Follow me, please."

She took them past Zadie's studio to a door that hadn't yet been stripped of its chipped paint. Natalya paused with her hand on the handle. "Zadie has her friends with her. They have come to help, but…"

"They're not making things any easier?" Dan suggested.

"They are good friends to Zadie," Natalya replied, but the look in her eyes said otherwise. She knocked once on the door, then swept into the room, Alan and Dan following in her wake.

Inside, Zadie was holding court from the centre of a huge, bright red sofa. Surrounded by her friends, she huddled amid a pile of colourful cushions, her feet tucked up beneath her. There was no glamorous dress for Zadie today. She wore a pair of faded jeans and a hoodie that was one or two sizes too large for her, the sleeves rolled up at the cuff.

Her four friends were probably around the same age as Zadie, and Dan decided that they'd all put considerable effort into choosing their outfits.

A pair of slim women had laid claim to one end of the sofa, and they sat at an angle to face the centre of the room, their posture very upright, all the better to show off their long, straight hair which cascaded down their backs. They wore near identical outfits comprising a simple blouse and a pair of dark trousers. At the opposite end of the sofa, a man in his early thirties lounged, his legs stretched out in front of him and his feet, shod in brilliant white Adidas basketball boots, resting on a footstool. He was dressed in faded jeans and a T-shirt, and his mop of tousled hair was in stark contrast to the smart coiffeurs of his companions.

A smaller sofa in a matching shade of red was arranged at right angles to the larger one, and a woman in a long dress sat on its armrest, leaning forward to face Zadie and looking uncomfortable, as though she might slip from her perch at any moment.

In front of the larger sofa, a long coffee table was strewn with magazines and books. Dan was surprised to see a brass ashtray which held the stubs of several hand-rolled cigarettes. He sniffed, but although there was a trace of stale smoke in the air, the windows were open and he couldn't tell whether it was plain tobacco or something else that had been smoked. The ashtray was closest to the man in the T-shirt, but apart from his slightly bloodshot eyes, Dan could see nothing that marked the man out as a smoker.

Dan looked back to the table, searching for another clue: a lighter or a pouch of tobacco. Instead, his gaze found a cafetière and five mugs, all empty. Damn it. He'd missed coffee time, and that was a shame; he could have used a good strong coffee before the investigation began in earnest.

"Mr Corrigan and Mr Hargreaves are here," Natalya announced. "Would you like to talk to them *in private?*"

"No thank you, Natalya. Anything we have to say can be said in front of my friends. You know how I feel about my support network. They're very important to me."

"Yes, I know," Natalya replied, then to Dan and Alan she added, "Would you like tea or coffee?"

"Yes please," Dan said. "Coffee would be great. I take it black."

"Me too," Alan put in.

"Decaffeinated?" Natalya asked, and both men shook their heads firmly.

"Oh dear," Zadie said. "Caffeine is so bad for you. You really ought to give it up. I can give you my five-point plan, and you'll soon wean yourself off it. I can guarantee it."

"Perhaps another time," Dan replied. "I'd like to concentrate on the case for now."

"Quite right," the man called out from the sofa. "Let's get to business, and Nat, could you bring me another cup? You know how I like it."

"Yes, I'll bring the coffee." Natalya scooped up the tray and marched stiffly from the room.

Zadie watched her go. "She's in a foul mood. Anyone would think it was her house that had been broken into."

"I'm sure she's found it upsetting," Dan said. "This might not be Natalya's home, but it's her workplace, and she was here when you realised someone had broken in. She probably doesn't feel safe."

"Nat's not afraid of anything," Zadie stated. "She's from Ukraine."

Dan didn't reply. Judging people by their origins was a trap he generally avoided, but something in Natalya's past had left her with a stern demeanour that seemed to arm her against the world. What had she seen? What had she lived through?

"Did Natalya stay with you last night?" Alan asked.

"Nat offered to stay, but I sent her home. She has a flat in Moretonhampstead, so she drives in every morning in the MG. It's my car, but I let her use it. In return, Nat ferries me about."

"You weren't alone in the house last night, were you?" Dan said. "I did suggest that someone should stay with you."

"Connor came over." Zadie indicated the man lounging beside her. "He was my knight in shining armour."

"It was no trouble," Connor said. "Always happy to help a friend."

"Did you drive here, Connor?" Dan asked.

"No, I walked," Connor replied. "I don't live far away. It's a nice little stroll, and anyway, I don't drive. We've got to respect the planet."

"Connor's very keen on the environment." Zadie's expression clouded but only for a moment, then she shook her head as if ridding herself of an unbidden thought. Focusing on Dan and Alan, she said, "Where are my manners? Please, have a seat. Make yourselves at home." Indicating the other sofa, she added, "Naomi, make some room for our guests. Fetch a chair or something."

The woman who'd been balancing on the armrest jumped to her feet. "Yes. Sorry. I didn't mean to… I'll go and find something."

"There's no need to move on our account," Alan said. "There's plenty of room." He sat down, gesturing to Dan to do the same.

Naomi shook her head. "Oh no, you'll be squashed."

"Not at all," Dan said, taking his place beside Alan, but Naomi lowered her gaze and hurried to the door, slipping out of the room without making a sound.

Zadie sighed. "You mustn't worry about Naomi. She's something of an introvert. I've been trying to help her, to bring her out of her shell, but it's an uphill struggle."

Perhaps she's happy as she is, Dan thought, but aloud, he said, "What's Naomi's connection to you? And what's her full name?"

Connor sat up, suddenly more alert. "Why do you want to know? Are we all suspects?" Connor grinned as though relishing the prospect.

"Not at this point," Dan replied, then to Zadie, he added, "I need to build a picture of the way you live, so I'll be asking a lot of questions, some of them quite personal. I'd like to know about your routines and your relationships."

The two women sitting beside Zadie shared a glance, then one of them said, "We should go. You obviously need some privacy, Zadie, and we can pop back later."

"Actually, I'd prefer it if you'd all stay," Dan said. "The more background information I can gather, the better, and you may well have seen or heard something important."

The pair of women looked distinctly uncomfortable, but the one who hadn't spoken yet said, "Okay. If you think it might help."

"Thank you." Dan took a moment to look at each person in turn. "I understand that this might feel awkward for everyone, but I'll try not to be too intrusive, and it's vital that we keep our goal in mind. I'm here for one reason only, and that is to find out who broke into this house. When I know that, I'll hand the matter over to the police and my work will be done."

"Ooh, yes, the police," Zadie said. "A couple of detectives called in yesterday. We had quite a long chat. They were okay. Very helpful."

Dan kept his expression neutral. "I see. You could've called and let me know. If I'm going to stay on top of this case, I need to be informed of any developments."

"There wasn't much point. They had a look around and took that nasty little note away in a plastic bag, the glass too. But it was mainly just a chat about safety. They advised me to get some window locks and have security bolt fitted to the front door, and they said there'd be someone coming to take fingerprints."

"Did they find the missing hand towel?" Dan asked.

Zadie shook her head. "They didn't find anything. They had a look around the garden, but they said there wasn't much chance of finding any footprints or anything like that. Too many people have been coming and going. They said it would be best to wait and see if there were any fingerprints in the house."

Alan had produced his notebook and pen. "These detectives, can you remember their names?"

"Detective Inspector Spiller was in charge, and the younger one, the Detective Constable, was called, erm…"

"Collins?" Dan suggested.

"Yes. That was it. They gave me a card, but I passed it on to Nat. She files everything away, and she handles all my contacts."

"Like a walking Rolodex," Alan said.

Zadie gazed at Alan in incomprehension, so he added, "Anyway, it's good to hear that Spiller and Collins are on the case. We've worked with them before."

"Yes, but to some extent, their hands will be tied," Dan said. "The police won't treat this as stalking unless they see a repeated pattern. They won't even class it as harassment. We can be more proactive, and I'd like to start by finding out a bit more about you and your friends."

"Go ahead," Zadie said. "Ask away."

Dan sat back. "First, let's go around the group and everyone can introduce themselves."

The assembled friends eyed each other as if anxious not to go first, but before anyone could speak, the door opened and Naomi appeared, struggling to manoeuvre a wicker chair through the doorway.

Alan jumped up and went to help, holding the door open and guiding the chair through.

Naomi sent Alan a grateful smile. "Thanks, but I can manage now."

"Are you sure? I can carry it for you."

"No, it's okay. I've got it."

"Be careful with that," Zadie called out. "It's vintage."

"I'm doing my best," Naomi muttered. Finally, she set the chair down heavily and took her place, smoothing down her dress and looking around the group nervously. "I had to go to one of the guest rooms. I couldn't find anything that was—"

"Never mind about that," Zadie interrupted. "We're all introducing ourselves to Dan and Alan, and it's your turn."

"Oh." Naomi clasped her hands together, her fingers intertwined. "Erm, there's not much to say. I'm Naomi. Naomi Smith. I'm a photographer, fashion mainly, though I'm still trying to get myself established. I've done some weddings and that sort of thing, but nothing major just yet. I live in Exeter, but my family are from the Midlands and… that's all I can think of."

The woman sitting closest to Zadie said, "That's plenty. They don't need your life story." The woman smirked as though she'd made a joke, then she laid a hand on her chest and launched into her introduction. "My name is Philippa Darley-Jones, and yes, let's put this out there since you're bound to find out sooner or later, I do have a title. Daddy was a baron, so I ought to add 'The Honourable' in front of my name, but let's not get into all that. You can call me plain old Philippa, okay?"

"Right," Dan said. It was tempting to refer to her as 'plain old Philippa' from that point onward, but he thought better of it. Instead, he added, "And what do you do, Philippa?"

"I'm completing a masters' degree in contemporary art."

"You're a mature student," Dan suggested, privately rejoicing at the way his remark made Philippa's nostrils flare.

"I'm undertaking a post-graduate research project at the University of Exeter," Philippa stated. "I take my work very seriously."

"Oh yes," Connor drawled. "We all know how seriously you take it, darling. Tell me, when did you last go into college?"

"I don't need to actually attend all that much. I'm writing my thesis, and I talk to my tutor online, but at least I'm doing something worthwhile with my time. What do you do, Connor?"

"I enjoy life," Connor replied. "I live off my inheritance and I don't care who knows it. It's what Mum and Dad would've wanted." Connor chuckled as though very pleased with himself. "Actually, what they wanted was a strapping, heterosexual son who left school with straight A's, became a heart surgeon and played rugby at the weekends, but what they got was me: an obsessive musician with a talent for making bad choices. I may have had a song in the charts, but in their eyes, that never counted for anything so long as I had anarchist tendencies and the moral breaking strain of a hot Mars bar."

In the silence that followed, Connor looked around his friends as though expecting laughter. When none came, he slumped back on the sofa, folding his arms and looking peeved.

"You didn't give us your surname," Alan prompted.

Connor pouted as though he might not oblige, but eventually, he said, "Griffiths. Two F's."

"Thanks, but I know how to spell it," Alan replied, making a note. "Out of interest, what was the song?"

"What?"

Alan looked up from his notebook. "You mentioned having a song in the charts. What was it called? Did you perform it yourself or were you in a band?"

"We had a band. There were four of us." Connor roused himself from his sulk. "We called ourselves The Idyllic Sirens. I was the lead guitarist. We made it to number three in the UK charts with *Bring it Down*. You might've heard of it."

Alan looked thoughtful, then he nodded. "Yes, that was about ten years ago, wasn't it?"

"More like nine," Connor replied. "Nine and a half."

"They used to play it on the radio all the time," Alan said. "That was you? Amazing. You remember it, don't you, Dan?"

Dan shook his head. "I'm afraid not. Did you have any other hits?"

"No, just the one, but that's enough, isn't it? It's one more than most people manage. It's fine."

"That's a healthy attitude," Dan said. "But going back to Sunday, how did you get to the pub in Doddiscombsleigh?"

"Philippa gave me a lift. She picked me up at around seven."

"Thank you." Dan turned to the one person who hadn't spoken yet. "You are?"

"Melody Reinhardt. I'm an old friend of Zadie's."

"Ah, yes, it was your birthday on Sunday," Dan said.

"My actual birthday was the day before, but Zadie was busy on the Saturday, so Sunday was the next best thing. Zadie treated me to a lovely meal."

Dan smiled. "That was generous of her, but you arrived late. Why was that?"

"Oh, I'd had my hair done especially, but it didn't turn out right. It looked awful." Melody pulled a face. "I had to try and fix it at home. It took ages."

Alan made a note then said, "Was anyone else invited to the party? Anyone who didn't turn up?"

Melody shook her head. "I don't have any family nearby, and my friends are all here in this room." She smiled sadly. "We had such a good time. It's awful to think that while we were enjoying ourselves, some horrible person was forcing their way into Zadie's home and poking around. It breaks my heart, it really does. I mean, what if we hadn't gone to my house afterward? Zadie might've come home when he was still here. It doesn't bear thinking about."

Melody had spoken quietly, her voice filled with passion, and Dan found himself hanging on her every word, nodding in agreement.

Alan also seemed to have been affected, and he made his voice soft when he said, "Melody, if you don't mind me asking, what do you do?"

"I run a clothes shop. Indiago. It's in Exeter."

Dan thought for a moment. "On Gandy Street?"

Melody smiled, showing her perfect white teeth. "Yes. Do you know it?"

"I've been past it," Dan said. "It caught my eye, but I haven't been inside."

"But you must," Melody said. "We have some fantastic summer shirts at the moment, and there's a pale-cream linen jacket that would suit your skin tone perfectly."

Zadie made a disapproving noise in her throat. "Melody, this is hardly the time for a sales pitch. I'm paying Dan for his time."

Melody's hand went to her chest in a close echo of Philippa's earlier gesture, and Dan studied her for a moment. It wasn't uncommon for close friends to pick up each other's little habits and patterns of speech, but Melody and Philippa seemed intent on becoming carbon copies of each other. Their hair styles were identical, their clothes and make-up strikingly similar, and even their speech patterns were the same. Which one was emulating the other? Or were they both conforming to a type they'd encountered elsewhere?

Dan's thoughts were interrupted by the arrival of Natalya with a tray, and as soon as she set it down on the table, Connor pressed down the cafetière's plunger and filled his mug. He swallowed a mouthful and then sat back with a sigh.

"That's better," he said. "Decaf just doesn't do it for me. I need my coffee with bullets in it."

Dan thanked Natalya, then he poured coffee for Alan and himself. After an appreciative sip, Dan addressed the group. "I'm sure you've all been mulling the situation over, and you may have formed some conclusions of your own. This is not the time to keep those suspicions private. If you're uncomfortable sharing your thoughts in front of the others, you can contact me at any time."

"In total confidence?" Philippa asked.

Dan hesitated. "I can't guarantee that. Alan and I will be as discreet as possible, but if someone were to disclose something that I have to pass to the police, I may have to explain where the information came from."

"That's fine," Zadie said. "We're all friends here. We share everything. None of us have anything to hide."

I doubt that very much, Dan thought, and though he smiled at Zadie, he watched Philippa from the corner of his eye. She'd been very quick to raise the issue of confidentiality, and even now, she was putting up a front, sitting very still, her hands in her lap. But her gaze had grown distant as if her mind was elsewhere, picturing some scene from memory.

"You know what?" Connor said. "You're dead right about one thing, Dan. We have been talking it over and trying to figure out what happened. To me, it's obvious. Some random nutter has seen Zadie online and decided to find out where she lives. He's obsessed, so he came over and broke in. We don't know what he was planning to do, but he could be dangerous. It shouldn't be too hard to find him. Look online. I'll bet he's made comments and sent messages."

"That's an avenue I've been pursuing," Dan replied. "And it takes me to another question. Who looks after your social media accounts, Zadie?"

Zadie raised an eyebrow. "I do. They're my livelihood. I can't entrust them to anyone else."

"You read every comment? Every tweet?"

"Of course. It's important for me to be authentic, to engage with my fans in person. I don't hide behind anybody else."

"I see." Dan looked at Natalya. She'd remained in the room, standing to one side, but she returned his gaze without giving anything away.

"Putting the idea of an unknown stalker aside, does anyone have any other ideas?" Alan asked. "Have there been any problems closer to home?"

"Such as what?" Zadie replied.

Alan looked as though he was hunting for the right turn of phrase, then he said, "For instance, have there been any romantic relationships that have gone wrong or ended badly?"

"Romantic relationships. What a nice way of putting it. I knew I was right about you, Alan." Zadie bestowed a smile on him. "But no, my relationships have always been very free, very open. We come together, we share our lives for a while, then we part as friends. No ties, no commitments and nobody gets hurt. It's very simple."

"How about unwanted admirers that you've turned away?" Dan asked. "Have any of them taken it badly?"

"That's a very loaded question. You're assuming some kind of power struggle, a battle of the sexes, but I don't accept that paradigm. I don't live by those rules."

Dan wasn't sure how to respond, and Alan stepped in to fill the silence.

Flourishing his notebook, Alan said, "The note that was left on Zadie's desk. *I'll see you soon.* It's ambiguous, isn't it?"

"I don't think so," Connor replied. "It means they're coming back. Someone wants to frighten her. It's horrible."

"It can be read that way, certainly," Alan admitted. "But it could simply be a message from a friend. Do any of you know anything about it?"

Dan watched carefully as fleeting glances were exchanged around the group.

Philippa spoke up. "If any of us had written it, we'd have said so."

"I'd have thought that was obvious," Connor put in. "Anyway, the note was in Zadie's studio, and we don't go in there."

"Never?" Dan asked.

"I've shown them around," Zadie replied. "But the studio is my inner sanctum. My friends respect that."

"In there, you're Zadie, the influencer," Alan suggested. "Out here, you can relax and be yourself."

Zadie pressed her hands together as if in prayer, then she bowed her head toward Alan. "I knew you'd understand, Alan. The identity that my followers see online is a creation. It's a version of me. Yes, it's authentic, but it isn't *all* of me. I have to keep something back. I need to be grounded, to replenish, to refill the well of my creativity."

Dan turned to Natalya. "You go into the studio though, don't you?"

Natalya blinked in surprise. "Of course. But I didn't see that note until Zadie showed it to me. Someone must've left it there while we were out."

"How can you be so sure?" Dan asked.

"I would've seen it. When we were on our way out to the car, Zadie wanted a scarf from her dressing room. I went to fetch it for her, and I would've noticed if anything had been on the desk. Zadie doesn't like any mess."

"Thank you, Natalya," Dan said. "That's very helpful." Looking back to Zadie, he said, "The timing of the note is a problem. All we know is that it was left between the time you went out for the evening and the time you arrived home again. Is there anything you can think of that might help to narrow it down?"

Zadie looked thoughtful, but before she could reply, Connor said, "He'll have waited until late at night, otherwise someone might've noticed him. It's a small town."

Dan kept his gaze on Zadie. "What do you think?"

Zadie sighed. "Connor's right. It must've been late. This is a quiet street, but people walk past now and then, heading into town or walking home from the pub. If someone had been hanging around in the early evening, they could've been seen, but after about half past eleven there's never anyone around."

"Would you agree with that, Natalya?" Dan asked.

"I don't know," Natalya replied. "I'm not usually here at night."

"And on that evening, you were at home in Moretonhampstead until it was time to pick Zadie up," Dan said.

Natalya nodded. "You know this."

"Yes, but you never told me what you were actually doing all that time."

"Do I have to?"

"No, but it might help," Dan replied. "I like to keep the facts straight."

"It's okay, Nat," Zadie said. "You don't have to say if you don't want to." Sending Dan an admonishing look, she added, "I don't want you upsetting Natalya. She's entitled to her privacy."

Dan raised a hand. "Of course. I'm simply being—"

"Reading," Natalya interrupted.

All eyes turned to Natalya.

"At home, I read. It helps with my English."

"What are you reading?" Alan asked, his voice bright.

"*Great Expectations*. I have seen the film, but the book is different. I try to understand, but…"

"Dickens can be hard work," Alan said. "I'm happy to help if you'd like to talk about it sometime, or I could lend you something that might be a bit more to your taste. I have loads of books at home. Too many really."

"I hate to interrupt your book group," Connor began, "but shouldn't we be talking about Zadie?"

"We're getting there," Dan replied. "You were saying, Zadie, that anyone hanging around would be spotted, and I was wondering about your neighbours. Do you get on with them?"

"I don't have any immediate neighbours," Zadie said. "As for the houses nearby, people tend to keep themselves to themselves, but I'm on good terms with everyone. They all seem very nice."

Philippa leaned forward to touch Zadie's arm. "What about that awful man? The American."

Zadie almost laughed. "John? He's a sweetheart. He wouldn't hurt a fly. Don't be so silly."

Philippa flinched, recoiling from Zadie as if she'd been slapped, her cheeks colouring. "But he was horrible to you about that footpath. You said he lost his temper completely."

"He apologised afterward," Zadie replied. "He came round personally, and he brought flowers. He cut them himself from his own garden. They were beautiful, and he's been so nice to me ever since. He still feels bad about it, I can tell."

Philippa dropped her gaze as if defeated, but even so, she said, "You can't trust a man who behaves like that to a woman. Never."

"Where does John live?" Alan asked.

"Not far away," Zadie replied. "He has a beautiful place along the lane."

Alan scribbled furiously in his notebook. "We should have a word with him. He might've seen something."

"His house is a good half mile away, but I don't think you'll get anywhere near him." Zadie smiled as if at a private joke. "I should've explained. He's John Callaway. The actor."

"*The* John Callaway?" Alan asked. "He lives in Devon? I had no idea."

"No one has any idea," Connor put in. "That's the way he likes it. You can try to talk to him if you want, but as he would probably say, good luck with that."

"You can't walk up to his house anymore," Philippa said. "The first thing he did when he bought the place was to put an enormous wrought-iron gate across his driveway. It's hideous and not in keeping with the town at all." She spread her hands wide. "I mean, this isn't Beverly Hills."

"Has he ruffled a few feathers?" Dan asked.

"Not at all," Zadie replied. "John is a lovely man, and he's very supportive of the community. He sent a scrumptious hamper for the harvest festival, and he always gives generously when the locals are raising funds. He practically paid for the entire school library."

"Oh yeah, he's very keen on throwing money to the peasants," Connor said. "At least, his PA is very good at splashing his boss's cash around. But you won't see Callaway popping in to the shops or propping up the bar in the pub."

"I've seen him walking in the fields," Zadie said. "And he goes to church every Sunday."

"With his minder," Connor shot back. "And he's a nasty piece of work. I don't know how he can squeeze into a pew."

"How would you know?" Naomi asked quietly, an edge of condemnation in her tone, and all eyes turned on her.

Lifting her chin in defiance, Naomi added, "Benny's not a minder, he's John's driver. He's a gentleman, and he kneels and prays along with the rest of us."

"Okay," Dan said slowly. "We'll pay a visit to Mr Callaway. He'll talk to us."

Connor grunted. "I wouldn't bet on it."

"We'll see," Dan said. "There are ways of approaching people like Mr Callaway."

"Maybe you should take Naomi with you," Philippa sneered. "That ought to do the trick."

Naomi bridled. "What do you mean by that?"

"You know perfectly well. You're all holier than thou, but you don't mind fluttering your eyelashes when a wealthy man comes along."

"I resent that."

"Resent it all you want, but it's true," Philippa said. "Are there no churches in Exeter you could go to? It seems a long way to come for no particular reason. Did you even go to church before you found out about John?"

"Of course I did. I come to the church here because I enjoy listening to Robert." Looking to Dan, she added, "Robert's the vicar here, and he's really good. Very down to earth."

"He's young too," Philippa said. "And not bad looking, if you like that kind of thing."

Naomi stood abruptly. "That's it! I don't know why you've got it in for me, Philippa, but you're being horrible, and I'm sick of it."

"Well, I'm sorry," Philippa replied without any trace of regret. "I'm just saying what I see. Anyway, aren't you supposed to turn the other cheek or something?"

Naomi kept her lips pressed tight but her eyes blazed as she glared at Philippa. In response, Philippa's superior smile was both smug and dismissive, and it was too much for Naomi. She turned on her heel and stalked from the room.

"For God's sake, Philippa," Melody said. "There was no need for that. You know she takes these things seriously." Melody rose to her feet. "I'll go after her and make sure she's all right, then I'd better head back to the shop." She sent Dan and Alan an apologetic glance. "It was nice to meet you. Sorry to dash off, but if you need to get in touch, Zadie has my number. Bye." Melody hurried to the door.

"Here we go again," Connor intoned. "Drama. Naomi was just the same last night."

It occurred to Dan that Connor had been deliberately vague to pique his curiosity, but he had to take the bait. "What happened last night?"

Connor grinned. "While the rest of us were tucking into our food, little Miss goody two shoes ordered a green salad, then she sent it back to the kitchen, complaining about something or other. She made such a fuss."

"They'd put parmesan shavings on it," Zadie said. "Like me, Naomi's a vegan. She's very strict."

"Maybe, but there was no need for her to be such a martyr," Connor replied. "She could've picked off a few bits of cheese, but no, she had to sit there with an empty space in front of her while we ate. It was very off-putting, but then, that was exactly what she wanted. Sackcloth and ashes. Honestly, that's no way to live. What's wrong with enjoying life?" Connor gave Dan a knowing look. "You know what I mean, don't you?"

"Actually, I almost always eat a plant-based diet myself," Dan replied, "so I understand Naomi's frustration."

Connor's dismay was outshone by Zadie's delight. She clapped her hands, a warm smile on her lips. "Dan, I had a feeling about you, and now I know why. The universe has sent you to me. You'll sort all this out. You'll find a way through."

"I'll do my best," Dan said. "In fact, it's time we were on our way. Unless there's anything you want to ask, Alan."

Alan put his notebook away. "No, I think we've gone as far as we can for the moment."

"Oh, but we've hardly got started," Zadie said. "Please, don't go on account of Naomi. She's sensitive, the poor thing, but you know how it is with friends. We have our little disagreements, but they don't mean anything. We always make up afterward, and then we're the best of friends again."

"It's not that," Dan replied. "We have plenty to be going on with. We'll get to work." Dan looked to Natalya. "Would you mind sending me contact details for everyone, Natalya?"

Natalya nodded. "No problem. I'll do it right away."

"Thank you." Dan stood and Alan followed suit. Looking around the group, Dan thanked everyone for their help, and Natalya stepped forward to show them out.

Outside, as soon as Natalya had shut the door, Alan said, "Well, they're an odd bunch, aren't they? I don't think I've ever seen so much bickering among adults. Could one of Zadie's so-called friends be the culprit, do you think?"

"I doubt it. They were all with Zadie on the night of the break-in, so they couldn't have been involved."

"True. So where do you want to start, with the famous neighbour who may or may not be bad tempered?"

"No, we'll save that pleasure for later," Dan replied. "It's more likely that we're looking for a stranger and this is a small town. Any outsiders or new arrivals will have stood out. Someone will have seen the person we're looking for." Dan started walking back to the car, Alan at his side.

"What's the plan?" Alan asked as they climbed into the car.

"We're going to do one of your favourite things," Dan replied. "We're going to take a look around and see what this town has to offer."

CHAPTER 8

D S Anisha Kulkarni parked her car in Diamonds Avenue
and climbed out, looking around. She didn't know
Teignmouth well, but this seemed like an ordinary urban
neighbourhood: a terrace of red brick houses, curtains at the
windows and well-kept front gardens. But as she headed for the
cluster of police vehicles parked at the end of the street, the
neighbourhood took a turn for the worse. Here, the houses were
larger and older—townhouses from a former and more prosperous
era—but they wore an air of neglect, their plastic window frames
spotted with grime, their walls stained brown from the rusted
gutters above, and their gardens paved over with concrete slabs
that had long since cracked.

Spotting the multiple doorbells beside each front door, Kulkarni
guessed these once grand houses had been divided into flats and
rented out to a certain type of tenant.

The acrid smell of smoke stung her nostrils before she reached
the nearest patrol car, and a moment later, Kulkarni could take in
the full horror of the scene.

43 Diamonds Avenue had been a three-storey townhouse, its
white painted walls boasting half a dozen tall windows, but every
pane of glass had gone, deathly black stains of soot trailing upward

from each gaping hole. The fire had raged through every floor, and Kulkarni hardly dared to think what it must've been like for anyone trapped inside. And there had been someone; that was partly why she'd been sent over to assist Teignmouth CID. Some of DI Spiller's case load had been transferred to her, and that included a string of arson attacks. If there was a connection, she was ideally placed to find it.

Kulkarni marched up to the cordon of police tape and introduced herself to the uniformed officer on duty, a grizzled constable whose expression said he'd seen it all and wasn't impressed by her rank or her sudden arrival on his patch. Nevertheless, he noted down her details without comment, then he pointed out the officer in charge. "That's DS Jo Winslow over there," he said. "She's on the phone."

Kulkarni spotted a woman in a long black coat, pacing up and down, a phone pressed to her ear.

"I expect she'll be with you in a minute, Sergeant," the officer added. He made no move to raise the police tape, as if he expected her to wait outside the cordon until she was invited in.

"Thank you," Kulkarni said and ducked under the tape, making straight for the woman she'd come to meet.

DS Winslow stopped pacing as she caught sight of Kulkarni, then she ended her call, striding forward to meet the new arrival. A good few years older than Kulkarni, and with a slightly severe manner, Winslow ran through the introductions quickly, adding, "Glad you could come over. We're going to need an extra pair of hands. We're up to our ears at the minute."

"It's always the way," Kulkarni replied. "Not enough hours in the day and never enough in the budget to do the job right. But I'm here to help, so let's get started."

"Sure. We've got a body in the basement flat. A male. We're treating it as a suspicious death. The SOCOs are still inside, but it's going to be a while before we get anything conclusive. It must've been like the ninth circle of hell in there. They say it's hard to tell what was what."

"Have you been able to look inside?" Kulkarni asked.

Winslow shook her head. "They're still processing the scene. We're lucky the body was in the basement. I'm told it's safe down there, but there's a lot of debris, a lot of rubble. It's good for us that the deceased was right by the front door."

"Trying to get out?"

"Impossible to know."

"Yes, of course," Kulkarni said. "I was just thinking aloud. Was there any ID on the body?"

"Not so far. I understand that his clothes and effects have been pretty much destroyed, but we don't think it was the occupier. A neighbour gave us a description of the usual resident, and it doesn't fit." Winslow gestured to the building opposite: a detached house with Venetian blinds at the bay windows. "Mr Leonard Franks. A senior citizen living on his own. He was the one who reported the fire, so I've talked to him already. He doesn't use the front of his house much, so he didn't spot the fire until he went into his front room to fetch something. He called right away, but by then the flames had taken hold."

"Did he see anything useful?"

"No one at the scene, but according to him, the usual occupier of the basement is a short guy, slightly built, and that doesn't tally with what the SOCOs are saying about the remains. It's early days, but they think the deceased was around the six-foot mark. I've been trying to get in touch with the landlord so we can get the tenant's name, but I haven't been able to get hold of the right person. The property, believe it or not, is run by a company registered in the Channel Islands."

"Interesting," Kulkarni said. "I could chase that up for you."

"That would be great. I'll send you the details. I've got my hands full organising the door-to-door. It's underway, but…"

"Not getting very far?"

"You could say that. It's not the most cooperative neighbourhood, not this end of the street, anyway. A lot of these big houses were bed and breakfast places at one time, then they were holiday flats, now they're full of people on benefits. People only stay here because they've got nowhere else to go, and none of them are what you might call early risers."

"So it was up to the man across the street to call the fire brigade," Kulkarni said. "Do we know how the fire started?"

"Early indications are that it started on or around the stove. It has all the hallmarks of a chip pan fire."

"Do people still have chip pans? I thought it was all electric air fryers these days."

Winslow gave her a withering look, and Kulkarni kicked herself. The resident of that basement flat wouldn't have been able to afford a fancy kitchen gadget; they would've made do with whatever they could lay their hands on. Moving on swiftly, Kulkarni said, "We've been looking into several cases of arson in Exeter. Empty buildings, chosen at random, petrol used to start the fires."

"We'll test for traces of accelerant, but the SOCOs say it looks like a classic chip pan fire. They can tell from the residue on the wall. We think the whole building was probably in a bad state of repair and that's why the fire spread to the upper floors so quickly. I'll be a lot happier when we find out who died down there, but it doesn't seem like the same MO as your arsonists."

"Even so, my DI wants me to keep an eye out for any connection."

"Is that Tim Spiller?"

"It was, but Jill Clements has taken over the case. DI Spiller has been temporarily reassigned."

"I don't like the sound of that," Winslow said. "Is he all right?"

"Yes, but he has other things on his plate at the moment. His wife has been unwell."

"That's a shame. I've met Sheila a couple of times. Tim and me go way back. I'll give him a call and catch up."

"He'd like that. He's all about the job. It's like family to him."

Winslow seemed to look at her with fresh eyes. "It gets you that way. At least, it does for the good ones, the ones who stay the distance. You'll see."

"I hope so."

They shared a knowing smile.

"Have you had anything to eat recently?" Winslow asked.

"Not properly. I'm running on coffee and snack bars."

"Same here, but we'll be no use to anyone if we don't get some food down us. They can spare us for a few minutes, and I know where we can get a mug of tea and something resembling a sandwich."

"Sounds like a plan."

"Good. I'll drive." Winslow led the way, taking out her phone and making a call as she went along. Kulkarni kept pace at her side, half listening as Winslow checked in with her DI. The exchange was short and to the point, but it didn't convey anything Kulkarni didn't already know.

Winslow pocketed her phone as they reached her car, a VW Touareg. "You'll meet DI Townsend later. He likes people to call him Thomas."

"Not Tom?"

"Don't go there. He's all right, but he's…" Winslow broke off and smiled. "I was going to say 'young', but that makes me sound like a grumpy old-timer. Let's just say he's done well for himself. He's probably not much older than you."

"A high flier."

"He seems to think so." Winslow unlocked the car. "Hop in."

Kulkarni did as she was asked, glancing over her shoulder as she fastened her seatbelt and noting the clutter on the backseat: a bright red hoodie, a single Vans sneaker and a pair of headphones. "Kids?"

"Teenagers," Winslow said. "A boy and a girl. You?"

"No. I'm single."

Winslow sighed and started the engine, setting off and driving swiftly through winding backstreets. She seemed content to drive in silence, and that suited Kulkarni fine. She needed a little time to get her thoughts in order.

Assuming the SOCO's first impressions were right, and the body didn't match the description of the regular resident, what was the connection between the two men? In a rundown neighbourhood, people sometimes made arrangements of their own, and the right paperwork wasn't always in place. Benefit claimants sometimes tried to beat the system, falsifying their address, while others unofficially sublet their flats without any documentation. And then there were the sofa surfers, moving from one address to the next, never leaving a trace in the records while being listed as living somewhere else entirely.

Who was the official tenant? Was it the deceased, or was it the slightly built man seen by the neighbour, Mr Franks?

The property's owners should be able to give her a name, and that would set her on the right track. The slightly built man must be out there somewhere, and if he didn't come forward, she'd track him down. He'd be on a computer somewhere, and she'd find him. It was only a matter of time.

CHAPTER 9

Standing outside the town's small supermarket, Dan and Alan surveyed Chagford's main street.

"Where next?" Alan asked. "There's a charity shop over there. It's just about the only place we haven't tried, so we may as well give it a go."

"No," Dan said. "I don't imagine our suspect would stop to browse the secondhand books. Besides, it'll be the same story there as everywhere else."

"I expect you're right." Alan adopted a Devon accent. "Well, m'dear, we get loads of day-trippers and then there's all the folks in holiday cottages, so there's people coming and going all the time." Alan sighed, dropping the accent as he added, "In other words, our outsider is a needle in a haystack."

"I ought to have known. It's an attractive little town, so there are bound to be plenty of people wandering around in search of tea and scones."

"Speaking of which, I'm a bit peckish," Alan said. "There's a cafe along the road, or…"

"Or what?"

"Well, there are several pubs, and it is almost lunchtime."

"So it is," Dan said. "I could do with a bite to eat, and while we're there, we can keep our eyes and ears open. We might learn something."

"Yes, there's bound to be a bit of gossip about Zadie by now, so there might be a useful rumour or two floating around. It's worth a shot, anyway. We'll try the Bull Inn. If memory serves, they have a decent menu, so you stand a chance of getting something vegan, and the beer's not bad either."

"That sounds ideal."

"Good. Motion carried." Alan set off at a brisk pace, and Dan fell in beside him.

DAN SMILED AS HE STEPPED INTO THE PUB. FROM THE OUTSIDE, THE Bull Inn had looked like any other pub he might've found on the high street of a British town, but inside, it was a different matter. Light and airy, the inn had been artfully decorated in the style of a modern gastropub, and the air carried the aromas of freshly cooked food and well-kept ale.

The place was moderately busy, the clientele sitting in small groups and chatting as they sipped their drinks or perused the menu.

"I haven't been here for quite a while," Alan said. "They've smartened it up. Let's get the drinks in. We can find a table afterward."

"Okay, but you must let me buy you lunch. It's the least I can do."

"It's all right. There's no need."

"Yes, there is. You're giving up your time to help me when you should be at home, working on your book and resting that leg."

"My leg's fine. I've got it strapped up, and I can catch up with my writing when I get home. Anyway, I wanted to come." Alan paused. "I'll tell you what, you can get the drinks in."

"Fair enough."

At the bar, the barman was busy pulling a pint, but he

acknowledged them with a nod and said, "I'll be right with you, gents."

"There's no rush," Alan replied, studying the row of gleaming beer pumps. To Dan, he added, "Since you're driving, I may as well have a pint. I fancy the guest beer: Tawton Session Ale."

"I'll have a half of the same."

While he waited, Dan watched the barman deliver a drink to a man sitting alone at the end of the bar. The customer seemed oddly out of place. He sat with his back very straight, and his dark-blue suit and tie, paired with a white shirt, gave him the appearance of a man in a uniform. He was broad shouldered and clean shaven, and his crew cut emphasised the broad dome of his skull.

As if sensing he was being watched, the man's head snapped around, and he focused on Dan, his gaze sharp.

Dan offered a smile, but the man did not return it, and when Dan looked away he had the impression that the man would continue to study him from the end of the bar.

"Making friends?" Alan asked in an undertone.

"I think not," Dan replied. "But I might've found someone we'll need to speak to later."

"Is he a stranger to the town, do you think? He looks like a nightclub doorman."

"No, that's wide of the mark. From the way he chatted with the barman, I'd say he's a regular customer. From his point of view, we're the outsiders, and he has good reason to regard us with suspicion."

"Us? We're not doing anything wrong."

"His opinion might differ, because I'd lay odds on that man being John Callaway's driver."

Alan's mouth formed an O, and lowering his voice, he said, "You could be right. We ought to introduce ourselves to him."

"Not yet. Let's keep our powder dry for a while. Don't stare at him. Relax. Try to blend in." Dan gestured to a stack of menus on the bar. "Could you pass me one of those?"

"Sure." Alan grabbed a couple of menus, passing one to Dan, and they studied the laminated pages in silence.

"Right, what can I get you?"

Dan looked up to see the barman eying him expectantly. Dan ordered their drinks, and as the barman began pulling the pints, Dan said, "It's a nice place you've got here. I'm surprised I haven't heard of it. We only live a few miles away."

"Is that right?" the barman replied, though it sounded as if that might be his stock answer to any remarks his customers might make.

"We live in Embervale," Alan explained. "Dan's my neighbour. I'm showing him the best pubs in the area. Are you the landlord?"

"That, I am. Andy Butcher. Name's above the door." He smiled, his eyes bright. "Always glad to meet a new customer, especially a thirsty one, and you gents look like you appreciate a decent pint, so you've come to the right place. You won't find better." He lifted their drinks as if offering them in evidence, then he placed them reverently on the bar.

"Looks good." Alan lifted his glass and held it up for inspection for a moment before taking a sip. He smacked his lips. "Excellent. I can see we'll have to drop in more often."

"Any time. We do a nice selection of food too. Are you ready to order, or do you need a few more minutes?"

"I'm ready now," Alan replied. "I'd like the ham ploughman's, please."

Andy tapped on the till's screen, then looked to Dan.

"I'll have the vegan salad bowl," Dan said. "And that's all for the moment."

"Can I tempt you to a portion of chips on the side?" Andy asked. "They're very good."

"Oh, I'm not sure." Alan glanced at Dan.

"Not for me, thanks," Dan said. "But you go ahead, Alan."

"No, I think I'd better not." Alan smiled wistfully. "Another time, perhaps."

"Right you are."

They paid for their food separately, and Dan asked for the drinks to be added to his bill. The transactions completed, Andy made to move away but Dan raised a hand to catch his attention.

"Before you go, I was wondering if we might ask you a couple of questions."

"What can I do for you?"

"Do you know Zadie Barrington? She lives in the town."

Andy's expression became instantly more guarded. "I've heard the name, but she doesn't come in here. Why do you ask?"

"We're working for her," Dan said. "We're looking into an incident that happened at her house on Sunday night."

"Are you with the police?"

"No, I've been hired by Ms Barrington to look into the case," Dan replied. "I'm acting as her representative."

Andy's expression immediately became more closed. "You're not reporters, are you? Because if you are, I've got nothing to say. I don't spread gossip."

"We're not journalists," Alan replied. "We're private investigators."

"In that case, you must have some ID. A card or something."

"I can give you a business card." Dan took out his wallet and offered a card. He'd ordered them recently, and it still gave him a thrill to see the words printed in bold type on the front: *Dan Corrigan, Private Investigator*.

Andy took the card and glanced at it, unimpressed. "No, I mean, don't you have something proper, something official."

"You don't need a licence in this country," Alan said. "But we're legitimate investigators. We have something of a track record."

"If you say so." Andy offered the card back, but Dan shook his head.

"Please, keep it. If something comes up later, you might want to get in touch."

"About what?"

"Someone trespassed on Ms Barrington's property, and she's concerned about it, we're—"

Dan was cut short by Andy's laughter. "Is that all? Someone traipsed through her garden by mistake, so she hired you to track them down. Blimey, who does she think she is?"

"That's not what happened," Dan stated, keeping his voice level. "A threat was made, and we suspect that the guilty party is not from around here. It's probably someone who travelled here specifically to bother Ms Barrington."

"Oh." Andy's laughter was gone now, and when he went on, his tone was grave. "I don't like the sound of that, but I don't reckon someone like that would come in here. We get a respectable type of customer: a lot of couples, families, people who've retired. Take a look around, you'll see what I mean."

"So if a man came in on his own, a man you hadn't seen before, you might notice," Dan said. "Especially if he seemed nervous or agitated."

"Blokes come in by themselves all the time. Tourists, usually. Hikers, campers, cyclists, birdwatchers. And I dare say we get a few holidaymakers who slip out while their wives are putting the kids to bed. Sometimes they like to chat, but they usually come in here for a quiet drink and maybe a bite to eat before they go on their way. If they want to be left on their own, that's fine by me. So long as they're happy, I leave them to it."

"Were you working on Sunday night?" Alan asked.

Andy studied Alan for a second, then he nodded. "I was here, and as it happens, we did have a few blokes on their own, but I didn't see anyone acting strange. Like I said, this is a respectable pub. Now, I have work to do, so if you don't mind, I'll be getting on with it."

"Just one more question." Dan leaned forward, lowering his voice. "The man at the end of the bar. Do you know him?"

Andy stood tall, folding his arms. "Yes, I know him, and he's all right, so leave him be. If I hear you've been bothering my customers with your daft questions, I'll have to ask you to leave."

Before Dan could reply, Alan said, "Don't worry, We wouldn't dream of disturbing anyone. We really just came in for some lunch."

"That's all right then." Having had the last word, Andy walked away, so Dan and Alan took their drinks and went to find somewhere to sit down.

Dan chose a table in a corner of the room, sitting with his back against the wall so he could keep an eye on the other customers. After a sip of beer, he said, "You know, Alan, we won't get far as investigators if you go around promising not to ask questions."

"There was no point in antagonising the man. Sometimes you have to pour oil on troubled waters."

"And sometimes you have to jam your foot into somebody's door or they'll slam it in your face."

"People who feel threatened never cooperate," Alan replied. "And you might want to bear that in mind, because we're about to have company."

"Oh yes. This could be useful." Dan watched as the man who'd sat alone at the end of the bar drew closer. Viewed while seated, the man had looked well built, but on his feet he was even more imposing, and he moved with purpose and precision, like a hunter closing in on his prey. There was no doubt about his destination; his hard-eyed stare flicked between Dan and Alan, defying them to move.

Dan sat back, his arms resting casually on the armrests of his chair, and from the corner of his eye he noted Alan attempting a similar show of nonchalance.

The man came to a halt in front of them, then he gave them a no-nonsense smile; the smile of a man who was used to taking charge of any situation.

A policeman's smile, Dan thought, and he did his best to match the man's expression, locking eyes with him. The man's silence was an implicit challenge. The first one to speak would lose, and Dan refused to break that deadlock.

"Hello," Alan said. "Can we help you with something?"

"That depends," the man replied, his voice gravelly and deep. "Mind if I join for a minute?"

Without waiting for a reply he grabbed a chair, clamping one hand on the chair's back and swinging the heavy wooden seat into position.

He sat, leaning toward them, his elbows on the table. "Forgive me for butting in," he said, sounding anything but apologetic, "but I couldn't help overhearing what you were saying, and we need to talk."

"I agree," Dan replied. "You're John Callaway's driver, yes?"

The man remained impassive, but his surprise was betrayed by a tiny twitch of his eyebrows. "I work for Mr Callaway, and it's part of my job to look after his security, so you need to fill me in."

We don't need to do any such thing, Dan thought, but he bit back the words. This man might have an attitude, but he could be useful. He was a man who kept his ear to the ground, and if they could get him on-side, he might provide a way for them to talk to John Callaway.

"Actually, we'd planned to have a chat with you later," Dan said. "But now is as good a time as any. I'm Dan Corrigan and this is Alan Hargreaves. You are?"

"Benny. Benny Washington."

"Nice to meet you, Benny." Dan extended his hand for a shake, and after a moment's delay, Benny shook hands.

"So what's happened over at Zadie's place?" Benny asked. "You mentioned a threat. Was anyone hurt?"

"Thankfully, no," Alan said. "The threat wasn't made in person, but we're taking it seriously nonetheless."

"Tell me what happened. Let's not beat about the bush."

"We have to consider our client's confidentiality," Dan replied. "But I don't think you need to worry about your employer's safety. This was a specific threat made against Ms Barrington."

"What kind of threat? Was it online?"

"No, it was in the form of a note."

"Delivered by hand or in the post?"

Dan hesitated. He wanted to keep a tight rein on the facts surrounding the case, but Benny wasn't going to help unless he was given something in return.

"Come on," Benny said. "You're keeping something quiet. Why is that? What's got Zadie so worried she called in a private investigator?"

"Okay," Dan replied. "If I tell you what happened, will you arrange for an—"

"I don't do deals behind my boss's back," Benny interrupted. "I'll make this simple for you. I'm paid to protect Mr Callaway, and if there's a problem affecting his nearest neighbour, I need to know about it. Do you understand?"

"Yes, I appreciate your concern," Dan said. "I can tell you that there was an intruder at Ms Barrington's home. She was out at the time, so no one was hurt, but a threatening note was left."

"Right." Benny seemed to think this over. "Has someone called the police?"

Dan nodded. "A couple of detectives have been out to take a look around. They're following it up."

"That's good," Benny said. "Any suspects?"

"Not as yet," Dan replied. "We've only just begun our enquiries, but we'll find the person responsible."

Benny grunted under his breath. "Well, you won't get far by asking the locals. They'll know you're not from around here and they'll clam up, believe me."

"We're locals ourselves," Alan protested. "We live in Embervale."

"That's miles away, but it's even smaller than this place, so maybe you'll understand. It's quiet here, and that's the way people like it. If there's trouble, they won't want to get involved."

"Perhaps you might have more luck," Dan suggested. "If you were to ask around, you might come up with something useful for us or for the police. After all, you seem to have settled into the community pretty well. You're a regular here, and I understand you attend the church every Sunday."

"Who told you that?"

Dan smiled. "We have our sources."

"And I have mine," Benny said. "I'll keep my eyes and ears open, but if I share with you, you've got to share with me. If there's some nutter prowling around, I need to know about it."

"Fair enough," Dan replied. "*Quid pro quo.*"

Benny held out his hand. "Give me your details, and if anything comes up, I'll be in touch."

Dan retrieved a card from his wallet, and as he offered it, Benny snatched it from his hand and stood up, stuffing the card in his pocket without so much as a glance.

"Here's my number." Benny rattled off a string of digits, and Alan hurriedly produced his notebook and scribbled them down.

"Got it," Alan said. "Thank you."

Benny focussed his stare on each of them in turn. "Do *not* call me unless absolutely necessary. Is that clear?"

"Understood," Dan replied.

"Good. See you around." Benny turned on his heel and strode away.

"That went better than I expected," Alan said.

"Do you think so? We told him all we know, but he didn't give us a single thing."

"Yes, but we've got his number and we've opened a dialogue. That's a start. You never know what might come of it."

"True." Dan took a sip of his drink. Alan had been right; the beer was good, very good. All in all, they hadn't had a bad morning. As well as making contact with Benny, they'd met some of Zadie's friends and witnessed some of the tensions within her social circle. They were making headway, and at this rate, it wouldn't be long before they could draw the net tighter, focusing their attention more closely. In the hunt for clues, it was always best to start with an open mind, gathering background information and putting the pieces together until the bigger picture emerged. Only then would he know where to look more closely.

Dan took another sip of beer, his gaze roaming around the

pleasant pub, and he spotted a woman backing out through a swinging door, a tray in her hands. She caught Dan's eye and smiled as she headed for their table.

Evidently, Alan had seen her too. He was sitting up straight, alert. "I think that might be our lunch. Things are looking up."

"Yes," Dan replied. "They certainly are."

CHAPTER 10

D I Spiller drew his car to a halt outside the wrought-iron gate and wound down the window. A stainless-steel intercom unit was set into the brick pillar at one side of the gateway, and Spiller reached out and pressed the button. Almost immediately, the speaker crackled and a male voice said, "Yes?"

"Detective Inspector Timothy Spiller, Devon and Cornwall police. I'm here to see Mr Callaway."

"Can I see some ID, please?"

Spiller spotted a small lens in the intercom's panel. He held up his warrant card and waited.

"Thank you, Detective Inspector. That's fine. I'm opening the gate for you now. You can drive right up to the house."

"Will do."

Somehow, Spiller expected there to be a buzz and a metallic clang as the gates opened, but they glided open silently. He drove through an avenue of stately chestnut trees, admiring the landscaped grounds as he passed. Perfect lawns were surrounded by flower beds, each one crowded with colour from blooms and foliage alike. Every hedge had been trimmed with geometrical precision, and beyond one of them he glimpsed the top of a tall chain-link fence. A tennis court, perhaps.

How the other half live, Spiller thought, but he had to admit that the grounds had a certain elegance. There were none of the gaudy flourishes that he might have expected from a Hollywood star: no faux Greek temples or mock Roman statues. The grounds had been made to look more like an idyllic English country garden than anything he'd ever seen: a picture book vision made reality.

The winding drive took him to a gravelled area, and as he left the shade of the chestnut trees, Spiller saw the house for the first time.

He'd expected the place to be grand, but nothing had quite prepared him for the Georgian splendour of Mr Callaway's house. The stone walls were pristine, as if they'd been laid just yesterday, but it was the windows that took his breath away. There seemed to be an impossible number of tall sash windows, each one glittering in the sunlight.

"They must take some cleaning," Spiller murmured. All that glass would let the heat out too, not that Mr Callaway would need to worry about that. A quick online search had been enough for Spiller to see that the man was worth millions.

There were no other cars parked on the gravel, so Spiller left his Volvo saloon in front of the main door and walked up the stone steps that led to the entrance. He'd barely reached the top step when the gloss black wooden door swung open, and a man stepped forward to meet him.

"Good afternoon, Inspector," the man said. "I'm Saunders, Mr Callaway's personal assistant. We spoke on the phone earlier."

"Ah yes. Thank you for arranging this interview, Mr Saunders. I appreciate that it was short notice."

"It was no trouble. Mr Callaway is always pleased to assist the police. But before we go on, if you don't mind, may I take a closer look at your ID? One can't be too careful."

"Very sensible." Spiller presented his card, and the man leaned forward to scrutinise it.

"Thank you, Detective Inspector. Much appreciated."

"No problem. Since we're being so formal, could you give me your first name, Mr Saunders?"

"William."

Spiller whipped out his notebook and scribbled down the man's name. "Thank you, Mr Saunders. If Mr Callaway is ready, we may as well crack on. That way, I'll take up as little of his time as possible."

"That would be appreciated," Saunders replied, but he showed no signs of moving from the doorway. He cleared his throat nervously. "On the phone, you weren't entirely clear about the purpose of your visit. We understand that there was a break-in at a neighbouring property, but for an inspector to come all this way, we began to wonder if it wasn't more serious. Should we be worried?"

"That's something I'd prefer to discuss with Mr Callaway in person."

"I see." Saunders' lips twitched as though he were searching for the right words. "There's just one more thing. On your way in, you didn't see any reporters or photographers waiting by the gates, did you? Only, Mr Callaway would prefer it if the press didn't know the police had been to call."

"There was no one there at all. Do you get many reporters hanging around?"

"Not usually. It depends on what else is happening at the time."

"I understand," Spiller said. "Reporters are like flies, aren't they? Nothing gets them buzzing like the whiff of scandal."

Saunders looked appalled. "There's never been anything like that. Mr Callaway is a committed Christian, and to him, that really means something. It's part of who he is, and he genuinely does his best to live a good life. All I meant was that Mr Callaway attracts attention from the press when there's something newsworthy, especially when it's awards season. He's been nominated for Academy Awards many times over."

"And he's won three," Spiller said. "I'd tell you the title of each film, but I'm sure you already know."

"Yes. I'm tempted to test you, but somehow, I think you'd be spot-on. You seem like a man who does his homework."

Spiller shrugged off the compliment. "I could say that I like to be prepared, but the truth is, I enjoy a good film as much as the next man, and Mr Callaway has made more than his fair share." Spiller gestured to the door. "Shall we?"

"Yes. Forgive me for keeping you chatting." Saunders offered a hesitant smile, then he ushered Spiller inside, leading him through a grand hallway and into a spacious drawing room.

A tall, silver-haired man stood in front of a marble fireplace, his head bowed slightly as though he was staring into the empty grate. He turned slowly, his gaze locking on Spiller, and there it was, the famous Callaway smile: blue eyes sparkling, and an instant sense of warmth and sincerity.

Spiller found himself grinning in return, but that wouldn't do. He wasn't a fawning fan waiting for the chance of a few words or even a selfie; he was here on official police business.

Spiller straightened his expression and said, "Good afternoon, Mr Callaway. I'm Detective Inspector Spiller of the Devon and Cornwall Police. Thank you for agreeing to see me."

Callaway held out his hands in an expansive gesture. "It's no trouble at all, Inspector. But please, call me John. And have a seat. Can I offer you anything? Tea, coffee, a glass of water? I'd offer you something stronger, but I know what you'd say." Adopting a convincing English accent, he added, "Thank you kindly, sir, but not while I'm on duty."

"That's very impressive," Spiller said. "If I didn't know better, I'd think you were a born Brit."

Callaway shook his head modestly. "Oh, it's nothing really. I've played a number of English parts, and I always try to get the accent right. I've made something of a study of it. Personally, I can't stand it when an actor goes over the top with all that 'cor blimey, mate' and 'gawd bless yer, guv'nor'; it grates on my ear." Callaway sighed. "But look at me, going on about nothing when you've come all this way to see me." He made a downward motion with his hands. "Please, sit. Make yourself comfortable. What about that tea?"

"Nothing for me, thanks." Spiller selected one of the high-backed armchairs that were arranged in a semicircle around the fireplace, and he sat carefully. The chair was clearly an antique, its upholstery embroidered with an elaborate design, and Spiller guessed it would be worth a significant portion of his annual salary.

"Interesting choice," Callaway said. "You took the chair closest to the centre of the room, and you have your back to the window. Now, whichever place I take, I'll be squinting into the light."

"It wasn't deliberate."

"Maybe so, but it's interesting nonetheless." Callaway perched on the seat next to him. "Don't mind my little observations, inspector. I don't mean to play games with you, but as an actor, I take notice of the people around me, especially professional people such as yourself. I like to see how they move, how they react, how they behave in a given situation. You might say I'm a student of human nature. I find it fascinating."

"You'd have made a good detective."

"I believe you're right," Callaway said. "I've played detectives several times, and I took pride in doing my research. I hung around with some real-life cops and I went out on a ride along or two. It was a real education and I've got a lot of respect for the work you do."

"That's always nice to hear, but it's a little different on this side of the Atlantic."

Callaway nodded thoughtfully. "I never got to play an English detective. I was always a man with a badge and a gun: a hero, striving for justice, fighting against the odds. That was a long time ago, of course, but it was great fun. Each movie was completely different, but I enjoyed them all."

"That's not quite true, is it, Mr Callaway? You played Detective Larry Bishop twice, once in *The Long Drop*, and again in *The Final Verdict*."

"You've got me there, Inspector. Guilty as charged. I can see I'll have to be careful what I say with you around. Wait, should I have my lawyer with me?" Callaway chuckled to show he was joking. "I know how you'd feel about that. Cops and lawyers are never going to get along, and that's true the whole world over."

Spiller forced a smile. "This isn't a formal interview, but if you'd like a legal advisor present, that's your prerogative."

"Okay, I get the message. No more fooling around." Callaway made his expression serious. "Tell me, Inspector, what can I do to help?"

"I'm following up an incident that occurred at the house of your neighbour, Ms Barrington."

"The break-in. Yes, I heard about that."

Spiller raised an inquiring eyebrow.

"I have a driver by the name of Benny," Callaway went on. "He tends to know what's going on around here, and he keeps me informed."

"I see. Were you also aware that a threat was made against Ms Barrington?"

"Yes. Benny said something about a note. It sounded pretty odd to me. Should I be concerned?"

"Not unduly. We believe that Ms Barrington was the only target. There's no evidence to suggest otherwise."

"Glad to hear it." Callaway's face fell and he corrected himself quickly. "I mean, I'm sorry to hear this has happened to Zadie—she seems like an admirable young woman—but I'm pleased that we're not dealing with some kind of maniac who might be a threat to everyone."

"I understand, but we are taking the threat against Ms Barrington seriously, so my reasons for visiting are twofold. First and foremost, we need to make sure that everyone is doing their best to keep themselves safe, so I'd like you to consider your personal security."

Callaway waved Spiller's concerns aside. "There are no worries on that score. I had a security firm go over the place with a fine-tooth comb. They upgraded all the locks and fitted an alarm system that's too smart for its own good. Fortunately, Will Saunders knows how it all works, so I leave that side of things to him. He assures me that the place is like Fort Knox."

"Nevertheless, this is a very large house and I presume you have outbuildings and so on."

"Yes, but they're all covered by the alarm system. Will is very detail oriented. He likes to cross every T and dot every I. His mantra is, you can't be too careful."

Spiller nodded. This thumbnail portrait certainly tallied with his impression of William Saunders, and that might be a cause for some optimism when it came to his next question.

"That brings me to the second purpose of my visit," Spiller said. "Do you have any CCTV on the premises?"

"No. I prefer to rely on good old-fashioned locks and bolts."

"How about the camera on the gate, does it record?"

"Again, no. There's no CCTV system here. I don't approve of it. If there's one thing I don't much like about this country, it's the goddamned cameras everywhere. I can hardly walk down the street without a camera following my every move, but everyone here seems to accept it." Callaway leaned forward in his seat. "I read that Britain has more CCTV cameras per head than any other country in the world. Is that right?"

"I couldn't say, but in the right hands—"

"And what do you call the right hands? Who decides?"

"There are rules and regulations. People are entitled to privacy in their own homes, but not in public places."

"What about civil liberties? It seems to me that it's a short walk from a surveillance society to a police state."

"Oh, I think we're a long way from that scenario," Spiller said. "But I can tell you that CCTV is incredibly useful when we're trying to track down criminals. If we could find footage of the person who broke into Ms Barrington's house, we'd be on our way to finding him or her."

"Well, I can't help you, and even if I had cameras all over the place, my answer would be the same. Whoever this clown is, he wouldn't dare trespass on my property. We have fences all around the house and garden, and floodlights in the yard and in front of the house."

"I understand that there's a public footpath that cuts across your land."

Callaway nodded. "I own a few acres of pasture, and you're right about the path, but it's some distance away across the fields. Do you think someone went that way to Zadie's house?"

"It's a possibility we're looking into, but it's too early to say."

"I see. Of course, I can't see the path from indoors, so I can't help you. All I can say is that no one came anywhere near the house that night. If they had, somebody would've spotted them."

"Were you at home on Sunday night?"

"Sunday night, I would've been working in my study. I like to work late into the night. I find the stillness very liberating." Callaway sat back in his chair. "I'm writing a memoir."

"What time did you go to bed?"

"It would've been about two in the morning. Before you ask, I didn't see or hear anything unusual, and I had the shutters open the whole time. Sometimes, when I'm trying to conjure a memory, I stare out into the darkness. It helps me to think."

"Who else would have been in the house that night?"

"Only Harriet. Mrs Yates. She's my housekeeper. She has an apartment on the top floor, but she would've been fast asleep."

"That may be the case, but you never know, she might've heard something. I'd like to have a chat with her while I'm here."

"Ah, she's not here at the moment," Callaway said. "This time on a Tuesday, she'll be out shopping."

"Does she have a mobile phone?"

"Yes, but…" Callaway waggled his hand in the air. "It would be better if you talk to her once she's finished her errands. Harriet's routine is set in stone, and God help anyone who stands in her way."

"I understand. No matter. We can talk later." Spiller pulled a business card from his pocket and passed it to Callaway. "If you could ask Mrs Yates to give me a call, that would be appreciated."

"No problem. I'll pass the message along." Callaway studied the card then tapped it against his fingers as if in thought.

"Is something the matter, sir?" Spiller asked.

"No, not at all. I was just thinking that it seems a shame to upset Harriet when I'm sure she won't be able to help. If she'd heard anything unusual, she'd have mentioned it, but as I said, she'd have been asleep on the top floor. As soon as my dinner things are cleared away, Harriet turns in for the night. If I'm an owl, Mrs Yates is very much a lark. She rises with the sun and has everything in order long before I tumble out of bed in the morning."

"There's no need to concern yourself, Mr Callaway. I won't keep Mrs Yates from her work for more than a few minutes. It's a formality, but a necessary one. I'm sure you understand."

"I guess so. Is there anything else, Inspector?"

"We're almost done. Does your assistant live in the house too?"

"Will? No, he works office hours. Most days he leaves around five, but he sometimes stays on for an hour or two, especially if he needs to talk to someone back in the States."

"Because of the time difference," Spiller suggested.

"Got it in one, Inspector."

"What about the driver you mentioned?"

"Benny is only here during the day. He'll stay late if I need him, but he likes to get back to his own home at night. On Sunday, I sent him home in the afternoon. I wasn't planning on going out, so there was no need for him to wait around."

"So apart from Mrs Yates, you're usually alone here during the evenings. No family?"

Callaway's expression tightened. "I'm divorced. I have a son and a daughter, but they're all grown up. They're back in the States."

"That must be hard, having your only family so far away."

"Not really. We have video calls all the time, and besides, they have their own lives. As a parent, you have to give your kids room to grow. They know where I am if they need me." Callaway smiled. "How about you, do you have kids?"

Spiller shook his head. "Going back to the matter in hand, how would you characterise your relationship with Ms Barrington?"

"We get along fine. We don't know each other well, but as a neighbour, she's perfect. I couldn't want for anyone better."

"I see." Spiller made a note in his book, taking his time, watching Callaway from the corner of his eye. The man seemed ill at ease, and when he'd spoken, his expression had been out of kilter with his fulsome praise of Zadie Barrington. There was something he wasn't saying, and in Spiller's experience, a pause in the proceedings often helped. Silence weighed heavily on people who had something to hide; it nudged them into saying more than they'd intended. But Callaway was apparently content to sit and wait without speaking, his blue eyes focused on Spiller and his lips firmly closed.

He's an old hand at this game, Spiller thought. *He's been interviewed more times than I've had hot dinners.*

Spiller closed his notebook and pocketed it. "That's all for now, Mr Callaway. Thank you very much." He stood, and Callaway followed suit.

"I'll leave you to it," Spiller said. "I can see myself out."

"No, I'll have Will show you the way."

"That's not necessary, sir."

"Perhaps not, but it's the way I'd like it." Callaway produced a phone from his pocket and tapped the screen before pressing it to his ear. "Will, Inspector Spiller is ready to go." A pause. "Thanks."

Smiling, Callaway lowered his phone. "He'll be here in a second. Will is nothing if not efficient."

"Okay. You have my contact details, Mr Callaway, so if you think of anything, or you see anything suspicious, please don't hesitate to get in touch."

"Naturally, I'll do anything to help, Inspector. Anything."

Callaway's tone was so overwhelmingly sincere that Spiller was lost for words. *This must be what it's like*, he thought, *to play a part alongside such an accomplished actor.*

The moment was broken by the appearance of Saunders, and Spiller nodded to Callaway then allowed himself to be led to the front door.

Outside, Saunders said, "You can drive up to the gate. I'll open it when you get there."

"There's a camera on this side?" Spiller asked.

"A motion sensor. I'll know when you're there." Saunders clasped his hands together. "I trust that you were able to find out everything you needed to know."

"We'll see. I'd like Mrs Yates to call me when she gets a moment, but otherwise, I think we're done. If the situation changes, I may need to come back, but otherwise, we shan't be bothering Mr Callaway again."

"That's great to hear." Saunders looked genuinely relieved. "I mean, you're welcome back at any time, Inspector, but Mr Callaway lives quietly, and he doesn't much like to be disturbed."

"Living here, I imagine he gets all the peace he could want. It's a long way from the glitz and glamour of Hollywood."

"Thankfully, yes."

"No more films in the offing?"

Saunders wagged a warning finger. "No fishing, Inspector. The film business is very secretive, so I couldn't possibly comment. It's more than my job's worth."

"Understood. What about this book he's working on? Is he really writing it himself? I thought most celebrities used ghost writers."

"You don't know Mr Callaway. He came from a poor background and climbed his way up by sheer determination. He's worked hard his whole life, and he doesn't mind getting his hands dirty. He's very self-reliant, and he has a stronger work ethic than anyone I've ever known. He puts me to shame."

"Rags to riches, eh? Good for him. He's obviously done well for himself." Spiller gazed up at the rows of impressive windows. "All those rooms for two people."

"Two?" Saunders' expression cleared as he understood. "Ah, you mean Mrs Yates. I rarely see her. She works so quietly we forget she's there. As for the house, it's all relative, isn't it? It may seem big to you and me, but Mr Callaway owns several properties, and I believe his place in France is even grander than this one."

"Does he spend much time here?"

"Quite a bit. I'm sure we'll continue to move around as the need arises, but for the time being, Mr Callaway is working on his book, and for that, he needs peace and quiet. Hopefully, you'll soon sort out whatever is going on with Ms Barrington, and then life will return to normal, and Mr Callaway will get back to his routine."

"Let's hope so. Thanks for your help, Mr Saunders."

Spiller glanced back at the house as he made his way to the car. A figure stood at an upstairs window, the tall outline unmistakeable. Mr Callaway was watching him leave.

Spiller raised a hand in acknowledgement, but the gesture wasn't returned, and Callaway backed away, slipping out of sight.

Had Callaway gone upstairs for the sole purpose of making sure his visitor left the premises? If he had, it was a slightly odd way to behave, but it was understandable. Callaway liked his privacy; he'd said as much, and Saunders had emphasised the fact. So why was Spiller suddenly uneasy?

There's something not quite right here, Spiller decided, but he couldn't for the life of him guess what that might be.

CHAPTER 11

D an followed Alan along the leafy public footpath, pushing through the bracken and nettles that seemed determined to slow them down. They'd been given directions to the path by a woman who worked in the pub. She'd come to clear their table and Alan had made several flattering remarks about the food. Basking in Alan's praise, she'd been more than happy to point them in the direction of the path, chatting cheerfully as she'd clattered the crockery. Her Devon accent had been particularly broad, and though Dan hadn't admitted it, he'd found her long series of instructions hard to follow. Still, Alan had apparently understood, so they'd set off in good spirits, buoyed up by their lunch.

But that had been a good twenty minutes ago.

"Is this definitely the right path?" Dan asked. "We're heading too far away from the town, aren't we?"

"This is the one, all right," Alan replied. "When we reach the river we'll turn back toward Zadie's house, and we'll cut through a field belonging to Mr Callaway."

"Are you sure?"

Alan glanced back over his shoulder. "Ye of little faith. I'll get you there."

"Okay. Maybe we'll be able to figure out where Zadie had a run-in with her famous neighbour. Ouch!" Dan stopped and rubbed the back of his hand. "Bloody thing."

"Bramble?" Alan asked.

"No, it was a dog rose." Dan inspected the scratch. The thorn had caught him where the skin was thin, and a trickle of blood oozed from the wound, but he wasn't going to let Alan see that.

"All right?" Alan asked.

"Fine."

Alan smiled. "A dog rose, eh? I'm impressed. When you came to Devon, you didn't know a dandelion from a daffodil."

"That's a bit of an exaggeration. Believe it or not, there are plenty of wild plants in London. When I was a kid, I was always getting covered in goosegrass or stung by nettles. We used to rub nettle stings with dock leaves. I'm sure you approve of that sort of thing."

"That's because it works, although some say the ribwort plantain is better."

"I doubt whether it makes any difference," Dan said. "The effect is psychological, or maybe it's the rubbing that makes it feel better. It's got nothing to do with the actual leaf."

"I disagree, but you have to use the back of the leaf. The rubbing releases the sap from the leaf's veins. Anyway, you must've thought it worked, or you wouldn't have kept doing it."

"Touché. It goes to show how we can convince ourselves of anything if we put our minds to it, especially when we want to feel better. It's a self-defence mechanism." Dan paused. "It makes me wonder about this case. Doesn't it strike you as odd that Zadie thinks *everyone* loves her?"

"She might be a little too naive for her own good," Alan said. "On the other hand, she seems like a very positive person, so when something negative comes along she can probably let it go, forget all about it. It's not a bad way to be."

"Perhaps, but the more I think about it, the more I'm convinced that Natalya, or someone else, is shielding Zadie to some extent. We both know what a cesspit the internet can be, but to Zadie, it's all hearts and flowers."

Alan nodded. "We ought to have a quiet chat with Natalya. She knows more about all this than she's letting on."

"Agreed. If we press on along this path, we should be able to find our way back to Zadie's house, shouldn't we?"

"Yes. I keep telling you, Dan, I know where I'm going."

"Just checking. I was thinking we could drop in and have a chat with Natalya and Zadie. With a bit of luck, Zadie's friends will have gone, and it'll be easier to talk."

"They're an argumentative bunch, that's for sure," Alan said. "Fortunately for us, they're all in the clear. They were with Zadie while the break-in was happening."

"That doesn't mean they don't know anything about it. We may have to talk to them again, but we'll tackle them one at a time. When they're together, there's too much going on, too much conflict. We'll come to them later. In the meantime, we'll concentrate on Zadie and her immediate neighbour."

"That sounds like a plan. Let's go." Alan marched onward, and Dan followed, surreptitiously taking out a tissue and then cleaning the blood from his hand.

The surrounding vegetation grew taller and denser as they went along, but Dan noticed that some of the fresh growth of bracken had been trampled flat, the young stems crushed. "Someone's definitely been this way," he said. "Dog walkers, I suppose."

"And anglers. The Upper Teign has its own fishing association. I believe there are salmon, but I've never seen any."

"So there could potentially be quite a few people heading toward Mr Callaway's property. I wonder how he feels about that. He was angry when he thought Zadie was trespassing on his land."

"He apologised afterward," Alan replied. "Personally, I'm withholding judgement until we meet the man. I've seen him interviewed on TV and he came across as rather waspish, but that's his public persona. In real life, he might be completely different."

"True, but according to Philippa, he's put a huge iron gate

across his driveway, so we can assume he values his privacy. He's unlikely to be happy with strangers tramping through his fields whenever they feel like it. And I suspect that Benny would dearly like to throw up a chain-link fence topped with razor wire."

"I'll give you that, but Mr Callaway must've known about the public footpath when he bought the house. His solicitor will have explained it to him. They always look into rights of way."

"Film stars have people to take care of paperwork," Dan said. "Callaway can afford to handle things at arm's length, and as an American, he might not have fully understood the implications. He wouldn't have known that people get hot under the collar whenever anyone interferes with a public footpath."

"The Ramblers Association don't like it, that's for sure," Alan said. "But Mr Callaway seems to be taking local sensibilities into account. He contributes to local causes, so I suspect he's trying to fit in."

"We'll find out when we meet him, but that may have to wait until another time. For now, I need to see the lie of the land. Zadie's intruder could've come this way, and if we're lucky, he'll have left a trail."

They resumed their progress, and it wasn't long before Dan heard the sound of running water. The path became easier as it followed the bank of the River Teign, the hard earth worn smooth by the passage of feet. Dan was used to seeing the Teign as a lugubrious stream, but here it showed a different face, splashing and foaming as it tumbled over the rocks. The noise of it filled his ears, and Dan found himself watching the gushing water, mesmerised by its glittering surface, the river ever-changing and yet somehow always the same.

As they followed the river's gentle curves, Dan said, "You can see why people come here. It's a beautiful spot."

"Yes, and this must be where the anglers come. The trout like to hide beneath the ripples, and all that churning oxygenates the water. They like that too."

"Who does, the trout or the anglers?"

"The fish, of course," Alan replied. "Lots of oxygen, lots of prey in the water. It's like a conveyor belt bringing food downstream. All the fish have to do is wait and snap up any juicy nymphs that come their way."

"They conserve their energy, take the path of least resistance."

"That's often the way with predators," Alan said. "It makes you think, doesn't it? Is that what we're dealing with here? Someone lurking beneath the surface, biding their time?"

"I wouldn't be surprised. It's interesting that the intruder broke in when the house was empty. That could mean they've been watching the house, but they didn't want a confrontation. Not yet, anyway."

Alan nodded thoughtfully. "You think they'll come back when Zadie's at home?"

"I'm afraid so. Leaving the note shows a degree of premeditation. They may well have written it before they entered the house, and that would imply they have a plan. They'll be back, but we have no way of knowing when or where. They might even try to catch Zadie when she's away from home. We'll need to talk to her about her routine."

"Good idea. The sooner the better."

They walked on, pausing briefly by a deep pool where the river widened, and the water ran slow. "Another good place to fish?" Dan asked.

"I'm not so sure about that. When the surface is so calm, any little splash spooks the fish, sends them racing to the bottom. You'd have to cast very gently." Alan studied the water for a moment, then he bent down quickly as if something had caught his eye. "Someone's been here."

"What have you found?"

"A bit of discarded fishing line. A leader. It probably got caught on something, so someone threw it away." Alan tutted as he extricated a length of thin nylon line from the low-growing plants on the river's bank. "It's irresponsible. This stuff doesn't break down naturally. It'll be here forever, and birds can get tangled in it." Alan rolled the line into a loop. "There's litter too. Some people have no idea." Alan plucked something from the vegetation and tucked it into his pocket along with the line as he stood up. "That's my good deed for the day. Ready to move on?"

"Sure."

A short while later they met a wooden fence that looked newly erected, the posts and rails still clean, the green wood preservative still fresh. There was a stile for walkers to continue on the path, and beside it a sign: *Please stick to the path. Dogs must be kept on a leash.*

"I think we can assume we're about to enter Mr Callaway's domain," Dan said.

"Yes, but you'd think someone would've told him we say *lead* over here, not *leash.*"

"Maybe they didn't want to contradict the boss. Would you have the nerve to tell the great John Callaway he's using the wrong word?"

"Probably not," Alan admitted. "But I don't mind cutting through his field. It's a public footpath after all. Shall we go and explore?"

"There's a stile. How's your leg holding up?"

"Not bad. It gives me a twinge now and then, but I think the exercise is doing it good. I'm ready when you are."

Dan and Alan climbed over the stile and found themselves in a lush meadow, emerald grass rippling in the breeze. A clear path ran along the field's edge, separated from the rest of the meadow by a low barbed wire fence. Like the stile, the fenceposts looked new and the wire still gleamed. Aside from that, there was not much else to see.

Dan searched in vain for a glimpse of John Callaway's house, but it must've been hidden by the tall, dense hedges that marked the field's other three sides.

"This must be where Zadie bumped into Mr Callaway," Alan said. "Presumably, before he had that fence put up."

"Possibly, but how would he have known she was here? She couldn't have been seen from the house, and there are no signs of animals being kept in here, so it's not as if he could've been tending to a horse or something."

"Maybe he was out for a walk around his estate," Alan suggested. "Taking the air, master of all he surveys. Lucky man." Alan took a deep breath as he gazed across the rolling expanse of perfect grassland. "An idyllic spot."

"Yes. Isn't it just?"

Alan caught Dan's eye and said, "No."

"What?"

"You were about to say, let's hop over the fence and take a look around, see if we can bump into Mr Callaway."

"It had crossed my mind," Dan admitted. "But I wouldn't like to meet him on those terms. We have to be smarter than that."

"Good lord. Is that a hint of subtlety creeping in?"

"I'll ignore that remark." Dan checked his watch. "Let's go. I want to see how long it takes to get from here to Zadie's house."

They set off at a brisk pace, exiting the field via another stile, and seven minutes later a wall of mellowed stone came into view. A low wooden gate was set into the wall, and above it, Zadie's thatched house was clearly visible across the large and untamed garden.

"We may as well go up to the house," Alan said. "I'm not sure what we gained by taking the footpath, but it's given me a thirst. I could do with a cup of tea."

"We're not done yet. Let's split up and search the garden. There could be a footprint or something."

"Okay, but we're being watched." Alan nodded toward the house, and Dan spotted a figure on the scaffolding: a man facing them and standing stock still.

"It's Shaun," Alan went on. "What do you make of him?"

"I'm not sure," Dan said in an undertone. "There's something odd about him, but I can't tell if he's being secretive or if he's a naturally reclusive character. He works on his own all day, so I wonder how much contact he has with others. You can bet he's never met anyone like Zadie before. I expect he doesn't quite know how to deal with her."

"Him and me, both." Alan looked around the garden. "I'll start over by that shrubbery while you take those old flower beds. Okay?"

"Why not? Keep your eyes peeled."

"Naturally," Alan said. "And you'd better watch yourself. There are some old-fashioned rose bushes that have gone a bit wild, and you don't want to get scratched. Again."

"Very funny."

"I do my best. I'll see you up at the house in five minutes."

"Make it ten," Dan said. "Our intruder will have left a sign somewhere. We just need to watch out for it."

"Will do."

Alan ambled across the garden and disappeared behind an untidy clump of overgrown shrubs, while Dan picked his way along a neglected gravel path. It took him on a winding journey between patches of earth that had once been flower beds but which now played host to an assortment of weeds and wild flowers. The gravel path was unlikely to hold any footprints, so he concentrated instead on the sprawling rose bushes. Anyone stumbling through the garden after dark could easily have caught their clothing on a thorn and left a trace. But Dan found nothing. He paused to look around, picturing the route an intruder might've taken. They'd have kept to the edge of the garden, sheltering in the shadows cast by the hedges on either side. There might be a footprint or two in the soft soil at the base of the hedges, but before he could check, Alan called out.

"Dan! Over here. I've found something."

Dan hurried to join Alan and found him crouching in front of a rickety wooden bench. Dan squatted beside him.

"Now that is interesting," Dan said. "Well spotted."

Three cigarette stubs lay on the ground, all of them hand rolled. Dan made to pick one of them up, but Alan held out his hand to shield them.

"We shouldn't touch them, Dan. They might be evidence. The police—"

"The police will leave it too late," Dan interrupted. "I'm only going to touch one of them. I'll leave the others, and I'll be careful."

Alan hesitated. "All right but use these." Alan fished in his pocket and produced his Swiss Army knife. He pulled a small pair of stainless-steel tweezers from its handle.

"Thanks." Taking the slim tweezers, Dan plucked up the nearest cigarette stub and sniffed at it. "I'm not an expert, but that's some form of cannabis, isn't it?"

Alan sniffed doubtfully. "I don't know much about these things, but it smells odd. I'll take a photo of it." Alan took out his phone and zoomed in on the cigarette stub, taking several photos.

"All done?" Dan asked.

Alan nodded. "The camera on this thing is amazing. Sharp as a pin. You can see every smear of mud on the cigarette paper. I'll share the photos with you. In fact, I'll make a shared album with a folder for each case, then we'll both be able to see any photos we take."

"Good idea." Dan carefully replaced the stub exactly where he'd found it. "I ought to carry gloves and plastic bags in future."

"Yes, I'll add that to my task list."

Dan waited while Alan tapped on his phone's screen. Where would he be without Alan's methodical approach? Alan was thinking ahead, putting a system in place that would serve them in the future. *He brought his own notebook for goodness' sake*, Dan thought. *He must've bought that before the case had even begun.*

"So who's been smoking in the garden?" Alan said. "It could've been one of Zadie's friends or Natalya. Perhaps Zadie won't tolerate it in the house, so she sends someone out here to indulge."

"I doubt it. There was an ashtray on the table earlier, and there were quite a few cigarette ends in it."

"We'll ask her about it. If her friends have left these stubs, they're not evidence of anything except carelessness." Alan pocketed his phone. "Shall we go inside?"

"Yes. We've spent long enough out here. We're not going to find anything else."

They stood and headed along the path, but before they reached the house, the quiet of the garden was split by a sudden scream: a yell of pain that ended in a deep-throated cry of anguish.

"Go!" Alan called out, but Dan was already running.

CHAPTER 12

D an reached the back door of Zadie's house in seconds. Another cry rang out, and Dan didn't hesitate. Barging in, he dashed along the hallway, calling Zadie's name.

A woman darted out from a doorway, and Dan almost collided with her. "Natalya! Where's Zadie?"

"Upstairs," Natalya said. "But you can't—"

"Call the police," Dan interrupted, and then he was off, racing up the stairs two at a time. At the top, he paused, listening. A woman's moan came from a door at the end of the passageway. Dan sprinted toward the sound, flinging the door open and bursting into the room.

The room was brightly lit, the walls startlingly white. In its centre, Zadie was laid flat on a padded bench, her arms stretched wide. She turned her head with a start, and something crashed to the ground. "My God!" she cried, sitting up sharply, her eyes wild. "What's happened? What's wrong?"

"I..." Dan stared stupidly, taking in Zadie's sports top and leggings, the sheen of sweat on her brow and the pair of dumbbells that lay on the floor where she'd dropped them.

A woman stormed toward him. Her athletic frame was emphasised by her sports gear, her blonde hair tied back in a ponytail. She squared up to Dan, her hands on her hips. "Who the hell are you, and what do you think you're doing, barging in like that? Someone could've been hurt."

"I thought," Dan began, but the woman wasn't about to let him speak.

"Zadie could've pulled a muscle, or if those weights had landed on her foot she'd have been in agony."

Dan held up his hands. "I'm sorry. I heard someone screaming, and I had to check if Zadie was all right."

"She was doing a workout," the woman said, emphasising each word.

"Yes, I can see that, but I didn't know at the time, and as I said, I'm sorry for charging in, but I thought it was for the best."

Zadie let out a sigh. "It's all right, Carly. Give him a break. This is Dan Corrigan. He's the private investigator I told you about, and he meant well." She smiled. "You have to see the funny side, I suppose. I do make a bit of noise when I'm really going for it. It's the chest presses that get to me." To Dan, she added, "This is Carly, my personal trainer. Is Alan with you?"

"Yes, he's right behind me, or he should be anyway." Dan paused, wincing in embarrassment. "I'd better go and talk to Natalya. I told her to call the police."

Dan started for the door, but there were heavy footsteps on the stairs and Alan appeared, his face flushed. Alan looked from Zadie to Carly, and he seemed to deflate, exhaling loudly. "I tried to catch you, Dan. Natalya stopped me downstairs. She explained what Zadie was doing, but I can see I didn't make it in time."

"It's okay," Dan said. "Was Natalya all right? She didn't call the police, did she?"

"She didn't, but she was quite angry with us for charging in."

"Ah, I'd better go and apologise."

"Don't worry about Nat," Zadie said. "She comes across as a bit fierce, but she's a sweetie really. She'll be fine, trust me."

Carly grunted in disapproval. "Whatever. You guys need to get out of here. Zadie won't be finished for at least another twenty minutes, and we don't want to be disturbed."

"Of course," Dan said. "If it's all the same to you, Zadie, we'll wait downstairs. We have a few things we'd like to talk to you about."

"That's fine," Zadie replied. "I won't be long." She stood, wiping a hand across her brow. "I'm done for today, Carly. I'm going to go and grab a shower."

"But we've got another set to get through, and then there's your warm down and stretches."

Zadie shook her head. "Not today. We've had a good session, but my arms are burning. I'm exhausted."

"You've lost your momentum, that's all," Carly protested. "You can't let Dan whatshisname and his mate put you off. We'll soon get you back into the zone, then we can push that bit further."

"Thanks, but no. I've already told you, I'm done."

"I see. Well, it's a shame, but if that's the way you want it, we'll skip straight to the warm down."

"I'll do some stretches in a minute, but you don't need to stay for that, Carly. Why don't you go home early? I'll still pay for the full session, but we'll call it a day, yes?"

"All right. That's no problem, I guess. I'll see you next time." Carly looked as though she'd have liked to say more, but she settled for casting a venomous glance at Dan before making her exit in silence.

Zadie turned to Dan with a smile, as if Carly had already been forgotten. "I won't be long. If you go downstairs, Nat will look after you. Okay?"

"Yes. There's no rush," Dan said. "I'm sorry about…"

"Never mind about that. I'll see you in a few minutes." Zadie made a shooing motion with her hands, but she did it in such a charming way that Dan and Alan smiled sheepishly and did as they were told.

Downstairs they found Carly waiting in the hallway, a small rucksack over her shoulder.

"Listen, about what I said up there," Carly began. "We got off on the wrong foot. It's just that when I'm working I get so caught up in it, you know? And Zadie, she's not just another client to me."

"How so?" Dan asked.

"Don't get me wrong. I look after all my clients. I do my best. This isn't just a job to me; it's my vocation. I try to help people, to give them the tools to break free and live their best lives."

"Very commendable," Dan said. "I'm all for self-improvement."

"Right. But it's not like that with Zadie. She's something else."

Dan nodded. "She's a unique character."

"Yes. That's it. She's unique. Special."

"And yet, someone wanted to frighten her," Dan said. "I presume Zadie told you about what happened the other night."

Carly's face twisted in disgust. "It's horrendous, isn't it? How could anybody even think of such a thing?"

"That's what we aim to find out. How long have you been Zadie's trainer?"

"For about four years now. Closer to five, actually."

"So you knew Zadie before she was famous," Dan said.

"Oh yeah. She wasn't always in such great shape, you know? I helped her to get where she wanted to be."

"When did Zadie come to Devon?" Alan asked.

Carly thought for a moment. "A couple of years ago, give or take. Before that she lived in London; we both did."

"Me too," Dan said. "Whereabouts?"

"Zadie had a flat in Fulham and I lived in Brent with my mum and dad. I couldn't afford to move out, not with London prices."

"What about now?" Dan asked.

"I live in Exeter. I have a little house in St Thomas."

"Very nice," Alan said. "But let me get this right. You upped sticks and moved from London to Devon just so you could work with Zadie?"

"You're damned right. I didn't think twice."

Dan heard the passion in Carly's voice, and it gave him pause for thought. Was Carly's devotion due to loyalty or was there a romantic element to their relationship? On the other hand, perhaps Carly saw Zadie as nothing more than a cash cow, her ticket to a better life.

Choosing his words carefully, Dan said, "Working together all that time, you must've become very close to Zadie."

"Yes and no. I'm her trainer, but we're not friends. I'm a professional. It's who I am."

"I see. Even so, you must talk about things while you're working together. Have you any idea who might want to harm or intimidate Zadie?"

Carly started to shake her head, but then she fixed Dan with a look. "Actually, there was something recently. She mentioned an argument with one of her friends. Who did she say? It was Margaret or Melanie. Something like that."

"Melody?" Alan asked. "Could that be the name you're thinking of?"

"No, I'd have remembered if it was Melody. Let me think. It might've been Mary. Yes, that was it. I'm pretty sure she said Mary."

"We haven't met anyone called Mary yet," Dan said. "What happened? What was the disagreement about?"

"Zadie didn't say, but they fell out over some little thing and this so-called friend turned nasty. Zadie was very upset by it. She's very sensitive to other people's emotions."

Alan whipped out his notebook and made a note. "We'll follow that up. Is there anything else you can think of, any hint of animosity toward Zadie?"

"No. I mean, how could there be? Everyone loves Zadie, don't they?"

Not everyone, Dan thought, but he kept it to himself. For all Carly's talk about professionalism, she seemed almost besotted with her employer, her pupils widening whenever she talked about her. Had her loyalty tipped over the edge into obsession? If so, Carly was someone to watch.

Thanking Carly for her time, Dan handed her one of his

business cards. "If you see or hear anything that makes you worry for Zadie's safety, please get in touch immediately. It might be nothing more than a suspicion or something that makes you uncomfortable, but I'd still like to hear about it. The smallest things can sometimes turn out to be significant."

"I will." Carly studied the card, then she unzipped a pocket on her rucksack and pulled out a phone. "I'll text you my details. We should stay in touch."

She began tapping on her phone, her lips moving as she worked. "There. All done." She beamed at Dan, her expression changing completely. Carly had perfect white teeth, and her smile was broad and warm. Dan guessed that Carly could turn heads if she so desired, and he couldn't help but return her smile.

"You're a runner," Carly stated.

"Yes. How did you know?"

"In my job, you get an eye for these things. What distance do you usually run, half-marathon?"

"I used to, back when I was running on flat pavements, but these days I do quite a lot of hill work, so I often make do with a shorter run."

"That's great for your cardio and your legs, but you could use some work on your upper body, especially your shoulders. Do you spend a lot of time sitting down? Do you work at a desk?"

"Sometimes."

"I thought so. Your posture isn't all it could be. Give me a few weeks and I'll straighten that out for you."

"Thanks but—"

"If you're thinking about the cost, that shouldn't stop you. It would be an investment. Getting into better shape will make you healthier and give you more energy. You'll be more productive, so my sessions will pay for themselves in no time."

"I'm sure you're right," Dan said. "Unfortunately, I don't think I can afford it at the moment."

Carly's smile slipped a little. "I can give you a special rate. Half price for your first couple of sessions. That way, you can try me out, see how well we can work together."

"I'll think about it."

"Great. You have my number. I'll look forward to hearing from you." Carly's gaze flicked to Alan, but not for long. "Well, I'll make tracks. It was nice to meet you both. We'll talk soon, Dan. Bye."

Dan and Alan said goodbye, though Alan's voice lacked its usual warmth.

"What's up?" Dan asked.

"Nothing."

"You're upset because Carly didn't try to enlist you as a customer?"

Alan huffed. "Nonsense."

"If you say so."

"I do," Alan insisted. "I expect she could tell I wasn't interested. I don't see why people need personal trainers at all. If you want to do some exercise, all you have to do is get off your backside and get on with it."

"You are totally right," someone said, and they turned to see Natalya watching them from the gloom at the far end of the hallway.

Dan hadn't seen her arrive. How long had she been there, listening?

Natalya advanced on them slowly, her arms folded across her chest and her gaze on Alan. She seemed to be studying Alan closely as if reforming her opinion of his worth.

"You have it exactly right, Alan," Natalya went on. "No one here needs Carly, but still, she comes all the time, like a fly buzzing around the place." Natalya grimaced. "And like a fly, she sniffs out the food, pokes her nose in the fridge, spoils everything."

"How do you mean?" Alan asked.

Natalya pointed an accusing finger, prodding the air as she acted out the scene. "Don't eat this, don't buy that, this is no good, that is disgusting. To her, everything is bad. We have good food, fresh fruit and vegetables, but Carly takes it all, throws it away.

Don't eat it, she tells Zadie. It is bad for you. Very bad. So it goes in the waste bin."

"That's a shame," Alan said. "I hate to see good food wasted. But presumably, this is part of Zadie's clean eating, isn't it?"

"It's worse than that. She leaves her with nothing. Instead, she gives her powder in a bag. Green powder, brown powder. It has protein and vitamins, she says, but it's not real food. How can these things be good for you?"

"That does sound a little extreme," Dan said. "But if Zadie goes along with it, it's not for me to interfere. Zadie's more than capable of making her own decisions. Earlier, she sent Carly home, and it was very clear who was in charge."

Natalya pouted. "Sometimes Zadie sends her away, but Carly does not care. She'll be back. She always comes back. 'I just popped in for a chat,' she says, but afterward there is an invoice. *Consultation*, she calls it. Ridiculous."

"Do you take care of Zadie's accounts?" Dan asked. "Do you pay her bills?"

Natalya jutted her chin as if the answer were obvious. "It's my job."

"Do you also manage her social media accounts?"

"No, Zadie takes care of all that. She insists."

Dan offered a conspiratorial smile. "Come on. We both know that isn't the whole story."

"Story?"

"You know what I'm talking about, Natalya. Someone gets to those sites before Zadie and filters out all the silly comments. It must be you."

"Why do you say that?"

"You're not denying it," Dan said. "That tells me all I need to know."

Natalya's eyes flashed, but she remained tight-lipped.

"Is it that you want to protect Zadie?" Alan asked. "That would be understandable; laudable, even."

"Laudable," Natalya repeated under her breath. "I don't know this word."

"Sorry," Alan replied. "It means praiseworthy. You want to shield Zadie from anything that might upset her, and that's a good thing."

Natalya remained stony faced, but after a moment she nodded slowly. "Some things, Zadie does not need to see. There are always bad people. Sick. I block them, report them, delete their stupid lies. It is necessary. If Zadie saw what they write, she would be very sad."

"These comments, have any of them contained specific threats to Zadie?" Dan asked.

"What do you think? Of course they make threats, but they are all gone. Deleted."

"You didn't make a note of them?"

Natalya shook her head firmly.

"Were there any repeat offenders, people who made threats more than once?"

"Not as far as I can remember. They all hide behind false names. I just get rid of them."

"That's a shame," Dan said. "Those usernames could've been very valuable evidence. Next time, please keep a record of anything that looks like a threat. Copy down the name they use and paste it into a document along with their comment and the date and time they made it. Can you do that for me?"

Natalya looked doubtful, so Dan added, "Any help you give will be in confidence."

"I could make a spreadsheet, but I don't want Zadie to see it."

"That's okay for now, but if we find anything that might be useful to the police, we'll have to share it with them, and then Zadie will find out about it."

Natalya's shoulders slumped. "Then she'll know I lied to her, and I'll lose my job."

"Not necessarily," Alan said. "It wouldn't be a lie exactly, more like a sin of omission. If necessary, we can have a word with Zadie, make her see that you've always had her best interests at heart."

"You'd do that?"

"Of course we would," Dan said. "You're going to help us, so we'll help you in return. It's the least we can do."

Natalya summoned a tiny smile. "While you wait for Zadie, maybe you'd like a cup of tea, yes?"

"Yes please," Alan replied. "That would be wonderful."

CHAPTER 13

P hilippa Darley-Jones walked purposefully across her kitchen, the heels of her Manolos tapping out a determined rhythm on the tumbled travertine floor tiles. Yanking the tall fridge door open, she pulled out a bottle of tonic and let the door swing shut. She grabbed a crystal tumbler from the wall cabinet and pressed it into the integral ice dispenser on her freezer. Two cubes were plenty. The Grey Goose vodka was on the counter, and she poured a good measure, adding a splash of tonic. She took a sip, then another, and she breathed out a sigh of relief.

Returning the tonic to the fridge, she scanned the sparsely stocked shelves. The tub of Kalamata olives had been open for a few days, but they'd be fine. She took out the tub and glanced at the use-by date. Was that yesterday or the day before?

"Who cares?" she muttered and set the tub on the counter along with her last hunk of dolcelatte. The cheese was a little riper than she liked it, but it would have to do. She couldn't afford to throw it out, that was for sure.

A few water biscuits completed her snack, and she took a small knife from the block and attacked her food, not bothering with a plate but smearing chunks of cheese onto the biscuits and shoving them into her mouth. Even with the olives, it was a poor meal, each bland biscuit forming a tasteless clump on her tongue, but she washed each mouthful down with the vodka and tonic. When her glass was empty, she made another drink and took it through to the lounge, leaving the counter covered in crumbs and specks of cheese.

Slumping on the sofa, she took a mouthful of her drink and let it sit in her mouth for a second, imagining she could feel the alcohol seeping into her bloodstream.

She'd added a little more vodka this time, but sod it, it was seven o'clock somewhere in the world, wasn't it?

Besides, she'd had a horrible day. Horrible. *It's all Zadie's fault*, she thought. *Crying wolf like that. She's going to ruin everything.*

So someone had broken into Zadie's tumbledown house and left a note. So what? It wasn't as if anybody had been hurt, and nothing had been taken. But now, thanks to Zadie's hysterics, the police were involved. They'd sent two detectives, one of them an inspector, and that would mean trouble. They wouldn't turn up once and then forget about the whole thing; they'd be back. They'd want to talk to everybody, and a word out of place would be enough to ruin her plans. Everything she'd put in place, everything she'd worked for, could be unravelled in an instant.

As if that wasn't bad enough, Zadie had insisted on hiring those ridiculous private investigators. *They won't get anywhere*, Philippa decided. *They didn't know what they were doing.* But she couldn't be sure of that. If they went around poking their noses into everything, they might stumble onto the truth.

The whole thing was a disaster.

Philippa sat back, letting her head rest on the hand-stitched upholstery, and she closed her eyes. She took a gulp of her drink, keeping her eyes shut, trying to visualise the course of action she must take, weighing up her options.

But she couldn't relax. Her stomach clenched, sending a pang of hunger to derail her thoughts. Philippa laid her hand on her stomach, massaging her abs. She'd barely eaten for three days. The last decent meal she'd had was on Melody's birthday in the pub, and she hadn't been able to enjoy that properly, not with a certain person leering at her from across the table.

Draining her drink, Philippa stood, a wave of dizziness washing over her. She took a moment to steady herself, lengthening her spine and regaining her poise as her mother had taught her all those years ago. *Dear Mummy*, she thought. *She'd never have left me like this*. Philippa pictured her mother, remembering the rows she'd had with Daddy, the pair of them fighting like cats and dogs over every little thing. Their bitterest arguments, though, had emerged whenever they'd discussed the kind of life they'd wanted for their only daughter.

Daddy had insisted she should follow in his footsteps, working for the family firm. He'd founded a property development company, and he was sure Philippa would learn to love it. It had been his dream that she'd take over one day, keeping the business alive.

Philippa had tried to show an interest, really she had, but she'd never been able to stomach it. It was not her destiny to sit in stuffy boardrooms, surrounded by dull, middle-aged men.

Thankfully, Mummy had been on her side, and between them they'd won in the end. Mummy had set up a trust fund that would grant her daughter a few years of independence. It wasn't a huge sum, but it was enough for Philippa to spread her wings, to learn and grow.

Philippa cherished the memory of that gift, even though the recollection was tainted by the sadness of what came soon afterward. Her mother hadn't told them about the cancer. She'd carried on, just as before, until the creeping disease robbed her of the things she'd loved to do. When she could no longer ride, she'd still tended to her beloved garden, and when she hadn't been able to do even that, she'd died quickly and quietly with the minimum of fuss. Her father had followed soon afterward, and his finances hadn't been as rosy as he'd always pretended.

He'd left everything to Philippa, but by the time the accountants and lawyers had finished untangling her father's finances, there was nothing much left except for the house she stood in. Meadow House: the simple name belied its size and grandeur. The place had been too large for a family of three, so it was far too big for one person. She ought to have sold it, especially since her trust fund had quickly dwindled, the money running through Philippa's fingers like water. But along with the garden, the house had been her mother's pride and joy, and there was no way Philippa would ever let it go.

Philippa could almost hear her mother telling her to be strong. "Yes, Mummy," Philippa murmured to the empty room. "I will."

She still had a few irons in the fire. She was trying to rent out Keeper's Cottage, the small house that sat at the end of the enormous garden. That would bring in a little money to tide her over, but there would be a much bigger payday soon. It was not without risks, especially now that Zadie's histrionics had involved the police, but the plan was still in place, and she would see it through to the bitter end. It was the only way.

CHAPTER 14

Natalya served tea to Dan and Alan in the surprisingly modern kitchen. The counter of polished black granite gleamed beneath the inset ceiling lights, and the fitted cupboards had doors of pale grey with black metal handles. The ceramic-topped stove looked brand new, and the larder fridge picked up the theme of gloss black. Even the kettle was in a matching shade, and everything was spotless. Dan found it hard to imagine that the kitchen had been used. It seemed more like a showroom than part of a home.

Only one item of furniture looked as though it had seen service: a solidly built Welsh dresser made from dark wood, its surface polished but its edges bearing the scars of age. A range of bone china crockery was displayed on its shelves, and an eclectic collection of mugs and cups hung from brass hooks beneath the lower shelf.

"Darjeeling?" Natalya asked. "It's organic."

"Lovely," Alan replied.

Natalya clearly knew her way around the kitchen, producing a teapot and mugs, and dispensing boiling water from a fitted tap. In no time at all, Dan and Alan had their steaming mugs of tea.

"I must leave you," Natalya said. "I have work to do, but I will come and tell you when Zadie is ready."

"Fine," Dan replied. "We'll wait here. No problem."

"Okay, but please, don't touch anything. Zadie is very fussy about her kitchen. She likes everything to be in order."

"We'll be on our best behaviour," Dan said. "Scout's honour."

Natalya regarded Dan from beneath lowered eyebrows as if unsure whether she could trust him, but after a moment's hesitation she left them alone.

The sound of her footsteps had barely faded when Dan began prowling around the room, opening cupboard doors and rummaging inside.

"What are you doing?" Alan hissed. "You heard what she said. We're not to touch anything. Natalya could come back at any second."

"Yes, so you'd better give me a hand. The sooner we finish, the better our chances of getting away with it."

"For goodness' sake," Alan muttered, but he joined in, opening a wall cabinet and peering inside. "This one's empty. What exactly are we looking for?"

"Anything unusual, anything out of the ordinary."

"That's not much help." Alan bent to open a cupboard. "There's nothing in here apart from a few jars of some kind of jam." Alan held out a jar full of a dark red substance. "What on earth is membrillo?"

"It's a Spanish preserve made from quinces. It's sometimes called quince cheese." Dan paused his search. "We haven't got time to look at each item individually. Use your intuition. See what's behind that door, will you?" Dan gestured to a white-painted wooden door at the back of the kitchen.

"My intuition tells me that it's a broom cupboard," Alan said, but he went to check it anyway, emerging a few seconds later. "It's an old scullery," he said. "Bigger than I'd expected, but there's not much there; nothing interesting anyway, unless you're interested in ancient wooden worktops and Victorian sinks. Oh, and there's one of those fancy rechargeable vacuum cleaners and a mop."

"The room doesn't lead anywhere else?"

Alan glanced back into the scullery. "Not as far as I can see."

"Okay. You can help me with the cupboards."

"We're wasting our time," Alan grumbled as he shut the scullery door. "There's probably nothing in this kitchen except a lot of fancy ingredients I've never heard of."

"I disagree. So far, all I've found are packets of protein powder." Dan opened another wall cabinet. "This one's the same. Tons of the stuff. Do me a favour and check the fridge, will you?"

Alan moved to the tall fridge. "Oh."

"What is it?"

"Come and see. There's hardly anything in it."

Dan joined him, gazing at the fridge's pristine glass shelves, all empty save for a small tub of dairy-free yoghurt, a carton of oat milk and a slim bar of organic dark chocolate.

"This must be down to Carly," Dan stated. "Natalya said as much."

"The fridge in Zadie's dressing room was even worse. Nothing in it but bottles of water. It makes you wonder what she lives on. A person can't subsist on yoghurt, protein powder and quince jelly. Not for long, anyway."

"I'm concerned about the sheer number of protein shakes. I haven't heard of the brand, but I'll check it out later. Some shakes are marketed as meal replacements. They're supposed to have everything you need."

"I doubt that very much," Alan said. "I don't think it's healthy. Zadie's already very slim, and with all that weight-training, she needs to eat properly, doesn't she?"

"Ideally, but in her line of work, people can become very conscious of their body image, and that can lead to some very dark paths."

"You're talking about eating disorders. I hate to say it, but I wouldn't be totally surprised."

"It's something to think about, but whether it has a bearing on our case is another matter." Dan shut the fridge door and scanned the kitchen, checking he'd closed all the cupboard doors. There were some drawers in the old dresser that he hadn't had time to check, but that was too bad; he could hear someone coming.

A second later, Natalya appeared, her gaze roving around the room before she nodded to Dan and Alan. "You can come up now. Zadie is waiting for you. You can bring your drinks if you wish."

"Thanks, but I've finished with mine." Dan took a sip and then wandered over to the dresser, setting his cup down on the surface.

He heard Natalya's sharp intake of breath and then she was at his side, scooping up the mug and bearing it away to the sink.

"We don't put things on there," she said. "It marks the wood."

"Sorry about that." Dan's fingers brushed the dresser's edge. Could he slide a drawer open while Natalya was occupied with pouring the remainder of his drink into the sink?

He let his hand rest on the drawer's knob, but Natalya wheeled around to face him.

"What are you doing?"

"Nothing. I was admiring this fine old dresser. It looks like it belongs here."

"It came with the house," Natalya replied. "An ugly old thing. I'd get rid of it, but Zadie likes it. I don't know why."

"It makes a statement, that's for sure," Alan said. "Do you still use it, or is it for display purposes?"

"Zadie uses it, but it's private."

Dan made a show of admiring the woodwork. "Look at these drawers. Beautifully made. I'll bet they still glide as smoothly as ever."

He pulled on the knob but the drawer didn't budge. "It's locked. Why is that?"

"That is none of your business," Natalya scolded. "This is Zadie's home. You have no right to go through her things. If you want to see something, ask Zadie. If she says it's all right, that's okay. Otherwise, leave things alone. Is that clear?"

"Perfectly," Dan replied. "I didn't mean any offence. I was curious, that's all, but next time, I'll ask."

Natalya tutted, holding Dan in an icy glare.

Alan sipped his tea and made a show of setting his mug down with a contented sigh. "I needed that. It really was a lovely cup of tea, Natalya. Thank you very much. It really was very good, wasn't it Dan?"

"Oh yes. Perfect. Thank you, Natalya."

"You're welcome," Natalya intoned. "But we must go upstairs. Zadie will be waiting."

"We're ready." Dan gestured to the door. "After you."

Natalya didn't speak as she led them upstairs to the lounge, but she did glance back sharply every few steps as though she didn't trust them not to wander off.

We're not off the hook yet, Dan decided. *Not by a long chalk*. It would take more than a few words of flattery from Alan to mollify Natalya.

In the lounge, Zadie sat in the centre of the huge sofa, an iPad on her lap. She wore a pale green sweater and a pair of faded jeans, and she looked relaxed, her eyes bright and her hair still damp.

"Please, sit yourselves down," Zadie said. "Has Nat been looking after you?"

"Admirably," Dan replied, taking a seat on the smaller sofa.

"We've been admiring your wonderful kitchen," Alan said, sitting beside Dan. "Did you have it installed recently?"

"Yes. We tried to manage with the old one, but it was a complete mess. It got to the point where I couldn't stand it for one more day." Zadie looked to Natalya. "Thanks, Nat, but you don't need to stay. I know you've always got such a lot to be getting on with."

"Okay." Natalya eyed Dan doubtfully, then she left without saying a word.

"Oh dear," Zadie said. "Nat's in one of her moods. I hope she hasn't been rude to you. She can be a bit blunt."

"She was fine," Dan replied. "She doesn't like the idea of us poking around. She's very protective of you."

"That's very true. Say what you like about Nat, but she's got my back, no matter what."

Dan nodded. "That's good to know, especially in the circumstances. While we're on the subject, we have a few questions we'd like to ask."

"That's fine. Go ahead."

Alan produced his notebook and pen, and Dan began. "You ran into Mr Callaway near the footpath that runs from here into town. Do you use the path often?"

"Every now and then, when the mood takes me."

"Parts of the path are quite overgrown," Dan said. "It's not the easiest way to get into town."

"No, but I love it just the same. I don't see it as overgrown or difficult to get through. It's nature, doing what she does best, growing wild and free. It's beautiful, don't you think?"

"There are some very attractive spots," Alan replied. "Especially by the river."

Zadie clasped her hands together and beamed at Alan. "Did you see the pool? It's heaven. It's one of my favourite places in the whole world. I go there all the time."

"To swim?" Dan asked.

"No, I don't go in the water. I like to sit on the bank and just *be*. Sometimes I meditate, sometimes I do some yoga, but mainly I sit on the grass and watch the water rolling gently by. It's very soothing."

"Do you go alone?" Dan said.

"Always."

"That's not a good idea." Dan adopted a solemn expression. "Until we find out who's threatened you, you ought to take more care. That path is very isolated. On your own, you'd be vulnerable."

"I don't know about that. I hardly ever see anyone while I'm out walking. I feel perfectly safe."

"It's just a precaution and it won't be forever," Dan insisted. "All I'm asking is that you be more careful for a few days. Don't go anywhere unless you really need to, but if you must go out, use the car and take someone with you."

"I'll think about it, Dan, but I won't live like a prisoner in my own home. I need to get out into the world and see people, interact."

"I understand," Dan said. "But you should be more cautious until we can clear this up."

"Not me. I'm not weak, you know. I can look after myself."

"That may be so, but can you fight? Can you fend off a physical threat, an assault?"

"Maybe." Zadie lifted her chin. "I'm willing to take that risk."

"Even against an armed assailant?"

Zadie's defiant expression faltered.

"I don't mean to alarm you, but we have to be realistic," Dan went on. "While there's a possibility that someone means you harm, it's best to avoid any situation that could leave you vulnerable. It's common sense."

"All right, I'll be careful. I'll try, anyway. I can't stay cooped up though. I'll need to get out in the fresh air, but I'll ask Nat to come with me."

"Thank you." Dan paused to marshal his thoughts, and his gaze rested on the coffee table. It had been tidied, the magazines rearranged into neat stacks and the books placed in a straight row. He searched for the brass ashtray he'd seen earlier, but it had been removed.

Looking up, Dan said, "Zadie, do you smoke?"

"No. It's disgusting. I can't bear it."

"I'm the same," Dan replied. "That's why I noticed the ashtray on your table when we talked earlier. I was surprised to see it."

"It wasn't an ashtray; I don't have one in the house. It was just a little dish. Nat fetched it from somewhere. I hadn't seen it before. It must be hers."

"It had been used," Dan said. "There were cigarette stubs in it, so who was smoking?"

"My friends were very upset when they heard what had happened. They asked if they could smoke, and I'm afraid I gave in."

"I see, but you haven't answered my question, Zadie. Who was smoking?"

Zadie met Dan's gaze. "Is it important? I don't like to talk about my friends behind their backs."

"It might be very important indeed. Alan and I found some cigarette stubs in the garden, beside an old bench."

"Oh, that's weird, but my friends wouldn't throw rubbish in my garden. They'd never do anything so awful."

"You could be right, but we need to be absolutely certain. If those stubs don't belong to your friends, they might've been left by the person who broke in. If you tell us which of your friends smoke, we can talk to them, if only to rule them out."

"I suppose you're right. Connor and Melody were smoking before you arrived. Connor doesn't smoke all the time, and Melody never does, but Melody was distraught and Connor said a smoke would calm her nerves. She was so upset, I gave in."

"Thanks," Dan said. "It looked to me as if they'd been smoking hand-rolled cigarettes. Were they just smoking tobacco, or was it something else?"

Zadie laid her hand on her chest. "Are you talking about drugs? Seriously, Dan, don't even think about it. My brand is based on healthy living. Do you honestly think I'd allow anyone to use illegal drugs in my home?"

"You wouldn't necessarily know about it. If your friends—"

"They wouldn't do that to me. They wouldn't be so dishonest." Zadie sighed in frustration. "Dan, I'm picking up some very negative energy from you, and I don't like it. It's obvious you don't like my friends for some reason, but please credit me with some intelligence. I know what goes on in my house, and I know my friends. We're like family. We have our silly rows, but we stand by each other."

"I don't dislike your friends," Dan said. "I don't have any strong feelings about them one way or the other. I have to remain objective."

Zadie looked at him, pity in her eyes. "That must make you very lonely."

"Not at all, but we're not here to talk about me."

"In life, every exchange goes two ways," Zadie said. "If you close yourself off, Dan, you miss out on so much. The world becomes a better place when you open up, invite others to share your experience."

"I'll try to remember that. In the meantime, I want to ask you about Carly."

Zadie raised an eyebrow. "Oh yes? What about her?"

"How long have you known her?"

"For years. She came with me when I left London."

"So she's seen you become rich and successful," Dan said. "Has that affected your relationship?"

"Not in the least. Carly's very down to earth. She keeps me grounded."

"She's not jealous of your fame?"

There was a split second of hesitation before Zadie shook her head. "Carly has always been very supportive. She's been a companion on my journey."

"But she doesn't share in your success," Dan said. "You've become a celebrity, but Carly is still a personal trainer."

"I don't see it like that."

"How does Carly see it?"

"I couldn't say. You'll have to ask her."

"We might do that later," Dan said. "Carly mentioned a disagreement between you and one of your friends. She said you'd had an argument with someone called Mary."

Zadie's posture stiffened, her gaze becoming colder, but she didn't reply.

"Is Mary a friend of yours?" Dan went on.

"I don't know what Carly's been saying, but she should know better," Zadie said. "I can't stand it when people spread gossip. It does nobody any good."

I've hit a nerve, Dan decided. *But if I push too far, I'll lose her.*

Alan seemed to sense the change in Zadie's mood. Putting down his pen, he said, "Forgive us if these questions seem intrusive. We've found that it's best to pay attention to all kinds of tiny details. We never know what will turn out to be important."

Zadie tilted her head on one side as she looked at Alan. "I understand, but you seem very interested in the people I have around me. Surely, you ought to be out there, looking for someone else. A stranger."

"I'm keeping an open mind," Dan replied. "We can't be sure that your intruder was unknown to you. Until we can establish that, we need to be circumspect."

"I disagree," Zadie protested. "I trust my friends and that's all you need to know. Trust is everything."

"It's important, certainly," Alan said. "What Dan means is, we're asking about your friends so we can see the bigger picture. We're simply trying to understand the way you live."

"That's right." Dan copied Alan's reassuring smile. "We're following a process. We'll narrow our search as soon as we can, but until then, we'll gather as much data as we can. Have you really no recollection of arguing with someone called Mary?"

Zadie shook her head, and Dan knew they were done for the day. Alan had tried to dig him out of a hole, but Zadie's defences were up and there was no point in quizzing her further.

"Okay," Dan said. "I think we've taken up enough of your time for one day. We'll leave you in peace."

Zadie let out a sigh. "Yes, that's a good idea. My work doesn't stop for anything. I have a lot of catching up to do."

"We'll be in touch." Dan got to his feet and Alan followed suit. "In the meantime, please be careful. Did you do anything about your locks? You said that the police advised you to have some extra ones fitted."

"Shaun's taking care of it. He said he'd pop into Exeter to buy some window locks. He's going to fit them later, before he goes home."

"Good." Dan looked to Alan. "Ready?"

"Absolutely," Alan said. "Thank you for your help, Zadie. I hope the rest of the day goes well. Try not to worry."

"We're on the case," Dan added. "We'll see ourselves out. We know the way."

"Okay. Bye." Zadie smiled wearily as though glad to be seeing the back of them, then her attention went back to her iPad.

Dan and Alan made their way downstairs. Perhaps hearing their footsteps, Natalya appeared at the foot of the stairs and ushered them out through the front door.

Outside, Dan paused. Might it be a good idea to have another word with Shaun? The man was certainly shifty, and it was unfortunate that Zadie had entrusted him with fitting the new locks. But before Dan could suggest it, a white Mercedes-Benz SUV pulled silently into Zadie's driveway.

"I wonder who that is," Alan said.

"I can't see from here, but it's an electric car. I didn't hear it coming."

The driver was indistinct, but his head snapped toward them, and the car purred to a halt.

"Hello," Dan murmured. "Let's go and see who's come to call."

They marched toward the car. The driver had turned as if to speak to a passenger in the back seat, but the rear windows were tinted, and Dan could see nothing beyond the dark glass. He lengthened his stride, but the car reversed back into the road and sped away.

"Damn it," Alan muttered. "I didn't think to get its number."

"Me neither. It happened too fast, but I recognised the driver. It was Benny."

"Interesting. Why did he scarper? Was it because he saw us?"

"I'm not sure. I couldn't see who was in the back, but if it was Mr Callaway, he might be wary of strangers. Then again…"

"What?"

"Something else may be going on," Dan said. "Either way, we'll have to have a word with Zadie's illustrious neighbour before too long, whether he likes it or not."

WEDNESDAY

CHAPTER 15

D an was brewing his mid-morning coffee when Alan passed by the kitchen window.

"It's open," Dan called out, but a moment later Alan tapped on the back door, beating out a familiar rhythm.

Dan let out a sigh and opened the door. "Morning, Alan. Didn't you hear me? I said you could come in."

"I preferred to wait," Alan said. "I didn't know if you had company."

"No, Sam doesn't stay every night. She has a pub to run."

"Of course. I didn't mean to pry."

"No worries," Dan said. "Thanks for coming over. I guess you must've seen my message about Zadie."

"Yes. She's busy all day. It's a shame."

"Never mind. It gave me a chance to do some more background research."

"Oh? Anything to report?"

"Not a lot. But we'll talk about it in a minute. Coffee?"

"Yes please. It smells terrific."

"I'll get you a cup. Make yourself at home."

Dan watched as Alan headed for the kitchen table. "How's your leg today? You're hardly limping at all. It's barely noticeable."

"Oh, can you still tell? I thought I was back to normal."

"Not quite, but so long as you're feeling better, that's the main thing."

"Definitely. I don't think I strained the muscle after all. It was just a twinge, a complaining ligament or something. I had a hot bath last night and I'm right as rain now."

"Glad to hear it."

Alan sat at the kitchen table and laid out his pen and notebook, opening it at a clean page and pressing it flat.

"You came prepared," Dan said as he measured out a scoop of freshly ground coffee.

"Always. It's one thing I learned from teaching. Preparation is everything."

"As in so much of life." Dan made Alan's drink, the ritual stilling his mind, giving him time to think.

Preparation. Had the intruder at Zadie's house prepared carefully before breaking in? It certainly seemed like a premeditated act.

Dan had been reading up on cases of celebrity stalking, and there was often an underlying obsession, an infatuation that slowly escalated, building from adoration to fanaticism before morphing into something darker: the desire to dominate, to control, to possess.

But this case doesn't feel like that, Dan thought. As far as he knew, there'd been no precursors to the break-in, no sense of an impending threat. And that note, *I'll see you soon*. The message wasn't threatening in and of itself, but it had been left in Zadie's studio, a place that was very special to her. The choice of room could be coincidental, but it felt intentional, calculated to cause fear and distress.

The more Dan thought about it, the more he convinced himself that the note had been written by someone close to Zadie, someone familiar with her routine. The intruder may well have been confident that the house was unoccupied, and they may have known that the scaffolding gave easy access to the unsecured upper windows.

Where's the evidence? Dan asked himself. *Where are the clues?* His intuition wasn't enough; not this time.

The drinks ready, Dan placed them on the table and then sat opposite Alan.

"Thank you, that looks great." Alan took a sip then set his mug down, swapping it for his pen. "So how did you get on this morning? What did you find?"

"I was looking at celebrity stalking. There are lots of news stories online but they're generally very sensationalised. It's hard to glean anything meaningful, but there does seem to be a pattern to these things, and Zadie's case seems different. I think there would've been warning signs, especially online."

"Maybe there were," Alan said. "You heard what Natalya said. She deleted any negative comments."

"Even so, I'm almost certain that if she'd seen something worrying, she'd have picked up on it. Natalya doesn't like to show it, but she's very protective of Zadie, and she's sharp as a tack."

"She's a force to be reckoned with."

"It's a good job Natalya is on our side," Dan said. "Well, she's on Zadie's side, at least. That's something."

"What other leads have we got? Has there been any news from Benny?"

"Actually, he did give me a call, but it was somewhat one-sided. He wanted to know if we were any closer to catching *the nutter who broke in*, as he put it, but he didn't give much in return."

"Oh? Did you ask him why he turned up at Zadie's house yesterday?"

"Yes. He said Mr Callaway had wanted to check in on his neighbour."

"So Callaway was in the car," Alan said. "But if he wanted to visit Zadie, why did they drive away as soon as they saw us?"

"Mr Callaway doesn't like strangers, apparently. According to Benny, he's a very private man."

"That fits with what we've heard about him," Alan replied. "I take it there's no chance of an interview with the man himself."

"Not at the moment. Benny said he'd given my card to Callaway's PA, but that was as far as I got. I wanted to ask if Mr Callaway would be prepared to talk over the phone, but Benny hung up."

"Where does that leave us?"

"We should look closer to home, for the time being anyway."

Alan cleared his throat. "Actually, I've been doing some research of my own, looking into Zadie's circle of friends."

"Excellent. What did you find?"

"Nothing much, I'm afraid. There was the usual nonsense on social media, especially on Instagram. All Zadie's friends, the ones we met anyway, are very supportive online. They follow her posts and they leave nice comments. Zadie follows them back, but that's where the similarity ends. Where Zadie has lots of snappy videos and carefully composed photos, her friends just share the usual snapshots you might see from anybody: cups of coffee, restaurant food, cocktails. Naomi's Instagram feed was a bit better, as you'd expect from a photographer. She shares some of her work, mainly wedding photos, and she has a website. It looked professional. I was quite impressed."

"How about Melody?" Dan asked. "Does she have a website for her shop?"

"Yes. Indiago. It was easy to find online, but there was nothing much on the site. It only had a couple of pages and it looked home-made, so I suspect her shop doesn't bring in enough to pay for a professional web designer. Melody uses Instagram to share photos of clothes and so on, but no other social media. Connor, on the other hand, is all over social media. He writes about music mainly. He's very scathing about anything mainstream. Some of his posts are actually quite funny, but he doesn't have many followers, so I'm not sure why he bothers."

"He's bored, I expect. Was there anything controversial or unusual?"

"Not unless you're a fan of Harry Styles." Alan smiled regretfully. "None of it amounts to anything much, I'm afraid. I pretty much drew a blank."

"It was good of you to try. Did you find any reference to the mysterious Mary?"

Alan shook his head. "It's a common name, so without something else to go on, we don't stand much chance."

"True, but we'll have to figure out who she is. I keep thinking about the way Zadie reacted when I mentioned the name. She didn't deny she knew someone called Mary, but she clearly wasn't going to be drawn on the subject."

"She was upset about something," Alan said. "Then again, you might be reading too much into it. It was Carly she was angry with. Zadie accused her of spreading gossip."

Dan let out an exasperated sigh. "You know, I've never had to deal with so many overheated egos at once. They're like children."

"Children are better behaved, but I know what you mean." Alan leafed back through his notebook until he found a page crammed with handwritten text, then he looked at Dan expectantly.

"I'll bite," Dan said. "What've you got there?"

"You know me. Once I get the bit between the teeth, there's no stopping me. I looked into those protein shakes Zadie seems so keen on, and this time, I fared a bit better."

"Go on."

"Arvitalize is a big company. They make a large range of so-called health products, but you won't find any of them in the shops."

"Are they online only? I'm surprised I haven't heard of them. I've spent long enough searching for shakes that weren't made from whey."

"I didn't know you used protein shakes."

"Not all the time," Dan said. "It depends my running. If I'm training hard, I like to keep my protein up, and since I don't eat meat, a supplement can make sense."

"Well, I don't think you'd approve of this particular brand. The company uses ordinary people instead of shops to sell their wares. If you sign up as a supplier, you'll earn a commission on every sale, but you can earn even more if you recruit someone else as a seller. That way, you can build up your own sales network and simply supply them with products which, of course, you buy from the company. Then all you have to do is sit back and count the money as it comes rolling in. It all sounds too good to be true. If you ask me, it's a pyramid scheme in all but name."

"It's called multi-level marketing," Dan said. "It's legal, but you're right to be wary. I always think that if the stuff was any good, you'd be able to buy it anywhere. These firms turn unsuspecting people into an underpaid sales force, then they motivate them to be underhanded. A friend once invited me to dinner, and the next thing I knew, he was trying to sell me boxes full of shower gel and shampoo."

"A strange kind of friend," Alan said. "Did you buy anything?"

"What do you think? I made my excuses and left. After that, we lost touch."

"That's a shame. Money can so easily come between friends."

"Yes, it can. Which is why you must let me—"

"Never mind about that," Alan interrupted. "I said I'd help on this case for free, and I meant it. This way, I can come and go as I see fit, and that suits me perfectly well. If you get this business on its feet and you need more help down the line, we'll work something out. A partnership, perhaps."

"Fair enough. A partnership. I hadn't thought of that."

"We'll cross that bridge when we come to it," Alan said. "In the meantime, let's concentrate on the few clues we have so far. I think the protein shakes might be significant. Zadie has a massive audience and a high level of influence. If she wanted to, she could sell an awful lot of protein shakes to a huge number of people."

"Very true," Dan replied. "We'll ask her about it, but there's another possibility. According to Natalya, Carly is very fussy about what Zadie eats. As her personal trainer, she could be pushing more than protein shakes. I wonder if there's an element of coercive control in their relationship."

"I didn't get that impression. Zadie spoke highly of Carly, but she was very much in charge when it came to sending Carly home. If they seem particularly close, it's because they've been together for a long time."

"Even so, it's something to follow up," Dan said. "I still don't know where this case is going, and until I do, we'll leave no stone unturned."

"So what's our next step?"

"I'd like to go back to her friends and speak to them one at a time. I thought we'd start with Melody."

"Why her?"

"Remember the clothes in Zadie's wardrobe?" Dan asked. "They'd been rearranged."

Alan nodded gravely. "That worried me as soon as I heard about it. I thought the intruder might have some sort of fetish."

"That's a possibility, but there could be a much simpler explanation. Designer clothes of the type Zadie wears are very expensive, and Melody runs a clothes shop."

"You think all this might be about stealing a few frocks? I doubt it somehow. Melody was with Zadie on Sunday night, and anyway, Zadie said nothing had been taken."

"I still think the idea bears looking into. If a dress was swapped for one almost identical, would Zadie know? Melody would, and don't forget that she lives in Doddiscombsleigh, the same village as the pub where they ate dinner together, but she arrived late."

Alan's lips formed an *O*.

"You see what I'm saying?" Dan went on. "Melody waited near Zadie's house until she saw Natalya and Zadie leave, then she popped inside and made mischief. The job done, she drove to the pub and made up some story about her hair." Dan clicked his fingers. "In fact, if her hair was less than perfect, that would fit very nicely. She'd just staged a break-in, so she wasn't going to look her best. Maybe one of her friends made a comment, but Melody was crafty. She turned it into an excuse for being late. After the dinner, she invited Zadie back to her place and plied her with drink, ensuring that Zadie would arrive home late and somewhat worse for wear. It was all part of her plan to unsettle Zadie and throw her off the scent."

"It's compelling, but it's a bit far-fetched. All that, just to steal some clothes? I don't buy it. Besides, it wouldn't work. Someone like Zadie would know instantly if one dress had been swapped for another; most women would."

"Okay, so Melody had some other motive. Jealousy, resentment, a grudge, a feud between friends: take your pick. But we can't ignore the fact that she turned up late for her own birthday celebration."

Alan nodded. "We need to talk to Melody. Shall we call her?"

"No. I know her shop in Exeter. It's a small boutique, so I doubt there's ever more than one person behind the counter. It's mid-week, so she'll be there. We can drop in unannounced and pretend we're looking for some new clothes." Dan cast a sideways glance at Alan. "Well, I can."

"I'm coming with you, aren't I?"

"Yes, if you like, but I'm not sure whether you'll pass for one of Melody's customers."

"Oh, one of *those* places is it? Trendy. Full of hipsters."

"Not exactly." Dan offered a smile. "Don't take this the wrong way, but it's pricey. I wouldn't shop there either; not these days anyway. You'll see what I mean when we get there."

"No offence taken. When are we setting off?"

"Soon, but there's no rush. You can finish your coffee."

Alan took a long draught from his mug and sighed. "One hundred percent Arabica. Am I right?"

"Spot on. You're on form today."

"You'd better believe it. It's the thrill of the chase. There's nothing quite like it for getting the blood flowing."

"I'll drink to that." Dan took a sip from his own coffee. In truth, the coffee he'd used was a subtle blend of arabica and robusta coffee beans, the former grown in Colombia and the latter from Brazil, but there was no need to burst Alan's bubble, especially when he was raring to go.

Alan was already pocketing his notebook, checking he had his phone and draining the last of his coffee. He looked at Dan expectantly. "Ready?"

"I'd better be. I'll drive."

"No need," Alan said. "I'm fine and it's my turn."

"Okay," Dan replied, happy to agree. The journey would give him time to collect his thoughts. If his suspicions about Melody were borne out, she was a much more slippery character than he'd imagined. When they met, Dan wanted to be ready.

CHAPTER 16

DS Kulkarni breezed into Teignmouth police station, exchanging smiles and a few words of greeting, a nod or two. She'd always had a gift for remembering names and faces, and at times like this, her quick memory came in very handy. Kulkarni needed to hit the ground running. This station was much smaller than Exeter HQ, and her success or failure would be instantly noticed by all.

There's nowhere to hide, Kulkarni thought. *I've got to get this right.*

Kulkarni stopped off at the kettle and made a couple of mugs of instant coffee, then she headed for the corner of the office reserved for CID. She found DS Jo Winslow hard at work at her desk, and Kulkarni presented her with a mug of coffee and a smile, saying, "A drop of milk and one sugar."

"Thanks." Winslow sat back and sipped her drink. "Not bad. You can stay."

"I have my uses."

"I'm sure. Take a pew." Winslow indicated the desk facing her own. "We've cleared that desk for you, but you'll need to find a spare chair."

"No problem." Kulkarni spotted a well-worn swivel chair nearby, so she wheeled it to her desk and took her place. But as she sat down, her chair's backrest gave way without warning. Kulkarni saved herself, but hot coffee sloshed from her mug and over her fingers. "Bloody hell!" she cried, setting the mug down and searching in her pocket for a tissue.

A ripple of laughter ran around the room, but Kulkarni raised her head, favouring her audience with a wry smile. It would take more than a dodgy chair to rattle her.

"Sorry about that," Winslow said. "We didn't leave it there on purpose, in case you were wondering."

"The thought hadn't crossed my mind," Kulkarni replied, although that wasn't entirely true. "How are we getting on with Diamonds Avenue? Anything new from the door-to-door?"

"Not a lot. We found a couple of people who thought they might've seen a black van, but no one seems to have noticed who was driving it, and as for the guy who lived in the basement flat…" Winslow shook her head. "He's a ghost. It makes you wonder whether he liked it that way, especially when you see this." Winslow slid a small plastic container across the desk, and Kulkarni peered inside.

The container held a stack of transparent evidence bags, all neatly labelled. Kulkarni took up the top packet. It contained a UK passport, and the bag underneath held another.

"There are twelve," Winslow said. "Each one with a different name, a different photo, a different date of birth."

"These were in the basement?"

Winslow nodded. "They were in one of those metal document safes, hidden under the floorboards. It's a miracle we found it. One of the SOCOs noticed the board had been cut. The heat had warped it out of shape, so she lifted it up. The metal box was just sitting there, not a scratch on it. It must be heatproof and waterproof."

"Fire damage can be very localised. It's amazing what can survive, even if it's close to the flames."

Winslow gazed at her levelly.

"But you already knew that," Kulkarni went on. "Sorry. I've

been learning a lot from the fire investigation team, and my head's full of it."

"That's okay. I wish this was the first fire I've had to deal with, but I've seen far too many. Mind you, I've never come across a stash of passports before, so there's always something new."

"Were there any prints on them?"

"Not a one. The chances are that we're looking at people who know what they're doing."

"Although they left the passports behind."

"My guess is, our unknown resident left in a hurry," Winslow said. "On the other hand, whoever set the fire might not have known where they were hidden. They couldn't find the passports, but they figured the fire would destroy them, along with any other evidence."

Kulkarni thought for a moment. "This case is all about these passports. It's very different to the arson we've been looking at in Exeter. I'd say we can rule out any connection between the two, so I suppose I'll be heading back to base."

"Actually, that's something we need to talk about."

"Yes?"

Winslow seemed to be weighing her words. "We could really use your help, Anisha, so I had a word with my DI, and he agrees."

"Oh, I see. I'd be happy to help, but we'd have to square it with DI Spiller, and—"

"Already done," Winslow interrupted. "I talked to Tim myself. He was pretty keen. He said it would be good experience for you."

"He hasn't said anything to me."

"I'm sure he will," Winslow said. "You know what it's like. He's got a lot on his plate, especially with his wife and everything."

Kulkarni nodded.

"Are you okay with staying here?" Winslow asked.

"Sure. I was surprised, that's all." Kulkarni gathered her thoughts. In this job, you had to think on your feet and deal with whatever it threw at you. Leaning forward on her desk, she said,

"We'd better crack on then. We could start by checking those passports, see if they've been reported as stolen."

"I put one of my DCs on that, and she drew a blank. The passports all came up as valid, so they were probably bought from the owners and altered. You buy an expired passport and apply for a renewal along with a photo of your paying customer, and you're in business. Some people will pay a lot for a valid passport."

"In that case, we need to consider whether an organised crime group was involved."

"I agree," Winslow said. "On the face of it, this has OCG written all over it. I've already flagged it for the DI, but he wants more than just speculation. Until we have evidence to the contrary, we're to treat this case as a suspicious death."

"Any news on the fire? Yesterday, you said it looked like a chip pan started it."

"We're still waiting for the full report. So far, they haven't found any accelerants, but that doesn't mean much. It's easy enough to stage a chip pan fire. It's the oldest trick in the book."

"How about the post-mortem? Has it been arranged?"

"Tomorrow morning," Winslow said. "I'll be attending, but you're welcome to come along."

"Thanks. That'd be great."

Winslow lifted an eyebrow. "You're keen, I'll give you that."

"I'm on this case now, and I'll pull my weight. Besides, like DI Spiller said, it's all good experience."

"Define 'good'."

Kulkarni smiled. "You know what I mean. It's useful. I may as well make the most of it."

"True. I just meant…" Winslow paused. "Have you ever been to a PM when the body was burned?"

"No, but I can handle it."

"Okay. That's tomorrow morning sorted. Now we need a plan of action for today. Any thoughts?"

Kulkarni nodded. "I'd like to swing by the scene, take another look around."

"Because?"

"Yesterday it was chaos over there; I'd like to see the place now it's had a chance to settle down, get a feel for the neighbourhood."

"That sounds all right in theory, but I'm not sure we can spare the time."

"It takes more than one man to run a forgery operation. The victim almost certainly had associates, and they might be sniffing around, wondering what happened to their passports."

"Returning to the scene of the crime? Come on, Anisha. They'll be lying low. They won't go anywhere near the place."

"I'm not saying they'll have been there yesterday, but once the SOCOs pulled out and the door-to-door was over, someone might've decided to take a look themselves. Was anyone left to guard the scene?

"Only until last night. The SOCOs said they'd got everything they were going to get, and the weather was closing in, so we called it a day. Did you see the rain last night? No one was going to be out in that if they could help it."

"The weather was okay in Exeter, but inland is often different to the coast, isn't it? I used to work in Newquay."

"Right."

"Still, the storm's blown over now, hasn't it? A nice day to take a trip to Diamonds Avenue." Kulkarni looked at Winslow expectantly.

"All right, Anisha, we'll give it a whirl. We can knock on a few doors, see if we can't scare up a lead or two." Winslow stood. "No time like the present. We'll take my car."

"Don't you want to finish your coffee?"

Winslow wrinkled her nose. "We'll grab something on the way."

"Let's go."

Winslow parked directly outside the burned-out remains of 43 Diamonds Avenue, and Kulkarni passed her the takeout cup of coffee she'd been cradling since their hurried stop at a coffee shop in town.

"Cheers," Winslow said, already unfastening her seatbelt. "Let's see what we can see."

They climbed from the car and stood beside the blue and white crime scene tape, sipping their drinks.

"What a mess," Winslow said, and Kulkarni murmured in agreement.

Without its roof, the house had fared badly in the overnight storm, and now it was little more than a skeleton. Parts of the outer walls had collapsed, and very little remained of the upper floors.

"It's going to be fenced off sometime today," Winslow went on. "When the council finally get their arses in gear."

"It's a shame we never got to go inside," Kulkarni said. "I'd have liked to look around."

"What for? The SOCOs know their job, and they do it better than we could. If you want to see something, there'll be a photo of it, that's for sure."

"Yeah, I know, but it's not the same as being in the place."

Winslow cast her a sideways look. "You won't get far in this game by standing around waiting for inspiration to strike. It might look good on all those Scandi crime shows, the moody copper staring into the distance, but in real life? Forget it."

"Okay, but there's room for a bit of intuition. Someone once told me to trust it, and you know what? He wasn't wrong."

"Who told you that? I'll bet it wasn't Tim Spiller."

"No, but DI Spiller isn't so different. He likes to get out on the street, keep his ear to the ground."

Winslow took a long drink of her coffee, draining her cup and crumpling it in her hand. Kulkarni did the same.

"Well, we won't find out anything by standing here like a couple of lemons," Winslow said. "Where do you want to start?"

Kulkarni looked around. "With him."

She pointed along the road to a man in a beige raincoat and a flat cap. He was shambling along the pavement, a wire-haired terrier trotting gamely at his side.

"He's the man I told you about yesterday, the one who called in the fire," Winslow said. "Len Franks. I talked to him myself. He wasn't holding anything back."

"Not intentionally, perhaps, but I think it's worth having another try."

"Okay," Winslow replied, her reluctance obvious from her tone. "After you."

Kulkarni strolled over the road to meet Mr Franks, but while the man merited only a brief hello, she kneeled down to make a much bigger fuss of the terrier.

The dog sniffed briefly at her outstretched hand then moved closer to her, its tail wagging furiously.

"He likes you," Mr Franks said. "You're honoured. He doesn't take to everyone."

"I'm a dog person," Kulkarni said. "What's his name?"

"Banjo. I'm not sure why we called him that. It just sort of suited him."

"Yes, it does. Hello, Banjo. Have you been for a walk? Yes? Good boy." Kulkarni stood up. "He's great, isn't he? But I'm sorry, I should've introduced myself. I'm Detective Sergeant Kulkarni, Devon and Cornwall Police."

"I figured as much."

Winslow joined them, and Mr Franks nodded to her. "You came around yesterday."

"That's right," Winslow said. "How are you doing today?"

"I'm all right. I mustn't grumble." Mr Franks hesitated. "On the news, they said there was someone in that fire. Is that right?"

"Perhaps we should talk about that inside," Kulkarni said. "I think Banjo might be ready to go home."

Sure enough, the dog was pulling its lead tight, its gaze fixed firmly on the street ahead.

"He wants his treat," Mr Franks replied. "I'm ready for a cup of tea, myself, so I suppose you can come in for a bit, if you really need to." He gave them a knowing smile. "Third time lucky, eh?"

"I'm sorry," Kulkarni said. "What do you mean?"

"Well, you talked to me yesterday, then those other two came knocking this morning, and now you."

"Who came to see you this morning?" Winslow said. "Were they in uniform?"

"No, they were like you: plain clothes. But they weren't so smart."

"Can you remember their names?" Winslow asked.

"They didn't say. I would've remembered if they had. Nothing wrong with my memory, nor my hearing."

"Did they give you a business card?"

"No. They weren't all that polite either. I had half a mind to make a complaint."

Kulkarni and Winslow exchanged a look.

"Let me get this straight," Winslow began. "Two people came to your house this morning, and they didn't identify themselves, but they claimed to be police officers."

Mr Franks nodded. "That's right."

"What did they want to know?" Kulkarni asked.

"About the fire, about the house. Had I seen anybody going in, did I know anything about a black van. All that kind of thing."

"Mr Franks," Kulkarni said gently, "we need to talk about this, but let's go inside and get you that cup of tea, yes?"

"All right."

Mr Franks walked briskly to his house and let them in the front door. "Wipe your feet as you come in," he said. "I like to keep it tidy." He let Banjo off the lead, and the dog raced along the hallway and disappeared through a doorway.

"He's gone to wait by his bowl," Mr Franks explained. "He won't be happy until he's had his treat. You go into the lounge and have a seat. I'll sort Banjo out, and I'll put the kettle on while I'm there."

"Thanks," Kulkarni said. "We've just had a drink, but you go ahead. Do you need a hand?"

Mr Franks waved her offer aside, then he looked pointedly at the crumpled paper cups they were holding. "I'll deal with those."

"Thank you," Kulkarni said.

Having relieved them of their cups, Mr Franks shuffled along the hallway, taking off his cap and shrugging out of his coat as he went.

Kulkarni and Winslow made their way into the front room and both of them looked around, taking in the photographs on the dresser, the ornaments on the mantelpiece. Kulkarni's gaze settled on a black and white wedding photograph, the happy couple beaming out across the decades, Mr Franks recognisable from the shape of his nose, the arch of his eyebrows. She recalled that Mr Franks had said 'we' when he talked about naming the dog, and she wondered what had happened to his wife, and how long he'd lived here alone. Because this house was heavy with silence. It was the house of a widower, the house of a man keeping up appearances: a man who dusted the mantelpiece and vacuumed up dog hair from the carpet.

The man himself appeared in the doorway, and without his hat and coat, Kulkarni could see that he was smartly dressed, his corduroy trousers clean and his cardigan neatly buttoned, as was his checked shirt. Kulkarni judged from the collar that the shirt had been carefully ironed; crumples and creases would not be tolerated. Mr Franks had combed his hair, and he was clean shaven. The message he sent to the world was clear: he could fend for himself.

"The tea's brewing," Mr Franks announced. "I know you said no, but I made a pot anyway. I can't very well have one myself without looking after my guests. It won't be long, but please, sit down. You're making the place untidy."

"Okay," Kulkarni said, taking up position on the sofa, and Winslow did the same.

Mr Franks nodded as if satisfied, then he disappeared from view.

"What do you think?" Kulkarni asked Winslow.

There was a pause before Winslow replied. "I think that, on this occasion, you were right. Someone's been sniffing around."

Kulkarni tried to hide her smile. "We'll see where it leads."

Banjo scampered into the room and made straight for Kulkarni, sitting down by her feet and looking up expectantly.

"Sorry, Banjo," Kulkarni said, "but I'm pretty sure you're not allowed on the furniture."

"I should think not," Mr Franks said as he bustled into the room bearing a tray, complete with teapot, milk jug, a stack of plates and three mugs. "Banjo might only be little, but his hair gets everywhere. You wouldn't believe it." He made for a small table beside an armchair, then he hesitated. "Er, could you move that book for me? I can't put the tray down."

Kulkarni jumped to her feet, picking up the hardback book. "Ian Rankin. They're detective stories, aren't they?"

"Yes. Inspector Rebus. I've read them all." Mr Franks set the tray down and took his seat, holding out his hand for the book.

Kulkarni passed the hardback to him, and after a moment's indecision, he slid it between the armrest and his body. "I'll get to that later." Rubbing his hands together, he said, "Now, do you both take milk?"

"Yes, please," Kulkarni said. "Just a splash."

"Right." Mr Franks poured the tea, then he frowned at the tray. "Drat. I forgot the biscuits."

He made to get up, but Kulkarni beat him to it. "I'll fetch them."

"There's no need."

"I'd like to help. It's the least I can do."

Mr Franks relaxed back into his seat. "Oh, all right. They're in a biscuit barrel by the kettle. You can bring the whole thing."

Kulkarni found the kitchen and it was, as she'd predicted, spotless. There were no dishes in the drying rack, and not so much as a crumb on the kitchen counters. She picked up the ceramic biscuit barrel and headed back to the lounge, hurrying in case Winslow had started without her.

As she entered the room, Mr Franks was saying, "Oh, about six foot two, but thin. Skinny as a rake. And the other one was a bit shorter say, five foot ten."

"Here we are," Kulkarni said brightly, setting the biscuit barrel down on the table, and glancing meaningfully at the notebook open in Winslow's hand.

"Mr Franks has just been telling me about the two men who called this morning," Winslow said. "He said they seemed very confident, very convincing."

"That's right. I asked for some ID, and one of them flashed his wallet at me. There was a card in the little window, but I didn't have my reading glasses on. It could've been anything. I suppose they took me for a fool. You must think I'm daft."

"Not at all," Kulkarni said. "At least you asked for ID. That's more than most people do."

"Maybe, but I'm still cross with myself." Mr Franks shifted in his chair. "The thing is, if they weren't police, who were they?"

"That's what we aim to find out," Winslow replied. "With your help, we can track these people down, stop them from pestering people such as yourself."

"I'll help if I can. I'll do my best." Mr Franks leaned forward and lifted the lid from the biscuit barrel. "Help yourselves. They're only digestives, but it takes me a while to get through them, so I only ever have one kind of biscuit on the go."

"Thanks." Kulkarni dutifully took a biscuit and passed the barrel to Winslow who took one almost without looking, her gaze focused on Mr Franks.

"You said they mentioned a black van," Winslow prompted.

"That's right," Mr Franks said. "I couldn't tell them much, but I saw it that day. I couldn't miss it. It was parked right outside."

Winslow made a note, and Kulkarni, forcing down her frustration at being reduced to dispensing refreshments, replaced the biscuit barrel and handed Winslow a mug of tea, picking up one for herself.

Taking her place beside her colleague, Kulkarni said. "I assume you didn't mention the van to my colleague yesterday. Why is that?"

"Well, I didn't know it was important. It only came up when those blokes started asking questions."

"That's perfectly understandable," Kulkarni replied. "Did you see the driver?"

"Not really. I might've caught a glimpse of him, but I'm not sure."

"When was this?" Winslow asked.

"Yesterday, in the morning." Mr Franks rubbed his chin. "It would've been about eight o'clock. I was going round the house, opening the curtains, and I saw him from the spare room."

"That would've been about an hour before you reported the fire," Winslow said.

"That's right, but I didn't think… I mean, I didn't put two and two together."

"Don't worry about that," Kulkarni said. "Can you describe the man for us?"

"I'll try. He was big, if you know what I mean. Like a rugby player or a boxer. A rough-looking type. I saw him crossing the road, that's all, but I figured he'd come in that van, otherwise, I'd have seen him walking along the street. But I didn't pay much attention to him. Like I say, I was just opening the curtains upstairs, and I caught sight of him going across the road. I didn't stop to see where he went. I didn't think anything of it. Sorry not to be more helpful."

"You're being extremely helpful," Winslow said. "What was the man's ethnicity?"

"He was white. Short hair, like a skinhead. I didn't see his face though. He had his back to me."

"Did you tell all this to the two men who called?" Kulkarni asked.

"No, I did not. Like I said before, they were rude. Ill mannered. I told them I'd seen the van, but that was all. They tried getting shirty with me, trying to bully me, but I wasn't going to stand for that. I told them they'd better go. I said I had the chiropodist coming round to do my toenails, which was true, as it happens. She wasn't due to come until much later, but they didn't know that. Anyway, they left soon after. They probably thought I was a daft old duffer, but I didn't care about that. I was glad to see the back of them."

"You did very well," Winslow said. "What about their ethnicity? Were these two white as well?"

"One of them was," Mr Franks replied. "Very pale, actually, like he didn't get out much. Unhealthy looking. You know, pasty. He was the smaller of the two."

"What about the other man?" Kulkarni asked.

Mr Franks glanced at Kulkarni then dropped his gaze. "He was… you know…"

"He was a person of colour?" Kulkarni asked.

"Is that the right thing to say these days? I never know."

"It'll do for now," Kulkarni said. "But we need to narrow it down if we can. How would you describe his skin colour?"

Mr Franks moved his lips as if chewing his words. "I don't know. I don't want to cause offence, but he was brown-skinned. Like his family were maybe from Pakistan or somewhere like that."

Kulkarni kept her tone level. "So his skin tone was something like mine, is that right?"

"Yes."

"How about accents?" Winslow asked.

"Oh, they sounded local. Both of them."

"That's very useful," Kulkarni said. "Have you seen either of these men before?"

Mr Franks started to shake his head, but then he stopped, his brow furrowed. "Come to think of it, there was something familiar about the tall one. I think I did see him before, but it wasn't here, it was somewhere else. Hold on…"

In the silence, Kulkarni leaned forward and sensed Winslow doing the same.

Mr Franks tutted. "No, it's gone. Sorry. Maybe it'll come back to me later."

"It might help if you come down to the station and look through some photographs," Winslow suggested. "We could take you there in the car and bring you back afterward."

"I don't know. I don't like to leave Banjo on his own."

"It needn't take long," Winslow said. "And we'd be very grateful for your help."

"Would it mean going to court and such?"

"Not necessarily," Kulkarni said. "It's highly unlikely that we'd rely on something like this for evidence. It's more a case of helping us with our enquiries, giving us a lead. If we can find these men, we can keep an eye on them and see what they're up to."

"Were they something to do with the fire and that poor bloke they found inside?"

"At this stage, we just don't know," Kulkarni replied. "But we need to find these people as soon as we can. Could you help us with that? We'd appreciate it, and you'd be making this street a bit safer."

"Oh, that's something we sorely need. We get too many youngsters making a nuisance of themselves. The trouble is, there's not much for them to do around here. So I'd like to help, but I don't know."

Kulkarni nodded and made sympathetic noises, waiting for Mr Franks to make his mind up.

He drew a sharp breath and lifted his chin, suddenly determined. "All right. I'll do it. Give me a minute to finish my tea and get Banjo settled in his bed, then we'll be off."

"Great. Thank you," Kulkarni said.

Winslow was taking out her phone. "I'll get someone to get the mugshots ready, and I'll make sure we've got a quiet room we can use."

"Well, well," Mr Franks said, then he took a drink from his mug of tea. "Helping the police with their enquiries. Me! Whatever next?"

Who knows? Kulkarni thought. *This could be just what we need to get this case moving.* But she tried to rein in her expectations. Mr Franks seemed like a reliable witness, but his memory wasn't infallible, and there was no guarantee that either of the men would be in the database. Only time would tell.

CHAPTER 17

Peter's nerves finally began to unwind as he drove the van into the Marsh Barton trading estate in Exeter. He'd made a good choice. Here, every second or third vehicle seemed to be a van of one kind or another, and he felt nicely anonymous. With no clear idea where he was heading, he chose a random route through the maze of small roads that led between car showrooms and squat, ugly industrial buildings. Some of the streets were named after small Devon villages such as Hennock and Trusham, and a plan began to form in Peter's mind.

He parked the van in a quiet side street and locked it before setting off on foot, his holdall dangling from his hand. Hopefully, he wouldn't see the van again. It had been useful, and it had given him a place to sleep the night before, but vehicles could be tracked and he couldn't afford the risk of keeping it for too long.

Passing a row of wheelie bins beside the street, he had an urge to lift a lid and drop the van's keys inside, but he'd learned his lesson. If things went wrong, he might need the means to get away.

Peter followed his nose until he met a main road, then he walked toward the city centre until he found a bus stop. Alone, leaning against the bus stop's concrete signpost, he mulled over his plan, and the more he thought about it, the more he liked it. It wasn't without potential pitfalls, but if he played his cards right he could be warm and dry for a while, somewhere out of the way, somewhere safe. The passport in his jacket was good. It was some of his best work, and he'd taken his time with it. It was his insurance policy, his way out. But how long would it hold up?

I'll soon find out, he thought. *When it all falls apart, it'll happen fast.* He'd have to be ready to run. Until then, he'd play it by ear.

It wasn't long before a bus grumbled to a halt in front of him, and the doors swung open with a muted hiss.

Stepping inside, Peter said, "City centre?"

The driver nodded, and Peter offered a ten pound note.

"Haven't you got a card?" The driver indicated a contactless card reader. "You can tap it on there. Much quicker."

"No, I left it at home. Sorry, mate."

The driver sighed and took Peter's money, issuing the ticket and dispensing his change.

Peter thanked him with a nod and a smile. He pocketed his ticket and change, then he found a place by a window, slumping into the seat and dropping the holdall onto the seat beside him. The bus resumed its rumbling journey, and Peter stared out as the dull trading estate gave way to endless rows of terraced houses.

The drone of the diesel engine and the warm, stuffy air in the bus sent Peter into a daze. His nerves had been strung tight for too long, and a wave of exhaustion washed over him. He let his eyes drift closed, and he laid his left hand on top of the holdall while his right hand drifted to the front pocket of his jeans, his fingers tapping at the bulge made by his wallet. He'd rifled through the wallet he'd taken from Ryan back in Teignmouth, keeping the cash and throwing the rest away. He had a bundle of notes that would last him a while, and despite what he'd told the driver, he had three credit cards, all in different names, none of which were his own. *I won't use them yet*, Peter thought. *Not until I have to.*

Peter didn't sleep, but he let his body rest while his mind buzzed busily, thinking ahead, running through his options one by one, concentrating on the details.

When the bus reached the city centre, Peter thanked the driver and stepped down onto the pavement, losing himself among the crowds. He walked aimlessly for a few minutes, changing direction often until he spotted a small shop selling secondhand electronics, its window crammed with used mobile phones.

Thankfully, it wasn't a branch of Fones and Gadgets. He'd had dealings with the owner of that particular chain, and he couldn't afford to show his face if there was even the slightest chance he'd be recognised.

This place is nothing to do with them, Peter told himself. *It'll be fine*.

He entered the shop and bought a decent Motorola, paying with cash. The phone was already charged, but after a brief bit of haggling, Peter persuaded the shopkeeper to throw in a power bank at a discount. That ought to last him until he could find a charging socket.

A charity shop yielded a jacket and a flat cap. Both were in a kind of tweedy material better suited to someone twice his age, and the jacket was at least one size too big, but when he looked in the mirror in the shop's fitting room, he could hardly recognise himself, and that was just fine.

Back on the street, Peter yanked the labels from his purchases and slipped them on, feeling better by the minute. A pang of hunger sent him to a small supermarket where he picked up a bottle of orange juice, an egg sandwich and a packet of crisps, along with a pay-as-you-go SIM card. Peter stuffed his shopping into the holdall, then he went to look for somewhere to sit down. He thought there were some benches by the cathedral, and his mood lifted when he saw that he was right. He found an empty bench and sat down, then he attacked his food, pigeons pecking around his feet in the vain hope he'd drop a crumb or two.

No chance, mate, Peter thought, stuffing the last crust into his mouth. He washed his meal down with a slug of orange juice, then he set about inserting the SIM card into the phone. A few minutes later and he was up and running.

Peter worked fast, keeping one eye on the phone's charge, but he needn't have worried. It took him less than fifteen minutes to set his plan in motion. He'd done the groundwork some time ago, so the identity he needed was already set up, complete with an email address and online profiles. He was ready to start his life anew.

All he had to do was find the perfect place.

CHAPTER 18

Gandy Street in Exeter was quiet when Dan and Alan strolled over the road's granite setts. A few tourists meandered aimlessly along the narrow street, pausing now and then to study a shop window, but there was little in the way of hustle and bustle. At the height of summer it would be much busier, especially at the weekends, but today Dan and Alan wandered along at a leisurely pace, and they found Melody's shop in no time at all.

"Here we are," Dan said. "Indiago. Does that actually mean anything?"

"It looks like a made-up word to me." Alan peered in at the shop window. "I can't see Melody, or anyone else for that matter. Shall we go in?"

"Absolutely."

Dan led the way inside, and as the door swung shut behind them, Melody appeared, stepping in through an archway at the back of the shop. "Good morning," she began brightly, but her smile slipped when she recognised them. "Oh, hello. It's Dan, isn't it?"

Dan stepped forward to meet her. "Hello, Melody. Yes, I'm Dan and this is Alan."

"I remember. What can I do for you?"

"We were passing, and we thought we'd pop in and take a look at those shirts you mentioned."

"Right. Okay." A weak smile fluttered on Melody's lips as she regained her composure. "Are you both looking for something?"

"Yes," Alan said firmly, at the same time as Dan said, "Just me."

Melody's gaze flitted between them. "Erm…"

"We're both looking," Alan explained. "I'd like something smart but casual. Dan?"

Dan nodded. "The same."

"Great. Wonderful." Melody looked them up and down. "I've got plenty to choose from, all excellent quality." She gestured to a rack on the wall. "Would you like some help, or shall I leave you to browse?"

"We'd appreciate your help," Dan said. "I'm told you have excellent taste."

"That's very nice to hear. Who said that?"

"Zadie," Alan replied. "She was talking about your home. Exquisite was the word she used."

Dan watched Melody's reaction carefully. At the mention of Zadie's name, her eyes had grown wider, and for a fraction of a second she'd frozen, her mouth slightly open as though she were holding her breath.

But then the moment was over and Melody smiled warmly, tossing her hair as if basking in Zadie's praise. "That was so kind of her. But Zadie's like that, isn't she? So generous, so thoughtful toward others."

"You get on well with her?" Dan asked.

"Always. She's been a great friend to me." Melody strode over to the rack of shirts, selecting a white shirt with thin, pink stripes. She held it out, the wooden hanger balanced on the tips of her fingers. "How about this one? It would suit you, Alan."

Alan went to her side. "Er, I like the stripes, but I'm not sure about the colour."

"Seriously? The colour's perfect for you."

"Is it?" Alan touched the shirt's sleeve, rubbing the material between his fingertips. "It's good quality fabric, I can see that right away."

Melody looked very pleased. "Thank you. You know, a lot of people don't know the difference between a handmade shirt like this and a cheap one from a supermarket."

"I've been well taught," Alan said. "Dan is the real expert."

Melody gave Dan an appraising look as he came over to join them.

"Don't give me too much credit," Dan said. "All I've done is show Alan a world beyond Marks and Spencer."

"You can find a few nice things in M and S, I suppose," Melody said. "But I'm offering a range that you won't find on the average high street. My little shop might seem pricey at first glance, but these clothes are made to last. All the materials are ethically sourced and I'm very choosy about the suppliers I use."

"That's very commendable," Alan said.

"That's not why I do it," Melody replied, and as she spoke her voice became stronger, her tone more urgent. "It's not about virtue signalling; it's about values. This shirt is a case in point. The fabric is one hundred percent organic cotton, and it was made by workers who were fairly paid. When you buy this shirt, you can be sure there were no sweatshops involved, no workers sleeping on the factory floor."

Dan found himself nodding along. Either Melody was quite the saleswoman or she was committed to a cause. But there was another possibility. She'd expertly steered the topic of conversation away from Zadie. Had that been a deliberate attempt to forestall any further questions?

It was time to find out.

"Are you a keen environmentalist?" Dan asked.

"I try. I do my bit, but there's always more we can do, isn't there?"

"Oh yes. Does Zadie share your convictions, do you think?"

Melody started to shake her head but then seemed to change

her mind. "In some ways. She sticks to her vegan principles. She won't even wear wool."

"On the other hand, she's paid by sponsors and advertisers because she can persuade people to buy lots of fancy products they probably don't need," Dan said. "And what about all those designer dresses? She told us that she usually only wears each outfit once. What happens to all those expensive clothes once she's used them?"

"I'm not sure."

"She doesn't give them to you to sell on, does she?"

"No, of course not. When people send clothes to Zadie, they generally specify what she can and can't do with them. There's usually some sort of contract."

"That's interesting," Alan said. "Like a non-disclosure agreement?"

"I think it depends on the company, but I'm sure no one would let her sell the clothes afterward. They may only have been worn once, but that makes them secondhand, and selling them off cheap devalues the brand. Zadie once told me that with some labels, she can't even throw the clothes out; she has to make them unusable. She literally takes a pair of scissors to them, rips them apart."

Alan tutted. "What a terrible waste."

"It is, but that's not Zadie's fault."

"But she goes along with it," Dan said. "Did that ever cause any friction between you or any arguments?"

"No. We've never argued. We're friends."

"It's always good to have friends," Alan said. "Have you known Zadie long?"

"Since she came to Devon, so for about two years. It might be a little longer." Melody nodded as if recalling a fond memory. "She came into the shop, actually. She stood right where you are now, Dan. She looked around and then she smiled. It was as if she lit up the room. We've been friends ever since."

"It must be handy to have a friend like Zadie," Dan said.

"How do you mean?"

"You know, a friend with links to the fashion industry. Someone with a high profile."

Melody's cheeks flushed, and a spark of anger flashed in her eyes. "I don't take advantage of her, if that's what you're implying. That would be awful, and it would be unethical. I could never do that."

Dan held up his hand. "Sorry. No offence intended. Please, forget I said anything."

"Easier said than done," Melody replied. "You know, I get tired of people assuming I ride on Zadie's coattails. I don't. I was running this business for a long time before I met her, and I've always stood on my own two feet." Melody curled her upper lip as she went on, "I'm not some kind of hanger-on, feeding on the scraps from Zadie's table. Not like…"

"Not like who?" Dan asked.

Melody shook her head, tight-lipped.

"Like Carly," Dan suggested. "She must've benefited from Zadie's rise to fame."

"I don't really know Carly very well, but Zadie swears by her. They seem to spend a lot of time together, so Zadie must be paying her a fair amount, but I've never had a personal trainer, so I've no idea what the going rate is."

"How about Connor?" Dan asked. "He seems like an unusual friend for Zadie. What do they have in common, do you think?"

"I couldn't say, but the other day, when you talked to Connor, he was being a bit weird. He isn't always like that. Connor can be good fun. He doesn't take himself seriously, and he likes to make us laugh."

"He doesn't have to work though," Dan said. "Would you describe him as a hanger-on?"

"No. He doesn't need Zadie's money; he has plenty of his own. He has a lovely house too. He never asks for anything. None of us do."

"Even Naomi? She's struggling to find work. And then there's Philippa: the student who doesn't go to college."

Melody stared at him. "I don't know what you're trying to imply, Dan, but if you're expecting me to say horrible things about my friends, you're wasting your time." Her expression became colder and more pinched as she added, "I think you'd better go."

"I know it must seem like we're being intrusive," Alan said. "But if we're going to find the person who's been bothering Zadie, we'll have to ask some awkward questions."

Dan nodded regretfully. "It's unavoidable, I'm afraid. But if there's anything you want to say, you can talk to us in confidence."

Melody shook her head firmly.

"Are you sure about that?" Dan went on. "To be frank, it seems as though you're holding something back. Maybe there's something that's been troubling you, something about one of Zadie's friends or acquaintances perhaps?"

"No," Melody said. "We might look like an odd bunch to you, but we look after each other. We don't think of Zadie as being famous. To us, she's just a friend."

Alan smiled. "That's good to hear. This must be a difficult time for Zadie. She's lucky to have such good friends."

Melody seemed to search Alan's expression, then she nodded slowly. "We're lucky to have Zadie, and each other." Her gaze still on Alan, Melody's tone softened. "You didn't come here looking for shirts, did you?"

"Not really," Alan admitted. "I'm sure they're very nice, but we wanted to talk to you. It might've been better if we'd explained that from the start."

"Yes, it would. But we are where we are, so…" Melody let out a theatrical sigh. "Go on then. What do you want to know?"

"Where do you get your hair done?" Dan asked.

"What? Why do you ask?"

"You said you'd had your hair done especially for the dinner with Zadie and the others, and I wondered which hairdresser you used."

Melody's hand went to her hair. "I go to Tony's. It's near the museum. But I don't see what that's got to do with anything."

"Your birthday dinner was on Sunday night. Is Tony's open on a Sunday?"

"Oh no," Melody said. "What I meant was, I'd had it done especially for my birthday, but that was on the Saturday. I'd already booked an appointment, so I shut the shop early and went off to treat myself. I had them put in a semi-permanent colour. I thought it was fine at first, but by the time Sunday came around, I hated it. I tried and tried to wash it out, and it didn't end well. In the end, I just had to make the best of it. You can still see the colour. Awful, isn't it?"

"Not at all," Alan said. "I think it looks very nice."

"Flatterer," Melody replied, though she looked secretly pleased. "Is there anything else, because if not—"

"Who's Mary?"

Melody squinted at Dan as though he'd spoken a foreign language. "Sorry? I don't…"

"We were told that Zadie had an argument with someone called Mary, and for obvious reasons, we need to find out who that is."

"Right." Melody looked thoughtful. "Who told you about this?"

"I'd rather keep that confidential," Dan said.

"I'll bet it was Carly. I hear she's a bit of a gossip."

Dan made his expression fixed and tried not to give anything away. "I won't comment on that, but you still haven't answered my question. Who's Mary?"

"I don't know why you're asking me about this argument Zadie's supposed to have had, but I can't see the point. She might've had some little spat with someone, but that doesn't mean a thing. Don't get me wrong, Zadie's great, but she can be difficult, demanding even. She likes to get her own way, and she'll argue over the slightest thing until she's blue in the teeth."

"Does she argue with you?" Alan asked.

"Sometimes, yes, but it's usually over something silly. She might make some offhand comment about what I'm wearing or my make-up or my shoes, and I'll admit, that kind of remark gets my back up. She knows what I do for a living, and she knows I do the best with what I can afford, so it's a bit tactless to criticise my taste in clothes, don't you think?"

Alan nodded. "Yes. Coming from a friend, that kind of remark can sting." He sent Dan a meaningful glance, then he returned his attention to Melody. "What happens when you fall out with Zadie?"

"We get carried away and say things we shouldn't, and then one of us storms off. But we don't stay angry for long. We call each other and apologise. Sometimes she'll send me a little gift: flowers or something. Then we'll get together and have a hug, and we're besties again. These little rows are nothing to get worked up about." Melody smiled. "Now, is that everything? Because I need to get on."

"Only one more question," Dan said. "Do you smoke?"

"No."

"Not ever? What about the day after the break-in?"

Melody grimaced. "Oh, that. Well, Connor persuaded me to try one, but I didn't like it. I didn't inhale, as someone once said."

"Is that because there was something other than tobacco it?"

"Seriously? That's your question?"

Dan nodded. "Seriously, and there's a good reason for asking it, believe me."

"I don't know what Connor gets up to, but I assumed it was just a normal cigarette. Why are you so interested in it?"

"We found cigarette stubs in Zadie's garden," Alan said. "Three of them."

"That might've been Connor, I suppose, but I doubt it. He always says that he only smokes when he goes out for a drink. He likes to stand outside with the other smokers; God knows why."

"Did he go outside when you were in the pub on Sunday night?"

"Erm, yes, he did. He finished eating before the rest of us, and he didn't want dessert, so he popped outside."

"Have you any idea how long he was gone for?"

Melody shook her head. "By that point in the evening, no one was looking at the time, and I hate to say it, but we didn't miss him. We all love Connor, but sometimes, it's nice if it's just the girls. We can let our hair down a bit."

"Right. It's a shame no one mentioned this before," Dan said. "It leaves Connor unaccounted for during the night of the break-in."

"Not for long," Alan replied. "As a cover story, smoking a cigarette wouldn't have bought him more than ten minutes or so. He didn't have time to nip back to Chagford. It takes a good half an hour in a car, and anyway, Connor can't drive."

"I think he *can* drive," Melody said. "He chooses not to. He says it's bad for the environment, but that doesn't stop him from begging lifts from the rest of us."

"We'll have a chat with him later. Thank you for your help, Melody. We'll let you get on." Dan handed her one of his business cards. "If you think of anything that might help, please get in touch."

"Erm, okay." Melody peered doubtfully at Dan's card as if unsure what to do with it, and Dan had the impression it would be in the waste bin as soon as he'd left the shop.

"We should be going," Alan said. "Thanks, Melody. I might pop back the next time I'm looking for a new shirt."

Melody's only reply was a weak smile, so Dan and Alan made their way outside and headed back along Gandy Street.

"What do you make of her?" Dan asked.

"I'm not sure," Alan replied. "She didn't answer all our questions, and I'm not sure I believed that story about her hair. Apart from that, she seems nice enough."

"But there's something not quite right. Melody tries very hard to fit in with Zadie and the others, but she doesn't quite manage it. She seems to be the only one to hold down a regular job, and that makes me wonder if she isn't jealous or resentful."

"If she was, is that a sufficient motive for her to harass Zadie?"

"It could be," Dan said, but before he could say more, his phone vibrated in his pocket. "Hang on, Alan."

Taking out his phone, he saw Zadie's name on the screen, and he took the call. "Hello, Zadie. Is everything all right?"

Dan waited with bated breath, but the terse response was not from Zadie. "This is Natalya. Zadie told me to use her phone. She's too upset to talk."

"What's happened? Is Zadie all right?"

"She isn't hurt, but while we were out, someone came into the house." Natalya paused. "Zadie found another note. It was worse."

"What did it say?"

"The same. The same words exactly. But there was…" Another pause. "This time there was a knife."

CHAPTER 19

S tanding at the kitchen sink, Philippa donned a pair of bright pink rubber gloves and plunged her hand into the bowl of soapy water. Finding the clump of wet fabric beneath the suds, she squeezed gently. You couldn't be rough with cashmere or it would be ruined, and the sweater was one of her favourites.

The scent of pure soap flakes conjured memories of her mother. She'd never trusted modern detergents, but she'd known how to eliminate all manner of stains, and she'd taught Philippa well.

A few minutes later, Philippa drained away the soapy suds and refilled the bowl with clean water. Rinsing was the most tedious part of the process, but it had to be done, over and over until all trace of the soap had been washed away. Philippa's mind wandered, the repetitive movements of her hands almost meditative. She thought of the house, deciding that it was in need of a thorough clean.

Sadly, she'd had to let the cleaner go. The poor woman hadn't charged a lot for all the work she'd done, but there'd been no money to pay even her meagre wage, so that was that. At first, Philippa had tried to keep on top of the housework herself, but it wasn't an easy house to keep in good order, especially when she was trying to concentrate on her studies. She'd make up for it as soon as she'd dealt with her sweater. She'd start by running the vacuum cleaner around every room. It wouldn't be quick, but it was necessary, and if she put her mind to it, it wouldn't be too bad.

There'll be better times ahead, Philippa told herself. *Much better times.* Philippa drained away the last of the water and laid the sweater on a towel before gently rolling the towel to soak up the excess water. After a few minutes, she took the sweater up to the airing cupboard and laid it flat on a shelf, singing softly to herself. The cupboard was warm and clean and filled with the comforting scent of lavender. There. She'd completed a task that had needed doing. Excellent.

Back in the kitchen, Philippa peeled off her rubber gloves. She'd have a little break before starting on the housework. A drink would go down well, but she banished the thought of an ice-cold G and T. She fetched a bottle of sparkling mineral water from the fridge and poured a glass. *That hits the spot*, she told herself, though she wasn't convinced. It really didn't do anything of the sort.

She needed a distraction, so she retrieved her phone from her bag, checking her messages and emails. *Boring. Boring. Boring.*

But what was this? Nestling among the spam and marketing materials was an email from Airbnb. Philippa smiled as she read it. Someone was interested in booking Keeper's Cottage, and they wanted to stay for a few days, although there was a possibility that the stay might be extended to several weeks.

Philippa tried not to get too excited. It was important to be cautious with these things. Even though the cottage was self-contained, it still felt like part of her home, and she couldn't have just anyone staying there. Philippa logged in to the site and checked up on her prospective tenant.

His name was Jack Devlin, and though he didn't have any reviews because he hadn't stayed in any other Airbnb properties, his message was very polite and well written. Apparently, he was from West Sussex, but he was living in Devon and studying at Exeter University. He'd been living in a shared house, but he needed somewhere quiet to work for a while. Philippa's spirits soared. Like her, Jack was a postgraduate student working on his thesis. It couldn't be better. She studied Jack's profile photo, and he looked nice. Not handsome by a long shot, but he had a kind smile, and you could tell a lot about a person from their smile.

Philippa composed a careful reply and sent it immediately. Setting her phone down on the counter, she went to make a cup of coffee, and as she took her first sip, a notification pinged on her phone. Jack had replied already. He was obviously keen, and a few minutes later an email arrived, confirming that Jack had booked the cottage for a whole week. He'd be arriving the very next day.

"Woohoo!" Philippa cried. With that money coming in, she could go out and buy some groceries and even pay off some of her credit card debt. Wonderful.

Philippa drank her coffee slowly, enjoying every mouthful. She'd have to give the cottage a once over to make sure everything was as it should be. She'd also need to pop to the shops so she could put some milk in the fridge and a loaf in the bread bin. She could even buy some scones along with a pot of clotted cream and a jar of strawberry jam. People enjoyed these little touches, and she wanted Jack to be happy. If he stayed for a while longer, the money would make all the difference.

Philippa rinsed out her empty mug and placed it in the dishwasher, then she went to fetch the keys for the cottage. When Jack Devlin arrived, everything would be ready.

CHAPTER 20

U pstairs in Zadie's studio, Dan and Alan stood with Zadie and Natalya, all of them staring at the desk.

Standing upright on the uncluttered surface of pale wood, the black-handled cook's knife seemed particularly incongruous, the tip of its stainless-steel blade buried in the desk. The knife had been driven into the desk with some force, stabbing through a small sheet of paper and pinning it in place. The paper's bleak message, spelled out in words cut from a magazine or something similar, was exactly the same as before: *I'll see you soon.*

The message may have remained unchanged, but the knife had lent it a chilling new significance, as if the blade implied an insidious addendum: *I'll see you soon. And then…*

Dan ran a hand over his jawline. The interloper was back and he was raising the stakes, but the chilling collage of cut-out words wasn't the only difference between the two notes.

"Look at the edges," Dan said. "The first note was torn from a book or a pad, but this one has been cut."

Alan leaned forward. "Oh yes. Could that be significant, do you think?"

"Yes. Along with the carefully cut-out letters, it suggests a greater degree of premeditation. This was planned." Dan turned his attention to Natalya and Zadie. "Who found the note first?"

"We both found it at the same time," Zadie said, her voice faint. "It was there when we came in."

"Since then, has anyone touched the note or disturbed anything in the room?" Dan asked.

"We touched nothing," Natalya replied. "I called the police, then you." Natalya looked uncomfortable as she added, "Also, Zadie asked me to call Connor. I don't know why."

"Because I need to have my friends around me," Zadie blurted. "This is hard for me. I don't... I don't know what to do."

"It's okay," Dan said gently. "You've every right to be upset, but you're safe now. We'll deal with this together. Take a couple of deep breaths, nice and slow, and when you're ready, in your own time, tell us what happened."

"I can do that," Natalya said. "We'd been out. Every week, I take Zadie into Chagford for her yoga class. It's in the town hall."

Dan raised a hand to halt Natalya's narrative. "When does the class start?"

"Twelve o'clock. It lasts for an hour."

"What do you do during that time?"

"I go to the shops," Natalya said. "I get some groceries. Zadie gives me a list."

"A paper list?" Dan asked.

Natalya shook her head, frowning. "It's on my phone. A shared note. What does it matter? Nothing happened until we got home. Everything was normal until we came back here."

"Nevertheless, I'd like to have all the details," Dan replied. "Who drove, and which car did you take?"

"We took Nat's car," Zadie said. "It's the same every week. Nat gives me a lift and drops me outside the town hall, then she picks me up when the class ends. Like Nat said, everything was fine until we got home. We came in the back door, and straight away Nat sensed something was wrong."

Dan looked at Natalya expectantly.

"I wasn't totally sure," Natalya said. "But the door into the hallway was closed, and when we went out, I thought we left it open."

"We usually just pull it to," Zadie explained. "If you shut it properly, the door sticks and that's a pain, especially if you're carrying a drink or something. When we came in, Nat spotted it was completely shut, so she pulled it open and we rushed upstairs. We found the note together. I was so glad Nat was with me, or I don't know what I'd have done."

"I didn't do a lot," Natalya said. "I checked there was no one here, then I made some calls, that's all."

"You did very well, Natalya," Alan replied. "Very level-headed."

"Yes, although it would've been safer if you'd gone straight outside," Dan said. "If you'd found someone—"

"I would've dealt with him," Natalya stated.

You would've tried, Dan thought, but he was not about to argue the point with Natalya. Changing tack, he said, "Are you both sure that all the doors and windows were locked when you left?"

Natalya's nostrils flared. "Of course. I checked everything. I am always very careful. Always."

Zadie made a noncommittal noise, and Natalya shot her a look. "What?"

"Well, the thing is, Nat, while you were getting into the car, Shaun asked if he could use the loo before we went out, so I let him in, and…"

"You didn't wait until he'd finished?" Natalya said.

"No, that would've been embarrassing."

"So what did you do about the door?" Natalya demanded. "Did you give him a key? Did you tell him to lock it?"

"Not exactly. I opened the back door for him and then I came out to the car. You were waiting, and I didn't want to be late for yoga, so I left him to it. I knew we weren't going to be out for long, and Shaun was going to be here the whole time."

Natalya muttered something under her breath in what Dan

assumed was Ukrainian, but he didn't need a translator to understand her displeasure.

"It wasn't my fault," Zadie said. "I didn't think anyone would be brazen enough to walk into my house in broad daylight."

"Let's not waste time apportioning blame," Dan said. "Did Shaun see anyone or hear anything? Was there a car or a passerby?"

Zadie waved his questions away. "You'd better ask Shaun. I can hardly get a word out of him."

"I'll find out what he knows," Dan said. "What about the knife, do you recognise it?"

"It's from the kitchen," Natalya replied. "From the knife block."

"Was anything disturbed in the kitchen, anything missing?"

Zadie looked thoughtful. "No, I don't think so. I didn't notice anything wrong."

"Perhaps you could check," Dan said. "There's nothing much else we can do. Hopefully, the police will send someone out soon. In the meantime, nobody must touch anything. It's best if no one comes in the room at all."

"But I have to work," Zadie protested. "I need my laptop and it's in the desk."

Dan shook his head. "You'll need to figure out an alternative. You must have another computer in the house."

"You can use mine," Natalya said. "It's practically brand new."

"But I was going to work on my book. I need my notes, my manuscript."

"They're in the cloud," Natalya replied. "I'll show you. You'll be fine. You can work at the kitchen table. I'll make some herbal tea, yes?"

Zadie's resistance crumbled. "A cup of tea would be very nice. Chamomile, please, that always helps. I suppose we'll muddle through somehow. Thanks, Nat. You're a lifesaver."

"Yes, well done, Natalya," Alan said. "I wish I had a PA like you to keep me organised. I'd get a lot more writing done."

Natalya looked Alan up and down. "You can afford?"

"Oh, I didn't..." Alan's cheeks coloured. "I wasn't trying to tempt you away from Zadie."

"I should think not," Zadie said. "That wouldn't be right at all. Anyway, you'd have me to reckon with. I wouldn't give Nat up without a fight."

"What are you saying?" Natalya demanded. "I am not a slave, Zadie. If I want to go and work for Alan, I can. You can't stop me."

Alan looked mortified and seemed temporarily speechless, so Dan intervened. "I'm sure my colleague was just trying to pay you a compliment, Natalya. Let's go downstairs and get that chamomile tea for you, Zadie. You ought to take a few minutes as well, Natalya. You've both had a shock. You need a moment to decompress."

Zadie acquiesced and she followed Natalya out of the room, but Dan tapped Alan on the arm, and they both hung back.

"I want to take a quick look around," Dan said. "It won't take a sec."

"Okay, but you mustn't tamper with any evidence. Be careful."

"I will."

Dan paced the room. Was anything out of place? The studio was as tidy as ever, and far as he could tell, nothing had been added to the meagre collection of items in the room.

"What are you doing?" Someone said, and Dan turned with a start to see Natalya watching him from the doorway.

"Nothing," Dan said. "We're just checking everything is okay."

Natalya was unimpressed. "If there was something wrong, I would've known. I would've told you already."

"Yes, of course." Dan started to turn away from the room, but his gaze snagged on the blue typewriter on top of the filing cabinet. "Hang on." Dan strode over to the typewriter.

"Wait," Natalya said. "You said we shouldn't touch anything."

"Just looking." Dan leaned over the typewriter. Yes. As he'd thought, the carriage was sticking out slightly on the left-hand side, and that wasn't right. It looked untidy, and Zadie liked everything in her studio to be neat and precisely aligned. It looked as if someone had tried to slide the carriage back to the centre and had pushed it slightly too far.

Alan joined him, Natalya hard on his heels.

"What's wrong?" Natalya asked.

"Does anyone ever use this typewriter?"

"No. It's just for show."

"So the carriage would normally be in the centre, yes?"

Natalya nodded. "There's a little catch. It keeps it in place."

"A carriage lock," Alan said. "It keeps the top part from moving during transit."

"Well, someone's disengaged the catch, that's for sure." Dan turned to Natalya. "Has anyone moved this typewriter recently, or dusted it?"

"No. I haven't cleaned the room this week. I usually do it on Fridays."

"You think the intruder used it?" Alan asked Dan. "The note wasn't typewritten."

"Somebody's been playing around with it," Dan said. "We'll need to check with Zadie, but if she hasn't used it, you must tell the police when they come. There could be fingerprints."

Natalya nodded. "I understand. We should go downstairs."

This time, Natalya made certain she was the last to leave the room, and she closed the door behind her.

In the kitchen, Dan asked Zadie about the typewriter, and she confirmed that she hadn't touched it and neither had anyone else.

"So it must've been the intruder," Alan said. "But why would they take the time to play with a typewriter? The longer they were inside, the greater the chance of them being spotted."

"There'll be a reason," Dan replied. "For now, all we can do is tell the police and hope they'll send someone to check for fingerprints."

Dan was about to say more when the back door opened and a broad-shouldered man breezed inside, closely followed by Connor.

"Tobias," Zadie cried. "What on earth are you doing here?"

"I called him," Connor said. "This is getting serious, Zadie. You need someone to—"

"I'm not helpless," Zadie interrupted. "I can look after myself, and I certainly don't need my brother to fight my battles for me."

"We'll see about that," Tobias said. "It seems to me that you should've called me ages ago, but first things first. How are you feeling? Are you all right?"

Zadie rolled her eyes. "I'm fine. There's no need for you to go into overdrive."

"I'm here to help, Sis."

"Don't call me that," Zadie said from between clenched teeth. "How many times do I have to tell you?"

"Sorry, er, Zadie, but I'm worried. This needs sorting out. Connor tells me there was a note left upstairs, along with a knife, and this is the second time it's happened. Is that right?"

"Yes, but there was just a note the first time, nothing else."

"And you have these notes?" Tobias asked. "Can I take a look at them?"

"You can look upstairs if you really must," Zadie replied, "but you can't see the first one. The police took it."

"Right. And who else has seen these notes?"

Looks were exchanged around the group, then Dan said, "We all have. Why do you ask?"

"Important to get the facts," Tobias said, adding in an undertone, "Such as they are."

His last remark seemed to sting Zadie, and she bridled. "You're not in the courtroom now, Tobias, and you can't just barge in here and start talking down to everybody."

"Come on, there's no need to overreact." Tobias made a downward motion with his hands. "Take a breath and calm yourself. You need help, otherwise you know what might happen, and we don't want to go there again, do we?"

"How dare you say that to me?" Zadie demanded. "I'm perfectly calm, Tobias. I'm in control and I'm dealing with this in my own way. I've been in touch with the police, and I have Dan and Alan; they're doing all they can.

"Yes, I heard about your private eyes." Tobias regarded Dan with a jaundiced eye. "It's okay, guys, I'll take it from here. You can go."

Dan smiled. "With respect, Tobias, we don't work for you. Ms Barrington is our client, and we take our instructions from her."

"Right, yeah, but things have changed. Perhaps I haven't made myself clear. I'm a lawyer, a barrister, actually, and if we want an investigator, I have people we can use. Professionals."

"Nevertheless, we'll stay until our client says otherwise." Dan looked to Zadie. "Would you like us to leave?"

"No," Zadie said. "Please stay, Dan. Take no notice of my brother."

"That will be my pleasure," Dan replied, favouring Tobias with an implacable smile.

"Now, look here—"

Zadie raised her hand to cut Tobias off. "Oh no, you don't. I'm not going to let you march in here and throw your weight about. This is my house, and I'll ask you to respect that."

"All right, let's not wash our dirty linen in public. Clearly we need to talk, but we'll do it in private, when these *gentlemen* have gone."

Zadie folded her arms. "I'll say this once, Tobias. If you want to help, that's fine, but you'll do it on my terms. Otherwise, you're the one who's going to leave."

A tense silence filled the room as the siblings stared at each other, then Tobias let out an exasperated sigh. "Seriously, Zadie, you're a piece of work, you really are. All right, have it your way. They can stay. They might even turn out to be useful, I suppose."

"Perhaps we can begin again," Dan said, offering his hand for a shake. "I'm Dan Corrigan, and this is my associate, Alan Hargreaves."

Tobias dutifully shook their hands. "Tobias Barrington, QC,

though I expect it'll have to be KC before too long, when Her Majesty finally shuffles off this mortal coil."

"Yes, that'll be a sad day," Alan said. "The end of an era."

"Quite." Tobias clasped his hands together and puffed out his chest as if about to address a jury. "Now, let's take stock. Has anyone had the sense to make sure there's no one lurking inside or out in the garden?"

"I checked the house," Natalya replied. "Everything was fine, but I haven't been outside."

"We can check the garden," Dan said. "And we'll talk to Shaun too, find out if he saw anything."

Tobias raised an eyebrow. "Shaun?"

"My decorator," Zadie said. "He was here the whole time, working outside."

"Do we trust him?" Tobias asked. "Do we know this wasn't an inside job?"

"That's just silly," Zadie replied. "Why would he do something like this? He's been working here for weeks, and we've had no problems with him whatsoever."

Natalya made a disapproving noise, and Tobias turned to her. "Nadine, isn't it? What's up?"

"Natalya. I was thinking about Shaun. There was one time, Zadie, when, you know…"

Zadie frowned but then realisation dawned. "Oh, I caught him peeping in through the window when I was filming. I didn't have much on, but it doesn't matter. It was nothing."

Tobias bristled. "I don't like the sound of that. I'd better have a word with him, set him straight."

"No, let Dan and Alan talk to him. It really wasn't a big deal. He just happened to be working outside the window. He didn't do it on purpose, and to be honest, he was much more embarrassed than I was. He apologised and then shuffled off with his tail between his legs."

"Even so, your brother is right," Dan said. "It needs following up. We'll take care of it."

"Right. Good." Tobias seemed to look at Dan anew. "While you're at it, I'll chase up the police and see if I can't make them move a bit faster."

"DI Spiller has been dealing with the case," Alan started to explain, but Tobias dismissed his words with a grimace.

"Never mind that, I'll go straight to the Chief Superintendent, and if that doesn't do the job, I'll talk to the Chief Constable."

Tobias appeared to be building up a head of steam, and when he took out his phone, Dan tapped Alan on the arm and gestured to the back door.

Outside, Alan puffed out his cheeks. "Tobias is very full of himself, isn't he?"

"You can say that again, but it's worth keeping him onside. It never hurts to have an ally with friends in high places."

"True. Shall we take a look around the garden, or do you want to start with Shaun?"

"Shaun. Let's go and get him."

They made their way along the back of the house and found Shaun working at the far end, standing on the highest level of the scaffolding, just below the level of the roof.

Dan yelled up to him, and a moment later Shaun's face appeared, his features partially concealed behind a dust mask.

"Could you come down for a minute?" Dan called out. "We need a word."

Shaun pulled up the dust mask. "What about?"

"I'll explain when you come down. It's important. The police will be here soon, and—"

"Police? Why, what's happened?"

"That's what we need to talk about," Dan said. "But we can't stand here shouting at each other. Come down, please. We won't keep you for long."

There was a pause before Shaun replied. "All right, all right, I'm coming."

Dan watched as Shaun made his laborious way down from the scaffolding. For a man who was probably used to working at height, he made heavy weather of his downward journey, his boots thudding on each rung of the aluminium ladders.

He really doesn't want to talk to us, Dan decided. *Is that because he has something to hide?*

Finally joining them, Shaun pulled a crumpled tissue from the depth of his boiler suit and blew his nose loudly. "Bloody dust. Gets everywhere. Now, what do you want that's so important?"

"You've been working here all day?" Dan asked.

Shaun nodded. "Since eight o'clock. Sanding woodwork mainly. Why?"

"You didn't pop out at all, at lunchtime maybe?"

"No. I had my dinner early. A sandwich in the van." Shaun screwed up his face as if losing his patience. "I had a mug of tea as well, if you really want to know. I bring a flask seeing as no one here's going to offer me anything."

Ignoring Shaun's surly tone, Dan said, "What time do you call early?"

"Half eleven. Listen, what's all this about? I've got work to do, and I'm behind as it is."

"Around midday, someone let themselves into Ms Barrington's house," Alan explained. "Did you see anyone?"

"No. I would've been up on the scaffolding by then, working."

"Did you hear anything?" Dan asked. "A car, maybe?"

Shaun smirked. "Couldn't have. There's a good reason I had my dinner early. I've been working here for weeks, and it's always the same. Every Wednesday, her ladyship toddles off just before twelve, so I can get some proper work done. See, she complains if I make too much noise. Sometimes it can't be helped, but today I waited until she'd gone."

"To do what?"

"To use my electric sander, of course. She wasn't here, so I cracked on with the window frames. You have to watch what you're doing, and it makes hell of a racket. You could've driven a truck down here and I wouldn't have seen or heard a thing."

Dan looked Shaun up and down. The man's boiler suit was

coated in dust, and the marks on his cheeks showed that he'd been wearing a dust mask for some time. His story rang true. Dan looked up at the scaffolding and saw a cable running from the kitchen window up to the level where Shaun had been working. "That cable; did you plug it in yourself?"

Shaun shook his head. "She did it for me; Natalie or whatever her name is. She doesn't like me going inside."

"Natalya," Dan corrected him. "But aren't you doing some decorating inside as well?"

"I started indoors, but that was a while back. I've been working outside for a few weeks. I've got to get on with the outdoor stuff while the weather's good. So if you've said what you're going to say, I'll get back to it."

"In a second," Dan said. "I was wondering if you decorated the studio. The room upstairs."

"Yeah. She wanted me to do that room first. There wasn't much to it. Why, is there a problem with it?"

"No, I was just interested," Dan replied. "Do you smoke, Shaun?"

Shaun shook his head indignantly.

"Never? You don't pop down the garden for a fag break?"

"Never." Shaun glared at Dan. "It was the fags that finished my dad off. They did for his lungs, and that was the end of him."

"I'm sorry to hear that," Alan said. "That must've been a hard loss to bear. You're very wise not to smoke."

"Yeah, well, it doesn't take much to figure out."

"Thanks for your time, Shaun." Dan said. "That's all for now. I expect the police will want to ask you the same questions when they get here, but for now, we'll leave you to it. Thank you, you've been very helpful."

"Right. Well, it's no trouble," Shaun said, though his tone implied otherwise. "I'll get on. Goodbye."

Shaun trudged back to the scaffolding and began climbing back up.

"What do you think of that?" Alan asked. "Was he telling the truth?"

"I think he would've left a trail of dust if he'd been inside. I suppose he could've taken his boiler suit off, and his boots too, but somehow, I can't see Shaun writing notes and making subtle threats. I'm inclined to believe him. It's a shame though. If he'd seen anything, it would've given us a break."

Alan nodded. "We could certainly do with a clue or two. Perhaps we'll find something in the garden."

"It's worth a try."

Dan and Alan made their separate ways around the garden, but when they met back at the house, neither had anything to report.

"Let's head back inside," Dan said. "If nothing else, we can have a word with Connor."

"Yes, it'll be good to cross another of Zadie's friends off our list. It's a pity we didn't learn anything worthwhile from Shaun. Zadie's brother won't be impressed. He's already taken a dislike to us."

"As far as I'm concerned, the feeling's mutual. Still, if he deals with the police, that ought to keep DI Spiller from breathing down our necks."

Alan stared at Dan in mock amazement. "What's this? Daniel Corrigan seeing the bright side? It must be Sam's influence. She'll have you reformed in no time."

"Ha, ha," Dan intoned, but something stopped him from dismissing Alan's remark out of hand, and he sent Alan a reproving look.

Alan held up his hands. "Sorry. I shouldn't have said that."

"It's okay, but…" Dan searched for the right words. "You know me better than most people, Alan, and you can make jokes at my expense all day long. I generally have it coming, and anyway, I know you don't mean anything by it. But when it comes to my relationship with Sam, that's different."

"Of course it is. I spoke without thinking. It won't happen again."

"Already forgotten. Water under the bridge."

Alan smiled. "I'd hate for you to think I'm resentful of you and Sam. I'm glad you've got together. I'm happy for you; for both of you."

"Thanks. Things will be different, but even so… you know."

"Yes. I know. Shall we go in?"

"After you," Dan said, and he followed Alan back to the house.

CHAPTER 21

S haun peered over the edge of the scaffolding boards and watched Dan and Alan until they made their way to the back door and disappeared from view.

"Why don't you two just bugger off, once and for all?" he muttered. "Asking stupid bloody questions. Nosy buggers."

Shaun shuffled back to the window and pulled his dust mask back into place. He resumed his work, sanding the window frame by hand, but his conversation with the two men kept coming back to his mind. *Those blokes are too full of themselves*, he thought. *Who the hell do they think they are?*

Shaun growled and ground his teeth together. They'd asked if he'd worked inside and wanted to know if he'd been in that room upstairs: the studio. A small voice whispered in the back of Shaun's mind: *They know.*

"No," Shaun murmured. "They know nothing. Nothing."

There was no way they could've found out what he'd done. It was impossible. But they had to know something was up, otherwise, why would they have asked him about that bloody room?

Shaun pressed hard on the sanding block, pushing it to the

window frame's edge, and it slipped, sliding from the wood and making him rasp his knuckles on the wall. "Bugger it!"

Shaun nursed his hand while he stared accusingly at the window frame. In truth, he'd made the wood perfectly smooth five minutes ago, but he'd carried on regardless. His mind wasn't on the job, and that was no good. It was no good at all.

He'd have to get his head straight and sort himself out, then he'd have to do something about those stuck-up blokes and their insinuating remarks. He'd sort them out once and for all. And that would be an end to it.

CHAPTER 22

Dan and Alan found Connor alone in the kitchen. He was resting his back against the edge of the counter, his arms folded and his shoulders slumped.

Before Dan could speak, Connor said, "They've all gone upstairs. Toby wanted to see the scene of the crime."

"You didn't want to go and see for yourself?" Dan asked.

Connor rolled his eyes. "Toby had other ideas, and there's no use trying to get him to change his mind."

"Yes, he seems to be a forceful character," Dan said.

"As a steamroller." Connor offered a faint smile. "It's his job to argue over every tiny detail, and he's damned good at it. Be grateful he's on our side. You wouldn't want to go up against him, take it from me."

"You've had a run-in with him yourself?" Dan asked.

"Me? No, thank God, but I... I know what he's like." Connor gestured to the back door. "How did you get on with the decorator, did he see anything?"

Dan shook his head. "He was working up on the scaffolding with an electric sander, so he didn't hear or see a thing, and we had a look around the garden, but we didn't find anything of interest."

"Oh well. Nothing to do but wait for the cops. Fat lot of use they'll be." Connor seemed deflated, his eyes dull as he gazed at Dan. "I suppose you'll be wanting to join the others, get in on the action."

"Actually, we wanted to speak to you," Alan said.

"Really? Why?"

"We've been speaking to all of Zadie's friends," Dan explained. "You're next on the list, and this is as good a time as any. If you don't mind, that is."

"No, I don't mind. It's fine." Connor perked up, pushing himself away from the kitchen counter and speaking rapidly. "What do you want to know? Not that I can tell you very much, not about this anyway. I mean, that would be weird, wouldn't it? But I'll try to help if I can. Of course I will." Connor's face fell. "Sorry, I'm babbling. I'm just a bit on edge. This business with poor Zadie, it's affected us all. I know it's worse for her, much worse, but it makes you think, doesn't it? I always used to feel safe around here, but not anymore."

"These things can be very unsettling," Alan said. "But I don't think there's any reason for you to be concerned for your own safety."

"That's right," Dan added, watching Connor carefully. "Unless there's something else that's worrying you, Connor. Is there something you haven't told us about?"

"No."

"That's all right then," Dan said. "So what made you call Zadie's brother?"

"I thought Zadie needed someone in her corner, someone who works with the police and knows how to get things done."

"That's perfectly reasonable, but why didn't Mr Barrington come straight here?" Dan asked. "I'm sure he was worried about his sister, but he stopped to pick you up on the way. Why did he do that?"

"I asked him to give me a lift."

"I see," Dan said. "What's your relationship with Mr Barrington?"

Connor looked put out. "How do you mean? He's not gay, if that's what you're implying."

"I wasn't implying anything. I simply wanted to know whether you're friends or acquaintances. It's helpful to know these things."

"Okay. I've known Toby for a while, but I wouldn't say we were friends."

"Thanks for clearing that up," Dan said. "You're a smoker, aren't you, Connor?"

"Yeah. Sometimes. It's not great, I know, but I try to keep it down to a few smokes a day. I could do with one now, come to think of it."

"Something to take the edge off?" Dan asked. "A little cannabis, maybe?"

Connor stared at him. "I don't do drugs. I saw too much of that in the music biz, and I swore I'd never go down that road. So yeah, I roll my own smokes, but it's tobacco. Gold Leaf. I get it at the newsagent in town. Here, I'll show you." Connor fished in the pocket of his denim jacket, his collection of enamel badges catching the light as he pulled out a plastic pouch of tobacco. "Look. This is what I use. Is that good enough for you?"

"Okay, fine. I believe you, Connor."

"I should bloody well think so."

"You must understand, we sometimes have to ask difficult questions, but that's all we want to know for now." Dan said. "If you want to pop out for a smoke, I'm sure Zadie wouldn't mind. You could go into the garden."

Connor shook his head.

"There's a nice old bench down there," Dan went on. "That's where you usually go, isn't it?"

"What are you talking about?"

"We found some cigarette ends," Alan said. "We thought they might've been yours."

"You thought wrong," Connor stated. "I don't know who's been smoking down there, but it wasn't me and it wasn't any of Zadie's friends. We'd never throw fag ends in Zadie's garden. We all know how much it would upset her. She loves nature and plants and all that. When she goes for a walk, she'll pick up litter from the side of the road, take it home and recycle it. That's the kind of person she is, and we all know that."

"Nevertheless, someone has been smoking in the garden, and it wasn't just tobacco," Dan said. "It smelt like cannabis to me."

Connor wrinkled his brow. "Really? Are you sure?"

"I can't be completely certain, but I'm as sure as I can be."

"You must've made a mistake. If any of us were smoking that stuff, I'd know it. I can smell it a mile off and I've already told you, I don't like it. It's a slippery slope, and I've seen too many people throw their lives away."

Dan and Alan looked at each other. In Alan's eyes, Dan saw genuine belief in Connor's story and a hint of concern for the man. Dan wasn't so sure. Connor had sounded sincere. He'd spoken with the conviction of someone who'd learned the hard way he had to abstain, but Dan couldn't quite see Connor as the holier-than-thou convert. On their first meeting, Connor had been flippant and devil-may-care. Perhaps that had all been bluster and bravado, a way of concealing his own insecurities, but it was hard to know. Was there a sensitive side to Connor's character, or was he a chameleon, changing his colours to blend in with the background?

Even now, Connor was putting on a show, his jaw falling open as though he'd experienced a sudden revelation.

"Hang on a minute," Connor said in hushed tone. "Don't you get it? We're on to something. Those cigarettes weren't mine, so they must be from *him*; they must be from whoever's been pestering Zadie. They're *evidence*."

"That had occurred to us," Alan said. "The police will be following it up. Some things are best left to the authorities."

"Exactly," Dan added. "In the meantime, we can be moving on. If you think of anything that might be useful, Connor, please give me a call. Do you still have my number?"

"Yeah, sure, but you're not going, are you? You can't just walk away."

"Yes, we can," Dan said. "It's for the best. Somehow, I think Tobias will get his way and the police will be here very soon. It would be better if we weren't here when they arrive."

"Too many cooks?" Alan asked.

"Yes, but it's not just that. You know what the police are like. We could be tied up for hours while they run through their endless procedures. We'll achieve a lot more on our own, and I'd like to talk to Philippa next."

"Why?" Connor asked. "This has got nothing to do with her."

"We're talking to everyone," Dan replied. "Is there some reason why we shouldn't talk to Philippa?"

Connor pouted like a petulant child, but Dan met his gaze, smiling patiently.

"She doesn't like people to turn up unannounced, that's all," Connor said. "She's a very private person. It would be better if I talk to her first and pave the way. I'll call her and see if I can arrange a meeting."

"That won't be necessary," Dan replied. "Natalya gave us her address, so we'll pop around there now. If you wouldn't mind telling Zadie where we've gone, that would be great."

Connor lifted his chin in acknowledgement, but his weary mood was back, and he was already slouching against the kitchen counter.

Dan and Alan let themselves out and headed for the car.

"He's a strange one, isn't he?" Alan said. "He's hard to figure out."

"Yes, but I'm surprised to hear you say it," Dan replied. "I thought you'd swallowed his story hook, line and sinker."

Alan shook his head. "I didn't like the way he kept gabbling about nothing much in particular. I'm not sure if he was deliberately being theatrical or if he was just nervous and letting his mouth run away with him."

"Agreed. But I wonder whether there might be more to it than that. Looking back, I can't help wondering if he was playing for time, trying to distract us with irrelevant information. His little speech about the perils of illegal substances didn't ring true to me. And there was something else. He lied about his relationship with Tobias."

"What makes you say that?"

"Mr Barrington introduced himself as Tobias, and that's what Zadie called him too, but to Connor, he's always Toby."

"I didn't notice," Alan said. "it's interesting, but it doesn't necessarily mean they're friends. I can't imagine Mr Barrington QC ever referring to himself as anything other than Tobias, so perhaps Connor does it to annoy him."

"Even when Tobias isn't there? Connor told us that *Toby* was upstairs, remember? Anyway, he uses the name lightly as if it comes easily to him, and that familiarity speaks volumes."

"Okay, so there's something there. The question is, what do we do about it? We could try talking to Mr Barrington, but I don't think we'd get very far. He's taken part in more interrogations than you've had hot Americanos. He'll run rings around us."

"We have a trick or two up our sleeves ourselves," Dan said. "But it might be better to approach him from an indirect angle. Could you do some digging online? You're so much better at it than me."

"Flatterer. But yes, I'll run some searches as soon as I get home. Mr Barrington's name will be all over the internet in court reports and so on."

"That's a good place to start." Dan clicked his fingers. "I wonder if he's ever prosecuted someone for stalking or harassment. If he put someone away and they've been released, they could be trying to get back at him; taking revenge by targeting his sister."

Alan looked doubtful. "That's a shot in the dark, but I'll bear it in mind. What about Connor, shall I look into him too?"

"Yes please. You know the drill. We want anything unusual, anything that stands out."

"No problem. Is there anyone else I should be looking for?"

"That's plenty to be getting on with," Dan said. "I don't want to put too much on your plate. We need to keep a bit of bandwidth in reserve. Something else might turn up when we talk to Philippa, and let's not forget Naomi."

"At least we're working our way through the list." Alan rubbed his hands together. "This is more like it. We're finally beginning to get somewhere."

"Do you think so? All we've done so far is chase down a series of dead ends and followed leads that went nowhere."

"But that's where the magic happens," Alan said. "It's only by working through the useless questions that we get to the good ones. It's exactly the same when I'm working on a book. Sometimes I have to write thousands of words just to find out which way the story is going. I know from the outset that I'll have to delete those words, but even so, they're invaluable. They're part of the process, a necessary step into the darkness."

"Very poetic," Dan said. "Let's hope you're right, because so far, there's been an awful lot of stumbling about in the dark."

"Well, you never know. Perhaps Philippa will tell us something illuminating."

"I hope so, Alan, I really do. At the risk of overextending your metaphor, it's about time we found the light switch."

CHAPTER 23

Philippa wasn't proud of herself. She lay huddled on the couch in her lounge, hiding in her own home like a frightened child. But they were still out there, Daniel Corrigan and Alan Hargreaves, and she didn't want to talk to them; not today, not ever.

Thank God for Zadie. Her call had come just in time, letting her know that Dan and Alan were on their way. It had given her just enough time to make sure the doors were locked and all the lights were off.

That done, Philippa had meant to go upstairs, but at the sound of a car approaching, she'd panicked and thrown herself onto the big sofa that faced away from the lounge window. Sinking into the cushions, she'd pulled in her arms and legs, curling into a foetal ball, determined not to move a muscle.

It would be fine. All she had to do was wait. The doorbell chimed, and after a few seconds it chimed again. The brass knocker rang out, once, twice, three times, the sound echoing in the empty hallway.

Why don't they just go away? Philippa thought. *Why don't they get the message?* The doorbell chimed once more and then footsteps crunched back and forth across the gravel driveway.

She couldn't be sure, but it sounded as though someone had come right up to the lounge window. They'd be peering in, searching for her.

Dammit! She'd left an empty wine glass and the unfinished bottle on the side table. She'd meant to tidy them away, but in all the flurry of checking the doors, she must've forgotten. *How could I have been so careless?* she thought. *They'll see them and they'll know I'm here.*

No. That was silly. It was just a wine glass and a bottle; they could've been there for hours, days even. She was getting jittery.

I should never have opened that bottle, she decided. *I've been drinking far too much.* But she'd only had a couple of glasses — a little celebration after she'd made Keeper's Cottage ready for her Airbnb guest. Okay, maybe she'd had three glasses of wine, and she hadn't held back when filling her glass, but it was only sauvignon blanc; it wasn't like she'd been hitting the vodka again.

A voice came from the window, startlingly loud: "There's no one in."

Philippa tried to picture who was speaking, but she couldn't tell; she didn't know their voices well enough.

"Her car's here," someone replied. "The bonnet's still slightly warm. She's been out recently."

"Maybe she's in the back garden. Shall we try going around?"

A pause.

Oh no, Philippa thought. *No.* She kept the bi-fold doors between the lounge and the dining room open, so anyone looking in from the back of the house would see right through into the lounge. They'd spot her cringing on the sofa.

Had she locked the side gate to the garden? Had she?

The silence stretched on forever. But then: "It's no good. The gate's locked, and no, don't even think about climbing over."

"Okay. Let's go. We'll try another time."

"We haven't got much choice, but I'll leave a note and make sure she's got your number."

Another agonising second and then the flap of the old brass

letterbox clattered, the metallic sound loud enough to make Philippa wince. She pulled her legs close to her chest, hugging them tight, and waited for the men's footsteps to fade away. She heard a car engine start, the rising whine of a car reversing, and then the unmistakeable sound of someone driving away.

But still, Philippa waited. What if they'd only pretended to leave? What if one of them had driven away while the other stayed outside?

Philippa closed her eyes, trying to listen hard, but as the adrenaline drained from her system, it left her dizzy and weak. A headache crept across her forehead, pulsing behind her eyes. God, it was all too much. With everything that was going on, she was shattered. She needed to rest. She needed to... She really ought to...

PHILIPPA WOKE WITH A START. WHAT TIME WAS IT? THE ROOM WAS swathed in gloom, and when she looked through to the dining room window, the panes were dark. How long had she been asleep?

It must've been hours. Not that it mattered. She'd obviously needed it.

Slowly, her limbs stiff and her back complaining, Philippa levered herself up from the sofa and crept toward the lounge window. Keeping low she peeped out, her gaze darting left and right across her front garden.

Her house was set back from the road, and the streetlights did little to dispel the gathering darkness. It was almost impossible to see anything against the dark background of the front hedge, and the old cherry tree cast a deep shadow that shifted as the breeze stirred the branches. Philippa blinked and forced her bleary eyes to focus.

"There's no one there," she whispered. "No one."

The two men had gone, but even so, she couldn't shake the feeling of being watched. *I'm being silly*, Philippa thought.

Frightening myself. She got like this sometimes when she was alone in the house. It was as if the emptiness of the place somehow made itself known, all those unused rooms crying out to be filled with life and warmth. It had been different in her parents' day: raucous laughter echoing through the hallways, the babble of conversation filtering from the dining room, the unfamiliar voices of weekend guests. But not anymore. It was just Philippa and her memories, her hopes and regrets, her half-forgotten dreams and uncertain plans.

"Come on, Philippa," she murmured. "Pull yourself together."

Straightening her spine, she stood and switched on the lamp, then she hurried to close the curtains, dealing with the front windows first and then the back, shutting out the dark. But as she glanced out at the sliver of light escaping from the window to illuminate a small patch of the gloomy back garden, something caught Philippa's eye and she froze. Had she seen something moving over by the shrubbery or had it been her imagination?

Her fingers still gripped the curtain. Dare she pull it back and check?

Philippa drew a steadying breath. *There's nothing to worry about*, she told herself. *It was probably just a cat or something.* There seemed to be scores of cats in the neighbourhood, and while she was fond of cats in an abstract way, it was no fun having the little buggers using her gravel paths as a latrine.

Philippa cocked an ear and listened. Nothing. She finished shutting the curtain, then she closed her eyes and exhaled. Why was she so jumpy?

You know why.

The thought came unbidden and she pushed it aside. This wasn't the time to dwell on such things. What was done, was done. The die was cast, as her father used to say, though as often as not, he'd said it in Latin: *Alea iacta est*.

Thinking of her father, Philippa wandered from room to room, closing all the curtains, switching on the lights. Daddy had been brave, she'd give him that. He'd had a kind of unbending courage that had carried him through the hard times. Surely, she must've inherited his streak of dogged determination, otherwise she'd never have had the presence of mind to put her plan into action.

She could be tough when the need arose, so she had nothing to worry about. She was in control. It was others who had something to fear, not her. She was strong, and she'd live life on her own terms.

She closed the last few curtains, and she didn't even look outside. She didn't so much as glance at the shadowy depths of the back garden, nor at the darkness that lay beyond.

CHAPTER 24

Peter pressed himself further into the dark embrace of the tall shrubs. *Philippa*, he thought. *A nice name*. With the room's soft light behind her, Philippa's hair seemed to glow, and her figure was enough to make his heart beat faster. Peter's gaze was glued to her as she made to shut the curtains.

He licked his lips and inched to his left, desperate to hold on to that fleeting glimpse until the last possible moment. *Shit!*

Philippa froze, her face framed by the curtains, and stared outside. An icy fear squirmed in Peter's gut. Could Philippa see him? No. He was too well hidden. He'd be okay.

She peered out for an agonising second, then the curtains slid shut and Philippa went from room to room, turning on lights, closing the curtains, shutting the house up for the night.

Peter waited a while, then he crept from his hiding place and retrieved his holdall from beneath an ornamental shrub.

Time to take a look around, he thought. *Time to find a way out*. You never knew when you might need to make a hasty exit.

The garden at the back of the house was surrounded by a high brick wall, and it hadn't been easy to climb inside, but he'd been helped by a nearby tree in the neighbouring woodland, its lowest branch providing a valuable handhold. Getting out again would be a different matter. So far he'd seen nothing so useful on the inside of the wall, and he felt like a rat in a trap.

He found several places where plants crept up the wall, but some were roses with savage thorns, while others had masses of thin stems and delicate flowers, but nothing substantial enough to take his weight. There wasn't even a sturdy trellis he could clamber up. The plants were held in place by lengths of thin wire that would surely snap if he tried to stand on them.

Peter cursed under his breath. He was almost at the garden's back wall, and he'd had no luck. But then he spotted a door set into the wall. *Perfect.*

The door's metal bolt was secured with a padlock, but that needn't be a problem. The padlock was very old and it had never been strong. It wouldn't put up much of a fight, but he wouldn't tackle it until he needed to. A broken padlock would give the game away.

In the meantime, the night was growing cold and the air felt damp, the chill creeping into his bones. He needed shelter, and there ought to be a shed somewhere, or at least a dry corner where he could huddle and wait for the dawn. Now that he'd found an escape route, it would be safe to stay.

Peter began his search by following the line of the brick wall. The far corner of the garden was screened off by a stretch of wooden fence panels, and Peter's hope's rose. Behind the fence he found a couple of wood-framed compost heaps, an old wheelbarrow, and something covered by a plastic tarpaulin. A peek beneath the plastic revealed a stack of logs. *My need is greater than yours*, Peter thought, and he pulled the tarpaulin free from the lengths of timber that had been used to weigh it down.

The plastic flapped and crinkled noisily as Peter draped it over his shoulders and wrapped it around his body, but it had to be done and he worked quickly. Cocooned in his makeshift robe, he sat down next to the logs, leaning his back against a wooden fence panel. It wasn't ideal, but he had something between himself and the ground, and that was something. *There were times when I'd count myself lucky for this*, he thought. *Very lucky indeed.*

Memories of his time on the streets came unbidden, but he shied away from them. This was very different. He was here by choice. He might have an uncomfortable night ahead of him, but it was necessary. He had to be cautious and do everything he could to let his trail grow cold. And here, tucked up in the corner, he was invisible. For now, at least, he was safe.

THURSDAY

CHAPTER 25

Immediately after breakfast, Dan called on Alan and found him bright-eyed and bursting with energy.

"Come in, come in," Alan said. "I'll put the kettle on. Tea? Coffee?"

"I'm fine, thanks. And it looks like you've had one or two already."

Dan nodded at the kitchen table, where Alan's laptop was surrounded by empty mugs.

"I woke up early and thought I may as well get up and get cracking. Are you sure you don't want a drink? I'm making tea."

"Okay, I'll have a cup, but what've you been working on? Is it your book?"

"No, no. Research. For the case." Alan busied himself at the kettle. "I was right about Tobias Barrington. His name crops in hundreds of court reports. He's been busy."

"Right. "

Dan sat at the table and ran his eyes over a large pad of paper, the top sheet covered in handwritten notes. "Do you mind if I have a look?"

"Be my guest, but you won't make much of it. I have my own

way of making notes, and they're indecipherable to anyone but me."

Dan pulled the pad closer and murmured in agreement. "I see what you mean. I'll let you break it down for me. Give me the edited highlights."

"No problem. Here's your tea." Alan placed a steaming mug in front of Dan, then he retook his seat, pushing the empty mugs aside to make room for the full one. "I'm going to have to do some washing up."

"Later," Dan said. "What've you unearthed about our friendly, neighbourhood barrister?"

Alan picked up his pad, flipping back through the pages, then he cleared his throat. "Tobias Barrington had an illustrious career in London before moving to Devon and settling down. Sound familiar?"

"Hm. Was there a particular reason he left London?"

Alan smiled triumphantly. "Love."

"Really? How did you figure that out?"

"When you move in certain circles, your engagement gets announced in the press, and as I said, Tobias Barrington was a high-flyer. At some point, he must've met an aristocratic family and taken a shine to their charming daughter. Their engagement made it into *The Times*."

Dan leaned forward. "It wasn't Philippa, was it?"

"Well, yes." Alan looked a little deflated. "You've spoiled my big reveal. How did you guess?"

"It wasn't a guess. When we met Philippa, she told us she had a title. You gave me the rest."

"I ought to have known you'd work it out. Anyway, four years ago, Tobias and Philippa planned to marry, so he moved to Devon and set himself up in Exeter. What happened after that, I don't know, but it makes for an interesting timeline. I can't help but wonder if Tobias planned to set up home with Philippa in Chagford, so he bought The Old Manse intending to renovate it.

When his engagement fell through, he persuaded Zadie to take the house on. That would explain a lot."

"We can ask about that," Dan said. "One way or another, it's another link between Philippa and Zadie, and that could be interesting. I'd like to know why Philippa and Tobias broke up. If it was anything to do with Zadie, Philippa might be holding a grudge."

"I wondered about that, but you're always telling me not to go too far beyond the evidence. For all we know, they might've parted amicably. It does happen."

Something in Alan's tone made Dan give him a sharp look. "You sound as though you're speaking from experience."

"Well, I haven't always been single you know. I've had my moments."

"I'm sure you have, but…"

"What?"

Dan hesitated. "I don't intend this to sound like a criticism, Alan, but you're hardly typical. You do *everything* amicably. For us ordinary mortals, breakups are miserable and packed with blame and bitter recriminations."

"Okay. Let's say they had a messy breakup and went their separate ways. What does that have to do with Zadie? If Zadie was in any way involved in the breakup, why would Philippa choose to keep her as a friend? Surely she wouldn't want anything to do with her."

"If we were talking about two men, I'd agree with you, but women are more subtle than that. Philippa and Zadie might appear to be friends, but they could still be holding on to some unresolved issues. Resentment can be dangerous when it's allowed to fester. It can easily turn to anger, or perhaps something worse."

"Hell hath no fury like a woman scorned?" Alan suggested.

"It's a cliche, I know, but that doesn't mean it isn't true. You're always telling me that Shakespeare knew what he was talking about."

"He did, but that line was from a play called *The Mourning Bride* by William Congreve. But don't feel too bad; it's a common mistake."

Dan sighed. "Let's stick to the point. There was a relationship between Philippa and Zadie's brother, and we should follow that up. We need to speak to Philippa, and it seems to me that she's been avoiding us. Yesterday, Connor knew we were on our way to see her, so he could've tipped Philippa off, giving her time to make herself scarce."

"We can try again later. Meanwhile, do you want to hear what I've found on Connor? It won't take long."

"Go ahead."

Alan turned the page of his notebook. "As you might expect with someone who was a celebrity in his day, there are lots of references to Connor online. Unfortunately, it's hard to sort the wheat from the chaff."

"Is there anything recent? His moment in the limelight was a while back, wasn't it? What was his song called?"

"It was 'Bring it Down', and it hit the charts nine years ago, apparently. I was quite shocked when I read that. It made me feel old."

"Things move fast in popular culture," Dan said. "Nine years might not seem long to us, but in the music industry, Connor's fame is ancient history."

Alan smiled. "I wouldn't be so sure. It turns out that in some corners of the internet, Connor has something of a cult following. He was the front man, the figurehead of the band, and his song might not be in the charts, but it has struck a chord with all kinds of protest groups. There's one part where Connor sings 'Bring it down' over and over, almost shouting it, and that one phrase has caught on with Extinction Rebellion. They chant it on protest marches and demonstrations. It's even a hashtag. It's popular with anti-capitalist groups too."

"I had no idea."

"Me neither. I've seen the protests on the news, but I never paid much attention to what they were chanting, so I certainly didn't connect it to the song. Unfortunately for us, Connor's newfound notoriety means that once you start looking, you find references to him all over the internet. People tweet about him, make memes and little videos of him singing those words. He's everywhere. Trying to find anything useful is like wading through treacle."

"Did you come across anything relevant?" Dan said. "Were there any hints of potential conflict between him and Zadie?"

"Not that I've been able to find. I can keep trying, though. I might dig up something worthwhile if I stick at it."

Dan shook his head. "Let's put Connor to one side for now. I think we should head back to Chagford. We can try Philippa again, and if she's not in, I'll persuade Zadie to give her a call and arrange a meeting. Also, I'd like to take another look around and see if we can spot anything."

"We've already tried that."

"I know, Alan, but you never know who we might bump into. Someone knows more than they're telling, so all we can do is keep asking questions until we get results. We'll solve this case. The answers are out there somewhere."

"Agreed, and we won't find them by staying at home," Alan said. "Shall we take my car?"

"Yes, please."

"Say no more." Alan closed his laptop and jumped to his feet. "Let's see what we can find out."

CHAPTER 26

D S Kulkarni swallowed the lump in her throat. She'd been to plenty of post-mortem examinations before, but never when the deceased had been so badly burned.

In the centre of the room, the pathologist, Dr Helen Bunting, and her assistant, an unprepossessing man introduced only as Ben, were busy at their work.

Kulkarni released a slow breath. She thought she'd exhaled quietly, but beside her, DS Winslow turned in her seat. "Are you okay, Anisha?"

Kulkarni nodded. "Fine."

"Are you sure? Because, if you want to pop out…"

"No, I'll be all right. The smell got to me for a second, that's all."

"Yeah. Thankfully, I'm lucky that way. I hardly have any sense of smell at all. My kids tease me about it, especially when I'm making dinner, but at times like this, I'm grateful."

Dr Bunting looked over at them. "This isn't a conclusive cause of death, but I can tell you what almost certainly killed him."

"Smoke inhalation?" Kulkarni asked.

"Not likely," Bunting replied. "Remarkably, a significant proportion of his lungs are still intact, and I can say with some confidence that at the time of the fire, this man was breathing very little or not at all."

"He was dead or dying," Winslow stated. "Did he have any other injuries?"

"He certainly did. Blunt force trauma to the frontal bone of the skull. There's a fracture that's consistent with a blow from a solid object, and in my view this was a perimortem injury. In other words, it was given at or immediately prior to death." Bunting paused for a moment. "He was hit very hard indeed, and he almost certainly lost consciousness. There would've been severe swelling in the brain, and I doubt he could've survived it, even if he'd received immediate medical attention."

"Somebody set the fire because they wanted to be sure," Kulkarni said. "And they wanted to destroy as much evidence as possible."

"As always, I leave that kind of explanation to you." Bunting looked down at the human remains on her slab. "We still have some way to go, so I'll proceed. Okay?"

"Fine," Winslow replied. "Please, carry on. I'll stay, but do you want to step outside, Anisha?"

Kulkarni shook her head firmly. "I'll stay."

BACK AT TEIGNMOUTH POLICE STATION, WINSLOW INSISTED IT WAS HER turn to make the coffee.

"Fine," Kulkarni said. "But make it strong, okay?"

The first sip of coffee almost stripped the tastebuds from Kulkarni's tongue, but she swallowed it gratefully.

Winslow, meanwhile, was studying her computer's screen. "Here's something. We've got the e-fits back. I'll forward them to your email."

"Thanks." Kulkarni opened the email and studied the two images: portraits generated from the descriptions provided by Len Franks. These were the two men who'd posed as detectives and questioned Len about the man who'd lived in the flat across the street. Both men had close-cropped hair, but while the white man looked heavyset with a square jaw and a broad nose, the other man had a slimmer face and finer features. Mr Franks had seen only a man with brown skin, but to Kulkarni's eyes, the man's ethnicity seemed more Middle Eastern than South Asian. There probably weren't all that many people of colour in Teignmouth, but even so, it wasn't much to go on.

"They're not exactly distinctive," Kulkarni said. "It's a shame he couldn't pick out anyone from the mugshots."

"We can only work with what we've got. I'll circulate these, and you never know, they might jog someone's memory."

Kulkarni nodded thoughtfully. "Mr Franks thought he'd seen one of the men somewhere else. I wonder where. He probably doesn't get out much, and I don't suppose he goes far."

"It could've been anywhere, and we can hardly go around trying to retrace his every step. If the memory comes back to him, I expect he'll let us know, but we can't clutch at every straw, Anisha."

"I know. So what's next?"

"We still need to track down the man who rented the flat. Did you get anywhere with the landlord?"

Kulkarni shook her head. "Not yet. I finally got hold of someone in the property company, but they weren't keen to help. They kept putting me on hold, and I got the impression there were discussions going on. Finally, I was told that they didn't give out that kind of information, and since the company's based in the Channel Islands, they weren't obliged to answer any questions."

Winslow rolled her eyes. "I'll pass it on to the DI and see if he can set the wheels in motion. Meanwhile, we have plenty to be getting on with. For a start, we need to identify the deceased."

"Any news on the DNA?"

"No, that'll take a while. I'm hoping he'll be reported as missing before too long. He must've been someone's partner, someone's son, maybe even someone's dad."

"I've been checking MisPers, but I'll look again today," Kulkarni said. "That shouldn't take long, then I can try looking for the black van."

"No need. I've got Pat Clarke checking CCTV. She's one of my DCs."

"I met her yesterday. She seemed great. Very bright."

"Oh, she's sharp, is Pat," Winslow said. "She'll go far. And if that van has been past a camera, she'll find it. If we can get the registration, I'll be chuffed to bits."

"Like the man who was run over by a steam train."

Winslow groaned. "Don't give up the day job, Anisha. Either that, or get promoted to Commissioner, then we'll *have* to laugh at your jokes."

"That's the plan."

Winslow simply nodded as if unsure of what to say.

"Now that *was* a joke," Kulkarni said. "And I got you fair and square."

"Okay." Winslow held up her hands with a smile. "Let's get back to work."

"Sure." Kulkarni turned her attention back to her screen. There was plenty to keep her busy for a while, and she was looking forward to it. There was a nice buzz of activity in the office, the feeling of a team working together, and it reminded her of her days in Newquay. She hadn't missed her old station when she'd moved to Exeter. She'd been thrilled to be based in headquarters: the bigger office, the newer building, the prospects of promotion. Truth be told, there'd been some things she'd been pleased to leave behind in Newquay, including a failed relationship with a colleague. But there was something about Teignmouth that made her feel at home.

Don't get too settled, she reminded herself. *This is only temporary.* She thought of Jo Winslow, still a DS and seemingly happy to stay that way. There was nothing wrong with that. Jo was good at her job, and she'd made her home in the town, raising her kids and settling down. A husband and a house by the sea. That sounded pretty good.

It's not for me, Kulkarni decided. She'd joked about making it to Commissioner, but there'd been a grain of truth in the heart of it. She wanted promotion, and she wanted it fast. There was still a long way to go, and she wouldn't get there by settling for a posting in a small town. The sooner she could clear this case up and get back to Exeter, the better.

CHAPTER 27

P hilippa hurried to answer the front door, but she stopped herself in the hallway, pausing to check her hair in the mirror and smooth down her skirt. *Take a deep breath,* she told herself. *Be friendly and polite, but don't go overboard.* There. She was ready. She'd greet her new guest in a welcoming manner, but she'd keep her composure. There was nothing worse than someone trying too hard and coming across as needy.

Philippa opened the door and smiled down at the man on the doorstep. "Hello. Mr Devlin?"

The man bowed his head and looked up at her shyly through his lashes. "Please, call me Jack."

"Delighted to meet you, Jack." Philippa ran her eyes over Jack, weighing him up. He wasn't quite as she'd imagined from his photograph, but perhaps that was down to his designer stubble. Along with the flat cap worn at a rakish angle and his tousled hair, he looked every inch the mature student. Philippa presumed that the holdall at Jack's side would be full of library books and unwashed laundry.

For some reason, Philippa had thought he'd be taller. In person, Jack was slim and narrow shouldered, but maybe that was down to the fact that his jacket was at least one size too big. He'd turned the sleeves up in an attempt to make it fit, but still, it was a tweed jacket and they weren't cheap, so he may well have chosen it deliberately. *He's going for the little boy lost look,* Philippa decided. *Never mind, we've all made mistakes.*

Aware that her welcoming expression had slipped, Philippa hoisted her smile back into place. "So you found the place okay? Were the directions all right?"

"Yes. Fine, thank you. Very helpful."

"That's good." Philippa peered past Jack. "Is your car out on the road?"

"It's in the garage, actually. There's something wrong with the brakes, so I came on the bus."

"From Exeter? Oh, you poor thing. That must've taken ages."

Jack chuckled. "It took an hour, believe it or not, but it was a scenic route: plenty of pretty villages to admire along the way."

"Yes, I suppose so," Philippa said, her voice growing faint. When Jack had laughed, his hand had gone to the side of his chest, and though he'd tried to hide his reaction, he'd definitely winced.

"Are you okay?" Philippa went on. "Are you hurt?"

"What?" Jack quickly lowered his hand. "Oh, yeah, it's nothing. An accident. It's a bit embarrassing. I had a couple of pints with a mate the other night, and I fell over on the way home. I think I bruised a rib or something. It was stupid of me. I don't really drink, you see."

"Me neither," Philippa said. "It's terribly bad for you, isn't it?"

Jack nodded regretfully. "Lesson learned. So you needn't fear for your carpets. I won't be spilling beer or anything."

Philippa shook her head as if completely unconcerned. "It's all stripped floorboards anyway, and I had them all sealed, so you must make yourself at home."

"Right. Well, I'm completely housetrained. I take my shoes off at the door and everything."

"Good to know." Philippa glanced down at Jack's shoes, and she tried very hard not to frown. The canvas shoes might be Vans, but they'd definitely seen better days. Still, if Jack was as good as his word, she needn't fear for the new rug she'd installed in the lounge. Cream hadn't been the best colour choice to entrust to paying guests, but the rug suited the room, so she'd have to take the risk.

"Er, do you think I could see the cottage?" Jack asked.

"Of course. Silly me, keeping you waiting. Let's go."

Philippa stepped down to the driveway, closing the front door behind her.

"Don't you need to grab the keys?" Jack said.

"I knew you were coming, so I left it unlocked. It's very safe out here. Very quiet. The cottage is tucked out of sight behind the house, and you need the combination to get through the garden gate. You won't be disturbed."

"Perfect. Just what I need."

Jack lifted his holdall and Philippa led the way to the side gate.

As she punched the code into the lock, she said, "I sent the combination in the email. Do you still have it?"

"Oh yes. It's on my phone."

"Great."

They walked through the rear garden together, Jack making a show of admiring his surroundings.

"Beautiful garden," he said. "It's huge. You can't even see to the end of it."

"Yes. I think the garden was the main reason my parents bought the place. My mother was a keen gardener. More than that, really. It was her great passion, along with riding."

"That sounds idyllic. Is she still with us?"

Philippa shook her head. "Both my parents passed away."

"I'm sorry for your loss."

Jack sounded sincere, his voice soft with genuine sadness, and Philippa cast him a glance. Beneath his raffish exterior, there was a man in touch with his emotions, a man with a heart.

"What are you studying?" she asked.

"At university? Oh, it's nothing exciting. Sociology."

"Oh, I have a friend in that department. Brian Feldman. Maybe you know him."

Jack looked thoughtful. "No, but I tend to keep my head down, focus on my thesis. I don't really mix with the other students."

"Dr Feldman isn't a student. He's a lecturer."

"Oh, yeah. *Dr* Feldman. Sorry. It threw me when you used his first name. You don't think of the lecturers as having first names, do you? It's like they live in some ivory tower, surrounded by stacks of dusty books. Or is that just me and my overactive imagination?"

Philippa laughed. "No, I know what you mean. They're a weird bunch. But Brian was a friend of the family. He knew my father."

"Right."

Jack seemed reluctant to talk, so they walked the rest of the way in silence.

Keeper's Cottage had its own small garden, and once Philippa had opened the garden gate, she gestured to the cottage with a sweep of her arm. "What do you think?"

Jack let out an appreciative sigh. "I think it's idyllic. Perfect. Like something from a postcard or a jigsaw puzzle."

"Do you do many jigsaws?"

Jack grinned. "Not anymore. My mum liked them, and when I was a kid, I'd try to help her. I wasn't much good at it, but she always said I was doing a good job. She said I had sharp eyes."

"Aw, that's so sweet. Is she…?"

Jack shook his head. "She passed away a few years ago."

"I'm sorry. How about your father, is he still with us?"

"No, he died when I was little. I don't really remember him."

"That's a shame." Philippa found herself taking half a step toward Jack. "You must've been very close to your mum."

"Yeah. I was. How did you know?"

"I can tell." Philippa smiled sadly. "I'll bet you were her whole world."

Jack nodded and pinched the bridge of his nose. "Erm. Sorry. I… I never really talk about this stuff."

"It's okay." Philippa laid her hand on his arm. "It's okay, Jack. I understand."

"Thanks. I…" Jack wiped his eyes on the backs of his hands and exhaled noisily. "Sorry. Here's me, getting all emotional. I didn't mean to. It came out of the blue."

"Grief can be like that. You think you're over it and getting on with your life, but then some small thing will remind you, and before you know it, it all comes rushing back."

"I guess so." Jack looked her in the eye, his gaze soft. "Thanks. You're very easy to talk to, but I shouldn't burden you with my troubles. I expect you've got more important things to do."

"It's okay, Jack. I don't mind. It's good to have someone to talk to, someone who understands. So while you're staying here, if there's any time you want to talk, just pop up to the house, okay? We can have a coffee or something."

"Thanks, that's very kind of you, but I'm sure your husband won't want me turning up."

"I'm not married," Philippa said. "And before you ask, there's no boyfriend or partner or anyone else. I'm on my own, and I'm perfectly happy."

"Good for you. I'm an independent sort of person myself."

"I thought as much."

They looked at each other in silence for a moment, then Philippa said, "I'll let you get settled in. There's a folder on the dining room table, and you'll find all kinds of information in there, but if there's anything you need to know, give me a call, okay?"

"Sure, but aren't you coming in?"

"No," Philippa said. "You don't want me standing over you while you search through the kitchen to see if there's a sharp knife and a cafetière. The answer is yes, by the way, to both questions. You'll also find a bottle of milk and a loaf of bread, plus some tea and coffee and a few basic provisions in the kitchen. Hopefully that's enough to tide you over until you can get some supplies. You'll find some shops in town, so you should be okay."

"Yes, thank you. I'm sure I'll be able to work it out. Thanks for the milk and bread, too, that was very kind of you."

"No problem. I'll leave you to unpack. Bye for now." Philippa turned and strolled away, her steps feeling lighter than of late.

She felt as though she knew Jack already. They'd made a connection, and that wasn't always easy, especially with a man. *Yeah, it's going to be good to have him around,* Philippa thought as she let herself back into the house. *It's going to be great.*

CHAPTER 28

D an and Alan waited patiently outside the broad front
door of Meadow House, Philippa's home.

"It's a marvellous building, isn't it?" Alan said. "Just
look at that stonework." He leaned forward to inspect one of the
stone pillars that framed the doorway. "Are these original, do you
think, or were they added afterward?"

"I have no idea," Dan replied. "As you well know."

"All right, I was just making conversation." Alan fidgeted,
checking his watch. "Maybe I should try the bell again."

"Give it another minute."

"Okay, but I'm beginning to think she's not at home."

"We'll see," Dan said. "I have a feeling she was here the last
time, and our impatience did nothing to help. Let's just wait."

A moment later, the door swung open and Philippa appeared,
smiling. But her smile vanished when she saw who was waiting on
her doorstep.

"Oh, it's you. What do you want?"

"Just a few minutes of your time, if you wouldn't mind," Dan
said. "We'd like to ask you a few questions."

"What kind of questions?"

"We'd like to talk about what's been going on at Zadie's house," Alan replied. "I'm sure that, as her friend, you'd like to help."

The corner of Philippa's lips twitched. "I'd help if I could, but I don't see what I can do. I've already told you everything I know. I don't have anything to add."

"Not even a word or two about Zadie's brother?" Dan asked. "Did you know that Tobias came over to help Zadie?"

"Tobias is here?"

"He was at Zadie's house yesterday," Dan said. "We had a little chat. It was most illuminating."

The colour rose in Philippa's cheeks. "What do you mean by that? Did he say something about—" Philippa seemed to bite back her words. "What did he say?"

"It would be better if we discussed it indoors." Dan glanced meaningfully at the high wall that separated Philippa's front garden from that of her neighbour. "You never know who might overhear if we talk out here."

Philippa looked very much as though she'd like to slam the door in Dan's face, but she stepped back, one hand still on the door knob. "All right. You can come in, but only for a minute. I've got a lot of things to do."

"Thank you," Dan said, and he stepped into the hallway.

Inside, the house was every bit as impressive as the exterior had implied. The broad hallway gave onto a grand staircase that led Dan's gaze upward, and he found himself turning around to take in the oil paintings displayed on the walls, and the crystal chandelier overhead.

"You have a beautiful home," Alan said. "It's breathtaking."

Philippa almost smiled. "Thank you. Yes, it was my mother's pride and joy, and my father loved it here too. They liked to entertain."

"Are they still with us?" Alan asked.

Philippa shook her head. "It's just me. They left the house to me, and I decided to stay. I wanted to keep it in the family."

"A place like this must cost a great deal to maintain," Dan said. "That can't be easy."

"I do what I can. My parents owned quite a bit of land. My mother kept horses and ran a small stable, but I didn't share her passion, so I sold it."

"Where was the land?" Dan asked.

"On the edge of town, near the river."

"It wasn't, by any chance, bought by John Callaway, was it?"

Philippa blinked. "Actually, yes, it was. Why?"

"It's just an interesting coincidence, that's all," Dan said. "We walked along the public footpath the other day, and we passed through a large field belonging to your famous neighbour."

"I'd hardly call him a neighbour; there's at least a mile between his place and mine, but yes, that would've been one of our fields originally. The old stable blocks have gone, of course. Demolished. It was one of the first things he did. Typical, isn't it? I'm surprised he hasn't put in a golf course."

Philippa aimed a disapproving stare at Dan as if defying him to disagree. "Now, what did you want to ask me about?"

"A couple of things," Dan said. "To begin with, do you smoke, Philippa?"

"No."

"You didn't have a cigarette at Zadie's house on the day after the break-in?"

"No. I think Melody had one, but that was only because everyone was so…"

"Upset?" Dan suggested.

"Yes. Everyone was so on edge. Melody thought it might settle her nerves."

"Did it?"

Philippa shook her head. "If anything, it seemed to make her more jittery. Is that all you want to know? Hardly worth your while coming here."

"Oh, there are a few other things you might like to help us

with," Dan said. "I understand you were engaged to Tobias Barrington."

"That's right. What of it?"

"I was wondering if that's how you met Zadie, through her brother."

"Yes. My father met Tobias at a dinner in London: one of those awful affairs where businessmen give speeches and pat each other on the back. Anyway, he invited Tobias here for a weekend, and we got together, which I suspect was exactly what Daddy intended. Later on, Tobias introduced me to Zadie, and we were friends right from the start."

"You didn't fall out with Zadie when you separated from Tobias?" Dan asked.

"No."

"There were no hard feelings?"

"Are you trying to suggest there was some kind of rift between Zadie and me?" Philippa shook her head in disbelief. "When I separated from Tobias, Zadie was on my side all the way, but even if she'd been angry with me, it wouldn't make any difference. Zadie is my dearest friend, and I wouldn't hurt her for any reason, least of all to get back at Tobias. You know, the world doesn't revolve around men and their fragile egos, at least, mine doesn't anyway."

Dan fought the urge to protest; Philippa had caught him out on a lazy presumption, and there was no point in denying it. Instead, he held up his hands. "Apologies. I know these questions might feel intrusive, but I'm trying to understand the relationships within Zadie's circle of friends."

"Why?" Philippa demanded. "What's been happening to Zadie has absolutely nothing to do with any of us."

"Not directly, perhaps," Dan replied. "But if a stranger is harassing Zadie, they've been remarkably well informed, don't you think? And that leads me to suspect that the stalker is someone who is known to at least one of you."

Philippa folded her arms. "Don't you think we've all considered that possibility? It was the first thing we asked each other. Who could have done this? Did we know anyone who might've harboured a grudge against Zadie? Had any of us let slip some piece of information about her: something that could've found its way to the wrong person?"

"Nothing came to mind?" Dan asked.

"No. If it had, we'd have told the police, and I dare say Zadie would've kept you in the loop. But there was nothing."

Dan waited a beat, then: "If one of you was involved, you're hardly likely to admit it."

"Now you're being ridiculous. None of us have anything to hide."

"That's all right then," Dan said. "So you won't mind answering a few more questions. Did Zadie approve of your engagement to her brother?"

"Totally. She was over the moon. She used to call me her sister, although she stopped doing that when I split up with Tobias, for obvious reasons."

"Do you know if Tobias found Zadie's house for her?"

Philippa started to shake her head, but then she seemed to reconsider. "It was Tobias who introduced her to Devon, and she fell in love with it, but I had something to do with her buying The Old Manse. It came up for sale and I mentioned it to Zadie, more as a joke than anything. I knew it was in a state, and I didn't think Zadie would ever dream of taking it on, but she jumped at the chance. She got it for a good price too. Zadie's not just a pretty face, you know. She's an entrepreneur, running a business with a huge turnover. None of that has happened by accident."

"I looked up her books online," Alan said. "They're all over the bestseller lists. She's done very well for herself, and that must've taken a great deal of hard work and determination."

Philippa gestured to Alan, her palm held flat and her fingers spread wide. "Exactly. Someone finally gets it. Zadie might not fit with your ideas of what a businesswoman looks like, but make no mistake, she knows exactly what she's doing."

"I understand that," Dan said. "I was a business consultant for years, and I've worked with a lot of entrepreneurs, so I can appreciate Zadie's achievements. But someone out there doesn't feel the same way. Someone has taken a dislike to Zadie, possibly because they resent her success. They want to bring her down, and I use the phrase with good reason."

"What are you trying to say?"

"*Bring it Down*," Dan said. "Surely you recognise it."

"Are you talking about Connor's silly song? What's that got to do with anything?"

"It's not silly to some people," Alan replied. "It's become something of an anthem to some movements, including some groups who are anti-capitalist."

"That's ridiculous. Connor lives on inherited wealth. He's loaded. He's the most conservative person I know." Philippa let out a bark of dismissive laughter, and when she went on, her voice grew louder, more strident. "He spends half his time twiddling about with the stocks and shares his father left him, then he sits back and does nothing while the money comes rolling in. He doesn't give a damn about where it comes from. He's got money tied up in fossil fuels and weapons manufacturers and God knows what else. If Zadie knew, she'd—"

Philippa stopped herself abruptly, clamping her lips shut.

"Go on," Dan prompted.

"Never mind," Philippa said. "I was getting carried away. Forget it."

"I can't do that," Dan said. "I'd like to understand Connor's relationship with Zadie. If she found out about his investments, what would she do?"

"She'd be angry with him, but not for long. She'd give him a lecture, I expect, and she'd try to make him see the error of his ways, but then she'd let it go. Zadie's never been one to let arguments drag on. She's too kind-hearted for that."

"Can we say for certain that Zadie doesn't know the nature of Connor's investments?" Alan asked.

Philippa seemed to weigh this up. "No, I suppose not."

"So Zadie might've given Connor a dressing down, and he might not have been so keen to let the matter drop," Alan said. "That's a possibility, isn't it?"

"I doubt it," Philippa replied. "Connor's an overgrown schoolboy. If Zadie had a go at him, he'd sulk and blame it on her. He's been like that for as long as I've known him. When things go wrong, he'll pout and whinge, but he never takes responsibility for his actions. He's never had to face the consequences of anything he's done. Nothing touches him. Nothing sticks." Philippa wrinkled her nose in distaste. "He sneers at the upper classes, but he has absolutely no sense of *noblesse oblige*. He's had every privilege, but he's never looked out for anyone other than himself."

"That's an interesting observation," Dan said. "Connor certainly comes across as rather devil-may-care, but in your opinion, might he have been involved in the incidents at Zadie's house?"

"No. He doesn't have it in him."

"Might it be his idea of a prank?" Alan asked. "A way to get back at Zadie?"

"I really don't think so. Frankly, he doesn't have the backbone to do something like that. Connor likes to portray himself as an artist, a wounded genius who never quite got what he deserved, and it works. People are taken in and they misjudge him. They think he must have hidden depths, but he doesn't. He really is that shallow. What you see is what you get." Philippa opened her mouth as if about to say more, but then she changed her mind.

Choosing his words carefully, Dan said, "Life would be simple, wouldn't it, if everyone were so transparent? But most of us choose which side of ourselves to show the world, don't we?"

"You could put it that way."

"If, hypothetically, I was looking for someone among Zadie's friends who wasn't all that they appeared to be, who would I start with?"

Philippa hesitated. "Hypothetically?"

"Yes."

"Okay. If I had to come up with a name, I'd go for Melody."

"That's an interesting choice," Alan said, "but we've already spoken to her."

"That's as may be, but you asked for a name, and I've given you one. Are we done?"

"Almost," Dan said. "Could you tell us where you were yesterday around noon?"

"Shopping. In Exeter. Waitrose. Do you want to see the receipt? I'm sure I still have it, and there's always the date and time marked on them somewhere."

"It would be useful," Dan said. "If it's not too much trouble."

"It's in the kitchen. Wait there."

Philippa marched from the hallway and disappeared through a doorway.

"Is this really necessary?" Alan asked. "You don't seriously suspect her, do you?"

"Not at this stage, but I never like to turn down the chance of finding more detail. You can tell an awful lot from a receipt."

Philippa reappeared, bearing down on them with a slip of paper in her hand. She thrust it at Dan. "There. At the top. Do you see it? I went through the checkout at quarter past twelve."

"I can't quite make it out from here. May I?"

Philippa offered him the receipt and Dan took it from her, stretching it out and running his eyes over the items. "I can see you have excellent taste. I like the nocellara olives at Waitrose, and I've tried the crab salad too. Very nice. Even so, that's a lot of groceries for one person."

Philippa snatched the receipt back from him. "What's that got to do with you? Absolutely nothing. But if you must know, I have a guest. He arrived yesterday, and I wanted to make sure I had plenty of food to offer him when he got here."

Dan looked past her, his gaze flitting across the doors that led from the hallway. "Is he here now?"

"No. There's a small cottage at the back of the house, and I've started renting it out. Like I said before, I do what I can to keep this house in a reasonable state, and that means I have to find ways to bring in some money." Philippa drew a haughty breath. "We've talked for long enough, and I have things I need to be getting on with, so we'll leave it at that, shall we?"

"Yes, we've taken up enough of your time," Dan said. "What have you got planned for the rest of the day? College work?"

"No. Housework. Not nearly so much fun, but it has to be done. I'll see you out."

Philippa showed Dan and Alan to the door. She said goodbye, then she shut the door firmly before they could reply.

"Blimey," Alan said as they made their way back to the car. "That's given us a lot to unpack."

Dan nodded. "For a start, we've just found out that Philippa does her own housework. That must be unusual for someone who owns a house like this."

"That's what you're focusing on, the fact that she does a bit of dusting?"

"It's probably the most significant thing she said, and I bet she's cursing herself for letting it slip out. It tells us that, despite all outward appearances, Philippa is in dire straits. She's been living beyond her means, and that's a dangerous place to be."

"Still, she's renting out a cottage," Alan said. "If it's a nice place, and I'm sure it will be, she'll make a decent income from it."

"Yes, but one glance at her clothes tells me that Philippa has expensive tastes, and there's something else, something I didn't want to mention in front of her."

"What's that?"

"I couldn't help noticing what was on her Waitrose receipt, and besides all the sourdough and artichoke hearts, there were a few bottles of booze: gin, tequila and vodka."

"Maybe she likes cocktails. They're enjoying a revival at the moment, aren't they? Perhaps Philippa takes after her parents and she likes to entertain. After all, she has the perfect place for it."

"Yes, that could be one explanation," Dan said. "For her sake, I hope it is."

They reached the car and Alan unlocked the doors, but before he opened them, he said, "What did you think to her remark about Melody? Should we talk to her again?"

"It's worth doing a bit of digging, but Melody knows us now, and if we reappear, she'll be on her guard. We can't tackle her ourselves."

Alan raised an eyebrow. "What else can we do?"

"It's simple." Dan pulled the car door open. "We enlist the help of someone else."

With that, Dan climbed in and slammed the car door shut.

CHAPTER 29

P eter strolled through the garden toward the house. *I'm Jack Devlin*, he told himself. *I mustn't slip up.* The name didn't feel right to him; he'd have preferred something similar to the one he was born with. But Jack's age had been right, and when you're putting together a fake identity, you play with the hand you're dealt, looking for as many matches as you can find between the other person's details and your own. *The work's hard enough*, he reminded himself. *There's no sense in making it harder.*

The garden path took him close to the tall wooden gate at the side of the house, and as he passed, something made him stop in his tracks, just in time. He heard footsteps on the gravel, and voices: two men, their voices low but growing clearer as they drew near.

Jack looked to the house, scanning the windows, but he saw no sign of Philippa, so he crept closer to the gate, listening.

"Just look at that stonework," one of the men said. "Are these original, do you think, or were they added afterward?"

The other man said that he didn't know, then they discussed whether they should try the doorbell again.

Who were they? They didn't sound like door-to-door salesmen. There was something strange in the way they spoke to each other.

They didn't bicker, exactly, it was more as if they were sparring, each sharpening his wits against the other.

Not coppers then, Peter decided. *They're far too cheerful to be coppers.* In his experience, coppers were a bunch of miserable bastards, barely speaking except to take the mickey out of some poor sod.

But when Philippa finally answered the door, Peter's mind filled with doubts.

The two men didn't identify themselves, so Philippa already knew them, but they certainly weren't friends or close acquaintances. They launched straight into a series of questions, interrogating Philippa on her own doorstep, and that was exactly what coppers would do.

Slowly, Peter began backing away from the gate. He heard Philippa saying the men could come inside, and as soon as the door thudded shut, Peter turned and hurried away.

He headed for the clump of shrubs he'd used the night before, sidling in among the leafy branches, then he waited. He could see most of the downstairs windows, and he already knew which one offered a view of her dining room and lounge.

Peter stared at the dining room window, but the men never appeared and neither did Philippa. So she hadn't invited them in as she might've done with friends. *Who are they and what do they want?* Peter asked himself, but he had no way of knowing. Surely, they couldn't be looking for him, could they?

No. He'd been careful. Very careful.

Peter chewed at the inside of his cheek. As long as no one came out into the back garden, he'd be okay. If someone did come out to look for him, he had to hope he'd hear them coming. He could back out from his hiding place without being seen, so long as he took it slowly. Then he'd be off, leaving his bag behind if need be.

But it wasn't long before he heard the slam of a door, and then the distant sound of a car driving away. Had the two men finally gone?

Yes. Philippa appeared at the dining room window, looking out into the garden, and she was alone.

Peter held his breath and kept perfectly still. Philippa seemed to be looking straight at him, but that must be his imagination working overtime, because she didn't recoil, didn't react at all.

She ran her hands through her hair, pulling it back from her face, and then she pressed her fists against her temples and closed her eyes. She bared her teeth and let fly with an incoherent roar of rage. Peter flinched, but he couldn't look away. Philippa's full-throated yell was muffled by the window pane, but even so, her heartfelt anger was all too clear. Her body trembled with the force of it.

Finally, Philippa grew quiet and she hung her head, her shoulders sagging as if all her energy was spent. She dabbed at the corners of her eyes with her fingertips, and then she turned and moved away from the window.

Bloody hell, Peter thought. *She's a dark one*. There was more to Philippa than he'd thought. She might be upper class, but underneath her nice manners and her posh accent lurked something powerful, something strong. And that might be useful.

Peter checked the windows, then he extricated himself from the branches and headed back to the cottage. He had a lot to think about.

CHAPTER 30

Jay Markham leaned one elbow on the bar in The Wild Boar and gazed around the room. There weren't many customers but that was to be expected on a Thursday. It would be busier tomorrow, the crowd a bit more lively, but for now this was fine. A nice relaxing pint or two after a hard day spent retiling a bathroom in Christow. A good job he'd made of it, too, so he deserved a night in the pub.

From behind the bar, Sam caught his eye and flashed him a smile. He smiled in return. She was a grand lass, that was for sure. Why she'd taken up with Dan Corrigan, he'd never know, but she was always in a good mood these days, and when you could rely on a warm welcome and a cheerful smile in the pub, all was right with the world.

The front door opened and a tall man stepped in, his sharp eyes narrowing as he scanned the room, studying the faces of each customer in turn. His gaze alighted on Jay and lingered for a moment before flitting away.

The man was past middle age, but there was something oddly striking about him, and Jay searched his memory. As an ex-copper, he reckoned he had a good memory for faces, and he'd never lost the police officer's habit of instantly weighing people up, checking them against his internal database of convicts and suspects. That said, it was getting harder to put names to faces as his days on the force receded into the past. The people he'd had dealings with had grown older and changed, but it didn't hurt to keep his eye in. There were some old faces he'd rather not see again, but if any of them should reappear, he'd do well to be ready.

The new arrival, though, did not pose a threat. As he made his slow, shuffling way toward the bar, Jay decided that the man was older than he'd first appeared. His posture was slightly stooped, his left shoulder held lower than the other, and he walked with a slight limp, his left foot dragging across the carpet as he moved. The combined effect lent the poor bloke a curiously lop-sided gait that must've made his life difficult.

Perhaps he'd suffered a stroke and been left with some residual weakness, though Jay couldn't detect any irregularity in the man's expression. In fact, beneath his generous beard and bushy eyebrows, the man might well be considered handsome. His features were sharp, his cheekbones well defined, and there was something else about him that Jay couldn't quite put his finger on.

Distinguished, Jay decided. That was the word. Perhaps it was something to do with his blue eyes which were bright and clear, his gaze missing nothing.

The man perched on a stool along the bar, and once he'd settled himself, he returned Jay's inquiring look.

"Now then," the man intoned, his voice deep and his accent distinctly northern. "All right?"

Jay's eyebrows shot up. "Aye. Not so bad. Always pleased to meet another Yorkshireman."

The man nodded.

"Where are you from?" Jay asked.

"Pickering," the man said. "It's between—"

"York and Scarborough," Jay interrupted. "Aye, I've been a few times. I like the steam railway. It's a grand day out is that."

"Right."

"I bet that's what everybody says, eh? Name's Jay, by the way.

This is my local." He extended his hand for a shake and the other man took it, his grip firm.

"Andrew. I'm just passing through, like. For work. Thought I'd take a break, have a beer or two."

"You do right. As it happens, I'm from Leeds myself. It's only about fifty miles from Pickering, so I know that bit of Yorkshire pretty well. What line of work are you in?"

"Nowt worth talking about." Andrew turned his attention to the bar, studying the beers on offer. "What's good?"

"If it's bitter you're after, I can't say. I'm a lager man myself." Jay raised his glass in evidence. "Sam will set you straight. She knows her beer."

"Did someone mention my name?" Sam asked, strolling toward them. "Nothing too bad, I hope, Jay?"

"No, I was just singing your praises to Andrew here," Jay replied. "I was about to say that this is the best pub for miles around. Well, the best pub in Embervale anyway."

Sam made a show of being displeased. "Cheeky beggar." Turning to Andrew, she added, "In case you hadn't realised, this is the *only* pub in the village. But still, we do our best, and we pride ourselves on our beer. What can I get for you?"

Andrew hesitated, shifting on his seat. "Do you have something gluten free?"

Jay was stunned into silence, but Sam didn't miss a beat. "Yes, we have a nice little ale called Sun Drop from Salcombe Brewery here in Devon. It's only in cans, but it's very good. It won an award."

"That'll be fine. Thanks."

"Right you are." Sam fetched a can from the chiller and poured the beer into a glass with practised ease.

"Gluten free beer," Jay muttered. "What will they think of next?"

Sam cast him a glance. "Alcohol free, that's the next big thing. They taste all right, and it's what the younger drinkers like. We've got some in if you fancy it."

"Get thee behind me." Jay crossed himself, chuckling. He looked to Andrew for support, but the man didn't so much as crack a smile.

Suit yourself, Jay thought. *Miserable bugger.* He took a swallow of his lager while Andrew paid for his drink, using cash and sifting through his wallet, hunting through the wad of notes before presenting her with far too much money.

"Have one for yourself," Andrew said, and Sam thanked him, rewarding him with a warm smile as she handed over his change.

For a while, the two men sat and sipped their drinks in silence. That would've been all right with Jay, but he couldn't help noticing the way Andrew kept gazing around the room, keeping a watchful eye on the other patrons as if any one of them might suddenly jump up and do something extraordinary.

What's his game? Jay asked himself. This man had some kind of hidden agenda, that was for sure, but what could it be? *Wait and see,* Jay decided. *Keep an eye on him.* But he couldn't sit there and do nothing. This was his patch, dammit.

Jay put his pint down heavily, the bang of glass on wood making Andrew turn with a start.

Jay fixed him with a stare. "Looking for someone, pal?"

"What?"

"You're looking for someone or something. Which is it?"

Andrew shook his head. "Just having a drink. Same as you."

"Oh no, that's not true, is it, Andrew? Come on. Out with it."

"I don't know what you mean." Andrew exhaled noisily as though flabbergasted. "I'm having a drink, minding my own business, and—"

"What business would that be?" Jay interrupted. "You never did say."

"I'm in sales."

"Selling what?"

"Why do you want to know? What's it to you?"

Jay pulled himself up to his full height. "What do you sell?"

"Bugger off. I don't answer to you."

"No, but I've never known a sales rep miss a chance to talk about what he's selling. Generally, you can't shut them up. They'll bang on about boots to a one-legged man."

"Everything all right, gents?" Sam was bustling toward them, a smile fixed on her lips. "I hope you're being polite, Jay."

"You're all right, Sam," Jay replied. "We're just having a friendly chat, that's all."

Andrew sent Jay a side-eyed glance, but he didn't say a word.

"Well, that's all right then." Sam tilted her head and turned to Andrew. "How did you get on with the beer? Like it?"

"Fine. It was all right."

"Good. Can I get you another?"

"No, thanks. I'm, not stopping."

"I can see if any of our other beers are gluten free," Sam said. "It's no trouble."

"No, it's all right. I prefer something colder. Besides, I ought to be going."

Andrew downed the rest of his drink, then he slid from his stool and faced Jay. He stared for a moment, his mouth a grim line, then he lifted his chin and said, "Tractor parts. I sell parts for agricultural machinery. Satisfied?"

Jay nodded, though it cost him to do it.

"Right." Andrew sent Sam a smile. "Thanks. Nice place you've got here. Shame I can't say the same about…" His voice trailed away and he sighed. "Never mind. Least said, soonest mended."

His head held high, Andrew walked to the door and left without a backward glance.

"Odd bloke," Jay said, but when he looked to Sam for agreement, he found only a glare.

"What the hell was all that about?" Sam demanded, hands on her hips. "The poor man came in for a drink, and you drove him away."

"You don't want his sort in here. Trust me, there was something off about him. He wasn't right. I could smell it."

"Rubbish. He was a nice, ordinary bloke. He even bought me a drink, which is more than I can say for you."

Jay scowled. There was nothing he could say to Sam's accusation without stirring up more trouble.

"You know, it's hard enough to keep this place going without you scaring off the customers," Sam went on. "I've a good mind to bar you, once and for all."

"Oh, come on," Jay said. "I wasn't being—"

"Yes, you were," Sam interrupted. "You were being rude and obnoxious for the sake of it. I don't know what it is with you, but every time you see someone from up north, it brings out the worst in you. You're like a grumpy old rooster, squawking and flapping your wings. You're always making fun of Alan, calling him a southerner because he comes from Liverpool. What does that make the rest of us, eh?"

"I don't mean anything by it. Me and Alan have a bit of banter, that's all. He doesn't mind."

"Maybe, but I do, and I'm the one running this pub, so you'll sort yourself out, Jay, or you'll find somewhere else to drink."

"All right, point taken. It won't happen again." Jay summoned a hopeful smile. "What do you say? Let bygones be bygones?"

"I don't know."

"Go on. Let me buy you a drink, make it up to you."

"All right, but only if you say sorry."

"I apologise," Jay said. "Unreservedly. I made a mistake. So I'll have another lager, and…" Jay paused, furrowing his brow. "That beer you sold him. What was it?"

"Sun Drop."

"What is it, though? IPA?"

"Not exactly. It's an ale."

"But you keep it in the fridge," Jay said.

"Yeah. It says on the can: best served chilled."

"But he said it wasn't cold enough. What kind of Yorkshireman wants his ale served cold?"

"A lot of people like it that way," Sam argued. "We're not all stuck in the past, Jay."

"He wasn't a youngster though, was he? He was older than me, by the looks of him. A man of his generation doesn't complain about his beer being too warm, especially when it's just come out the fridge."

Sam's stern expression was back. "What are you on about, Jay? Are you buying me a drink or what?"

"Hang on," Jay said. "Pour me a lager, Sam, and have one for yourself. I won't be a sec."

He made for the door.

"I'm not pouring anything until you come back with your wallet," Sam called after him.

"Fine. Whatever." Jay barged out through the door and hurried onto Fore Street. There was no sign of Andrew, but some distance away, a large white car was pulling out almost noiselessly from a parking space.

Jay could make out the registration number, but just in case, he plucked his phone from his pocket and took several photos as the car drove away.

"Got you," Jay murmured. Because he'd seen the outlines of two people sitting in the front of that car, one of them tall and the other shorter. He was almost certain that the tall man was Andrew, and he'd been in the passenger seat. So who had been driving? And why had Andrew made up that cock and bull story about being a salesman?

I knew he was a wrong'un, Jay told himself. *I've not lost my touch.* Jay headed back inside for a celebratory pint, but he kept his phone in his hand. Once he'd paid for the drinks, he had a call to make. He knew someone who'd be very interested in the evening's events, and with a bit of luck, the story might even be rewarded with a drink. Possibly two.

CHAPTER 31

"What do you think he wants?" Alan asked as he and Dan walked toward The Wild Boar.

"We'll soon find out," Dan replied. "With Jay, there's always an angle, but for once, I don't mind. I wanted to talk to him anyway."

"Oh? Have you got some more work lined up for him?"

"Yes, but not the kind you're thinking of. I'll explain inside, but we won't be talking about painting and decorating."

A few minutes later, they arrived at the pub and Dan made straight for the bar, Alan at his heels.

Sam looked up in surprise and treated him to a smile. "Hello, stranger. I wasn't expecting to see you this evening."

"Hi," Dan said. "I couldn't keep away."

"Is that right?"

Sam looked into his eyes, but the moment was spoilt by a voice booming across the room. "Dan! Over here."

Dan turned to see Jay beckoning to him from his seat at a table beside the fireplace.

Sam sighed. "You'd better go and see what he wants. He's in a funny mood tonight. Full of himself."

"He can wait," Dan replied. "How have you been? Had a good day?"

"Not bad. You know, the usual routine."

"If you're ever shorthanded, I'm happy to come and help."

Sam shook her head. "You need to stick to what you're doing. I'm all right. I can manage this place with my eyes shut."

"Okay, but the offer stands."

"We'll see." Sam peered past him to where Alan was standing awkwardly, looking around the room as if pretending he couldn't hear every word they were saying. "All right, Alan? Pint of Jail Ale, is it?"

Alan stepped up to the bar, smiling. "Yes, please. That'll be just the thing."

"The same for me, please," Dan said. "And we'd better get a pint of whatever Jay's drinking."

"Right you are, but I wouldn't give Jay too much encouragement if I were you." Sam lowered her voice to add, "He's been putting it away a bit too fast for his own good. It'd be a shame if he went back to... well, you know what he used to be like."

"Don't worry," Alan said. "We'll keep an eye on him."

Sam smiled gratefully then busied herself with their drinks.

"You go and talk to Jay," Alan said to Dan. "I'll bring the drinks over."

"But I was going to pay."

"Never mind. I'll get these. You can get the next round in."

Dan hesitated. He'd hoped to treat Alan to a few drinks in return for all the time he'd put into the case, but he hadn't yet been paid by Zadie and cashflow was becoming a problem.

"Go on," Alan added firmly. "You can get the drinks another time."

"Okay. Thanks." Dan picked his way between the tables and pulled up a chair to join Jay. "Hi, Jay. Alan's bringing you a pint."

"Very decent of him," Jay said. "I won't say no."

It never occurred to me you would, Dan thought, but all he said was, "So what did you want to talk about?"

"Ah, something right up your street. A mystery."

"Here we are." Alan arrived with the drinks, and he slid them onto the table. "The lager's for you, Jay."

Jay rubbed his hands together. "Ta very much." He drained the remains of his drink and pulled the fresh one toward him, but he didn't take so much as a sip. He seemed to be preparing for something, his expression growing serious as he gazed at Dan and Alan in turn, his eyes alight with a purposeful gleam.

"Tonight, there was a fella in here," Jay began, then he recounted the events of his evening so far.

"The white car you saw," Dan said, "was it a Mercedes-Benz SUV? Electric?"

Jay had been about to take a mouthful of lager, but he froze with his glass halfway to his lips. "Bloody hell. How did you know that?"

"It ties in with a case we're working on. I've a pretty good idea who it might've been."

"Oh." The gleam in Jay's eyes dimmed and he looked put out. "Well, that didn't turn out to be much fun, did it? I thought we'd work it out between us. I was looking forward to it."

"You've been very helpful," Alan said. "Besides, we can't be one hundred percent sure about the car. You didn't happen to get its registration number, did you?"

Jay perked up. "Of course I did. What do you take me for? I memorised it, *and* I took some photos too." He pulled out his phone. "Here, I'll send them to you."

"That'd be great." Dan took out his phone, and a few seconds later he showed the photos to Alan.

Alan nodded. "It looks like the car we saw the other day."

"Definitely," Dan said. "It was the fact that he had a driver that gave it away."

"But what did he want here?" Alan asked. "Was he looking for us?"

"Probably, but if he wanted to get in touch, he could've done it any number of ways, so why would he come all the way over here?

And once he'd made the effort, why didn't he just ask for us? Then there's the false name, the phoney accent."

"It's a strange way to behave," Alan said. "Maybe he's a bit eccentric. We know he's a reclusive sort of character."

Dan shook his head. "This wasn't eccentricity, this was somebody carrying out a plan."

Jay had watched their conversation carefully, his head turning from side to side like a spectator at a tennis match. But now, he let out a groan of frustration. "What the bloody hell are you on about? Who was he?"

"You'll like this, Jay," Dan said. "You've had a brush with a world-famous American actor: one of Hollywood's finest leading men."

Jay's expression froze, then he laughed. "Get on with you. You almost had me going for a second. I told you, the bloke was from Yorkshire. I wouldn't get that wrong now, would I? Who was it really?"

"I hate to break it to you, but you've had the wool pulled over your eyes," Alan said. "That was John Callaway, and he's played many an Englishman. He's well known for it."

"Don't talk rubbish. I know who John Callaway is and this wasn't him. He was older for a start, and he walked with a limp, and his shoulder was..." Jay's defiant expression faltered. "All of which could've been faked," he went on. "Bloody hell fire! It was him. How did I not notice?"

"Don't be too hard on yourself," Alan said. "He was in that remake of *Look Back in Anger*, and he was very good, so he's got the northern accent down pat. I think he won a BAFTA for that. And he's done some theatre too, so he knows how to play to a live audience. I wonder if he's done any Shakespeare. That limp and the shoulder sound straight out of Richard III."

"But I was stood right next to him, as near as I am to you, and I didn't recognise him at all."

"A fake accent and a few mannerisms can work wonders," Dan

said. "To be fair, you did notice that something wasn't quite right about him, and you said he was distinguished looking."

"He might've been wearing a false beard," Alan put in. "We haven't seen him in person, though we did try calling on him."

"Is he working around here?" Jay asked.

"He has a house in Chagford," Dan replied. "A big place, so I'm told, although we haven't actually seen it. We couldn't get past the front gate."

Jay shook his head in disbelief. "Wait until I tell my ex-wife. She goes mad for him. She'll be over there like a shot."

"I wouldn't advise that," Dan said. "She won't get near him. He values his privacy, and he has a minder: Benny Washington. That's who would've been driving the car. He's a tough-looking character. I wouldn't be surprised if he's an ex-cop like you."

"The name isn't ringing any bells," Jay replied. "But that doesn't mean much. He could be from anywhere."

"Benny's background isn't important," Dan said. "The main thing is to figure out why Callaway came here. I gave Benny my name and details, and he said he'd passed them on to Callaway's PA. Chances are that Callaway knows I live in Embervale, so he must've come here to look for me, but why?" Dan thought for a moment. "Callaway has something to hide, and he's worried I might be on to him, otherwise why would he go to all the trouble of posing as someone else?"

"Maybe he just likes to go around *incognito*," Alan suggested. "It must be very tiring to have unwanted attention everywhere he goes. I wouldn't be surprised if he just fancied a quiet pint in a country pub. Your card gave him the idea of trying Embervale."

"I'd already thought of that, and I don't buy it," Dan said. "He had some other purpose in mind. Why else would he have his minder sit in the car outside?"

"It obvious," Jay said. "He was going to try and nobble you, simple as that."

"In the pub?" Alan asked. "In front of witnesses?"

"No, he'd have made an excuse and got you outside, then he'd

A MUST-HAVE MURDER

have whacked you on the head." Jay rubbed his hands together. "Or more likely, he'd have told his minder to do it. They could've made it look like a fight outside the pub, or maybe a mugging gone wrong. Then they'd have driven away."

"That's a bit of a stretch," Dan said. "If he wanted Benny to beat me up, Callaway wouldn't have come along as well."

Jay leaned forward. "That's where he was clever. When the police turned up, we'd all have said we'd seen a middle-aged man from Yorkshire by the name of Andrew: a man with a limp and a bushy beard. Nobody would be looking for this Benny character."

Dan made a noncommittal noise in his throat. "I'll keep it in mind, but my instincts tell me there's something else going on here. Whatever it is, it's going to be bad news for somebody. Very bad news indeed."

The three men sipped their drinks in silence, alone with their thoughts.

"Any empties?" Sam asked as she marched toward their table.

"Just the one." Jay held up his empty glass. "Thanks, Sam."

Sam took his glass and paused to look around the group. "Blimey, you're a gloomy bunch. Who died?"

"No one," Dan said. "Not yet, anyway." He attempted a smile to show he wasn't serious, but he clearly didn't pull it off because Sam looked concerned.

"That was Dan's idea of a joke," Alan explained. "We were just talking about the case, thinking it through."

"Not going well?"

"It could be better. We've hit a roadblock, but we'll get there."

"We were talking about that bloke who was in here earlier," Jay said. "You'll never guess who he was, Sam. He was only John blooming Callaway."

Sam's expression clouded, but then she chuckled. "Right, and I've got Robert DeNiro in the back room, taking all night to drink a pint of Guinness. We get all the big names in here. Natalie Portman came in the other day and asked for a pint of bitter and packet of pork scratchings."

"Actually, I think she's a vegan," Dan said, the words out of his lips before he could stop them.

Sam cocked an eyebrow. "Good for her, but that was *my* idea of a joke, Dan. There's no need to pick holes in it."

Dan raised his hands in surrender. "I know, but we weren't kidding about John Callaway. He was in here, pretending to be from Yorkshire."

"All right, have it your way. To be fair, that bloke did look a bit like John Callaway. He had the same blue eyes, and a nice smile, but he was far too old."

"It really *was* him," Dan started to say, but Sam wasn't listening.

"I do like him though, John Callaway. He was amazing in that film… what was it called? The one where he was stuck on a desert island and everything went wrong."

"*Castaway*?" Alan asked. "That was Tom Hanks."

"No, no. I'm talking about a really old film. It was all a bit weird, but he was amazing. I'm not so keen on his new stuff. He's not as good as he used to be, but then, he's been through a lot. I feel sorry for him. It's terrible, all that business with his daughter."

"I didn't know you were such a movie buff," Dan said. "But what happened with his daughter?"

"You must've heard about it, surely."

"No, I didn't even know he had a daughter."

Sam's gaze flitted upward. "That's what you get for listening to Radio 4 all day. You lose touch."

"I like to keep up with current affairs," Dan protested. "What's wrong with that?"

"Nothing. I listen to headlines, then I get up and get going. I can't sit around listening to politicians moaning and scoring points off each other. They're like kids in a playground. It's all a game to them, and I'm just not interested. I like a bit of entertainment on the radio; most people do. But you, you've no idea what ordinary folk talk about, have you?"

"I'm not interested in celebrity gossip, if that's what you mean.

But I'm not the only one who doesn't like soap operas and *Strictly Come Dancing*. You feel the same, don't you, Alan?"

Alan cleared his throat. "Well, erm, actually, I was just going to pop to the, er…"

He made to stand, but Sam held out her hand to stop him. "Don't go on my account. I'll leave you three to your wild stories while I get back to work. You never know, DeNiro might be ready for another Guinness."

Dan bit his lip. He'd done it again, putting his foot in it. He couldn't take back the last couple of minutes, but he couldn't let Sam leave like this.

"I'm sorry, Sam," Dan said. "I didn't mean to be so dismissive." From the corner of his eye, he saw Jay sitting back with his arms folded, a smug grin on his lips as he relished the scene, but Dan ploughed on. "I think it's great that we like different things, and I value your opinion, Sam, you know I do."

Sam raised one corner of her lip as if not entirely convinced.

In the silence, Jay tutted under his breath, then he looked from Dan to Alan. "You don't watch *Strictly?* What, neither of you?"

"I'm afraid not," Alan replied. "It's lost on me."

"Me too," Dan said. "I don't see the appeal."

"Millions of people watch *Strictly* every week," Sam stated. "Millions. If you got down from your high horse once in a while, you might learn a thing or two about what's popular, and you might've known who John Callaway's daughter is."

"You're probably right," Dan said. "Please, tell me the answer, Sam. Who is she?"

"Adriana Perez."

The three men exchanged blank looks.

"She's an actor too," Sam said. "Or she was. She was in that big series on Netflix: *New York Homicide*. She played one of the detectives."

"Like father, like daughter," Alan said. "It must've helped to have her old man in the business."

"Not one bit," Sam said. "Not at first, anyway. She didn't tell anyone who she was. That's why she used her mother's maiden name. She didn't want everyone thinking her dad had given her a leg up."

"But the secret's out now," Dan said. "Is she still working? Just now, you said she *was* an actor."

"That's right. She was good, really good, but she hasn't been in anything for ages."

"What happened?" Dan asked.

"Do you really want to know?"

Seeing the gleam in Sam's eyes, Dan sensed a story and sat up a little straighter. "Definitely."

"Hold on." Sam pulled up a chair and settled in, leaning forward and lowering her voice.

"You've got to go back a bit to get the full picture. John Callaway married young. He was supposed to go to college, but he met a girl called Isabel Perez. Her family were from somewhere in South America, and they were strict Catholics. John Callaway was from the other side of the tracks, so they didn't think much of him."

"Very *West-side Story*," Alan put in. "Life imitating art."

Sam nodded enthusiastically. "I know, right? Anyway, very soon after they married, they had Adriana, so you can join the dots."

"Oh yes," Jay said. "I know that story. There's a last-minute wedding at one end of it and a divorce at the other, with nothing in-between but arguments and accusations."

Alan sent him an uncertain glance. "Is that what happened with you and your ex-wife?"

"More or less. I should never have gone through with it, but believe it or not, I wanted to do the decent thing. More fool me."

An awkward silence fell over the group, the others watching as Jay took a long draught from his pint. He put his glass on the table and looked up, scanning their faces. "What are you lot staring at? I haven't always been the happy-go-lucky type, you know. I've had my moments."

Dan wasn't sure how to respond, and the others seemed to feel the same way. No one spoke, and Jay laughed as if enjoying their disquiet.

"It's all right," Jay said. "I'm not going to start crying into my beer. On you go, Sam. Let's hear about the great John Callaway and his disastrous marriage."

After a moment's hesitation, Sam resumed her tale. "As it goes, you've got it more or less right, Jay. It wasn't long before they split up, and soon after that, Callaway had his break. He started getting parts, and suddenly, he was flavour of the month. He was in the money, and Isabel reckoned he owed her. When he'd been struggling to find work her family had put food on the table. He'd never have made it big if it weren't for her. But Callaway could afford a top lawyer, and Isabel didn't stand a chance. She was left out in the cold. They say she never forgave him."

"I'm not surprised," Alan huffed. "What a terrible thing to do. I had no idea the man was such a…" He pursed his lips as if biting back his words.

"Self-centred bastard?" Dan suggested.

"It'll do," Alan replied. "I suppose that's nothing new in Hollywood, but even so, I've a good mind to go through my DVD collection and throw out anything with his name on it."

"You still have DVDs?" Jay asked. "Blimey. Why don't you just stream everything?"

Alan looked ready to debate the point, so Dan made a downward motion with his hands. "Let's stay on track, shall we? I want to concentrate on what Sam has to say."

"Sorry, Sam," Alan said. "Please, carry on."

"Well, Isabel and her daughter got on as best as they could, but later on, when Adriana was a teenager, she got into acting. She was a natural, and one thing led to another. Before long, she was landing parts in big TV shows, and everything was going great. But that's when all the trouble started."

"What kind of trouble?" Alan asked.

"John Callaway came back for her. He reckoned he'd found

God, and said he wanted to put things right. He wanted to take her in."

There was a collective murmur of concern from the three men.

"Typical," Jay said. "After leaving the poor lass to fend for herself for all those years, her dad finds out she's a chip off the old block, and suddenly he's interested."

"Something tells me Adriana was having none of it," Dan suggested.

Sam nodded. "Big time."

"I'm not surprised," Dan said. "She'd changed her name and built a career on her own. She was bound to kick back against the father who abandoned her."

"She kicked back, all right," Sam replied. "Drink, drugs, wild parties and more besides."

"That wouldn't go down too well with her newly evangelical father," Dan said. "How did he take it?"

"Hard to say. He stopped talking about his daughter, but then things got even worse; for her, anyway."

The three men sat very still, hanging on Sam's every word.

Alan broke the silence. "What happened? Is she all right?"

"Not really." Sam let out a sorrowful sigh. "She's in a clinic: one of those posh, private ones. That's all anybody knows for sure, but the rumour is, she's got an eating disorder. I don't know if it's true, but there must be something wrong with her. It's very sad."

"Perhaps that's something we can look into," Dan said. "What do you think, Alan? It could be useful background information."

"Agreed. I'll get on it tomorrow morning." Alan took a sip of his drink and then smiled at Sam. "It's a good job you steered us in the right direction."

"That's all right," Sam replied. "It's all out there if you know where to look. But I'd better get back to work." She stood and put her chair back where it belonged. "I'll see you later."

"Sure," Dan said. "Thanks, Sam."

As Sam made her way back to the bar, he realised Jay was regarding him with disapproval.

Dan arched an eyebrow. "Something on your mind, Jay?"

"You don't know you're born," Jay stated. "You need to talk nice to a woman like that, give her a few compliments, turn on the charm."

"Relationship advice, Jay? Seriously?"

"Aye. I'm dead serious. I tell you, if you don't look after that lass, she'll be gone in the blink of an eye. And if you upset her, you'll have me to answer to."

"I don't see what it's got to do with you," Dan protested. "But—"

"I'll tell you what it's got to do with me. Sam's been a good friend of mine, and she's kept me on the straight and narrow, so I'll stand up for her any day of the week."

"All right. I get it. You're looking out for her, and that's fine, but Sam and I are okay. We're good. You don't need to tell me how special she is. I know that already."

"Come on, you two," Alan chipped in. "Let's not argue. I'll get the drinks in. Same again, Jay?"

Jay looked down at his pint. "No, you're all right, Alan. I've had enough for one night. Time to go. I'll finish this one at the bar, leave you two in peace."

Jay climbed to his feet, pint in hand. "Thanks for the drink, lads. I'll get you one next time."

"Before you go, there's something I wanted to ask you," Dan said quickly. "It's about some work."

"Oh aye? If it's another bit of decorating, I've got to warn you, I'm booked solid for the next couple of months."

"No, this is more in your old line of work," Dan replied. "I think you might be interested."

"I doubt it. I'm done with all that."

"This is just a little surveillance job. It needn't take long, and I'll pay for your time."

Jay looked doubtful.

"It's a local job," Dan went on. "I want you to follow someone from their place of work, and see where they go, who they meet."

"Why don't you do it yourself?" Jay pointed a finger at Dan. "They've already clocked you, haven't they? You need a fresh face."

"Got it in one," Dan admitted. "Are you up for it?"

"I'll think about it. Give me a call tomorrow, and I'll see if I can squeeze it in. See you later."

Jay turned and marched toward the bar.

"I take it you want him to follow Melody," Alan said. "Do you think he'll do it?"

"I'll make it worth his while. Besides, whatever he may say about his days in uniform, Jay secretly misses it. He won't be able to resist."

"We'll see, and in the meantime, I'll have a go at digging up some more background info on John Callaway." Alan leaned his elbow on the table, cupping his chin with one hand. "I have a feeling we've stumbled onto a promising lead. I don't know how someone like John Callaway could possibly be connected to Zadie, but his name keeps cropping up, and that stunt he pulled tonight is very peculiar indeed. I think we've found a new suspect."

"Me too," Dan said. "Now all we have to do is find a way to get our hands on him."

FRIDAY

CHAPTER 32

I t was early morning when Dan knocked on the front door of The Wild Boar, but it wasn't long before Sam appeared, smiling at him from the doorway. "Hello. What's brought you here at this time of day?"

"I wanted to see you," Dan said. "I couldn't keep away."

"You ought to have warned me." Sam glanced down at her clothes. She had her hair tied back and she was dressed in a baggy T-shirt and a pair of faded jeans with a rip at the knee. "I must look a sight."

"You look wonderful," Dan said and meant every word. "Can I come in for a minute?"

"Of course." Sam stepped back, inviting him in. "I can't stop long though. Lots to do this morning."

"I'll give you a hand."

Sam shut the door and looked around the room. "All right. I've finished hoovering, so you can go around taking the chairs off the tables, and I'll get on with wiping everything down."

"No problem."

As they worked, Sam said, "Are you coming in tonight?"

"I expect so. I owe Alan a pint or two. He's been helping me all week."

"Your first full week as a private eye. That's something to celebrate."

"It's a bit early for celebrations, but we'll see how it goes today. You never know when something's going to turn up."

"That's true, right enough." Sam finished wiping a table and looked at him. "Do you get weekends off?"

"I'm self-employed, so I can take time off whenever I want. Why?"

"I just wondered." Sam went back to her task, and Dan resumed his efforts, arranging a couple of chairs before moving to the next table. Sam obviously had something on her mind, but there were times when it was best to wait until she was ready to talk.

After a long minute, Sam said, "I was thinking, it probably won't be very busy tomorrow lunchtime, so I reckon I could get Jordan to cover the bar."

"Really? I thought he only worked in the kitchen."

"He does a bit of all sorts. I've been training him up."

"That's good, but didn't you say he was a bit dippy?"

Sam frowned as she rubbed at an obstinate stain on a table. "I might've said it one time, but that was ages ago. Jordan's coming on really well, as it goes. He just needed a bit of time to settle in, that's all."

"He's had a good teacher."

"I don't know about that. There's not much to this business when you get down to it. Smile and give folks a nice glass of beer, and they're happy. Anyone could do it."

"But not everyone could run a place like this," Dan said, carrying a chair to its proper home by the fire. "Don't do yourself down, Sam. You've turned this place around, and that takes a lot of skill. You've taken a down-at-heel pub and turned it into a thriving business."

"It was never that bad."

"It was okay, but it wasn't great. It was tired and stuck in the past. I'm willing to bet it wasn't turning much of a profit."

"That's right enough," Sam admitted. "When Kevin was in

charge, there was barely enough coming in to pay the bills. He left the books in a right old mess, but I soon sorted that out. You've got to see where you're losing money and put a stop to it. There's no point trying to fill a leaky bucket."

"You know, I've met people who've spent years in business, but they still haven't grasped that idea."

"It's just common sense, isn't it? Nothing special."

"You'd be surprised. In my experience, common sense is in short supply."

"You might be right." Sam said. "If you haven't got a level head on your shoulders, no amount of fancy degrees can make up for it. Anyway, speaking of people who don't catch on too quick, what do you think to my idea?"

"Erm, which one?"

"My plan about you and me going out for lunch tomorrow."

"Oh, sorry, I didn't hear you say anything about lunch."

"That's because I didn't think I'd have to spell it out for you. I thought you might offer."

"Right. I'm afraid that passed me by." Dan laughed quietly, shaking his head.

"Are you laughing at me, Dan Corrigan, because if you are…"

"No, I was laughing at myself for being such an idiot. I should be better at spotting these things by now."

"Yes, you should. So what about it? Are we going out for lunch tomorrow or not?"

"I'd love to take you out for lunch," Dan said. "Do you have anywhere in mind, or shall I surprise you?"

"I don't mind really. You can choose, so long as it's not somewhere too posh."

"We could head to the coast. There are plenty of places I haven't explored yet. I'd like to find a decent seafood restaurant. Do you know where we might find one?"

Sam stopped working for a moment. "There used to be a nice place in Brixham. I don't know if it's still there."

"I'll ask Alan."

"Why? He's not coming as well, is he?"

"No, but he can tell me where to find the best pubs and restaurants in a fifty-mile radius. He's better than Google maps any day of the week."

"That's all right then. Don't get me wrong, I like Alan, but…"

"Three's a crowd." Dan lifted down the final chair and brushed his hands together. "Job done. Speaking of Alan, I ought to get back home. He's going to help me out today, and he'll be champing at the bit."

Sam sent him a look, hands on her hips. "What about the back room?"

"Oh." Dan checked his watch. "I would stay and help, but I was supposed to be at his house five minutes ago, and you know what he's like. He's probably waiting, boots on and coat at the ready."

"It's all right, I was only teasing." Sam walked over and stood facing him. "Thanks for helping. I usually have to do it all on my own." She smiled. "I reckon you've earned a kiss."

"If I'd known that, I'd have come around every morning."

Sam moved closer, and they held each other, but before their lips met, Sam pulled back, her eyebrows raised. "Ooh, I almost forgot. I remembered the name of that film: the John Callaway one where he's on an island."

"Okay. You can tell me later."

Sam playfully slapped his chest. "No, I'll tell you now. I'm trying to help. I thought you'd be pleased."

"I am, but you mentioned a kiss?"

"In a minute. Let me tell you about this film first. It was called *Wild Yonder*. I don't know about wild, but it was definitely weird."

Dan felt a shiver run through Sam's body, and something told him their kiss would have to wait.

"What is it, Sam? What's the matter?"

"I was just thinking about that film. It was so strange."

"In what way?"

"It was very dark. Menacing, you might call it. John Callaway was quite scary. When he looked into the camera, it gave me chills.

I remember, I had bad dreams after watching it, and just now, it came back to me."

"Really? I thought Callaway was usually Mr Nice Guy: the cop with a heart of gold."

"That's all he does nowadays, but back when he was younger, he was tall, dark and handsome; all mean and moody. A lot of women liked him. They'd go on about Mr Rochester and all that, but I never saw the attraction. He scared the life out of me."

"This is interesting stuff," Dan said. "I know he's an accomplished actor, but that performance must've come from somewhere. I wonder if there's a darker side to his nature; a side he keeps away from the public eye."

"If you like that bit of news, you'll be amazed at what else I've got to show you. Hang on."

"Wait a minute," Dan started to say, but Sam was already moving away from him.

Sam hurried across to the bar and returned a moment later, clutching a magazine. Holding it out to him, she said, "Here. Take a look at this."

The issue of *Hello!* was creased as if it had been well thumbed. Dan took it from her. He vaguely recognised the photo of the actor on the cover, though he couldn't recall her name, and the accompanying headlines weren't particularly illuminating. He could see that there had been a big wedding, a singer had thrown a birthday party, and a couple of actors were in the midst of a divorce.

"Thanks," Dan said as enthusiastically as he could manage, but then he noticed the date on the cover. "This is over a year old. You don't keep all your old magazines for that long, do you?"

"Not exactly. Every now and then, I throw a load of them out, but I keep a stash for when I haven't got anything else to read. They bring back memories." Sam's cheeks coloured. "I was reading a magazine in the shop when we first met. I'd seen you before, of course, but not like that."

"Like what?"

"You know. All sporty and sweaty. I could see your muscles through your top."

"Well, I used to spend a bit more time in the gym and a lot less time in the pub. I'm not in such good shape anymore."

"I wouldn't say that. You look all right to me. But…"

"But what?"

Sam grinned. "Don't get distracted. You're meant to be looking at that magazine."

"Why?"

"You'll see. After we talked last night, I remembered reading something, so I had a rummage through my old mags, and there it was. Mind you, it took me long enough to find it. I had a hard job keeping my eyes open by the end of it."

"You needn't have troubled yourself. You need your rest."

"I don't mind. I wanted to help."

"That was very thoughtful of you, Sam. Maybe I'll look at it later when I've got more time and I can read it properly."

"Oh no, you don't get out of it that easily. There's something in there that you need to see, so let's see if you can find it."

Dan flipped open the magazine and half-heartedly scanned the first page. "Nope, I'm not getting anything."

"Some investigator, you are. Look for the contents page. Start with that."

"Okay." Dan did as she asked, but he saw nothing that grabbed his attention. "I know you're trying to help, Sam, but I don't see the relevance. I mean, it's all much the same, isn't it? Celebrities behaving badly. I'm sure it's entertaining, but it's not exactly earth-shattering."

Sam sighed in exasperation. "Give it here."

Dan held out the magazine, and Sam plucked it from his fingers. Turning it around, she rapidly flicked through the pages, then she pressed it flat and handed it back to him.

"Okay. What have we got here?" Dan said. He did his best to appear interested as he read, but he wasn't sure he was carrying it off. The page was a compilation of celebrity news, each item very brief, but the headlines alone were enough to make him grimace.

"Come on," Sam urged him. "Are you a slow reader, or what?"

"No, it's just not my cup of tea. Why don't you just tell me what I'm supposed to be looking—"

Dan broke off as his gaze came to rest on a heading that nestled near the bottom of the sidebar: *Callaway Lashes Out*. His eyes widened as he read. The piece was short, little more than a teaser, but it concluded with another phrase in bold text: **Full Story on page 43.**

Dan flicked quickly through the tatty magazine, ripping the corner of a page in his haste. "Sorry about that," he muttered, but he didn't slow down until he found the right place.

The promised story was brief and lurid. Dan read it from start to finish, then he looked up at Sam. "My God, Sam. This is amazing."

"I thought you might like it. You see, you're not the only one with a good memory and a sharp pair of eyes."

"But I had a look online when I got home last night, and I didn't pick up on this."

"I thought Alan was going to do all that."

"Yes, but I couldn't wait. I decided to have a go on my own, but I missed this completely."

"That's because you didn't know what you were looking for, and I did. What do you think?"

"I think you're brilliant. Amazing. Wonderful."

"Stop it. You know what I mean. What do you think of the article?"

"I think, Sam, without fear of exaggeration, that this changes everything."

CHAPTER 33

The barbed wire fence ran at waist height, but Dan had no difficulty in pressing the wire lower. To Alan, he said, "After you. I'll hold it down."

Alan looked unimpressed. "This is your grand plan? Turn up at Chagford, trespass on Callaway's land and see what happens?"

"More or less."

"No wonder you didn't tell me beforehand. I'd have said no."

"I know. But we're here now, so…"

Alan huffed. "Honestly, Dan, you distinctly said we weren't going to do this. The last time we were here, you said, and I quote, 'We have to be smarter than that.' Isn't that so?"

"Yes but needs must. We haven't found any other way of getting to Callaway. What other option do we have?"

"I don't know, but there must be something."

Dan let go of the wire. "Such as what? The only contact details we could find were for Callaway's agent in LA, and they were no help. I called Benny, but he told us to forget it."

"We could try the front gate again. Maybe someone else might answer the buzzer this time, someone a bit friendlier."

"No. You heard the man. He was in charge of the gate, and that was an end to it. A real jobsworth." Adopting a disdainful tone, Dan recounted the terse reply they'd received at the gate, "It is not our policy to discuss interview requests in person. Kindly submit a request in writing via the appropriate channels. Goodbye."

"You rubbed him up the wrong way. If you let me speak this time, we might get somewhere."

"I don't think so, Alan. I get the impression he gives the same reply to everyone. He sounded like an officious little man, hiding behind his intercom and laying down the rules as if he owns the place." Dan gestured to the fence. "This is our only chance at getting nearer to Callaway."

Alan folded his arms, but he didn't say a word.

"Okay," Dan said. "I shouldn't have led you up the garden path, but I'm going over the fence to try my luck. You don't have to come with me if you don't want to. You could stay here in case I need help."

"What good can I do from back here?"

"You never know. Anything could happen."

"Precisely," Alan said. "We've been down that road before, and I swore I'd never hang back again. I'll have to come with you."

"But you said—"

"Never mind about that," Alan interrupted. "Hold the wire and let's get this over with."

Dan pressed the wire down, and Alan stepped over in an ungainly fashion.

"That wasn't too bad," Alan said, straightening his clothes. "Not too bad at all."

He held the wire while Dan followed.

"What now?" Alan asked.

"We wander toward the house, and we'll see what we can see."

They set off across the field, leaving a trail of flattened grass in their wake.

"Just like old times," Alan said. "Do you remember when we ran across the lawns at Knightsbrook House?"

"Yes. We were like a couple of school kids."

"Looking back, it was a strange thing to do. We'd only just met."

"I needed a problem to solve," Dan said. "I needed something I could make sense of. I sometimes wonder if you knew that at the time."

"I might've had an inkling."

"It was very good of you to go along with it. It earned us a telling off. Ever since that day, one way or another, I've had a habit of getting you into trouble."

"No, we keep getting each other *out* of trouble. That's how I see it. I wouldn't have it any other way."

"Me neither. Thanks for coming along. I should've asked you properly."

Alan waved his words away. "It's my turn to say water under the bridge."

They walked on, and before long they spotted a gate set into the tall hedge that bordered the field. Beyond the gate they caught a glimpse of a broad lawn and a series of formal flower beds.

They slowed their pace, and soon the house came into view, its tall windows reflecting the sky.

"A beautiful house," Alan murmured. "But look at all those windows. If anyone looks out they'll spot us for sure."

"That's not necessarily a bad thing. If someone comes out, we can at least talk to them."

When they reached the gate, Alan grabbed Dan's arm. "Let's wait a minute, see if we can spot anything from here."

"All right. We'll give it a few minutes."

But they didn't have to wait long before a figure emerged from the house, a man striding toward them across the lawn.

"You there!" the man called out. "This is private property. You have no right to be here."

"Be careful what you wish for," Alan muttered darkly. "I don't think he wants to chat, do you?"

"Let me handle him." Raising his voice, Dan said, "I'm dreadfully sorry. We must have taken a wrong turning."

"There's a barbed wire fence."

"Yes, but we thought the landowner might've put a fence across the footpath. It happens all the time, some farmer or other objecting to people crossing his land."

"That's not the case here, I can assure you of that. The footpath is clearly marked."

"Look, I'm sorry, Mr…"

"That's no business of yours."

"Perhaps not, but it's always good to resolve matters in a civilised manner. I'm Dan Corrigan and this is Alan Hargreaves."

"Corrigan?" The man stared at Dan. "You came to the gate."

"Yes, and you sent me away. I recognise your voice. But we're here with good reason. If you'll allow me to explain, I think you'll be pleasantly surprised." Dan wore his most charming smile. "But first, it would be nice to know who we have the pleasure of addressing."

"All right. My name is Mr Saunders, and now you know that, you can leave."

Dan extended his hand for a shake. "Nice to meet you, Mr Saunders."

Saunders glanced at Dan's outstretched hand but didn't take it. "This isn't a garden party, Mr Corrigan. I've asked you to leave."

"Surely, that's for Mr Callaway to decide," Alan suggested.

"Mr Callaway pays me to keep people like you away from his property. I assume you're reporters, so you'll understand when I say that we have no comment to make at this time. Please, go back the way you came."

"We're not journalists," Dan said. "I'm a private investigator. We're looking into what happened at a nearby property. We've already spoken to Benny, and we agreed that cooperation would be in everybody's best interest."

"I don't believe you."

"We met Benny in the pub in town: The Bull Inn," Dan replied. "We had a chat and he saw the sense in us helping each other. He gave us his number."

Saunders lifted his nose as though detecting a foul odour. "This is nonsense. You saw someone in the pub, you got a name, and you expect me to take that as some kind of testimonial?"

"Why don't we go up to the house and ask Benny?" Dan suggested "I'm sure he'll confirm what I've just told you. After that, perhaps we could have a chat with Mr Callaway."

"That's not going to happen. I'm Mr Callaway's personal assistant, and I can tell you in no uncertain terms that he won't want to be bothered by a private investigator, especially one who has come onto his property without permission."

"And yet, he sought me out," Dan said smoothly. "He came looking for me yesterday. Benny drove him to Embervale to look for me. Were you aware of their little expedition?"

Saunders didn't deign to answer, but a flicker of doubt crept across his expression, and that was all Dan needed.

"I see you weren't in the loop," Dan went on. "So it's safe to say you didn't know that Mr Callaway wore a disguise and pretended to be a salesman from Yorkshire; a salesman of tractor parts."

Saunders suddenly seemed to have difficulty meeting Dan's eye. "What a ridiculous story," he grumbled, but his strident tone had gone. "I've never heard such a load of rubbish."

"By all accounts, he put on quite a performance," Alan put in. "I'm told he was very convincing although, personally, I think the limp was a bit over the top. It was a bit too theatrical. It was from his Richard III, I suppose."

Saunders shook his head, but the fight had gone out of him.

Dan pressed home their advantage. "Mr Callaway's misfortune was that he ran into a friend of ours who happens to be an ex-police officer. He became suspicious and followed Mr Callaway outside. He saw the car and noted down the registration. It won't be too hard to check who owns the car. As I said, our friend is an ex-policeman. He has contacts."

"That would be against the law," Saunders said. "A clear breach of privacy. Our legal team would—"

"Do nothing unless the car we saw belonged to Mr Callaway," Dan interrupted. "So you admit that it was him."

"I... I admit no such thing."

"Come on," Dan said. "You've painted yourself into a corner. I'll tell you what, I'll show you some photos of the car. My friend took them outside the local pub." Dan retrieved his phone and hunted for the photos.

"Don't bother," Saunders said, a note of resignation in his voice. "There's no need."

Dan looked up from his phone. "You accept that Mr Callaway went over to Embervale?"

"I accept that it's a possibility, but don't read too much into it. I expect he was just... curious."

"You don't seem surprised," Dan said. "He's done this kind of thing before, hasn't he?"

Saunders nodded wearily. "It wouldn't be the first time."

Dan and Alan exchanged a look.

"It would be awful, wouldn't it," Dan began, "if news of Mr Callaway's little jaunt was to make it into the public eye?"

"The tabloids would be all over it," Alan said. "It would probably go down well online too. It's the kind of story that goes viral."

Saunders sighed heavily. "Okay. What will it take to keep this between ourselves?"

"Answer a few questions," Dan replied. "That's all. We have no axe to grind with your employer. Our case isn't about him, but by looking for us in such a suspicious manner, he's raised a number of questions that need answers."

"Look, there's nothing sinister about what he did," Saunders said. "It's a foible of his. Every now and then he likes to go around without attracting too much attention. That's not easy when you're so recognisable, so he changes his appearance, puts on an accent, and off he goes. Sometimes he spends the day at the races— Newton Abbot or Exeter—and he likes to mingle with the other punters. Where's the harm?"

"That depends on his motive," Dan said. "It's a risky thing for him to do, so why do it?"

"It's for research. He says it helps him when he's developing characters for the screen, and I believe him. He's a great actor, and they all have their own ways of preparing for a role."

"You do hear of these things," Alan said. "They say Daniel Day Lewis spent all day in character when he was playing Abraham Lincoln."

"Is Mr Callaway preparing for a film at the moment?" Dan asked. "A film in which he plays a tractor parts salesman from Yorkshire?"

"No," Saunders admitted. "No, he isn't. In this instance, I think his curiosity got the better of him. I know Benny had said something to him about a private investigator, and Mr Callaway was…"

"Worried?" Dan suggested. "Concerned?"

"Not at all. I think he was intrigued, and to be honest, he gets bored when he's not working on a film."

"He misses the adrenaline," Dan said. "The excitement of being on set, the thrill of giving a performance."

"It's something like that. Whatever the reason, I've given up trying to talk him out of it. Mr Callaway can be very stubborn when he wants to be, so when he gets these ideas into his head, it's better to let them play out. It's not as if he does it all the time, and it only lasts for a few hours. He gets it out of his system, then he goes back to his usual routine."

"There's one thing I'm unclear on," Alan said. "You said it was a *possibility* that Mr Callaway came to our village yesterday, but you're his PA, so I assume you manage his diary. Did you not know what he was up to?"

"I knew he was going out with Benny in the evening, but he didn't say where, and he certainly didn't say anything about concealing his identity."

"You didn't ask?" Dan said.

"No, I did not." Saunders pursed his lips in disapproval, and Dan sensed that here was a thread worth tugging on.

"Is that unusual?" Dan asked. "Does Mr Callaway routinely plan a trip with his driver, but without informing you?"

For a moment, Saunders looked as though he wasn't going to answer, but his expression soured and he said, "It happens. It's a bit maddening, but sometimes they're as thick as thieves, those two. It's odd. I—" Saunders stopped himself abruptly, looking slightly chastened as though he'd said too much. Clasping his hands together, he said, "Right, I've answered your questions and fulfilled my part of the bargain. I trust you'll honour your side, and we'll say no more about it. You'll be able to find your way back to the path. Goodbye."

Saunders turned on his heel and made to march away, but Dan wasn't ready to let him off the hook. "When did Callaway last speak to his daughter?"

Saunders froze, then he turned back to face them. "What?"

"You heard exactly what I said," Dan replied. "And trust me on this, the answer is important. I wouldn't have asked otherwise."

"Trust you? Seriously? Why would I? You come barging in here without—"

Dan cut him short, raising his voice. "We have every reason to be here, Mr Saunders. We're investigating a crime. Serious threats have been made against my client, Zadie Barrington, who, as I'm sure you're aware is a social media influencer. And we all know how Mr Callaway feels about people in that line of work, especially in regard to his daughter."

"His daughter, who happens to be in a clinic being treated for an eating disorder," Alan added. "And we know that Mr Callaway lays the blame for her illness on social influencers such as Zadie."

"Oh no, not this again," Saunders muttered. "For God's sake, this has all been dealt with. I won't have this nonsense dragged up all over again."

"You have no choice in the matter," Alan said. "We've made the connection, so it's only a matter of time before the police come to the same conclusion."

"The police aren't interested in tittle-tattle and rumour, and that's all you've got."

"I wouldn't be so sure," Dan replied. "We found the interview in which Mr Callaway said, and I quote, 'these people ought to be flogged in the street.' He was referring to social media influencers, people exactly like his neighbour, Ms Barrington, was he not?"

"No. Mr Callaway was quoted out of context. That's what they do, these gossip column journalists. They say something outrageous to provoke a reaction, then they print one snippet of the reply."

"Then perhaps you can set us straight," Dan replied. "Please, put the phrase 'flogged in the street' into a context that sounds sane and rational."

"I don't know exactly what Mr Callaway said at the time. I wasn't there. If I had been, I would've controlled the situation and that story would never have appeared. But I can tell you that he was extremely upset when he found out that he'd been so badly misrepresented."

"Did he sue the magazine for libel?" Alan asked.

"No. No one else ran the story, so we decided to let it go. It seemed the safest option."

Dan studied Saunders, watching his body language. The man's bluster and bumptiousness had gone. He was no longer sticking out his chest and his shoulders had slumped, his neck craning forward. This was the real Mr Saunders: an administrator, a man who wanted nothing more than to serve his employer. He took his job seriously, and he hadn't been afraid to march out and confront Dan and Alan, but he was a sensible man, mild mannered even. With a nudge in the right direction, he might be persuaded to cooperate.

"I sympathise," Dan said. "I've had some trouble with the press myself, and I know how upsetting it can be. I'm only small fry, so it was nothing on the scale of what happened to Mr Callaway. It must've been a very trying time."

"Yes. Yes, it was, but it's in the past, and hopefully we can move on and forget all about it."

Dan sent Alan a meaningful glance, and Alan took his cue. "Naturally, we wouldn't want to cause any embarrassment to Mr Callaway," Alan said. "That would be in no one's interest."

"Well, that's good to hear. Thank you."

"There are a couple of things we'd like to clear up though," Dan said. "If that's all right with you, that is."

"Such as?"

Dan offered a friendly smile. "It would help us enormously if we knew that Mr Callaway has never harboured any resentment toward social media influencers such as our client."

"I can assure you of that."

"That's good, but I'd like to focus on the facts. In that interview, what did Mr Callaway actually say?"

"Unfortunately, he wasn't able to recall his exact words."

Dan made a show of looking surprised. "That seems strange. Had he been drinking?"

"No. He was tired, that's all, and he'd been going through a difficult time, and the journalist would've known that. She knew what buttons to push."

"I take it that mentioning his daughter would be a sure-fire way to get Mr Callaway's back up," Alan suggested.

"Very much so. Mr Callaway does his best to be supportive of his daughter, but as I'm sure you know, they don't have an easy relationship."

"I see," Dan said. "So in the interview, Mr Callaway lost his temper, did he?"

"I wouldn't put it like that. He doesn't have a bad temper, not at all. He simply isn't that kind of person."

"He was acting out of character then?"

"Yes, you could say that. He's normally a very courteous man. This was a momentary lapse, a blip."

Saunders attempted a smile, but there was no warmth in it. It was a deflection mechanism, but if he'd expected Dan to be taken in, he'd misjudged him entirely.

"You're lucky to have such a good-natured employer," Dan said. "I expect some of the big Hollywood stars can be difficult to handle, but you've obviously fallen on your feet."

"Yes. I've had worse jobs, that's for sure."

He chuckled and Alan joined in while Dan smiled indulgently.

"Mind you, it has its moments," Saunders went on. "Mr Callaway is a decent chap, he really is, but he can be a bit prickly."

"There but for the grace of God go all of us," Dan said. "We all have our pressure points. He's probably a bit fussy, isn't he?"

"No, it's not that. But he has some strong views, and he doesn't like to back down, so if he's pushed into a corner he can become quite combative. He tends to give as good as he gets." Saunders gestured to the house. "I've told him to get some cameras installed to cover this approach to the house, but he refuses point blank. He's against them on principle, he says they're an invasion of privacy, and he won't listen to reason."

"Maybe we could have a word with him," Dan suggested. "Make him see sense."

Saunders wagged a finger. "Nice try, Mr Corrigan, but that's not going to happen. Now, I hope I've been able to put your mind at rest. Take it from me, Mr Callaway bears no grudges whatsoever against people who work with social media, and he speaks very highly of Zadie Barrington. We were all deeply upset when we heard her house had been broken into, and I'm sure Mr Callaway would be pleased to offer any help she might need. He likes to keep on good terms with all his neighbours. He's very invested in the local community." Saunders smiled, and this time it seemed sincere. He watched them, waiting for their response.

"I understand," Dan said. "It was very good of you to clear that up for us. Please accept our apologies for the unusual way we arrived. It won't happen again."

"Apology accepted. Least said, soonest mended. Consider it forgotten."

"Thank you. We'll be on our way, but before we go, can I give you this?" Dan took out a business card and offered it to Saunders, who eyed it doubtfully.

"It might come in useful," Dan went on. "I could come around and audit your security measures. Mr Callaway might not want cameras, but there are other steps he could take. Motion-triggered floodlights, perhaps, or a good old-fashioned fence, solid wood and tall enough to deter unwanted visitors. It wouldn't take me long to walk around the property, and I needn't disturb Mr Callaway. He wouldn't know I was there."

"You don't give up, do you, Mr Corrigan?"

"It's my only saving grace." Dan extended his arm further. "It's only a card, Mr Saunders. You can throw it away when I'm gone."

"Okay." Saunders took the card and slid it into his pocket. "Goodbye."

"Bye for now." Dan turned to Alan. "Ready?"

Alan nodded. "Absolutely." To Saunders, he added, "Thank you for your help. Much appreciated."

They took their leave, and as they walked back toward the path, Alan said quietly, "Do you buy all that stuff about Callaway being as nice as pie?"

"No, I do not. Not for a second."

"The question is, what do we do about it?"

"Well, I do have one idea, but I'm not sure you're going to like it."

"If it involves more trespassing, count me out," Alan replied.

"No, I was thinking that while Jay is busy on our behalf, we could run a little surveillance operation of our own."

"On Callaway? I don't see how. He's firmly ensconced in his mansion."

"He's got to come out some time," Dan said. "We could move the car a bit further along the road, somewhere where we can keep an eye on Callaway's front gate and sit tight."

"A stakeout?"

"Yes, you could call it that. If Callaway comes out, we can follow him and see what he gets up to."

"It could take a while. Isn't there anything more pressing we should be getting on with?"

"Not that I can think of," Dan said. "What do you say? Are you up for it?"

"Let's do it. Only…"

"What?"

"I wish we'd known beforehand," Alan said. "I'd have packed some sandwiches and a flask of tea."

CHAPTER 34

I t was a bright day in Teignmouth, and DS Kulkarni took deep breaths of sea air as she walked into town. She passed through a pedestrianised high street, taking little notice of the shops and cafes. The place she was looking for was in a side street, and she found it easily enough, only stopping once to consult her phone's map.

Somerset Place held a curious collection of shops, selling everything from fishing tackle to electrical goods. How these small businesses held on in the face of competition from Amazon and the like, Kulkarni had no idea, but here they were, stubbornly open for business.

Kulkarni found the shop she wanted and cast her eye over its window. Fones and Gadgets sold secondhand electronic devices, and the window display teemed with games consoles, tablets and phones. Had any of those devices been stolen before they found their way onto the shelves? It was more than possible, but that wasn't why she was here.

A man appeared in the doorway. "See anything you like?"

Of average height and narrow shouldered, the man was probably in his thirties, but his prime had passed him by. His oily hair had been combed across his scalp in an attempt to conceal a receding hairline, and he was in need of a shave. The waistband of his jeans did battle with a burgeoning paunch, and though his polo shirt was clean and boasted the shop's logo, it stretched tight over his stomach. Clasping his hands together, the man grinned, adding, "If you're looking for something particular, I've got loads more stock inside, and I can always do something with the price."

"Thanks, but I'm not looking to buy."

"Something to sell?"

"No, not that either. I'm looking for a Mr Whelan. Is that you?"

"Who wants to know?"

"I'm DS Kulkarni, Devon and Cornwall Police." Kulkarni showed her warrant card. "You are Mr Whelan, aren't you? Your name badge says Harry, and I'm looking for a Harold Whelan."

The man's grin vanished. "What's this about?"

"I'll discuss that with Mr Whelan, so if you aren't him…"

The man seemed to deflate a little. "All right. I'm Harry Whelan. What's the problem?"

"There's no problem, sir. I'm following up on the van you reported as stolen. A black VW Transporter T30."

Whelan exhaled noisily. "Why didn't you say that in the first place? Have you found it?"

"Not yet, no."

"Oh well. To be honest, I'd more or less given up hope of seeing it again. I only reported it so I could get the crime number for the insurance." Whelan smiled sadly. "My premiums will go through the roof, but what can you do?"

"There's a chance we'll recover your vehicle. We're pursuing a line of enquiry."

"Are you? CID looking for a nicked van? I wouldn't have thought it'd be worth your while."

"We take every crime seriously, sir." Kulkarni paused. "Perhaps it would be better if we talked inside."

"I don't much see the point, but you're welcome to come in. I've got nothing to hide."

"Pleased to hear it."

Whelan led the way inside, Kulkarni looking around as she followed. Glass cases lined the wall, and as Whelan had said, the shelves were crammed with stock: laptops and digital cameras mingled with phones, tablets and a few devices Kulkarni didn't recognise.

Whelan took up position behind the counter and stood a little taller, a man in charge of his domain. Gesturing to the shelves, he said, "I've got paperwork for everything in here. It's all legit. We don't touch anything dodgy."

Kulkarni gazed at him levelly. "I'm here to talk about your van, nothing else."

"All right. I'm just saying."

"Understood. Now, you reported the van missing this morning. When did you last see it?"

"That would've been last night." Whelan made a show of thinking, his gaze flicking upward. "It was parked behind the shop as per usual. We've got a loading bay."

Kulkarni studied Whelan's expression, noting the film of sweat on his brow, the way his eyes refused to stay still. He'd just lied to her, and she could think of no good reason for him to do so. "Are you sure about that, sir? Last night?"

"Yeah. It was in the yard last night, but this morning, it had gone."

"Is the van always parked behind the shop overnight?"

"Sure."

"Is there anyone who can confirm that?"

Whelan pulled a face. "What?"

"It's very simple, sir. I'd like to know if there's anyone who can confirm that the van was on your premises last night."

"No, there's only me here. I run the place on my own."

"Do you have CCTV covering the loading bay?"

"No, we've never bothered."

"That's not very wise. The back door is probably the easiest way to break in and you have a lot of valuable stock."

"We've got steel shutters. We've never had any trouble."

"Until now," Kulkarni corrected him.

"Yeah, until now."

"Mr Whelan, whenever you talk about the shop, you say 'we', but you've told me that you work here on your own."

"I do, but I don't own the place. I'm just the manager."

"I see." Kulkarni took out her phone and opened a new note. "Who's the owner?"

Whelan looked distinctly uncomfortable. "He's a businessman, but he's not from around here. He has a whole string of places like this. Plymouth, Exeter, Taunton. All over."

"Trade must be booming. What's his name?"

Whelan shook his head.

"You don't know or you don't want to say?" Kulkarni asked.

"I'm not supposed to give out details like that. He doesn't like people bothering him. If there's anything to do with the shop, I deal with it myself."

Kulkarni stared at him, waiting.

"What do you want his name for? It was my van that got nicked, not his, so there's no need to bring him into it."

"That's for me to decide, Mr Whelan. It will help if you cooperate, but if you don't, it won't take me long to find the owner's name. I assume he pays business rates on his retail empire, so he won't be hard to track down."

"Do that, then."

Kulkarni stifled a sigh and looked pointedly at the nearest display case. "That Sony camera looks brand new. It's an Alpha 7, but is it the M2 or the M3?" She stepped closer to the case. "Ah, the M3. Very nice. We had a report of an M3 stolen from a holiday cottage in town." She looked Whelan in the eye. "Maybe it would be best if we went through your inventory, after all. It'll take hours, but I can call in a few uniforms to help."

"That camera is totally legit," Whelan spluttered. "A guy brought it in last week. He had a receipt and everything."

"Well, there'll be nothing to worry about then, but it'll still take a long time to check everything else."

"Come on, do me a favour. I've had my van nicked, and now you're breathing down my neck. That's not right. I haven't done anything wrong."

"We'll see." Kulkarni smiled sweetly. It was time to step things up. "Let's rewind a bit, shall we? When did your van go missing?"

Whelan looked taken aback as if thrown by the sudden change in topic. "I told you. Last night."

"Who has keys for the van?"

"Me, obviously, and there's a bloke who helps out with deliveries. Ryan. He's got the spare keys."

"What's Ryan's surname?"

"Hallett."

"Okay. Do you have contact details for Ryan?"

"No. He doesn't work for me. He—" Whelan cut himself short.

"Go on, Mr Whelan. Who does Ryan work for?"

"The owner."

"Describe Ryan for me."

"Why?"

"It's important," Kulkarni stated. "I need to establish who used the van and when, okay?"

"All right." Whelan puffed out his cheeks. "He's about my age, I'd say, but he's a big guy."

"As in tall?"

"He's a bit taller than me, but I mean he's muscly. He's always going on about the gym, saying how much he can lift. Weights and all that."

"Is he white?"

"Yeah."

"How about his hair colour?"

Whelan grinned. "He shaves his head. Reckons he looks tough."

"And is he?"

"I wouldn't know. He's always been all right with me, but I wouldn't like to get on the wrong side of him."

"That's an interesting observation," Kulkarni said, "because a man matching Ryan's description was found dead recently, just a short drive from here. He was murdered."

Whelan paled, and his lips moved silently before he murmured, "What?"

"I'm afraid it's true. You might've heard about the fire on Diamonds Avenue and the body we recovered."

"Yeah, but that can't have been… I mean, it wasn't Ryan, was it?"

"We can't be certain yet, but a witness saw the victim shortly before his death, and from what you've told me, it sounds like Ryan. And here's the thing: the dead man appears to have arrived at the house in a black van; a van that matches the description of the one you reported as stolen."

"No. That can't be right."

"I'm afraid it is. That's why I'm here."

Visibly shaken, Whelan ran his hands through his hair. "Listen, I don't know anything about any of this. This is all some kind of mistake. It probably wasn't even my van. I mean, they all look alike, don't they?"

"Yes, but since you gave us the registration number of your van, we've been checking CCTV, traffic cameras, ANPR. Do you know what that is?"

Whelan shook his head.

"It stands for Automatic Number Plate Recognition. It's a way of looking for vehicles we need to trace, so we'll find your van, and we'll know where it's been. And we'll be able to see whether your van was really in your yard last night, or if it was out on the streets. If you've lied to me, I'll be coming after you, and I'll charge you with perverting the course of justice, insurance fraud and one or two other things besides, such as wasting police time."

"But I haven't done anything."

"You've deliberately made a false statement to the police and now you're wilfully withholding evidence. Mr Whelan, this isn't about your van anymore, this is a murder inquiry, so I advise you to start telling the truth. *Now*."

Whelan's bluster had burned out and he looked spent, his jaw slack and his eyes dull. He licked his lips then said, "I think I might've made a mistake about the dates. I got muddled, but now I think about it, I reckon my van might've gone missing on Monday night. That's the last time I saw it. It was the Tuesday morning when I realised it had gone."

"Why didn't you report it straight away?"

"I was going to but…" Whelan wrung his hands together. "At first, I thought Ryan might've taken it, but I couldn't get hold of him, so I called the owner, just in case he already knew about it. He didn't have a clue, so I said we ought to report it, but he told me not to. He said there might be a problem; something to do with liability on account of the van getting nicked from his premises. He said he needed a while to get the paperwork together. I had no reason not to believe him, so I didn't argue. I just went along with it, but after a few days, I thought…"

"You thought you'd better report it anyway."

"Yeah. I paid for that van out of my own pocket. I can't afford to lose it, so I had to make a claim. I had no choice."

"Did you tell the business owner what you'd done?"

Whelan shook his head rapidly. "Best not to bother him."

"Okay. I need the name of the business owner, and let's not go all around the houses this time. You know I can find it anyway, so just tell me."

"All right, all right. It's Dave. Dave Whitehead."

Kulkarni didn't pause to write the name down; it was important to keep Whelan talking. "And where does Mr Whitehead live?"

"I've no idea. Honestly. I think he's in Plymouth somewhere, but I couldn't say."

"What's the best way to get hold of him?"

"I don't usually try. Like I said, he doesn't take kindly to being bothered. Anyway, he comes here about once a week. He likes to see how things are going."

"But you must have a phone number for him."

Whelan nodded wearily, then he picked up a phone from

behind the counter. "I'll give it to you, but…" His head bowed, he looked up at her like a whipped dog. "Can you, maybe, keep me out of it? You could say you found his name by yourself and you figured out about the van. No need to mention me."

Kulkarni pursed her lips.

"Please?" Whelan said.

"It doesn't work like that, Mr Whelan, but I'll see what I can do. It depends on how helpful you are." Kulkarni's finger hovered over her phone. "The number, please."

Whelan closed his eyes for a second, then he read out the number and Kulkarni tapped it into her phone.

"Thanks for that," Kulkarni said. "We're almost done, but before I go, I'd like you to look at a couple of photos."

Kulkarni swiped her phone's screen and located the two e-fit images of the men who'd questioned Mr Franks. Holding the phone out to Whelan, she switched from one image to the other.

Whelan glanced at the images, expressionless, then he shook his head, his lips clamped tightly shut.

"Look again," Kulkarni insisted. "Closer."

"There's no point. I don't know them." Whelan looked away as if trying to appear disinterested. "You're wasting your time."

"I don't think so." Kulkarni moved the phone back into his field of vision. "You know these men, don't you?"

A muscle twitched in Whelan's cheek, but he shook his head.

"You seem nervous, Mr Whelan."

"No. I'm upset. You come in here, telling me something awful might've happened to Ryan, and then you expect me to answer all these questions. It's not right. I've told you everything I know."

"Is that so?"

"Yes." Whelan gestured angrily at Kulkarni's phone. "I don't know those people, all right? I've never seen them before in my life."

"Okay, we'll leave it at that for the moment." Kulkarni put her phone away, but she made no move to leave. "I may need to speak to you again, Mr Whelan. Next time, I advise you to be straight with me from the start, otherwise, we'll have to take you to the station and interview you there."

"Fine. Whatever." Whelan attempted a smug smile, as if he didn't give a damn either way, but the worry lines creasing his brow told a different story. He was on the ropes and he knew it.

Kulkarni almost felt pity for the man. "Goodbye for now, Mr Whelan. We'll be in touch."

Taking a last look around the shop, Kulkarni stepped out onto the pavement and scanned the street. It might be worth talking to neighbouring shopkeepers. The e-fit images might ring a few bells, and if there'd been any unusual comings and goings at Fones and Gadgets, anyone working nearby might've noticed.

The shop next door was empty, its windows obscured by white paint while refurbishment work went on inside, but a little further along the street, a charity shop, Age UK, was clearly open for business. Kulkarni strolled up to the shop window and looked inside.

The displays of clothes and household goods were bright and cheerful. A lot of the stock would've been donated, but some of the items were obviously new, and everything looked as though it had been laid out thoughtfully. Several customers were browsing the shelves, and as she watched, an elderly man took something to the counter and was served by a middle-aged woman who was all smiles. The woman laughed as she handed the man his change, and she seemed very bright and alert. *Definitely worth talking to,* Kulkarni thought. She made for the door, holding it open for the gentleman who was preoccupied with placing his purchases into a cloth bag.

"Thank you," the man said, before bustling away, and something in his manner put her in mind of Leonard Franks.

Kulkarni paused, then she let the door fall closed without going inside. The man had bought three or four paperbacks, so like Mr Franks, he was a keen reader. Mr Franks had kept an Ian Rankin book by his chair, and he said he'd read all the novels starring DI Rebus. That would've cost him a pretty penny, especially since he seemed to favour hardbacks. What were the odds that he'd built up his collection of novels by buying from charity shops?

Kulkarni grabbed her phone and retrieved Mr Franks' number.

He answered the call promptly: "Hello?"

"Hello, Mr Franks. It's Detective Sergeant Kulkarni. We met the other day."

"Yes. Is there any news? I hope those pictures came out all right. It wasn't easy, trying to say what someone looks like, but the young lady was very nice, and it's amazing what she could do on the computer."

"That's good to hear. You've been a great help, but actually, I just have a couple of quick questions to ask."

"Go ahead."

"Mr Franks, do you tend to buy your books at charity shops?"

"Well, yes. I pop in about once a week."

"Do you go to Age UK?"

"That's one of them. I generally check the Heart Foundation too. They have a decent selection: all very organised. Alphabetical order."

"Right. I also need to ask about the two men who called on you. You said you'd seen one of them before. Might that have been while you were visiting a charity shop?"

"Oh, it might've been. Hold on. Let me think…"

Kulkarni bit her lip. It was all too easy to ask leading questions, and recollections were a lot less reliable than most people realised. She could only wait while Mr Franks trawled his memory.

"Are you still there, miss?" he asked.

"Yes, I'm here."

"Ah, good." Mr Franks sounded relieved. "You know, I think you're right. I saw that chap hanging around outside a shop. I'd been in to donate a few books. I sometimes give them back when I've finished with them; I can't keep them all. Anyway, he was standing by the shop, smoking, and as I went past, he threw his fag end on the pavement and then he went inside. I'd a good mind to call out and tell him to pick it up. We don't all want to live in an ashtray, do we?

"You're right, of course, but are you sure it was the same man?"

"Definitely. It's come back to me now, clear as day. I don't know why I couldn't remember it the other day. My memory's not what it was."

"You seem sharp enough to me, Mr Franks. Can you remember which shop he went into?"

"That one with all the phones and whatnot in the window. Silly name. Now, what do they call it? Phones and Gadgets, that's it, only they spell phones with an F." He paused. "Is that useful?"

"It certainly is, Mr Franks. Thank you very much. I'll let you go now, but I might come back to you later if that's okay."

"Any time. Give me a call first, and I'll make sure I'm in."

"I will. Thanks again, Mr Franks. Bye."

"Bye."

Kulkarni smiled as she put her phone away. Harry Whelan had lied. He knew at least one of the men who'd called on Mr Franks, but he'd been too scared to admit it. Later, she could use that fact against him, but she wasn't ready to bring Whelan in for an interview under caution. That could wait until the van had been traced. Whelan was a small fish, but the shop might easily be a cover for something much more sinister.

If we could just find the damned van, life would be a lot easier, Kulkarni thought. Unfortunately, the odds were stacked against her. The van would've been dumped by now, probably burnt out.

She considered heading back to the station to check if ANPR and CCTV had yielded anything new, but since she was here, it might still be worthwhile to canvas the local shopkeepers. Kulkarni made her way into the charity shop and was greeted with a cheery hello from the woman behind the counter. This would be a much more pleasant encounter than the one she'd just had with Harry Whelan. And even if no new information came to light, it wouldn't be a waste of time. It was always good to get law abiding citizens onside. They had a tendency to keep their eyes open, and you never knew what they might see.

Kulkarni had her warrant card ready. A five-minute chat, and then she might have a quick browse around the shop. Somehow, she felt pretty sure she'd find a bargain. This might just be her lucky day.

CHAPTER 35

There was a measured hurriedness in Jay's stride as he made his way through Gandy Street. An observer might take him for a workman on his way home through the streets of Exeter at the end of a working day. He'd dressed to blend in: jeans and a zip-up fleece, a pair of well-worn trainers. No one would look twice, and that was fine with him.

He spotted the place he was looking for and slowed his pace as he passed Melody Reinhardt's shop. Indiago: what kind of name was that for a clothes shop? He couldn't recall ever seeing the place before, but that was no surprise. He didn't waste time on the fancy little boutiques and craft shops in the city centre; they were for tourists and people who had more money than sense.

As far as Jay could see, there was only one person inside: a young woman with long straight hair. He couldn't get a good look at her, but Dan had given him a detailed description of Melody, and this person seemed to fit the bill. What was more, she appeared to be tidying the place up, getting ready to close for the day. Dan had told him that Melody usually ran the shop alone, so this was almost certainly her.

Jay took a few more strides along the street and then crossed to the other side, stopping in front of a small cafe and pretending to read the menu displayed in the window. The reflection in the glass gave a reasonable view of the other side of the street, and by angling his body, he could make out the doorway of Melody's shop.

Come on, he thought. *Don't take all day.* Jay checked his watch, and as he looked up, he realised a man was watching from inside the cafe. The man shook his head and then tapped at his watch, mouthing a phrase that was probably, 'We're closed'.

Jay nodded to show he'd understood, but he stayed put, returning his attention to the menu. From the corner of his eye, he saw the man return to his work, wiping down tables and straightening the chairs.

The distraction lasted no more than a few seconds, but it was almost disastrous. In Melody's shop, the lights were off, and a woman was walking away from the door, heading back the way Jay had come.

Dammit! The woman had her back to him, so he couldn't be sure this was Melody, but she was smartly dressed in a pale raincoat and high heels, her long, dark hair flowing out behind her as she marched away. He could be mistaken, but this woman carried herself with a certain poise and elegance, strutting as though she owned the street. Yes, this was Melody; it had to be.

As casually as he could, Jay set off on her trail, keeping a safe distance. He smiled to himself. *This beats the day job,* he decided. He liked decorating well enough, and it paid the bills, but it didn't exactly set his heart racing. Maybe, if he played his cards right, Dan might hire him to do a bit more of this line of work.

Jay had never wanted to be a detective. He'd been happy in uniform, out on the streets where all the real work was done. But he'd always had a keen eye and knack for guessing what people would do in a given situation. Watch and wait, that had been his motto. Read the signs and stay mentally prepared, thinking two or three moves ahead, and always, *always* watch your back. The rules of the street were baked into his DNA.

Today, he was ninety-nine percent certain he knew exactly what

Melody was going to do next. Yes, she'd caught him off guard by her sudden emergence from the shop, but he knew exactly where she was heading, and he'd prepared accordingly.

Dan's description had been enough to tell Jay that Melody would park in the Guildhall car park. It was expensive, but it was the closest to Melody's shop, and pretty young things like her did not walk far unless they really had to.

Jay had scoped the car park earlier. A quick circuit had confirmed that there were at least three black Audi saloons in the parking bays. Of course, Corrigan hadn't been able to supply the registration number of Melody's car, nor even the year and model, which was what you got for working with a civilian, but at least he'd provided the make and colour, and that was enough to tip the balance of probability.

Sure enough, Melody turned left at the end of Gandy Street, and the car park came into view. A minute later, Melody marched in through the entrance and took her keys from her handbag. Jay lingered in the shadows near the entrance and saw the indicators on a black Audi A8 flash as she unlocked it.

I knew it, Jay thought. *There are no flies on me*. He strolled over to his truck and climbed inside, ready to follow. He'd parked near the only exit, so all he had to do was wait.

The Audi swept past him, its driver paying him no heed, and for the first time, Jay got a proper look at his quarry.

Very glam, Jay thought. Melody was a looker, if you liked the haughty, upper-class kind of woman. She was all cheekbones and arched eyebrows, her nose in the air. Naturally, she didn't deign to glance in his direction, but that was fine.

The Audi exited the car park and Jay pulled into the traffic directly behind her. Later, he'd drop back and allow a couple of cars to pull in and hide his truck from Melody's view, but for now, he'd stick to her like glue.

Jay let his gaze run over the Audi. The A8 was a luxury model and practically brand new. Cars like that didn't come cheap, and he wondered if Melody could afford it from the proceeds of her little shop. Of course, she could've taken out a loan, but then again, she might've had some help from the bank of mummy and daddy. Melody looked like a person who could lean on a rich family. There she was, all dolled up, a young woman living beyond her means.

You don't know that, Jay scolded himself. *All assumptions are dangerous*. He chuckled darkly at his own stupidity. When had he become such a grumpy old man?

For all he knew, Melody was a hardworking young woman with a head for business and a string of shops to her name. He could ask Dan about that later. In the meantime, he'd kick his prejudices into touch and keep an open mind. *Watch and wait*, he reminded himself. *That's all I've got to do.*

The rush-hour was well underway, and they moved slowly through the city in fits and starts, from one red light to the next. Jay relaxed. Melody lived in Doddiscombsleigh, and she was clearly on her way home. Jay knew both the main routes she could take, so even if he lost sight of her for a second, he'd soon pick her back up.

Once clear of the city, Melody made for the stretch of the A38 that would take her home. The dual carriageway was relatively clear, and the Audi accelerated away. Jay's pickup didn't have the same kind of power, but he looked after his vehicle well. It didn't let him down, matching Melody's speed in a matter of seconds.

But when they reached the notorious Splatford Split, climbing a steep hill as the road briefly gained two extra lanes before separating into two dual carriageways, the Audi sailed across all four lanes at the last second, and Jay had to put his foot down to follow suit.

Where was she going? This route would take her away from home and toward the coast. She was heading in completely the wrong direction, and she seemed to have chosen to go this way as an afterthought.

Jay's pickup was directly behind the Audi now, and Melody tilted her head as though looking into her rear-view mirror.

Had she noticed the way he'd followed her? Had the sudden change in direction been an attempt to shake him off?

No. Melody didn't know him, and he was sure she hadn't clocked him in the car park.

Jay kept his eyes on the traffic, drumming his fingers on the steering wheel like any bored commuter heading for home. After a moment, he risked a glance at Melody, and she appeared to be looking straight ahead. Jay breathed a sigh of relief, and as they crested the hill, Jay slowed his truck for a few seconds, hanging back to gain some space before matching the Audi's speed.

"Now then, young Melody," Jay muttered under his breath. "Where are you headed?"

It wasn't long before he found out.

The exit for Teignmouth approached, and unlike Melody's earlier change in direction, she indicated in plenty of time and took the junction smoothly. Jay followed at a discreet distance. The road was narrower here, and much quieter. If she spotted him now, there was a chance she'd put two and two together.

Jay took it easy, letting the Audi disappear around bends in the road now and then, and they made it into Teignmouth without incident. In town, Melody seemed to know exactly where she was going, driving carefully and keeping below the speed limit.

Jay looked around as they went. He knew the streets reasonably well, and his sense of direction had always been good, but Melody led him into a maze of residential streets he didn't recognise. Terraced houses of pale brick stood shoulder to shoulder, each one identical to its neighbour. The road was potholed here and there, and the place had the cramped feel of a council estate. Still, it looked like a decent place to live, by and large. There were curtains at the windows, and the small front gardens were well tended, the fences painted and the hedges trimmed. He passed a small park and saw a few children playing on the swings while half a dozen others were having a kick around with a football.

The Audi slowed to a halt and reversed into a parking space. Jay drove past without turning his head, but he kept an eye on his mirrors.

This was Melody's destination. She climbed from the car and

headed straight for a terraced house, letting herself in through the front gate without hesitation.

Jay found a parking space and squeezed his truck in between a white van and an SUV, then he sat for a minute, thinking.

He couldn't march up to the house and start asking questions, but he could have a wander and get a feel for the place. On the other hand, he could try something a little more direct.

Jay rummaged in the glovebox and found an old, padded envelope. It was a bit crumpled and tatty but it would do. He stepped out from his truck and looked around as though searching for an address, then he took out his mobile phone as though checking he was in the right place.

Walking quickly, he spotted the gate Melody had used, and he took note of the number displayed beside the front door: 37. Tapping the number into a note on his phone, he made for a house two doors down.

Jay rang the doorbell and stood back. Somewhere inside the house a dog began to bark, and by the sound of it, it was a big one. *Just my luck*, Jay thought.

A shadow fell across the dimpled glass of the front door, and a woman's voice snapped, "Quiet! Get back!"

Jay braced himself, but when the door opened, an older woman appeared, her hand on the collar of a large golden retriever, and though she looked mildly surprised to see someone standing at her door, she seemed friendly enough.

"Don't mind the dog," she said. "He makes a lot of fuss, but he's all right."

"So I can see." Jay held out his hand for the dog to take a sniff, and the retriever obliged.

"Anyway, what was it you wanted?" The woman looked at the packet in Jay's hand, adding, "I haven't ordered anything."

"Oh? Have I not got the right address? This is for a Miss Reinhardt."

The woman shook her head. "No, that's not me."

"Oh dear, they must've made a mistake at the depot. This must be for one of your neighbours."

"I doubt it. I've lived here for more than twenty years, and I know most people. There's no one with that name, not around here."

"That's a shame. I'll have to take it back. Sorry to have bothered you." Jay made to move away, but he hesitated, pretending to consult his phone. "Ah, I was supposed to go to 37. My mistake."

"You must be in the wrong street. There's no one called Reinhardt at 37."

"Oh? What's their name then?"

"That's not for me to say, but it's definitely not Reinhardt."

"Okay, well, I'm sorry to have troubled you." Jay offered a smile. "I'll go and check at number 37 and see if I can sort out what's happened. Maybe this Melody Reinhardt is a relative or something. Bye." Jay turned away.

"Hang on," the woman called out, and Jay looked back. The woman's expression had brightened. "Did you say Melody?"

"That's right. Melody."

"I reckon you had the number right, after all. It's where her parents live anyway."

"I see, but you said they aren't called Reinhardt."

"They're not. They're the Robinsons, but their daughter changed her name. She calls herself Melody, or so I'm told." The woman chuckled. "She always was a headstrong little maid. Pretty as a picture, but a bit full of herself, if you know what I mean."

"Oh yes," Jay said. "Youngsters, eh?"

"She's not so young now. A grown woman. But she's too good for the likes of us, or so she thinks. Anyway, problem solved. You can deliver your parcel now. When you find her, say hello from me."

"I'd be happy to, but I don't know your name."

"Just say Joan." Another chuckle. "Say, 'Joan says hello, Mary Robinson.' That'll shake her up."

"Right, I'll do that," Jay said. "Thanks for your help."

Joan nodded in acknowledgement, then she retreated indoors, pulling her dog away from the door with some difficulty.

Result, Jay thought as he made his way back to his truck. He'd head for home and report back to Dan later. Maybe they could meet in the pub. Dan would be very interested to learn that Melody Reinhardt had gone to some lengths to conceal her humble origins. Surely, such a nugget of information was worth a small bonus, preferably in the form of a pint or two. If there was one thing better than a beer after a job well done, it was a beer that someone else had paid for.

CHAPTER 36

L ate in the afternoon, DS Kulkarni leaned her elbows on her temporary desk in Teignmouth police station and read through her notes from the day. The threads were coming together, and a case was emerging. Harry Whelan had known Ryan Hallett, and Whelan's VW van might link both men to the fire on Diamonds Avenue and to the body found in the ashes. Even so, looking back over her carefully composed concise sentences, Kulkarni frowned. Where was the solid evidence? She hadn't been able to positively identify the body, and they hadn't found the van. What's more, the resident of the burned-out house was still unaccounted for. The only witness, Len Franks, had described the missing man as being small built, but that wasn't a lot to go on.

And then there was Fones and Gadgets.

Kulkarni's visits to the neighbouring shops had yielded little. The assistant in the Age UK charity shop, a lady by the name of Enid, had been helpful, but her account hadn't added up to much. Yes, Enid had long harboured suspicions about the activity at Fones and Gadgets, lowering her voice as she'd muttered darkly about there being a lot of 'comings and goings', particularly in the alley that ran behind the row of shops. But she hadn't been sure about the men in the e-fit images. Perhaps she'd seen them before, but maybe not, and didn't one of them look a bit like that chap from Eastenders?

Kulkarni had thanked Enid and made sure to buy something from the shop before leaving. But what next?

She'd already tried calling Dave Whitehead, but the owner of the Fones and Gadgets empire wasn't answering his phone. Routine background checks had revealed nothing interesting. The Fones and Gadgets shops appeared to be legitimate businesses, and there was no reference to Dave Whitehead on the Police National Computer.

It was time to try a different approach. According to Harry Whelan, Mr Whitehead was based in Plymouth, and Kulkarni had a contact in Plymouth CID: DI Russ Blakey. They'd worked together and got on well, so Kulkarni was hopeful as she placed the call, but her optimism didn't last long. *Voicemail*. Kulkarni left a message, asking Blakey to call back when he had time, then she rang Plymouth Police Station and asked to be put through to CID.

This time, she got an answer: "DS Simon Trevor here. How can I help you today, DS Kulkarni?"

Kulkarni gritted her teeth at the man's condescending tone. DS Trevor was an acquaintance from a previous case, but they hadn't hit it off on first meeting, and it seemed the situation hadn't improved.

"I'm looking into a guy called Dave Whitehead," Kulkarni began. "He's a businessman based in Plymouth. He owns a chain of shops selling—"

"Sorry," DS Trevor interrupted, sounding anything but. "No can do."

"But I haven't explained what I want yet," Kulkarni protested.

"It really doesn't matter. We're up to our eyeballs over here. I only took your call because I remembered your name from that carjacking case."

"All I want is for you to ask your colleagues and see if Dave Whitehead is on anybody's radar."

There was no reply.

"Hello?" Kulkarni said. "Are you still there?"

"Yeah, but I really can't help. We're short of resources as it is. We can't handle your workload as well as our own. You know how to run background checks, don't you? Look him up on the PNC."

"I've done that already. There's nothing there."

"There you go then. Job done."

Kulkarni felt her blood beginning to boil, but with some effort, she kept her tone civil. "Listen, all I want to know is whether the name Dave Whitehead is ringing any bells for anyone."

"I understand, but I'm not going to bother anybody with such a vague question. If there's something concrete, we might be able to help, but—"

"I have e-fits for two of Whitehead's associates," Kulkarni said. "I'll email them over to you, okay?"

"I'll take a quick squint at them if I get time, but I'm not promising anything."

"Thank you," Kulkarni said, but DS Trevor had already ended the call.

That's just rude, Kulkarni thought. Would he have hung up on a male colleague? Kulkarni didn't think so, but it was the way he'd spoken to her that rankled. DS Trevor was the same rank as her, but he'd been deliberately disrespectful, and what was worse, he'd enjoyed every moment.

Kulkarni checked the time and glanced around the office. It was getting late, and most people had left, some of them heading out to a nearby pub. Kulkarni had been invited, but she'd given it a miss. She hadn't wanted to leave until she'd completed her notes, but now she wondered whether she'd made the right decision.

One look at her inbox was enough to convince her. There were dozens of messages awaiting her attention, but she was in no mood to tackle them. Kulkarni saved her notes and logged off, grabbing her bag and heading for the door without a backward glance.

She wasn't quite sure where her Teignmouth colleagues had gathered for a drink, but she'd figure it out. She was, after all, a detective.

CHAPTER 37

Zadie woke suddenly, staring up at the ceiling. The blackout blinds in her room made it hard to tell if it was day or night, but her mind was busy, buzzing with half remembered snippets from disjointed dreams. She'd had an early night, so she ought to be feeling good: rested and refreshed. She definitely shouldn't be dazed and disorientated. Something wasn't right.

Zadie checked her Apple Watch, and as she suspected, it was still the middle of the night. That wasn't good. If her REM cycles got out of sync, she'd be a mess in the morning, her mood and energy levels all over the place. She'd need to change her alarm and wake up a little later to make up for her disturbed night's sleep.

Zadie rolled onto her side and reached out for her phone. Her fingers found the disc of its wireless charger, but it was empty. *Weird.* She always left her phone to charge overnight. Always. She patted her hands across the nightstand, groping for the familiar oblong of smooth aluminium and glass, but there was only her bottle of water and a couple of paperback books.

Zadie sat up and pressed the switch for her bedside lamp. Its soft glow bathed the room in a dim, pink-tinted light, the shade chosen to aid relaxation as she wound down each evening.

Her phone was clearly not on her nightstand, and when she leaned over and peered at the floor, it wasn't there either. Zadie sat back against the upholstered headboard, searching through her memory. Her bedtime routine was unchanging, a ritual preparation for restful sleep. She'd put the phone in place the night before, so it had to have fallen down. Never mind, she'd solve the puzzle easily. Zadie found the icon on her watch that would ping her phone, and she pressed it.

Immediately, a muted ringtone sounded from somewhere below her. Somehow, her phone had ended up underneath her bed. Perhaps she'd reached out for water in the night and inadvertently swiped the phone from its place. That was odd, because the charger was magnetic, but nevertheless, the phone had become dislodged somehow.

Zadie clambered out of bed, glad of her satin pyjamas, and knelt on the floor, peering under the bed. There was no sign of her phone, but there was something else: a box pushed under her bed. Made from polished wood, the box was perhaps thirty centimetres across, and its sides were angled as if it were hexagonal, but she couldn't see any identifying marks nor guess what it might contain.

Zadie pinged her phone again, holding down the icon to activate her phone's flash. She could see no pulse of light beneath her bed, but her phone's ringtone seemed to be coming from inside the box. Zadie pictured her phone slipping down the back of the mattress and through the wooden slats of her bed's frame. In a way, it was a good job the box had been there to cushion her phone's fall, but if the box was open, why hadn't she been able to see her phone's flash?

It's fallen in among a load of old clothes or something, Zadie thought. *Nat must've bundled up some unwanted items instead of throwing them out.* She'd have a word with Nat later and remind her of the rules on clutter. If something was necessary, it was kept close at hand, but if it wasn't needed, it went out. It was as simple as that.

Zadie stretched her arm toward the box. Her fingertips brushed its surface, and Zadie felt smooth wood, cold to the touch, but she couldn't get any purchase on it. She shifted position, lying down on her back and pushing her shoulder under the bed. She gazed up at the ceiling while her hand groped for the box. At first she felt nothing but dust devils and indeterminate particles that fell apart as she touched them. Zadie tried not to picture the crumbling corpses of long-dead insects as she stretched out her hand to reach further. There. Her fingertips brushed against smooth wood, and she held on to a corner and pulled the box toward her.

The wooden box was much longer than she'd anticipated—roughly three times its width—and it was heavier too, its smooth sides resistant to her grip. It slid slowly over the waxed floorboards, and it kept slipping from her fingers as if reluctant to leave its hiding place. If it wasn't for the fact that her phone seemed to be inside the box, she'd leave the damned thing where it was and have Natalya clear it up. But there was nothing for it; she'd have to continue.

Zadie half rolled over and stretched her other arm under the bed, clamping the box between her hands, then she edged away from the bed, dragging the box after her. And when it finally emerged into the light, Zadie's heart lurched.

This was not a box but a miniature coffin. Crafted from highly polished dark wood, its sides angled into an elongated hexagon, it was too well made to be a Halloween novelty. This was either the real thing or a perfect replica. Either way, it was a sick joke to leave this dark symbol of death beneath her bed. Who would do such a thing, and when had they done it?

Zadie froze, staring at the coffin's lid. It was closed, so how the hell had her phone ended up *inside*?

Slowly, Zadie lifted the lid to peep inside. Her phone was there, nestling on top of a small stack of papers. She set the lid on the floor and retrieved her phone, but when she saw what lay beneath it, her breath caught in her throat.

The photograph was small, but its subject was clear: Zadie working at the desk in her studio. She picked up the photo, revealing another, also of her, this time relaxing on the sofa in her lounge. Setting down her phone, Zadie plucked the stack of photos from the box, rifling through them, tossing them aside, one by one. Zadie on a deckchair in the garden, Zadie sipping a drink in a coffee shop, Zadie walking along a leafy lane. On and on, each photo of her and her alone, snapshots from unguarded moments when she was clearly unaware she was being photographed, watched, spied upon.

Zadie's mind reeled, a swirl of panic seething in her stomach. And as she dropped the last photograph to the floor, she found a sheet of plain paper, its surface covered with typewritten text, the same sentence again and again: *I'll see you soon.*

Zadie clamped her hand over her mouth, stifling a scream as she let the note flutter from her fingers.

She had to get away from that grotesque box. Zadie scuttled backward, hands and feet flapping clumsily at the floor, a low groan escaping from her lips. Her back thudded against the bedroom wall, and the shock startled her into silence. Zadie scrambled to her feet, her legs shaking, then she backed to the door, her gaze fixed on the box beside her bed.

"Oh my God," Zadie whispered, and a shudder raced the length of her spine as a cold realisation formed in her mind. Someone had stage-managed this moment, going to great lengths to make her suffer.

The whole thing had been planned, the photos collected over time, the box bought, the note written. But worst of all, someone had been in her room, creeping in while she'd slept, baiting their trap with her phone.

Was the intruder still nearby? Was someone in the house, listening, waiting for her to scream, taking some kind of twisted pleasure from her misery?

Zadie tried to take a deep breath, but her chest was too tight. She had to think. If she panicked, she was lost.

Phone for help, she thought. *Call 999.* But if she was in immediate danger, help might come too late.

Zadie fumbled for the door handle and made sure the door was shut tight, then she leaned her back against it. Why hadn't she had a lock fitted? She'd been foolish, carried away by her own confidence, but this house was supposed to have been her refuge, the one place where she could finally feel safe.

So much for that.

Zadie took a slow breath and cleared her mind as best she could. What now? What was the next logical step?

If someone was still in the house, they might come back to her room at any moment. If they tried to barge in, she could put up some resistance, but she wouldn't be able to keep them out for long. She could shove her bed against the door, barricade herself in. Her phone was on the floor by the bed. She could call the police and wait for them to arrive.

The nearest police station was in Exeter, wasn't it? A thirty-minute drive away, some of it through country lanes. Could she wait that long?

No. She had to get out of the house, get away. Zadie's gaze went to the blinds. She'd had locks fitted to the windows, so an intruder couldn't have come in that way, but the window might provide an escape route. The scaffolding was right outside. She could climb out, creep across the scaffolding and climb down. Outside, she'd be free. Her car keys were in the kitchen, and that was a damned shame, but she could run to the road or hide in the garden. There'd be choices.

All she needed was time. And something else.

Zadie glanced down at her bare feet. Her Birkenstock sandals were on the floor by the nightstand. She could run while wearing them, but there was no way she could tackle the scaffolding.

Zadie scanned the room. Her shoes were all downstairs or stored neatly in her dressing room. Although…

She backed away from the door, placing her feet carefully, every step silent. A small wardrobe stood in the corner, and she opened its door slowly, taking care not to let it swing wide and hit the wall.

Crouching, she found the cardboard box in the bottom of the wardrobe, the distinctive logo unmistakeable. The Nikes had been an unwanted gift from Carly, but Zadie hadn't had the heart to throw them out or give them away. Now, she pulled the shoes from their wrapping of tissue paper and slid them onto her feet, her trembling fingers fumbling with the laces.

Her shoes on, Zadie crept across the room and retrieved her phone. She was ready. Her breathing was slower now, but as she moved toward the window, the floorboards creaked beneath her feet, and with every tell-tale sound her chest tightened as though a metal band had been clamped around it, squeezing the breath from her body.

The key was still in the window lock, and a moment later she had the window open. It swung outward silently. Shaun had done a good job of restoring the woodwork.

Zadie leaned out and looked down at the scaffolding. She knew the planks were only a short distance below her window, but in the dark, they looked further away, the rough lengths of wood loosely balanced on the metal pipes. And beyond, there was the dizzying drop through the darkness. She could just make out the ground, but she forced herself to look only at the wooden planks directly below her window.

You can do it, Zadie told herself. *You've got this.* After all, Shaun had been clambering about on the scaffolding for weeks, so it must be solid enough. If he could rely on it, she could too.

Zadie hoisted herself up so she sat astride the sill, legs dangling either side. The window was narrow and not tall enough to accommodate her height, but if she ducked her head and twisted her body, she ought to make it through. She was slim and supple, and all she had to do was slide through, lowering herself down until her foot reached the scaffolding.

But Zadie hesitated. It wasn't the height, it was the thought of falling, of being out of control. She couldn't trust her life to a bunch of rickety planks. It was dark, and she'd never set foot on scaffolding in her life. She could so easily slip or miss her footing. What if she was making the wrong choice, letting her fear overrule her head?

Yes, someone had been in her house and played a trick on her, but if they'd wanted to hurt her, they would've done it by now. She'd been asleep, an easy target, but they hadn't laid a finger on her. Was it rational to climb out of the window if she wasn't in danger?

And then she heard something.

From beyond her bedroom door, echoing through the stillness, came the groaning creak of a footstep on the stairs. Zadie stayed perfectly still, listening, straining her ears. The silence stretched out, achingly long, but then there was another footstep, and another. Heavier now, the next footstep rang out, and then there was a louder snap of wood: a resounding crack, sharp as a gunshot; the damaged fifth tread shifting beneath someone's determined tread.

The sound electrified Zadie, urging her muscles into action. Hardly knowing what she was doing, she clambered out and clung to an upright metal pole as she looked frantically from side to side. Which way should she go? Where was the ladder that would take her down to safety?

It was at the far end of the house, wasn't it? Yes. Of course it was. Moving as fast as she dared, Zadie hurried along the uneven boards. They shifted a little each time she transferred her weight from one foot to the other, but despite their ominous rattling, they held firm. She'd be okay. She could make it.

In no time at all, she reached the end of the boards. There was a short metal gate, painted yellow, and Zadie remembered it now. The ladder would be on the other side.

But when she looked down, there was nothing there. She leaned over the gate, but there was no sign of the ladder.

Zadie hissed a curse under her breath. She should've remembered. Her brother had told her about this. She'd only half listened, tuning out the inevitable lecture, but it came back to her now in startling clarity. Tobias had instructed Shaun to remove any and all ladders at the end of each working day, insisting that it simply wasn't safe to leave them unattended. They were to be taken down and made secure with padlock and chain.

"Oh God," Zadie whispered. "What the hell am I going to do?"

She looked back to her window and saw that she'd left it wide open. The intruder would know instantly what she'd done. All they had to do was to look outside, and they'd see her, cowering like a caged animal.

No. She couldn't allow that to happen.

Summoning every last scrap of courage, Zadie opened the yellow gate and stepped to the scaffold's edge. The metal pipes formed a simple framework. She could place her feet on one of the diagonals and that would be a start. After that, she could lean across and grab onto the nearest vertical. From there, she'd shimmy down to the next level of planks, then she'd repeat the process until she was within jumping distance of the ground. She was strong enough; all those workouts had made sure of that. She could do this.

She sat on the edge of the boards. She'd need two hands for this, but she had no pockets, nowhere to keep her phone. Reluctantly, she set her phone down on the boards, then she turned, taking her weight on her arms as she lowered herself down.

The board's rough edges bit into her fingers, but she held on tight while she moved her legs tentatively from side to side, searching for a foothold.

Where was that damned diagonal pipe? It must be further away than she'd thought. She lowered herself a little more. Her arm muscles burned, but there was nothing she could do about that. Until she could find a safe place to rest her feet, she had no choice but to cling on. And in that moment, she heard the sound of her bedroom door creaking open.

SATURDAY

CHAPTER 38

D an woke early and got straight out of bed. Today would be better. He'd work hard in the morning, then he'd take a break and go out for lunch with Sam. If everything went according to plan, he'd take the afternoon off, but only if he could achieve enough in the morning to make up for lost time. And there was a lot of wasted time to recoup.

Yesterday, he and Alan had spent hours parked near John Callaway's house, but it had been a complete waste of time. The gate across Callaway's drive had remained stubbornly closed. As the afternoon had turned into evening, they'd given up and driven back to Embervale, tired and hungry.

Really, he shouldn't have been surprised. As Alan had pointed out, this was real life, not a detective drama in which the bad guys always appeared at the right moment.

It had been a disappointment, but what was done, was done. After a setback, you picked yourself up and forged ahead. A brisk morning run would clear his head and help him to think about the case. After that, he'd make a few notes and do some background research, then he'd take a couple of hours off to have lunch with Sam. That would be his reward for a morning's work, and it would keep him on track.

He hadn't got around to searching for a seafood restaurant, so he'd found a vegetarian place in Exeter called Herbies, and he'd booked a table. A good lunch, a stroll around the cathedral, and they'd take it from there.

I'll have to get a move on, Dan told himself as he hurried downstairs. *Lots to do.* He breakfasted quickly, wolfing down a piece of toast with a mug of coffee, and he hummed a tune to himself as he cleared away his breakfast things.

Dan's phone rang out, cutting short his wavering rendition of 'Lovely Day', but that was okay. It might be Sam.

Dan grabbed his phone, but his smile vanished when the caller's name was unknown. *It's probably nothing*, Dan decided, but he accepted the call, making his voice neutral as he said hello.

A muted hiss came from the speaker as if someone had exhaled on the microphone, and when the caller spoke, the voice was a man's: "Dan. It's Tobias Barrington. Could you come and meet me? I'm in Exeter. It's important or I wouldn't ask."

"What's happened? Is Zadie okay?"

A pause, then: "No. No, she isn't. She's in the hospital, but I can't talk about it like this. Can you come over?"

"Of course. Which hospital?"

"RD and E. Do you know it?"

"The Royal Devon and Exeter. Yes, I know where it is. But how's Zadie? Is she ill or has something happened?"

"We don't know the circumstances, but she's unwell. It seems as if she had some kind of episode last night."

"Oh no. Was it sudden?"

"That's hard to say, Dan. It looks like she collapsed. Nat found her this morning. Outside. We think Zadie must've been out there for hours, the poor thing."

"Was she awake? Had she lost consciousness?"

"We think she must've blacked out, but what she was doing outside, God only knows. She was in a pretty bad way when they brought her in. The doctor said they've made her comfortable. They want to keep her sedated while they run some tests."

"What are they saying?" Dan asked. "Is she going to be okay?"

"They're not giving much away. Physically, I think she's okay apart from a few cuts and bruises, so that's something. We're waiting for a consultant to come in. We'll find out more then."

"Did Zadie say anything? Was she able to say what happened?"

"Not really. Apparently, she tried to say something in the ambulance, but she was incoherent." Tobias let out a heartfelt sigh. "Listen, we might know more by the time you get here. We need to talk in person about this, Dan. With everything else Zadie's been going through, I'm worried."

"I understand. This could be related to the break in and the—"

"Yes, but not in the way you might think," Tobias interrupted. "We'll talk properly when you get here."

"I'll be there as fast as I can. Is it okay if I bring Alan?"

"I don't think—" Tobias stopped abruptly, and Dan heard a woman's voice in the background. When Tobias spoke again, he sounded on edge. "Got to go. The consultant has arrived and she wants a word. Meet me in A and E. Bye."

Tobias ended the call, and Dan set his phone down on the kitchen table. He'd get Alan in a second, but he needed a moment to think, to let his mind adapt to this new turn of events.

This was his first proper case as a private investigator, and from the start he hadn't got a grip on it. He'd been slow to react, distracted by false trails and spurious clues.

I have to do better, Dan chided himself. *I have to* be *better.*

Until now, it was as if he'd been playing the part of a PI, swaggering about and handing out business cards. That wasn't good enough. Zadie had placed her faith in him, but he'd let her down, and now she was in hospital.

It was time to step up to the mark. He'd help Tobias and Zadie in any way he could, and then he'd damned well find out who'd done this and make them pay for it. He owed that much to Zadie.

Dan grabbed his jacket and his phone, then he headed for the door. He'd pick up Alan and then he'd drive to the hospital as fast as he dared.

He just had to hope he wasn't too late.

CHAPTER 39

T aking a quick break from work, Benny slipped into the kitchen and put the kettle on. There was a fancy coffee machine, but he didn't want to muck about. Besides, he couldn't tell the difference between the fancy stuff and instant. He spooned granules into a mug and stared at the kettle, drumming his fingers on the counter while he waited for it to boil. "Idiot," he muttered. "You put too much water in." Finally, the kettle gurgled to a stop, and he poured water into his mug, then he took a slurp, scalding his tongue. "Bloody hell!"

Benny ground his teeth together. He didn't have time for this. He shouldn't even be indoors. The car needed cleaning, inside and out, and Mr Callaway wouldn't hear of the damned thing being taken to be valeted. No, Benny had to do the job himself, and he'd better do it thoroughly or there'd be complaints.

No wonder he's divorced, Benny thought. Callaway was a decent employer, but he was picky for the sake of it. It was enough to drive a man to drink.

Benny blew on his coffee and took a cautious sip. It was still too hot, but it would be okay in a minute. He looked over his shoulder, listening carefully. You could usually tell when Mrs Yates was around. The woman was never still, her presence accompanied by the buzz of a vacuum cleaner or the clattering of crockery. And when she went from room to room she had a habit of humming, on and on, with no tune as far as he could tell. Stupid woman. If there was one thing Benny couldn't stand, it was the endless drone of that humming. *One of these days, I'll make her shut up*, he thought. *I'll stop her bloody noise*.

Still, she wasn't around, so he'd grab a few minutes peace, and no one would be any the wiser.

Benny pulled out a stool and perched beside the counter, then he took out his phone. A scroll through the football results and a quick browse through the local news; that took no time at all. His thumb hovered over the screen. There was a certain website he liked to visit now and then. Why not? There was no harm in it. He typed in the URL, and the website loaded quickly. There. He felt better already. There was a new video, and the thumbnail looked very promising indeed. He was just about to play it when he glimpsed a movement from the corner of his eye.

Benny looked up with a start to see Mr Callaway standing in the doorway.

"Oh, here you are," Callaway said. "Found you at last."

"Yes, sir." Benny jumped to his feet, automatically swiping away the web browser with his thumb and stashing his phone in his jacket's inside pocket. "Sorry, I was just, erm, taking a break."

"That's all right, Benny. I thought you were outside, that's all. Did you finish cleaning the car already?"

"No, sir. I haven't got to it yet."

"Okay. When you're done cleaning it, let me know. I want to head out this afternoon, run a couple of errands."

"Of course, sir. It won't take me long: half an hour at most."

"To clean the car inside and out? I don't think so, Benny. I think I trod in some mud last night, and it's all over the footwell. It'll come clean with a little effort, and you know what I always say. When you do a job, you may as well do it right. Take your time, Benny, and clean it properly, okay? We want that car spotless, don't we? We want it to look as good as new."

"Of course, sir. No problem. I'll get right on it."

"Thanks, Benny. I know I can rely on you." Callaway smiled and left the room, leaving Benny standing there with a grin on his face.

It's strange, how he can do that, Benny thought. Mr Callaway could ask you to do anything, and you'd not only do it, but you'd feel good about it. He had charisma, and as far as Benny could tell, it worked on pretty much everyone. There was one exception, of course, but that person was never to be spoken of, not in Mr Callaway's hearing. A single mention of a certain person was enough to push the boss into one of his dark moods, and when the storm clouds gathered around Mr Callaway, you never knew what the man might do.

Why do I work in this madhouse? Benny asked himself, but he knew the answer. The money was good, and the work might get tedious, but it wasn't by any means hard. It was a cushy number, and it gave him a certain amount of freedom. There was a lot to be said for that.

Benny sighed, then he straightened his jacket and set off to the garage. It was a shame he hadn't had time to enjoy that video, but he could always take a peek at it later.

He was looking forward to it already. He could still picture her in his mind. He'd found her. He'd found her, and she was perfect.

CHAPTER 40

D an and Alan strode quickly into the Accident and Emergency department of the Royal Devon and Exeter Hospital. Rows of plastic chairs filled the centre of the waiting room, the seat pads upholstered in blue vinyl. About half of the chairs were occupied, men, women and children looking tired and anxious.

A few faces turned toward Dan and Alan, hoping perhaps for the arrival of a loved one, but most looked away quickly as if disappointed. Only one person acknowledged them with a nod.

Tobias Barrington stood and shuffled over to meet them. "Dan, Alan, thanks for coming."

"Think nothing of it," Alan said. "How is she?"

Tobias screwed up his face. "They've moved her from A and E, thank God. They've admitted her to a ward, so I suppose she'll be here for a while. I'll go up there in a bit, but I thought I'd better wait here for you."

"Thanks," Dan said. "We're here if you need us, but don't let us keep you from your sister."

"It's all right. Zadie's sedated at the moment, so she doesn't know whether anyone's there or not. They say she's stable, but they're still running tests, and they're going to take her for a scan. They're worried about the risk of swelling in the brain, but until the results come back, there's nothing I can do. Nothing at all." Tobias looked around the room, his eyes glazed with worry. "Shall we talk outside? I can't stand being in here for a second longer."

"Whatever you want." Dan led the way to the door, and they headed outside.

"Is it all right if we walk and talk?" Tobias asked. "There are some things that need to be said, and the sooner the better. That's why I wanted you to come, so we can talk face to face."

"Sure," Dan replied, and the three of them set off along the paved path, passing clusters of brick buildings, each one adorned with a collection of brightly coloured signs, not all of them intelligible to Dan's untrained eye. A few grassy areas and flowerbeds had been provided to break up the monotony, and there were benches, but Tobias seemed intent on marching along as fast as possible, his energy needing an outlet.

That was fine by Dan. He could already feel the fresh air sharpening his wits, and a question came to him.

"Tobias, has this kind of thing happened to Zadie before?"

Without breaking stride, Tobias stared at him. "How did you know that?"

"When we talked on the phone, you sounded as though this wasn't the first time you'd been down this road," Dan said. "You described what had happened to Zadie as an episode, and that makes me wonder if she suffers from an ongoing condition. Also, you said that her collapse might be linked to the break-in but not in the way I might think, so I knew there was an alternative explanation to consider."

"You're perceptive, I'll give you that," Tobias replied. "And you're right, my sister has had some health issues in the past. That's why I can be a bit overprotective."

"That's only natural," Dan said. "What kind of issues are we talking about?"

Tobias exhaled noisily. "Everyone says you're meant to talk

about this kind of thing, don't they? Mental health. There's always someone on the telly opening up about their depression or whatever, but still, it doesn't make it any easier, not as far as I'm concerned anyway."

"Was Zadie depressed?" Alan asked gently.

"No," Tobias said as if the idea was ridiculous. "It was something different, something harder to explain. I don't quite know where to start."

"Go from the beginning," Alan suggested. "When did you first think that Zadie might be having a problem?"

"Oh, a long time ago. Ever since she was a little girl." Tobias pressed his fingers against his forehead as he talked, rubbing as if to ease a headache, his fingertips leaving white trails on his flushed brow. "At first, everyone said she had a vivid imagination. There were always imaginary friends, and she'd come out with all kinds of strange tales, saying things that couldn't possibly have happened and swearing they were true."

"What did your parents do about it?" Dan asked.

"They went along with it at first. We all did. But then…" Tobias took a breath. "Then Zadie became worried. Anxious. She'd always been full of life, bright and bubbly. She'd have a go at anything: climb the highest tree, jump off a rope swing, dive into the sea. Nothing scared her. But when she became ill, it was as if her spirit had been taken away."

"That must've been very worrying," Dan said. "Did your parents take her to see someone?"

"Oh, endless doctors, specialists, therapists, you name it. Mum and Dad did everything they could, but nothing seemed to help. Eventually, when she was a teenager, they took her to a private clinic in Harley Street. I don't know how they found the money for it, but they managed somehow, and I think it helped for a while. Zadie seemed to level out, though she wasn't quite her old self."

"What was the diagnosis?" Alan asked. "If you don't mind sharing it, that is."

"BPD. Borderline Personality Disorder, though I didn't know

that at the time. Mum and Dad tried to shield me from what was going on. They were probably worried in case I went the same way. Silly of them really. I'd have been better off knowing the truth from the start. As it is, I didn't find out what really happened until years later, when Zadie felt able to tell me."

"I've heard of BPD, but I can't say I really understand it," Alan said. "When did she tell you?"

"Not until relatively recently. It was only a few years ago, back when Zadie lived in London. She'd been in trouble, making a nuisance of herself, shouting in the street at all hours. The police had been out to see her more than once. Some damned neighbour must've complained. Anyway, she was cautioned, which is a bloody disgrace."

"She needed you to defend her," Dan suggested.

"No, she didn't tell me about it until it was all done and dusted, otherwise I'd have gone in with all guns blazing. But Zadie didn't want a fuss. She accepted the caution and I suppose one good thing came out of it. She was determined to make a fresh start, and she said she needed a quieter place to live. She'd been up to Scotland for a break and loved it. The hills, the wide-open spaces, the fresh air: it did her the world of good, gave her a new lease of life."

"The countryside can do that to people," Alan said, glancing at Dan.

"It certainly helped Zadie," Tobias said. "She loved the scenery up there, and she really took to the people, but Zadie's never been keen on the cold. She wanted somewhere a bit milder. I was already in Devon, so I dropped a few hints. To be honest, I jumped at the chance. I thought, if I could keep her close, I'd be on hand to help. I thought I might be able to keep her…"

"Safe?" Dan suggested.

"Yes. It sounds patronising, I know. I mean, Zadie's an adult and she knows her own mind, but even so…" Tobias looked from Dan to Alan. "Do either of you have brothers or sisters?"

Alan shook his head, but Dan said, "A sister. She lives in the

States now, but she's always looked out for me, so I think I understand how you feel."

"Families, eh?" Tobias smiled sadly. "I think it was Freud who said all family life is organised around the most damaged person in it. Well, ours certainly revolved around Zadie. But still, we couldn't make her better."

"Don't blame yourself," Dan said. "You tried to help, and I'm sure your parents did their best too."

"We tried, but in the end we failed."

For a few seconds no one spoke, and Dan replayed the conversation in his mind. It was a lot to take in, and there was something nagging at him. That was it. The consultation with the Harley Street doctor and the odd change in Zadie's personality that followed.

Catching Tobias' eye, Dan said, "When Zadie saw the private doctor, do you think she might've been given medication?"

"She was, but they weren't for the BPD. They were for the anxiety that came with it. Antidepressants. It was the only way to…" Tobias shook his head as if admonishing himself. "Zadie hates people talking about this, and I've been trying to figure out how to tell you, but I can't go on like this, beating around the bush. You need to know the full story."

"It would help to know all the facts," Dan said slowly. "But I wouldn't want you to say anything that might upset Zadie. If it's a confidential matter, it might have to wait until Zadie can say it's okay."

"No, it can't wait. There's no choice. Remember, I didn't understand all this at the time, but I now know that, when she was a teenager, Zadie used to hear voices. That's why Mum and Dad took her to Harley Street."

"That's awful," Alan said. "At that young age, it must've been very frightening for her."

"Yes. She had a rough time, and it made her very anxious. Hence, the medication."

With a heavy heart, Dan said, "These voices, what did they say?"

"They'd tell her to do all kinds of odd things. The whispers, that's what she called them. She'd hear them when she was on her own, and they'd tell her to wreck her bedroom or break all the plates in the kitchen, and she'd go and do it. She felt compelled. The whispers, you see, would threaten her."

"Oh dear," Alan murmured. "Poor Zadie."

Tobias nodded gravely. "As you can imagine, when she said people had been threatening her, sneaking into her house and leaving cryptic messages, I couldn't help but wonder if it was real. I gave her the benefit of the doubt, partly because it doesn't do any good to contradict her, but I've been quietly suggesting that she see someone."

"Did she take your advice?" Alan asked.

"Unfortunately not. She's been insisting that she's okay. She said she wanted to handle things in her own way. I've told her that it's all very well doing yoga and meditating and all that lark, but some problems can't be solved that way. And the damned thing is, it looks like I was right."

"You think her condition is getting worse," Dan said.

"I'm afraid so. The doctor said they'd found drugs in her system, so it looks as though Zadie was back on the antidepressants."

"Maybe Zadie felt she needed them," Alan replied. "She might not have wanted to admit it to anyone, but she was trying to deal with the problem herself."

"Maybe so. That would be typical of my sister; she has to do everything on her own terms. But it makes you wonder about the break-in, doesn't it? And those notes. Did she invent the whole thing?"

"I don't think so," Dan said. "I've seen the notes myself. They're genuine."

"How can you know?" Tobias demanded. "Zadie wouldn't

deliberately mislead anyone, but if the voices told her to write those notes, she'd do it. She might not be aware of what she was doing, or she might have repressed those memories, but either way, the result's the same."

Dan looked down at the ground as they walked, his mind reeling. Could Zadie have written those notes herself? It seemed unlikely, but so far he'd found precious little evidence of the intruder. Yes, he'd gathered a list of suspects, but for all he knew, he could've been proceeding from a false premise.

Alan might have been having the same thoughts, because he said, "I wish Zadie had explained all this from the start."

Tobias cast them a sharp look. "Would you have taken the case if she had?"

"No, I wouldn't," Dan replied. "I would've suggested that she seek help and see a doctor or a therapist."

"Even if she'd offered to pay you handsomely?"

"That wouldn't have made any difference. I'd never take advantage of someone who might be vulnerable."

"You know what? I believe you," Tobias said. "Sorry for the cross-examination, but old habits die hard, and in my line of work, it's easy to become cynical. I spend a lot of time sifting through lies and half-truths. I deal with people who are trying to gain the upper hand, exploit the system, manipulate the facts. But I misjudged you. I think you two might well be on the side of the angels. You came here today and that says a lot."

"That's appreciated," Dan said. "But I wouldn't be too quick to dismiss Zadie's account of recent events. She's always struck me as being in full control of her faculties."

"Didn't you think she was a bit erratic, a bit flighty?"

"Maybe a little," Dan admitted. "But I still think that someone has been trying to intimidate her." Dan stopped in his tracks. "Oh my God!"

The others halted, turning to face him.

"What is it?" Alan asked.

Dan stared at Tobias. "Who else knows about Zadie's past, about her condition?"

"No one. She keeps it to herself. She gets angry with me if I mention it, and I'm her brother." Tobias lowered his eyebrows. "You don't think someone is doing this deliberately, do you? Trying to push her over the edge?"

"That's precisely what I'm thinking," Dan said. "But they'd have to know her medical history."

"She has a very close relationship with her circle of friends," Alan suggested. "Might she have confided in them?"

"That lot?" Tobias sneered. "Those people are hangers on. They're not real friends, but they don't mind basking in her reflected glory, and Zadie knows that. She's nobody's fool. She likes to keep them around because she enjoys their company, but that's all there is to it."

"What about Carly?" Dan asked. "She seems to have some kind of influence over Zadie, and they've known each other for a long time."

"Why would Carly do something so awful?" Alan replied. "I got the impression that Zadie's her best client. According to Natalya, Carly visits often, and she always charges for her time."

"I don't know," Dan said. "Maybe Carly wants to be needed. She was certainly keen to pick up more work. She tried to enlist me, and she looked very disappointed when I turned her down."

Tobias raised a hand to stop them. "This isn't going to get us anywhere. I know you mean well, but I have to think about Zadie. I need to concentrate on her."

"You're right," Dan said. "But if it's all the same to you, we'd like to continue with the case. If there's even the slightest possibility of foul play, we need to find the culprit."

"I don't know about that. It might be better to wait until I hear from the doctors. The consultant wants to bring in the neurology team, and she said something about referring her to a psychiatrist later on. After that, who knows?" Tobias gazed into the distance, looking lost. His voice softened as he went on, as if he could hardly believe what he was saying. "They said the scan will tell them if there are any anomalies in Zadie's brain. I suppose that's a roundabout way of saying growths or tumours. If that's what happened, I…" He looked back at them, his gaze dimmed. "I really don't know what I'll do."

"I know this is hard, but please try not to dwell on the worst possible outcome," Dan said. "It does no good, and it'll wear you down. You need to look after yourself, or you'll be in no shape to help Zadie."

"Zadie's in the right place," Alan put in. "She's young and strong, and that has to be in her favour. With a bit of luck, she'll be home before long."

Dan looked Tobias in the eye. "When Zadie goes home, we want to be sure that it's safe for her. You can leave that with us. We'll work *pro bono*. Whatever it takes."

"*Pro bono*. Those are words that haven't crossed my lips for a while." Tobias seemed to weigh up Dan's offer for a moment, then he added, "All right, Dan. You can carry on, but there's no need to waive your fee. If someone's responsible for this, I'll hang them out to dry. All you have to do is find them for me."

"We will," Dan said. "But I want you to do something for me."

"Name it."

"I want you to keep very quiet about the fact that Zadie's in hospital. Tell no one."

"That's easily done," Tobias replied. "I wasn't going to tell anybody anyway."

"There's more to it than that," Dan said. "I need to give the impression that Zadie is at home, so if anybody asks, that's what you must say."

"All right. Is that it?"

"For now. Who else knows where Zadie is?"

"Natalya, obviously, but no one else. I don't imagine that Natalya will have told anyone, but you'll have to check with her."

"We will," Dan said. "Hopefully, no one saw the ambulance.

Zadie doesn't have any close neighbours, so we should be okay. What about the police? Have they been to the house?"

"They're going to send someone over. A detective."

"That's good. They'll come in plain clothes and use an unmarked car."

Tobias sent Dan a shrewd look. "What are you planning to do?"

"It's very simple," Dan replied. "We're going to set a trap."

CHAPTER 41

D an rang ahead to make sure Natalya would be in, then they drove straight to Zadie's house. Natalya opened the door before they'd had time to knock, so she'd obviously been watching for their arrival.

"Any news?" Natalya asked.

"Sorry, not yet," Dan replied. "Okay if we come in? There's something we need to discuss, something that will help Zadie."

"Of course." Natalya ushered them inside and led them upstairs to the lounge. "Please, sit."

Dan and Alan took the smaller sofa and Natalya settled herself at the centre of the larger one. "I feel so bad," she said. "Poor Zadie. If only I had stayed with her, this terrible thing would not have happened."

"You weren't to know," Alan replied. "Besides, we don't really know what happened. Not yet."

"We aim to put that right," Dan said. "And we'd like your help."

Natalya pressed her hands together and leaned forward. "What can we do?"

"First things first," Dan replied. "Have you noticed anything suspicious around the house, anything that looks out of place?"

MICHAEL CAMPLING

Natalya shook her head. "Nothing. Everything seems the same as always."

"We'll take a look around ourselves," Dan said. "Have the police been yet?"

"No. They say they're sending someone, but it is Saturday, so not many detectives at work." Natalya held out her hands, palms upward. "I said, what are they thinking? Do criminals not work at the weekend in the UK?"

"Good for you," Alan said. "What did they say to that?"

"They put me through to someone else, but she was no help at all. It isn't urgent, she said. It might have been an accident. I will have to wait." Natalya tutted. "There is always waiting in this country. You wait for everything. Nothing ever happens straight away."

"Well, you won't have to wait for us," Dan said. "We're here and we have a plan. To begin with, we'll see if we can find any clues, and we'll try to piece together what happened last night—"

"Or early this morning," Natalya interrupted. "I came at seven o'clock, but I don't know how long Zadie had been there."

"Good point." Dan paused. "You arrived very early. Is that usual?"

"Zadie was going to shoot a video this morning and she asked me to help. I had to get everything ready."

"Do you always work on Saturdays, Natalya?"

"No, but Zadie pays me extra money if I work at the weekend, so if she asks I always say yes. I am glad I did, otherwise…"

"It was very fortunate for Zadie that you arrived when you did," Alan said. "Your prompt action may well have saved her life."

"It was nothing," Natalya replied, but she seemed pleased, her expression mellowing when she looked at Alan.

Dan cleared his throat. "When we've finished looking around, we'll put the next part of our plan into action."

"What are you going to do?" Natalya asked.

324

"We're going to pretend that Zadie is still here," Dan said. "We want everyone else to think that things are going on as normal."

Natalya looked at him as though he were a naughty child. "What are you talking about? This is no time for silly games."

"I know that," Dan replied. "We're setting a trap. We want to find out who did this, and I think they might turn up."

"That doesn't make any sense. The person who did this knows what happened. He left her for dead. He won't come back."

"He or she might turn up *if* we can make people think that Zadie is at home and feeling much better."

"How do we do that?"

"This is where you can really help, Natalya," Dan said. "I want you to pretend to be Zadie."

"I know it sounds difficult," Alan put in, "but Dan and I have talked it over, and we think it really could work."

Natalya looked from Dan to Alan in stark disbelief. "In case you hadn't noticed, Zadie is a beautiful woman. I am just me. Ordinary, nothing like her."

"You're both slim," Alan said. "And you're about the same height."

Natalya's laughter was cold and mocking. "Listen to yourselves. You are talking… I can't even think of the right word. Have you lost your minds?"

"No one needs to see your face," Dan said. "You could cover your hair and wear some of Zadie's clothes, preferably something that will really stand out. If you walk around the place, preferably upstairs, no one will know the difference. If people see someone moving around in Zadie's studio, they'll assume it's her. After all, hardly anyone else goes in there."

Natalya made a dismissive noise in her throat, but she didn't look quite so appalled at the idea.

"It's worth a try, isn't it?" Dan went on. "If it doesn't work, we'll think again, but at this point, we really don't have anything to lose by giving it a go."

"I don't know," Natalya muttered. "It still seems silly to me, but…"

"You'll try?" Dan asked.

"Maybe. I won't wear her clothes, but I can stay out of sight. If someone comes to the house, I could play some of her old videos on the computer with the sound turned up. That way, it will sound like she is upstairs, filming. No one comes in when she is working."

"That's a brilliant idea," Dan said. "Come to think of it, if you can find a suitable video, you could post it online and make it look as though Zadie is still working."

Natalya shook her head. "It wouldn't be live. People make comments in the chat."

"You can answer them as if you're Zadie," Dan replied. "You already help out with her social media accounts, so this would be easy."

"I don't write the replies though. I can't sound like Zadie. My English is good, but I can't write like her. People would know."

Alan sat up straight. "I can help with that. I'm a writer, so it's no problem at all. A quick look at her older comments and I'll soon pick up her style. I'd like to help you. It would be my pleasure."

Natalya gazed at Alan, a slow smile forming on her lips. "Well, I think that might be okay."

"Excellent. That's settled." Dan jumped to his feet. "I'll leave you two to iron out the details. I need to go and make a couple of calls."

"Are you going to call Zadie's brother?" Alan asked.

"Not yet," Dan said as he made for the door. "First, I need to call Sam and deliver the bad news, then I need to cancel our table. I'll see you in a few minutes. I'll come and find you."

DAN HEARD THE BUZZ OF CONVERSATION AS HE CLIMBED THE STAIRS and approached the studio door. Natalya and Alan seemed to be getting on well. *A little too well?* Dan put the thought from his mind. Natalya and Alan? No. Surely not.

But some instinct stopped Dan from marching straight into the room. He knocked on the door, and the conversation stopped abruptly. A moment later, Natalya opened the door.

"All right if I come in?" Dan asked.

"Yes, of course."

Dan followed Natalya into the studio where Alan was perched on a round-topped stool, a laptop in front of him. Beside him there was a mesh-backed office chair that hadn't been in the studio the last time they'd visited, and Dan guessed that Natalya had fetched it for Alan. But of course, Alan would've offered to take the less comfortable option, leaving the chair for Natalya.

"We were working," Natalya said, at exactly the same time as Alan said, "We were talking about books."

Alan and Natalya locked eyes and then laughed.

"We are talking while we work," Natalya insisted, gesturing to the laptop. "There has been a lot to do."

"We're getting through it though," Alan said. "Natalya knows her way around all the social media channels. It's quite an education. How did you get on? Is everything all right with Sam?"

Dan nodded. "She's fine. She was a bit disappointed to be missing lunch, but she understood. I'll make it up to her another time."

"Sam is your partner, yes?" Natalya said. "Or maybe she is your wife."

"No, we're not married."

"You missed seeing her because you are working," Natalya said with a hint of a sigh. "That is a shame. Would you like to have lunch here? I can go and make something."

"That would be very kind," Alan replied. "I'll eat anything, but Dan is a bit fussy. He tends to eat plant-based stuff."

"I remember, and it's all right. If I can make food for Zadie, I can make food for anyone." Natalya started to smile, but her lips quickly turned downward. "I keep forgetting she's not here. I'm not used to being in the house without Zadie. It's strange."

"Let's hope she'll be better soon," Alan said. "Then you'll be able to visit her. She'd like that. I'm sure you'd cheer her up."

"Yes, that would be nice. Thank you, Alan. You always know what to say."

"I, erm… well…"

Dan stopped himself from pointing out the irony in Alan's sudden inability to form a sentence. Instead, he said, "Lunch would be very welcome, but before we get to that, we'll take a look around. There must be some clues around here somewhere."

"Okay," Natalya replied. "Where do you want to start?"

Dan thought for a moment. "What was Zadie wearing when you found her?"

"Pyjamas and training shoes."

"That's a bit odd, isn't it?" Alan said, but Natalya's only answer was a resigned shrug, as if there were no accounting for the strange outfits chosen by her employer.

"We'll start with her bedroom," Dan stated. "Can you show us where it is, Natalya?"

"Yes. We'll go now."

Natalya took them along the corridor to a pine door that had been stripped and sanded smooth. "In here." She pushed the door open and stepped back, but Dan and Alan lingered in the doorway.

"We mustn't disturb anything," Alan said. "Should we even go in?"

"I was just thinking the same thing," Dan replied. "We'll leave trace evidence as soon as we walk in, but we don't have much choice. The police might not get here for days. So long as they think Zadie might've had an accident, they won't do a thing. We know better, and we have to do something about it."

"It's a dammed shame I never got around to ordering those gloves. I haven't had time."

"Don't worry about it. We'll be careful, and we have Natalya as a witness. She can back us up if the police start asking awkward questions."

Alan nodded slowly. "Okay. After you."

"Okay." Moving carefully, Dan crossed the floor, Alan following.

The room was sparsely furnished: a double bed with a heavy wooden frame, a wardrobe and a nightstand. A lamp and two paperback books sat on the nightstand, and a couple of small ceramic dishes had been arranged on the window ledge. Apart from those few items there was nothing on display, and there was no clutter, no clothes left on the floor.

Dan crossed to the window. It was shut, and he could see that the window lock was securely fastened. The key to the lock lay in one of the small ceramic dishes on the window ledge. Dan leaned close to the window pane and peered down. The scaffolding was outside, and that could've been a way for someone to come in, but Zadie had been warned about the importance of keeping her windows closed and locked.

Dan turned around to see Alan kneeling on the floor to look under the bed.

"Anything?" Dan asked.

"No. Not a thing." Alan stood, brushing his hands together. "Is it always so neat and tidy in here, Natalya?"

"Yes. Zadie likes things to be this way."

Dan pointed to the ceramic dishes which were evenly spaced along the ledge. "What about these? Are they always here?"

"Yes, although…" Natalya tilted her head to one side. "No, they don't look right. They're usually together in the middle. I think maybe they have been moved."

"That's something," Alan said. "Someone might've moved them when they opened the window."

"It's possible, but one of them is in front of the only part of the window that opens. If you were opening the window to climb out, you'd move the dish out of the way. This looks more like someone has arranged them after closing the window." Dan stepped over to the wardrobe. It struck him as being particularly small for someone who was so keen on clothes, but then he remembered the dressing room next to the studio. Zadie was someone who had a place for everything, and the bedroom was the place where she slept. "We'd better take a look inside."

"Be careful," Alan said. "There could be fingerprints."

"I know." Dan used the cuff of his shirtsleeve as a makeshift barrier between his fingertips and the edge of the wardrobe door. Touching the door as lightly as he could, he swung it open.

Inside, a few nightdresses and sets of pyjamas hung from hangers. On the wardrobe's floor, a small collection of cardboard boxes were carefully stacked. One of them bore the Nike swoosh. Squatting down in front of it, Dan said, "What kind of trainers was Zadie wearing?"

"I don't know. I didn't think about it, I just called the ambulance." Natalya's expression sharpened as if at a sudden memory. "When they put her on a stretcher and lifted her up, it was so sad, seeing her lying still like that, and her trainers were sticking out from the blanket. I thought they ought to wrap her up properly because her feet would be very cold. And those shoes… I'm sure I hadn't seen them before. I'd forgotten about that until now."

"You've been through a traumatic experience," Alan said. "At times of stress, memories can become very muddled."

Natalya said something softly in reply, but Dan's attention was on that shoebox. "New shoes on Zadie's feet and a brand-new shoebox in the wardrobe. I'm going to take a peek inside." Using only the tips of his fingers, he opened the cardboard flap and lifted it gently. The box was empty apart from some tissue paper. "Interesting. We know where the shoes might've come from, but it doesn't explain why she was wearing them with her pyjamas." Dan left the box as he found it, and then he stood, carefully closing the wardrobe door.

"Doesn't she have a pair of slippers?" Alan asked.

"Not everyone wears slippers," Dan said. "But I take your

point. What does Zadie normally wear around the house, Natalya?"

"She has a pair of Birkenstocks. They're in the bathroom."

"I guess she walked from the bathroom in bare feet," Alan suggested. "I don't think we can glean anything from that."

"Except, she doesn't do that," Natalya said. "When she isn't working, and there's no one but me around to see her, Zadie wears those sandals all the time. She says she only takes them off when she goes to bed. She loves them. She tells me I should get some, but they're very expensive."

"That's an extremely useful observation," Alan replied. "It's beginning to look as though there's something not quite right about this room."

Dan nodded. "It's as if the scene has been deliberately set. Someone has tidied up, but they've made a few mistakes. Zadie's sandals should've been near her bed, but instead, she unboxed a new pair of trainers. She must've had a good reason to do that. She has loads of shoes in her dressing room, but either she couldn't get there, or she was in a hurry. Either way, having taken the trainers, she wouldn't have bothered to close the box afterward; someone else did that. Also, the dishes have been moved, so we know that something happened near the window. Someone put them back in the wrong place." Dan clicked his fingers. "The window might've been opened, and someone wanted to give the impression that it had stayed closed."

"I think you're on to something." Alan moved over to the nightstand and bent over to examine the paperbacks. "Non-fiction, both by someone named Marc Reklau. *Change your Habits, Change Your Life* and *The Productivity Revolution*." Alan leaned closer to the nightstand. "I didn't notice this. It was hidden by the books, but there's a gadget. I think it's one of those wireless chargers."

Dan joined him. "Yes, it's a phone charger. Dammit! I should've asked straight away. Do we know what happened to Zadie's phone?"

"No, but I'll call it now." Natalya produced her phone, and Dan and Alan waited in silence. Dan half-hoped to hear a buzz or a ringtone, but that was almost too much to hope for.

"I'm sorry," Natalya said. "It went to voicemail."

"That's a shame, but we can look for it later," Dan said. "Does she have one of those apps you can use to find your phone?"

Natalya started to shake her head, but then she gasped, her hand on her chest.

Alan moved to her side. "What is it?"

"Her bottle of water." Natalya pointed to the nightstand. "It is always just there. Always. Every night."

"One of her special bottles?" Dan asked. "The ones with her initials on?"

Natalya nodded.

"You didn't find the bottle next to Zadie?"

"No, I would've noticed it. She has quite a lot of them, but she always puts them away. She's very proud of them."

"Any idea how many she has?"

"Twelve. They sent a whole box, different colours."

"Could you find the others and count them for me?" Dan asked. "It's important."

"Is it though?" Alan said. "Maybe she just forgot to bring her water when she went to bed."

"I don't think so. Zadie's one of those people who likes to keep hydrated. We'll know more if there's a bottle missing."

Natalya made to leave. "I can check now."

"That would be great," Dan said. "We'll come too. There's nothing else to see here."

They made their way back to the studio, then Dan and Alan waited while Natalya hurried from room to room in search of the metal bottles.

It wasn't long before she returned, her cheeks a little flushed. "I checked everywhere, outside too, next to where I found her, but I can only find eleven. There's one missing. The black one."

"That settles it," Dan said. "Someone went into Zadie's bedroom, and whatever they did in there, it left them nervous and on edge, desperate for a drink of water. Remember the glass on the kitchen table after the break-in?"

"Of course," Alan replied. "Although that was different. They left that in place for all to see."

"Things have moved to a different level since then. This time, the intruder came while Zadie was in the house. The stakes are much higher. They knew Zadie was hurt, so they had to remove the evidence. After they'd had a drink, they took the bottle with them."

"I wonder what they did with it," Alan said. "If they were in a hurry, they might've disposed of it nearby. If we could find it, we could give it to the police. There might be fingerprints or DNA."

"It's a nice idea, but there's too much ground to cover. For all we know, the bottle is at the bottom of the river Teign. When the police finally turn up, they can look for it, but we don't have their resources." Dan paused. "Natalya, can you show us where you found Zadie?"

"Yes, but there's nothing there."

"We need to see for ourselves," Alan said. "If you don't mind, that is. It wouldn't be too upsetting for you, would it?"

Natalya shook her head firmly. "It's okay, Alan. I'm not afraid. What happened in the past can't hurt us if we don't let it. This is something I have learned."

Before Dan or Alan could say anything, Natalya led them outside. She stopped beside the corner of the house and gestured at the ground. "Here. This is the place."

Dan looked up at the house. "Where's her bedroom window?"

"Right over there." Natalya pointed to a window some distance away. "That is Zadie's bedroom."

Dan looked from the ground to the window and back.

"What are you thinking?" Alan asked. "Do you reckon someone might've climbed up to her bedroom?"

"No, I'm certain she'd have locked the window before she went to bed, and there were no signs of a forced entry. I was wondering if she'd climbed from the window and fallen. She might've moved along the scaffold before she fell."

Alan grimaced. "Dear God. If that's the case, it's a wonder she wasn't more badly injured. She must've been lucky in the way she landed. She might have been able to crawl along the ground for a short distance."

"I doubt that. It's more likely that she lost consciousness when she hit the ground, otherwise she'd have called for help."

"Poor Zadie. What's our next step?"

"I need to think. We're not looking at a case of harassment anymore. Someone drove Zadie to the point where she risked her own life. It was deliberate."

"I'm inclined to agree," Alan said. "But let's take a minute. It may seem frivolous, but I think we should take a break and have something to eat. Brains need fuel, and we can discuss the case while we eat."

Dan smiled. "Okay, let's grab a quick lunch then we'll see what we can do."

"I'll go and make something," Natalya said. "You can go upstairs and wait in the lounge. I'll call you when it's ready."

"A sandwich is fine for me," Alan said. "Do you need any help?"

"No, thank you. It won't take long."

Natalya went inside and they trailed after her. At the bottom of the stairs, Natalya turned to face them. "Alan, maybe you could check the social media accounts and reply to the comments."

"Yes, I'd be happy to," Alan replied. "I could post a few tweets while I'm at it."

"Thank you, Alan. You're very kind." Natalya headed back toward the kitchen.

"Are you sure you can write Zadie's tweets?" Dan asked. "I imagine her followers are used to a certain style."

"Ye of little faith. Natalya's shown me the ropes, and I know what I'm doing. It'll be like writing dialogue for one of my characters. There's nothing to it once you capture their voice."

"I'll come with you," Dan said. "I can take another look in the studio while you work."

But as they started up the stairs, a jangling ringtone stopped them short, and Natalya hurried back into the hallway, her phone in her hand.

"It's him again." Natalya held the phone out to Dan, and he saw the video feed from the camera at the front door.

"Well, well," Dan muttered. "I wasn't expecting that. You'd better let him in."

"Yes." Natalya opened the door, and they heard a familiar tone.

"Hello, madam. You might remember me from before. I'm Detective Inspector Spiller."

CHAPTER 42

Having made himself comfortable on a large sofa in Zadie Barrington's lounge, DI Spiller favoured Dan Corrigan with a piercing look, holding his gaze in a way that would make most people squirm. But facing him from a smaller sofa, Corrigan looked calm and relaxed. Ah well, there was nothing for it but to press on.

"Mr Corrigan," Spiller began, "I've had a good look around, and I've listened very carefully to everything you've had to say, and if this house were to be considered a crime scene, I should be angry with you right now. Very angry indeed. As it is, I am in no way convinced that we have a crime scene, so you've been lucky."

"I disagree," Corrigan stated. "Taken together, the events leading up to last night point to foul play."

"Why?"

Finally, Spiller had scored a point. Corrigan looked nonplussed. "What do you mean?"

"I'll rephrase," Spiller said. "Why would a person or persons unknown construct such an elaborate way to intimidate Ms Barrington?"

"I haven't worked that out yet, but I will."

"That doesn't seem likely." Spiller sighed and adopted a more open posture. "Look, we've been through these hoops before, you and I, and I'll admit that you've had some success, but that doesn't mean you're correct in this instance. It's like they say on all those adverts for saving accounts: past performance is no guarantee of future results. You've done well in the past but—"

"You think I'm headed for a crash," Corrigan interrupted.

"Not to put too fine a point on it, yes. You're out on a limb here, and if I were you, I'd climb back down before the branch breaks and it takes you down with it."

"An unfortunate metaphor in the circumstances."

"Is it?" Spiller asked. "I may not be as nicely spoken as you, Mr Corrigan, but I'm talking common sense. What happened to Ms Barrington is very sad, but there are good reasons to believe that it's a tragic accident. I have information that I can't disclose to you, but it leads me to believe that Ms Barrington's account of recent events can't be relied upon."

"You've been talking to her brother."

Spiller kept his expression fixed. "There's more to it than that. There is an incident on our database, an incident that involves Ms Barrington, and although it was some time ago, it gives me cause for concern."

"Are you talking about the caution she was given?"

"You know I won't comment on that, Mr Corrigan. Let's not play games."

"I'm in deadly earnest, Inspector. Whatever troubles Zadie may have had in the past, they're nothing to do with this case. I'm convinced that Zadie is in danger. Someone has been in this house on more than one occasion, and their intentions are not good."

"We've looked into that allegation, and so far we've found nothing to support it. Let's look at what we've got, shall we?" Spiller raised a hand for emphasis, lifting a finger as he counted off each point. "We've got a couple of ambiguous notes, a glass that no one can remember using, a door that might've been left unlocked by accident, a missing towel, for goodness' sake, and a water bottle that might've been misplaced. I'll admit that the kitchen knife stuck in a desk is concerning, but it strikes me as being theatrical rather than threatening. That's about it."

"What about the fact that Zadie was found unconscious? Where does that figure in your assessment?"

"As I said, that was almost certainly an accident. We'll look into it, but there's not much we can do at the moment. We'll know more when Ms Barrington regains consciousness, but until then, we have nothing much to go on. There's no concrete evidence, no CCTV, no footprints or fingerprints, no sign of damage to windows or doors, and nothing seen by witnesses, even though this is a small town."

"That's because the intruder has taken a lot of trouble to conceal the evidence."

"That's one way of looking at it, but there's another," Spiller said. "Do you know the old joke about the man spreading white powder along a railway line?"

"No, and I don't—"

"It goes like this," Spiller swept on. "There's a man spreading white powder all along the railway tracks, and someone says to him, 'What are you doing that for?' And he replies that the powder is to keep elephants from straying in front of the trains. 'But there are no elephants around here,' the other man says, to which the other chap replies, 'I know. It's good this powder, isn't it?' Do you see what I'm getting at?"

"Very droll," Corrigan said. "But if I'm completely wrong and there's no case to answer, why have they sent a detective inspector to investigate? Here you are, on a Saturday no less, so you must have some cause for concern. Unless…" Corrigan paused, a smug smile spreading across his features. "Oh, I get it. You're only here because Zadie has such a high profile. You've been told to show your face and make it look as though her case is being taken seriously."

Spiller felt himself bridle, but he was damned if he was going to let it show. "Mr Corrigan," he said slowly, "I can assure you that we always take it seriously when someone reports or alleges a crime, of course we do. But this case is unusual. I'm concerned for Ms

338

Barrington's state of mind, and it seems to me that your activities may well make matters worse. She is a vulnerable person, and there are safeguarding issues here."

"I appreciate that, and I've got her best interests at heart. You're not the only one who's spoken to Tobias Barrington. He knows what we're doing, and he's authorised us to carry on, so that's exactly what we'll do."

Spiller sat up straighter, squaring his shoulders. "I've warned you before about overreaching yourself, but this time, that warning counts double. Ms Barrington is a troubled woman, and it will do her no good to have her delusions reinforced. If I think your presence here is causing her any distress or anxiety, we'll be having a very different conversation."

"That goes without saying," Corrigan protested. "I'd never do anything to upset Zadie."

"Then you'd better think very carefully before you proceed. At the moment, Ms Barrington is in a safe place, and she'll get the care she needs. When she's ready to talk to us, our investigation will step up a gear. At that point, I don't want you anywhere near this case."

Spiller stood, pulling himself up to his full height. "I'm going to have another look around, then I'm heading back to Exeter to write up my report. After that, I shall be going home to spend some time with Mrs Spiller. Don't you have someone you should be spending the weekend with, Mr Corrigan?"

"Yes, but I have work to do here."

Spiller shook his head. "I disagree. If you insist on staying here, do not go into Ms Barrington's bedroom again. In fact, try to go in as few rooms as possible, and stay away from the garden. This house and its surroundings may yet become a crime scene, and we don't want you trampling all over it with your size nines. Is that clear?"

"Perfectly."

"Right. Goodbye for now, Mr Corrigan. I expect we'll be calling on you before too long."

Spiller marched for the door, but Dan Corrigan called out something that made him stop and turn on his heel.

"What about her phone, DI Spiller? Will you at least try to find that?"

Spiller paused before replying. He didn't owe explanations to Dan Corrigan, but the question irked him and he had to reply. "Naturally, we tried to locate Ms Barrington's phone, and all I can tell you is that it is probably somewhere in or around this house. We're retrieving her phone records, so we'll see if her messages or calls can shed any light on what happened. In the meantime, if you come across her phone, do not touch it. Call us and we'll come and collect it."

"Understood. Thanks. I was careful when I went in Zadie's bedroom, by the way, but if I've contaminated the scene, or whatever you call it, I'm sorry. I was trying to help."

Spiller tried to hide his surprise. Still, it was nice to have an apology, and he had to admit that Corrigan looked contrite. He acknowledged Dan with a nod, then he went on his way.

That man, Spiller thought as he trudged down the stairs, *will one day drive me to distraction.* And not for the first time that day, the thought of retirement came creeping into Spiller's mind.

CHAPTER 43

In Zadie's studio, the doorbell triggered an app on Natalya's phone. The next visitor had arrived at The Old Manse.

We didn't have to wait for long, Dan thought. *But who will it be?*

Natalya studied her phone to check the camera feed from the front door. "It's Melody. I'll go and see what she wants."

"Thanks, but it would be better if you stayed here," Dan said. "It's important that we keep up appearances, and our story is that Zadie is working. Speaking of which, have you found a video to post?"

Natalya looked doubtful. "I've found an old recording. I don't think she ever used it, so it should be okay, but…"

"It'll be fine," Dan said. "It only has to hold up for a while. You can always take it down later, but post it now. I'd better go and talk to Melody."

"Do you think she knows something's up?" Alan asked. "I replied to one of her Facebook comments earlier, and I don't know if I handled it well enough to convince her."

"We'll know in a minute."

"I'd go easy on her if I were you," Alan advised. "Somehow, I don't think Melody is the villain of the piece, otherwise she wouldn't have commented on Zadie's page in the first place."

"Let's not make assumptions, Alan. I'll find out what I can."

Dan hurried down the stairs and answered the door.

"Oh," Melody said. "I wasn't expecting you."

"Who were you expecting?"

"Nat generally answers the door."

"She's busy at the minute, but please, do come in."

Dan ushered Melody inside and offered a welcoming smile. "Can I get you anything? Tea, coffee, a glass of water?"

"No. No thanks." Melody looked around nervously. "Where is Nat, anyway? And where's Zadie?"

"They're upstairs in the studio, working."

"Okay. I'll just go and—"

"You can't," Dan interrupted.

"I beg your pardon?"

"You can't go upstairs just yet. Zadie's filming."

"Okay, I'll wait here."

"Fine." Dan looked Melody in the eye. "Why did you come here today?"

"Obviously, I came to see Zadie. What's it to you?"

"I'm checking all Zadie's visitors," Dan said, and even to his ears, his excuse sounded lame.

Melody looked distinctly unconvinced, but before Dan could come up with something better, his phone rang and he plucked it from his pocket. The screen showed Jay's name and photo.

In the aftermath of his rush to the hospital, Dan had forgotten all about the task he'd set Jay. Now, with the subject of Jay's surveillance standing in front of him, this call couldn't have come at a better time.

Inclining his head apologetically, Dan said, "I'm sorry but I have to take this."

"Go ahead. I'll wait outside." Melody made to turn toward the door.

"Actually, it would be better if you'd wait here," Dan said quickly.

Melody sent him a quizzical look. "Why?"

"Because after this call, I need to say something to you. It's about Zadie."

Melody took half a step back, but Dan raised a hand, his fingers spread wide. "Please, Melody. It's important. I won't be a minute."

"All right," Melody huffed. "But you'd better not be wasting my time. I had enough of that nonsense in the shop."

"Thanks, and I won't waste your time. I promise."

As soon as Dan accepted the call, Jay said, "Where were you last night? I waited for you in The Boar but you never turned up."

"We popped in later, after the meat raffle was done and dusted."

"That explains it. We must've missed each other. Never mind. I've got some news on your friend Melody."

"Go on."

"For a start, she doesn't go by the name she was born with. She started life as Mary Robinson but changed it later."

"That is interesting. Anything else?"

"Oh yes. Melody might have a fancy little boutique or whatever you want to call it, but she's not as posh as she makes out. After she shut the shop, she drove over to visit her mum and dad. They live in a council estate in Teignmouth. According to a neighbour, it's where she grew up."

"So she's not quite as she appears."

"It looks that way. I got the impression she fancies herself as a cut above, so she changed her name to fit in. You said she has some posh friends, didn't you?"

"Yes, I'd say they're well-off. Do you have anything else for me?"

"Not yet, but if you want any more of these little jobs doing, let me know. It was like old times."

"I'll see what comes up. Let me know how long it took, and I'll settle up later."

"Will do. There'll be no invoice though. We'll keep this cash in hand if you don't mind. The taxman has swiped more than enough of my hard-earned cash; there's no need to give him any more."

"No problem, Jay. I'll catch you later. Bye."

As Dan pocketed his phone, Melody's patience seemed to have worn out, and she headed toward the hallway, but Dan moved to intercept her. "Where are you going?"

"Upstairs, to see my friend."

"I've already explained, you can't do that. Zadie's busy."

"I don't care. I want to see her for myself."

"That's an interesting choice of words. Why do you have to actually see her?"

"Are you serious? Do you expect me to justify myself to you?"

Dan opened his mouth to reply, but Melody didn't give him time.

"Look, I'm worried for my friend, and I demand that you let me see her."

"What are you worried about?"

"You, for a start. You're behaving very strangely. What are you, her jailer?"

"Not at all," Dan said. "But you can't go and see Zadie at the moment. She's filming a special show as we speak. If you interrupt her now, she won't be pleased."

"We'll see about that." Melody took out her phone and began tapping on the screen, her thumb moving fast.

"What are you doing?" Dan asked. "She won't answer the phone while she's filming."

"I know that, but I can watch her livestream and send her a message. She always keeps an eye on those."

"Okay. Go ahead." Dan said no more. He had to hope that the video was playing and Natalya and Alan were poised and ready to respond.

Melody watched her screen for a few seconds, then she put her phone away, glaring at Dan.

"Satisfied?" Dan asked.

Melody didn't deign to reply.

"You won't see much of Zadie over the next couple of days," Dan went on. "She has a lot of work to do."

"But it's the weekend."

"The internet never sleeps. Whatever the time of day, there are viewers somewhere in the world, wide awake and looking for something to watch."

"Nevertheless, Zadie usually takes some time off at the weekends. She likes to keep a work-life balance, and we help her with that."

"We?"

"Her friends, of course. We promised Zadie we'd help her stay fresh. Burnout is real, and Zadie needs time out to relax, to replenish her energy. Otherwise, she'll become creatively blocked."

"Fascinating." Dan said. "You should write a book on the subject. After all, you have a ready-made pen name."

"What are you talking about?"

"Melody Reinhardt. Now that really sounds like a writer's name. So much more sophisticated than Mary Robinson."

"How...?"

"How did I find out? I'm a private investigator."

"I was going to say, 'How dare you?' You have no right to go poking into my private affairs. No right at all."

"I have a duty to protect my client, and when one of her friends is not who she claims to be—"

"Nonsense," Melody interrupted. "Melody Reinhardt *is* my real name. I changed my name legally, and I don't have to explain the reason why; not to you, nor to anyone else."

"No, but I wonder whether it shines a light on your motives."

"Motives for what? Are you implying I've done something wrong?"

"You haven't exactly been forthcoming," Dan said. "And you glossed over the argument you had with Zadie."

"No, I didn't. I told you we sometimes bicker over nothing, but that's what happens among friends."

"This was different. Zadie told someone about the argument afterward, and she wouldn't have done that unless it had affected her."

Melody shook her head. "You don't know Zadie. She loves drama."

"There's more to it than that. I specifically asked you about it when I came to your shop. I told you that Zadie had argued with someone called Mary, and you could've explained that it was you, but you didn't."

"That's because it was between Zadie and me. It was a private matter, and I won't betray her confidence. If you want to know more, you're free to ask Zadie."

"I already have, and she deflected the question, rather expertly in my opinion."

Melody stared at him, her gaze cold, but her cheeks flushed.

"Something's just struck me," Dan said. "When Zadie told someone about your argument, she referred to you as Mary, and I wonder if that was something she did while she was still angry with you. Did she do that sometimes? Did she call you Mary, even though she must've known it would needle you? Did she call you Mary to put you back in your place?"

"You think you're so clever, don't you? But you have no idea."

"I'm prepared to be proved wrong. If you want to explain, I'll listen."

"Why should I?"

"Because at the moment, you look guilty. You look like someone who harbours a longstanding grudge against Zadie, and you might've finally found a way to get your own back. Notes, threats, a knife stabbed into a desk."

Melody's expression sharpened. "What knife?"

"Come on, your friends must've told you."

"No, I don't know anything about a knife, but if I've been kept in the dark, it's no big surprise. They don't tell me everything, and unlike Connor and the others, I work for a living. I'm too busy in the shop to sit around gossiping. I can't afford the time. How could I? I work twelve hours a day, more sometimes, but still…"

Melody held out her hands in exasperation, and the spark of anger that had lit her gaze dimmed. Her accent faltered, reverting to a softer Devonian tone, as she added, "Still the books don't balance. But what do I know? Nobody's ever given me something for nothing, and they're not bloody well going to either."

Melody lowered her gaze, her indignation replaced by disappointment, disillusionment.

Softening his tone, Dan said, "Talk to me. Tell me about it."

Melody shook her head. "There's nothing to tell." She looked up at him. "It was me you were talking about on the phone, wasn't it? I'm the one who's not what I appear to be."

"Yes."

"So you know a bit about me. So what?"

Dan took a moment to reply, rapidly revising his opinion of Melody. She was self-employed and doing everything in her power to make ends meet; he knew how hard that could be. And like him, Melody was doing her best to find her place in the world. "I owe you an apology," Dan said. "I was far too hard on you. For what it's worth, I think I understand some of what you've been going through, but I'd like to ask about something."

Melody sighed. "Go on. You might as well."

"Thanks. There's nothing wrong with wanting to improve your lot in life, but your background is part of your identity; why hide it?"

"Because with some people, if your face doesn't fit, you may as well be invisible. I didn't want that. I'm trying to make something of myself, but… you were right about one thing. Zadie knew my old name. I confided in her one night over a bottle of wine, and she said she'd keep it between us. I thought that was the end of it, but I should've known better."

"Did she tell the others?"

"Not as far as I know, but she'd use it sometimes, just to remind me. And yes, she used it that day, when we had that stupid argument. There's no sense in denying it anymore. If I don't tell you, Zadie will, so I may as well give my side of the story."

"That would be very helpful. What were you arguing about?"

"It was to do with my business, such as it is. I ought to have had more sense, but I was desperate. I asked Zadie if she'd wear some of the clothes from my shop and give me a mention in her show. She turned me down flat."

"The other day, you said that you'd never take advantage of Zadie. You said it would be unethical."

"I'm not proud of what I did; I was hardly going to tell someone like you. Besides, I wasn't trying to take advantage of Zadie. I offered to pay her. It would've been a business arrangement, and I was totally upfront about the whole thing, but she… she was horrible to me."

"What did she say?"

"She told me that the clothes I sell aren't good enough. Not in so many words, naturally. She talked about style and flair and uniqueness, but we both knew exactly what she was saying. Poor little Mary. She tries but she just doesn't get it. She's out of her depth, out of step, out of luck. She doesn't make the grade."

Dan folded his arms and made his expression serious while he hunted for the right thing to say. Melody's heartfelt speech could've been carefully planned, rehearsed even, but it hadn't come across that way. *She meant every word*, Dan decided. *She held back the truth, but who can blame her?*

Melody had lingered on the fringes of Zadie's little group for a couple of years, but she'd never make it to the inner circle and she knew it. That might be a cause for bitterness, but it didn't make sense as a motive. Melody had nothing to gain by intimidating Zadie, but everything to lose if her high profile friend was out of the picture.

Dan made sure he had her attention, then he asked his initial question once more, this time with added emphasis. "Why did you come here today, Melody?"

Melody's expression grew pinched as though she might refuse to answer, but she let out an exasperated sigh and said, "If you really must know, I'm worried about Philippa. She isn't answering her phone or replying to any messages. I called Connor and Naomi, but they both say the same. None of us have been able to get hold of her. Connor even went around to her house, but she didn't answer the door." Melody took a breath, and her voice wavered as she went on.

"It's not like her. Philippa's always very good at getting back to people. If we have a group chat, she's usually the first to reply, but there's been no response all day. That's why I'm here. I'm hoping Zadie can help. I thought we could go around to Philippa's house together. I even shut the shop so I could do this. That's how much my friends mean to me. They may not think much of me, and I know I'm not like them in lots of ways, but we're friends. You can understand that, can't you?"

Dan nodded. "Yes. Yes, I can." He hesitated. "Listen, I really can't let you in to see Zadie just yet—"

Melody started to protest, but Dan swept on. "But I will do everything I can to help you. If you like, I'll go over to Philippa's house with you. If she's at home, we'll find her and make sure she's okay. If she isn't there, I might be able to find some clues and work out where she's gone. I am a private investigator, after all."

"Really? You'd come over with me?"

"Yes. Maybe it'll make up for being so heavy handed when you arrived. I really am sorry about that."

Melody seemed to weigh this up. "I suppose it might help if you came with me, but you can only come if we take my car."

"That's a good idea. Give me a second to tell Alan what's going on, then we'll go."

"I'll get the car started. It's the—"

"Black Audi A8," Dan interrupted. "I know."

Melody narrowed her eyes as though putting two and two together, perhaps wondering to what extent Dan had been checking up on her, but all she said was, "I'll see you out there."

"Sure." Dan bounded up the stairs to the studio. He'd fill Alan in, then he'd dash off and get this business with Philippa cleared up. Hopefully, he'd be back before long, and until then, Alan could hold the fort, watching out for anyone else who might turn up. It would all be fine.

CHAPTER 44

W*hat would Dan do?* Alan thought as he made his way down to the front door. No answers came to mind, but if he kept Zadie's visitor talking, something might occur to him.

Alan opened the door and smiled. "Hello, Carly. It's nice to see you again. It looks like you're ready for action."

Carly glanced down at her leggings and training shoes, her Adidas hoodie. "Well, yeah. I'm here for Zadie's session, and I'm a bit late, as it goes, so excuse me." Carly stepped forward, forcing Alan to move back, then she barged past him into the hallway. "Is she upstairs?"

"Yes, but there must've been some mistake," Alan blurted. "You can't go up there now."

Carly halted, turning back to face him. "Is Zadie not ready? That doesn't matter. I'm used to hanging around while she gets changed."

"No, it's not that." Alan moved past Carly, placing himself between her and the stairs. Clasping his hands together in front of him, his fingers intertwined, he said, "You see, Zadie won't be needing you today. She's working in her studio, making several shows back-to-back, and as I'm sure you know, she can't be disturbed during filming."

Carly let out a growl of frustration. "She could've told me. I've come all the way over here."

"I'm sorry about that. It must've been an oversight, but I'm sure–"

"It's Natalya's fault," Carly interrupted. "She's supposed to tell me if Zadie cancels a session. Where is she anyway? Where is the ice queen from the frozen steppes or wherever?".

"If you mean Natalya, she's assisting Zadie at the moment. She'll be free later today, so if you want to make an appointment with Zadie, you could call in a few hours."

"No thanks. I'll wait until Zadie gets in touch. I won't waste my time talking to Natalya; I know what she thinks of me. I wouldn't mind, but she's so bossy, isn't she? She shouldn't talk to people like that, it's just rude."

"I've always found her to be polite."

"Yes, but you're a bloke. Some women are like that: all cow-eyed when they're talking to men, and snarky as hell with women."

Alan felt his expression hardening. Locking eyes with Carly, he said, "Carly, where were you last night?"

"Why?"

Bluffing had never been Alan's strong suit, but he had to say something. "Zadie mentioned something about trying to cancel her session with you. She tried to get hold of you last night, but she didn't manage it."

"Really?" Looking worried, Carly whipped a phone from her bag and checked the screen, shaking her head as she swiped. "Nope, nope, nope. No missed calls, no messages, no emails. Nothing. Are you sure she tried to reach me?"

"I think so. Maybe you were out of range."

"No, I had a marathon session at the gym last night. I was there all evening, and they have great wi-fi. After that, my legs were destroyed, so I went straight home and collapsed into bed, but I always check my phone before I crash out. I'd have got a message or a call, even when I was driving. There's nothing wrong with my signal in Exeter, it's only when I come out here it gets spotty."

Carly moved closer to Alan. "What did Zadie say? Was she in a good mood, or was she, you know, in one of her grumps?"

"She was fine. Zadie's never struck me as being a grumpy person."

Carly sent him a patronising smile. "You don't know her like I do. I've seen her have hissy fits like you wouldn't believe, but then, we've been together for years."

"So I understand, and it makes me wonder if you know about Zadie's medical history."

Carly's smile froze. "That's not something I would discuss with you or anyone else."

"That goes without saying, but there are some aspects of Zadie's history that Dan and I already know about. We had a full and frank discussion with Tobias, Zadie's brother."

"That doesn't make any difference. My lips are sealed."

"Fair enough." Alan raised a finger as if a thought had just struck him. "Oh, I wanted to ask you about the protein shakes Zadie uses."

"Are you looking to buy some for yourself?"

Alan nodded. "I was thinking about it. I need to get myself into better shape. I've started running."

"Okay." Carly looked him up and down. "You might want to start gently. If you're interested in a proper training programme, I can book you in for a few sessions."

"Not at the moment. It was just the protein shakes I was interested in."

"I can bring over some samples. They're not cheap, but they're very good."

"Great. Would they be the same brand as the ones you sell to Zadie?"

Carly's expression became guarded. "I advise Zadie on nutrition, and she chooses to buy a few products from me."

Alan couldn't stop himself. "A few? Her kitchen cupboards are crammed with the stuff."

"That's up to Zadie. She orders products and I deliver, but I don't force anything on her."

"Not force, perhaps, but you persuade her, don't you?"

Carly shook her head firmly. "I advise, I make recommendations. The rest is entirely up to her."

"That's interesting, because I've been doing some research into Arvitalize, and they're a multi-level marketing company."

"I'm not sure what you're getting at, but they make a range of products, and they're all excellent. The quality is great, and they're good value too."

"You said they're not cheap."

"They're not, but you need less of them." Carly folded her arms. "What's this really about? It's obvious you're not really interested in buying some, so why did you ask?"

"Because I know you get a commission on each product you sell, and that makes me wonder what you'd do if Zadie stopped buying them."

Carly's cheeks paled as she stared at Alan. "Wait, are you implying I had something to with what happened here?"

"That depends. What are you referring to?"

"You know perfectly well. Someone's been leaving notes for Zadie, trying to frighten her, make her freak out."

"The notes. Is that all?"

"Yeah." Carly searched Alan's expression. "Listen, I know your friend, Dan whatshisname, is a bit strange, but I thought you were more normal. I thought you were okay. Why are you being weird all of a sudden?"

"I think you might know what I'm getting at, Carly. I think you were here last night."

"No, of course, I wasn't. I've already told you where I was."

"Yes, but I don't know whether to believe you," Alan said. "The problem is, I'm concerned about your relationship with Zadie. You seem to exercise a degree of control over her."

"What? No one can control Zadie, least of all me."

"What about her diet? You tell Zadie what she can and can't eat. That sounds very controlling to me."

"Hold on, where are you getting this?"

Alan didn't reply, but Carly laughed scornfully under her breath. "It was Natalya, wasn't it? But that doesn't mean a thing. You can't believe a word she says. She's had it in for me since she got here."

"Natalya is extremely loyal to Zadie, and—"

"That proves it was her," Carly sneered. "Oh, I get it. She's turned on the charm for you, hasn't she? And you fell for it."

"That's nonsense."

"Is it? You must've wondered why a young woman like Nat would come after you. Well, I'll tell you. She wants a visa, Alan. She wants to stay here, and once she gets her hands on the paperwork, you'll be kicked out without a second thought."

"What are you saying?" someone called out, and Alan turned to see Natalya storming toward them, her gaze fixed on Carly.

Alan made to say something, but he didn't get the chance. Natalya stood beside him, her hands on her hips. "I have indefinite leave to remain. This is my country now."

"Ah, but that's not the same as having citizenship, is it?" Carly said. "You need to apply for that, and I'm sure it would be handy to have a nice, sensible husband in tow."

"You had better stop talking," Natalya snapped. "Zadie doesn't want to see you today. Maybe she's had enough of you. She's been looking for a new trainer, somebody better."

"Rubbish. You're just jealous because I'm Zadie's friend and you're an employee. You're nothing more than a dogsbody."

"That's enough." Alan held up his hands, one palm facing Carly, the other toward Natalya. "There's nothing to be gained by this. Carly, I think you'd better leave."

"I'm going, don't you worry." Carly tutted in contempt. "I'll leave you two alone. You deserve each other." Carly turned to leave, but then she paused, hunched over her phone, her hands busy.

Before Alan could ask what she was doing, Carly turned back, holding out her phone, the screen facing Alan. "Do you know what this is?"

"I can see you've got an app of some kind, but I don't recognise it. Should I?"

"It's an app by Exeter University," Carly said. "I use it to book my gym sessions, and it shows the time when I arrived and when I left." Carly indicated the top of the screen. "See that? Three minutes past eight: that's when I got there. I scan my phone when I go in, and again when I leave. I was there for two and half hours. And another thing, your story about Zadie trying to call me is a pack of lies. I'd know if she called me. It would be in my call log and there's nothing there. Nothing whatsoever."

Playing for time, Alan peered at the screen, taking in the university's logo and the timestamps showing Carly's attendance. Carly was telling the truth, and it was clear that she was a regular at the gym, getting a session in almost every day. Still, he had a question. "Why do you use the gym at the university? There must be lots of them in Exeter."

"Because it's the best and I'm registered to use it. I go there all the time. Call them up if you don't believe me. They know me. They'll back me up."

Alan blinked, suddenly feeling very stupid. He'd overplayed his hand and made a fool of himself. *I should leave this kind of thing to Dan*, he thought. *I can't carry it off.*

"Well?" Carly demanded. "What do you say to that?"

"I say that I've made a mistake," Alan replied. "I put two and two together and made five, and I'm sorry for that. I shouldn't have accused you. It was wrong of me."

"Whatever."

"I mean it," Alan said. "I really am sorry."

In the tense silence, Carly regarded him with a cool gaze. "Prove it."

"How?"

"Do something for me," Carly said. "Talk to Zadie and put in a good word for me."

Alan's disquiet must've shown, because Carly added, "I'm not asking you to lie. Just tell Zadie I was here and I was ready for our session. Say she cancelled it too late, but I won't bill her for it, okay?"

Natalya let out a dismissive hiss, but Alan kept his gaze on Carly. "All right, but can I ask one small favour in return?"

"Seriously? You're almost as bad as your friend. What do you want this time, my fingerprints?"

"No, I was wondering, would you mind if I took a photo of your phone's screen? I'd like to show it to Dan so that he doesn't make the same mistake."

"Yes, I do mind," Carly said. "I shouldn't have to make excuses for myself when I've done nothing wrong, but what the hell. Knock yourself out."

"Thank you."

Carly held her phone still while Alan took several photos with his.

"That ought to do it." Alan studied the images and something snagged in the back of his mind, but before the memory had a chance to resolve, he noticed something else that one of his images had captured. He'd taken the first shot too wide and included Carly's hand.

Looking back at her, he said, "That's a fine gold ring you have. Are you engaged?"

"Good God no. It's nothing like an engagement ring, and anyway, it's on the wrong hand."

"Oh yes. Silly of me. Still, it's very impressive. Are all those diamonds real?"

Carly's lips formed a petulant pout. "Definitely. It's from Cartier. Actually, Zadie gave it to me. It was her way of saying thank you for everything I've done for her." Carly's pout became a smirk as she turned to Natalya. "You see? Whatever you might

357

think, Zadie has always been grateful to me. She understands all the work I've put in, all the sacrifices I've made. Did she ever buy you a diamond ring?"

"No, and if she did, I wouldn't keep it," Natalya said. "I don't need such things. I work hard, I get paid, that is all I want."

"Yeah well, good luck with that if Zadie ever gets tired of you, and she will. It's only a matter of time."

"If that day comes, I will find another job. It is not so difficult. But now, you had better go."

"Fine. Goodbye." Carly flounced from the house, slamming the door behind her.

"Good riddance," Natalya said. "Let's hope she does not come back."

"I suppose that's up to Zadie." Alan thought for a moment. "Did Zadie really say she was looking for a different personal trainer?"

Natalya sent him a stern look. "She mentioned it once. I don't make things up, Alan. I am not a liar."

"I'm sure you're not, but there's such a thing as a white lie. You know, a falsehood said for a good reason."

"No, there isn't. There is truth and there are lies. That is all. It doesn't matter why you say it, a lie is a lie."

"You're a very principled young woman."

"Not so young." Natalya's frown turned into the suggestion of a smile. "But you are being kind, I think."

Under Natalya's watchful gaze, Alan found himself floundering. "Yes, but I wasn't trying to flatter you or anything. I just meant that you seem young to me, because you're so…" Alan circled a hand in the air as if the right words could be summoned, but nothing came to him, at least, nothing he could say out loud.

"It's okay, Alan. More than okay." Natalya hesitated. "In this house, I hear kind words sometimes, but people don't mean what they say. With you, it is different."

"Thank you, but what do you mean about the people in this house? Has someone said something to upset you?"

"No, not to me, but they say such things to each other all the time. They talk about each other's clothes, their shoes, their hair. They say words like divine and gorgeous, and you think they are being nice, but really, they are being hurtful, laughing behind each other's backs."

"Ah, that doesn't surprise me. It's what we call a barbed compliment. That's when you intend to insult someone, but you dress it up as flattery."

Natalya nodded slowly as though storing this information away.

"Is there someone in particular who says hurtful things?" Alan went on. "Someone who might seem as though they have a cruel streak?"

"Not really. They all do it, except for Naomi. She's the only one who is okay."

"Right. We haven't talked to Naomi yet, but I expect we'll get around to it soon."

"Shall we go upstairs now, Alan?"

Alan swallowed. "Er…"

"We have lots of work to do," Natalya said. "If we don't keep up with the comments, we'll get behind."

"Yes, of course." Alan gestured to the stairs. "After you."

And when Natalya turned away, Alan took the opportunity to wipe a hand across his brow. Somehow, it seemed to have grown suddenly hotter in the house. *Get a grip*, Alan chided himself, then he headed for the stairs.

CHAPTER 45

Peter sat in the front room of the cottage, his head in his hands.

I shouldn't have done it, he told himself. *I should not have done it.* He massaged his eyeballs with his fingertips, but still, he saw her: Philippa's face as she'd stared at him, the disgust in her eyes.

She'd rumbled him. She'd tried to hide it, but he'd known exactly what she was thinking and he'd realised what it meant.

He should've walked away. He should've grabbed his few possessions and headed for the bus stop, but he'd reacted out of instinct. He'd said the wrong things and made matters worse. *Idiot!*

He'd been on to a cushy number for a while, and he'd ruined everything.

"It doesn't matter," Peter muttered to the empty room. "I've got to go."

Wiping his palms on the front of his shirt, Peter stood and took a long, slow breath.

There. He could cope now. All he needed was his phone, his wallet and his holdall. In a few minutes time, he'd be gone.

It took Peter no time at all to gather his few possessions, and he left the cottage without a backward glance. He marched across the lawn, his holdall banging against his legs.

But what was that noise?

Peter halted and cocked an ear. Voices. A man and a woman. They called out Philippa's name, and he heard dull thuds. They were hammering on Philippa's front door.

Peter took a few faltering steps back. The voices were growing closer now. They were at the garden gate.

"I know the combination," the woman said, and Peter turned and ran.

The cottage was the best hiding place on offer, and he sprinted to the front door, barging inside and locking the door behind him. Breathing hard, he stepped back, keeping away from the windows. The old-fashioned mortice lock would keep them out. Even if they had a key, it would do them no good while the keyhole was in use from the inside.

Peter took a couple of deep breaths, trying to stop his heart from hammering against his ribs. He'd be okay. He was locked in. He was safe.

Who was out there? And what did they want?

Whoever it was, they'd known the code to unlock the gate, so they must be close to Philippa: friends or family. Either way, their arrival spelled trouble.

They were calling out Philippa's name again, their shouts growing more urgent. It sounded as though they were pounding on the back door of Philippa's house, the hollow thuds echoing in the garden's still air.

It'll be all right, Peter told himself. *I'll sit tight until they go.*

"I'll check the cottage," the man called out, and Peter recognised his voice. It was one of the men who'd come to see Philippa before: one of the pair who'd acted like cops, asking questions.

"Wait for me," the woman said.

"Come on then," the man replied, his voice nearer now.

They're coming. Peter's nerve failed and he made for the back door, but the man called out again: "I'll go around the back."

No, no, no. Peter dropped to the floor and crawled on all fours to the front door. He sat, huddled on the floor, his back pressed against the wooden door.

No one would see him there. He reached up and checked the key was still in its place. It was fine, but the backdoor only had an old Yale lock. If the man outside had a key, he'd be inside in a second. Failing that, the guy might put his shoulder to the door, and the old lock wouldn't offer much resistance.

If he comes in the back, I'll run out the front, Peter told himself. There was no way he was going to hang around and tackle that bloke, not without a weapon.

Someone banged on the front door, the noise impossibly loud, the vibrations reverberating through his chest.

Why didn't they give up and go away? He wasn't going to answer. He wasn't going to move a muscle.

The back door's handle rattled, then the man tapped on a window pane, calling out: "Hello. Anyone home? We need to speak to you. It's important."

The cry was taken up by the woman at the front. "Hello! It's Jack, isn't it? Are you in, Jack?"

No, he isn't, Peter thought. *Jack doesn't exist. I made him up.* Peter stared straight ahead, waiting. If he heard a key in the lock of either door, or if they tried to force their way in, he'd have to act. Until then, he had to stay calm, think only of what came next.

He *would* get away. No one could stop him.

But there was no rattle of keys, no thump of a boot against the door.

A pause, and then the voices came together at the front of the house.

"We'll try again later," the man said. "For now, let's go back to the house and have another look around."

"Wait," the woman replied. "Maybe we should call the police."

"Not yet. Let's see what we can figure out first."

The woman said something else, but her voice was soft, little more than a whimper, and besides, they were moving away.

Peter exhaled slowly, then he stood.

The danger was over for a while, but he'd almost blown it. He'd panicked and acted without thinking. He couldn't afford to make the same mistake again. His luck was already stretched paper thin.

He needed to change the situation. It was time to take action.

CHAPTER 46

A lan hit the return key and sat back. *Done it*, he thought. *I'm finally up to date.* It wouldn't be long before a new batch of comments appeared on Zadie's various social media channels, but he'd deal with them later. *It's a full-time job*, he thought. *It's a wonder Natalya manages to get anything else done at all.*

Come to think of it, where had Natalya got to? She'd made a cryptic remark about having something to deal with, then she'd left him on his own. Immersed in the dizzying world of Zadie's adoring fans, Alan had lost track of time, but surely, Natalya had been away too long. Dan too.

Alan stood, stretching his back and looking around Zadie's studio. The Olivetti typewriter on the filing cabinet caught his eye and he wandered over to it. It was a curious coincidence that Zadie owned exactly the same model as him, the Lettera 32. Natalya said she'd bought it for its pale blue finish, but that, too, seemed odd. It was almost as if the typewriter had been put there to draw him in. So much of this place called out to him. The studio would make a perfect room to sit and write. Nicely proportioned and free from distractions and clutter, it exuded an atmosphere of calm productivity. The house itself would be lovely when the renovations were complete, and the garden, with its views of rolling fields and wooded slopes would be perfect. All in all, The Old Manse was his idea of heaven: a dream home.

And then there was Natalya.

Alan let his thoughts turn to daydreams for a while. It was silly of him to imagine any romantic entanglement between them, but that didn't stop his heart from beating a little faster at the thought of it.

Without really intending to, Alan found himself opening the door and making for the stairs.

In the hallway he was about to call out Natalya's name, but something made him hesitate. A faint noise echoed through the almost empty house: a hollow tapping of something hard against a solid surface. Alan tilted his head and half turned, listening. There it was again, and this time, he was certain where the sound came from.

Alan strode through to the kitchen and halted. There was no one there.

What had he heard, and where on earth was Natalya?

Alan's gaze rested on the antique pine dresser that stood against one wall. Whereas all the other cabinets and cupboards had their doors firmly closed, forming an uninterrupted expanse of glossy pale grey, one of the dresser's wooden drawers had been left half open.

A sudden memory sent a chill to chase down Alan's spine. After the first break-in, Zadie had said that one of the dresser drawers hadn't been closed properly. Had the intruder returned?

His heart in his mouth, Alan moved stealthily to the dresser. And when he saw what filled it to the brim, his eyes went wide.

Another tapping sound, followed by the scrape of metal against metal. The sound seemed to be coming from somewhere at the back of the kitchen, but there was nothing there except for the old scullery.

A thought forced itself to the front of Alan's mind: someone was trapped inside the scullery, trying to escape, tapping on a pipe to send out a signal, desperate for help.

Natalya!

Alan charged toward the white-painted wooden door, but before he could reach it, the door swung open.

And then everything happened quickly.

Natalya appeared in the doorway, her arms laden with tins and packets. Alan tried to stop his headlong dash, but he was too late, and he collided with Natalya, wrapping his arms around her in an instinctive embrace. Natalya let out a yelp and dropped what she was carrying, grabbing Alan with both hands to stop herself falling backward. Packets and tins clattered to the floor, a plastic bag bursting open to send rice scattering over the tiles.

For a moment, Alan and Natalya stared at each other in silence, their faces close, then they both started speaking at once.

"Hang on," Alan said firmly, and he disengaged from her embrace, stepping back and straightening his clothes.

Natalya had stopped talking, and she stared at him, wide-eyed.

"I am so sorry," Alan began, "I wanted to help. I thought you were in trouble."

"Trouble?"

"I heard a noise and I thought…" Alan gestured to the scullery. "I thought you might be trapped in there."

Natalya shook her head. "It's just a storeroom. How could I be trapped?"

"Someone might've broken in. I was worried about you."

Natalya's expression lost some of its incredulity. "You were coming to rescue me?"

Alan had never felt so foolish in his life, but he nodded. "It was silly of me, I know. You're more than capable of looking after yourself, but even so, in the heat of the moment…"

"That wasn't silly, Alan. It was brave."

"I don't know about—"

"It was very brave," Natalya interrupted. "Thank you." Natalya surveyed the mess on the floor, then she squatted on her haunches and began to retrieve the fallen groceries.

Alan joined her, scooping up a couple of tins of chopped tomatoes.

"You don't have to do this," Natalya said, but Alan kept going.

"I want to help," Alan replied. "It's the least I can do. This was all my fault."

"An accident." Her arms full, Natalya stood and placed her burden on the kitchen counter. "You can put those tins here."

"Sure." Alan did as he was told. "What are we going to do about all this rice?"

"I'll clean it up. I'll fetch something." Natalya returned to the scullery, and Alan stood by the doorway and peered inside.

While Natalya retrieved a brush and dustpan from its hook on the wall, Alan said, "Where did you get all that food?"

"It was in the cupboard. Why?"

Alan hesitated. "When we first came in the kitchen, Dan asked me to look around. I told him we shouldn't, but he insisted, so I peeked inside. I thought it was only used as a broom cupboard."

Natalya was fetching a plastic bin liner from a shelf, but she stopped and looked at him. "I remember. I asked you not to touch anything."

"I know, but we didn't mean any harm. We were looking for clues." Alan wanted to say more, but Natalya had cast her gaze downward as though she couldn't bear to look at him. Without a word, she snatched up the bin liner and swept past Alan without sparing him a glance. In the kitchen, she began sweeping up the rice and pouring it into the bin liner.

"Can I help?" Alan asked.

Natalya shook her head. "You have done enough."

While Natalya worked, Alan watched helplessly. Natalya was upset, not only because he'd joined Dan in rifling through the cupboards, but by the fact that they'd ridden roughshod over her perfectly reasonable request to leave things alone. They'd treated her as a servant, a second-class citizen, and Alan had no idea how to make up for that. He didn't know where to begin.

Her tidy up completed, Natalya washed her hands, then she marched back to the scullery, returning a moment later with an onion and a couple of carrots. Drawing a knife from its block and a chopping board from a drawer, Natalya placed the onion at the board's centre, but she didn't begin cutting. Instead, she drew a long breath and then turned to Alan. "Did you find any?"

"Sorry, what?"

"Clues. Did you find anything?"

"No, not really," Alan said. "We noticed all those protein shakes, but apart from that, there was nothing interesting."

Natalya glanced at the groceries she'd placed on the counter. "You think this is strange, me bringing food from in there." She nodded to the scullery door.

"Now that you mention it, it does seem a bit odd to keep food elsewhere when there's plenty of room in here. Some of the kitchen cupboards are empty."

"I know. It's Carly; she throws everything away. But I've found a place she doesn't look."

"The scullery?"

"That's what Zadie calls it, but it is like a pantry. It keeps things cool. The floor is stone, and there are some old cupboards. I keep food in there and I cook for Zadie and me."

"I see," Alan said. "That's very good of you, to look after Zadie, but you shouldn't have to hide things."

"It's complicated."

Alan gestured to the pine dresser. "Like that drawer?"

"Ah." Natalya's cheeks coloured. "Zadie calls it the naughty drawer. We usually keep it locked."

"I must admit, I was surprised. That's a lot of chocolate and snack bars."

"She doesn't want anybody to know," Natalya said. "You won't tell anyone, will you?"

"That depends. Does Zadie have a problem with food? Does she have a condition?"

"No, Zadie has no problem like that, but she's very fussy about her image. She tells everybody to stick to the rules, but…"

"But every now and then, she likes a treat, the same as everyone else," Alan suggested.

Natalya nodded. "We only open the drawer once a day. We choose something then we lock it until the next day."

"Hang on a minute. After the first break in, you thought a drawer wasn't shut properly. Was it that one?"

"Yes, but I don't know if it was locked. Sometimes, Zadie…"

"She helps herself to an extra treat?"

"Yes. Only sometimes, not every day. This is not so bad, I think."

"It's not bad at all. If anything, it's good to know that Zadie is like the rest of us. We all have our little weaknesses. Personally, I find it hard to resist a good pint of ale in the evening."

"Ah, but for men it is different."

"Maybe, but it shouldn't be." Alan risked a smile. "Besides, you don't need to worry about your weight. You're very slim and you keep yourself fit, I'm sure. Anyone can see that."

"Not so much. I am always busy here. There is never enough time." Natalya gazed at Alan levelly as if his flattery had gone unnoticed, but there was the hint of a smile on her lips, and that was enough.

"I'm sorry about charging into you earlier," Alan said. "We must've looked comical, practically falling over, food all over the floor and rice flying everywhere. It's a good job Dan wasn't here."

"Yes, that would've been very bad." Natalya pressed her lips tight shut, but a snort of laughter escaped and Alan joined in, the tension melting away as they giggled like mischievous children.

Alan wiped the corners of his eyes with his fingers, and he smiled hopefully at Natalya. "I've made a mess of things. Can you forgive me?"

Natalya waved his apology away. "You didn't mean any harm,

and there were things I could've told you. I should've explained about Zadie's food. I let you think she doesn't eat properly."

"I must admit, we were concerned about all those protein powders. We wondered how she coped, but it all makes sense now." Alan glanced at the chopping board. "Were you going to cook something?"

"Yes. I promised you lunch. It was going to be a surprise."

"Well, you surprised me, that's for sure."

"We surprised each other." Natalya hesitated. "I was going to make you a chilli. Would you like that?"

"I'd like it very much, but I wouldn't want to put you to any trouble."

"It's no trouble. I'd like to do it. You are working hard, trying to make this place safe again, and that means something. I know what it's like to be afraid in your own home."

Alan bit back the sympathetic words on the tip of his tongue. Natalya would have no time for glib commiserations; she was too strong-minded for that.

While Alan searched for the right thing to say, Natalya appeared to make her mind up.

"So I will cook a hot meal for you and Dan. Chilli, yes?"

Alan nodded enthusiastically. "Yes please. That would be wonderful."

"Good. It will be okay for Dan, all plant based. But you eat meat, Alan, yes?"

"Yes, I'm afraid so."

"There's no need to be sorry about it. I eat meat too, but don't tell Zadie."

"Your secret's safe with me."

They shared a grin.

"I'd better get started or lunch will be very late. How do you like your chilli, Alan? Do you like it hot?"

"I do. How did you guess?"

"I know how you Englishmen like spicy food." Natalya smiled. "It will be nice to have a man to cook for. You men, you like your food, don't you? You have a good appetite, Alan?"

"Guilty as charged. Really, I ought to cut back a bit." Alan patted his stomach, his abdominal muscles making a brave attempt to spring into action.

He felt foolish, but Natalya was shaking her head, smiling. "You are just right, Alan.

"That's very flattering, but I need to get fitter. I've taken up running, and I'm thinking about trying weight training. I might even join a gym."

"That's good, but you don't need to do these things. You're a proper man, not one of these skinny boys with their big beards and their floppy hair."

Natalya stepped closer to Alan, laying her hand on his upper arm and pressing his bicep. "You see? Plenty of muscle there. Very firm."

Alan seemed to have forgotten the English language.

"There's no need to look so worried, Alan. I don't bite. Not usually, anyway."

Alan managed a nervous chuckle. "I wasn't worried."

"No?" Natalya moved even nearer, so close now that she filled Alan's field of vision. "How about now?

Alan shook his head. "Natalya—"

"Shush. There's no need to say anything, Alan. I see the way you look at me."

"I didn't mean to, erm…"

"It's all right. I don't mind. I look at you too, and I think you are a good man. Kind."

"I try."

Natalya nodded slowly. "Alan, if you ask me to go out with you, I will say yes."

"Oh. I see. I'd like that. Maybe after this case is over—"

"It will be over soon," Natalya interrupted. "You will find this man; I know you will."

"We'll give it our best shot."

"Yes, and when it's over, everything will be back to normal. But not for me."

"How do you mean?"

"All this trouble has made me think," Natalya said. "It's made me wonder if I am happy working for Zadie. She was good to me when I came here, but sometimes, she is very…"

"Difficult?"

"Yes. I was going to say crazy, but your word is better. She makes things hard when they should be easy. For me, life is simple. I work, I do my best and I try to do things right. You understand this, I think."

Alan nodded. "You put it very well, and I'm sure you do a good job. I know Zadie depends on you."

"I like Zadie, but this job is not enough. I know my English is not perfect, but that doesn't mean I'm not clever. Back home, I went to university. I have a degree, an MBA. I should not be running errands and putting makeup on someone like Zadie or helping her with her hair. It's time to move on."

"But you'll stay in this country, in Devon?"

"I'm not sure. It depends."

"I see."

Natalya shook her head. "No, you don't."

Alan met her gaze and saw the glimmer of hope in her dark eyes. This was one of those moments: a split second in which the course of his life would be changed forever. Ridiculous as it was, his heart called out to Natalya. All he had to do was string a few words together, and he knew how to do that. He was supposed to be good at it, wasn't he?

Alan swallowed. "Natalya, when this case is over and everything settles down, would you like to go out for dinner with me?"

"Erm…" Natalya made a show of thinking it over, her eyes raised and a finger against the corner of her lips.

"Oh, have I misunderstood?" Alan blurted. "I'm sorry, I thought you were serious before."

Natalya laughed and pressed her hands to either side of his cheeks. "You are very sweet, Alan. Of course, I would like to go out to dinner with you. I would be delighted. We'll make plans later, but here is something just for you." She leaned in and planted a kiss on Alan's lips. He placed his hands gently on her arms and closed his eyes. For a dizzying second, he thought he might sway backward and make a complete fool of himself, but his worries melted away in the sheer, wonderful warmth of Natalya's kiss. And then it was over.

Natalya stepped back from him. "There. Now you understand, yes?"

"Yes."

"Good. But it is time to cook, so you'd better go." Natalya laughed, shooing Alan away. "Go on. Out of my kitchen."

"Okay, but are you sure you don't want any help?"

Natalya's eyes flashed. "Never. When I cook, I work by myself. Go upstairs and make sure everything is okay. Check YouTube and Instagram, and don't forget Facebook. When the food is ready, I'll bring it up to you, yes?"

"That would be great. Thank you."

Natalya looked pleased, then she moved back to the counter and picked up the knife. She looked back over her shoulder with a seductive smile. "Off you go, Alan. I'll see you soon. Okay?"

"Okay."

Alan strolled to the door, looking back just once. Natalya was already chopping an onion, making short work of it, wielding the gleaming knife with accuracy and precision.

What an amazing woman, Alan thought, and he sauntered along the hall and up the stairs, scarcely registering the bare boards beneath his feet. He was in a world of his own, his head spinning. For a few short minutes he forgot about the case, about Zadie, about Dan.

There was room for only one person in his mind, and she was in the kitchen. He heard Natalya's voice drifting up from below, and he stopped to listen. In a lilting voice, bright and pure, Natalya was singing. Alan couldn't understand the words, so he supposed she was singing in her native tongue. He was hearing her true voice for the first time. It was a beautiful sound, her voice growing stronger as she went along, and Alan didn't have to understand the language to know it was a song filled with joy. Natalya was happy, and suddenly, that was the most important thing in the world.

CHAPTER 47

Peter stood in the street and stared at his phone, willing the bus timetable to change before his eyes. *Cancelled,* he thought bitterly. *How in God's name could they cancel it?* It was bad enough that there was only one bus going to Exeter that afternoon, but to cancel it at a moment's notice was plain stupid. Peter ran a hand through his hair, then he turned around, scanning the street.

He could hitch a lift, but it wasn't without risks. People who picked up hitchhikers tended to remember their passengers. He might get lucky and be picked up by someone who didn't pay him much attention, but most drivers didn't like to pass the journey in silence. They generally wanted to talk and ask questions, and he wasn't sure if he could face that.

A car approached, a red Kia with a single occupant, and before he'd had time to think, Peter stuck his thumb out.

The car slowed to a halt in front of him and the passenger-side window whirred down.

Peter leaned in and smiled at the driver: a man about his own age but better dressed, better groomed, better fed.

"Are you all right?" the man asked, concern in his eyes.

"Yeah, but thanks for stopping. The bus has been cancelled, and—"

"Hello!" The cry from the backseat cut Peter's speech short, and he leaned in further to see two young children strapped into car seats, the oldest probably around five, the other a couple of years his junior. Both were grinning.

"Hi," Peter said. "You two look snug back there."

"We're going for ice-cream," the youngest child announced.

"And pizza," the older one added. "With ham on it. And cheese. Lots and lots of cheese."

"Wow," Peter said. "That sounds amazing. Pizza and ice cream. What's not to like?"

"Got to keep them entertained," the driver said. "You know how it is."

"Yeah, right." Peter's smile was hurting his cheeks, but his spirits slumped. *No, I really don't*, he wanted to say. *I haven't the faintest idea.* He couldn't imagine what it would be like to have a nice family, a decent car, a life that involved pizza and ice cream; not even from memory. He hadn't had that kind of childhood.

"I'm headed to Exeter," the driver added. "Is that any good to you?"

"Yeah, I was planning to go there myself." Peter glanced at the children, at their carefree smiles, their plump faces alive with hope and excitement. And their happy faces hollowed him out and left him standing like a shop window dummy, an empty shell.

"But you know what?" Peter went on. "I'm sorry to mess you about, but I've just remembered something I have to do. Thanks for the offer, but I think I'd better stay here."

"Are you sure? I mean, don't let the kids put you off. They're as good as gold really, and I wouldn't have minded a bit of adult company for half an hour." The man laughed as if he'd just made a joke, but there was a faint tinge of desperation in his voice. Peter almost felt sorry for him.

"No, no, it's not that," Peter said. "Honestly, there's something that slipped my mind, something I have to deal with."

"Okay, mate, but are you sure you're all right? You look a bit pale."

"Yeah, no, that's just me. I don't get outdoors much. Seriously though, thanks for stopping, but I'd better head back, and I'll let you get on. It sounds like you'll have fun." Peter sent one last smile to the kids in the backseat. "Have a nice time. Don't forget to eat some salad with all that pizza."

"Fat chance," the man said. "All right, kids, let's go."

The window wound up as the car pulled out and drove away.

For some reason, Peter lifted a hand to wave. He waited until the car had vanished from sight, and it felt good to let them go. If he'd accepted the lift, there was always the chance the driver would've been tracked down and questioned. If the guy was lucky, it would've been the police who came knocking. The alternative was much worse. Peter's old gang were still out there, and they'd be looking for him, wanting to teach him a lesson, to set an example for anyone looking for a way out.

It would've been wrong to inflict that kind of risk on an innocent family, to drag them into his world of violence and chaos. He didn't have the stomach for it.

You're getting soft, Peter chided himself, but it wasn't like that. He had to be careful, but he didn't know which way to turn. His nerves had been stretched too tight for too long, and he wasn't himself anymore. He could hardly think straight.

What if I stay put? he thought. *What's the worst thing that could happen?*

Philippa's friend and that nosy bloke might come back to knock on his door, but he'd hidden from them before and he could do it again. Sure, there was the problem of what to do about Philippa; that situation wasn't about to get better on its own. He'd have to pull himself together and come up with some fancy footwork if he was going to tread that path. Was he up to it?

The image of Philippa, her face when he'd last seen her, sprang into his mind, and Peter's stomach churned.

It was all her fault, he told himself. *She shouldn't have led me on like that.*

The day before, he'd waited until late in the afternoon, then he'd headed out, figuring the streets would be quiet. But as he'd made his way past Philippa's house she'd appeared at a downstairs window.

He'd waved and smiled, of course he had, but he hadn't meant anything by it. He was being friendly, that was all, putting on a show.

But Philippa had beckoned to him, pointed to the back door, so he'd gone along with it, smoothing down his hair as he'd ambled up to the house. A moment later she'd ushered him in, and he'd trotted inside like a lamb to the slaughter. She'd wanted to chat, she'd said, but he'd known that look in her eyes; she wanted something more.

At first, he'd kept his distance. Philippa had been drinking, and it looked like she'd started early. Vodka. He'd known the signs. Hell, he'd learned the smell of the stuff at his mother's knee. Vodka might not taint the breath, but if someone had enough of it, the scent of over-ripe apples followed them around the room, as if the stuff was seeping from their pores.

Peter had noticed the smell as soon as Philippa had stood close to him; too close. She'd been wearing perfume and the musky scent mixed with the odour of stale booze, the combination sickening. But she'd looked so good, so beautiful, her pupils dark with desire. He'd wanted her so much, he hadn't been able to resist.

But then it had all gone wrong. He'd ruined it. He'd given the game away and spoiled everything.

Why did I have to try and be clever? Peter thought.

Philippa had said she had a gift for him, and she'd told him to wait while she fetched it. Alone in Philippa's lounge, he'd thought of sneaking out, but she'd come back too soon, sweeping into the room and presenting him with a long, striped scarf. He'd guessed that the colours signified Exeter University, and he'd grinned like a fool, saying that he'd finally fit in with the other students, proud to wear the university's colours. And Philippa's smile had vanished.

She'd stared at him as if he were from another planet. The scarf's colours, she'd told him, were the blue, black and white of Exeter Chiefs, the local rugby team.

Peter had claimed he was kidding, winding her up, and he'd moved in for a hug, holding out his arms, but she'd pushed him away.

Her gaze sharp, she'd asked him again about that Doctor Feldman character, and he'd piled one mistake on top of another. He should've deflected the question, but instead, he'd made some remark about him being quite cool for an older guy. It ought to have been a safe bet. Philippa had made Feldman sound old, with all her talk of him being a friend of her father's. After all, her father had been dead for years.

Peter cringed at the memory of Philippa's cold tone as she'd set him straight. Brian Feldman wasn't old. Her dad had been a father figure to young Brian, helping the lad to reach his potential, and it had paid off. These days, Dr Feldman was a high flier, a university lecturer while still in his twenties.

Peter had tried to bluff it out, saying something glib about age being just a number, but he'd lost all confidence. Philippa had seen right through him, accusing him to his face, calling him a liar, a cheat and more besides.

He'd tried to explain. He'd pleaded, begged, taken hold of her arms and tried to make her see sense. That was when she'd broken free and lashed out, hitting him hard, her fist connecting with his cheekbone to send a jolt of pain through his skull.

What came next was hard to remember. It was as if it had happened to someone else, and he'd only witnessed it from a distance, the scene made indistinct by a veil of tears.

Oh God, Peter thought, still standing on the pavement, staring at the empty road where he'd let his hope of escape disappear. He turned around and started walking, looking only at the ground. He couldn't remember deciding where to go, but somehow he found himself back at Philippa's house and marching along the drive, letting himself in at the garden gate. Philippa had given him the code, of course she had; she'd trusted him.

How the hell was he going to straighten out this unholy mess? He couldn't make things right, it was too late for that, but there was still unfinished business, and that was no good.

This has to be sorted out, Peter decided. And this time, he would do it properly.

CHAPTER 48

His lunch break over, Benny nodded to Andy Butcher behind the bar of The Bull Inn and made his way outside, buttoning his jacket as he stepped onto the street. And he collided with a woman passing by. Instinctively, he put out his hands to steady her, and she latched onto his arm.

"I'm sorry," Benny blurted, and he was about to say more, but then he saw who he'd walked into, and he stepped back smartly, lowering his hands. "Naomi. I'm sorry about that. I didn't see you."

Naomi smiled. "It's all right, Benny. It was my fault. I was marching along in a world of my own, as usual. I should've been looking where I was going. I really am silly."

"No, that's not right. It wasn't your fault, and you're not silly, you're…" Benny's mouth was suddenly dry, and he had absolutely no idea how to finish his sentence. It didn't help that Naomi was looking up at him expectantly, her dark eyes locked on his. *She's gorgeous*, Benny thought. *Amazing.* Naomi's dark hair fell in loose curls to her shoulders, framing her lovely face and accentuating her perfect skin. She'd definitely been to the hairdresser, and her clothes looked new too. She wore a knee-length summer dress with a pattern of delicate blue flowers, and she'd draped a silky wrap over her shoulders. A handbag and strappy sandals completed the picture, and everything went together beautifully. She looked incredible.

Naomi smiled, the tips of her white teeth nipping the corner of her lips. "Go on, Benny. What were you going to say? That I'm a dreamer, my head always in the clouds?"

"No. You're not silly, and you shouldn't do yourself down. I think you're a good person. Really good." Benny cringed at the sound of his own voice. Somehow, he'd sounded lame and patronising at the same time. But Naomi was still looking at him, waiting. He had no choice but to blunder on. "Well, you've always been, you know, very nice to me. You made me feel welcome, part of the community."

Naomi sighed. "That's me: good old Naomi. She's very nice, people say, as if I'm a particularly disappointing dessert or something: sweet but a bit plain."

"Oh no, please don't say that. There's nothing wrong with being a kind person. You don't know how rare that is. And you're not plain; you're anything but. You're..." Benny swallowed, his lips twitching as he tried to form the right words. Was he going to make a fool of himself? He'd been thinking about Naomi for ages, but was he really going to come out and say it, right here in the street?

Naomi seemed to sense his discomfort. She cast her gaze at the pavement, her cheeks colouring. "It's all right," she murmured. "You don't have to say anything. I know what people think about me, and it's fine, really, it is."

"But I want to. I want to tell you..."

Naomi looked up, her eyes round.

"I think you're lovely," Benny went on, and then the words that had previously eluded him came all at once. "You're kind and caring and generous and gentle, but there's more to you than that. You make people happy. You make the world a better place, and you're pretty too. Very pretty. I probably shouldn't say it, but I think you're lovely. I hope... I hope you don't mind me talking like this, but it's all true."

"Oh, Benny, of course I don't mind, but you really don't have to—"

"I'm not just saying it," Benny interrupted. "I mean it. You're the most beautiful woman I've ever seen."

Naomi stared at him, and then a smile curled her lips. "No one has ever said that to me. It's very…" Naomi laughed, covering her mouth with her hand. "Oh dear, I was going to say *nice*." She stopped laughing and took a breath. "It's very sweet of you to cheer me up, Benny. You made my day, but I think I'd better go before I get all emotional and embarrass both of us."

"Please don't," Benny said. "Stay for a second. There's something I want to ask you."

"Oh?"

"Yes." Benny took a breath then said, "Naomi, would you like to go out with me one night? We could go for a meal or just a drink. Anything you wanted."

"Well, I…" Naomi held his gaze. "Do you really mean that?"

Benny nodded firmly. "How about tomorrow? We could go out for dinner. Somewhere nice. In Exeter, maybe. We could go to the Hotel du Chambray. That's where Mr Callaway goes. He knows the chef."

"That's a bit expensive, isn't it?"

"I don't care about that. If you'd like to come with me, I'll take you there. My treat."

Naomi shook her head gently. "I usually prefer somewhere simpler. There's a pizza place I quite like by the Cathedral. That's if…"

"I know it. Carlo's. I like it there too. I can book a table. Is seven okay? Half-past?"

"Either is fine."

"Right. I'll sort it out, and I'll give you a call." Benny took out his phone. "Do you mind, only I haven't got your number."

"Sure. No problem." Naomi reeled off her number and Benny tapped it into his phone, his thumbs clumsy.

"I'll call you later," Benny said. "Shall I pick you up?"

"Erm, no, I'll drive and meet you there. I don't drink much anyway, so it's no trouble."

"Okay. That's fine. Whatever you want." It crossed Benny's mind that Naomi might prefer to arrive under her own steam in case the evening turned out to be a disaster, but that was understandable. After all, they hardly knew each other.

"Well, this has been a lovely surprise, but I really ought to be going," Naomi said. "I'll see you tomorrow."

"It's a date." Benny felt the blood rushing to his cheeks. "Not that I mean a *date* date, just, you know…"

"Yes, but I think we can call it a date, can't we? I'd like that."

"Okay. It's a date."

Naomi laughed gently. "Bye, Benny. I hope you enjoy the rest of your day."

"Yeah, you too."

"I will." Naomi turned in an elegant way, her dress swirling, then she strolled away, her head held high and her hair bouncing with each step.

She's so light on her feet, Benny thought. *Like a dancer*. The thought brought him down to earth. What could a beautiful young woman like that see in him? He'd liked her from the first moment he'd seen her, but he'd known she was out of his league. If he hadn't physically bumped into her, he'd probably never have asked her out.

But he'd done it. He'd punched above his weight and won. All he had to do now was to make the date a success, and he'd give it a damned good try.

Benny walked tall as he headed back to the car. It didn't occur to him until he was buckling himself into the driving seat that he'd never asked Naomi what she'd been doing in Chagford. *Nipping to the shops, probably*, he thought. *Grabbing something for lunch*. But an unbidden question popped into his mind. Which way had Naomi been walking when he'd run into her? Because it seemed to him that, when she'd left, she'd headed back in the direction she'd come from, walking away empty handed.

No, I must've got that wrong, Benny decided. After all, he hadn't been looking where he was going, so there was no way he could be sure which way Naomi had been headed. He must definitely have made a mistake.

CHAPTER 49

Dan returned to The Old Manse and trudged up the stairs to find Alan alone in the studio, still perched on the wooden stool and working away at a laptop.

"Has Melody gone?" Alan asked.

"Yep."

"How did you get on? Any sign of Philippa?"

Dan shook his head, then he sat heavily on the office chair at Alan's side.

"No clues as to where she might be?" Alan went on.

"No. Sorry, by the way, I was much longer than I intended, but I wanted to take a good look around. Unfortunately, I didn't see so much as a footprint. I looked in at all the windows I could get to, but there was nothing. Everything inside looked clean and tidy."

"Perhaps she's gone away for a day or two."

"Without telling any of her friends? I don't think so. Something's wrong, but I don't know what."

"How about her paying guest, the chap who's renting her cottage?"

"No sign of him," Dan said. "Nothing."

"We could try again later or tomorrow. We might have better luck next time."

"Maybe. Did anything happen while I was out?"

Alan ran his hand along his jaw. "You missed a bit of excitement. Carly came, and I made a bit of a hash of it, but I did find something out."

"Go on."

Alan related his encounter with Carly, explaining that, according to Natalya, Zadie might've been looking for a new personal trainer. Finally, he showed Dan the photo of Carly's phone, zooming in to show the times displayed on her app.

"As you can see," Alan said, "Carly was at the gym until half past ten on Friday night."

"We don't know what time Zadie fell," Dan replied. "Carly could've been here by eleven o'clock, and I'm interested in the possibility that Zadie was letting her go. On its own, it's not much of a motive, but it could form part of a bigger picture."

"I told her I'd put in a good word."

"That's up to you, but we need to keep an open mind. Carly is a suspect until she isn't."

Dan let his gaze drift lazily around the room, taking nothing in.

"There's one bit of good news," Alan said. "Natalya's making us lunch: a veggie chilli."

Dan looked up. "That's kind of her. I thought I smelt cooking when I came in, but I didn't want to get my hopes up. The last time we looked, there was barely any food in the house."

"Natalya has a hidden store of supplies in the scullery. She cooks for Zadie all the time, apparently. And that's not all. I've discovered the secret of the drawer in the old dresser."

Dan leaned forward. "Go on."

"Treats," Alan announced with a smile. "Chocolate, snack bars and biscuits."

"For Zadie?"

"And Natalya too. They call it the naughty drawer."

"Well, well. So Zadie isn't quite as puritanical about food as she makes out, but she keeps that fact under wraps."

"Exactly," Alan said. "I found it quite reassuring."

"It could be significant. Let's say we're dealing with an obsessed fan: someone who's latched onto Zadie and everything she stands for; someone who is so desperate to get close to Zadie that they break into her house. How would they feel if they'd opened that drawer and discovered that their hero doesn't practise what she preaches?"

"Bitter? Resentful?" Alan suggested.

"Betrayed," Dan said. "Angry. Vengeful."

Alan looked doubtful. "How would they have known to look in the drawer? I only saw it today because Natalya left it open."

"Where do they keep the key?"

"Good question," Alan said. "I think it must be in the kitchen somewhere. Natalya said they open the drawer once a day, so it stands to reason the key would be nearby."

Dan sat back in the chair. Maybe, at last, they were on to something. This case was closely tied to Zadie's public image. Her online identity had made her famous and brought financial rewards, but it wasn't who she really was. There was a disconnect, a rift between her public profile and her real life, and somewhere in the middle of that murky grey area were her closest friends: Connor, Naomi, Melody and Philippa. They all clung to Zadie in the hope of reflected glory, but they'd seen her with her guard down. They'd looked behind the curtain, but had they liked what they'd seen?

Dan's train of thought was interrupted by his phone ringing. Accepting the call, he'd barely had time to say his name before the caller began speaking.

"Mr Corrigan, it's Will Saunders. I need to speak to you."

"Okay. Go ahead." Dan mouthed the word 'Saunders' to Alan, then he stood and paced the floor as he listened.

"I'm concerned," Saunders began, and as he went on, his words almost tumbled over each other in their haste to be heard. "But it's no good beating about the bush. I'm very worried. It's Mr Callaway. He hasn't been himself, and I know there's something going on. I've tried to talk to him about it, but he brushes me aside. That's not like him at all."

"Are you saying he's preoccupied? That might not—"

"It's more than that," Saunders interrupted. "He's usually a creature of habit, but he's become erratic. I never know what he's going to come out with next." Saunders hesitated. "And there's something else, something much more troublesome."

"Go on, but Mr Saunders, do you mind if I put you on speaker? Alan's here, and I'd like him to hear what you have to say."

There was a pause before Saunders replied. "All right, but there won't be any recording, will there? I couldn't have that."

"I wouldn't dream of it." Dan activated his phone's speaker and nodded to Alan.

"Hello, Mr Saunders," Alan said. "Alan Hargreaves here. Please, tell us how we can help."

"I don't know if you can," Saunders replied, "but I have to talk to someone."

"What makes you so worried about Mr Callaway?" Dan asked.

"He's been a bit odd for a few days, but things came to a head yesterday. I went into Mr Callaway's study, hoping to chat with him about the menus for the following week. As a rule, Mrs Yates likes to have his approval by Friday at the latest, but he's been too preoccupied to talk to her. He says he's focusing on his book, but I don't know that he's produced many actual pages."

"Have you read any of his work in progress?" Alan asked.

"I've glimpsed the odd bit now and then, when I've been in to speak with him, but it always looks as though he's on the same page." Saunders paused. "I don't know if I should tell you this, but he seems to be stuck on the section about his daughter."

"That's understandable, isn't it?" Dan said.

"I wouldn't say so. You mustn't give any credence to what you see in the gutter press. Mr Callaway is extremely fond of his daughter. Yes, they've had their ups and downs, and their relationship is complicated, but he's a very caring father."

"I understand," Dan replied. "Let's go back to what happened when you went into Mr Callaway's study."

"Yes, of course. The thing is, he wasn't alone. He and Benny were standing behind the desk, huddled over the computer as though they were looking at something extremely interesting. But when I came in, they stood back suddenly, almost as if…"

"As if they felt guilty about something?" Alan said.

"Yes. That's it. They looked like two little boys who'd been caught misbehaving."

"Did you manage to see the screen?" Dan asked.

"No. Mr Callaway clicked the mouse and closed down whatever they'd been looking at. He didn't tell me what it was, and I could hardly ask."

"Okay," Dan said slowly. "I can see why you might be concerned, but there could be any number of explanations."

"That's what I thought, but it's what happened next that was odd. You see, I went ahead and asked him about the menus, but he barely glanced at them. He just said everything would be fine, which is odd because he's normally a very fussy eater."

"Does he have coeliac disease?" Alan asked.

"Yes, but how did you know? That detail hasn't made it into the gossip columns, has it?"

"Not as far as I know," Dan said. "But I told you about the time he came into our local pub. I'm told that he asked for gluten-free beer."

"Oh, I see. That was a regrettable incident, but perhaps it was the first sign of something going on with him."

"That's possible," Dan replied. "So you showed him the menus. What happened next?"

"Mr Callaway seemed eager for me to go, so I left the room, but I… I hardly like to admit it, but I eavesdropped outside the door. I think they went back to whatever they'd been doing before. Mr Callaway said something like, 'It looks like a lot of work.' Then Benny said, 'Don't worry about it. I'll take care of all the hard stuff.'"

"That could mean anything," Alan said.

"Yes, but then Benny said, 'What do you think of her?' And Mr Callaway said, 'She's gorgeous, Benny, that's for sure.' The way they were talking made my flesh crawl. I heard Benny chuckling, and he said, 'What do you say, shall I see if we can get her?' And Mr Callaway said, 'Take care of it, Benny. The sooner the better.'"

"That does sound odd," Dan admitted. "Was there anything else?"

"That's all I heard. I crept away as quietly as I could. I didn't know what else I could do."

"Have you talked to anyone else about this?" Dan asked.

"Definitely not. I still think I might've got the wrong end of the stick. If they hadn't looked so guilty when I went in, I probably wouldn't have thought anything of it."

"Your instincts told you something was wrong," Dan said. "That's why you listened at the door. I presume that's not something you'd usually do."

"Never. That was the one and only time, and part of me wishes I'd never done it. But I heard what I heard, and the question is, what should I do about it?"

"Leave it with us," Dan replied. "We'll look into it, but if anything strange happens in the meantime, write down as many details as possible and then call me as soon as you can, okay?"

"I'll do my best, but I won't be doing any more snooping. I haven't the stomach for it."

"That's for the best," Alan said. "We don't want you to put yourself in any danger."

"You don't think…?"

"We don't know what to think, not yet," Alan replied. "Until we know more, it's best to play it safe."

"We need to talk to Mr Callaway," Dan said. "Is he at home today?"

"He should be, but he's not receiving visitors. He gave everyone strict instructions that he's not to be disturbed this weekend. He says he's close to making a breakthrough on his book. Although…"

"What is it?" Dan said.

"He does have one appointment over the weekend. Tomorrow morning he'll be going to church with Benny, so if I went over to the house and let you in while he was out, he need never know."

"That's a tempting invitation, but I need to see the whites of his eyes," Dan replied. "And you've just given me an idea."

SUNDAY

CHAPTER 50

Quite a place, Dan decided as he followed Alan through the churchyard in Chagford. The square tower of St Michael the Archangel's Church seemed particularly impressive with the early morning sunshine bathing its ancient stones in soft light. From beyond the mighty wooden door came the strains of organ music.

"We'd better nip inside," Dan said. "I hope we're in time."

But Alan halted in front of the door and turned to face Dan, his expression dour. "Are you sure you want to go through with this?"

Dan nodded. "We need to change things up. I've had enough of sitting around and waiting for something to happen."

"It was working though, wasn't it? Carly turned up and so did Melody."

"That was all in the morning, and then everything went quiet. We wasted the whole afternoon."

Alan looked distinctly put out. "I wouldn't say that. Natalya and I worked non-stop."

"While I got nowhere." Dan hesitated. "What's the matter? Don't you want to go in? I can handle it on my own, if you—"

"It's not that," Alan interrupted. "I'm happy to go in, but…"

"What?"

"I don't ask much of you, Dan, I really don't, but please, whatever happens, do not make a scene in this church."

"That goes without saying."

Alan raised an eyebrow and regarded him for a moment. "You'll keep quiet and be respectful?"

"Of course. I may be an atheist, but—"

"Not so loud," Alan hissed.

"Okay." Dan made a point of lowering his voice as he went on. "I'll be on my best behaviour."

"Glad to hear it. Come on then. Let's get this over with."

Alan pulled open the door and led the way inside. The service hadn't begun, and the congregation were settling in, a few of them bending their heads together to exchange whispered words.

"There's no sign of him," Alan murmured. "Shall we wait?"

Dan scanned the rows of pews. "No. We'll take that empty row at the back."

"Really? Callaway will want to sit near the front, won't he?"

"I don't think so. He'll keep a low profile, then he'll make a quick getaway as soon as the service is over. As you were so keen to point out, this isn't the place to make a scene."

Alan cocked an eyebrow, but he took Dan's advice and made for the back row. Dan sat beside him, and a moment later, Benny appeared in the doorway, closely followed by John Callaway.

Benny's expression didn't alter when he saw Dan and Alan, but he halted, half turning to exchange a few words with his boss.

Callaway smiled, his eyes twinkling as he turned his gaze on them, then he gestured to the empty space beside Dan.

Benny was clearly displeased, but he stepped forward and made to sit next to Dan.

"Hold up a second," Callaway said, laying his hand on Benny's arm. "I'd prefer it if you'd take your usual place by the aisle."

"I don't think that's a good idea, Mr Callaway" Benny murmured.

"Nevertheless, that's what we're going to do," Callaway replied. "I'm sure I'll enjoy sharing this morning's service with these fine gentlemen."

Benny looked as though he'd like to argue, but he stood aside, and Callaway settled himself next to Dan while Benny squeezed into the narrow pew to take the aisle seat.

Callaway nodded to Dan and Alan in turn. "Welcome. Tell me, what brings you here today?"

"I'm seeking enlightenment," Dan said.

"Aren't we all, my friend, aren't we all?" Callaway smiled, offering his hand for a shake. "I'm John."

Dan shook Callaway's hand. "I'm Dan Corrigan, and this is my friend, Alan Hargreaves."

Callaway's smile didn't falter, but a flicker of alarm flashed in his eyes. It was there for a fraction of a second, and then it was gone. "Dan, Alan, glad to make your acquaintance. But goodness me, you must forgive my manners. I've neglected to introduce my companion. This is my good friend, Benny."

"We've met," Benny said.

"Well, isn't that wonderful?" Callaway said. "Then you'll know, Dan and Alan, that Benny served with your gallant Royal Marines."

"No, he never mentioned that," Dan replied.

Callaway glanced at Benny with mock horror. "You know, Benny, you're just too darn modest." Leaning closer to Dan, Callaway added, "As a matter of fact, Benny has had the most distinguished career. He's served with the best, and distinguished himself in the field of battle, rising to the rank of captain. What was the name of your unit, Benny?"

"Four-two Commando," Benny stated.

"That's right. Four-two Commando," Callaway said. "It has a ring to it, doesn't it? I believe it's something like our Green Berets back home. Special Forces. That's right, isn't it, Benny?"

Benny nodded once, his expression grim.

"There he goes again," Callaway went on. "Modesty itself. Benny won't tell you, so I will. He was decorated three times for bravery: once while serving in Iraq, and twice in Afghanistan. Isn't that something?"

"Very impressive," Dan said. "I had no idea."

"Well, you do now," Callaway replied. "Benny might look like a peaceable kind of guy, but he could snuff out a man's life, just like that." Callaway clicked his fingers. "At the first sign of trouble, Benny can move in the blink of an eye. Can you imagine that, Dan? Because let me tell you, I've seen Benny in action, and it's quite spectacular, it really is. Forget about all those fight scenes you've seen in the movies; I'm talking about the real deal. Swift, silent, deadly."

Callaway's smile had remained throughout his homily, but his voice had steadily grown stronger, edged with steel, and the message was clear: Do not step out of line.

Dan held eye contact with Callaway, but before he could formulate a reply, a woman entered the church, and Dan's gaze flicked to the new arrival.

Naomi was the picture of serenity as she strolled into the church, her smile broad and yet reverent, her eyes alight with expectation as she looked at the back row. But her gaze landed on Dan, and she halted, her smile vanishing.

Benny started to stand up, but Callaway made a downward motion with his hand, and Benny retook his seat, his reluctance plain in his expression.

To Naomi, Callaway said, "I'm sorry, my dear, but this row is full. Perhaps you wouldn't mind sitting across the aisle just this once. I see there's plenty of room."

"Yes, that's fine," Naomi replied. "One place is as good as another."

The organ music faded and Alan nudged Dan with his elbow. The vicar had already taken his place, and Dan dutifully paid attention as the service began. At least, he tried. Dan sensed someone watching him, and he turned sharply, but Callaway and Benny were both watching the vicar in rapt attention. Benny's gaze flicked to Dan, a silent warning in his stare. Dan responded with a cheery grin, and Benny turned away, none too pleased.

Dan looked over to Naomi, but her head was bowed as if in silent prayer. She was the only other member of the congregation who wasn't paying attention to the vicar. Why was that? Did she simply want to be alone with her thoughts, or had she been the one who'd been staring at him, averting her gaze to avoid being caught in the act?

The vicar said something about fellowship and peace, and everyone else apparently knew how to respond, saying, "And also with you." Dan joined in, half a beat behind, and Alan nudged Dan's arm once more.

Dan lowered his voice to a whisper and said, "Are you going to do that the whole time?"

"If necessary," Alan murmured. "Grab a hymn book. I hope you're in fine voice."

Oh dear, Dan thought as he picked up a hymn book from the narrow shelf in front of him. The organ struck an introductory chord and the congregation stood, hymn books at the ready. Dan hastily found the right page just in time, and as everyone else burst into song, he did his best to keep up. Every now and then his voice faltered, and he attracted a few sideways glances from the other members of the congregation, but he kept going nevertheless, and as the hymn ended, he sat back down, feeling pleased with himself.

The sermon was on the subject of worship. The vicar, who looked young to Dan, delivered it with a mixture of warmth, sincerity and good humour and Dan found it quite compelling. He listened carefully, and for a few minutes, he forgot about Callaway and Zadie and the others. The rest of the service passed quickly, and in no time at all, Callaway and Benny were standing up and heading for the door.

"We'd better try and catch up with them," Dan said. "We can have a quick word outside."

Alan sighed, but he followed Dan from the church without protest.

Standing by the doorway, the vicar was intent on exchanging a few words with them, but Dan thanked him for the service and made his excuses, saying he wanted to catch up with a friend.

On cue, Alan asked the vicar about the church's history, and Dan made his escape with an inward sigh of relief; he'd stumbled through the service, but it was only a matter of time before he said the wrong thing, and despite what Alan thought, he had no wish to cause offence.

Dan found Callaway, Benny and Naomi still in the churchyard, standing to one side of the path. They were chatting among themselves, but they stopped talking as Dan approached.

"Well, well, if it isn't our latest addition to the congregation," Callaway began. "Did you enjoy the service, Dan?"

"Yes, it was interesting," Dan replied.

"That's good to hear. I have to say, that was quite a spirited performance you put on in there, Dan. The way you tackled those hymns, it was quite something."

"I'm afraid I've never been much of a singer. I haven't sung a hymn since my schooldays, and even then, the choirmaster gently suggested it would be okay for me to mime."

There was a brief pause before Callaway laughed. "The famous self-deprecating British humour. It still catches me out from time to time, doesn't it, Benny?"

"Oh yes, we've had a misunderstanding or two." Benny summoned a reluctant smile. Only Naomi looked unsettled, her wounded gaze lingering on Dan; he was trespassing on hallowed ground and she wanted to let him know how she felt about that.

Alan arrived, beaming as he looked around the group. "Hello again. That was a very enjoyable service, wasn't it?"

Naomi looked taken aback. "Do you really think so?"

Alan nodded earnestly. "Of course."

Naomi arched an eyebrow as she regarded Dan. "What about you, Mr Corrigan? What did you get from the service?"

"I think I gained something from the experience." Dan conjured an inscrutable smile and left it at that, tossing the ball back into Naomi's court.

Naomi's cheeks tightened, but before she could reply, Callaway said, "You two have already met?"

"Yes," Dan replied. "We have a mutual friend, don't we, Naomi?"

"I wouldn't put it quite like that." Turning to Callaway, Naomi added, these gentlemen work for Zadie. They're private investigators."

"Ah, so that's it." Glancing at Benny, Callaway added, "When we arrived, I thought my friend had spotted a couple of fans, but I figured you looked harmless enough, and I was right."

"Nevertheless, you warned us off," Dan said. "All that stuff about Benny's time in the forces; some might call that a veiled threat."

"Oh, that's a bit strong, isn't it, Mr Corrigan? I introduced you to my friend, that's all, and if I laid it on a bit thick, you can understand my reasons. Movie fans can get a bit overzealous, but they tend to quieten down once they see the lay of the land."

"I can imagine. But you quickly found out we weren't fans, didn't you? As soon as you heard our names, you reacted."

"I don't think so."

"I'm afraid you did," Dan insisted. "You tried to hide it, but you recognised our names straight away. I'm sure you were told that we came to your house. Well, we tried, but we didn't make it to the front door. Mr Saunders turned us away."

"Good. That's his job."

Naomi tutted. "You know, Mr Corrigan, you shouldn't be hounding people like this, especially not here of all places. It's not right. It's not right at all."

Callaway patted Naomi's arm in a fatherly way. "Now, now, my dear, there's no need to upset yourself. I don't like deceit any more than you do, but at least these two listened to the sermon, and they joined in the hymns, albeit with a certain disregard for the melodies. Maybe, in the spirit of Christian fellowship, we ought to give them the benefit of the doubt."

Naomi looked up at Callaway, her expression transformed by a doe-eyed smile. "You're right, John, as usual. Your generosity puts me to shame."

"You have nothing to be ashamed about, my dear. Nothing at all." Turning to Dan, Callaway said, "It was nice meeting you gentlemen, but it's time for us to be going."

"It was good to finally meet you in person," Dan replied. "It was a shame we missed you when you came to our village."

Callaway blinked in confusion. "I don't believe I've had that pleasure."

"Is that so?" Dan said. "I have to hand it to you, Mr Callaway, you're nothing if not consistent. I suppose it's part of your skill set. As an actor, you have to really believe in the parts you play. It must take a certain mental agility to keep up the pretence."

"I work hard at my craft, but I don't quite see what you're getting at."

"It's just an observation," Dan said. "It's quite an achievement to switch from one role to another, even though you might be playing the part of an American police officer one day, and the next, you might appear as, oh I don't know, a tractor parts salesman from Yorkshire."

Callaway's puzzled smile remained for a moment, and then it gave way to laughter. "Darn it! I thought I'd gotten away with that one, but I can see I've been rumbled. I'm sorry, Mr Corrigan, you must forgive me my foibles. When I first heard about you, I fell to wondering what kind of man becomes a private investigator in the heart of the English countryside where hardly anything ever happens. I must confess, my curiosity got the better of me. I hoped I might catch a glimpse of you in your environment, and maybe gain some insight into what makes a man like you tick."

"You could've simply picked up the phone and called," Dan

replied. "There was no need to go about it in such an elaborate way, so why go to all that effort?"

"I didn't want to sit down for a formal interview; that would've defeated the object."

"Which was?"

"To learn. As an actor, I've become a student of human nature, but in this day and age, it's hard for me to meet people as equals. There's always someone with a cell phone, asking for a photo, and that's nice but it's a distraction. It takes me out of the zone and destroys any chance of creativity. So I slip out on these little trips from time to time. I like to sit and watch the world pass by, and it does me the world of good. So when I called in at Embervale, it was purely out of interest. I meant no harm by it."

"Of course, you didn't," Naomi chipped in. "You don't have a mean bone in your body, John. You're a true gentleman." She aimed a look at Dan that seemed to say, *Unlike some people.*

"I suppose fame can be inconvenient," Dan said. "Having these secret projects must help to ease the burden."

Callaway looked bemused. "Why do I get the impression you're talking about something else?"

"I don't know. What do you think I might be referring to?"

"I've no idea. I've explained why I sometimes travel *incognito*, but I don't have any *secret projects*."

"You're not working on something with Benny?"

"Of course not." Callaway glanced at Benny. "Do you know what he's talking about, Benny?"

"No, sir," Benny replied. "Not an inkling."

"My apologies," Dan said. "I must've got my wires crossed."

"I expect so." Callaway clapped his hands together. "It's been nice talking with you, but I have a fine lunch waiting for me at home so, I'll say goodbye."

"Yes, I'd hate to keep you from your Sunday lunch," Dan replied. "It's been nice talking to you. Thank you for your time."

Callaway nodded, then he started to turn away.

"Good luck with your book," Dan added.

Callaway stopped in his tracks and looked back at him. "You know about that?"

"We've heard rumours," Dan replied.

"Where from? I don't think there's been anything in the press."

Dan wasn't sure how to reply, but Alan came to his rescue.

"Blame me," Alan said. "To some extent, we move in the same circles, Mr Callaway. I'm a writer too, and you know how it is: we writers like to talk among ourselves. Mostly it's gossip, but I do pick up the odd snippet of interesting news, like the fact that you're not using a ghost writer. That's a bold choice."

Callaway affected a modest expression. "It's always been a dream of mine to write, and this seemed like the perfect opportunity to fulfil my ambition."

"Good for you," Dan said. "I couldn't do it. I tried once, but I got hopelessly stuck halfway through chapter one. Does that happen to you? Do you get stuck at all?"

Callaway's modest smile slipped. "From time to time, but I work through it."

"That's the only way," Alan said. "I've never tried my hand at a memoir, but even so, when I'm writing my stories, memories come to the surface. I recall the good times as well as the bad, and sometimes those memories can be very vivid, painful even."

As Alan spoke, Callaway watched him intently as though taking in Alan's every word, but it seemed to Dan that Callaway's gaze had grown distant as if clouded by a memory of his own.

Making his voice gentle, Dan said, "Do you find it difficult to write about your daughter?"

Callaway's head snapped toward Dan, his expression utterly changed. "What kind of question is that? Mind your own business, why don't you?"

Dan raised his hands, his fingers spread wide. "I was simply asking if—"

"Well don't," Callaway snapped. He looked as though he was about to say more, but Benny interrupted him.

"It's time for us to go, sir."

"Yes, Benny, I believe you're right." Regaining his composure, Callaway added. "Mr Corrigan, Mr Hargreaves, goodbye. Enjoy the rest of your day."

"I didn't mean to cause offence," Dan replied. "Please, let's not part on these terms, especially given where we are."

Callaway's expression remained distinctly dour, so Dan quickly added, "I spoke out of turn, and I'd like the chance to apologise, if I may."

"Fine. Apology accepted. Now—"

"I really am sorry," Dan swept on. "My tongue ran away with me. I must've been star-struck. It's not often we get to meet our heroes, and it can be difficult to know what to say."

"That's understood, but I'm nobody's hero, Mr Corrigan. I'm just a guy who's been fortunate enough to have a job I love, and I've stuck at it for a long time. I do the work, and I like to think I've improved as the years have gone by, that's all."

"But you have a special talent," Dan insisted. "Even in your early films, your star quality shone through. You were amazing in Wild Yonder."

"Huh. Wild Yonder." Callaway looked thoughtful. Begrudgingly, he added, "It's odd you should mention it. It was a long time ago."

"Yes, but in some ways it's a classic," Dan said. "The piece still has something to say to us today."

"Does it? I don't think so." His mood lightening, Callaway waved his hand in front of his face as though wafting away a bad smell. "That movie was a stinker. Thankfully, almost everyone has forgotten it."

"Surely not," Alan said. "It was a fascinating drama."

"A flop is what it was. Oh, it played in all the art house theatres, and some of the critics raved about the lighting or the sound design. Heck, the colourist won some kind of award, but that movie was never going to make it into the mainstream. I'm not complaining. It paid the bills for a while, and when you're a young actor that's the best you can hope for, so it was all good."

"It was a remake wasn't it?" Dan asked.

"They called it a reimagining at the time, but there was a much earlier, and much better, version of the film. Vincent Price was the star."

"Yes, he said it started his career as an onscreen villain," Alan said.

"Did he? I did not know that." Callaway studied Alan as though reappraising him. "Of course, to get to the heart of the drama, you have to go back to the original material."

Alan nodded. "*Gaslight*. The play was a big hit in its day, wasn't it?"

"It certainly was, and with good reason. It was quite a piece of work. Genre-defining."

"It also gave us a word to describe a certain kind of behaviour," Dan put in.

"True, but I hate to see a piece of art hijacked in that way. That wasn't the playwright's intention. He wasn't a crusader; he was trying to entertain the audience, to give them a thrill, to show them something they hadn't seen before, and it worked. The play ran for years. It was a huge success. It's a shame I can't say the same about my awful movie, but that was never going to end well. The play relied on a very specific effect, dimming the lights on the stage as the gaslights went down. You needed a big, old gloomy house to get the atmosphere. You can't scoop the whole thing up and set it somewhere else. It doesn't work, as the producer of my movie found to his cost."

"There are no gaslights on a desert island," Alan suggested.

"Exactly. They tried to make do with weird noises from the jungle, but that didn't have the same impact. Have you ever seen the play performed?"

"I'm afraid not," Dan admitted. "I've never been much of a theatre goer."

"But there are plenty of beautiful theatres where you come from. You're from London, right? Somewhere north of the river."

The surprise must've shown on Dan's expression, because

Callaway laughed. "There's no need to look so surprised. I can hear it in your accent. I've been told I have a keen ear."

"Well, you're right," Dan replied. "I lived in London for most of my life."

"But you didn't go to the theatre? What were you doing that was so important you missed out on all those wonderful experiences?"

"Working."

Callaway nodded wisely. "I get it. You were one of those city types, dashing around, barking into your phone, getting irate if someone walks too slow on the sidewalk. Do I have it right?"

"More or less."

"I figured as much." Callaway was smiling now, pleased with himself as he went on. "So like me, you escaped to the countryside, and why not? It's a gentler pace of life out here. Still, it's a pity you never saw *Gaslight* for yourself. It's terrific. Let me set the scene for you." Callaway lowered his voice, and Dan found himself meeting the man's gaze, transfixed.

"You're sitting in the dark," Callaway went on, "and the only light is coming from the stage. A woman paces back and forth across a gloomy old-fashioned living room, distraught. You know she's scared, and you know something bad is going to happen. She says that when the gaslights go down, it means there's someone in the house, someone who shouldn't be there, but her husband tells her she's imagining the whole thing. But when she's all alone, the gaslights grow dimmer, and you're *there*. You're in that room, holding your breath, waiting, wondering what the hell's going on. Is someone in the house with her, or is she losing her mind? Let me tell you, when I saw it, there were times when a chill ran very slowly down the full length of my spine."

Callaway chuckled, and the spell was broken.

"You paint a very vivid picture," Dan said. "And in *Wild Yonder*, you played the husband who tormented his wife in that way. It must be hard to portray such evil without letting it get under your skin."

"Not really. Acting is my bread and butter. I'm a storyteller of a kind. I'm no more a villain than I am a cop or any of the other parts I've played. Now, you've expertly waylaid me once again. You did it with a certain charm, I'll give you that, but you've kept me talking long enough. No more, Mr Corrigan." Callaway smiled as he wagged a finger. "You know, I get the feeling there's more to you than meets the eye, but we really must be on our way."

"Yes, we should go now," Benny said to his boss. "Mrs Yates will be put out if we're late for lunch, and we have… an appointment this afternoon."

"True, true. You're right, Benny, we're behind schedule." Nodding politely to Dan and Alan, he added, "Gentlemen, it's been a pleasure."

"Thanks for taking the time to talk to us," Alan said. "It was kind of you."

"Not at all, Alan. It was good to meet you." Callaway shook hands with Alan before turning his attention to Dan. "Goodbye, Dan. Somehow, I don't expect we'll be seeing you again at our church, or any place else, so I'll wish you a good day, and may God bless you."

Dan acknowledged him with a nod, and this seemed to satisfy Callaway. The actor smiled before turning and walking away, Benny and Naomi by his side.

As Dan watched, Benny said something to Callaway, his voice low, but there was an edge of excitement in his tone. Dan couldn't quite make out his words, but he heard Callaway's reply.

Dan stood stock-still, staring after them.

"I wonder what they were talking about just then," Alan said. "Benny seemed very excited about something. It sounded very much as if he said, 'I can't believe it.'"

"Yes, I think you're right, but did you catch what Callaway said?"

Alan shook his head. "He was facing the wrong way. I missed it completely."

"I heard him," Dan replied." He said, 'We're going to get her. We're going to get her today.'"

CHAPTER 51

Like most of her CID colleagues, DS Kulkarni only worked at the weekends when absolutely necessary. Weekends were for relaxation, so she'd made herself comfortable on the sofa at home, wireless earbuds in place, listening to the meditation session playing on her phone. It was supposed to help her to unwind, to take her mind off her job. So why was she scrolling through her work emails?

In her earbuds, the man with a gentle voice said something about clouds drifting through an endless blue sky, but Kulkarni wasn't listening.

"Oh hell!" Kulkarni whispered. Why hadn't she seen this email before? True, it was buried among a slew of workaday messages, but even so, it ought to have grabbed her attention earlier.

She checked when it had been sent. Friday, 4:30pm. She'd still been at work at that time, but she'd been irked by her conversation with DS Simon Trevor, and she hadn't been able to face her inbox, opting instead for a quick drink with her Teignmouth colleagues.

And this was the result. A break in the case, and she'd missed it.

The email was from DC Pat Clarke, and it contained a list of ANPR hits for the missing VW van. DC Clarke was nothing if not efficient, and each row of tabulated text contained a location, along with a date and time, starting with the earliest.

Kulkarni scanned to the bottom of the list. The van's registration number had been picked up on Wednesday as it entered the Marsh Barton trading estate in Exeter, and then there was nothing, suggesting two possibilities. Either the van exited the trading estate via one of the smaller roads, avoiding any cameras, or it was still there.

If it was still in Marsh Barton, it might be hard to find. It could be hidden in a garage or outbuilding, or it might be tucked away in one of the many small side streets. She'd need to draft in a few uniformed officers from Exeter and have them scour the area. The search would have to wait until the following day, and it would take some time to organise, but it would be worthwhile if they found the van.

On the other hand, it was a Sunday, and the trading estate would be relatively quiet, with most of the business units closed for the weekend.

How long would it take her to drive to Marsh Barton? *Fifteen minutes*, Kulkarni decided. *Maybe less if there isn't much traffic.* But she shouldn't go on her own. It was a fool's errand, with too much ground to cover and little chance of success. She should wait until Monday and run it past DS Winslow in Teignmouth before liaising with Police HQ in Exeter. That was the way to get things done properly.

Kulkarni sat back, closing her eyes and tuning back in to the meditation session. As instructed, she took a long, slow breath, then she opened her eyes and yanked the earbuds from her ears. Jumping to her feet, she tossed the earbuds onto the sofa and shut down the meditation app.

Three minutes later, she was driving away, alert and energised, buoyed up by a new sense of purpose. *Meditation really works*, she thought. *All you have to do is ignore it.*

———

KULKARNI CHECKED THE REAR-VIEW MIRROR IN HER HONDA ACCORD and took the second exit at a mini roundabout, trying to recall whether she'd already been that way. Marsh Barton trading estate was a labyrinth of winding roads, the layout presumably chosen to bewilder the traveller and keep them driving around until they gave in and bought something.

Kulkarni noticed a street sign and realised she'd turned on to Trusham Road. Again. Still, she might have better luck this time.

She ran her eyes over the parked vehicles as she passed. There were vans by the score, but most of them were white, many of them emblazoned with the names of builders or decorators. No surprise there; this was the place to come if you wanted to buy power tools, building supplies or paint in commercial quantities. Kulkarni's gaze went to her wing mirror, drawn there by something moving fast. Cyclists, dozens of them, all clad in the same bright colours, their heads down and pedalling hard. These were no casual Sunday cyclists, but the members of a local club, out for a morning ride and all doing their best to keep up with the pack.

Kulkarni smiled to herself. That was the type of thing she ought to be doing, getting fresh air and exercise, though she preferred a nice long run rather than perching on a narrow saddle for hours at a time, and she had no intention of joining a club and wearing its colours. She'd said goodbye to her uniform years ago, and she had no desire to adopt another.

Still, give the cyclists their due, they were going for it, racing along under their own steam and getting fit into the bargain. Kulkarni pulled her car over to the side of the road and halted to let them pass. The cyclists whizzed past her car, a few riders acknowledging her with a nod, their streamlined helmets dipping, their eyes hidden behind futuristic mirrored sunglasses.

As the last cyclist raced away, Kulkarni looked to her right in readiness to pull out, and her gaze landed on the entrance to a narrow side street on the other side of the road. The side street was narrow and there was no sign to give it a name nor to indicate where it might lead. An anonymous road to nowhere, it looked little used, its tarmac rough around the edges and dotted with potholes. What better place to hide a vehicle?

Kulkarni waited for a gap in the traffic, then she pulled out, driving across the road and into the side street. She drove slowly, checking each parked vehicle and peering past metal fences to peek into neglected concrete forecourts. Nothing. The vans she spotted were white or silver or blue or red: every colour but black.

But then she caught sight of a dark outline. The van was partly hidden by a large pickup truck, but it was the right shape for VW T30 and it was definitely black.

Kulkarni halted her car alongside the van, blocking the road, then she jumped out, scarcely believing her eyes as she stared at the van's number plate. This was it. She'd done it. She'd actually found the very thing they'd been hoping to find for days.

Smiling, Kulkarni took out her phone and began making calls. A few minutes later she'd arranged for the van to be recovered. A team from Exeter would bring out a low-loader and shroud the van in plastic sheeting before taking it away to be examined. With a bit of luck, there'd be trace evidence aplenty, including DNA. If DNA from the van matched the body from Diamonds Avenue, it was a strong indication that the dead man was indeed Ryan Hallett. And if there were other DNA profiles present, and at least one of them scored a hit on the database, it might belong to the unknown man who drove the van away from Diamonds Avenue. They might at last be able to identify the slightly built man who'd disappeared after the fire.

It was a lot to hope for, and forensic tests took time to complete, but Kulkarni was feeling positive. Finally, this case was going somewhere, and she'd been the one to get it moving. Now all she could do was wait.

CHAPTER 52

Back at Zadie's house, Dan and Alan listened carefully as Natalya stood with a phone in her hand and read out the messages and voicemails that had appeared while they'd been at church. Connor, Melody and Naomi had all sent messages to Natalya, asking why their messages to Zadie had gone unread. And there was, at last, a message from Philippa.

"She says she is okay and has gone away for a few days," Natalya reported.

"That's a relief," Alan said. "It's one piece of good news, isn't it Dan?"

"Maybe." Dan was watching Natalya. At first, he'd found Natalya a little distant and hard to read, but the more time he'd spent in her company, the more he'd come to respect her judgement. Right now, unless he was mistaken, something was bothering her. There was the tiniest tightness around the corners of her eyes, and the suggestion of frown lines on her forehead.

"Natalya," Dan said, "is there something wrong?"

"Not really," Natalya replied. "Maybe something, but... I don't know.

"Was it something to do with Philippa's message?" Dan asked. "You didn't sound too sure about it."

Reluctantly, Natalya nodded. "I worked hard to learn English. There are rules, a lot of rules, and I think they are important, but most English people do not seem to know this."

"That's very true," Alan said. "I'm afraid that a lot of us are quite lazy with our grammar."

"But not Philippa," Natalya replied. "She is educated. She writes very well. Even in a text message, she uses commas, full stops. But this message is different. Here, let me show you."

Natalya passed her phone to Alan.

"Thank you." Alan scanned the screen. "I see what you mean. Listen to this, Dan. She says, 'Sorry not to be in touch,' then there's a broken heart emoji instead of a full stop. After that, she wrote, 'I'm all good,' followed by a smiley face, then she added, 'Have gone away for a few days,' and there's a string of kisses." He looked up at Dan. "There isn't a single full stop in the whole thing, and she's put an apostrophe before the s in days. That's certainly not right."

"It's interesting, but there could be a reasonable explanation," Dan said. "Philippa might've been overtired or she might have had a drink or two."

"Maybe you are right," Natalya said slowly. "Sometimes, Philippa likes to drink. No one else seems to notice, but I know when someone has been drinking vodka."

"I'd wondered about her drinking habits," Dan said. "I saw some spirits on her receipt, remember?"

Alan nodded, his expression sombre as he passed the phone back to Natalya.

"Let's see if we can find out where she is," Dan went on. "Natalya, can you call Philippa and see what you can find out?"

"Yes, but what should I say?"

"I'll leave that to you, but try not to sound too worried," Dan replied. "Keep it light, and ask her for some small details, such as what the weather is like where she is. If we can get her talking, we can get her to open up and she might tell us where she's gone and why."

Natalya placed a call and held her phone to her ear, but her frown deepened as she waited for a reply. She lowered her phone and said, "It's gone to voicemail. Shall I leave a message?"

Dan heard the anxiety in Natalya's tone and shook his head. "Could you send her a text message instead? Perhaps you could say that you hope she's having a good time, then you can ask if she's gone somewhere nice."

"Yes, I can do that." Natalya busied herself with the phone, concentrating as she composed a reply.

Dan thought for a moment. "It's interesting that *all* of Zadie's friends tried to get in touch with her this morning, even Naomi. We know Naomi attended the church service, but she still took the time to keep in touch with Zadie."

"They're all carrying on as normal, so they obviously don't know Zadie's in hospital," Alan said. "Is that enough to put them in the clear?"

"Not at all. We're dealing with someone devious enough to plan a subtle campaign against Zadie; they'd think nothing of sending a message to make themselves appear innocent."

"Good point, but I thought we were concentrating on Callaway now."

"Yes and no," Dan said. "He has a grudge against influencers, and he's displayed some distinctly odd behaviour, but I'm still not sure about him. He's a hard man to pin down."

"I know what you mean. When we talked outside the church, it was as if he was putting on a show, and I came away wondering what he's really like."

"He was playing the part of John Callaway, the Hollywood legend. It's a role he's created for himself and he wears it like a comfortable coat."

"So what do we do? How do we break through his defences?"

"I honestly don't know," Dan replied. "We're not going to get any further with him today, so there's no point in beating our heads against a wall. Something will come to me, but in the meantime, we have other matters we can attend to."

"Such as what?"

"For a start, I'm still concerned about Philippa. Let's go round to her house and see what we can find out. Even if there's no one home, we might be able to catch her lodger."

Alan nodded firmly, his mouth a grim line. "There's something about the mysterious lodger that I don't like the sound of. Although, if they've both disappeared at the same time…"

"You think they might've run off together?" Dan asked. "I doubt it. Philippa wouldn't do something so impulsive. She only met the man a few days ago."

"There's one way to find out," Alan said. "Shall we set off right away, or do you want to grab a coffee first?"

"Coffee can wait," Dan said. "We'll go now."

DAN RECALLED THE CODE TO UNLOCK THE GARDEN GATE BESIDE Philippa's house, and he wasted no time in letting himself in, Alan at his side. They marched across the lawn, and as they approached Keeper's Cottage, Dan caught a suggestion of movement behind a downstairs window: a shadowy figure darting out of sight.

"He's there," Dan said. "You take the front, I'll take the back." Dan made for the back of the cottage, breaking into a run and putting on a burst of speed. He rounded the corner just in time to see a man emerging from the back door.

"Hey," Dan called out, and the man turned with a start, his gaze sliding past Dan as though checking whether he'd come alone. The man didn't speak, but he looked to the garden wall, perhaps measuring his chances of reaching it before Dan could stop him.

Dan jogged to a halt, putting himself between the man and the wall. "You must be Mr Devlin. Jack Devlin, yes?"

The man nodded, his eyes beetling from side to side. "That's right."

"Great." Dan plastered a friendly smile onto his features. "I'm

Dan, a friend of Philippa's. We dropped in for a chat. It won't take long."

"We?"

"My friend, Alan, and me. He's around the front."

"Another time perhaps," Devlin said, "I'm heading into town."

"Shopping?" Dan asked.

Devlin nodded. "I'm going to pick up something to eat."

"It's Sunday. Most of the shops around here are closed."

"There's a convenience store. It's got the basics. There's not much choice but what can you do? It's a small town."

"It is, and country living can take some getting used to," Dan said. "Where's home?"

Before Devlin could reply, Alan's voice rang out: "No answer here. Any luck?"

"He's here," Dan called back. "Come and join us."

Alan jogged into view, his jaw set and his gaze fixed on Devlin. He joined Dan, and the pair of them faced Devlin as a unified front: friendly but barring his way.

"You were about to tell me where you live," Dan prompted.

"Yeah. Erm, Exeter. I go to the university."

"So you're a mature student," Alan said. "Student life must've changed since my day. I couldn't have afforded a cottage in the country when I was at uni, especially one like this. It must be expensive."

"I had some money from a relative, and I needed a break, so…"

"Lucky you," Dan said. "And you're here on your own?"

Devlin nodded.

"I expect you're used to a shared house or a flat," Dan went on.

"Yeah."

Dan raised an eyebrow. "Which is it, a flat or a house?"

"A flat. It's on the ground floor of an old house. It's small but there are only three of us, so, you know, it's okay."

"That sounds good," Alan said. "Whereabouts in Exeter is it?"

"Trusham Road."

Alan tilted his head as though thinking. "As it happens, I know Exeter pretty well, which is more than I can say for you."

"What?"

"If you knew Exeter at all, you'd know that Trusham Road is in the middle of a trading estate," Alan replied. "I doubt whether there are any flats there at all. Car dealerships, yes, and a few DIY outlets, but not much in the way of residential properties."

Devlin cracked a smile and held up his hands. "My fault. I should've said it's *just off* Trusham Road. The house is on a side street. It's a very small road, more of an alley really. You'd miss it if you didn't know it was there, so when people ask, I always say Trusham Road. It's easier than trying to explain."

"I see," Dan said. "Listen, I know you're headed out, but if you could spare us a few minutes of your time, we'd appreciate it."

"It depends. What do you want?"

"Nothing much," Dan replied. "We have a couple of questions we need to ask, that's all."

"Is that right? But you're not police, are you?"

Dan shook his head. "We're private investigators. You don't have to talk to us, but if you don't, we'll have no option but to call in the authorities."

"Why would you do that?" Devlin looked from Dan to Alan. "Is your friend okay? I mean, listen to him. *Call in the authorities?* Who does he think he is?"

"This isn't a joke," Alan replied. "We're serious, and we have excellent contacts with the police."

Devlin raised his hands in mock surrender. "Okay, okay. What do you want to know?"

"When did you arrive in Chagford?" Dan asked.

Devlin's gaze flicked momentarily to one side. "Wednesday."

"You don't seem sure," Alan said.

"I lose track of the days out here. I'm on holiday. My timetable is out the window. Whoosh! There it goes."

Devlin's gaze roamed skyward, but Dan kept his attention fixed firmly on the man. "How did you find this cottage?"

"The usual way. Online. Airbnb."

"Why Chagford?" Dan asked. "It's a bit out of the way, isn't it?"

"I wanted somewhere quiet. I'm working on my thesis. Sociology."

Dan suppressed a snort of disbelief. Devlin was like no academic he'd ever met, and what's more, he was a poor liar.

"A thesis," Dan said as if impressed. "A moment ago, you were here on holiday."

"Well, I meant a break—a break from the routine. No lectures, no timetables, no… seminars."

And now Dan knew. No student would have to search for the word 'seminar'. Devlin was up to no good; Dan had never been more sure of anything in his life.

Still wearing a smile, Dan said, "Do you drive, Mr Devlin?"

"Yeah, but my car's in the garage at the moment. It needs quite a bit of work."

"Oh dear. But if your car's out of action, how did you get here?"

"The bus. It was cheap, and it's environmentally friendly too."

"Very true," Alan said. "But it's inconvenient if you're carrying a lot of luggage."

"Yeah, but I travel light."

"Right." Dan tried to stop himself from reacting to Devlin's dismissive attitude, but it was getting harder as time went on. It was time for a change in pace. Squaring his shoulders and fixing Devlin with a stare, Dan said, "When did you last see Ms Darley-Jones?"

"Philippa? Erm, that would be yesterday, in the evening. I saw her through the window. She was in the garden. I waved, but I don't think she saw me."

"Why do you think that?"

"Isn't it obvious? She didn't wave back."

"She might've had reasons of her own for ignoring you," Dan said. "Do you know where she is now?"

Devlin's smug grin vanished. "What are you implying? I don't know why she'd ignore me, and I haven't got a clue where she is right now. Isn't she at home?"

Dan shook his head slowly. "Philippa hasn't been seen for several days."

"No, that's not right. I've just told you, I saw her yesterday."

"So you did," Dan stated.

Devlin's cheeks flushed. "Don't you believe me?"

"That depends," Dan said. "Is there anyone who can corroborate your story?"

"It's not a story, it's the truth," Devlin replied, his tone hardening as he went on. "And no, I'm here on my own, so of course there isn't anyone who can back me up."

"Okay, there's no need to get upset," Dan replied. "I have to ask these questions."

"Do you? Do you really?"

"If we seem brusque, it's with good reason," Alan said, his voice calm. "We're here because we're concerned for Philippa's safety."

Devlin raised a hand to his cheek as though he'd been slapped. "Philippa's all right, isn't she?"

"We don't know," Dan said. "We haven't been able to get in touch with her."

For a moment, no one spoke.

Devlin lowered his gaze, staring at the ground while he ran a hand across his face. When he looked up, he took a sharp breath, like a man trying to pull himself together. "Okay. First things first. Have you tried her phone?"

"Yes, several times," Dan replied. "We've had a text message, but Philippa hasn't responded to calls or messages. Do you have any idea why that might be?"

"No. I'm sorry but I can't help you. If Philippa's gone away, I didn't know anything about it. There's no reason she'd tell me. I've hardly seen Philippa since I got here. I'm just renting the cottage, that's all."

"Were you here yesterday morning?" Dan asked.

"Some of the time, but I went for a walk. Why?"

"I knocked on your door, but apparently, you weren't in."

"Like I said, I was out for a walk."

"Where did you go?" Alan asked.

"Nowhere much. I wandered into town, picked up a couple of things."

"But you still need to go shopping today," Dan said. "Why is that?"

"I've run out of milk."

"It's easily done," Alan said. "Do you always use the back door when you go out?"

"Sometimes. So what?"

"Come on, Jack," Dan said. "When I caught you just now, you were trying to run away from us. Why else would you slip out the back?"

"No particular reason. I went out by the nearest door. There's nothing wrong with that." Devlin made an attempt to stand taller. "I've answered your questions, but enough is enough. I don't know what you're trying to accuse me of, but I've done nothing wrong. Now, if it's all the same to you, I'm going into town, and since you say Philippa's not here, I think you'd better leave. You know where the gate is." Devlin hooked his thumb in the general direction of the garden.

Dan's only reply was a hard stare, but Alan nudged his arm and said, "Come on, Dan. I think we've seen enough."

"More than enough." Dan kept his gaze locked on the man in front of him. "It was nice to meet you, Mr Devlin. If I were you, I wouldn't stray too far. Unless Philippa turns up very soon, the police will need to talk to you, and if you run away, it will make you look guilty. Very guilty indeed."

"Guilty of what?"

"That remains to be seen," Dan said. "Goodbye, Mr Devlin. Until next time."

Dan's tread was heavy as he made his way back across the lawn with Alan. Devlin had guilt written all over him. He'd veered from smug to defensive and back again, but somehow, Dan had learned nothing much from all his questions. There was only one certainty in Dan's mind: Devlin was trouble.

As if chasing down the same train of thought, Alan said, "Shifty."

"Very," Dan replied.

"What do we do about it?"

Dan hesitated. "It's time to call an old friend."

"Do you mean Jay?" Alan asked. "I suppose he could follow Devlin, see where he goes."

"No. The situation has changed," Dan said. "I'm worried about Philippa, and we need to inform the police. It's time to talk to DI Spiller."

CHAPTER 53

Sitting on the sofa in his front room, DI Spiller put the phone down. "Blooming man," he muttered. Not the first time, he wondered at the gall of Dan Corrigan. The man had a nerve, that was for sure. Brass-necked, that was the only word for people like Corrigan. No shame, no embarrassment: he ploughed ahead and to hell with the consequences.

That's not how we do things, Spiller thought. *Not in this game.* Police work was all about consequences. Everything he did as a police officer left its mark, affecting the lives of others for good or ill. The majority of ordinary people lived their lives with a blithe disregard for the criminal activities happening around them. So long as they weren't affected, they didn't want to know. But when the forces of law and order came knocking on the door, innocence was stripped away, certainty replaced by doubt, security replaced by suspicion.

In his working life, Spiller had learned not to do anything lightly, and there was no way he could be impulsive, haring around the countryside on a whim.

He thought of Philippa Darley-Jones, recalling their brief meeting. He'd called at her house when he'd been doing the rounds, talking to everyone who might be involved in the Zadie

Barrington case. Philippa had been polite and cooperative, but he'd detected a certain frostiness in her manner. He'd put it down to her background; she'd introduced herself as The Honourable Philippa Darley-Jones. Her father, apparently, had been a baron.

Spiller had been unimpressed, and from that point on she'd kept their conversation formal, referring to him by his full rank at every opportunity. *Yes, Detective Inspector. No, Detective Inspector.* Looking back, he wondered if her condescending manner had been meant to discourage him from asking too many questions. Had she been using formality to erect a barrier between her and the lowly police officer? If so, why had she done that? What had she been trying to hide?

Spiller got to his feet and strode over to the window, looking out at the quiet street. Sunday afternoon and not a soul in sight. Earlier, people had been out in their gardens or walking their dogs. The man across the street, Ken Tanner, had washed his car, and it sat gleaming, surrounded by a patch of damp tarmac. Ken was retired. He'd been a firefighter once, but you wouldn't guess it when you looked at him now. Ken had lived across the road from Spiller for over a decade, and in that time he seemed to have shrunk. Ken was a decent bloke. He'd smile and nod if you passed by, but these days there was always that look on his face: a crestfallen expression of sadness, like a lost dog.

He's got nothing to do, Spiller decided. *No purpose in life.*

Spiller checked the time on his watch, then he went through to the hallway and stood at the foot of the stairs.

"Sheila," he called up. "Are you all right, love?"

"Yes," she replied. "I'm having a go at the bathroom, giving it a thorough clean."

"Well, don't overdo it, love. Do you want a cup of tea or anything?"

A pause and then Sheila appeared, peering down over the banister. "What's brought this on?"

"What? I was just offering you a cuppa. Got to look after you, haven't I?"

"I don't need mollycoddling. I can make a cup of tea."

"I know, but I thought it would be nice. You ought to put your feet up for five minutes."

Sheila smiled. "Go on then. A cup of tea would be lovely."

"Right. I'll make you one before I go out."

"Oh, I thought…" Sheila shook her head. "I should've known. It's work, isn't it? Have they called you on a Sunday *again?*"

"No, but there's something I need to check."

"Can't it wait until Monday?"

"I don't think so, love."

"Can't you send someone else? You're a DI now. You don't have to go traipsing around all over the place."

"I know, but this is complicated. It's not work, exactly. It's something I want to chase up."

Sheila sighed. "You won't be happy until you've done something about it. You may as well go."

"Thanks, love. I'll pop the kettle on."

"Don't bother. You get on. The sooner you go, the sooner you get back."

"You're the boss. I won't be long."

"Make sure you're not late," Sheila said. "You need *some* time off."

"Okay. If you like, I could pick up a takeaway on the way home."

"We'll see. It depends what time you roll back."

"I won't be late. We'll have a nice evening together."

"That would be nice."

They shared a smile, then Sheila said, "Go on then. Take care."

"I will. And you mustn't work too hard either. See you later." Spiller grabbed a coat and headed out.

As he drove, he made a hands-free call, and it was answered immediately. "Text me the address, Mr Corrigan. I'll meet you there in half an hour."

CHAPTER 54

D an walked to Philippa's house and found Spiller's Volvo saloon already parked in the driveway, the detective standing beside it, gazing up at the house.

"Thanks for coming," Dan said as he went to join the policeman.

"Just doing my job." Spiller watched him approach. "On your own, then?"

"Yes. Alan's staying over at Zadie Barrington's house."

"Right. Let's see what we can find out. I've tried the door already. No sign of anyone in."

"I'll show you how to get around to the back," Dan said. "It's through that gate."

"Go ahead."

Dan led the way, unlocking the gate and opening it.

"You know the code?" Spiller asked.

"I came over yesterday with one of Philippa's friends—Melody —she gave me the code."

"And you remembered it. Of course you did." Spiller paused. "This friend, Melody, she was the one who raised the alarm, yes?"

Dan nodded. "As I said on the phone, Melody is a close friend of Philippa's and she said it's very unusual for Philippa to be out of touch. According to Melody, Philippa is normally very good at

426

answering calls and messages, but that's changed suddenly. Apart from one strange text message, she hasn't replied to anyone. It's as if she's disappeared."

"That's why I'm here. Something about this is ringing alarm bells for me, but I don't know if we've got a good reason to report Philippa missing. I need to talk to the lodger." Spiller gestured to the garden. "The cottage is down there?"

"Yes. It's hidden by the trees, but I'll show you the way."

"Heck of a garden," Spiller observed as they followed the path to the cottage. "I've seen smaller parks. It must take a lot of upkeep."

"That might be part of the problem. I have a feeling that Philippa isn't as wealthy as she might appear, otherwise, why would she rent out her cottage?"

"Hard to say," Spiller replied. "Her idea of wealth might not match up to ours. As someone said to me recently, it's all relative."

"True." Dan hesitated. "Before we get to the house, I should tell you that when Alan and I came down, the guy renting the cottage, Jack Devlin, saw us coming and tried to make a run for it. I caught him sneaking out the back."

"Okay. Perhaps you could cover the back, and I'll try the front."

"Sure." Dan stopped walking and looked over his shoulder. "Did you hear that?"

Spiller nodded, then he said quietly, "The garden gate?"

"I think so," Dan whispered. "It might be Philippa, but somehow I don't think so. It's more likely that she'd go in through her own front door and out the back. Why would she go around the side?"

"Wait and see." Spiller tilted his head toward a shrubbery, and Dan understood. Moving silently, they crept close to the dense evergreen shrubs, mingling with the shadows.

A moment later, Jack Devlin walked into view, trudging along the path as though dog-tired, his head down. As he neared the cottage door, he took a keyring from his pocket and let out a heavy sigh.

Spiller sent Dan an inquiring look, and Dan nodded.

As Devlin fitted a key to the lock, Spiller strode from the shadows, Dan at his side.

"Hello," Spiller called out, and Devlin hissed a curse, his fingers still fumbling with the key.

"No need to panic," Spiller went on. "I'm Detective Inspector Spiller, Devon and Cornwall Police, and I'd like a word if I may."

Devlin stopped scrabbling at the lock and turned around, his back against the door. "Why? I haven't done anything wrong."

Dan and Spiller were close to him now, and Devlin's suspicious gaze settled on Dan. "What's he been telling you?"

"Shall we talk inside?" Spiller asked.

Devlin stayed stony-faced for a second then he said. "Sure. Why not?"

Devlin renewed his efforts with the lock, sliding the key out and trying again. This time, the lock turned easily. "There's a knack to it," Devlin muttered. "It drives me crazy."

Devlin stepped inside, holding the door open. "Come in, have a seat. Make yourselves at home, why don't you?"

"Thanks, but I'll stay standing," Spiller replied as he marched inside, and Dan followed, content to let Spiller handle things for a while.

The front door opened directly into a lounge, and Dan scanned the room quickly while Spiller made a more obvious show of looking around.

Spiller nodded in approval. "Nice place."

"Yeah." Devlin sat heavily on a sofa and regarded Spiller balefully. "So what can I do for you?"

"Just a few questions," Spiller said. "Have you been somewhere interesting?"

Devlin shook his head. "Stretching my legs."

"Anywhere in particular?"

Devlin pursed his lips then said, "Look, I guess this is about Philippa, so before you get started, I have no idea where she is. As a matter of fact, that's what I've been trying to find out. I went out to look for her."

"That's very public-spirited of you," Spiller said. "What made you do that?"

Devlin pointed at Dan. "Him. He came around, asking questions about Philippa, and he got me worried. He said her friends haven't seen her for a while. Is that right?"

"That's something we need to establish," Spiller said. "We'll check."

Dan's patience wore thin, and despite himself, he said, "Where exactly have you been looking?" Spiller looked annoyed at the interruption, but Dan pressed on. "How did you even know where to start?"

"There's a path on the other side of the garden wall," Devlin replied. "I went down there."

"Did you have reason to believe that Philippa had gone that way?" Spiller asked before Dan had a chance to speak.

"Yeah. I think that's where Philippa was headed when I last saw her. That was on Saturday." Devlin hooked a thumb over his shoulder. "There's a door in the wall, but there's a padlock and I don't have the key."

"Is it locked now?" Dan asked.

Devlin nodded, then his brow wrinkled as though a thought had struck him. "Oh, it's locked from the inside, so she must've come back without me seeing her."

"Unless someone else locked the gate," Dan said. "Someone who knew about the padlock; someone who was covering his tracks."

Spiller made a non-committal noise in his throat. "Let's not jump to conclusions." Focusing on Devlin, he said, "If the door's locked, how did you get to the path?"

"It's easy enough to pick it up from the road if you know where to look. There's no sign or anything, just a gap between the bushes, but it's right next to the front garden."

"Where does this path lead?" Spiller asked.

"Through the woods and toward the river. I went quite a way along it, but there are loads of little paths branching all over the place, so I don't know, maybe I went the wrong way." Devlin lowered his gaze and shook his head as if admonishing himself. In a quiet voice, he added, "There was no sign of her anywhere." He looked up, his eyes moist. "I tried. I really tried. But..."

For a moment, the room was silent, then Spiller said, "Mr Devlin, I'm going to take a few details. Okay?"

"Sure. Whatever. If there's anything I can do to help, I'll do it."

"That's good to hear." Spiller took out his phone and asked Devlin a series of brusque questions, entering the answers into his phone.

Dan fought the urge to take out his own phone and record the information himself; there was no sense in putting Spiller's nose any further out of joint. Instead, he committed Devlin's address and phone number to memory.

It struck Dan that Devlin had given his address in Exeter promptly and without preamble, which was very different to his manner earlier in the day. In fact, he answered all Spiller's questions smoothly and without hesitation, almost as if his answers had been rehearsed.

Devlin didn't seem the type to be awed by authority figures, so there had to be some other reason for his sudden change in attitude.

He's polished up his act, Dan decided. *I wonder if he's been interviewed by the police before.*

There were many questions Dan wanted to ask, but to his surprise, Spiller said, "Right, that's it for now, Mr Devlin. Thank you for your time."

"What about—" Dan began, but Spiller cut him off.

"We've got what we came for, Mr Corrigan. Time to go."

Dan heard the warning in Spiller's tone, and he nodded. "Okay. Fine. Thanks, Mr Devlin."

Devlin stood, seeming a little shaky on his feet. Wringing his hands together, he said, "What are you going to do? Will you send out a search party? If you do, I could help."

"All in good time, Mr Devlin," Spiller said. "We haven't quite reached that stage yet. In a case like this, family and friends are the first port of call, then we'll decide if we're dealing with a missing person. With a bit of luck, we'll find Philippa visiting someone she knows, but you can leave it with us. There's no need to worry yourself."

"Okay. Okay. But please, if you find her, will you let me know? It would put my mind at rest."

"Of course, sir." Spiller said gently. "I'll give you a call, but it'll probably be tomorrow, okay?"

Devlin nodded gratefully. "Great. Fingers crossed, eh?"

"Yes. The best thing at the moment is for you to get some rest. You look worn out." To Dan, Spiller added, "Come along, Mr Corrigan. We'll leave Mr Devlin in peace."

"Sure."

Outside, Spiller's smile disappeared in an instant, and he set off at a brisk pace.

When Dan fell in beside him, Spiller said, "I'm glad you called me, Mr Corrigan, but you've done your part now. I'll make sure this is followed up."

"You think something's happened to Philippa?"

"Let's say I have cause for concern. What I want from you is very simple. I need contact details for Philippa's family and friends, as many as you can provide."

"No problem. Will you check up on Devlin?"

"Oh yes. You can be sure of that."

"And you meant what you said about setting up a search party?"

Spiller grimaced as if irked by the question. "I'm a policeman; I don't say things for effect."

"Of course. Sorry."

They walked in silence for a second.

"Thank you for coming, by the way," Dan said. "It's a weight off my mind, knowing that you're on the case."

"That's all right." A pause, and then Spiller added, "You did the right thing, calling me. If you'd rung the station, I doubt whether anyone would've come out until tomorrow, and that wouldn't have done at all. Between you and me, I have a horrible feeling that I'm coming to this too late."

MONDAY

CHAPTER 55

"Come here!" Benny shouted, then he turned around on the spot, staring between the trees. It was early, the dew still clinging to the undergrowth, and the damp had seeped in through Benny's dark trousers where he'd brushed against the bracken.

"Where the hell is she hiding?" he muttered. "For God's sake."

There. The crackle of dead twigs snapping underfoot, a frond of bracken swaying. Benny fixed his eyes on the place.

"Come on, you silly girl. Come out. I know you're hiding in there."

Benny waited. "This isn't a game. I'm getting angry."

A rustle of dry leaves, then the bracken parted and she blundered out, racing toward him, tongue hanging out, ears erect.

"For goodness' sake, Lucy," Benny muttered, though he couldn't keep the fondness from his voice. "What am I going to do with you?"

Lucy bumbled up to him and leaned against his leg, looking up at him adoringly with her big brown eyes. A long-coated German shepherd and not quite a year old, Lucy still carried the remnants of puppyish charm. Her coat was fluffy, her dark ears looked a little too large for her head, and her snout was shorter than it would become when she was more mature.

Benny ought to be cross with her for taking so long to come back, but he couldn't do it. Instead, he clipped the lead onto her collar and stroked the top of her head before rubbing her ears.

Really, he shouldn't have let her off in the woods. It was far too soon. They'd only picked her up the previous afternoon, and he'd barely begun to train her. Lucy certainly hadn't had the chance to get used to her new life, her new surroundings. But she'd been so keen to explore the woods, her nose working overtime to sniff the air, and he hadn't had the heart to keep her on the lead.

"Next time, I'll bring a couple of treats with me," Benny said. "You'd come back for a biscuit, wouldn't you, girl?"

At the word 'biscuit' Lucy licked her lips and stared at him with renewed intensity.

"No, I haven't got anything for you." Benny held out his hand, his palm open, and Lucy sniffed it briefly before resuming her stare.

"Nope. Nothing. You can have a treat when we get home. Come on, I'll take you down to the river. You liked it down there yesterday, didn't you?"

Lucy huffed as if disappointed, but as soon as Benny stepped forward, she fell into step beside him.

"Good girl," Benny said absentmindedly, heading for the path that led down to the river.

As they walked together, Benny breathed deep, savouring the fresh scent of damp earth and that unidentifiable aroma that somehow smelled green. Lucy would know precisely where the smell came from; she had levels of sensory perception that Benny could only guess at. And she was smart as a whip, there was no doubt about that.

The dog had been his idea. He'd wanted one for years, and it hadn't been hard to convince Mr Callaway. With the recent troubles at Zadie's house, getting a dog had been a sensible precaution, and yes, as it happened, Benny had seen the perfect animal. Mind you, he'd spent long enough poring over The Dog's Trust website; it had been almost like an addiction.

The Dog's Trust looked after unwanted dogs, and they ran a dogs' home near Exeter. As chance would have it, they had a female German Shepherd in need of a caring owner: someone who could provide all the time and attention this highly intelligent animal needed in order to thrive.

One look at the website had been enough to sway John Callaway. A visit to the dog's home had been arranged, and John and the dog had taken to each other from the outset. The charity's staff had clearly been bowled over by Mr Callaway's easy-going charm, and the wheels of the adoption process had rolled swiftly into motion.

There were times, it seemed, that having a famous film star as an employer brought particular privileges, especially when that employer owned a very large, enclosed garden and a country estate.

The dog's name was Loki, but Mr Callaway hadn't been impressed by that. For a start, Loki was a male character, and for another thing, the name suggested that mischief might be allowed or even encouraged, and that wouldn't do.

Benny had suggested Diana, named after the huntress, but Mr Callaway had laughed aloud at that idea. No, it was to be Lucy and that was that. The name was near enough to Loki that the dog might adjust quickly, but Mr Callaway had privately admitted to having a different reason. When his daughter, Adriana, had been a little girl, she'd invented an imaginary dog and named it Lucy. She'd bought a collar with a name tag, and even kept a bowl of water on the floor, the name written on the side.

Whatever the reason, Benny grudgingly admitted that the name suited Lucy down to the ground.

The only fly in the ointment was that Will Saunders was by no means a dog person. So what? Saunders didn't like anything much. Besides, it turned out that the feeling was mutual. When Saunders had arrived for work that morning, Lucy had jumped to her feet and padded toward him, following his every move with her gaze. And when Saunders had stood close to John, Lucy had advanced on him, a low and distinctly disapproving growl building in her throat.

Not that Lucy was aggressive. She was cautious, that was all, and she knew how to pick a side. A word from Callaway or Benny would silence Lucy immediately, but when Saunders had tried to pat her, she'd seen him off with a barrage of warning barks. As far as Lucy was concerned, Saunders didn't belong. He was not one of the pack and he was not to be trusted.

"You're smarter than most people, aren't you girl?" Benny said, and Lucy looked up at him, bright-eyed.

They neared the river, and Benny prepared to hold Lucy back. The day before, she'd taken her first look at the river and tried to charge full tilt into the water, almost dragging Benny with her. She was surprisingly strong, but today, there was no lunge forward; quite the reverse. Lucy stopped sharply, digging her paws into the soft earth, and Benny was forced to a sudden halt as the lead reached its limit.

"Lucy, what are you doing?"

Lucy lowered her head and stared into the distance. Benny tried to follow her gaze, but he could see nothing.

"What is it, did you see a squirrel or something? Because you'll have to get used to—"

Lucy's loud bark cut him short. It was a warning, and Benny scanned the forest. Was someone out there?

Lucy pawed the ground, her front legs stiff. Her head was even lower now, and a huff turned into a plaintive whine. Something had spooked her, but she'd never make a guard dog if she lost her nerve at the slightest hint of danger.

Benny stood close to her, his hand on her head. "It's okay, Lucy. I'm with you. It's all right."

Lucy barked again, but she didn't back away. "Come on," Benny said. "Let's go and see what's bothering you."

Benny made to move onward, patting the side of his leg and saying, "Heel."

After a moment's hesitation, Lucy did as she was told. "Good girl," Benny said. "You'll see, there's nothing to worry about."

Lucy trotted beside him, but she still held her head low and her gaze was fixed on the path.

"Here we are," Benny said. "Maybe you could try a swim in the —" But it was Benny's turn to stop short.

They'd arrived at the place where the river widened to form a pool, the water almost still and its surface smooth. And there, floating close to the opposite bank, was the body of a woman, face-down and fully clothed, her long coat rippling gently in an unseen current.

Lucy began to howl and whine, the sound shaking Benny to the core.

"Shush," he murmured. "Lucy, shush." He wrapped her lead around the nearest spindly tree, forming a clumsy knot with shaking fingers, then he stripped off his jacket as quickly as he could.

Every instinct told him the woman was dead, but he had to get her out of the water. His training kicked in and he knew what to do. Even if he was too late, he had to try.

CHAPTER 56

D I Spiller and DC Collins made their way along the path
through the woods. Spiller was in no mood for talking,
and thankfully, Collins seemed to understand this
without being told. Spiller had only been assigned to this case after
a prolonged discussion with DCI Montague. She'd wanted to give
the job to someone else, but Spiller had insisted that he was better
suited. He was already working a case in Chagford, so he knew the
area, and it made no sense to have two separate teams trailing back
and forth to the same small town. Eventually, Montague had given
in, but their encounter still rankled. *I shouldn't let it get to me*, Spiller
told himself. *The DCI means well.* Still, he didn't need anyone's
sympathy. Yes, Sheila needed a little help while she recovered from
her stroke, but she was determined not to give in. She wanted life
to carry on as usual, and that meant Spiller had to go out and do his
job. Besides, he wasn't ready for retirement yet, and this case was
his chance to prove it. He was raring to go.

As if picking up on his boss's determination, Collins said,
"We're almost there, guv. Time to get stuck in."

Spiller nodded. He could hear the quiet bustle of activity ahead,
and the first band of crime scene tape came into view: the outer

cordon. Beyond it, there was another band of tape, and within that, a white and yellow forensic tent.

Collins gave their details to the uniformed officer controlling access to the scene. A fresh-faced young man, the constable was all bright-eyed enthusiasm as he noted down their names. "You're clear to go through to the inner cordon, sir," he said. "The SOCOs have done what they can out here."

Spiller thanked the constable, then he ducked under the tape, Collins following behind. Together, they approached the cluster of white-suited SOCOs, all of them working at their tasks with an industrious solemnity. Nicola Haig, one of their best Crime Scene Managers, came to meet Spiller and Collins at the inner cordon.

Pulling down her face mask, Nicola wasted little time on greetings before launching into her report. "The victim is female, and she had plenty of ID in the pocket of her jeans: driving licence, credit cards and an ID card from the University of Exeter. The photo on her licence matches well with her appearance, and it's in the name of Philippa Darley-Jones."

Spiller sighed. "I've met her. We talked not long ago, in relation to another case not far from here. Harassment, possibly stalking. Ms Darley-Jones was a friend of the victim."

"A possible connection?" Collins said.

"That remains to be seen," Spiller replied. "I tried to call on Ms Darley-Jones just yesterday. I'd been told she'd gone missing, and I knew something wasn't right. What are we looking at?"

"I'll take you through what we've found," Nicola said. "The deceased's hands were tied behind her back. The rope was still around her wrists. It's a synthetic rope, blue, not what I'd call heavy duty. It could be polypropylene, but we'll check that later. If it is, it's unfortunately very common."

Spiller nodded. "Somebody wasn't taking any chances. Was she tied up and then put in the water, or is it too early to tell?"

"First indications are that she drowned, but we'll know more after the post-mortem examination. There are some marks around her throat that I need to look at more closely."

"Rope marks?" Spiller asked.

Nicola shook her head. "They weren't made by any kind of narrow ligature. They look more like friction burns, so they could've been made by a piece of fabric or an article of clothing that had been pulled tight around her throat. Whatever it was, we haven't found it yet, but we'll keep looking. I'll let you know if we find anything."

"Thanks," Spiller said. "Any other signs of violence?

"There are abrasions on her knuckles, especially on her right hand, as though she put up a fight. Apart from that, she has no obvious injuries, but she's fully clothed, so I won't speculate on that."

Collins cleared his throat. "Is there any evidence of a sexual motive?"

"I've seen nothing to suggest that, but at this stage I can't rule it out."

"Okay." Spiller stared down at the slow-moving pool of cold, clear water, its mirror-like surface reflecting the lush green canopy of leaves overhead. Drowning: he had a horror of it, but he couldn't let that show, especially not in front of Collins.

"We've not had much luck with footprints," Nicola went on. "The undergrowth makes it hard, and the ground was churned up before we even got here, but we'll persevere. We'll do our best."

"I know you will," Spiller said. "Was there anything missing, anything we might expect to see?"

"Yes, her phone. It might turn up, but it certainly wasn't in her pockets. Also, we haven't come across any cash, although that's not unusual these days. And we haven't found a bag."

Spiller cocked an eyebrow. Nicola had placed an odd emphasis on her last sentence, and he knew there was more to tell. "Go on."

"Well, it's not my job to come up with theories, but she seems like the kind of person who'd carry a handbag. Her clothes have designer labels, her nails were manicured, and her shoes are interesting: leather loafers made by a brand called Toteme. Quite expensive. I'd guess that a woman who wears kitten heels for a walk in the woods carries a bag everywhere she goes."

"It's something to bear in mind," Spiller said. "Is there anything else I should know?"

"No, that's it for now. I'll get a preliminary report to you as soon as I can."

"Thanks, Nicola. I'll let you get back to work."

"No rest for the wicked." Nicola pulled her mask back into place and picked her way carefully across the crime scene, being careful to step on the small metal platforms that had been laid down for the SOCOs to walk on.

"Right, Collins," Spiller said. "There's a lot to do. For a start, I'd like to find the deceased's bag, if she had one, and her phone as well."

"I'll organise a search of the surrounding area," Collins replied. "I'll get on it right away."

Spiller cast him a sharp look, and Collins added, "If that's all right with you, guv."

"It's more than all right, Collins. I wasn't going to complain. It's good to see you so keen."

"It's an interesting case, guv, and like you say, it could tie in with your stalking case. Both victims live in the same small town, they're both female, and they knew each other. The cases could be linked."

"The thought had occurred to me, Collins, but we'll reserve judgment for now. Later on, you can hop over to Zadie Barrington's house and see what you can find out."

"I thought she was in hospital."

"She is, but you might find her PA there, and she's worth talking to. Natalya Rudenko. She's one of those people who always seem to know what's going on. Find out when she last saw the deceased and ask about any recent changes in Philippa's behaviour. Was Philippa worried about anything or nervous? Did she say anything about being followed or harassed? And don't forget to check if there were any disagreements among Philippa's friends or associates. Someone came prepared with a rope, and that means premeditation. It might also mean someone held a grudge, the tension building up over time. Maybe Philippa had split up with a partner or had an unhappy relationship. You know the drill, Collins. Chances are, Philippa was killed by someone she knew."

"Maybe she was killed by Zadie Barrington's stalker. He couldn't get to Zadie because she was in hospital, so he picked another target, choosing one of her friends so it would hurt Zadie indirectly. At the same time, his behaviour escalated from harassment to murder."

"It's one thing to be keen, Collins, but it's another to go chasing your own tail. We'll stick to the here and now, and we'll follow procedure. I'll set up a team and get the door-to-door inquiries underway. Meanwhile, we'll focus on victimology. When we know how she lived, we might be able to figure out why she died. I'll get hold of the deceased's phone records and financials, and we'll need to search her house too. There are lots of boxes to tick, lots of calls to make, and lots of people to see, including the Chief Superintendent."

"You're going back to the nick, then?"

"Yes. Believe me, I'd rather be down here, knocking on doors, but unless I go back and set the wheels in motion, we won't get anywhere."

"Fair enough. I can go over to Zadie Barrington's house now if you like."

"Later, Collins. Your first job today is to pick someone up and persuade them, as nicely as possible, to come in for an interview."

Collins perked up. "Who?"

"Philippa Darley-Jones had a paying guest: a man renting the cottage at the back of her house. Name of Jack Devlin. I spoke to him yesterday, and I wasn't convinced by what he had to say."

"Do you think he might've seen something or is he a suspect?"

"He's a general suspect, but don't let him know that. Not yet.

Persuade him to come in as a potential witness, and we'll take it from there."

"No problem, guv," Collins said. "I'll go and get him now."

CHAPTER 57

DS Winslow looked up as Kulkarni took her usual seat in Teignmouth's CID office. "New blouse?" Winslow asked.

"Yes. It's River Island, but I got it at a charity shop."

"Why not? I'm more of an Asos girl, myself. Order it online, next day delivery, and if you don't like it, you can send it back. I haven't got time to go trailing around the shops."

Kulkarni studied Winslow's expression. "You're doing this deliberately, aren't you?"

"Doing what, Anisha? I don't know what you mean."

"Yes you do. You're not mentioning the fact that I found the van. I thought congratulations might be in order."

"Well, you did okay on that score, but a little bird tells me you had the ANPR report before close of play on Friday, so we could've sent a team over to Marsh Barton before the weekend."

"Okay, I'll hold my hands up to that. I didn't see the email, and with one thing and another, it fell through the cracks."

"So that's why you decided to deal with it on your own at the weekend," Winslow suggested.

Kulkarni nodded. "It was the least I could do."

"That's fair enough, I suppose. Anyway, it all worked out in the end. For what it's worth, what happened on Friday wasn't all on you. Ordinarily, Pat would've passed the info on herself and made sure you saw it, but she had to dash off early. Her eldest boy came a cropper playing rugby after school."

"Is he all right?"

"Nothing broken, but he injured his knee. He'll mend." Winslow paused. "Pat feels pretty bad about the whole thing."

"I'll talk to her later. It wasn't Pat's fault. I'm usually on top of my emails, but on Friday…"

"Something on your mind?"

"You could say that." Kulkarni hesitated before going on. "I called Plymouth CID to ask about Dave Whitehead, and I was brushed off in no uncertain terms. I spoke to a DS, and I did not like the way he talked to me at all. I can take a few knocks, and I can stand up for myself, but somehow, this guy got under my skin. At the time, I thought it was the usual sexist nonsense, but now I wonder if there was something else going on."

Winslow's expression grew instantly more sombre. "You think he was being racist?"

"No, that's not it."

"What then?"

Kulkarni took a moment to choose the right words. "I believe he was being deliberately obstructive. He could easily have helped, but he refused. He was holding something back."

"That's odd. I know a couple of people over there. I can make some calls if you like."

"Thanks, but I've already left a message for DI Blakey. We've worked together before, and I think he'll get back to me and straighten it out."

Winslow nodded. "I know Russ. He's all right. He'll help if he can."

"I hope so."

"In the meantime, I've got something that'll cheer you up." Winslow sat back in her chair, a smug grin on her face.

"What?"

"Harry Whelan told you that Ryan Hallett uses a gym. It's about time we followed that up."

"I've already tried. I've called every local gym I could find. No one had him listed."

"That's because there are gyms and there are gyms. I know one in town that isn't in the phone book. Do you fancy a trip out there? I happen to know they open early."

"Sure. I'm ready when you are."

WINSLOW PARKED IN AN ALLEY THAT BOASTED NO NAME, RAMPING TWO wheels of her VW Touareg onto the pavement to allow other vehicles to pass. Not that the prospect of incoming traffic seemed likely to Kulkarni as she climbed from the car.

The road was lined on both sides by what had once been small industrial buildings of some kind. Now, the doors were secured by steel shutters that seemed destined never to reopen, and in many of the windows the broken panes behind the iron bars had been shored up from the inside by sheets of wood.

Winslow joined her in the road. "What do you think to the neighbourhood?"

"I think it's a shame. What was down here?"

"Small businesses, mainly to do with the fishing industry, but that's all had the bottom knocked out of it. Whatever you do, when you're talking to the locals, don't mention the EU or fishing quotas. It never ends well."

"Noted," Kulkarni said. "But is there really a gym down here?"

"Yes, for the time being anyway. The word is, all this is going to be knocked down to make room for retirement flats. Just what we need." Winslow inclined her head toward a squat windowless building. "Come on, I'll introduce you to Mickey."

Kulkarni followed Winslow to the steel reinforced door, surprised to see her colleague turning the handle and marching in without so much as knocking.

447

Inside, the wide space was well lit by overhead fluorescent tubes, the glare of the lights contrasting with the black painted concrete floor. Pride of place had been given to a boxing ring, its canvas currently unoccupied. The only customers were two men, stocky and clad in vests and shorts, both knocking seven bells out of punching bags and oblivious to the new arrivals.

Kulkarni gazed around in wonder. It was as if she'd slipped into an alternate reality, a world away from the genteel shops and cafes of the seafront. Here, the scents were not of sea air and freshly fried fish, but body odour and stale sweat.

"All right, Winslow."

Kulkarni turned to see a man in a wheelchair emerging from a partitioned area in the corner. With close-cropped hair and a muscular upper body, the man had the look of a prize fighter, and he propelled himself toward them at speed.

"All right, Mickey," Winslow said. "This is my colleague, DS Kulkarni. We popped in for a chat."

Mickey halted in front of them, his eyes fiercely bright as he gazed at Kulkarni. "Always a pleasure." He smiled, and it transformed his features, taking him from rough to ruggedly handsome. "Are you new to the patch, Detective Sergeant?"

"I'm here temporarily," Kulkarni replied. Finding it hard to maintain eye contact with the man, she looked around the room. "This is quite a place you have here."

Mickey followed her gaze. "It's not bad. We get by, but we can always use a few new members if you're interested. I'm happy to charge a special rate for key workers such as yourself."

"Thanks, but it's not really my thing," Kulkarni said. "I run and lift a few weights, but that's about all I've got time for."

"We've got weights. Dumbbells, barbells, kettlebells, you name it. And you wouldn't be the only woman. We have quite a few female members, especially for the kickboxing. You ought to give it a try. We can do a couple of sessions for free."

Kulkarni smiled. "You're an excellent salesman, but I'll have to say no."

"Pity. Still, you'll bear it in mind, won't you? I know you will. Once you've been to my gym, nothing else matches up."

"Once seen, never forgotten," Winslow said.

"Absolutely." Mickey turned his intense gaze on Winslow. "Anyway, you're not here for a chat about the old days, so what can I do for you?"

"We're trying to trace a man called Ryan Hallett," Kulkarni said.

Mickey affected a nonchalant shrug.

"Does the name ring a bell?" Kulkarni went on.

"That depends. I don't give out personal details about our members."

"So Ryan was a member?"

"Ah, you're not going to catch me out as easily as that. But why do you say '*was*'?"

"We don't give out details of an active investigation," Kulkarni countered. "Do you know Ryan Hallett or not?"

"You're hard work, aren't you?" Mickey looked to Winslow. "Is she always like this?"

"Come on, Mickey, you know the drill," Winslow replied. "We've got a job to do, and it'll make life easier if you can help us out."

"I know, and I'll do my best, but first, you've got to tell me one thing. Is Ryan all right or has something happened to him?"

"A man matching his description was found dead recently," Winslow said. "We have reason to believe that the man was murdered, but we haven't been able to confirm his identity."

"Bloody hell." Mickey hung his head and exhaled loudly. When he looked up, some of the light had gone from his eyes. "Yeah, Ryan was a member. Maybe he still is, if this bloke turns out to be someone else. But the thing is, Ryan was always a regular. He came most days, but I haven't seen him for a while. I thought he was working, but now…"

"Do you know where he works?" Kulkarni asked.

"Not really. I know he drives a van, and sometimes he's away for days at a time, but he never said who he works for. All I know is, he's got a girlfriend. He talked about her sometimes. Sandra, I think her name was."

"We'll need to talk to her," Winslow said. "Do you know if they lived together?"

"I think so. I'll fetch Ryan's address. It should be in the office."

Mickey turned his wheelchair around, and Kulkarni made to follow, but Winslow laid a hand on her arm to stop her. "Give him some space."

"What if he calls someone?" Kulkarni asked. "What if he tells Ryan's partner we're on our way?"

"Mickey wouldn't do that. I've known him for years, and he might look a little rough around the edges, but he's straight as a die. Trust me."

"Okay." In the brief silence that followed, Kulkarni noticed that the gym's customers were taking a break, both men loitering at the far end of the room where metal lockers stood against the wall. The men were watching the proceedings while swigging from large plastic bottles.

Kulkarni lowered her voice and said, "Ryan was a regular, so those two might've known him. It could be worth asking them a few questions."

Winslow glanced at the men but shook her head. "They won't give us the time of day. Besides, Mickey won't like it if we start annoying the members. He's going to give us the best lead we've had. The last thing we want is to turn him against us."

"Good point. I was wondering, was Mickey one of us?"

"No. I can't see him taking orders from anyone." Winslow smiled as if entertaining the absurd notion of Mickey in uniform. "He was in sales, actually, but he had an accident in a warehouse. A load fell from a fork-lift truck and put him in a wheelchair. He used the compensation to pay for this place."

"Oh. So when I said he was a good salesman, it was a bit tactless."

"Don't worry about it," Winslow said. "Mickey's got broad

shoulders, and anyway, he is good at selling stuff. I suppose he might have to go back to it if all this gets knocked down."

"That would be a shame."

"It would."

Kulkarni watched as Mickey emerged from his office and sped toward them. His wheelchair was more sophisticated than she'd first realised, its wheels set at an angle and its lightweight frame seeming stripped down and built for speed.

"Admiring the wheels?" Mickey said as he halted in front of her.

"Yes," Kulkarni admitted. "It's quite a piece of engineering."

"You've got a good eye. It's custom made. Although this isn't the one I use for matches. That's even better."

"Mickey goes in for wheelchair basketball," Winslow explained. "He's a star player for the Exeter Otters."

"You should come and see us play," Mickey said. "You'd enjoy it."

"I might do that."

Mickey produced a folded piece of paper from the breast pocket of his shirt and held it out to Kulkarni. "My number's on there."

Kulkarni took the paper and found it was a flier for Knight's Gym, the name apparently taken from Mickey's own. "Thank you, Mr Knight." Flipping the paper over, she saw an address written out in neat capitals. "Is this Ryan's address or yours?"

"Ryan's, of course." Mickey puffed out his chest in indignation. "I don't go around giving my address to every woman I meet, you know. I'm not that kind of bloke." With a disarming smile, he added, "That can come later, when we've been out a few times."

Kulkarni couldn't help but smile. "You're quite the gentleman."

"Okay, you two, that's enough of that," Winslow said. "Mickey, thanks for your help. I appreciate it, but we'd better get going. We've got a visit to make."

Mickey's smile disappeared. "Listen, joking aside, I hope Ryan's all right. Can you let me know?"

Winslow nodded. "I'll give you a call, Mickey."

"Thanks."

Kulkarni and Winslow took their leave and headed back to the car.

"The address is fourteen Portland Road," Kulkarni said. "Do you know it?"

"Yeah, we can be there in ten minutes. Are you good to go?"

"Sure. Let's get it done."

To Kulkarni, the drive to Portland Road took no time at all. Mentally preparing for a meeting with Ryan's partner, she barely registered the succession of terraced houses as Winslow wove a path through a rabbit warren of residential streets.

"Here we are," Winslow said, pulling the car into a space at the side of the road. "Number fourteen is over there."

"I see it."

They made their way to the house and Winslow rang the bell. While they waited, Kulkarni stood back and looked around. The house was small and nondescript, but it seemed as though someone cared for it. There were net curtains in the windows, and small potted conifers beside the door. The small front garden had been replaced with pale gravel except for the footpath, which was built from brick pavers laid in a herringbone pattern.

Neat and clean, it was the kind of house you could find in any suburban setting, and it had been home to Ryan Hallett. But the news they brought was about to disrupt all that.

Kulkarni saw someone approaching through the door's partially obscured window, and she steeled herself, adopting what she hoped was an expression of sympathy.

The door was opened by a woman in her thirties, smartly dressed. She was wearing a coat, and she eyed them cautiously, a slightly harried expression on her face. "Yes? Can I help you?"

Winslow identified herself and introduced Kulkarni, causing a flicker of concern to pass over the woman's face.

"What's this about?" she asked. "Only, I'm on my way to work."

"We're looking for Ryan Hallett," Kulkarni explained. "Is this his house?"

"Why?"

Winslow's voice was heavy as she said, "I think it would be better if we talked inside."

The woman shook her head. "I told you, I'm on my way out. Whatever it is, it'll have to wait. Ryan isn't here. He's out on a job, and I don't know when he'll be back."

"I'm sorry, but it can't wait," Winslow replied. "Are you Sandra?"

The woman's nervous gaze went from Winslow to Kulkarni, and her face fell. Kulkarni had seen the same thing happen on far too many occasions. People knew when bad news might be on its way, and they went into a strange, trance-like state, their brains shutting down as they braced themselves for the worst.

"What's happened?" the woman murmured. "Is he all right?"

"That's what we're trying to establish." Winslow said. "Before we go on, can you confirm that you're Sandra, Ryan's partner?"

"Yes, I'm Sandra. I live with Ryan. Is he…?"

"Let's pop inside, Sandra," Kulkarni said. "Will that be okay?"

Sandra nodded, then she took them into a tidy front room.

"Let's sit down for a minute," Winslow said, and Sandra perched on the edge of an armchair, her coat still on.

Winslow and Kulkarni took the two-seater sofa, and Kulkarni tried to keep her posture upright even though she was sinking into the soft sofa cushions.

"Okay, Sandra, what's your full name?" Winslow asked.

"Why?"

"It's just a formality," Kulkarni replied. "You're not in any trouble."

"What if I don't want to give it?" Sandra said. "I don't have to talk to you if I don't want to, do I?"

Winslow sent her a thin-lipped smile. "No, you don't have to say anything, Sandra, but remember, it's Ryan we're interested in, not you."

"Well, I can't help you there. I haven't seen him since last Tuesday. He left for work early."

"So almost a week ago," Kulkarni said. "Is it unusual for him to be away so long?"

"Not really. Sometimes he goes away for a week or so. He's a delivery driver. He goes all over, but…"

"But he usually tells you when he'll be away," Winslow suggested.

"Yeah, but not this time. I suppose he must be busy."

"Have you had any contact with him since last Tuesday?" Kulkarni asked. "Any calls or messages?"

"No. I tried ringing him a few times, but he didn't pick up. I thought…" Sandra's voice trailed away. "Something's happened to him, hasn't it? Has he been in an accident?"

Kulkarni leaned forward. "Sandra, we don't yet know whether Ryan was involved, but there has been an incident, and we're trying to find him so that we can eliminate him from our enquiries."

"I don't understand," Sandra said. "What do you mean, *an incident*?"

"Ryan drove a black VW van, didn't he?" Winslow said.

"Yes, I think so. It was black anyway."

"Okay. Does he have access to another vehicle?" Kulkarni asked.

"He has a Ford Focus. It's parked outside. He bought my Astra for me, so it's in his name, but he never drives it."

Kulkarni took out her phone and made a note. "Do you know the registration numbers?"

Sandra shook her head. "Sorry. My mind's gone blank."

"We'll check them later," Kulkarni said. "How about Ryan's phone number. You must know that."

"Yeah, no." Sandra looked bewildered for a moment. "I mean, I don't know it off by heart. It's in my contacts." She stood shakily. "My phone's in my bag. It's by the front door."

"That's okay," Winslow said. "We'll wait."

454

Sandra left the room, and Winslow turned to Kulkarni. "Keep an eye on her."

"Is that necessary? She seems very—"

Kulkarni's sentence was cut short by the sound of the front door closing.

"Hell!" Kulkarni jumped to her feet and dashed out the room, Winslow right behind her. The hallway was empty.

They ran outside, looking up and down the road, but Sandra was nowhere to be seen. A little way down the street, an engine revved and a silver hatchback pulled out and drove away.

Kulkarni stepped out into the road. The car was a Vauxhall Astra, and Kulkarni just had time to get the number before it sped out of sight. Tapping the details into her phone, she heard Winslow cursing under her breath.

Kulkarni looked up. "I'm sorry. I should've reacted quicker."

"Well, I did tell you to keep an eye on her, Anisha." Winslow heaved a sigh of frustration. With some effort, she added, "Never mind. These things happen."

"I misread her completely," Kulkarni said. "I really thought she was distraught. She seemed so upset."

"I had the feeling she wasn't as innocent as she made out. My guess is that whatever Ryan was up to, she was part of it, otherwise, why run?"

"She knew bad news was coming, and she couldn't face it. Grief can do strange things to people."

"Maybe, but we hadn't even told her about the body." Winslow shook her head. "No, I reckon Sandra saw the writing on the wall. She must've known we'd turn up on her doorstep one day, and she'd already decided what to do."

"We can track her down," Kulkarni said. "I got the car's registration. We'll find her on ANPR."

"We can try, but she'll probably ditch it, then she'll go to ground."

"I'll find her. In the meantime, we could take a look around the house. She invited us in."

Winslow looked doubtful. "It's a grey area. We know nothing about Sandra, and as for Ryan, we don't know for sure it was his body in Diamonds Avenue. Until we get the forensic report on the van, we're fishing in the dark."

"There'll be plenty of trace evidence in the house, and that ought to be enough to identify the body."

"Yeah, but let's do it properly and get a team in. We'll run it past the DI and get him to authorise it. We need to tread carefully. After all, as far as we know, neither Sandra nor Ryan have committed a crime."

"I'll put in a request when we get back," Kulkarni said. "The sooner we can get a search organised, the better."

"Agreed. I'll leave it with you, but make sure you dot the i's and cross the t's. Tom's a good DI, but he can be a stickler."

"Oh, I'm used to that," Kulkarni said. "If I can get along with DI Spiller, I can deal with anyone."

They talked little on the drive back to the station. Kulkarni had let a potential witness slip through their fingers, and they both knew it. She'd questioned the decision of a more experienced colleague, and her lapse of judgment would cost the inquiry in terms of time and energy. She'd have to do better, and she'd begin by making up for her mistake.

CHAPTER 58

Dan was brewing a cafetière of coffee in Zadie's kitchen when someone knocked on the back door. "Come in," Dan called out, and the door opened slowly as if pushed by a cautious hand.

Shaun stood on the threshold, wiping his hands on a scrap of rag. "Oh. I saw the light and thought maybe it was…"

"Ms Barrington?"

Shaun nodded.

"She's busy at the moment, up in the studio."

"No, she isn't. I've just been up on the scaffold, and I saw she wasn't there."

"She's probably in another room. Perhaps I can help," Dan said.

"Thanks, but I'd better talk to her direct."

"Come in and we'll work something out. Can I offer you a cup of coffee?"

Shaun brightened, and he stuffed the rag in the pocket of his overalls. "Maybe just a quick one, if it's no trouble."

"No problem at all."

Shaun stepped inside and closed the door behind him.

"Milk and sugar?" Dan asked.

"Yes please."

"I'll see what I can find."

Dan located a carton of oat milk in the fridge and decided that Shaun wouldn't know the difference once the sugar had been added. He found some demerara sugar in a cabinet, the packet pushed to the back of the shelf like a guilty secret, half hidden by bags of dried lentils and pulses.

"I just need another mug," Dan muttered as he hunted through the cabinets.

"They're in that one."

Dan turned to see Shaun pointing at a cabinet on the far wall.

"Top shelf," Shaun added.

"Thanks." Dan closed the cabinet door and moved to the one Shaun had indicated. Sure enough, Shaun was right about the mugs. How had he known such a thing?

While Dan prepared their drinks, he kept half an eye on Shaun, but the man stood still, his expression blank but his body language tense.

"There you go." Dan passed Shaun a mug of coffee, noting a slight tremble in the man's fingers as he gratefully accepted it.

"Thanks." Shaun took a slurp and smacked his lips, seeming to relax a little. "That's all right, that is."

"Good. Now, what did you want to talk to Zadie about?"

"Well, I found something up on the scaffolding, and I think it's hers."

Dan's breath seemed stuck in his chest, and he forced himself to let it go. "It's not a phone, is it?"

"Yeah, it is." Shaun fumbled in a pocket and produced a phone, wiping the screen with his sleeve. "It got a bit damp. I don't know if it still works."

Dan held out his hand. "Please, don't wipe it any more. Just pass it to me."

"All right." Looking slightly affronted, Shaun handed the phone to Dan.

"Where was it?" Dan asked.

"At the end of the scaffolding by the gate. Up on the top. It was just sitting there. I almost stepped on it."

"Thank goodness you didn't." Dan tried to activate the phone, but it was dead. That was no surprise; it had been left outside for the whole weekend. Looking up, he said, "You can leave this with me, Shaun. I'll see that Zadie gets it."

"All right. I suppose I'd better get back to work then."

Dan set the phone down on the counter and studied Shaun. The man was definitely on edge but why? Something wasn't quite right. It wasn't just the fact that Shaun had known where the mugs were kept. There was something else, but what was it?

"Stay a while," Dan said. "At least finish your coffee."

"All right. Thanks."

While Shaun was occupied with his drink, Dan's gaze roamed around the kitchen, instinctively seeking out an answer.

And there it was. Hanging from a wooden rail by the kitchen sink was a hand towel, the lime green fabric adding a splash of colour to the largely monochromatic kitchen.

"Can I ask you something, Shaun?" Dan said. "How did you know where the mugs are kept?"

"I dunno. I didn't think about it. I suppose someone must've given me a drink before."

"But you recently said that no one ever offers you anything. You told me that you have to bring your own flask of tea for that very reason."

"Well…"

"You also said that Zadie and Natalya don't like you coming inside."

"They don't, as a rule."

"Is that what's making you nervous?"

"What are you talking about? I'm not nervous." Shaun attempted a light-hearted chuckle, but it was far from convincing. As if anxious to get away, he drained his mug and set it on the counter. "Anyway, thanks for the drink. I'll get back to work."

"In a minute. I have to ask you a couple of questions."

Shaun's good humour evaporated. "I haven't got time to stand around chatting."

"This is important. That rag you were cleaning your hands on when you came in, where did you get it?"

"I brought it from home. I've got a bag stuffed full of old rags."

"Really?" Dan marched over to the sink and plucked the towel from its rail. While he searched for its label, he said, "Where do you buy your towels, Shaun?"

"My wife takes care of all that."

"And where does Mrs Brown usually do her shopping?"

Shaun's expression became more guarded. "The usual supermarkets. Asda. Tesco."

Finding the label at last, Dan smiled. "This one is from John Lewis. Does Mrs Brown get her towels there?"

"No. That place is for people with more money than sense."

"Not necessarily," Dan replied. "They have some nice things. This towel, for example, is Egyptian cotton, and it's good quality, isn't it? It'll last for years."

Shaun screwed up his face. "What are you on about? What's a towel got to do with anything?"

"I'll tell you. This towel is a distinctive colour. As a decorator, I expect you're pretty good with colours, aren't you?" Dan waited, but when Shaun didn't reply, he added, "Could you show me that rag in your pocket?"

"What for? It's just an old rag."

"Then you won't mind showing it to me."

"I haven't got time for all this," Shaun growled. "I'm going back to work."

Shaun made for the door, but Dan moved quickly and stood in his way. "You'd better wait. I need to see that rag and then I need to look inside your van."

Shaun stared at him. "Why?"

"I'm almost certain there'll be some evidence in there; something to link you with the threats that have been made against Zadie."

"Where's all this coming from? I've never heard such a load of old rubbish in my life. You're just making stuff up as you go along.

"No, I'm deadly serious, but we can clear this up right now. All it'll take is a quick check of your van. That shouldn't be a problem, should it? Not unless you have something to hide."

"There's nothing in my van that shouldn't be there, but you'll have to take my word for it. That van is how I make my living. It's not for people to go poking around in."

Dan made a show of looking thoughtful. "That's an interesting choice of words: *Nothing in my van that shouldn't be there*. It all comes down to your opinion, doesn't it? So what *should* be inside your van, Shaun?"

"It's obvious. Tools, brushes, rollers, paint, that sort of thing."

"What about a notebook, one with lined pages?"

"I haven't got one," Shaun stated. "I put everything in my phone these days."

"But you used to have a notebook?"

A spark of indignation flashed in Shaun's eyes. "Why are you asking all these daft questions? What difference does it make one way or another whether I had a bloody notebook or not?"

"No need to get angry, Shaun."

"I'm not. I'm not bloody angry, but I'm not stupid neither. You're accusing me and I don't like it." Shaun took a few steps toward Dan, pointing. "You've no business talking to me like this, do you hear me? No business at all."

Dan locked eyes with the man. Shaun was losing control, teetering on the edge of a full-blown outburst. A swift change in tack would catch him off guard, push him into making a mistake.

"Why did you do it?" Dan demanded. "Why did you frighten Zadie out of her wits? Did you want her to climb out the window? Did you want her to fall to her death?"

Shaun came to a sudden halt, his face blanching before Dan's eyes. His lips moved but no sound escaped.

"Were you trying to kill her?" Dan went on. "Did you want her dead?"

461

"Dead?" Shaun whispered. "She's not..." He gazed at Dan in bewilderment. "I don't understand. You said she was upstairs."

"Zadie is in hospital, seriously ill, but then you knew that, didn't you? You left her for dead."

"No. I didn't. I swear." Shaun's eyes seemed to lose focus, and he swayed on his feet, reaching a hand to the kitchen counter as if seeking support. "I can't believe this."

Dan watched him carefully. Shaun didn't look like a man who was ready to confess, but neither was he protesting his innocence. Instead, he seemed genuinely stunned. It was time to push him further.

"Shaun, I know how it started. You saw Zadie getting changed while she was filming one day, and you became obsessed with her, so much so that you came into the house one evening when Zadie was out. That's right, isn't it, Shaun? That's what happened."

Shaun lowered his gaze and made grumbling noises in his throat as if arguing with himself, until finally, a murmur escaped from his lips: "It wasn't like that."

"Then you'd better tell me what it *was* like."

"I don't know." Shaun looked up at Dan. "Did you mean what you said, about Zadie being in hospital?"

"Absolutely. She's unconscious, but when she comes around, she'll be able to tell us what happened, so I suggest that you stick to the truth."

Shaun breathed heavily for a moment, his face ashen.

"Sit down," Dan said, pushing a stool toward him, and shakily, Shaun sat down, his breath still ragged.

Dan fetched him a glass of water and placed it in his hand. "Drink this. Take your time."

Shaun took a swift gulp of water, then he heaved a wretched sigh, defeat etched in the lines on his face. "What started it all was those bloody cigarettes. If I hadn't found them..."

"You found a packet of cigarettes? Where?"

"It wasn't a packet; they were in a little tin. It was on the drive, sort of under the hedge. I spotted it, so I picked it up and had a look inside. And there they were: a few little cigarettes already rolled. And I was tempted. It had been a long day."

"So you smoked them, presumably in the garden."

"No, that weren't me. When you asked me about it, I might've made out like I don't smoke. I didn't like to admit it on account of how Miss Barrington doesn't like it, but it wasn't true. I've had a smoke around here, right enough, but I wasn't lying about those fag ends you found in the garden. That was nothing to do with me."

Dan wanted to argue, to scold Shaun for daring to persist in this fiction, but something stopped him. He could see no logical reason for Shaun to lie about where he'd smoked a cigarette, so he gestured for him to go on.

"I never went down the garden," Shaun said. "But I did take one out of that tin, and I smoked it. Not right away, though. That was later."

"Tell me what happened."

"I'll try." Shaun took a deep breath. "I was sitting in my van, and I only smoked one cigarette. It made me a bit light-headed. I thought it was because I'm not used to smoking roll-ups. I felt a bit odd, truth be told, and I wondered afterward if there wasn't something funny in it. If I'd known at the time, I wouldn't have touched it. I've never had anything to do with drugs. Never."

"Do you still have the tin?"

Shaun shook his head firmly. "I threw it away. Lobbed it in the wheelie bin back at my place."

"Might the tin still be there?"

"No, the bin men came the other day. It'll have gone to the tip."

"That's a damned shame," Dan said. "How many cigarettes were left?"

"Two. There were three to start with, and like I said, I only had one."

Dan thought for a moment. Shaun seemed in earnest, but he could be making this up as he went along, and with no evidence to back it up, Shaun's story might be just that: a fiction from start to finish.

"What did the tin look like?" Dan asked. "Can you describe it to me?"

"The bottom part was plain metal, sort of silvery, but the top was dark orange—that's how come I spotted it—and it had a sort of symbol on it. It was black, but I don't know what it meant."

"Was it a logo?"

"Maybe, but it didn't mean anything to me. It was just a circle with two triangles in it, one on top of the other."

"Let's put that to one side for now. When did you smoke the cigarette and where were you?"

"I'm not sure when exactly." Shaun's gaze flicked away for a second. "I didn't look at the time."

"Shaun, you came back here a little over a week ago, didn't you? You came here on a Sunday evening."

"I hadn't planned to, but I'd left something behind. My power supply was up on the scaffold, and I needed it at home. When I realised what I'd done, I had to come back and get it. They're not cheap."

"But you didn't realise you'd left it until the Sunday?"

"I didn't need it until then."

"Okay. So you drove to Chagford. When did you arrive?"

Shaun pushed out his lower lip. "It was late afternoon by the time I got here."

"But you didn't park on Zadie's drive, did you? Nobody reported seeing your van."

"That's because I didn't want to bother anybody. I parked in that little lay-by down the road and walked along. But… I don't know. When I got to the gate, I couldn't face going in. I saw their cars parked up front, so I knew they were home. They were bound to collar me, and I'd have to explain why I was there. If I do anything wrong, that Natalya woman gets cross, and Zadie gets all uppity. I didn't want them going on at me, so I went back to the van for a bit. I thought they'd go out sooner or later, and while I was waiting, I remembered that tin, and I thought, sod it, and I lit up."

"Was there a lighter in the tin?"

Shaun nodded. "One of those plastic ones. Disposable."

"Okay. Then what happened?"

"I finished that cigarette, and after a while, I saw them drive out the gate. Natalya was driving and her ladyship was in the passenger seat. Anyway, they came past and Zadie was staring out the car window, but she didn't see me. She looked straight through me, like I was invisible. I think that's what gave me the idea."

"It was you who came into the house that evening, wasn't it?"

Shaun ran his tongue over his lips. "Yes."

"Zadie didn't go out until the evening, so you must've been sitting in your van for quite a long time."

"Happen I dozed off a bit, but I was wide awake when they drove past. I saw them clear as day."

"So you walked back here once the coast was clear, but your power supply was on the scaffold, so you could've fetched it without coming inside. Why did you break into the house?"

"I didn't break in, as such. When I was up on the scaffold, I saw they'd left a window open. I was feeling all fuzzy headed and I had a powerful thirst, so I went in through the window and popped downstairs to get a drink from the kitchen."

Dan nodded, picturing the scene. "You came in here and you went through the cupboards until you found a glass; that's how you knew where the mugs were. You had a drink and washed up your glass, then you left it on the draining board."

"I meant to put it back in the cupboard, but I must've forgotten."

"What else did you do?"

Shaun looked blank. "Nothing. Nothing really."

"Come on, Shaun. You took the towel."

"Oh, that. Yeah. Erm, I was hot, so I splashed some water on my face, and I must've been dusty from all the work I'd been doing at home. The towel got all mucky, so I took it with me. I was going to put it in the machine and bring it back all clean, but on the Monday, it all kicked off. Zadie called the police, and you turned up. I didn't know what to do."

"So you destroyed the evidence," Dan said. "You panicked and you tore the towel into rags."

"I'd have thrown it away, but it seemed a shame to waste it."

"Indeed. Did you take anything else?"

"No. Although…" Shaun sighed. "I was powerful hungry, see, and when I first came here, Zadie gave me a fancy snack bar from the drawer, so I knew where they were. Anyway, I helped myself, but I only took the one."

"Even so, that's a poor way to repay her generosity."

"I know. It wasn't right, and I felt bad afterwards, especially about taking the towel. I'm not a thief. I was going to knock a few quid off the bill to make up for it."

"Maybe you didn't take anything else, but you were tempted, weren't you? Zadie said that some of her clothes had been moved. Was that you?"

Shaun bowed his head and there was the suggestion of a nod.

So that was it. Shaun had fetishised Zadie's clothes, wanting to touch them, to paw them with his grubby fingers. Now he was full of remorse, but his shame didn't make up for the trouble he'd caused. And there was more to tell. They hadn't yet dealt with the threatening notes and the campaign of harassment that had driven Zadie to risk her own life.

"What else did you do?" Dan demanded.

"Nothing. I went home, kicking myself all the way. I couldn't believe what I'd done, but I thought maybe nobody would know. I'd forgotten about that glass, and I shouldn't have gone out the back door. I couldn't lock up because they never gave me a key, so I should've gone out the way I came in, but I was all jittery, and I had to get away. I wasn't thinking."

Dan let the silence hang in the air.

Shaun sniffed, utterly dejected, and when he put the glass of water down, he almost missed the counter's edge, saving it just in time, water splashing onto the worktop.

"What about the note?" Dan asked. "Where does that fit in?"

"I don't know, but I didn't write it. I don't know where it came from."

"Do you expect me to believe that? Does it seem likely there were two intruders wandering around Zadie's house on the same evening?"

"I didn't see anyone. Someone must've come around after Zadie left, while I was still in the van."

"No. You came to the house as soon as you saw Zadie and Natalya driving away. Why don't you just admit that you wrote the note? You've told me everything else."

"I'm not lying, really I'm not," Shaun protested. "I never wrote that note. I just moved it."

Dan stared at him. "You did what?"

"While I was washing up that glass, I heard the letterbox, so I went to look. There was a bit of paper on the floor by the front door, so I picked it up."

"Did you see who left it? Did you hear anything, a voice or a car?"

"No, but I didn't go looking. I stayed away from the windows. I just took the paper upstairs and put it on the desk where I thought someone would notice it. I didn't mean any harm by it."

A cold anger stirred in Dan's stomach. "Have you any idea of the trouble you've caused? Why the hell didn't you tell me all this in the first place?"

Shaun ran his hand over the side of his face. "You didn't ask."

"That's not good enough. You knew damned well that Zadie was frightened when she found that note."

"Not at first. I knew something was going on, but it never occurred to me it was about that bit of paper. I thought…"

"You thought it was about the fact that you sneaked in through the window," Dan said.

Shaun offered a feeble nod.

"You do know that the police have the note, don't you?" Dan said. "Detective Inspector Spiller is not going to be pleased when he finds out you've lied and withheld important evidence."

"But I didn't mean for all this to happen."

"That's beside the point, Shaun. You're going to be in trouble over this. The best thing you could do is to tell the police what you've just told me. If you come forward voluntarily, they might go easy on you. I can't guarantee it, but it's your best chance."

"They won't arrest me, will they?"

"I don't know, but they'll need to interview you and get everything on the record. After that, I really can't say what they'll do. They've got bigger things to deal with right now, so you might be lucky and get away with a warning."

Shaun hung his head, staring unfocussed at the floor.

"If you don't call the police, I will," Dan said.

"All right. I'll do it. I've got the number. He gave me his card."

"You'd better do it now, and don't think I won't check. I know DI Spiller, so you'd better give him the full story."

"I will." Shaun looked up at Dan, his eyes moist. "You'll have to tell Zadie, I suppose. You'll have to tell her what I did."

Dan waited a moment, letting the man squirm. Despite his remorseful expression, Shaun hadn't been totally honest. His story about forgetting an expensive power supply didn't ring true. Shaun might not be the fastest worker in the world, but he was the kind of tradesman who looked after his tools. Certainly, Dan hadn't seen so much as a paintbrush out of place on the scaffold or in Zadie's house. The conclusion was clear: Shaun had come back to the house for reasons of his own, reasons that he refused to admit.

There may have been mitigating circumstances. The cigarettes Shaun had found might have contained a drug, and that could've spurred him on, but there was no evidence to back that up, only Shaun's claim that he'd felt light-headed.

I'd like to get my hands on that cigarette tin, Dan thought, but it was no use wishing for the impossible. Here and now, he had to face one key question: was Shaun dangerous?

It's a moot point, Dan decided. *He can't be trusted.*

"I'll have to tell Zadie what you did," Dan said. "Even if the police let you go, we can't have you anywhere near this house. Is that clear?"

"Yes. I'll collect my tools and go. I'll be as quick as I can."

"That's for the best."

Shaun made for the door, but a nagging thought made Dan call out to him. "Before you go, there's one thing I need you to do."

"What's that?"

"The logo on the cigarette tin, could you draw it for me?"

"I don't know. I suppose, I could have a go."

"Hang on." Dan hunted in his pockets and found a scrap of paper, holding it out to Shaun.

Shaun took the paper and produced a pencil from a pocket on his overalls. He placed the paper on the worktop, then he made a few pencil strokes before sliding the paper back toward Dan. "There. It's the best I can do."

"Thanks." Dan took the paper, his gaze fixed on the hurried drawing. Without looking up, he added, "You'd better go and make that call now, Shaun. Talk to the police and get it over with."

"All right." Shaun hesitated. "Is it important, what I drew? Does it help?"

"Oh yes. It helps a great deal."

Shaun's expression brightened a little. "What does it mean?"

"It means, Shaun, that there's someone I need to take a good look at, and the sooner the better."

CHAPTER 59

D an was sitting on the large sofa in Zadie's lounge while Alan sat at the smaller one, Zadie's laptop balanced on his knees. Connected to the laptop by a white lead was Zadie's phone.

"Any luck yet?" Dan asked.

Alan glanced at the phone. "It's charging, but we shouldn't be doing this. DI Spiller specifically told us not to touch it."

"It's a bit late for that. Now that Shaun's had his grubby hands all over it, there's not much chance of retrieving any fingerprints. Besides, it was still where Zadie left it. If the culprit had seen it, he would've taken it. He certainly wouldn't have touched it and then left it lying around."

"Even so, we ought to call Spiller and tell him we've found it."

"All in good time," Dan said. "The police are already looking at Zadie's phone records. I'd like to take a quick peek before we hand it over. I expect Natalya will have the PIN."

"We'll ask her later," Alan said. "If she agrees, Natalya ought to be the one who reads any messages. We don't have the right."

"Okay."

Alan blinked. "That's it? No arguments?"

"No, I happen to think you're right," Dan said. "Anyway, we

have plenty to be getting on with. I'd like you to have another look at Connor Griffiths."

"I didn't get very far last time. Is there something specific you want me to search for?"

"Not at the moment. I'd rather give you a free hand and let you follow your instincts."

Alan looked unimpressed. "My instincts say it'll be a waste of time. Why the sudden interest in Connor?"

"It was something Shaun said to me, but it'll take a while to explain."

"Go ahead. I can listen while I type." Alan focussed on the laptop, tapping away on the keyboard while Dan relayed his conversation with Shaun. Dan paid particular attention to the sequence of events leading up to Shaun creeping into the house uninvited.

Alan tutted a few times, but otherwise listened without comment until they came to the moving of the note.

"Oh no," Alan said. "That makes a mess of everything, doesn't it? If it just came through the letterbox, the message isn't threatening at all."

"I agree, but that first note was just the start. Think about the second note that came with a knife. And what caused Zadie to climb out the window?"

Alan massaged his temple as though warding off a headache. "I'll leave the theorising to you. I'll stick to what I'm good at."

Alan resumed typing. "What has all this got to do with Connor?"

"It all comes back to those cigarettes," Dan said, but Alan wasn't listening.

Alan's hands had frozen over the keyboard, and he was staring at the screen. "Oh my God." He turned to Dan, his face pale.

Dan sat up straight. "What is it?"

"I went to the BBC news site, looking for old stories about Connor, but..." Alan glanced back at the screen. "It's Philippa. She's dead. She was found in the river."

"No."

"It's true. They're treating her death as suspicious."

Dan jumped to his feet and crossed the room to sit at Alan's side. Both men stared at the screen in silence. Philippa's body had been found by a dog walker not far from her home. An ambulance had been called, but Philippa had been pronounced dead at the scene. An investigation was underway.

"This is terrible," Alan muttered. "I can't believe it."

Dan said nothing. He'd been worried when Philippa had apparently gone missing, but this… This changed everything.

"What do we do?" Alan went on. "They're appealing for information. It says that anyone who's seen Philippa recently should come forward. Do we call in? We might be able to help."

"I've already talked to DI Spiller and told him everything we know, and he has my number. I'm just sorry I didn't call him earlier. Maybe he could've found Philippa before it was too late."

"It's no use thinking like that. We couldn't have known this would happen."

"Couldn't we? We knew Philippa was upset about something, and neither of us trusted Jack Devlin, but what did we do about it?"

"You called the police," Alan said. "What else could you have done?"

"I don't know, but I was too slow to catch on. Spiller knew that. He said he was coming to this too late, and he was right."

"We're only human, and we've had other things to deal with. Zadie was our priority."

"Yes, but we're taking too long to find the culprit," Dan said. "What if Philippa was killed by the same person? If we'd caught him earlier, Philippa might still be alive."

Alan started to say something, but Dan didn't give him the chance. Standing up, he said, "I'm sorry, Alan, but I've got to get out of here for a while. I need to think. I need to move. Do you want to come?"

"I'd better stay here. Someone has to tell Natalya about

Philippa, so it may as well be me. I'll break it to her gently, but she's bound to be upset. I don't want to leave her on her own."

"You're right. You'll handle the situation better than I would, so I'll go, but I won't be long." Dan headed for the door. "I'll see you later."

Alan said something in reply, but Dan didn't hear properly. He was already walking quickly, making for the stairs and the outside world. Dan's brain was buzzing, clouded by conflicting emotions, and he needed to get it clear. He needed movement, the faster the better. If he'd been at home, he'd have gone for a run, but the best he could manage for the moment was a brisk walk.

Dan marched toward the town, his head down and his senses shuttered from the world around him. His footsteps fell into a regular rhythm, and he allowed his thoughts to flow where they may, waiting for fresh connections to emerge from the chaos.

He heard nothing, saw nothing. Until it was almost too late.

A huge white shape swerved silently across the road, heading straight for him. The car was travelling fast, and Dan jumped back, pressing himself against the wall of a house, every nerve firing as his body prepared for action. The car ramped one wheel onto the pavement, skidding to a halt, and Dan recognised the Mercedes-Benz SUV: Callaway's car.

The driver's door opened and Benny emerged, scowling as he advanced on Dan. "Stay there, Corrigan. I want a word with you."

Dan pushed himself away from the wall, squaring his shoulders. "Go ahead."

"Not out here. Get in the car."

"No thanks, I'm fine where I am." Dan tilted his head to see into the car's backseat but there was no one there. "On your own today?"

"We don't need anyone else. I want you all to myself. Now, do what I tell you and get in the car."

"I can't do that, Benny, so you'd better say what you came to say, and then be on your way. You're blocking the road, and there's a car coming."

473

The road was narrow here, and Benny had parked at an angle, obstructing the traffic. A Vauxhall MPV pulled up behind Callaway's car, the driver peering at Benny expectantly.

"Get in the bloody car," Benny growled.

Dan shook his head, and the driver of the MPV gave a toot on his horn.

"He's getting irate," Dan said. "You'd better move your car."

"In a minute." Benny raised a hand toward the MPV, smiling. "Bloody tourists," he muttered. "No patience."

"Maybe he has an urgent appointment."

"So do we. Very urgent. And I'm not finished with you yet." Benny squared up to Dan. "What the hell did you think you were doing on Sunday? We were at church. Does that mean nothing to you?"

"I meant no disrespect, but I had to talk to Mr Callaway and there was no other way. I asked for your help but you refused. You gave me no alternative."

"Don't try and pin this on me. You were out of order. You've got no right to harass Mr Callaway. I know about you sneaking onto his property the other day. Saunders told me all about it, and let me tell you, you got off lightly. If I'd seen you, it would've been a different story. I have my own way of dealing with trespassers, and you would not have enjoyed it."

"How about Philippa, did she trespass?"

Dan didn't have time to react. The man's face was suddenly millimetres from his own, the front of Dan's shirt held tight in Benny's fist.

"You listen to me, Corrigan. I found that young woman, and I tried to save her. I pulled her out of the water for God's sake. I called for an ambulance, tried CPR, I did everything I damned well could. But still, it was no bloody use, so I'm in no mood for your bullshit. I've had more than enough."

"I didn't know that," Dan said. "They said a dog walker found her."

"That was me, you idiot. So don't you dare accuse me of hurting her. Don't you dare!"

Dan's mind raced. Here was a man with a temper, a man who'd been trained to kill. Had he really found Philippa and tried to help her, or was that just a convenient cover story? He wouldn't be the first murderer to report finding a body in the hope of diverting suspicion from himself. And then there was the fragment of conversation he and Alan had overheard in the churchyard. 'We're going to get her,' Benny had said. Could he and Callaway have been plotting to murder Philippa, even as they'd been walking away from their place of worship?

No. It didn't fit. Dan had known Philippa was missing on Saturday, the day before the church service, and there was something else: an inconsistency that had almost slipped past him. And then Dan glimpsed the truth, and he knew what he had to do.

"I'm sorry," Dan said. "I shouldn't have said that."

"You're damned right." Benny held onto Dan's shirt for a second longer, his fierce stare filled with pure anger, then he pushed him away.

Dan straightened his clothes, and with as much dignity as he could muster, he said, "Did they get it wrong on the news, or do you have a dog?"

"It's Mr Callaway's dog, a German Shepherd, but I was walking her."

Dan hesitated, a sinking feeling in the pit of his stomach. "Am I right in thinking you picked her up on Sunday?"

"Yes. Why?"

"That was what you were talking about, wasn't it? When you came out of the church."

Frowning, Benny nodded. "Why, what did you think I was…?" Benny sneered in disgust. "We weren't talking about that poor woman. How could you even think that?" Benny raised his hands to waist height, his fingers formed into fists. "I don't know why I'm wasting my time on you. You're beneath contempt."

"I wasn't to know you were talking about a dog. I was suspicious, that's all, and I admit, I made a mistake."

"Make another and see what happens."

The driver of the MPV honked his horn again, and Benny sent him a glare so fierce it made the man blanch.

"I think you'd better go before he calls the police," Dan said. "He looks the type to make a fuss."

Benny grunted under his breath, then he turned on his heel and marched to the Mercedes, climbing inside and speeding away, the car's electric motor almost silent.

The MPV did not follow. The driver was sitting motionless, staring out through the windscreen, his worried gaze fixed on Dan.

"It's okay," Dan called out. "I'm fine. It was a misunderstanding, that's all. Nothing to worry about." Dan waved and smiled.

The driver puffed out his cheeks, and then he too, drove away.

What a disaster, Dan thought, but it was over, and he'd got off lightly. If he'd got in the car with Benny, things might well have been worse. The man might've tried to save Philippa, but that didn't mean he was okay. Benny was a time bomb, primed and ready to explode, and if that day should come, Dan did not want to be around.

CHAPTER 60

"Dratted thing!" sitting at the desk in Zadie's studio, Alan pushed the laptop away from him, sliding it gently across the smooth wooden surface. A dedicated PC user, Alan was being slowly driven to distraction by the Apple MacBook Pro, but it wouldn't do to be rough with it. Zadie treasured the infernal machine, and it had probably cost a small fortune, but why were some of the keys in the wrong place while others were labelled with odd squiggles? Natalya had told him about the command key, but what was the option key for? And what had happened to all the keyboard shortcuts he knew and relied upon?

Alan turned in his seat, gazing around Zadie's studio. It wasn't right to be sitting on his backside when there was so much going on. His thoughts returned to Philippa, but there was nothing he could do for her now. His best bet was to concentrate on helping Dan. If they could nail the person who'd persecuted Zadie, they'd have achieved something worthwhile.

I'd better get back to it, Alan told himself, and he squared up to the MacBook for another round.

He typed in another search query, one in a long line of queries relating to Connor Griffiths. Unfortunately, the results so far had been very much as expected. There was far too much information about Connor online, almost all of it irrelevant and much of it bogus.

Alan's eye landed on a quote from an online magazine, and he read it aloud, muttering under his breath: "Connor Griffiths fathered my love child."

Alan sighed. There was a lot of that kind of thing. In his heyday, Connor had been adored by young women, but as far as Alan could see, it was unlikely that their affections had been reciprocated. Connor had never made any secret of his sexuality. Even before his brief time in the spotlight, he'd campaigned for gay rights and appeared on stage at Pride events up and down the country, singing protest songs and making speeches. He'd been a prominent figure in the LGBT+ community.

At one time Connor had wanted to stand up and be counted, but those days had gone. As far as Alan could tell from their meetings so far, Connor was smug and self-satisfied, content to sit back and make snide remarks from the sidelines, but he didn't seem to *do* anything. What had happened to all that energy and zeal?

Alan recalled the way Connor had introduced himself at their first meeting, bragging about his wealth while sniping at his deceased parents. Maybe all that money was the root of Connor's problems.

Embittered at the mayfly shortness of his musical career, he'd fallen back on his inherited wealth. No romantic life on the road for him, but a big house in the country and the quiet stability of life in a small town. The rebel had become entangled in the trappings of the establishment.

Alan wondered what Connor's parents had made of their son's rise to fame. A quick search revealed their names, but there weren't many links to pursue. His mother, Eleanor, was almost absent from the results, but his father, William, had been on the board of a merchant bank. Such a man would not have seen eye to eye with a son whose only hit was an anti-establishment anthem. And hadn't Connor claimed to have left-wing sympathies?

A champagne socialist, Alan thought. Had Connor's whole career been an attempt to hit back at his father? If so, he wouldn't be the first to spend his early adulthood railing against the previous generation. It was something of a cliché.

Alan ran a hand across his chin. How could he find out what Connor had been like before he'd found fame? How could he get past the hype?

"It's obvious," Alan muttered, and his fingers went to work on the keyboard. Naturally, Connor's erstwhile bandmates would've seen him in a different light, and they might have tales to tell. Within a minute, Alan was reading an article titled *The Idyllic Sirens: Where Are They Now?*

If Connor had fallen on his feet, his old friends hadn't fared quite so well. The bass player, Malcolm Richards, had become a secondhand car salesman in Swindon. The drummer, Maurice Potter, had emigrated to Canada where he worked in a bank. Alan learned that Maurice had joined the band shortly before they'd become famous. The original drummer, Stuart O'Neill, was known as Spud. He was a key figure in the bands' early days, credited with writing several songs. Sadly, Spud had died in a road traffic accident twelve years earlier, so he hadn't lived to see The Idyllic Sirens enjoying their moment in the sun.

Lastly, the rhythm guitarist, Jeff Dawkins, made and sold guitars constructed from cigar boxes and reclaimed materials.

At least he's local, Alan thought. According to the article, Jeff Dawkins was based in Devon, so this was a lead worth chasing.

Craftspeople generally had a website, and it didn't take Alan long to find the online home of Mr Dawkins, where apparently he was known as Turkey Bone Jeff. The site was comprehensive, including an online store and pages filled with videos: tutorials on how to make and play guitars. The boxy little guitars looked distinctly odd to Alan, but he skimmed past them in search of contact information. He found a phone number and tried it immediately.

The woman who answered the call sounded out of breath, as though she'd dashed to the phone. "Hello?"

"Hello," Alan said. "My name is Alan Hargreaves. I was hoping to speak to Mr Dawkins, or should I say, Turkey Bone Jeff?"

"Jeff's not in the workshop at the moment. Is it about a guitar? Because if it is, I'm sure I can help you."

The temptation to spin a convincing story sprung to Alan's mind, but he hadn't touched a guitar since his university days, and he had no idea what to say. Besides, the woman had a soft Irish accent and she sounded friendly; he couldn't possibly lie to her. "No, it's about a more personal matter. I'd like to speak to Mr Dawkins, preferably in-person if that's possible."

"How do you mean *personal?*" The woman's voice hardened. "You're not a reporter, are you?"

"No, I can assure you that I'm not a journalist of any kind. I'd just like a chat with Mr Dawkins."

There was silence on the line. "Hello?" Alan said. "Are you still there?"

"Yes, I'm still here, but I'm in the middle of something, and Jeff isn't here. You can try again tomorrow."

"Is there any way I can reach him before then? Does he have a mobile I can call?"

A pause, and then: "What's this about?"

"I'd rather discuss that with Mr Dawkins."

"And I'd rather be in Tenerife, but we are where we are, and I have half a dozen boxes to sand down, so you can tell me what you want or you can hang up and let me get back to work."

"I see," Alan said carefully. "When you say you're sanding down boxes, would that be cigar boxes for making guitars?"

"That's right."

"Fascinating," Alan said with as much enthusiasm as he could summon. "So you work together as a team. Are you husband and wife?"

"Yeah. It's a family business. I make the parts and Jeff puts them together, does the finishing touches. He's the craftsman. He knows what he's doing."

"But he wouldn't get far without all your hard work, Mrs Dawkins. Preparation is everything when you're working with wood, isn't it?"

"You're right there." Mrs Dawkins' tone softened as she went on. "We do everything properly, starting from scratch. Our guitars are precision-made. They're guaranteed to sound good or your money back, and they're perfect for beginners, if you're interested."

"I see, but I'm not a total beginner. I did have an electric guitar for a while, although it was a long time ago.

"You never lose the knack. You'd pick it up again in no time."

"You're very persuasive," Alan said. "I'm almost tempted."

"Come up to the workshop, Mr…"

"Hargreaves, but please, call me Alan."

"Okay, Alan. Come and see us and try out a guitar. Are you in Devon?"

"Yes, I live in Embervale in the Teign Valley."

"A local. We're based in Newton Abbot, so it'll take you no time."

"Thanks, but I won't make any promises unless Mr Dawkins is going to be there. I really need to speak to him."

Mrs Dawkins sighed. "In regard to what? And don't beat about the bush. Anything you can say to him, you can say to me."

"Okay, Mrs Dawkins, I'll come to the point. It's nothing for you or your husband to be concerned about, but I'm working with a private investigator. We're running a background check on one of your husband's old associates, and—"

"Connor Griffiths," Mrs Dawkins interrupted, the word loaded with disapproval. "I might've known. It's about Stuart, isn't it?"

"Yes, it is, in part."

"Well, Jeff knows nothing about it and neither do I, so there's no use asking."

"Actually," Alan began, but Mrs Dawkins had already hung up.

"Curious," Alan murmured. Setting down his phone, he pulled the laptop closer and began to type.

CHAPTER 61

Back at Zadie's house, Dan and Alan conferred in the kitchen over a mug of tea. Natalya was upstairs in Zadie's studio. She'd remained stoic when Alan had given her the news about Philippa, and she'd insisted on taking a shift at the computer, maintaining the pretence that Zadie was still at home.

"We should get Connor over here," Dan said. "We want him on our ground."

"Easier said than done. Connor's not the most cooperative person."

"I'll get him here."

Dan made the call, but it took four attempts before he got past Connor's voicemail message and received a response from the man himself.

"Who's this?" Connor croaked, his voice thick.

Dan introduced himself and Connor groaned, muttering something under his breath.

"Is there any chance you could pop over to Zadie's house?" Dan went on. "There's something I'd like to discuss."

"Like what?"

"This isn't something we can talk about on the phone. It's a

483

delicate matter, regarding Zadie, and as her closest friend, I'd value your input."

Suddenly sounding more alert, Connor said, "Is she all right?"

"Yes and no."

"What's that supposed to mean? Is she okay or isn't she?"

"That's a more nuanced question than you might imagine, Connor."

"Bloody hell, man. What are you on about?"

"It's simple really," Dan said. "A person can seem okay on the surface, but underneath it all, there can be something very wrong. Only someone's closest friend would know the difference."

"You keep saying that. *Zadie's closest friend*. That's not me."

"I'm only repeating what she said."

"Really? She said that?"

"Of course. That's why I called. It's you that we need."

There was a brief pause.

"Okay then," Connor said. "I'll come over, but it'll take me a while to walk. I'll be there in half an hour or so. "

"Thank you," Dan replied. "I'm sure Zadie will appreciate it. We'll see you soon."

Ending the call, Dan met Alan's incredulous gaze. "What?"

"That was a bit much, wasn't it?" Alan said. "He'll be expecting to see Zadie, and he can't."

"Don't worry about it. We can handle Connor."

"Does he know about Philippa, do you think?"

Dan shook his head. "He was half asleep. I doubt whether he follows the news."

"Do we tell him?"

"We'll play it by ear," Dan said. "We've got half an hour to figure out our tactics. More tea?"

"Why not? I think we're going to need it."

Almost an hour later, Connor arrived, letting himself in at the front door.

"Zadie," they heard him call out. "It's only me. Where are you hiding?"

Dan went to the kitchen door. "We're in here, Connor. Come through."

"Okay. I'll be right there."

Dan took up position beside Alan, standing with their backs against the counter, facing the door.

Connor strode into the kitchen and stopped, looking around with a bemused grin on his lips. "Where's Zadie?"

"Working," Dan replied. "Hopefully, we can talk to her soon."

Connor's hand went to his mouth. "Oops. If I'd known she was working, I wouldn't have shouted." He paused. "On the phone, you said something wasn't right with Zadie, so how come she's working? Has something come up?"

"In a manner of speaking." Dan said.

"In a manner of speaking, eh? No offence, Dan, but that sounds like bullshit, so unless there's a national emergency, I'm going upstairs to see Zadie." Connor started to turn away, but Dan called his name sharply enough to stop him.

"What now?" Connor snapped.

"If you wouldn't mind, we'd like a moment of your time," Alan said. "It won't take long."

"Not right now. If Zadie needs me, I'd better go up."

"Actually, I wasn't totally honest with you on the phone," Dan said.

"Ah, you were buttering me up. All that stuff about being her closest friend. I should've known." Connor looked from Dan to Alan. "Go on then. Why am I really here? And no lies, this time."

"It was only a white lie," Dan replied. "You see, Zadie's been working too hard, and we don't want her getting burnt out, do we? She needs someone to take her out of herself, so I invited you over. I may have exaggerated a bit, but you are one of her best friends, and I thought a visit from you would cheer her up."

"Fine. I'll go and do that."

"If only it were that simple," Alan said. "We need to tread carefully. You know Zadie. She throws herself into her work, and she's told us in no uncertain terms that she mustn't be interrupted. If we go barging in, the whole plan will backfire."

Connor nodded reluctantly. "That sounds about right. Zadie's the most driven person I've ever met. When she gets into the zone, there's no talking to her. She hasn't even been answering my messages."

"You're welcome to wait here for a while," Dan said. "You never know, she might come down for a break in a minute."

"Maybe." Connor looked doubtful, but he sighed, adding, "I'll give it ten minutes. If she's still tied up, I'll head back."

Dan smiled. "Good idea. Would you like tea or coffee?"

"No, I'm fine thanks." Connor pulled up a stool and sat down. "So what have you two sleuths been up to since I last saw you?"

"We've been busy," Dan replied. "As it happens, there are a couple of things you can help us with."

The corner of Connor's lip lifted in a cynical smirk. "Really? Like what?"

"For a start, I've got a simple question for you," Dan said. "Are you a member of Extinction Rebellion?"

Connor guffawed. "Me? No way. I don't join things. Never have."

"Like Groucho Marx," Alan suggested. "He said he'd never join any club that would have him as a member."

Connor laughed. "Yeah, that's about right. Non-conformists, Marx and me both."

"How about the other Marx?" Dan asked. "Karl."

"Do you mean, am I now or have I ever been a communist?" Connor laughed again, shaking his head. "I was born into money, and I live quite happily off the proceeds. I'm all for equality, but I'm not about to give away what's mine."

"I see," Dan said. "So what do you think of Extinction Rebellion using your song as their anthem?

"What about it? They're a bunch of nutters."

"They seem to think you're on their side," Alan said. "Are they wrong?"

"Yeah. They're misguided. They don't know anything about me. They like my song and that's fine. If they want to stream it or go out and buy it, I'm happy with that. I get the royalties either way, and it all adds up."

"But you're profiting from their anti-capitalism beliefs," Alan said. "That's not very ethical."

"Who cares? Not me. I'm completely and utterly relaxed about the whole thing. They've got a good cause, but when all's said and done, it's up to them how they spend their money. Nobody's making them buy my record. If they'd rather spend it on lentils or donate it to Greenpeace, I'm not standing in their way."

"You do think they have a worthwhile cause though," Dan suggested. "You support their goals?"

"Sure, in principle. There's a climate emergency and somebody's got to do something about it, but that doesn't mean it's okay to glue yourself to the road or whatever. That's just stupid. It won't change a thing."

"And yet you have one of their badges on your jacket," Dan said.

"Oh yeah." Connor looked down at the enamel badge on the left breast pocket of his denim jacket. "I'd forgotten that was there. I think someone sent it to me. I get all kinds of stuff in the post. People know I like badges. I'm usually wearing a few when I take a selfie, so they send me one or two. I don't mind."

"Do you have any other merchandise from Extinction Rebellion?"

Connor wrinkled his brow in an exaggerated frown. "I don't think so. Like I said, I'm not exactly a fan. I thought the badge was cool though, so I pinned it on. It's about time I changed it for something else."

"Why would you do that?" Alan asked.

"I dunno. I like to change things up." Connor favoured them

with a puzzled smile. "Pretty weird questions. What's my badge got to do with anything?"

"We'll get to that," Dan replied. "Do you ever roll a few cigarettes and carry them around in a tin?"

"I have done, in the past."

"Do you have some with you now?" Dan asked.

Connor's left hand twitched toward his chest as if to check the right breast pocket of his jacket, but he stopped himself, his hand going to his sleeve instead, brushing away an imaginary speck of dust. "I don't carry them around all the time. I hardly smoke at all. I explained that to you the other day."

"You certainly did," Dan said. "As a matter of fact, you've already told us a great deal, and probably more than you intended to."

"Have I? Good for you. You've wheedled my secrets out of me. Connor Griffiths is an occasional smoker." Connor mimed a slow handclap. "You've got me bang to rights, Mr Holmes. The master detective strikes again."

"It's a flattering comparison," Dan replied with a smile, "but Sherlock Holmes is fictional, and I'm very real. I have my own way of working things out, and here's an example. I can tell you exactly what happened to your tin of cigarettes."

"I already know. I left it at home."

"Are you sure about that?" Dan said. "Or is there a chance that you've lost it?"

"It'll be at home somewhere. I forget."

"Did you also forget that the tin has a logo on the lid?" Dan asked. "It's the same symbol you have on your badge: Extinction Rebellion."

"I don't think so," Connor replied. "It's just an old tin I use sometimes. I've had it for ages. I don't really pay much attention to stuff like that. A tin's a tin."

"When did you last see it?" Dan asked.

"I don't know, and to be honest, I've had enough of this game, so let's call it a day, shall we?"

"Okay," Dan said. "But first, my colleague has something he wants to ask you."

Connor smirked at Alan. "Oh, it speaks, does it? Go on then. I've crossed swords with the organ grinder, I may as well have a word with the monkey."

"There's no need to be rude," Alan replied. "All I want is the answer to a simple question. What happened to Spud?"

Connor's smirk slipped. "What do you want to know about that for? It was years ago."

"I'm interested," Alan said. "I was looking up your old bandmates, and when I called Jeff Dawkins, Spud's name came up."

"Jeff talked about Spud?" Connor asked sharply.

"No. It was Jeff's wife who mentioned Spud. She wouldn't give me Jeff's number."

Connor almost laughed. "She's a piece of work. Now there's a whole can of worms you don't want to open."

"Are you talking about Spud's death?" Alan asked.

"No, I meant Jeff's love life. Back in the day, he was a heartbreaker, but you wouldn't know it to look at him now. Too fond of a pie and a pint, is Jeff." Connor glanced pointedly at Alan's midriff before adding, "Obesity. It's an epidemic."

Undeterred, Alan said, "Spud's real name was Stuart O'Neill, wasn't it?"

"Yeah, but nobody called him that. Poor old Spud. He was a good friend. It was terrible what happened to him, but it was an accident. He was driving and took a corner too fast. The car skidded off the road and hit a tree. Spud went through the windscreen. He didn't have his seatbelt on, the stupid sod."

"Why didn't you tell him to wear it?" Alan asked. "You were in the car with him at the time."

"Who told you that?"

"It was mentioned in the local press," Alan said. "It was only a short piece, but your fans are very good at ferreting out old stories and posting them online. They're extremely thorough."

Connor nodded slowly. "I probably did tell him to put his belt on, but he wasn't going to listen to me. It turned out Spud was off his head, doped up to the gills. He shouldn't even have been behind the wheel."

"Are you sure he was driving?" Dan asked.

"What? Of course I am. You don't forget something like that."

"It must've been a traumatic experience," Alan said. "But it's true, isn't it, that your friend's death was initially treated as suspicious?"

"That was a formality. Everyone knew it was an accident."

"But there *were* some suspicious circumstances," Alan insisted. "The car left the road for no discernible reason. There were no other vehicles involved and no one around to witness what happened."

"I bloody well witnessed it," Connor shot back. "I was right next to him. He drove straight into a tree. I could've died."

"Is that why you don't drive?" Dan said.

"Partly. Having a near-death experience tends to put you off."

"*Partly*," Dan said, letting the word hang in the air. "It's a weasel word, isn't it? It conceals more than it reveals. In this case, it's hiding the real reason you don't drive. It's hiding a lie."

The colour rose in Connor's cheeks. "What the hell are you talking about? How dare you stand there and say that to my face?"

"Because I know the truth," Dan stated. "What name was on your driving licence?"

"I haven't got one."

"Not anymore," Dan said. "But when you did have one, what name did it carry?"

"My full name."

"Connor is your middle name, isn't it?" Alan said. "Your first name is William."

"I've never used that name. It belonged to my father. It isn't me."

Alan nodded as though taking this in. "An interesting choice of words. Some might say it *is* you. William is your legal name, I believe, but there's precious little trace of it online. It's not even on your Wikipedia page."

"Someone removed it," Connor replied. "I didn't ask them to, but I was happy about it. As I said, that name isn't me. I'm not going to be defined by a piece of paper."

"How convenient," Dan said. "It must've been handy to have a means of obscuring your identity, especially when you were in trouble with the police."

"I've no idea what you mean."

Dan tilted his head to one side. "Really? You've forgotten that you had your driving licence taken away? At the time of your arrest, you had three times the legal limit of alcohol in your blood and traces of cocaine too."

"I was stupid and I paid the price, but no one got hurt. I made a mistake, but I wasn't myself back then. I'd been going through a hard time, but this was nothing to do with Spud. It was six months before the accident, so don't go putting two and two together and making five. I hate it when people do that."

"So explain it to us," Alan said. "Tell us what happened."

Connor exhaled, and when he spoke, his voice was calm. "It's the same story for most people when they're starting out. We were all mates in the band, so we kidded ourselves we'd be okay, but it wasn't a great time for any of us. We worked hard and tried to be good at what we did, but we weren't getting anywhere. We spent all our time driving from one crappy gig to another, barely getting paid. We were all feeling the strain, getting on each other's nerves.

One night, we played a gig in some godforsaken pub near Finsbury Park. We stayed behind after and had a few drinks. We all lived in London back then, so we were going to get the night bus then come back the next day to pick up our cars and our gear. But we missed the bus and we had no money for a taxi, plus it was pouring down, so we decided to drive. I didn't get far. The cops pulled me over. And that was that."

"When we met, you led us to believe you didn't drive by

choice," Dan pointed out. "You claimed it was for environmental reasons."

"So what? I don't want to shout my mistakes from the rooftops; who does? I'm not proud of what I did, but it's not like some dark secret. I was young and I was stupid and I lost my licence. It happens all the time, and maybe some people don't learn their lesson but I did. I haven't driven since, and I don't intend to. End of story."

"And yet, six months later, you were in a car with another intoxicated driver," Dan said. "Was that bad luck or bad judgement?"

"Neither, but there's no point trying to explain it to someone like you. You wouldn't understand."

"We might," Alan said. "We've all made mistakes in our youth, even me. Tell us what happened with Spud, and we'll listen."

Connor studied Alan for a moment. "Have you ever met an addict? I mean a real addict, not someone who likes a buzz now and then; somebody who can't live without getting another hit."

Alan nodded. "Sadly, yes. I've known a couple of people who were alcoholics. In both cases it led to poverty and an early death."

"Then maybe you'll get it. It wasn't booze with Spud, but he was an addict. Pills, I think. I don't know what he was taking, but he was good at hiding it. We were close friends, but I had no idea what he was doing to himself. The pills were his way of getting through the day, and in the end, they took their toll."

"I'm sorry to hear that," Dan said. "But if you don't know what he was taking and when, how did you know the drugs were to blame for the accident?"

"I didn't put it together until later. There was an inquest, and they found drugs in his system. When I heard that, it all made sense. He'd been acting weird for a while. He'd get jittery and nervous. Maybe he was seeing things or hearing voices. I don't know what was going on in his head, but something made him drive off that road, and then it was all over."

"It's a sad tale," Alan said, "And like your full name, it's not easy to find references to the accident online, which is odd, don't you think?"

"No, it was years ago, and accidents happen all the time."

"You could be right," Alan replied. "But I looked back through all the archive material I could find, and there wasn't much to see, and that surprised me. The story would've been red meat to the tabloids: a pop star in a tragic accident, the death of a young musician who could've made it big, the drug angle and the rock and roll lifestyle. But for some reason, the accident was hardly mentioned in the press. It took quite a bit of digging to find it."

"Maybe I was never as big as you seem to think. I had one hit record; I'm not George Michael. As for Spud, he never had the chance to get famous. As far as the press were concerned he was a nobody, but not to me. To me he was a friend." Connor rubbed a knuckle against the corner of his eye as if dabbing away a tear. "You needn't have wasted your time trawling through the internet. You could've just asked. I'll talk about this to anyone who'll listen. There but for the grace of God and all that. Spud was a friend, and we lost him far too young, but it was an accident. I've had to accept that and move on. It was a senseless accident. No one was to blame. No one."

While Connor pulled a tissue from his pocket and blew his nose, Dan and Alan exchanged a look. Alan seemed downcast, as if affected by Connor's display of emotion. Perhaps Alan was regretting the way they'd broached such a sensitive topic with Connor, forcing him to relive a painful episode from his past, but Dan wasn't ready to take Connor's story at face value.

Connor claimed he was happy to talk about his friend's death, citing it as a cautionary tale while painting himself as the sinner who'd turned toward the light. But they'd had to drag the story out of him. Connor hadn't admitted the details until he'd realised the game was up. He was no one's idea of a modern-day saint.

And then there was his unfortunate history on the roads. Two

493

incidents within six months of each other, both involving driving while intoxicated. Was that simply the by-product of a chaotic lifestyle, or was there a more sinister connection? And there was something else: a question Connor had evaded.

Dan gave Connor a moment to pull himself together, then he said, "It still seems strange to me that you were barely mentioned in the coverage of the accident, even though you were the only other person present."

"I was a passenger, as much a victim as poor old Spud."

"But the police looked into the accident, didn't they?" Dan said. "They were obviously suspicious, so you must've been formally questioned. I'd have thought that would be significant enough to hit the news."

"I was interviewed more than once, and I told them the truth, but I was never arrested, never charged."

"Lucky for you," Dan said. "But maybe it wasn't luck. You come from a wealthy family, and no matter how much you resented him, your father must've had connections in the right places. What was he, a mason? Or did he play golf with the Chief Constable?"

Connor grimaced. "You're talking absolute bollocks. My father was a pain in the arse, but he never broke a rule in his life. He was the straightest person you could ever meet. He never asked favours of anyone."

"Not even to help his own son?" Alan said.

"*Especially* not to help me. If he'd known I was in trouble, he would've told me to be a man, to tough it out and find a way to fix it."

"And did you?" Dan asked. "Did you find a way to *fix* it?"

"You're deliberately twisting my words, but you know what I meant. Spud's death was an accident and it was all dealt with at the time. As far as I know, the inquest was a formality. There was no question of anyone *fixing* anything." Connor sniffed and looked down at the tissue he still held in his hands, his fingers twisting it back and forth as if to wring it out. He lifted his gaze to Alan, and in a quiet voice, he added, "There are some things that can't be fixed, like losing a friend."

"It's okay," Alan said gently. "I think we've asked enough questions for one day. I'm sorry to have brought back what must be a painful memory."

Connor sent Alan a grateful smile. "Thank you, Alan, but it's all right. I suppose you had to ask. I understand, but it doesn't make it any easier."

"We appreciate you taking the time to answer our questions," Dan said, "but there's just one more thing."

Making an obvious effort, Connor hoisted his smirk back into place. "Who are you, Columbo?" Connor laughed bitterly. "Oh man, I've got to stop watching daytime TV. I'm losing my mind. But go on, what do you want to know?"

"It's only a quick question. I wondered how many cigarettes were in the tin when you lost it?"

"I didn't lose it."

"I beg to differ," Dan said. "I think you dropped it in the driveway not far from this room. Zadie doesn't like anyone smoking near her, so you waited until you were leaving. You took a cigarette out of the tin, lit it, and then missed your pocket when you went to put the tin away. It landed on the soft earth underneath the hedge, so you didn't hear it fall, and you didn't miss it until you needed it, maybe the next day."

Connor's face fell. "You know what? I sometimes have a smoke on the way home; it makes the walk go faster. I hate to admit it, but you're right. If I'm going to smoke, I usually light up as soon as I'm out the door. I suppose I could've dropped my tin and not noticed. It's possible."

"There's not much doubt about it," Dan replied. "It all fits, and my question stands. How many cigarettes were in the tin when you last saw it?"

"About half a dozen, something like that."

Dan tried not to let his excitement show. At last, they were getting somewhere. Meeting Connor's gaze, he said, "On the day we first met, you'd been smoking in the house, but there was no tin on the table. Had you already lost it?"

"I didn't have it on me, but I thought I'd misplaced it. I was pretty sure it was still at home. Anyway, I had my tobacco and papers with me, and everyone was very uptight, so I rolled a couple. I was going to go outside, but Zadie said it was okay, for once, so I made the most of it."

Dan smiled, sharing a conspiratorial look with Connor. "Between ourselves, what was in those cigarettes, Connor? Was it something special? Something to, as you said, make the time go a little faster?"

"I smoke tobacco these days, nothing else. Does that answer your question? Are we done?"

"Yes," Alan said. "Thanks, Connor. You've been very helpful."

"Good, but I've waited a lot longer than ten minutes. Maybe I'll pop upstairs and see if Zadie can take a break." Connor made to move toward the doorway, but Dan reached out and laid a hand on his arm.

"I'm sorry," Dan said, "but I was telling the truth when I said you can't go up and see Zadie at the moment. It's impossible."

Connor glanced down at Dan's hand and looked distinctly put out. "That's a shame."

"Yes, but I'm sure you can catch up later," Alan suggested. "When she's ready."

"That might be for the best. I'm in no fit state." Connor puffed out his cheeks. "I may as well head home, if you've finished giving me the third degree, that is." He looked once more at Dan's hand, making a point, and Dan let go of his arm.

"Yes, we're all done for the time being," Dan said. "Thank you for your help, Connor."

"We really appreciated you taking the time," Alan added. "I'm sorry if it felt like we were interrogating you. That wasn't our intention."

"Yes, it was," Connor replied. "To be honest, I'm beginning to wonder if you invited me over just to give me a grilling. All that stuff about cheering Zadie up — that wasn't true, was it?"

"We may have bent the truth a little," Dan admitted. "But—"

"Spare me your excuses," Connor interrupted. "But do me favour, yeah? Next time you want to talk to me, just ask, okay? Keep things simple." Connor shook his head as if disappointed, then he headed for the door, letting himself out without another word.

CHAPTER 62

S piller was at his desk when DC Collins appeared at the
door.

"I've brought Jack Devlin in for you, guv," Collins said.
"He's waiting in interview room three."

"Excellent. Did he take much persuading?"

"Not really. He was anxious to help. Mind you, I caught him at
the right time. He was half asleep and not quite with it. He's very
pale, and he's got bags under his eyes as if he hasn't slept for days,
so maybe he's feeling guilty. He's definitely twitchy, and there's
something else."

"Go on."

"While I was waiting for Devlin to get himself together and put
his shoes on, I looked around and spotted a notebook on the table.
It was a posh one with a nice cover, and I thought it might be a
visitor's book for the cottage, so I opened it up in case Devlin had
written something. Anyway, some of the pages had been cut out:
you could still see the stubs where they'd been. The rest of the
pages were blank, but there was something written inside the
cover. I'm pretty sure it's not Devlin's writing, but we can check
that out later. I took a few photos. Here."

Collins produced his phone, tapping the screen a few times, then he passed it to Spiller.

"Interesting," Spiller said. The photo showed the inside cover of a hardback notebook and two lines of text written with a blue biro. The first was a mobile phone number, and below it was a simple message in small capitals: *DO THE RIGHT THING*.

"It's Philippa's phone number," Collins went on. "I checked."

"Good work." Spiller handed the phone back to Collins. "*Do the right thing*. That suggests something going on between Philippa and Devlin. We'll follow it up, but not until we've got him warmed up. Before we go pulling the rug from under his feet, we want him to feel relaxed. From what you said, he sounds a bit wobbly. Is he hungover, or has he been taking anything, do you think?"

"There was no smell of alcohol, but he might've been popping pills. I can't be sure, but my guess is that he's just stressed out. He's a bag of nerves."

"Okay, so long as he's fit for questioning, we'll get started. I'll grab a tea, then we'll see what we can winkle out of him. I'd like you to sit in, okay?"

"Sure, guv. Happy to."

"Good. I want you to ask him about the time he's spent in Philippa's company. Find out when he was last in the house, that kind of thing. And you can go through their past communications. We're looking for any hint of a relationship. It'll be better coming from you; you're closer to his age than I am."

"Got it."

"Right. Do you want to grab a drink?"

"I've got my water, thanks." Collins brandished a metallic bottle. "You ought to get one of these. They keep your drink cold, and you've got to stay hydrated."

"So I'm told," Spiller replied. "I can't see the appeal myself, all this glugging down water. Give me a nice hot cup of tea any day of the week."

A few minutes later, Spiller and Collins entered the interview room. Jack Devlin was already seated at the table, leaning one elbow on the surface as he gnawed at his thumbnail.

"Everything all right, Mr Devlin?" Spiller asked. "Can we get you anything?"

Devlin sat up straight. "I'm fine thanks."

"Excellent." Spiller took the seat immediately opposite Devlin, placing his mug of tea on the table, while Collins sat at Spiller's side, arranging his tablet computer and bottle of water with exaggerated care.

Spiller gestured to the recorder on the edge of the table, and Collins started it.

For the benefit of the recording, Spiller introduced everyone present, then he said, "OK, Mr Devlin, I understand that you refused the offer of having a legal adviser present for this interview, is that right?"

"Yeah," Devlin muttered. "But I thought we were going to talk about Philippa. I didn't think this was an interview."

"That's just what we call it, Spiller explained. "It's a formal term, but we're having a chat, hoping to piece together what happened to Ms Darley-Jones."

"Right, yeah. I'm still gutted about what's happened. I can't believe it." Devlin rubbed at his forehead with his fingertips while he stared down at the table.

"Are you all right, Jack?" Spiller asked. "It is okay if I call you Jack, isn't it?"

"Sure." Devlin looked up, squinting at Spiller as though trying to bring him into focus. "I'm fine, but you mentioned a lawyer. I'm here to help you, so why would I need a lawyer?"

"You don't necessarily *need* one, but I always advise people to have legal advice, even when we're talking informally. Police procedure can be confusing, so a legal adviser can be very helpful."

"Okay. I get it, but I don't think I want a lawyer right now." Offering a hesitant smile, Devlin added, "I'm not under arrest, am I?"

"No, you can leave whenever you want, and it's your prerogative to turn down legal advice. Is that all clear to you?"

Devlin nodded as if trying to look casual, but Spiller wasn't fooled. The man was nervous, scared even. What was bothering him? If he felt guilty about something, he'd been particularly foolish to refuse legal advice. Then again, guilt could express itself in strange ways, and Spiller had interviewed suspects who'd been worn down by remorse, almost eager to unburden themselves.

Spiller made his tone friendly. "Jack, would you mind confirming that you understand? It's best if we can make things clear on the recording."

"Sure. I'm here for the interview, but I haven't done anything wrong, so ask your questions. All I want to do is help so you can find out what happened to…" Devlin sniffed, then he took a breath, pulling himself together. "Sorry. I still can't take it in."

"Do you need a minute?" Spiller asked. "A glass of water?"

"No, no. I'll be all right. It's just the shock, you know?"

"I understand. It's difficult, but if you don't mind, we'll get through this as fast as we can." Spiller nodded to DC Collins. "This would be a good time to show Mr Devlin those messages."

"Yes, sir." Collins tapped on his tablet's screen to locate the first file, then he turned the tablet around so that Devlin could see it. "I am showing Mr Devlin the file labelled EC-301 which is a PDF document containing the messages exchanged between Mr Devlin and Ms Philippa Darley-Jones. Do you recognise those messages, Jack?"

Devlin glanced at the screen. "Yeah. They're from the Airbnb site. That's how I booked the cottage."

"Thanks for confirming that," Collins said. "In those messages, you state that you are a mature student studying at the University of Exeter, correct?"

"I said that, yeah." Devlin shuffled in his seat. "But I know what you're going to say. I'm not actually a student."

"So it would seem," Spiller replied. "As you've apparently

guessed, we've already checked at the university, and they have no record of you ever being a student there. So why did you lie, Jack?"

"I'm unemployed at the moment, okay? It's no big deal, but I needed somewhere to stay, and I didn't think she'd let me rent the place if she knew I was out of work."

"What line of work are you in?" Spiller asked.

"This and that. Odd jobs. I've been doing a bit of manual work, moving stuff around."

"Casual labour," Spiller suggested.

"Yeah, that's right."

"This stuff you've been moving around, what kind of thing are we talking about?"

"I don't know. It was in a warehouse, all packed in boxes. I didn't take much notice."

"You weren't curious?" Spiller asked.

"Not really. It was hard work and we had to move fast, but I think it was electrical stuff. Heaters, things like that."

"I see. Where is this warehouse?"

"Exeter."

"Come on, Mr Devlin," Spiller said. "You'll have to be more specific than that."

"Okay, yeah, obviously." Devlin chuckled as though he'd made a silly mistake.

Playing for time, Spiller thought.

"It's in a trading estate," Devlin went on. "Marsh Barton. It was on Trusham Road."

"I know the area," Spiller said. "This warehouse, does it have a name?"

"Not that I know of."

"No signpost, nothing on the building to say who owns it?"

Devlin shook his head. "It was a crappy place. Old. Built of bricks. It looked like it had been something else at one time. A factory maybe."

"Thank you, that should make it relatively easy to find. We'll check it out."

"Go for it, but I don't think you'll get anywhere. I worked there for a bit, that's all. I don't suppose they'll even remember me." Jack lowered his voice. "It was all cash in hand. There was never any paperwork or anything like that."

"Nevertheless, we'll follow it up," Spiller said. "Now, my colleague has some questions for you."

Collins smiled. "Jack, how often have you been in Philippa's house?"

"A couple of times. Once when I rented the cottage, and again when she invited me in for a drink."

"That was nice of her," Collins said. "When did you pop in for a drink?"

"Erm, that would've been Saturday, in the afternoon."

"Why not, eh? It was the weekend. Did you stay long?"

"No. Twenty minutes, maybe a little bit longer."

Collins looked unconvinced. "Twenty minutes. That's not long for a drink."

"I only went in to be polite, but I didn't want to stay. It was a bit… awkward."

"In what way?" Collins asked.

Devlin's lips moved wordlessly for a moment, then he said, "I don't want to speak ill of Philippa, but we weren't alike. She was posh and I'm not. I felt like a fish out of water."

"I know what you mean," Collins said. "So you had a quick drink, then you left."

"Yes."

Collins paused before moving on. "While you were inside for this quick drink, which rooms did you go in?"

"The kitchen, the lounge."

"Is that all?" Collins asked. "You didn't go upstairs?"

"No. Why would I?"

"That depends, doesn't it?" Collins leaned forward. "A woman invites you in for a drink, and there's only the two of you there. Maybe there's a spark between you, if you know what I mean.

She's taken a shine to you, and one thing leads to another. It happens, right? Nothing wrong with that."

"It wasn't like that," Devlin spluttered. "My God. We chatted for a bit, that's all. I had one drink, then I left."

"If you say so." Collins sat back. "What did you drink?"

"A glass of white wine. Philippa opened the bottle for me. It was all a bit desperate, like she wanted someone to drink with. She offered me gin, vodka, tequila, whiskey, but I said no. She was drinking vodka, I think, but I don't much like spirits. I said I'd prefer a beer, but she didn't have any, so she fetched out the wine and poured me an enormous glass. I didn't even finish it."

"How many drinks had Philippa already had?" Collins asked. "Did she seem drunk to you?"

"Sadly, I'd say she was completely inebriated. I felt sorry for her. I thought maybe she'd asked me in because she was lonely. There's something pathetic about someone drinking on their own, isn't there?"

Collins didn't comment; he simply stared at Devlin, letting the silence hang in the air.

"Is that it?" Devlin asked. "Is that all you wanted to know?"

Spiller cleared his throat. "What I want, Mr Devlin, is for you to think very carefully about each and every statement you've made in this interview. Bear in mind that we're going through Ms Darley-Jones' house with a fine-toothed comb, looking for tiny pieces of trace evidence: fingerprints, fibres, strands of hair and so on. If we find, say, one of your hairs in the bedroom or in a room you say you've never visited, we'll have to ask ourselves why you lied to us."

Devlin attempted a smile but his lips quivered, and when he spoke, his voice had lost any hint of confidence. "But I haven't lied. I've told you the truth."

"You've given us something, but I'm interested in the parts you've left out," Spiller said.

"I don't know what you want me to say. I've told everything I know."

"We'll see about that," Spiller said. "Over to you, DC Collins."

"Thank you, sir." Gazing intently at Devlin, Collins said, "*Do the right thing*. Do those words mean anything to you, Mr Devlin?"

"What's that?"

"I'll rephrase it for you," Collins replied. "Does the phrase, 'Do the right thing' have any special significance to you?"

"I understand the idea, obviously, but I don't see what you're getting at. I *am* doing the right thing. I'm trying to help, and you two are acting like I've done something wrong. I don't get it."

"There are good reasons for the questions we ask," Collins said. "You see, Jack, while I was waiting for you today, I noticed you had an item in your possession, an item that may have belonged to Ms Darley-Jones."

Devlin simply stared, his face blank with incomprehension.

Come on Collins, Spiller thought. *Be more specific.* Spiller waited for a moment then cleared his throat. When Devlin looked at him, he said, "Mr Devlin, do you know which item DC Collins is talking about?"

Still staring, Devlin shook his head.

"Please answer verbally for the recording," Collins intoned.

Devlin took a breath and let it out slowly. "No. I don't know what you mean. Unless… do you mean the scarf?"

Spiller couldn't help but exchange a glance with Collins, and he knew they were both thinking of the marks on Philippa's neck: the marks that might've been made by an item of clothing pulled tight.

Speaking slowly, Collins said, "Tell us about the scarf, Jack."

Devlin's expression crumpled. "Wait. I made a mistake. It's all your questions, muddling me up. I didn't take the scarf. I left it behind."

Well done, Collins, Spiller thought. Aloud, he said, "Tell us what happened with Philippa's scarf."

"She tried to give it to me. It was something to do with a rugby team, but I told her I wasn't into all that. She wasn't best pleased with me, turning down a gift like that, and…"

Spiller leaned forward. "Please, go on, Jack. You're doing so well."

"We got into an argument, but it was nothing. Silly really. Just a misunderstanding."

"You argued and tempers flared," Spiller suggested.

"No. Listen, I got confused when you said I had something of hers. I haven't got anything. She offered me the scarf, but I turned it down, then I left her alone. I remember now, she was wearing the damned thing when I last saw her."

"Can you describe the scarf for us?" Collins asked.

"Sure. It was striped, blue and white, and a dark colour, maybe dark blue."

"That sounds like an Exeter Chiefs scarf," Spiller said. "Blue, white and black. I have one at home."

"Yes, that was it. Exeter Chiefs. That's what she said."

"And you're sure Philippa was wearing it when you saw her through the window on Saturday evening?" Spiller asked.

Devlin nodded. "It was tucked into her coat, but you could see the stripes."

"That's very helpful," Spiller said, "but actually, we were talking about a notebook. It's in the cottage and it has Philippa's name and phone number written inside."

"Oh, she'd put some pens and paper and stuff in the cottage. She thought I was a student, but as you know, I'm not. I never touched them."

"So you didn't use the book at all?"

"That's right. I never touched it."

Spiller paused. "Did you know that Philippa's phone number was written inside the book?"

"No. I didn't open it. I didn't need it, so why would I look inside?"

"Curiosity," Spiller offered. "You saw the book and opened it, and you saw what she'd written. Maybe it put an idea into your head; the idea that Philippa had given you her phone number for a reason. You might have seen it as an invitation."

"That's not what happened. I didn't see it."

"What about the message from Philippa?" Collins asked. "In the book, it said, 'Do the right thing'. How do you explain that?"

Devlin's face was a mask of bewilderment. "I can't. If Philippa wrote it, I have no idea why she would've done that. Maybe it was meant for someone else, or it could've been a reminder to herself."

Spiller stayed silent for a while, watching Devlin all the while. The man sat still, perhaps making an effort to give nothing away, but a vein throbbed on his temple, and his cheeks were pale. Although…

Spiller leaned forward. "Have you been in an accident, Jack?"

"No."

"A fight then?"

Devlin's hand went self-consciously to his left cheek.

"Yes, that's what I was looking at," Spiller said. "The lights are bright in here or I might not have noticed it, but there's a bit of a bruise on your left cheek. You've been in the wars, haven't you?"

"I knocked it somewhere. I forget how I did it. I think, maybe, I hit a branch when I was walking through the woods."

"When was this?" Collins asked.

"Erm, yesterday?"

"Are you asking us or telling us, Jack?" Spiller said.

"I'm telling you. It was yesterday."

Spiller arched an eyebrow. "When I saw you yesterday, you'd just come back from a walk, but you didn't have that mark then."

"No? Well, it must've been later then. I went out twice, both times to look for Philippa. The second time was after you'd been around with that other bloke."

Spiller sensed Collins looking at him, but he didn't react. He'd explain about Dan Corrigan's involvement later.

"You're making something out of nothing," Devlin went on. "I went into the woods for the second time but it started to get dark. I could hardly see where I was going and I walked into a low branch. It didn't really hurt, so I forgot all about it."

Keeping his expression neutral, Spiller said, "The thing is, branches are rough, and if you walk into one you get a scratch. Your skin isn't broken. It looks more like somebody gave you a punch or a very hard slap."

"No," Devlin protested, but Spiller swept on regardless.

"They're very interesting, bruises. They can tell us a lot. It's a fact that some bruises take a while to show up, so you could've been hit *before* I saw you on Saturday. The injury could've happened while you were talking with Philippa."

"That's ridiculous."

Spiller held out his hands, the fingers spread wide. "Is it? You've already told us that you and Philippa had an argument. Did it go further than that? Did she lash out at you?"

"No."

"We know that Philippa hit someone, Jack" Spiller said. "We found abrasions on her knuckles. Philippa struggled, and she got lucky. She landed a blow on your cheek. But it wasn't enough, was it? It wasn't enough to stop you from taking her life."

"I didn't…" Devlin covered his nose and mouth with his hands, and he shook his head violently. He mumbled something, his voice cracking up, but Spiller bided his time; he could wait.

Devlin sniffed and wiped at his eyes with his fingertips.

"Jack," Spiller began, "it's important to give your side of the story. Tell us what happened between you and Philippa."

Devlin lowered his hands and swallowed. "I didn't kill her. I didn't. You have to believe me. We had an argument, but it was nothing. Philippa gave me the scarf, and I didn't recognise it. I thought it was from the university, so she figured out I wasn't a student. She got angry. I tried to explain, but she wouldn't listen. She was drunk, out of control, and she hit me, so I… I didn't mean to do it, but…"

"What did you do, Jack?" Spiller asked.

Devlin pressed a hand against his chest. "I want that lawyer now. You said I could have one."

"Okay," Spiller said. "But first, I have to tell you that I'm arresting you on suspicion of the murder of Philippa Darley-Jones.

You do not have to say anything, but it may harm your defence if you do not mention when questioned something that you later rely on in court. Anything you do say may be given in evidence. Do you understand?"

Devlin stared at him like a deer frozen in the headlights of an oncoming truck.

"Do you understand what I've just told you?" Spiller said again.

"Yes." Devlin's voice was thin and his eyes had lost focus. "I understand."

To Collins, Spiller said, "Take Mr Devlin to the custody suite and get him booked in. See that he gets access to a legal adviser or a lawyer as soon as possible."

"Yes, guv." Collins gathered his things and stood. "Come on, Mr Devlin. Let's get this done."

Devlin stood slowly as though his legs were unsteady. "I didn't kill her. I didn't. You can't have any evidence, because I know I didn't do it. I *know*."

"Save that for your next interview," Spiller said. "We'll talk again soon."

Spiller ended the recording but remained sitting as Collins led Devlin from the room. *Twenty-four hours*, Spiller thought. *That's all I've got*. At the end of that time he'd have to charge Devlin or let him go, so the investigation team would have their work cut out. Devlin had been right; there was no real evidence against him. But Spiller had been compelled to arrest him. If Devlin had gone free, he'd have set about destroying any evidence, and if they'd prevented him from leaving, technically he'd have been under arrest anyway. It was better to keep everything formal and in accordance with procedure. This way, the team had a clear shot at Devlin's residence and belongings, including his phone, plus they'd be able to take his fingerprints and swab him for DNA.

There had to be something linking him to Philippa's murder. There had to be. All they had to do was to find it.

CHAPTER 63

Dan turned to face the door as Alan came back into Zadie's kitchen.

"He's gone," Alan said. "I watched until he was out of sight."

"You mean, Connor has left the building?"

Alan smiled. "What did you think of his performance?"

"Performance is the operative word. For my part, I found it most instructive."

"Careful. I know he compared you to Holmes, but that doesn't mean you have to start talking like him."

"I couldn't resist it," Dan replied. "Still, I meant what I said. Connor told us a lot more than he intended."

"Go on then, dazzle me with your deductions. Did you learn something by studying his shoe laces, or was it the scent of his shampoo that gave the vital clue?"

"I think we've tortured that bit of banter for long enough. Let's put it out of its misery and focus on the case."

Alan held up his hands. "I'm all ears."

"Okay. Connor told us one thing loud and clear: he's a liar. Shaun found Connor's cigarettes, and we both know what happened next. Shaun had one cigarette and felt light-headed.

Before he knew what he was doing, he was breaking into Zadie's house and wandering around. We'd wondered whether there was more than just tobacco in that cigarette, and now I'm certain."

"It would make sense," Alan said. "If Shaun was high, it could explain a lot."

"Exactly. Some time ago, Shaun saw Zadie through the window while she was getting changed, and I think he fixated on that memory. The drugs in the cigarette affected his impulse control, and he acted out his fantasy. Connor might be used to smoking cannabis, or whatever it was, but Shaun wasn't, and it tipped him over the edge."

Alan nodded. "Those cigarette stubs in the garden, we thought they smelt of cannabis."

"Yes, they almost certainly came from Connor. He could've been lurking in the garden, waiting for Zadie to go out. A sensible person would've cleaned up the evidence, but he's too lazy and too entitled to do even that."

"You've really taken against Connor, haven't you?"

"I don't trust him," Dan said. "He does and says whatever he wants. He has no job, no responsibilities and no principles. He doesn't seem to care about anything very much."

"He was upset when we talked about the accident. Losing his friend obviously had a profound effect on him."

"I didn't buy that sudden show of emotion. It was put on for our benefit, and he directed his performance at you because he figured you were an easier audience."

"I showed a little empathy," Alan replied. "There's nothing wrong with that."

"No, but it's wasted on the likes of Connor. He's a liar and a layabout."

"You've taken a dislike to him because he inherited his wealth. You get a chip on your shoulder whenever you have to deal with people who were born into money."

"I wouldn't say that," Dan replied, but without much conviction.

"Don't take it to heart," Alan said. "I've never had much patience with the overprivileged either. Still, it feels like we're finally getting somewhere, doesn't it?"

"We're building some momentum, but we're not out of the woods yet. We know Shaun moved the first note, but we still have no idea who wrote it and why. There must be connections we haven't found yet. We need to keep an open mind and go back to the beginning."

"Surely we've come further than that. We have made *some* progress, haven't we?"

"Yes, but starting again isn't necessarily bad," Dan said. "From the start, we made a dangerous assumption about the original note. We believed it had been left late at night, and who suggested that?"

Alan thought for a moment. "Connor. He put the idea into our heads and Zadie agreed, so we didn't pursue it. At the time, it seemed like a reasonable idea to work with."

"Exactly. Like all good lies, it was instantly believable and we swallowed it hook, line and sinker. But the game's up. Thanks to Shaun, we know the note was posted through the letterbox shortly after Zadie and Natalya left the house. At that point, Zadie's friends almost certainly hadn't arrived at the pub, so we have no idea where they were."

Alan whipped out his notebook and flipped through the pages. Stopping to read, he said, "Connor was quite vague about the time Philippa picked him up. He said it was about seven, but even so, he couldn't have left the note and then been home in time for Philippa to collect him, especially since he doesn't drive."

"Unless Philippa was in on it."

"My God," Alan murmured. "That could make sense."

"They worked together to terrorise Zadie, but something went wrong," Dan said. "Perhaps they never intended Zadie to be so seriously hurt. Philippa had an attack of conscience and wanted to confess, so Connor decided to silence her."

"It's a bit melodramatic, isn't it? I can't help feeling there's a simpler explanation."

"I've just laid it out for you. It doesn't get much simpler than that."

Alan shook his head as if unconvinced. "A minute ago, we said the note was ambiguous at best. It's open to interpretation." Alan looked back at his notebook, turning the page as he read. "The first note could've been left by Melody. She knew she was going to be late for the meal, so she dropped in to explain. She saw Natalya's car was in the driveway, so she assumed they were still at home. She didn't know they'd already set off in Zadie's Tesla."

"So why not simply ring the bell? Why not knock on the door?"

Alan tapped his notebook. "Her hair was a mess, remember? Her new hair colour was a disaster, and she didn't want to be seen."

"I remember. I also remember that she'd had her hair done the day before, so she'd had all of Sunday to deal with it. Why would she wait until the last moment?"

"I don't know," Alan admitted. "But women can be very sensitive about these things. Imagine if you had a friend as glamorous as Zadie; would you want her to see you when you were feeling bad about the way you look?"

Dan pursed his lips. "So you think this whole thing is a simple misunderstanding. You think the note was harmless and everyone misinterpreted it."

Alan hesitated. "It started out that way, but then Melody thought it might be fun to keep it going, and she got carried away. Remember, Melody isn't quite who she appears to be. She's changed her name, and she's done all she can to fit in. But Zadie knew about Melody's past, and she used that knowledge to put Melody in her place. That's enough to make anyone resentful."

"Resentful, yes, but vindictive?" Dan said. "We've talked to Melody, and I can't see her as cruel or manipulative. My money is still on Connor, and I think he may have dragged Philippa into his plan."

"Hang on a minute," Alan said. "Connor told us there were half a dozen cigarettes in the tin when he last saw it, but Shaun said there were only three when he found them. I don't see why Connor would lie about such a small detail, so who smoked the missing cigarettes?"

Dan stared into space as his thoughts tumbled over each other. Alan's argument wasn't conclusive, but some instinct told Dan it was important. They were missing something, but what?

"Alan! Dan!" The call came from the hallway, and a moment later, Natalya hurried into the kitchen, breathless. "There is someone at the door. A policeman. He came before."

"DI Spiller?" Dan asked.

Natalya shook her head. "No. The other one. Younger."

"DC Collins," Alan said. "You'd better let him in."

"Okay. I'll bring him in here." Natalya composed herself then strode from the room, returning a moment later with DC Collins trailing in her wake.

If Collins was surprised to see Dan and Alan, he didn't let it show. After a brief greeting, he turned his attention to Natalya.

"You might like to sit down," Collins said. "There's something we need to talk about."

Natalya froze. "Is it Zadie? Is she all right?"

"As far as I know, Ms Barrington is doing okay," Collins said hurriedly. "DI Spiller has been checking with the hospital, and the last we heard, Ms Barrington was stable."

Natalya let out a breath. "That's good."

"Yes," Collins replied. "But I'm here about another matter. Please have a seat, Ms Rudenko."

"Okay." Natalya pulled out a stool and perched on it. "Is it about Philippa?"

Collins nodded, his expression grave. "What have you heard?"

"I know… I know Philippa is dead. It's terrible. She was found this morning, yes?"

"I'm afraid that's right," Collins said. "I appreciate that this is a difficult time, but we're doing our best to find out what happened. If you don't mind answering a few questions, it'll help."

"Of course," Natalya replied. "What do you want to know?"

Collins took out his phone and began. "Philippa was a friend of Zadie's, wasn't she?"

Natalya nodded. "Philippa came here all the time."

"When did you last see her?"

"She hasn't been here since Tuesday."

"Almost a week ago," Collins said. "Is that unusual or did she sometimes visit more often?"

"Usually she came two or three times in a week, but I think she was busy. She had a holiday cottage. She was getting it ready."

Unable to wait any longer, Dan blurted, "DI Spiller knows about this. The lodger's name is Jack Devlin, and if you haven't already, you really need to talk to him."

Collins turned his patient gaze on Dan. "Mr Corrigan, I understand you were concerned about Philippa at the weekend."

"Yes. Her friend, Melody, told us she'd been trying to get in touch with Philippa, but there was no reply. She was worried, so we went to Philippa's house, but there was no one home. I've already told all this to DI Spiller."

"Yes, he's filled me in," Collins said. "Was there a particular reason you didn't go through the usual channels and report Philippa as missing?"

"At first we thought she might've gone away for a few days," Dan said. "Philippa isn't tied to a regular job, and I don't think she has any family, so there's nothing to stop her taking a break."

"So why did you call the DI?"

"We went to the holiday cottage and talked to Jack Devlin. He seemed like a suspicious character to us, and we were worried. We thought he might've played a part in Philippa's sudden disappearance."

Collins expression remained fixed. "We?"

"Alan came with me," Dan replied.

"That's right," Alan said. "And I agreed with Dan: Devlin seemed very shifty."

"What gave you that impression?"

"For a start, he lied to us," Alan replied. "He told us he lived in

Exeter, but the address he gave us was nonsense. It was in the middle of a trading estate."

"That wouldn't happen to be the Marsh Barton estate, would it?" Collins asked.

Alan nodded. "Yes, it was actually. He said he lived near Trusham Road."

"That is interesting. Was there anything else that Mr Devlin said to you, anything that seemed suspicious?"

"He told us he'd been out looking for Philippa," Dan said. "He said he was worried, but I didn't believe him. He hardly knew her, and I doubt whether he'd do anything so selfless."

Collins looked unimpressed.

"Also, we'd seen an odd text message," Dan went on. "It was from Philippa's phone, but it wasn't written in her style and we think someone else sent it."

"Who was the message sent to?"

"Me," Natalya said. Her cheeks coloured and she looked only at Collins, avoiding eye contact with Dan and Alan. "But we have done the wrong thing."

"In what way?" Collins asked.

"We found Zadie's phone, and I switched it on. I know the PIN and…"

"You'd better tell me all about it," Collins said.

Her voice faltering, Natalya explained how Shaun had found Zadie's phone, and they'd decided to check it before handing it over.

Natalya finished by saying, "I thought it might help, but then there was another message on Zadie's phone, and I didn't know what to do. I didn't want to get into trouble."

"You should have told us about the phone straight away," Collins said. "But you won't get into trouble for reading a message."

"But it was from Philippa," Natalya blurted. "And that can't be right. It only came a couple of hours ago, and she was… she was dead."

"Ms Rudenko, could you give me that phone now?" Collins asked. "I need to see it."

"Yes. I'll go and get it." Natalya left the room, and Dan watched DC Collins carefully. He was tapping notes into his phone, and though his expression had remained impassive, his body language had changed completely, his upper body tense, his elbows pinned tight against his side as he worked.

"You've got someone in custody, haven't you?" Dan said.

Collins' head snapped up, his gaze sharp. "I beg your pardon."

"I'm right, aren't I?" Dan said. "You've arrested someone already, but this message must've come from Philippa's killer, so you've got the wrong man."

"I'm not going to comment on that," Collins said. "I'm not here to answer your questions, Mr Corrigan. I'd have thought that would be clear to you."

The brief silence was broken by Natalya coming back into the kitchen, Zadie's phone cradled in her palm. "Here. I've unlocked it." She passed the phone to Collins, and he scanned the screen, his expression tightening.

"Thank you for this," Collins said. "I'll have to take the phone with me. It's an encrypted message, so that's the only way we can see it."

"Yes, take it," Natalya said. "I wish I hadn't looked at it. I'm sorry."

"If you didn't know about this message, that means you haven't found Philippa's phone," Dan stated.

Collins looked as though he might not reply, but then he said, "Not yet, but we will."

"I wouldn't bet on it," Dan replied. "Someone will have taken the sim out and the battery too. They probably put them back in for a few seconds, just long enough to send a text. This was a couple of hours ago, so they were trying to throw you off the trail. At the time, they obviously didn't know you'd found Philippa, but they'll have heard the news by now, so they'll have destroyed the phone and got rid of it."

517

"We're actively pursuing a number of leads," Collins replied. "Our digital forensics team are already hard at work and it's amazing what they can do. We'll find the person responsible." Looking at each of them in turn, he added, "If any of you can think of anything that might help, we need to hear it. Don't hold back. If there was anything that was upsetting Philippa, or anyone who might've wished her harm, we need to know."

"We've already told you about Jack Devlin," Dan said. "Wait. Is that who you've arrested?"

Collins looked uncomfortable. "I can't comment on that, sir. We don't give out details of an active investigation, and there's no point in speculating; that won't help anyone. Leave this to us now. We'll do everything we possibly can. In the meantime, here are my numbers."

Collins produced some business cards and handed them out. "If you think of anything that might help, please get in touch."

"We'll do that," Dan said. "We'll call you or DI Spiller."

"It's best if you call me. The DI is a busy man, and he has a lot of responsibilities. If you think of something, call me and I'll be sure to pass it on."

"Yes, we will," Natalya said. "Is there anything else you want to know?"

"Not for the moment, but I'll be in touch."

"Thank you. I'll see you out." Natalya led Collins from the room.

Alan's watchful gaze followed Natalya and Collins as they left the room together, and Dan thought he detected a jealous gleam in Alan's eye. It was out of character, but then, emotions were running high and they were all on edge. Whatever the reason, Dan wasn't going to comment.

There was room for only one train of thought in his mind, one burning question: who killed Philippa Darley-Jones?

CHAPTER 64

Zadie fell through the soft darkness. *It's not real,* she told herself. *It's the dream again.* The pattern was familiar; she recognised it all too well. But this time, when she hit the ground, her body jerked and a sudden wave of disorientation swept through her: a dizzying sensation of reality clashing with her nightmare, like stepping onto a stair that wasn't there.

Bright light filtered through her eyelids. From somewhere, a wavering hum droned on and on, like a fan or a vent, and she tasted something bitter on her tongue. Then suddenly, she was aware of something else.

Someone stood near to her. She could hear them breathing. And her nightmare wasn't a dream, but a memory.

They're here. The intruder stood over her, gloating. Zadie swallowed hard. *Why?* she wanted to demand. *Why do you hate me so?* But her tongue was heavy and she couldn't speak.

To hell with that!

Zadie screamed, her eyelids flying open. The light dazzled her, but at least the figure standing over her recoiled.

"Christ, Sis! You practically gave me a heart attack."

Zadie stopped screaming and blinked rapidly. The figure swam into focus. "Tobias? What are you doing here? What's going on? Where…?"

Tobias moved closer. "It's all right, Zadie. You're in hospital but you're going to be okay. You've had a fall, but the doctors are really pleased with how you're doing."

"Hospital?" Zadie tried to push herself up, but her body was heavy and sluggish, waves of pain shooting up from her feet and through her calves. She slumped back on the pillow. "My legs. What's wrong with me? I'm not…"

"Don't worry, there's no permanent damage. Your ankles and knees have taken a pounding, and you banged your head, so it'll be a while before you're up to full strength, but they say you're healing remarkably fast. It must be all those veggies you eat. I ought to try it. Knock the meat on the head for a bit."

"You? Never. You think a lemon twist in your gin is one of your five a day."

Tobias grimaced in mock horror. "You mean it isn't? You'll be telling me olives don't count in a minute."

He wiped his hand over his face and chuckled. "I can't tell you how good it is to have you telling me off again."

"You know me, always happy to help." Zadie tried to move but the pain in her legs made her wince. "Can you give me a hand to sit up?"

"I'll call someone. A nurse."

"No, I can do it. I just need a hand." Zadie took her weight on her arms and struggled to pull herself up, but it was much harder than it should've been.

"Hang on, let me fix the bed." Tobias moved to the side and did something out of Zadie's eyeline.

Slowly, the bed began to tilt upward beneath her shoulders, moving her gently into a sitting position.

"That's far enough," Zadie said, and Tobias stepped back.

"I figured out the buttons a while back, and I've been dying to have a go. I haven't had much else to occupy my mind for the last few days.

"Days? How long have I been here?"

"Don't worry yourself, Zadie. I'll get a doctor to come and—"

"Tobias, tell me. How long have I been here?"

Tobias bowed his head slightly. "You've been here for three days. It's Monday and you fell on Friday night."

"Yes. It was Friday." Zadie stared into space, her eyes growing round.

"Zadie, what's the matter? Listen, I'm going to get a doctor."

But before Tobias could move, Zadie reached out with a sudden surge of strength and grabbed his arm. "I got away," she said, her voice hoarse. "I escaped."

"From whom?"

Zadie shook her head. "I don't know. I climbed out the window."

"Why did you do that, Zadie? What were you afraid of?"

"I don't know who it was, but he was in the house."

Tobias seemed to be studying her. "Did you *see* someone?"

"I heard him. But he'd been in my room before. I don't know when, but he must've been there before."

"Why do you say that?"

Zadie hissed in frustration. "Because of the pictures. Where did he get the pictures?"

"What pictures?"

"The photos of me," Zadie stated. "They were in the coffin. They were under my bed."

Tobias nodded slowly. "I think you need to take a deep breath or two and calm down. You mustn't upset yourself."

"I am calm. I'm not making this up. There were photos of me. Lots of them. Someone hid them under my bed. Lots and lots of photos in a weird little coffin. It freaked me out. You must've seen it."

"Zadie, that doesn't sound likely. I really don't think there was a coffin under your bed."

"It wasn't a real one. It was like a toy. A model. I pulled it out but it must still be there."

Tobias pursed his lips. "Zadie, the police have been to your house, and no one has said anything about a toy coffin or any photos."

"That's ridiculous. Talk to…" Zadie let go of Tobias' arm and circled her hand in the air as if groping for a word. "Dan. Talk to Dan. Ask him about the coffin and the photos."

"Okay, I'll do that." Tobias looked down at her, concern in his eyes. "Zadie, are you sure you didn't imagine all this? You've had a head injury, and even before then, you were a bit anxious."

"I didn't *imagine* anything, Tobias. There was a little wooden coffin under my bed. Someone had put my phone in it, and when I took it out, there were photos underneath. Lots of them. They were all pictures of me, pictures taken without me knowing about it. Don't you understand? Someone has been spying on me, trying to frighten me."

"Okay, okay," Tobias said. "I believe you, and I'll talk to Dan, but first, we need to get a doctor to come and check you out." Tobias edged back from her bed. "I'm going to get someone." He took another step back. "I won't be long, just try not to worry. Don't overexcite yourself."

"I'm not," Zadie began, but Tobias had turned his back on her and was already hurrying away. "I didn't imagine it," Zadie whispered to the empty room. "It was real. All of it was real."

CHAPTER 65

Alone in the kitchen at Zadie's house, Dan ended the call from Tobias Barrington. He gathered his thoughts for a second, then he went to find Alan. Upstairs in the studio, Alan sat at Zadie's desk, typing on the laptop, but there was no sign of Natalya.

"Hello," Alan said without pausing in his task. "I'll be with you in a second." He rattled off a few decisive keystrokes then smiled wearily. "There. I can take a breather. Zadie's social media takes some keeping up with. I don't know how Nat does it."

"Dedication," Dan replied. "Where is she?"

"She popped out for a few minutes to get some fresh air. I said I'd take over for a bit while she…" Alan's voice trailed away as he took in Dan's expression. "What's up? Not more bad news."

"No, it's good actually. I had a call from Tobias. Zadie's awake. They're checking her over, but he thinks the doctors are satisfied. It sounds like she's doing well."

Alan let out a sigh of relief. "That is good news. Thank goodness."

"Apparently, she was able to tell Tobias something of what happened."

"Oh? What did she say?"

Dan relayed the information Tobias had given him, and Alan listened, his expression growing graver by the second.

When Dan finished, Alan said, "A coffin? That's very strange, very macabre."

"Yes, at least it would be if it really happened."

"Do they think Zadie's memory was affected? I wouldn't be surprised. She's been in a coma for days. That's enough to leave anyone confused."

"It's not just that," Dan said. "Remember what Tobias told us about Zadie's past?"

Alan nodded. "Anxiety, BPD, hearing voices. But that was a long time ago."

"Even so, Tobias is worried she's had some sort of relapse, brought on by the stress of everything that's happened."

Alan looked thoughtful. "We certainly didn't find any photos in her room, and there was definitely no sign of a miniature coffin. Everything looked as neat as the rest of the house."

"Someone could've tidied up afterward, and let's not forget that Zadie climbed out of the window. She wouldn't have done that unless she was seriously scared."

"Are you suggesting that we take what she said at face value?"

"I'm saying we need to consider it. It could be an extreme form of gaslighting."

"In that case, we'd be looking for someone who has access to the house, and someone who'd go to great lengths to construct an elaborate plot to scare Zadie out of her wits."

Dan nodded. "Also, someone who knew about Zadie's previous issues with her mental health."

"What about motive? Why on earth would anyone do something so despicable?"

"I don't know," Dan admitted. "That's the problem with this case. The motive has been missing from the start, so we've been going round in circles, suspecting everyone."

"*Qui bono?*" Alan said. "Who benefits? Zadie is wealthy, and if she wasn't able to manage her affairs, who would take over? Tobias?"

"I expect he would be next in line, but he's a barrister so he won't be short of cash. On the other hand, he's keen to put this latest episode down to Zadie's mental health. That's the very definition of gaslighting, isn't it? And he knows Zadie better than anyone. Plus, it was his idea that she should come and live in Devon. He helped her to find this house. Is that because, as he says, he wanted to keep her safe, or was he trying to control her?"

"To what end?" Alan asked.

"Aside from getting his hands on her money, there could be some kind of simmering resentment dating back to their childhood. Maybe Tobias felt starved of attention while his parents fretted over Zadie. It could be that simple."

Alan thought for a second." Tobias didn't turn up until the second note was left, and he only came because Connor called him."

"Yes, but the first thing Tobias did was to try and take control. He gave us our marching orders."

"He changed his tune later though," Alan said. "Tobias can be bossy and overprotective, but I think he genuinely cares about Zadie. Also, he has a lot to lose. If he was caught breaking the law he'd be disbarred, and that would be the end of his career and his reputation."

"What about his link with Philippa?" Dan said. "At one time, they were together. Now Philippa is dead, and his sister is in hospital. Is Tobias really just an innocent bystander in all that mayhem?"

"No smoke without fire?" Alan sent Dan a reproving look. "You always say that kind of speculation is lazy thinking."

"You're right. Let's take a step back, but we'll assume Zadie's version of events is correct. Someone came into the house and left a small coffin full of photos beneath her bed. We'll go from there."

"Agreed," Alan said. "For a start, I want to know who could've taken those photos. It must've been someone who knew her schedule, someone who could get close enough to take pictures without raising suspicion. Does that mean we're still looking at Zadie's friends?"

"Naomi is a photographer," Dan replied. "She'd be the obvious candidate."

"Naomi? She wouldn't say boo to a goose."

"I'm not so sure about that. Think back to Sunday. When we met Naomi at the church, did you notice anything different about her?"

"Not particularly," Alan said. "I hadn't realised she was quite so attractive. The more formal attire really suited her, and her blouse brought out the colour of her eyes."

"Trust you to notice that. But that's not what I meant. I was thinking about her manner. She was quite forthright with us, and she wasn't going to stand for any nonsense."

"Yes, but I'd have thought the reason was obvious. I imagine she takes her faith seriously. I did try to warn you against bothering people when they're in church. It was bound to upset somebody."

"There was more to it than that. Naomi was like a different person. She scolded us in no uncertain fashion. I have a feeling she showed her true colours that day."

"You're being too quick to judge her," Alan said. "We were in the wrong, and Naomi was within her rights to set us straight. I don't think a few stern words amounts to much."

"On the other hand, we know that Naomi can be quite dramatic," Dan replied. "When we first met her, Naomi stormed out of the room like a highly strung actor flouncing from the stage. That fits with the pattern of harassment we've seen so far. The notes, the knife, the coffin: they were all carefully placed, setting the scene for a piece of theatre."

Alan shook his head. "Naomi left the room that day because the others were belittling her, ganging up on her. She had good reason to be upset."

"But she didn't stay and defend herself," Dan insisted. "Rather than face up to her friends, she marched out. She suppressed her anger, and a person can only do that for so long."

"That's true, I suppose. I can see where you're going with this. I'm not sure I believe it wholeheartedly, but there could be another side to Naomi, and we caught a glimpse of it outside the church when she stood up to us and told us off."

"Believe it," Dan said. "And here's another fact: since we set our trap, Naomi is the only one of Zadie's friends who hasn't come to visit."

"Connor didn't show up until we invited him," Alan pointed out.

"Yes, but when we asked him, he came straight away, and he acted as if he expected to see Zadie at home. Naomi hasn't come because she knows Zadie isn't here."

Alan tilted his head from side to side. "It's thin, but we'd better follow it up. We could invite Naomi over and see if she accepts. I still have her contact details."

"If we do that, she'll be on her guard and she'll have time to prepare. I'd rather drop in on her and see what we can find out."

"Naomi lives in Exeter, and we're supposed to be waiting here. We can't leave Natalya to deal with everything. What if someone turns up?"

"I think our pretence has run its course, don't you?" Dan said. "We're not going to learn anything new by staying here. Besides, Natalya can manage perfectly well. She's more than capable."

Dan hesitated. "If you'd rather stay here, I could go to Exeter on my own."

"There's no question of that. If it turns out Naomi is behind all this, she's more devious than she seems. You need backup."

"I can handle Naomi."

"Physically, yes," Alan said. "But what if she tries to get you into trouble? One allegation is all it takes, and then you'd be the one taken in by the police."

"Okay, we'll go together," Dan said. "Do you want to go and tell Natalya where we're going?"

"Yes." Alan jumped to his feet. "I'll meet you in the car."

"Fine. You won't be too long, will you?"

"Credit me with a little professionalism," Alan said, then he strode from the room.

Dan stayed where he was for a few seconds, thinking. Was Naomi capable of harassing Zadie, gaslighting her, making her fear for her life and her sanity? If she'd been behind the notes and the veiled threats, what was her motive? Did she hate Zadie so utterly and completely? If so, why?

But no answers came to Dan. Not one.

CHAPTER 66

The sign was shiny and brand new. *Welcome to Exebrook*, it read. *Mason Homes, Building Communities.* Dan took the correct exit from the roundabout, which also looked as though it had only recently been completed. In the centre of the roundabout was an artfully arranged heap of stone blocks, its surface dotted with small pockets of vegetation.

In the passenger seat, Alan tutted. "I don't know what that pile of rocks is supposed to be."

"At least it's neat," Dan said. "Perhaps it'll look better when the plants have grown."

"I doubt it." Alan had been in an unusually dour mood since they'd left Zadie's house, but Dan hadn't dared to ask why. Alan would confide in him if and when he was ready. Dan kept quiet as he drove into Exebrook, following the winding road, his mind on the case.

On the edge of Exeter, Exebrook had been easy to find, with plenty of signposts along the road. *Executive Homes*, the first one had read, closely followed by, *3- and 4-Bedroom Houses for Sale.* Finally, the series ended with: *Affordable Housing.* Dan had wondered at the developers' understanding of the word 'affordable', but he mentally acknowledged their marketing efforts.

They were plainly keen that no potential customers should pass them by.

Now they were here, Dan looked forward to seeing where Naomi lived.

"Exebrook," Alan muttered. "There's a contrived name if ever I saw one. We're nowhere near the river Exe, and if there ever was a brook, they'll have built over it."

"People need places to live," Dan replied. "You can't blame them for wanting to get away from the city centre."

"No, but you can blame the planners for allowing this kind of thing. This was all fields and farms once. Now look at it."

It's really not that bad, Dan thought, but there was no point in antagonising Alan. Although not a native of Devon, Alan had adopted it as his county, and he was fiercely protective of its wild moorland, its wooded valleys and its rolling farmland.

Here, the only patches of green were the grass verges alongside the road, and they looked as though they'd been laid as fresh grown turf. The rest of the space was filled with modern detached houses, some larger than others, but all were almost identical in design, laid out in uniform rows that followed the curved roads.

"They call this a community?" Alan grumbled. "Where are the shops, the school, the post office, the pubs and cafes?"

"Not everyone can live in a village like Embervale," Dan said. "Most people can't afford it. We're lucky."

"Yes, I know. Ignore me. You've had enough of me banging on about housing estates, I'm sure. I'm a bit out of sorts, that's all."

"It's something to do with Natalya, isn't it?"

Alan sighed. "I should've known you'd guess. It's nothing, really, but when I went to say goodbye to her, she was quite offhand with me. It's not like I was expecting some grand emotional scene, but I thought she might've been a little disappointed to see me go."

"Alan, I hope you don't mind me making an observation. I have no idea what Natalya's life was like in Ukraine, but I imagine there were some hard times, and she got through them by being self-reliant. She's hardly going to get upset over you popping out for an hour."

"Maybe so, but she's not as tough as people think," Alan replied. "She's…"

"Yes," Dan said. "She is, isn't she?"

"You've no idea what I was going to say."

"Haven't I? When you can't put something into words, Alan, I know it must be very important, and that's good enough for me."

Alan nodded thoughtfully. He didn't speak again until he pointed through the windscreen and said, "That's it. Next left. Yew Tree Avenue." Under his breath he added, "Not a yew nor any other tree in sight."

Dan smiled and took the turning. A minute later, he parked the Toyota outside one of the smaller detached houses. There were curtains at the windows, and a small potted shrub beside the front door. A red Mazda 3 sat on the drive.

"That's the hatchback we saw outside Zadie's house the other day," Alan said. "It looks as though Naomi might be at home."

"Yes. Let's go."

They exited the car and marched to the front door. Dan rang the doorbell, and while they waited, he stepped back and studied the windows.

A few seconds later, the door opened and Naomi appeared, smiling at them uncertainly. Dressed in faded jeans and a T-shirt, and with her dark hair tousled, she looked younger than Dan had remembered.

"Hello, Naomi," Dan said. "Sorry to disturb you. Have we come at a bad time?"

"No. I was working, that's all. Can I help you with something?"

"I hope so," Dan replied. "Do you mind if we come in for a minute? We wanted to ask you a couple of things."

"About what? If it's anything to do with John, I've got nothing to say."

"It's not about Mr Callaway," Dan said quickly. "We want to talk about Zadie."

"It'll only take a minute," Alan added. "We wouldn't ask if it wasn't important. We're just trying to keep your friend safe."

"Oh, all right. You'd better come in."

Naomi ushered them into her front room, where the two-seater sofa took up the lion's share of the floorspace. Swiping a fleecy throw from the sofa, she said, "Have a seat."

"Thank you," Alan said, taking one end of the sofa while Dan positioned himself at the other.

Naomi pulled up a beanbag and sat looking up at them, her elbows on her knees and her chin on her hands.

Looking around the room, Alan said, "It's a nice place you have here. Very cosy."

"It suits me," Naomi replied. "For the moment anyway."

"You said you were working," Dan said. "Where do you do that? Do you have a studio?"

Naomi let out a wry laugh. "There's no room for anything like that." She gestured to a small table where a silvery laptop sat, its lid closed. "That's where I do most of my work. Almost everything I do is digital."

"Adobe Photoshop?" Dan asked.

"Sometimes, but I mainly use Lightroom, especially when I'm dealing with RAW images."

"Raw?" Alan said.

"R, A, W," Dan explained. "They're uncompressed files so the images are much higher resolution, better quality."

"The man knows his stuff." Naomi favoured Dan with a smile. "Do you take photos yourself?"

"A few snaps with my phone, that's my limit," Dan replied. "But I am interested in computers, so I know a brand-new MacBook Pro when I see one. How are you finding it?"

"It's great. My old Mac was on its last legs, so this one is like a breath of fresh air."

"Expensive though," Dan said. "How much did it set you back?"

"It was an investment. It's very fast, so I get a lot more work done. It'll pay for itself in no time."

Dan nodded as if convinced, but he noted that she hadn't answered his question.

"Anyway, you didn't come here to talk about photos," Naomi went on. "You said something about Zadie."

"That's right," Dan replied. "I was wondering if you've ever taken photos of Zadie."

"Yes, quite a few."

"Professionally?" Alan asked.

Naomi sat upright, clasping her hands in her lap as if attempting to look indignant, though it was a hard effect to achieve while sinking into a beanbag.

"I take a professional approach to all my work, but Zadie didn't pay me to take them if that's what you mean."

"So why take the photos?" Dan asked.

"You've seen her. Zadie's a fantastic model. Any photographer would want to shoot her."

"So you took the pictures for practice," Alan suggested. "To develop your skills."

"Yes, and to build up my portfolio. I've put some of them on my website."

"Does Zadie know you've done that?" Dan said.

"Yes, at least, I told her at the time. I wouldn't dream of taking advantage of her. I always give her a credit, and I link back to her website. You can have a look if you want."

"That would be great," Alan said. "Actually, I did glance at your website the other day, but I didn't see any photos of Zadie."

"You looked at my site? Why?"

"I was curious," Alan replied.

Naomi kept her gaze on him as if expecting more, and Alan crumbled.

"We looked into all Zadie's friends when we took the case, so naturally, I came across your website."

"Right," Naomi said. "What did you think of it?"

"I was impressed. Was it expensive to have it built?"

Naomi summoned a smile. "I did it myself. It's good to have more than one string to your bow. But I can see how you might've missed Zadie's photos; my portfolio is pretty big. I'll show you."

Naomi sprung up from the beanbag and fetched her laptop, opening the lid and cradling it with one arm while she tapped on the keys and touchpad with her other hand. "Here."

She passed the laptop to Alan, and he rested it on his knees, angling the screen so that Dan could see it.

On the screen was a large photo of Zadie sitting at a table in a coffee shop or a cafe, a vibrant green smoothie in a tall glass in front of her. The photo was razor sharp and composed beautifully, the light from a window falling softly on Zadie's face, giving her an almost angelic glow.

"It's very good," Alan said. "You have an excellent eye."

Naomi looked quietly pleased. "Thank you. There are more. You can scroll through the thumbnails."

Alan obliged, and they sat in silence for a while, flicking through one photo after another, all of them with Zadie as the only subject, her striking beauty captured over and over again.

"These are excellent," Dan said. "But I can't help noticing that Zadie is never looking at the camera."

"It's a collection of candid shots. That's where the subject appears to be unaware they're being photographed." Naomi smiled modestly. "It's something of a speciality of mine."

"Did Zadie know you were taking them?" Alan asked.

"Oh yes. At the time, she was aware of every shot. She gave me permission to use them, but she's probably forgotten. Most of them are from a couple of years ago, when Zadie first came to Chagford. I showed her my website, or I tried to, but she…" Naomi hesitated. "She was busy."

"Zadie's always busy, isn't she?" Dan said. "I don't mind telling you, I find it quite exhausting being around her."

Naomi seemed to look at Dan with fresh eyes. "She's a

whirlwind. The rest of us are like leaves, being blown around in her wake."

Dan made a show of nodding in eager agreement. "Zadie's great, but I sometimes feel as if she isn't listening to a word I say."

"I thought that was just me," Naomi said. "Zadie doesn't pay any attention to me at all, unless I do something stupid, that is." Naomi looked down, a wry smile on her lips. "It's funny."

"What is?"

Naomi looked up. "Nobody has asked about my work for ages, but this is the second time I've shown those photos to someone in the last month."

"Who was the other person?" Dan asked.

"Tobias. Zadie's brother. He asked if I could get him some prints. He was making an album, he said. A present."

Dan's pulse quickened. "Did you make the prints? Did you give them to him?"

"Yes. I wasn't sure whether Zadie would appreciate the album, but he paid me, so I thought, why not?"

"Couldn't he just have downloaded them from the website himself?" Alan asked.

"He could try, but they wouldn't have been good enough quality to print. The files on my site might look okay on a small screen, but they're low-res, and I watermark everything on my website."

"I see." Dan looked closer at the images on the screen and saw that each one had Naomi's name written across some part of it in translucent lettering. The watermarks had been carefully positioned so as not to distract the eye too readily, but they would spoil the photo for anyone who downloaded them.

"Anyway, why are you so interested in photos of Zadie?" Naomi asked. "Is there a problem with them?" Naomi's eyes widened. "She doesn't want me to take them down, does she? Oh hell, she's not angry with me, is she?"

"No, it's nothing like that," Dan replied. "We're simply

following up on a lead." He offered a reassuring smile. "Out of interest, what size were the prints you made for Tobias?"

Naomi tilted her head to one side. "Ten by eight. That's in inches. We still use old-fashioned print sizes for some reason. Don't ask me why."

"Did you print them yourself or order them from somewhere else?" Dan asked.

"I had them done at a lab. I use the same place for all my prints. They're not cheap but they do a much better job than I could." Naomi sent Dan a quizzical look. "You still haven't explained what the problem is."

Dan framed his reply carefully. "Someone had photographs of Zadie, and they were using them in a way she didn't like."

"It happens. Welcome to the age of the internet. People think that if something's online, they can do what they want with it. There's no respect for copyright anymore." Naomi sighed in exasperation. "But listen, about those prints I made for Tobias. You won't say anything about them to Zadie, will you?"

"Why's that?"

"Tobias said they were going to be a surprise. He was very secretive about it. I thought it was quite sweet of him. He obviously thinks a lot of Zadie. He often talks about her, and he's always sung her praises, even before she came to live here."

"Did you know him back then?" Dan asked.

"Yes. You know he used to be with Philippa, don't you? I've known Philippa for ages."

Dan and Alan glanced at each other. Gently, Dan said, "Have you heard about Philippa?"

"How do you mean?" Naomi's face fell. "Is she okay?"

"I'm afraid not," Alan replied. "I'm sorry to tell you this, but Philippa has been found dead."

Naomi's hand went to her mouth, but she didn't make a sound.

"Philippa was found this morning," Dan said. "She was in the river, fully clothed."

"I don't understand," Naomi mumbled, her cheeks deathly

pale. "How could this happen? I've been working all day, but why did nobody tell me? Why?"

Alan stood. "Please, Naomi, sit down for a second." He gestured for Dan to get up, and he obliged.

"Alan's right," Dan said. "Please sit down."

Naomi nodded meekly then sat on the couch, perching on its edge, her lips trembling. "Not Philippa. Not her."

Alan set the laptop down on the table. "Naomi, you ought to have a glass of water. Is the kitchen along the hall?"

"Yes. I'll show you." Naomi started to stand, but Alan waved her back down.

"I'll get it," Alan said, "or I can make you a cup of tea or coffee."

"Just water. Thank you." Naomi stayed quiet until Alan left the room, then she looked up at Dan. "Was it an accident, what happened to Philippa?"

"We don't think so. The police are treating her death as suspicious."

"Of course." Naomi looked away, her gaze losing focus.

"Naomi, do you know something about Philippa, something that might have put her at risk?"

Before Naomi could answer, Alan bustled back in with a glass of water and handed it to her. "Here we are. It's nice and cold. Take a sip."

"Where did you get it?" Naomi asked, her voice growing stronger. "Is it mineral water?"

"No, I used the tap, but I ran it for a few seconds first," Alan said. "Do you want mineral water instead? I can go and get it."

"No, there's no need." Naomi attempted a smile, and when she spoke again, her voice was softer. "Tap water's fine, thank you." Naomi took a sip, the colour returning to her cheeks. "I feel better now. If you don't mind, I'd like to be on my own for a bit."

"That's perfectly understandable," Alan replied. "Will you be all right?"

"I'll be fine. I need to sit quietly for a while, and I've got some calls to make."

"We'll be on our way," Dan said. "But just now, you were just going to say something about Philippa."

"Was I?"

"Yes. When I said her death was suspicious, you said, 'of course,' and it sounded almost as if you expected it."

Naomi simply stared into the middle distance, tight-lipped.

"You don't have to answer," Alan said. "We understand. You've had a shock, and the last thing you need is us pestering you. We'll go." Fixing Dan with a look, Alan inclined his head toward the door.

"We'll leave in a sec." Dan squatted down in front of Naomi. "I don't want to upset you, but if there's anything that's worrying you about what happened to Philippa, please tell us now."

"Worried?" Naomi blinked at Dan. "It's too late to be worried. She's gone."

"Yes, but have you any idea who might've wanted to harm her?"

Naomi let out a long breath." No, but I do know she was frightened sometimes. I don't know what was on her mind; she was never going to confide in me. Truth be told, Philippa didn't like me very much, but I can tell when someone's scared. When you've felt that way yourself, you recognise it in others."

What frightened you, Naomi? Dan thought, but this wasn't the right time for such a question. Naomi was holding it together, but her eyes gleamed with freshly formed tears. She'd need time to come to terms with the bombshell they'd just dropped, but for now, she'd need the space to express her grief.

"I'm sorry for your loss," Dan said. "And I'm sorry for the way we sprung it on you. We'll go now, but before we leave is there anything we can do for you?"

"No," Naomi said. "Thank you, but I'll be all right. You can see yourselves out, can't you?"

"Of course." Dan stood, then he and Alan said their goodbyes and made their way out.

As Dan closed the front door softly behind him, he heard a sob echoing through the quiet house.

"Come on," Alan said. "Let's leave her in peace."

On the drive out through the housing development, Alan stared out of the car window but he made no comment, and Dan was glad of the quiet. Naomi had given him a lot to think about, and he needed the headspace to mull it over.

It was only when they'd left Exeter a few miles behind them that Alan spoke.

"Ten by eight-inch prints," Alan said. "Would they fit into a small wooden coffin, do you think?"

"Yes," Dan replied. "I believe they would."

"You have a number for Tobias Barrington, don't you?"

"I do, but before we speak to him we need to be prepared. He's an experienced barrister, and he won't be fooled by my attempts at interrogation."

"I wouldn't be so sure," Alan replied. "You have a way of needling people, and I mean that as a compliment. At times, it can be extremely useful."

"Thanks, I think. But you know what I mean. We need some ammunition to use against Tobias, something that might trip him up."

"I'm happy to help, but I've already looked into his past, and all I found were records of his glittering career."

Dan thought for a second. "A bit of background information won't be enough. We need something more."

"Such as what?"

"Connections," Dan said. "We're looking for connections."

"That's easy. He's Zadie's brother and an ex-partner of Philippa."

"There'll be more to find. This case is a tangled web, and we're missing at least one of the most significant strands."

Alan heaved a sigh. "I don't mean to be dismissive, but if we've missed these connections so far, how do we know they exist?"

"Intuition. In other words, we need to apply the thought patterns we've learned through experience. And my experience tells me that when I run into a problem I can't solve, it's because I'm looking at it in the wrong way. I need to redraw the parameters and start again."

There was a pause before Alan replied. "Okay. Tell me what you need."

"I need," Dan said slowly, "to go back to Embervale and go to the pub."

"Now that," Alan replied, "is the kind of problem-solving I can get on board with."

CHAPTER 67

DS Anisha Kulkarni should've gone home hours ago, but here she was, sitting in her car and staring at an empty street in Teignmouth. She looked at the detritus on the passenger seat beside her. The empty packets and the crushed plastic bottle told a tale of their own. *Not exactly what you'd call a balanced meal*, Kulkarni thought. Vegetable samosas, crisps, a Mars bar and a bottle of water. What would her Mum think? She'd roll her eyes at the shop-bought samosas, but she wouldn't say much. Her mum had almost given up the fight against her daughter's eating habits. *I'll go to the gym later*, Kulkarni decided. A workout would burn off all those excess calories, and a slim figure was excellent ammunition against her mother's disapproval.

Outside, the sky was growing dim and Teignmouth's town centre had been growing progressively quieter for a while. Now it was deserted save for the occasional lone pedestrian. The shops had long since shut their doors, and the steel shutters had been rolled down over the front of Fones and Gadgets. Still, Kulkarni hadn't seen Harry Whelan leave, so she'd stay a while longer. *He could've slipped out the back way*, she thought, but there was nothing she could do about that.

If this had been an officially sanctioned surveillance operation, she'd have covered all the exits, but she'd decided to come on her own, going the extra mile to keep the inquiry moving along. After all, she had some making up to do.

Kulkarni glanced at her phone's screen and checked the time. It was almost eight o'clock, and she heaved a resigned sigh. No one was going to turn up now.

She turned the ignition key, but as she went to turn on the headlights, she caught a glimpse of movement in the rearview mirror. A grey SUV was slowing as it approached. Kulkarni watched from the corner of her eye. The car was a BMW X5 and it had slowed to a crawl. Quickly, she pressed her phone to her ear, talking to a non-existent caller while looking straight ahead. She was aware of the BMW passing by very slowly. Kulkarni laughed as though someone had just told her a joke, but the subterfuge wasn't working. The BMW stopped, and Kulkarni turned to see its passenger staring down at her, a pale face framed in its side window. The man had wound down the window, all the better to get a good look at her, and Kulkarni's heart skipped a beat. It was him: the pasty-faced man Mr Franks had described.

Feigning annoyance, Kulkarni waved him away, mouthing, "What are you looking at?"

The man bared his teeth in a leer, then he said something to the driver and the BMW moved away.

"That's right, my friend," Kulkarni whispered. "Do what you came here to do. Let's see what you're up to."

The BMW ramped two wheels onto the pavement and pulled up right in front of Fones and Gadgets. Two men got out, and Kulkarni almost punched the air. The stocky pale man was accompanied by a taller man of Middle Eastern appearance.

The pair headed for the alley that led to the back of the shop, and they moved with a certain swagger: men with a sense of purpose.

By now, the owner of the Fones and Gadgets stores, Dave Whitehead, probably knew that Whelan had disobeyed his orders. Whelan had been told not to report the loss of the black VW van, but he'd done it anyway. His actions had aroused the interest of the police, and Mr Whitehead would not be best pleased. Now, his associates had come to make that displeasure felt in a very real way.

Kulkarni placed a call to Jo Winslow, and it was answered quickly.

"Anisha? What's up?"

"Jo. I'm in town, outside Whelan's shop, and—"

"What the hell?" Winslow interrupted.

"I haven't got time to explain. Listen. Two men answering the descriptions given by Mr Franks have just arrived in a grey BMW X5." She gave the registration, certain that Winslow was memorising it. "I think they might've—"

Kulkarni stopped abruptly as three figures emerged from the alley: Whelan flanked by the two men, one holding each of Whelan's arms.

"They've got him," Kulkarni went on. "They're going to take Whelan, and it doesn't look good."

"I'll send backup," Winslow said. "Stay in the car."

"I can't do that. I've got to stall them."

Winslow started to argue, but Kulkarni ended the call. If she let those men drag Whelan away, he might never be seen again. Her first duty was to preserve life, and she couldn't stand by while Whelan was dragged to an uncertain fate. If she didn't act now, the BMW would drive away, and any backup would arrive far too late.

Kulkarni stepped from her car and strode toward the three men. They already had the back door of the BMW open, and as she watched, the men let go of Whelan only to shove him toward the car.

"Going somewhere, Mr Whelan?" Kulkarni called out, and all three men turned to stare at her.

"What's it to you?" the pasty-faced man demanded. "Jog on, love. Mind your own business."

"Oh, but it is my business." Closer now, Kulkarni flashed her warrant card. "It seems to me as though Mr Whelan isn't exactly keen to get in your car, but maybe we can straighten this out."

The taller man raised a hand. "Apologies, officer. My friend here has no manners, but I'm sure he didn't mean to cause offence. Of course, we'll be happy to help you in any way we can."

"That's good, but it's Mr Whelan I'd like to hear from. Are you all right, sir?"

"He's fine," the taller man said. "There's no problem here. We're friends of Harry's, and we've come around to take him out for a pint after work."

"Is that right, Mr Whelan?"

Whelan opened his mouth, but once again, the taller man didn't let him speak. "He doesn't need to answer that. I've already told you, we're going to the pub. That's all there is to it."

"Maybe, but I'd like to hear it from Mr Whelan."

The taller man nodded to Whelan, who cleared his throat and said, "That's right. We're going for a drink."

Kulkarni fixed her gaze on the taller man. "What's your name, sir?"

"I don't see why you need to know," the man replied with a smile. "We haven't broken any law, have we?"

"We'll see. Your name, please."

The man's smile remained, but it had lost any trace of good humour. "I'm sorry, but I make it a rule never to talk to the police without my solicitor present. That is my right, is it not?"

"Yes, but if everything's all right, as you say, then there's really no reason not to give me your name, is there?"

"Nevertheless, I prefer not to give it."

Kulkarni looked to the other man. "How about you, sir? Do you have a name?"

The man shook his head slowly, his lips fixed in a scowl.

"I see." Turning her attention to Whelan, she said. "These are the men in the images I showed you, aren't they?"

As one, the two men glared at Whelan.

"I never..." Whelan began.

544

"Shut up," the taller man snapped. "Don't say a word, Harry. You've done nothing wrong."

Whelan nodded unhappily.

"Okay, if that's the way you want to play it." Kulkarni beckoned to Whelan. "Come on, Mr Whelan. You're coming with me. Let's go."

"What?" Whelan spluttered. "Why?"

"I warned you about withholding information, but you lied to me, so I'm going to take you to the station for an interview under caution. There are patrol cars on their way, but it's better if you come with me willingly."

The pasty-faced man stepped forward, but Kulkarni faced him, squaring her shoulders and standing her ground. "Stay right there. That's the only warning you're going to get."

The tall man took hold of his stocky friend's arm. "Calm down. If the officer wants to talk to Harry, that's okay." To Kulkarni, he added, "You're going to the local police station?"

"That's right."

"Okay." The tall man turned to Whelan. "I'll send a lawyer to meet you there, Harry. Don't say anything until he arrives, okay? I would hate for you to get yourself into trouble. You don't want any trouble, do you, Harry?"

"No," Whelan replied.

"I'm waiting," Kulkarni stated. "Let's get this done."

Whelan meekly stepped toward her, and Kulkarni gestured to where her car sat at the roadside. "On you go, Mr Whelan."

Whelan shuffled toward the car like a man in a dream, but Kulkarni didn't immediately follow. She pointed to each of the two men in turn. "Watch your step. Keep away from Diamonds Avenue. We've got patrols running through there all the time, and if we see either of you around there, your feet won't touch the ground."

The taller man looked faintly amused. "Why would we go there?"

"You know why."

Kulkarni delivered a warning look, then she turned away and

caught up with Whelan. While Whelan was climbing into the back seat, a patrol car pulled up behind, and two uniformed constables climbed out.

"DS Kulkarni?"

"That's right. Thanks for coming, but it's all under control now. Unless you want to give those guys a ticket for parking on the pavement."

"What guys?" The officer peered past her, and when Kulkarni looked back, the BMW was already driving away.

"Never mind," Kulkarni said. "Thanks again. Hope you have a quiet night."

"Not much chance of that," one of them said, and his colleague offered a wry grin.

A minute later, Kulkarni was driving back to the station, Whelan sitting quietly in the back. With a bit of luck, his silence wouldn't last. Once she had him in the interview room, he'd crumble. *He must know I've saved his skin*, Kulkarni thought. *Without me, he'd be in a very dark place by now*. Kulkarni shuddered to think what might've happened to Whelan if she hadn't stepped in. He was a weak link in the chain, and his associates knew he'd talked to the police. He'd have been lucky to get away with a beating; the alternatives could only have been much worse.

Ideally she'd let Whelan stew in the interview room for a while, giving him a chance to appreciate the full horror of the fate his so-called friends had in store for him. But there was a lawyer on the way, and Whelan would almost certainly be advised to make no comment; the interview would be over before it began. She couldn't let that happen, but as things stood, there was little she could do to prevent it.

Her only hope was to persuade Whelan to start talking before his lawyer arrived. There wasn't a moment to lose.

CHAPTER 68

I t was late when Dan finally left The Wild Boar and headed for home. Fore Street was deserted. Alan had gone home a little while before, giving Dan some time to stay and chat with Sam. Dan had invited Sam back to his place, but she'd gently declined, saying she was tired and had a lot to do the next day: a delivery of beer was due first thing in the morning, and it would have to be dealt with.

Dan had tried not to feel too disappointed. It wasn't as if they lived together; that was a prospect they hadn't even discussed. *Give it time*, Dan thought. *There's no rush.*

As he walked, Dan replayed the discussion he'd had with Alan in the pub. *We went round in circles*, Dan decided. *We talked each other to a standstill.* Each time Alan had put forward an idea, Dan had shot it to pieces, and Alan had been only too keen to return the favour. Alan had been in a good mood, buoyed up by the promise of a date with Natalya, but Dan had felt himself growing more and more frustrated. In the end, they'd run out of ideas and called it a night.

There's still something missing from the case, Dan thought. *There's an angle I'm not seeing.*

He was still deep in thought when a sudden sound made him

halt. Dan began to turn, but someone barged into him from behind, thudding into his upper body with enough force to knock him from his feet. Dan tried to save himself, but he was too slow, and the next thing he knew his face was being pressed against the pavement. A sharp pain jabbed in the centre of his spine, crushing the breath from his body. Dan's arms flailed for an instant but then they were grasped tight at the wrists and pulled sharply back and up, twisting his shoulders. Agony shot through Dan's arms, bleaching all thoughts from his mind. He gasped for air, his throat tight as panic flooded his senses.

The weight above him shifted, lessening the pain in his arms. Dan tried to turn onto his side, struggling to break free, but he was still pinned to the ground. He grunted in pain and tried to yank his arms from his assailant's grip, but they were held too tight. Something cold was pushed against Dan's fingers, and then came the voice: a hissing whisper from lips pressed far too close to Dan's ear, the breath caressing his cheek, making his flesh crawl.

"I've got your fingerprints, Danny boy. Stay away from Chagford, stay away from Zadie's friends."

The voice was a man's but was too quiet to recognise.

"Who are you?" Dan growled. "Show your face."

There was no reply.

"I said," Dan began, but something hard collided with the side of his head, and the world turned white, pain blossoming in his skull. The weight vanished from Dan's back, and his arms fell free, flopping to his sides, but he never felt his hands touch the ground. He didn't feel anything at all.

A DRY COUGH RACKED DAN'S THROAT, AND HE OPENED HIS EYES. "Where?" he mumbled. "What?"

He was on the ground, lying in the street. He could make out the orange glow of a streetlight. Dan put his hands on the ground and started to push himself up, but everything hurt. His head felt as if it was splitting apart. His arms shaking, Dan slowly shifted into a sitting position. He touched his temple and was rewarded with a sharp pain, but there was none of the dampness of blood and his fingers came away marked only with dirt.

He must've lost consciousness, but for how long?

Dan staggered to his feet, nervously scanning the street, but there was no one in sight.

He patted his pockets and found that his phone, his wallet and his keys were all where they should be. No surprise there. He hadn't been mugged; the attack had been a warning, pure and simple.

Dan started for home, holding one hand against his head. He'd been hit by someone who knew what they were doing. They'd taken him down, knocked him out and disappeared without a trace. He hadn't even caught a glimpse of the man.

Who the hell could have done that? And what had the man said about his fingerprints? Dan had been forced to touch something cold and smooth. That could've been enough to capture his prints, but why? Was someone going to try and incriminate him?

Possibilities spun through Dan's mind as he covered the short distance to home. He wanted nothing more than to clean himself up and lie down, but head injuries could be tricky, couldn't they? Was he supposed to go to the hospital and get himself checked over?

The lights were still on at Alan's house, and Dan stood outside for a moment, swaying as he looked up at the windows. Lifting his head made him dizzy, but that might've been the beer he'd had earlier. On the other hand, he could have concussion. How would he tell the difference?

Ask Alan, Dan thought. *He'll know what to do.*

Dan went to Alan's front door and knocked. He didn't have to wait long. Alan opened the door, took one look at him and said, "Go through to the kitchen. Sit down. Let's get you sorted out."

Dan nodded, and for once, he did what he was told.

TUESDAY

CHAPTER 69

Dan woke with a start, blinking in the light from an unfamiliar window. Where was he?

He took a breath and memories rushed back: the unknown assailant in the street, the whispered warning, the blow that had stunned him.

Afterward, Alan had been as good as his word, cleaning him up while gently but firmly asking a series of questions: Did he feel nauseous? Was he dizzy? Did he have blurred vision?

Dan had answered no to the first question but was hesitant about the rest, so Alan had insisted on calling 111 for advice. By then, Dan had begun to feel better, but Alan had spoken to a nurse and was freshly armed with strict instructions. On no account was Dan to go home on his own. There could be a delayed reaction to his head injury, so he was going to sleep in Alan's spare room and that was the end of it.

Alan had reverted to teacher mode, issuing instructions with the clear expectation they would be followed. At such times there was little point in arguing with Alan, so Dan had given in, and here he was.

Dan rolled onto his back with a sigh. It was a lot of fuss over nothing, but Alan had acted for the best; he generally did.

Sitting up, Dan carefully touched the side of his head. It was sore, but it wasn't swollen. There'd be a bruise, but apart from a few twinges from his shoulder muscles, he was okay. All things considered, he'd got away lightly.

There was a knock at the door.

"You can come in, Alan," Dan called out.

Alan appeared, already dressed and shaved, concern in his eyes. "How are you feeling?"

"Fine. I actually slept really well. I think your spare bed is better than mine."

"It rarely gets used. It's mainly for when my mum and dad come to visit, which isn't often these days." Alan studied him for a moment. "No headaches or anything like that?"

"Nothing that a cup of strong coffee won't cure. I'm all right, honestly, but thanks for last night. I appreciate it."

"It was nothing. You'd do the same for me. Anyway, while you're here, you may as well have some breakfast. I'll put some coffee on."

"That's kind, but there's no need."

"Maybe not, but I can't send you home without breakfast. I'll see you downstairs in a few minutes."

"Okay. Thanks. That would be great."

Alan nodded as if satisfied. "Right. You know where the bathroom is. If there's anything you need, give me a shout." Alan exited the room, leaving Dan to get dressed and sort himself out. There was something slightly bizarre about being an overnight guest at the house next door to his own, but it was nice to think of coffee being made downstairs, and with a bit of luck Alan might've baked a loaf of bread recently.

Dan was suddenly hungry, and he made himself ready as quickly as possible.

In Alan's cheerful kitchen, the table had been laid for two and the rich aroma of hot coffee mingled with the tantalising scent of freshly toasted bread.

Busy at the counter, Alan said, "Sit down and pour yourself

some coffee. I'm making some extra toast. I thought you could do with it."

"Thanks. It smells great. Is it some of your famous home-baked bread?"

Alan looked pleased. "Yes, I made it a couple of days ago, but it came out really well. It's perfect for toast."

"I'm sure it is." Dan sat down and poured a decent measure from the cafetière, filling his mug almost to the brim. The first sip almost scalded his tongue, but he savoured it nonetheless.

Alan placed a plate of toast on the table and joined him, pouring a mug of coffee for himself. "There's vegan spread, and some of Marjorie's hedgerow jelly, or you can have marmalade, but the butter is for me; it's dairy."

"Thanks." Dan took another sip of coffee, then he tucked in, and for the next few minutes they didn't talk much, pausing only while Alan fetched more toast.

When they'd finished, Dan sat back, patting his stomach. "That was great. Thank you."

"No problem. I'm just glad you're okay. Have you had any thoughts about who might've done it?"

"Lots. At first I thought it must've been Benny, because I didn't hear a thing until it was too late, and he's had the training. But then, he's not the sort to sneak about. I've already had one confrontation with him, and it was very much in the open. If he'd wanted to warn me off, he'd have done it face to face."

"Also, there's the problem of motivation," Alan said. "Benny works for Callaway, but your attacker said something about Zadie's friends, didn't he?"

Dan nodded. "Stay away from Chagford, stay away from Zadie's friends, that's what he said."

"Right. I don't see why Benny would say that. John Callaway and Zadie aren't friends."

"It could be a smokescreen," Dan said. "Someone wants us to drop the case, but mentioning anyone by name would've given the game away, so they kept it general."

"Okay, but a beating in a dark alley doesn't seem like the tactic of a rich film star. They go in for restraining orders, don't they?"

"That's true, and we laid ourselves open to that when we tried to sneak into Callaway's garden."

"I told you that was a daft idea."

Dan tilted his head to concede the point. "Okay, so let's leave Callaway out of it for now. What if Benny jumped me for reasons of his own?"

"I can't see any connection to the case. Benny doesn't really know Zadie, so why would he want to intimidate her and threaten you?"

"I don't know," Dan admitted, "and since we can't hang it on Benny, we'd better look for a simpler explanation."

"Okay, what about Tobias? I wouldn't put it past him to sneak up on someone from behind."

"I'm not so sure. Tobias is heavier built than me, so he could've pinned me down, but why would he warn me off? He was the one who told me to keep working while Zadie was in hospital."

"If he's the one gaslighting Zadie, he must be extremely devious. Who knows what he's capable of? He might do anything."

"That's a good point," Dan said. "And Tobias is clever enough to think of taking my fingerprints."

"Yes, that was strange. Do you really think someone would try to plant evidence with your prints on it? Surely, that wouldn't hold up in court."

"I've been wondering about that, and I think they were just trying to frighten me. There was something theatrical about the whole thing. It was like a scene from a thriller."

"Such as the many detective dramas starring John Callaway," Alan said. "I expect he's learned a thing or two from the various stunts he's performed over the years. He's been to the village before and he knows you go to the pub. Saunders will have given him your card, so Callaway knows where you live, and he knows better than anyone how to mask his voice."

Dan pursed his lips. He checked his mug but it was empty.

"I can brew some more," Alan offered.

"Thanks, but I've had plenty."

"What's up? You've gone very quiet."

"It's silly, but it's one thing to have been jumped by an ex-commando, but another to have been knocked down by a barrister or a retired actor. I can't help thinking that if it was either of those two, I didn't give a very good account of myself."

"Don't be too hard on yourself," Alan said. "They caught you unawares. Besides, Tobias Barrington is a hefty chap, and he seems like the public-school type. I'll bet he used to play rugby or row for the team or something. As for John Callaway, he looked very spry for his age. For all we know he could have a fully equipped gym in that great big house of his." Alan paused. "But aren't we forgetting someone? What about Connor?"

"No. It wasn't him. I could handle Connor."

"You didn't get the chance, and it doesn't take much physical strength to knock someone down if you time it right and charge straight into them. All you need is momentum, and don't forget, Connor is younger than you."

"But this person held me down easily. Connor's lightly built, but it felt like a bear was on my back."

"A knee pressed hard to the spine; painful if you do it right. And you said he twisted your wrists. That's the kind of thing they teach in self-defence classes and martial arts, but you can look it up online. Anyone can learn it."

Dan raised an eyebrow. "How would you know that?"

"Research for my books. Fight scenes are hard to get right."

"Even for children's books?"

"*Especially* for children's books. Your average eleven-year-old knows a thing or two about unarmed combat. I blame all those video games."

"Okay, Connor is another suspect," Dan said. "Moving on, let's assume that the person who knocked me down and the person who's been harassing Zadie are one and the same. Where do we go from there?"

"I take it you're not deterred by the mysterious warning."

"What do you think? If anything, I'm more determined to catch him."

"I thought as much," Alan said. "But it might pay to be a bit more cautious for a while. Next time, they might do something more drastic."

"Let them try. I'll be ready."

"Good. Me too." Alan rubbed his hands together. "There's one way to look at your late-night encounter; it's narrowed the list of suspects down nicely. We're looking for a man and we only have four prime candidates. That's a definite improvement."

CHAPTER 70

D I Spiller leaned back in his office chair and stared at the ceiling. His eyes needed a break from staring at the computer screen. He'd always known that a certain amount of admin came with the role of inspector, but he'd assumed he'd get used to it. He was wrong. Instead, the forms and reports and spreadsheets seemed to get more onerous with every passing day. Some might call it modern police work, but he called it a complete waste of time.

Spiller didn't intend to close his eyes, but it happened just the same. His mind buzzed, his thoughts jumbling. Sheila hadn't slept well, so neither had he. Since the stroke, Sheila had trouble getting comfortable at night. Last night, she'd tried not to disturb him but he'd lain awake, waiting for her to fall asleep. Silly really. Sheila wasn't ill, as such. She was doing well, getting stronger all the time. Her energy and quiet determination put him to shame. Still, he worried. He couldn't help it.

The knock on the door made Spiller sit up with a start. He hadn't dozed off, had he? Surely not.

Clearing his throat and running a hand over his hair, he called out, "Come in."

Nicola Haig, the best Crime Scene Manager in the county, let herself in.

"Is this a good time? I've got a preliminary crime scene report for the Darley-Jones case."

"Excellent. Pull up a chair."

Nicola made herself comfortable, facing Spiller across the desk. She was carrying a tablet computer, but she laid it on her lap and looked at Spiller. "How are you?"

"I'm absolutely fine," Spiller said, his voice gruffer than he intended. "Why?"

Nicola tilted her head to one side. "I was just being nice. No need to bite my head off."

"Sorry, Nicola. I didn't mean to be tetchy. People keep talking to me like I'm on my last legs, and I don't much like it. But since you ask, I'm fine thank you. And yourself?"

"I'm good. Busy, but good." Nicola looked pensive. "I heard you had to let your prime suspect go."

"For the time being. His twenty-fours were up, and we didn't have enough to hold him."

"The deceased's phone was used while you had the guy in here, is that right?"

Spiller nodded. "We've tried to trace the phone, but someone will have ditched it or destroyed it by now. There's no signal from it anyway, although we did find where it was last used, and it was somewhere in the Chagford area."

"How far can you narrow it down?"

"We're looking at miles rather than metres. Unfortunately, Chagford isn't replete with phone masts, so it makes it difficult to be precise."

"A pity," Nicola said. "How was the post-mortem examination?"

"Much as I expected. The cause of death was almost certainly drowning. There'll be some more tests, but there's not much doubt about it. There was alcohol in her system, and not much food in her stomach, but apart from a few bumps and bruises there wasn't a mark on her."

"That fits with what we found at the scene." Nicola raised her tablet and referred to it. "There were some signs of a struggle on the river bank. The earth is soft and it had been significantly disturbed. There were some deep footprints that matched the deceased's shoes. It looked as though she may have dug her heels in."

"Any other shoe prints?"

"We found some eventually. The ground was churned up, and the undergrowth made things difficult, but we spotted a couple of decent shoe prints and took casts. We're looking at something with a pattern of square grips, perhaps a training shoe. They're size nine, so they probably belong to a man."

"That's something, but it doesn't narrow it down much," Spiller said.

"No, but you'll be pleased to know I was right about the handbag. We found it downstream, washed up against some rocks. It's a black leather handbag. Dior. It looks like the genuine article, so quite expensive."

"Anything useful inside?"

"I've listed everything in the report, but there was a library card from Exeter University, and it was in the name of Philippa Darley-Jones, so that was helpful. There were a few items of makeup, all posh brands, and a small hairbrush. We also found a packet of tissues and a couple of tampons. Nothing unusual. Unfortunately, we couldn't recover any usable prints or trace evidence. It had been in the water a while, and with the current and the rocks and the mud, it was impossible to retrieve anything useful. We can do more tests if there's something specific we should be looking for. We can take it apart and check the seams for particles or traces of drugs if you think it might be worthwhile."

"We'll hold off for now," Spiller said. "There are better uses of our time. Did you find her scarf?"

Nicola shook her head. "Someone may have taken it from the scene. If it had been in the river, it probably would've got snagged on something, and it certainly wasn't on the bank or on the path. We searched as thoroughly as we could."

"I'm sure you did a good job, as always. What about her clothes? Did we get anything interesting?"

"We're still processing them," Nicola said. "You know how long it can take. I know we have some fibres, and I'm hopeful we can learn more as we go on. If you can find something to match them against, we'll be ready."

"Thanks, Nicola. Anything else I need to know?"

"Not yet. What's next for you?"

"I'm popping over to Chagford this morning. Forensics have finished with her house, and I want to take a look around."

"Weren't there enough photos?" Nicola asked. "I believe we were pretty thorough."

"You were, but it's not the same as seeing it for myself. I want to get a feel of the place."

"Okay, then I'll let you get on." Nicola stood. "Tim, you can tell me to mind my own business, but why don't you let Ben drive you over there."

"I'm quite capable of—"

Nicola raised a hand to cut him short. "There's no question about your abilities, but I know you, and you can be your own worst enemy. Use the privilege of rank now and then. You've earned it."

"We'll see."

"Okay, I won't say any more. Look after yourself, Tim, and give my regards to Sheila."

"I will. Bye."

As soon as Nicola left, Spiller jumped to his feet and grabbed his jacket from the back of the chair. A few strides took him into the main office, and a moment later he was standing beside Collins.

"Come on," Spiller said. "We're off to Chagford to have a look at that house."

"Sure." Collins logged out of his computer and gathered his things.

It took Collins only a few seconds to get ready, but Spiller tapped his foot on the carpet while he waited, an impatient frown on his features.

"Come on, lad," Spiller muttered.

"I'm ready. Shall we take my car?"

"No," Spiller said. "I'll drive. It'll be quicker."

SPILLER WALKED QUIETLY THROUGH THE EMPTY ROOMS AND HALLWAYS of Meadow House, his hands in his pockets, DC Collins trailing behind him. Here and there, Spiller saw the patches of fine black dust where the SOCOs had lifted fingerprints, but apart from that, there was no sign that anything out of the ordinary had happened in Philippa's handsome home. The deep-pile carpets were clean, the antique furniture dusted, the ceramic vases and porcelain figurines neatly arranged. Large oil paintings hung on the walls, and pristine silverware was displayed in glass-fronted cabinets.

The whole place had the air of a museum or a stately home, everything arranged to give the impression that nothing had changed since the house was in its heyday. The only modern items were the appliances in the kitchen and utility room, and a large screen TV in the lounge. Philippa had owned a laptop, but it had been taken in for analysis. Everything else bore the patina of antiquity, from the polished wooden flooring in the hallway to the sparkling glass of the chandelier in the lounge.

What would happen to this splendid house now? As far as he knew, Philippa had no living relatives, so there was no one to preserve all this grandeur, but that made his job simpler. He could almost certainly rule out a disputed inheritance as a motive for her murder.

Spiller strolled up to the lounge window at the back of the house and looked out over the generous garden. Only a couple of days ago he'd marched through the garden with Dan Corrigan and questioned Jack Devlin. Now, he wondered what more he could've done. If he'd gone looking for Philippa, might he have been able to save her, or had she already been murdered? He'd probably never know.

Spiller heard Collins mooching about behind him. The lad had no idea how to be still and quiet, alone with his thoughts. Something metallic screeched and Spiller turned on his heels, a rebuke on his lips. But Collins wasn't there. Another screech, and Spiller realised that the sound had come from the other half of the lounge; the part of the room that faced the front of the house. Collins must've wandered off on his own. What was he up to?

Spiller marched through and found Collins crouching in front of the fireplace. The door of the cast iron stove stood open, so its hinges had probably been responsible for the screeching, but what on earth was Collins doing?

"Getting a bit chilly, are you?" Spiller asked. "Thinking of lighting a fire?"

"I was just checking something," Collins said. "I thought someone might've tried to burn some evidence."

"The SOCOs think of all that. They know what they're doing."

"Yeah, but I noticed a bit of ash in the grate, and it's too warm for a stove at this time of year."

"It could've been left there for months."

"I know, but the rest of the house is very tidy, so I reckon she'd have cleaned it out before now. Anyway, hang on a sec." Collins leaned closer to the fireplace and put both hands into the stove. There was clunk, and Collins moved back, an angular metal sheet in his hands. "Baffle plate. Stops the flames going straight up the flue."

"You're an expert on wood burners are you?"

"No, but Mum and Dad have one. Actually, this is a multi-fuel stove, so you could use coal in it if you wanted."

"Fascinating," Spiller intoned. "But what's the point?"

"The points is…" Collins leaned in again and appeared to be fumbling about at the back of the stove. "Ah, there's a little ledge. Got something." He retracted his arm, some small scraps of singed paper held gently between his fingertips. "Have you got an evidence bag handy, guv?"

"Always." Spiller pulled a plastic bag from his jacket pocket and crouched next to Collins, holding the bag open while Collins carefully placed the slips of paper inside.

"My dad always says you shouldn't put paper in a stove," Collins said. "It's not heavy enough, so the air from the vents can blow it up past the baffle plate before it's caught fire. If you're not careful, unburnt paper can build up in the flue and start a chimney fire."

Spiller didn't reply. He'd only half listened; his attention was on those pieces of paper. He stood and tilted the bag from side to side, trying to catch the light.

Collins got to his feet and stood close. "What do you think, guv? A good find, eh?"

"Yes. Very good."

"Looks like the same paper as the book we found in Devlin's cottage."

"It could be. We'll have it checked."

"I reckon it's the same handwriting," Collins said. "Same colour ink too."

"It's similar, certainly."

Stop prattling for a second and let me concentrate, Spiller thought, but he pushed the unworthy thought aside. Collins had done well; he'd earned his moment in the sun. "You did a good job," Spiller muttered while squinting at the scraps of paper. "Excellent instincts."

There were three pieces of paper, and though they were scorched, traces of handwritten text were visible, fragments of sentences scribed in small, neat capital letters with a blue biro.

One was illegible to Spiller's eyes, but a specialist would have more luck. On the second slip, he thought he could make out the phrase *RIGHT THING*. But it was the third note that made Spiller's heart beat a little faster. It was the best preserved of all, and its message was stark: *I KNOW WHAT YOU DID.*

CHAPTER 71

By the time Dan had popped home for a shower and a shave, he felt right as rain. True, the bruise on his temple was tender to touch, but it was nothing to worry about.

A fresh set of clothes and a snack of nuts and dried fruit, and he was raring to go. Dan was tying his shoelaces in the hallway when there was a knock on his front door, but before answering it, he checked his appearance in the hall mirror. In a certain light, the bruise made him look distinctly disreputable, but there wasn't much he could do about that. He opened the door to see DI Spiller and DC Collins waiting outside.

"Good morning, Mr Corrigan," Spiller said. "We'd like a chat. Have you got a minute?"

"Yes, but what's it about?"

"We'll come to that." Spiller gestured to the hallway. "Shall we…?"

"Okay. We can go and sit in the kitchen." Dan stood back to let Spiller and Collins in, noting that they both wiped their shoes on the mat in exactly the same way as they entered. The copied mannerism snagged at a memory in Dan's mind, though he couldn't quite place it.

"Through here?" Spiller asked, although he was already making for the kitchen door.

"Yes," Dan said. "Go ahead and grab a seat. I'll be right there."

While the detectives went into the kitchen, Dan checked the hall mirror again, tugging at his hair to coax it forward over the bruise. It wasn't great but it would have to do.

Hurrying through to the kitchen, Dan found the detectives standing, both facing the door as if awaiting his entrance.

"Please, have a seat," Dan said. "Can I offer you tea or coffee?"

"We don't need a drink, thanks," Spiller replied. "But we'll take a pew."

They sat on one side of the kitchen table and Dan sat facing them. The policemen seemed content to sit and wait in silence, so Dan said, "Right, what can I do for you?"

Spiller studied him for a second. "Have you bumped your head, Mr Corrigan?"

"Not exactly. Somebody jumped me on my way home from the pub last night. They gave me a thump."

"Did you report it?"

"No, and I don't think I will. There was no harm done."

"That's up to you," Spiller said. "We do take these things seriously though. Was anything taken?"

"I wasn't mugged. It was a warning. Someone told me to drop the Zadie Barrington case."

Spiller and Collins exchanged a look.

"Have you any idea who did it?" Collins asked. "Can you describe them?"

Dan shook his head firmly. "No to both questions. It was a man, but I didn't see a thing. They sneaked up on me from behind. It all happened very fast."

"Pity," Spiller said. "Whether you report it or not, I'll have to look into it. I'm still investigating Zadie Barrington's case."

"I see. Is that why you're here?"

"Actually, no," Spiller replied. "We've come to talk about Philippa Darley-Jones. You've heard what happened?"

"Yes. I know you're treating her death as suspicious. It's very sad."

"Indeed it is. And just before Ms Darley-Jones was found dead, you contacted me, saying you were worried about her."

"I was concerned. It was only natural."

Spiller nodded gravely. "Are you aware that Ms Darley-Jones had one of your business cards? We found it in her house."

"Yes, I gave her a card when we called on her. We were asking about Zadie."

"You and another man, presumably Mr Hargreaves, went to Philippa's house on two occasions," Spiller said. "Why was that?"

"Yes, and Alan was with me both times. When we first called, Philippa wasn't at home, so we tried again the next day, and on that occasion, we had a brief chat with Philippa. But how did you know we'd been there?"

"It's an exclusive neighbourhood in a small town," Spiller replied. "Neighbours can be very watchful, very suspicious of strangers."

"That makes sense," Dan admitted. "We weren't exactly subtle. When we first turned up, we probably looked shifty. We even peered in at a couple of windows, but that was because I wondered if Philippa was pretending to be out."

"Why would she do that?" Collins asked.

"I've no idea."

"But you formed the idea she was hiding from you," Collins suggested. "Why would Philippa do that? Was she frightened of you?"

Dan felt the blood drain from his cheeks. "No, not at all. That's ridiculous. At that point we'd barely spoken."

"So why wouldn't she want to talk to you?" Collins persisted.

"I really don't know. All I can tell you is that her car was in the drive, so I guessed she was home but didn't want to be bothered with visitors."

"So you made a return visit the next day," Spiller said, "and this time, you went inside."

"Only as far as the hallway. We talked about Zadie."

"Of course you did," Spiller said. "That's why you were there." He paused. "When you became worried about Philippa, why did you call me? Why didn't you go through the usual channels?"

"I thought you'd respond more quickly, and I was right."

"You decided that time was pressing," Spiller suggested. "What did you think had happened to Philippa?"

"I didn't have a specific scenario in mind. I feared for her safety, but that's what happens when someone goes missing, isn't it? You have no idea what to think, so your mind fills in the blanks. It's almost as if you're trying to frighten yourself. I've often wondered if it's a defence mechanism; your mind bracing itself to hear the worst."

Spiller sent him an inquiring look, and Dan shifted in his seat, suddenly aware that he'd been gabbling. *Slow down*, he told himself. *Breathe*.

"Listen," Dan went on, "I'm happy to help, but are you suggesting that I'm in some way responsible for what happened to Philippa? Because if you are, I'll call my solicitor right now."

"Relax, Mr Corrigan," Spiller said. "No one's accusing you of anything. We like to be thorough, that's all. If this was a formal interview, we'd have asked you to come back to the station."

"Right." Dan remained tight-lipped, and from the corner of his eye he spotted a familiar figure flitting past the kitchen window. A moment later, there was a knock at the back door.

"That'll be Alan," Dan said, standing up and making for the door. "You don't mind if he sits in, do you?"

"That's fine," Spiller replied. "We may as well speak to him while we're here."

Dan opened the door and gave Alan a meaningful look. "DI Spiller and DC Collins are here. They want to talk about Philippa."

"I saw them arrive," Alan said. "I thought I'd pop over and see if I can help."

"I'm glad you did. Come in."

Dan and Alan sat side by side, Alan placing his elbows on the table and leaning forward.

"Right," Alan said. "Ready when you are, Inspector."

DI Spiller smiled, and when he spoke his tone was altogether more genial than before. "You both knew Philippa Darley-Jones, yes?"

"Only through her friendship with Zadie Barrington," Dan replied. "We talked to all Zadie's friends in case any of them knew why someone might want to harass her."

"Did Philippa have anything useful to tell you on that score?" Collins asked.

"Not a lot," Dan said. "She suggested that one of Zadie's friends, Melody Reinhardt, wasn't quite who she appeared to be, and she was right. Melody was called Mary Robinson until she changed her name."

Spiller didn't react, and that gave Dan pause for thought. Watching Spiller carefully, he added, "But you already knew that, didn't you?"

"I can neither confirm nor deny that statement," Spiller intoned. "Was there anything else?"

Alan cleared his throat. Looking uncomfortable, he said, "We were concerned that Philippa may be drinking more than was good for her."

"Did she appear to be under the influence when you spoke to her?"

"No, she wasn't drunk," Dan replied. "But we saw a receipt from Waitrose, and there were quite a few bottles of spirits."

"Somewhat circumstantial," Spiller said. "But what was she like, as a person?"

"She was very formal in the way she spoke to us," Alan replied. "She came across as quite haughty."

Dan raised an eyebrow. "What Alan's trying not to say is that Philippa was a bit of a snob. She tended to look down her nose at people. She came from a privileged family, but she was living in reduced circumstances, and I think she resented the fact."

"Reduced circumstances," Spiller said. "That's an interesting remark considering the size of her house, the antiques, the paintings on the wall. You've seen inside, so you know what I mean."

"Yes, but she had to do all the housework herself," Dan replied. "Also, Philippa's parents had left her some land, but she'd sold it, and she was renting out the cottage at the bottom of her garden. Those aren't things she'd have done willingly. A house of that size is expensive to maintain, but Philippa didn't have a job. Put all those pieces together, and you get a picture of someone living beyond their means."

Speaking slowly as though choosing his words with care, Spiller said, "Did you come across any suggestion that Ms Darley-Jones had other sources of income?"

Dan met Spiller's gaze. There was something in the way the policeman had spoken, something that hinted at illicit activity, but what was he getting at? And what was he keeping back?

Chancing a bluff, Dan said, "There may have been something."

Spiller's eyes lit up. "Such as what?"

"It was probably nothing," Dan replied. "Just something she said one day."

"Nevertheless, I need to hear the details."

Dan made a show of looking thoughtful. "It's slipped my mind. Maybe if you tell me what you're looking for, it'll come back to me."

"Mr Corrigan, do not play games with me," Spiller snapped, all trace of geniality gone. "I'm conducting an extremely serious investigation, and if you withhold evidence, I'll have you down to the station before you know which way is up." Spiller drew a breath. "Do you know anything about any payments made to Ms Darley-Jones or not?"

"So she received payments," Dan replied. "That's interesting, but I don't know anything about that. Sorry."

A tense silence hung over the four men.

Eventually, Collins said, "What do you think, guv? Shall we take Mr Corrigan back to the station?"

"It's very tempting," Spiller replied. "But there's still a chance he might redeem himself." Straightening his posture, Spiller locked eyes with Dan. "Did Ms Barrington or any of her friends say anything about loaning or giving large amounts of money to Ms Darley-Jones, yes or no?"

"No, they didn't," Dan replied. "Most of them probably couldn't afford to do that."

"Who could?" Collins asked.

"Zadie earns a fair amount from her work, so she might've helped her friend out," Alan replied. "And Connor told us that he lives on money he inherited from his parents, so he's another candidate."

"That's Connor Griffiths," Spiller suggested. "The ex-pop star."

"That's right," Dan said. "There's also Zadie's brother, Tobias Barrington. He's a barrister, so I expect he's well paid, but I don't think he was on friendly terms with Philippa. At one time they were in a relationship, and Philippa wasn't best pleased when we mentioned his name, so I imagine they weren't on good terms."

"Moving on," Spiller began, "does the phrase, 'Do the right thing' mean anything to you?"

"Of course," Alan replied. "It's an excellent principle."

"I think DI Spiller meant something beyond the obvious," Dan said. "Am I right?"

"Please answer the question," Collins droned.

"Okay," Dan said. "As it happens, it means a lot to me. I have it written on a card in my wallet, although mine says, 'Please do the right thing'. It's a kind of psychological trick."

"How so?" Spiller asked.

"It was an idea I got from a YouTuber, actually. Casey Neistat. He wrote the same message on a wallet and deliberately dropped it on the subway in New York. He pretended to be asleep, but he'd placed a hidden camera, and it recorded someone handing the wallet back to him. He said he put the same words on his phone and so on, and he claimed it often worked. He even had stickers printed with the same message. You could send off for them."

Spiller stared at Dan. "Are you making this up, Mr Corrigan?"

"No, of course not. You can look it up online. And here, let me show you." Dan pulled his wallet from his pocket and opened it, showing Spiller the card displayed behind the wallet's plastic window. Along with Dan's phone number, there was his blood group, his parents listed as next of kin, and the phrase, 'Please do the right thing.'

"Dan's had that for as long as I've known him," Alan said. "He tried to get me to do the same, but I never got around to it."

Spiller blinked slowly as if restraining an emotion.

"Why are you asking about it?" Dan said. "Did Philippa have it written somewhere?"

Spiller's expression soured. "I'm not here to give you information, Mr Corrigan. Nor do I need to explain the reason for my questions."

"It might help though," Dan replied. "We know some of Philippa's friends and neighbours, and we know the area, but we're completely in the dark as far as your investigation is concerned. We don't even know exactly where Philippa was found."

"That's as it should be at this stage," Spiller said, but then he seemed to relent, his stern expression fading. "On the other hand, we'll be giving a statement to the press later, so some facts will be made public very soon."

"Guv," Collins began, but Spiller forestalled any objections with a wave of his hand.

"You may have seen the news that Philippa Darley-Jones was found in the river," Spiller said, "but what we won't be making public until later is the fact that she was drowned. Deliberately. Philippa was murdered."

"My God," Alan murmured. "Poor Philippa. It brings it home when you hear it like that. It's terrible."

Unwanted images came to Dan's mind and he swallowed hard, fighting down the surge of revulsion that rose from his gut. Making his voice steady, he said, "We've walked along the river all the way from the town to Zadie's house. Where was Philippa found?"

"There's a deep pool not far from her house," Spiller replied. "There's a path that leads from Philippa's garden gate and it goes all the way to the pool and beyond."

"So Jack Devlin might've been telling the truth," Dan said. "He told us Philippa was heading that way when he last saw her. He said he'd walked along the path to look for her, so how come he didn't find her?"

"There are a lot of paths through the woods," Alan replied, then his eyes went wide. "We've been there. The pool. We saw it."

"Oh yes," Dan said. "We talked to Zadie about it. She said it was a nice spot to sit."

Alan nodded. "I picked up a bit of litter. It was just a few days ago, but it feels like a lifetime has passed since then."

"What did you find?" Spiller asked.

"A bit of paper. No, actually, it was…" Alan paused, his eyes brightening. "Ah, this is what I was thinking of the other day when Carly showed me that app."

"I don't follow," Spiller said. "What app?"

"Carly has an app for the gym she uses. She uses a gym at the university almost every day, so I vaguely wondered what she did about parking. I went to the Northcott Theatre recently. It's on the campus, and whenever I go there, I have trouble knowing where to park. There must be at least half a dozen car parks, and the signage is very confusing."

"Mr Hargreaves," Collins intoned, "is this going anywhere?"

"Patience, Collins," Spiller said. "Let the man speak."

"Thank you. Anyway, I was thinking about parking at the university, and it reminded me of what I'd found by the river. At first, I thought I'd picked up a parking ticket, but actually it was a bus ticket, and the one thing reminded me of the other, if you see what I mean." Alan offered an apologetic smile. "Sorry, I'm rambling. The short version is, I found a bus ticket by the river. Do you think it might be important?"

Spiller seemed to speak through gritted teeth. "In a murder investigation, everything is important, Mr Hargreaves. Please tell me you still have the bus ticket."

"I'm not sure. I could look." Frowning, Alan muttered, "What did I do with it?"

"Recycling?" Dan suggested.

"No, it was grubby and they only like you to put clean stuff for recycling. Let me think. It was in my pocket when I went to wash my trousers. I always check the pockets. Anyway, it was all scrunched up and I'd forgotten what it was, so I opened it out. That's when I saw it wasn't a parking ticket after all, and…" Alan clicked his fingers. "It's in the waste bin at home. I haven't emptied it yet. It'll still be there."

Spiller and Collins jumped to their feet. "Let's go," Spiller said.

A minute later, Dan, Spiller and Collins crowded around Alan as he plucked a small plastic waste bin from beneath the kitchen counter. "It should be in here. I'll have a look."

Spiller raised his hand. "Leave it to us, please." Taking the bin from Alan, he added, "Collins, have you got a pair of gloves handy?"

"Always." Collins pulled a pair of disposable gloves from his pocket and snapped them on, then he removed the plastic liner from the bin. He held it up to the light and they could all see that it contained very little except for a few plastic wrappers and unidentifiable clumps of fluff.

"There are some things you can't recycle," Alan said as if an explanation was required. "But I do what I can."

"It's just as well," Spiller replied. "Have a look, Collins. See what you can find."

"Yes, guv." Collins delved into the rubbish and retrieved a strip of crumpled paper. Unfolding it, he read, "Chagford to Exeter City Centre, Service 173, Dartmoor Coaches. It was issued at five past ten in the morning, and the date was last Monday so it's over a week old."

"That's the day before I found it," Alan said. "But anybody could've dropped it."

"There can't have been that many passengers," Dan said. "Those Dartmoor buses are small, and we've been past the bus stops in Chagford; there's never more than one or two people waiting."

"But it was dropped *before* Philippa was murdered," Alan replied. "So what's the significance?"

Dan and Alan looked at Spiller expectantly, but there was no reply forthcoming. Spiller's expression remained neutral but his lips were drawn tight.

"Hang on," Dan said. "You think Philippa might've met someone at the same spot more than once. Why? Was she having an affair with someone?"

"You know better than to ask questions like that," Spiller replied. "Thank you for passing on the bus ticket. You can bag it now, Collins."

While Collins sealed the bus ticket in an evidence bag, Dan leaned closer to peer at it. "173," he said, "Where's the last stop on that route?"

Alan whipped out his phone. "Give me a second."

"Gentlemen, we always appreciate support from the public, but it only goes so far," Spiller said. "You can leave this with us."

"Cowick Street," Alan announced. "I know it. There are quite a few shops, a post office and several takeaways. It's not far from St Thomas Station, so someone might've taken a train as well as the bus."

"That doesn't matter," Dan said. "There'll be lots of CCTV coverage from all those shops, and we can find out what time the bus arrived and check—"

Spiller raised his hands to cut Dan short. "That's enough, thank you. This might be important or it might lead nowhere, but either way, we'll take care of it. We've got other calls to make today, so we'll be on our way."

"Let me say one thing," Dan blurted. "Jack Devlin took the bus from Exeter to Chagford. That's how he travelled to Philippa's house. He told us his car was in the garage."

Spiller didn't give much away, but there was a distinct twitch at the corner of his eye. "Goodbye for now," he said. "We'll see ourselves out."

The detectives left quickly and quietly, leaving Dan and Alan standing in the suddenly quiet kitchen.

"Blimey," Alan muttered. "Why do I feel like we've set the cat among the pigeons?"

"Devlin's already a suspect. DI Spiller's confirmation bias must be going into overdrive."

"But the bus ticket was issued in Chagford, not in Exeter, and the dates don't make sense." Alan fumbled in his pocket, retrieving his notebook. He flicked through the pages then said, "Devlin told us he arrived on the Wednesday, two days after the ticket was issued."

"But he could've lied about that. He seemed very shifty when we…"

Dan left his sentence unfinished as a thought shouldered its way to the front of his mind.

"What's up?" Alan asked.

"It's just occurred to me that we know someone else who might use the bus."

Alan thought for a second. "Connor?"

Dan nodded. "Connor."

"I can't see him riding the bus with the great unwashed. He can afford to take a taxi."

"Booking a taxi would leave a trail. Taking the bus is much more anonymous." Dan ran his hand over his chin. "I hate to torture your metaphor, but I hope we haven't aimed the cat at the wrong pigeon."

CHAPTER 72

As he drove out of Embervale, Spiller found himself talking rapidly while Collins listened quietly from the passenger seat. *This is more like it*, Spiller thought. *We're on the right track, I'm sure of it.*

"Think about Philippa's financial situation," Spiller said. "You saw those payments, all of them in cash and at fairly regular intervals. They weren't huge, but they were enough to keep her head above water. Philippa was blackmailing someone."

"Maybe, but she spent more than she had coming in, and she'd maxed out half a dozen credit cards," Collins replied. "Blackmail is risky. If she was going to do it, she'd have gone for it big time, wouldn't she? She hadn't even cleared her debts."

"Philippa was smart. She knew better than to bleed her victim dry at the first bite. Besides, large amounts of cash fall foul of anti-money laundering regulations, but split it into smaller amounts and pay it in bit by bit, and no one blinks an eye. And think about the notes you found. *I know what you did.* Philippa Darley-Jones had someone on the hook, but they didn't want to pay any more, so they killed her."

Collins was quiet for a second, then he said, "If Philippa was

577

blackmailing someone, why would she still have the notes? Surely she'd have given them to whoever she was blackmailing."

"She was practising. Philippa didn't want to leave anything to chance, so she tried out a few notes at home, then she tore out the pages and burned them. She was a careful person. You saw her house; the place was immaculate. She liked everything neat and tidy, even when she was up to no good."

"I'm still not seeing it, guv. Okay, she needed money, but blackmail? It's a bit of a leap, isn't it? She would've been better off selling a couple of paintings or some of her antique furniture."

"By that logic Philippa could've sold the house," Spiller said. "But she didn't because she was proud of her past, and she couldn't bear to let it go."

Collins shook his head in disbelief.

"Let me take you through it," Spiller went on. "Did her house look like it belonged to a fashionable modern woman? No, it did not. It was more like a museum. Philippa was stuck in the past, holding on to a way of life she couldn't afford, but she was desperate to keep up appearances. I bet she kept everything just the way it was when her parents were alive."

"Okay, so who was she blackmailing?"

"We'll find out. That notebook of hers is interesting, don't you think? The one that Devlin had."

"*Do the right thing,*" Collins said. "And one of the half-burned notes probably said the same thing."

"That's right. What did you think to Mr Corrigan's explanation?"

"It didn't smell right to me. He was very quick to come up with an answer. It was like he'd rehearsed it."

"I don't think so. I hate to admit it, but Corrigan might've been on to something. Philippa was the kind of person who wrote her number in a notebook in case she lost it." Spiller paused. "But that wasn't what I was getting at. I'm struck by the fact that Philippa, a careful person, tried to burn the notes but gave the notebook away, leaving her number inside for all to see."

Collins was silent for a moment, then: "You think she left her number on purpose. She could've crossed it out, but she didn't. She was coming on to Devlin."

"I doubt it. She was out of his class."

"Doesn't mean she didn't fancy him," Collins said. "There she was in that great big house, all alone, and Devlin came along. He's a smooth talker and he fancies himself as a bit of a charmer, so he gave her the eye and she fell for it."

"Actually, I've a different scenario in mind. I never seriously believed Devlin turned up by chance. Anyone can see the man doesn't have much going for him. He's unemployed, his clothes have seen better days, so how can he afford to rent a nice holiday cottage?"

"You think they're in it together?"

"It would make sense, wouldn't it?" Spiller said. "Blackmail is a dangerous business. Philippa needed an accomplice, so she went looking and found Devlin. God knows where she dug him up, but I don't think he'd have needed much encouragement. He was down on his luck, and a glamorous woman asked for his help in return for a cut of the proceeds. He would've bitten her hand off. That would explain why he was so worried when Philippa went missing. She could get him into trouble, and he knew it."

Collins nodded. "When she was found dead, he was keen to help all of a sudden. He figured someone was cleaning house, and he was next for the chop. He wanted Philippa's killer put away, the sooner the better, so he bent over backward to help. He even refused a lawyer until we started looking at him for the murder."

"I was thinking along the same lines," Spiller said. "As a theory, it hangs together, and I suspect one of Mr Corrigan's guesses was correct; Philippa had used that spot by the river on more than one occasion. She grew up in that house, so she knew the woods like the back of her hand. She told someone to leave the money in a hiding place, then she came along and picked it up while Devlin watched her back. It's a quiet spot but if anyone saw them, it didn't matter. There's a public footpath, so to all outward appearances they were out for a stroll."

"But the payments were going on long before Devlin arrived," Collins argued.

"That depends on whether you believe his story. He can't corroborate any of it, so we don't really know where Devlin has been recently. He's a ghost, and that would've suited Philippa very well. He could've come and gone easily enough. But something changed. Philippa knew she was in danger, so she wanted Devlin nearby. The cottage must've seemed like a good solution."

"If Devlin was her protection, he didn't make a good job of it."

"Don't forget, Philippa and Devlin had argued," Spiller replied. "There's no honour among thieves. They fell out and she gave him that bruise on his cheek. She didn't trust him anymore, so she went to pick up the money on her own and her victim grabbed the chance to be free of her. He'd come prepared, or maybe he'd left the rope nearby at an earlier date. That would tie in with the bus ticket."

Collins made a noncommittal noise in his throat. "We can't rely too much on one bus ticket. On its own, it doesn't prove anything. And Dan Corrigan got it wrong. He thought Philippa was having an affair, so I wouldn't set much store by anything he has to say."

"Don't be too quick to write Corrigan off. He has his uses."

"That's not what you said this morning," Collins said. "You told me we were going to push him and make out like he was a suspect."

Spiller smiled. "Like I say, Mr Corrigan has his uses, but we can't have him going around treating us like equals. He needs a nudge now and then to put him on the back foot."

"You wanted to put him in his place," Collins suggested.

"Exactly, and it all worked out beautifully. Mr Corrigan was reminded of the pecking order, and we have a new lead. All is well with the world."

"So what's the next step?"

"When we get back to HQ, I have a nice little job for you."

"Oh hell, it's going to be CCTV," Collins groaned. "You want me to find out who got off that bus in Exeter, don't you?"

"Got it in one," Spiller said. "We'll make a DS out of you yet."

CHAPTER 73

D an fobbed Alan off with an excuse, claiming he had some chores that needed his attention, but once Alan had gone home, Dan immediately prepared to head out for the day. He'd go to Chagford alone. He'd been attacked by an unknown assailant, and there was a killer on the loose. Dan had no intention of dragging his friend into a potentially dangerous situation, no matter how enthusiastic Alan might be.

But when Dan marched out of his back door, he found Alan waiting for him in the short alley that separated their two houses.

"I wanted to be ready," Alan said before Dan could speak.

"For what?" Dan asked. "I didn't say I was going out."

"I guessed you'd head to Chagford as soon as you'd got your shoes on." Alan looked Dan in the eye. "You weren't going to invite me along, were you? After all this time, you thought I'd sit this one out."

"Not exactly. I knew you'd come if I asked, but there's no need. I can check out the situation, see the way the land lies, and—"

"I'm not afraid," Alan interrupted.

"No, I know that. But we don't know who came after me last night, and they could be dangerous. Next time, they might do more than deliver a thump on the head."

"Then we'll do better by facing them together. I can make my own decisions, Dan, and I'm coming with you."

Dan saw the determination in his friend's eyes. Alan's mind was made up, and there was nothing to be gained by arguing with him.

"Okay, Alan, I expect you're right, as usual. Of course you can come."

"Good, then we'll say no more about it."

"We'll take my car," Dan said. "It needs a run. I think the battery's dying. Sometimes I can't get the windscreen wipers to come on."

"We don't want to be stranded at Chagford."

"It'll be fine. A quick trip ought to give the battery a boost." Dan headed for the car. Behind him, Alan muttered something about getting a new battery, but Dan didn't listen properly; he needed to get moving.

THE GRAVELLED AREA IN FRONT OF ZADIE'S HOUSE WAS ALREADY FULL, so Dan halted his Toyota RAV4 in the gateway.

"Visitors," Alan intoned. "Our ruse might've come to an end."

"We'll see. I recognise the BMW, that's Tobias Barrington's car, but I'm not sure about the little Honda."

"Whoever it is, they haven't left us enough space, and we can't park here; we'd be blocking everyone in."

"I'll find somewhere else."

Dan reversed back out into the street and found a roadside parking space a hundred metres away.

"Right," Alan said. "Let's go and see what's going on."

They exited the car and made their way to the house, opting for the back door.

Natalya answered their knock, greeting them with a weary smile. "Come in, please. I'm glad to see you."

"Are you okay?" Alan asked.

"Yes, yes, but Tobias is here, and Carly too. They are in the lounge, having an argument. Come and talk to them. They won't listen to me."

"No problem," Dan said. "We'll calm them down."

Natalya looked doubtful, but she led them through the kitchen and into the hallway.

Dan heard raised voices as soon as he reached the stairs, Tobias' booming baritone doing battle with Carly's strident tones.

"How long has this been going on?" Dan asked.

Natalya sighed. "Maybe twenty minutes. I'm not sure. It feels like a long time. I tried to say something, but it was no use."

"That's too bad," Alan said. "You shouldn't have to deal with this kind of behaviour."

"Who arrived first?" Dan asked.

"Tobias. He called this morning and asked about Carly. He wanted her address, but I could tell he was angry, so I didn't tell him; I thought he might go to her house and cause trouble. It didn't help. He said he'd come here. He knew Carly always comes to see Zadie on Tuesday."

"How did he know that?" Dan asked. "Did you tell him?"

Natalya started to shake her head, but she changed her mind. "A while ago, he called and I told him Zadie was with Carly. I might've said it was better not to call on Tuesday mornings, something like that."

Dan nodded thoughtfully. "When was this?"

"A month ago, maybe. I'm not sure."

"That's quite a while ago, but Tobias remembered," Dan said. "Interesting."

"Is it?" Alan asked. "Tobias is a barrister. He wouldn't get far without a good memory."

"It's a small detail," Dan replied. "And in my experience, small details often turn out to be the most interesting."

"I suppose so," Alan said. "In that vein, it's strange that Carly has turned up as if nothing has happened. When I last saw her, I as good as accused her of harassing Zadie."

"It is not so easy to get rid of people like Carly," Natalya replied. "I called her last night, and I told her not to come. I said Zadie was still too busy to see her, but she said she'd come anyway. She would not take no for an answer."

"But you let her in, knowing that Tobias was waiting for her in a bad mood," Dan said.

"Yes. I am not happy about it, but he gave me no choice." The corners of Natalya's lips turned down. "He is Zadie's brother, I am an employee. I must do what I am told."

Alan bridled. "Is that what he said to you?"

Natalya shrugged as if to say she was accustomed to such treatment.

Alan looked as though he was about to burst a blood vessel, so Dan said, "We'd better go up."

"Okay," Natalya replied. "Come."

They climbed the stairs, Natalya leading the way, but when they reached the landing she turned to face them. With the raised voices echoing behind her, Natalya said, "I don't like Carly, but I did not want this. I did not want anything bad to happen to her."

"That's understood," Dan said. "Let's go in. I'll see what I can do."

"Of course." Natalya opened the lounge door wide and stood back. Her grim expression made it clear she was not keen to enter the room herself, so Dan marched in, Alan hard on his heels.

Tobias was in full flow. "Where else could she have got them?" he demanded.

"For the tenth time, I don't know," Carly snapped back, enunciating the last three words slowly and clearly as if she were speaking to an imbecile.

"I don't believe you," Tobias shot back, the colour rising in his already florid cheeks.

Carly spread her hands wide. "I didn't even know Zadie was in hospital, for God's sake. Why did nobody tell me? What the hell has been going on here?"

"Don't pretend you don't know," Tobias thundered. "You're the one who's behind all this. You've tipped her over the edge, deliberately and with malice aforethought."

"I still don't know what's happened to her. *Why* is Zadie in hospital?" Carly raised a finger in warning. "Have you had her committed against her will? If you've had her sectioned, I swear I'll—"

Raising his voice, Dan said, "Time out!"

Carly and Tobias turned to glare at him.

"Oh, here we go," Carly sneered. "Reinforcements for the boy's club. What's the matter, Tobias, can't you face a little opposition on your own?"

"How dare you?" Tobias demanded. "I can take on people like you in my sleep."

"This isn't going to get us anywhere," Dan said, keeping his voice calm. "Tobias, what's the problem here?"

"Oh right, ask *him* first," Carly muttered. "Why do you assume he's in the right?"

"Actually, Carly has a point," Alan said. "Tobias is the only person losing his temper. Perhaps he's the one causing the problem."

Dan turned to Carly. "I wasn't assuming anything. We'll come to you in a second. First, I want to know what Tobias was asking about when we came in, so it's only fair to give him a chance to answer that question."

"Quite right, Corrigan," Tobias said. "It's a good thing you're here. I need you to witness this."

"Give me a break." Carly tilted her chin in defiance. "You know what? I'm out of here. I've had enough macho bullshit for one day. I'm going to visit Zadie. Which hospital is she in?"

"Please wait a moment," Dan said quickly. "I'll tell you exactly where Zadie is, and I'll explain everything. But I can hear you're angry and upset, so there's obviously an issue here. It would be best if we could resolve it before you go. You'd like to sort this out, wouldn't you, Carly?"

"What I'd like is for him to take back the ludicrous accusation that I've been poisoning one of my oldest friends." Carly pointed at Tobias. "What I'd like is for him to apologise."

Tobias pulled himself up to his full height as if preparing for battle, a gleam in his eyes. Before he could speak, Dan said, "Tobias, did you make such an accusation against Carly?"

Tobias grunted. "No, I did not. I'm simply trying to find out what's been happening to my sister, a job which, incidentally, you were hired to do, Mr Corrigan."

Dan wore an implacable smile. "What do *you* think has been happening to Zadie?"

"She's been poisoned, and I'm looking at the most likely culprit." Tobias glared at Carly, and she folded her arms, shaking her head.

"That's a terrible thing to say," Alan said. "In the first place, why on earth would you think Zadie's been poisoned?"

"I'll tell you why," Tobias replied. "I visited Zadie first thing this morning; I've been popping in whenever I can. But this morning, the consultant took me to one side. Remember I told you about the antidepressants in her system? Zadie is denying all knowledge."

"Did you ask her about it?" Dan said.

"Yes, but she's sticking to her guns. She swears she threw out all her meds ages ago, and I believe her."

"So you think someone has given her antidepressants without her knowledge," Dan suggested.

"It's worse than that. They ran more tests, and it turns out they'd got it wrong the first time. A false positive. There were no antidepressants at all."

"They looked at Zadie's medical records, saw she'd been prescribed antidepressants in the past and jumped to a conclusion," Dan said. "So were there drugs in her system or not?"

"Unfortunately, there were. Amphetamines. The consultant asked if Zadie ever used illegal drugs, and I said absolutely not. Then he started talking about diet pills. Some of them are similar to methamphetamine, apparently. He said Zadie wouldn't be the first celebrity to try them. I told him I was damned sure Zadie would never do something so stupid, not with her history."

"Hang on a minute," Alan said, "people take methamphetamine to lose weight?"

"The consultant said it's not uncommon, but we're not talking about the crystal meth they use on the streets; they think Zadie might've taken something called phentermine. It's supposed to be given under medical supervision, but the consultant said no doctor would give her that kind of medication, on account of her BPD."

"He was hinting that Zadie might've bought the pills illegally," Dan suggested.

"That's what he was getting at, but I set him straight. When Zadie says she didn't knowingly take them, I believe her. That leaves only one possibility: someone gave those pills to my sister without her knowledge. And we know who keeps giving Zadie all kinds of weird powders and potions."

"Okay, that's it." Carly unfolded her arms and squared up to Tobias. Lifting her hand, she began speaking, counting off each point with her fingers.

"One; I'm the person who weaned Zadie off all the meds she was on in the old days, not that I'd expect someone like you to understand, nor the male doctors who doped her up to the eyeballs because they thought women ought to be docile and compliant. Two; everything I provide for Zadie is plant-based and pure, made from brown rice, peas, soy and pumpkin seeds. It doesn't even have sugar in it. It couldn't be safer. Three; I actually know what I'm talking about because I have a degree in sports science and nutrition, so I'm the only person in the room who can tell you the side-effects of taking methamphetamine-based diet suppressants, which are: insomnia, high blood pressure, fast heart rate, palpitations and restlessness, followed by dependence and withdrawal symptoms if—"

She was cut short by Tobias pointing at her, his fingers jabbing the air, his face almost puce. "Where did you get that? That ring. Where did you… did you steal it? Is that what all this is about?"

The wind went from Carly's sails, and she lowered her hand, clutching it to her chest. "How can you even say that? Zadie gave this ring to me."

Tobias shook his head. "No. That ring belonged to my mother. It was her eternity ring. It was passed down from my grandmother on my father's side, and it was the only valuable piece of jewellery my mother ever owned. She held on to it through thick and thin, because she said it was all she had to pass on to her children. On her deathbed, she gave it to Zadie because she knew I'd be all right. Zadie would never give it away. Never."

"I…" Carly's lips moved soundlessly for a second. "No. You've made a mistake. This can't be—"

"It's from Cartier, yes?" Tobias interrupted. "Eighteen diamonds."

"Yes, but…" Carly looked to Dan and Alan. "I had no idea. Zadie told me it was vintage. I assumed she'd bought it. You can't think I'd steal from her. Zadie's my *friend*."

Dan held up his hands. "I'm not going to jump to any conclusions, and neither should anyone else. Let's all calm down." To Tobias, he added, "Surely, you know better than to accuse someone without proof. Do you really think Carly would be wearing that ring around the place if she'd stolen it?"

"That's a good point," Alan said. "I noticed the ring on Saturday, and Carly told me Zadie had given it to her as a thank you gift."

Carly nodded eagerly. "That's right. I remember telling you about it. You said Zadie was busy, but was she already in hospital? Were you lying to me?"

"It was necessary," Dan said. "We won't go into it now. One thing at a time. When did Zadie give you the ring?"

"For God's sake," Tobias blurted. "You're not going to be taken in by her, are you?"

"I've seen no evidence of Carly doing anything wrong," Dan replied. "For all we know, Zadie might've found a similar ring and decided to buy it as a gift."

"In that case, Zadie's ring will be in her room. I'll go and check, and if I don't find it, I'm going to call the police."

"You can check if you really want to, but if it isn't there, it doesn't prove it was stolen," Dan said. "Your best bet is to talk to Zadie. If she wanted to give it away, that was for her to decide."

"We'll see about that. You're all to stay right here while I have a look." Tobias stomped from the room, leaving the door wide open.

Dan heard his heavy footsteps thudding along the floorboards, and a moment later, a door creaked open.

Carly stood still in the centre of the room, the fingers of one hand twirling the diamond ring around her finger. Dan saw the muscles in her jaw working overtime, and he guessed she was trying very hard to keep a lid on her anger. *She's doing pretty well,* Dan thought. *She's spent the last half hour going toe to toe with an irate barrister.*

No. He'd got that wrong. Tobias Barrington wasn't behaving like a barrister; there was no trace of professional detachment in the way he'd laid into Carly. He'd simply thrown his weight around, trying to browbeat her, to bully her into submission. But Carly hadn't given in. She'd stood up for herself. *Good for her.*

Dan watched Carly for a little longer, seeing her with fresh eyes as he replayed their previous encounters. In that moment of reflection he saw a new role for Carly: a part she might've played. Dan smiled to himself as an assortment of disparate ideas slotted together in his mind.

He glanced at Alan, but Alan was occupied, peering through the open door, his head moving from side to side. He'd be looking for Natalya, but she'd made herself scarce.

Here we go, Dan thought, and making his tone warm and friendly, he said, "Carly, the day Zadie first received a note, she went out with her friends for dinner, but you weren't invited, were you?"

Carly shook her head. "I'm not... I'm not in that circle."

"You knew she was going out though, didn't you?"

"I can't remember. She might've mentioned it." Carly let go of her diamond ring and let her arms fall to her sides as she looked away. "I'm not her social secretary, for God's sake."

"Of course, you're her personal trainer. Nevertheless, I think you knew she was going out, but you came around that evening anyway."

"No." Carly looked at him. "Why would I do that if I knew she was going out?"

"So you *did* know she had plans for the evening," Dan stated.

"Yeah, no, I..."

Dan smiled. "Carly, you knew where Zadie was going and you wanted to be included. There's nothing wrong with that. You dropped in, hoping to catch her, because then Zadie would've invited you along, wouldn't she? Because Zadie is your friend, and she can be very generous, can't she?"

"When she feels like it, yes." Once again Carly began fiddling with the diamond ring.

"But that night, you missed them, didn't you? You turned up but they'd already left. Were you dressed up? Had you made an effort?"

Carly wrinkled her nose in exaggerated expression of puzzlement. "I don't know where you're getting this, but it's a fascinating story."

"I prefer to think of it as a scenario," Dan said. "It's hypothetical, I know, but you don't mind if I run through it, do you? It's the way my mind works."

"Knock yourself out."

"Thank you." Dan waited until Carly made eye contact with him, then he said, "People tend to underestimate you, don't they, Carly? They see someone who's into fitness and sport, and they think you conform to a certain stereotype. In a nutshell, they assume you're not particularly intelligent."

"Maybe."

"There's not much doubt about it. I'll confess, I stupidly fell into that trap myself. It was only when you mentioned your degree that I came to my senses and gave myself a talking to."

Carly mimed applause. "Well done, you've finally graduated from your boys' school and made it to the twenty-first century. The women of the world rejoice."

Dan bowed his head. "I had that coming, and for what it's worth, I apologise. I'm not usually so narrow minded.

"Good for you, Mr Corrigan. I hereby declare you fully woke."

"It's funny how you've remembered Dan's surname all of a sudden," Alan said. "Up until now, you've referred to him as Dan whatshisname."

"So?"

"So it was an affectation," Alan replied. "You've known Dan's name all along, but you were pretending not to have an excellent memory. You were playing down your intelligence to fit in with the expectations of others."

Carly sent them a patronising smile. "Is this all part of the service, this character assassination? If it is, you might want to rethink your marketing."

"Now we're seeing the real you," Dan said. "You're as sharp as a tack, aren't you, Carly? But Alan's right; you don't mind pretending to be a bit forgetful when it suits you, like the time you told us about the argument between Zadie and one of her friends. You claimed you couldn't remember who the friend was, but you gave us the name Mary in the end, and that was deliberate. You wanted us to find out about Melody and the fact that she'd changed her name."

"When was this?"

"Come on, Carly, you know exactly what I'm talking about."

"Well, I might've got the names muddled. Melody, Mary, anyone can make a mistake."

"But you didn't," Dan stated. "You wanted to throw suspicion on Melody, because you don't like her. You resent the fact that she's reinvented herself."

"Huh. She's fooling no one. You can take the girl out of the council estate, but... you know how the saying goes."

"I know that, in some ways, you and Melody are alike," Dan

replied. "She doesn't come from a wealthy family, and I suspect that you don't either. Am I right?"

"Okay, so I'm working class. So what? I'm not anything like her."

"You've taken different paths," Dan said. "Melody tried to escape from her background, but you've embraced yours. You wear it like an old, comfortable sweater, a layer of insulation between you and the world."

"Is that so? And here's me thinking I'm perfectly happy as I am."

"Most of us like to think we're normal and well-adjusted, but we all have our battles to fight," Dan said. "But you're clever. You pick your battles, saving your energy for when it really matters, like just now with Tobias."

"He doesn't frighten me."

"I can see that, but you've dealt with his type before, haven't you? I have the feeling you've been patronised and talked down to for as long as you can remember, especially by men."

Carly arched an eyebrow. "Like right now? Thanks for mansplaining the female psyche to me, Dan. I couldn't possibly have figured it out on my own." Carly's lips moved as though she'd like to say more, but she held back, settling for a hard stare and a dismissive shake of her head.

Dan smiled. He'd touched a nerve, and that was exactly what he wanted. He needed Carly to stop being defensive; he needed her to go on the attack. All she needed was one more push.

"You used to be equals, you and Zadie, didn't you?" Dan asked, but he didn't wait for a reply. "You've known Zadie for much longer than her new circle of friends. You've known her from when you were both struggling to get by. You came through the hard times together, and that kind of experience forms a bond, doesn't it? A strong bond. Unbreakable."

Dan paused for effect, then: "Or so you thought. But it was different for Zadie. She got what she wanted. She found a way to become rich and famous, and she didn't need you as an ally anymore. Zadie made a new life for herself, but you were a part of her past. She didn't even count you as a close friend. So when you came here that night, hoping to be invited to dinner, you discovered Zadie had already gone. You were sad and frustrated that your plan hadn't worked, and you were jealous of—"

"No I wasn't," Carly snapped. "It didn't bother me at all."

"I think you must've been a little upset, because you made a mistake when you left the note. You forgot to sign it. You just dashed it off and shoved it through the letter box. *I'll see you soon.*"

"No."

"You deny writing it?"

"There's no point, is there? You've tripped me up." Carly lips curled in a sneer. "But you're not as clever as you think. You've got it wrong. I *was* invited to dinner. Zadie asked me to come, so yes, I did make an effort. I do own a dress, believe it or not. But when I got here, they'd gone. She'd forgotten about me. That was what hurt."

Dan tried not to react. Now they were getting to it. After all his questions and fruitless speculation, they were finally glimpsing the truth. And Carly *was* telling the truth; he could see it in her eyes. She was unburdening herself, breaking free from the lies that had trapped her for too long, and Dan had to admit, her version of events made more sense than his.

Speaking gently, Dan said, "Someone else came into the house shortly after you left, and they moved the note. It was the fact that it was found in Zadie's studio that caused so much distress. When you realised what must've happened, why didn't you say anything?"

Carly gazed at him, her expression lifeless.

Dan nodded. "It's one thing to be undervalued by a man, but quite another to be scorned by a woman, especially someone you'd always thought of as a true friend."

Carly set her lips in a grim line.

"Maybe Zadie was more than a friend to you; she was like a sister," Dan went on. "But she cast you aside and you wanted to pay her back. So when Zadie was distraught after seeing your note, part of you thought she deserved it, so you kept going. You wrote another note, and this time you upped the stakes, adding a knife for good measure."

Carly shook her head. "That wasn't me. I wrote one note, and that was it. Yeah, Zadie was upset about it, but that wasn't my fault. I didn't break into the house like she thought. Anyway, I was going to tell her what happened, but she went overboard, calling the police and bringing you two in. It was too late to back out, so I let it go. I knew she'd get over it. Zadie loves a bit of drama, but it never lasts for long. I had no way of knowing someone else would start winding her up."

"Really?" Dan said. "You expect me to believe that someone else carried on where you left off?"

"Believe what you like, but that's what must've happened. When she had that second note, and all that business with the knife, I was in the same yoga class as Zadie. I go every week. Wednesday, twelve o'clock."

"You drive from Exeter to Chagford for a yoga class?" Dan asked. "There must be plenty of classes closer to home."

"There are, but I go to that session with Zadie." Carly drew a breath and let it out slowly. "For one hour a week we're students in the same class. Equals. It's nice. At least, it was. All that will have to end now. I'll be out in the cold once and for all, but that's my fault. I'll have to deal with it." Carly dabbed at the corner of her eye with the back of her hand. "It could be worse. At least I've got an alibi."

You have so much more than that, Dan thought. *You've had the key all along, you just didn't know it*. Carly's admission had turned this case on its head. All of Zadie's friends had an alibi for the evening when the first note was left at Zadie's house, but it was now clear that they'd never needed one. That note hadn't been a threat at all; it had only seemed sinister thanks to a couple of unfortunate coincidences. Since then, someone else had seized the opportunity to harass Zadie, and they'd driven her to tipping point. But who and why?

Dan let his gaze lose focus while his mind went to work, and another question begged an answer, a question that, until now, he'd neglected: How? How had someone given Zadie amphetamines on the night of her fall? Zadie had been home alone and on her guard, the doors and windows locked. But still, someone had got to her, someone who knew her house, knew her routine.

An idea began to form in Dan's mind. It was as if he'd been pulling at a tangled ball of string for ages, but he'd only just found the free end. When he pulled that one thread, the stubborn knots and twists would unravel at last.

He was ready, but before he could begin, Tobias appeared in the doorway, looking much more subdued than when he left. Dan, Alan and Carly looked to him expectantly.

Tobias cleared his throat. "There's no jewellery in Zadie's bedroom or her dressing room; nothing of value at any rate. There are a few bangles and trinkets but that's it. I know for a fact she had lots of gold earrings. I've been giving them to her for Christmas for years, but there's no sign of them, so I called the hospital, and they let me speak to her."

Tobias briefly bit his lower lip, but he quickly composed himself. "Zadie says the gold and the diamonds weren't ethical, whatever that means, so she's given all her valuable jewellery away. She confirmed that she gave the eternity ring to Carly." Tobias pushed out his chin as though preparing to say something that cost him a great deal of effort. "I was wrong to accuse you, Carly. Please consider this a full apology for everything I said."

Carly seemed to consider this for a second, then she nodded. "Okay. What about the allegation that I somehow poisoned your sister?"

"In the circumstances, I fully withdraw any and all allegations I made," Tobias stated. "I hope you can understand that I wasn't myself. I've been worried about my sister for a while, but that's no excuse. Again, I apologise."

"Looks like it's my day for receiving apologies," Carly said.

"But that'll all go out the window when you hear what Dan and Alan have to say."

Tobias cast a puzzled look around the group, but Dan wasn't about to launch into an explanation for his benefit. Instead, he fixed his gaze on Carly. "For what it's worth, I believe everything you've told me, but I have a few questions."

Carly nodded once in mute acceptance.

"Thank you," Dan said. "To start with, were you telling the truth about the side effects of those diet pills, or was that a bluff to win the argument with Tobias?"

"I wouldn't make that stuff up," Carly replied. "I'm a professional, and I take my work seriously. Of course I know about diet pills. I know all about the damage some people will do to their bodies for the sake of some weird concept of beauty. As it happens, phentermine came up in my work recently. I'm doing research for my thesis. It's all about body image and mental health. It's a serious problem for a lot of people."

"I'm sure it is," Dan said. "But you said you already have a degree."

"I'm a postgrad student at Exeter, that's how come I get to use their gym. I'm hoping to finish my master's this year, and unlike Philippa, I actually turn up and do the work."

Without warning, Tobias lunged toward Carly, his hands outstretched, a growl erupting from his lips.

Dan moved fast, closing the distance between them in one stride. He grabbed Tobias by the arm, pulling him back.

Tobias rounded on him, planting his hands on Dan's chest and shoving him hard, but Dan held on tight.

"Get the hell off me," Tobias snarled, grabbing the front of Dan's shirt with both fists. "I'll knock your bloody block off."

"Go ahead, but you'll be disbarred when I press charges for assault."

"Huh! You wouldn't do that."

"Try me."

"But *you* grabbed *me*," Tobias protested. I'll be the one pressing charges."

"No, I stepped in to prevent you from assaulting a woman. That's a fact, and I have two witnesses who can corroborate it. So ask yourself, Tobias, if that's a story you want people to know."

Tobias glared at Dan, but he opened his fists, releasing Dan from his grip, and he held his hands out to each side. "Back off, Dan."

"Are you going to behave yourself?"

"Obviously. I was never going to hurt her in the first place. You overreacted."

"Better safe than sorry." Dan let go of Tobias' arm and stood back. "Okay?"

Tobias grunted under his breath as he straightened his jacket.

"What the hell is wrong with you people?" Carly demanded. "You're worse than children."

"Carly," Dan began gently, "haven't you heard about Philippa?"

Carly shook her head, frowning.

"It's bad news," Alan said. "I'm sorry to tell you this, but Philippa was found dead yesterday morning. The police have started a murder inquiry."

Carly's face was a mask of incomprehension. "Philippa? Are you serious?"

"I'm afraid it's true," Dan said. "I'm surprised you haven't heard."

"I don't listen to the local news. I just… I didn't…" Carly's voice faded to a whimper as she looked down, breathing hard as though holding back a sob. All appearance of health and vitality had vanished. Carly seemed to have shrunk in stature, her shoulders rounded, her posture slack.

"Can I get you a glass of water or anything?" Alan asked.

"No, thank you." Carly looked up, her eyes moist. "I'll go. I'm sorry, Tobias. I'm sorry for what I said. I'm sorry for your loss, and I'm sorry for what I did. Dan will explain." Carly swallowed hard. "I'd better go."

"Please wait for a second," Dan said. "Tell me more about the diet drug. What did you call it?"

"Phentermine," Carly said. "What about it?"

"Is it soluble? Tasteless?"

Carly nodded slowly. "Yes to both questions, but I think what you're really asking is, could someone have given it to Zadie without her knowing. I'd have to say yes, and if the dose was high, it would've made her feel terrible: disorientated, anxious, panicky. With Zadie's history, if somebody did that to her... Well, I'd like to get my hands on them."

"Thank you. There's one more question. Did you take or find a small tin of cigarettes?"

"What do *you* think?" Carly replied. "I've never smoked and I can't understand people who do."

"Okay, but someone smoked three cigarettes in Zadie's garden, and nobody's owning up to it." Dan glanced at Tobias, and when he went on, he chose his words carefully. "On the night we talked about earlier, you were upset, so you might've broken the rule of a lifetime."

"No way," Carly stated. "I've never tried it and I never want to."

"Okay, thanks." Dan turned to Tobias. "I need to ask you something too. Did you ever ask Naomi to give you photographs of Zadie?"

"Certainly not. Why would I do that?"

"Naomi is a photographer," Alan said. "Have you met her?"

"Yes, but I've never asked her for photos of Zadie. That would've been very odd."

"I thought as much." Dan smiled at Alan. "Excellent. We've got almost everything we need to tie this case up."

Alan blinked. "Have we?"

"Certainly. We're one short step away from handing this case over to the police, and I know exactly what we need to do next."

"Let's go then," Alan replied. "I'm ready when you are."

"Are you going to explain?" Tobias asked.

Dan shook his head. "Not yet. Soon, but not yet. Come on, Alan. We need to go for a drive."

"I'll leave as well," Carly said, then she hesitated. "Tobias, do you think it would be okay for me to visit Zadie? It might be the last time I get to see her."

"I don't think it's a good idea," Dan replied. "Zadie needs rest, and if she sees you, she'll know something's wrong and that will only make her anxious. But there's no need for you to worry. Zadie's getting the best possible care. She had a fall and hit her head, but she's doing well, and she's going to make a full recovery."

Carly exhaled slowly. "Thank God. When I heard she was in hospital, I thought she might've had another breakdown. I mean, it's awful she's had a fall, but so long as she's doing okay, that's all that matters. Injuries heal, don't they? Some things aren't so easy to fix."

Dan wasn't sure what to say, and in the silence, Carly made for the door, her hands clasped over her stomach, her shoulders hunched. Carly moved slowly as if in a trance, but she made a detour toward the sofa. Her steps faltered, and for a fleeting moment, Dan thought she was going to sink onto the sofa, overcome with emotion, but Carly kept walking, slowing only to bend down and lay the diamond ring on the coffee table. That done, without another word, Carly left the room.

CHAPTER 74

I n Teignmouth police station, DS Kulkarni knocked on the door of Detective Inspector Thomas Townsend's office and stepped inside.

Townsend looked mildly surprised. Perhaps he preferred his visitors to wait for an invitation before they marched in, but Kulkarni was in no mood to wait. She'd been working at her desk for most of the morning, and she was ready for some action.

"Morning, sir," she began. "Have you got a minute?"

"Sure, but please, call me Thomas. Now, what can I do for you?"

"It's about Ryan Hallett's house. I'm hoping you can authorise a search."

"At this stage, that's doubtful, Anisha. What would be the aim?"

"For a start, I'd like to see if we can retrieve samples containing DNA, then we can match them against the victim from Diamonds Avenue."

"That's not going to achieve much. You'll find DNA in the house, but how would we know how it got there? We don't know who visited the house and when."

"It's about tipping the balance of probabilities, sir, I mean,

Thomas. If we get a match, we'll be one step closer to establishing the victim's identity."

"Not really. I'm sorry, Anisha, but it doesn't stack up. We don't have the time nor the resources to go hunting for evidence that would be, at best, circumstantial. We'd be clutching at straws. We have to do better than that."

Kulkarni bit her lip. Townsend's words stung, but she had no good argument to offer in return.

"Is there anything else?" Townsend went on.

"No, sir. Not at the moment."

"Okay. Since you're here, fill me in on this business with Mr Whelan. I understand that his interview was less than fruitful."

"Unfortunately, that's true. He wouldn't say anything until his legal advisor arrived, and after a brief consultation, Whelan answered 'No comment' to all my questions."

"Leaving us with egg on our faces," Townsend observed. "Frankly, I'm not surprised. You didn't have enough evidence to bring Whelan in for an interview under caution. You overplayed your hand, Anisha."

"In hindsight it looks that way, but at the time, I believed I was acting to preserve life. I honestly thought Mr Whelan was in danger."

"In danger from the men who you *believed* were the same two blokes seen by a witness on Diamonds Avenue."

"Yes. As soon as I saw them, I knew it was them. They were a very close match to the e-fits."

"I've never set much store by e-fits, and anyway, you were seeing them from a distance and on a dark street," Townsend said. "Any half-decent lawyer could drive a coach and horses through that kind of evidence. Added to which, you seem to have been carrying out an unauthorised surveillance operation."

"I realise that I didn't exactly follow procedure, but I had reason to believe Harry Whelan had lied to me, and as it happens, it was just as well I was there. It looked as though the two men were in the process of abducting him."

"Did Whelan say as much? Did he make a complaint against the two men?"

Kulkarni was about to answer, but Townsend plucked a piece of paper from his desk and brandished it at her. "No, he did not. Quite the contrary. In fact, Mr Whelan claims you brought him in for an interview against his will. He says you harassed him without provocation while he was trying to go to the pub with some friends. That *is* what he's claiming, isn't it?"

Kulkarni nodded, tight-lipped.

"We police by consent," Townsend swept on. "I don't know how you do things in Exeter, but around here we work hard to build trust in the community, and all our efforts are wasted if even one officer comes across as heavy-handed. Do you understand that?"

"Yes, sir."

"Good." Townsend tossed the sheet of paper to his desk, and his expression mellowed. "Anisha, anyone can see you're keen, but you've got to stick to the rules. Procedures are there to protect everyone. Do you understand?"

"Yes, sir."

Townsend studied her for a second. "Okay. End of lecture. Learn from it and move on. What are you working on today?"

"DS Winslow is in court, so I've been running checks on Harry Whelan, looking into his phone records and trying to trace his associates. There's a connection with a man called Dave Whitehead in Plymouth, so I've made contact with Plymouth CID to see if they can shed any light."

"Whelan again." Townsend sighed. "That line of inquiry is sketchy, and that's me being generous. I don't want you wasting your time and chasing shadows, Anisha. Move on, look for new leads, try approaching the case from a different angle."

"Yes, sir. I'll do that."

"Fair enough. You'd better get back to work." Townsend pulled a file from the stack in front of him, his attention already elsewhere.

Kulkarni let herself out quietly and returned to her desk. She slumped into her seat, staring at her computer's screen as though it held all the answers. *Clutching at straws*, she thought bitterly. *How dare he?*

But the truth was, Townsend wasn't entirely wrong. She'd stepped out of line, and there was nothing a criminal defence lawyer liked better than a police officer who'd bent the rules; as far as they were concerned, it was a get-out-of-jail-free card.

Kulkarni shook her head to dispel her dark mood. There was still a case to clear up, and she couldn't sit around, waiting for something to happen.

She'd had no reply from Plymouth CID, so Kulkarni grabbed a phone and called her contact: DI Russell Blakey.

It wasn't long before he answered: "Anisha. How's tricks?"

"Not bad. You?"

"Fine, fine. Listen, I can give you a few minutes, that's all. I was going to call you later, but now is as good a time as any." Blakey paused. "I got the e-fits and the info you sent over. Do you want the good news or the bad news?"

"The good news, definitely. I need something to brighten my day."

"Like that is it? Well, you'll be pleased to know you've struck lucky. The e-fits were pretty good, and along with your description, I'm almost certain I know who we're looking at. It helps that those two characters usually come as a pair, and they're both known to us. The tall one is Tariq Hamidi, and his associate is Lewis Crouch."

"That's great." Kulkarni scribbled down the names. "Whatever info you've got on them, I'd love to see it. Can you send it over?"

"This is where the bad news comes in. We need you to lay off them for now. They're being looked at by our Serious Crime Unit. It's an active investigation, and it's taken a long time to put together. The folks in SCU don't want anyone kicking the hornets' nest."

"They're looking at Dave Whitehead?" Kulkarni asked.

"He's part of the picture, but it's a complex case. A lot of moving parts."

Kulkarni's thoughts raced. "What's going on? Have you got someone undercover?"

"What kind of question is that? You know better than to ask, Anisha."

"Of course. Sorry. Are Serious Crimes looking at Harry Whelan as well?"

"He's on the list, but again, we need you to steer clear."

"That's understood, but I'm concerned for his safety. When I ran into Hamidi and Crouch, they were taking Whelan away, and he was frightened for his life."

There was a pause before Blakey spoke. "Tell me about it. What happened?"

"I saw them in the street. Hamidi and Crouch were holding on to Whelan, and he looked scared. I brought Whelan in for questioning, mainly for his own protection."

Blakey grunted in disapproval. "Did you get anything out of him?"

"No. He was too scared to talk, and then a solicitor showed up and it was all over."

"Serious Crimes are not going to be pleased with you, but they'll get over it. It's just as well that Whelan didn't give you anything. We want Whitehead and his pals to think they've run rings around us. That way, they'll carry on with business as usual. We mustn't spook them until Serious Crimes have enough evidence to grab them."

"Even if it means they decide to kill Whelan?"

"It won't come to that, Anisha. They know you've clocked Hamidi and Crouch, so if anything were to happen to Whelan it would come back to bite them. They've frightened Whelan enough, so they'll leave him alone for now."

"Let's hope you're right."

"That's all we can do. Listen, I know it's tough on you, Anisha, but you need to back away from this case."

"I understand, but I've got one more question. Does the name Ryan Hallett ring any bells?"

There was a pause, and Kulkarni heard the tapping of keys. "Yes. He's on our radar. Why?"

"We recovered a body from a house fire. It looks like the fire was started deliberately. We think the victim might be Hallett, but we can't be sure. All we've got to go on is a description of a man who was seen nearby at the time, plus the fact that Hallett seems to have gone AWOL."

"Is there no one to ID the body?"

"We went to Hallett's address and found a girlfriend, but she did a runner. She only gave us her first name: Sandra. I have the number of the car she drove, but it was registered in Hallett's name, not hers, and she's probably ditched it by now."

"What did she look like?"

"Thirties. About 1.6 metres tall. Blonde. Slim. Smartly dressed."

"Hm. Send me a full description and her details. I'll pass it on."

"What about Hallett? Is there anything you can give me?"

"Let me get back to you on that, Anisha."

"Okay, but I've got a murder inquiry here, Russ, and we still can't identify the victim. But you're telling me we can't pursue the only leads we've got. What am I supposed to do, sit on my hands?"

Blakey didn't reply immediately, and when he spoke, his voice had taken on an authoritarian tone. "If I were your superior officer, Detective Sergeant, I'd expect you to use your initiative and look for other avenues of inquiry."

"Yes, sir. Of course. Apologies. I didn't mean to sound so…"

"Disrespectful? Insubordinate?"

Kulkarni winced, but before she could say anything, Blakey added, "I get it, Anisha. You want results, and you're frustrated. We've all been there. It goes with the job. Solid police work takes time. Look for evidence, build a case. You said you've got Hallett's address. Do a search, get some DNA to match with the victim."

"I suggested that to DI Townsend, but he doesn't think we have reasonable grounds for a proper search."

"I see," Blakey said. "So you have a man answering Hallett's description seen near the site of the fire. How many witnesses?"

"Just one, I'm afraid, but he's reliable. He lives opposite, so he had a good view, and he mentioned a black van at the scene. Hallett drove a black van for work, and the owner has reported it missing."

"That's good enough. If you ask me, your DI is being a pain in the arse for the hell of it. I reckon he saw a bright young DS like you coming into his nick, keen as mustard, and he decided to take you down a peg or two. If I were you, I'd bide my time, get my ducks in a row, then I'd have another crack at talking to your DI. Show him a bit of respect and he'll come around."

"I've got to massage his male ego, you mean?"

"Not as such, no," Blakey said. "It takes a lot of work to make it to DI, and most of us don't get here by flashes of inspiration and following our instincts. We do it by steady police work and following the rules, and we don't like it when people act too big for their boots. If you want your DI to be on your side, let him know you're ready to play it by the book. Put a decent case together, and he'll go along with it."

Kulkarni felt her jaw clenching. One more lecture from a superior officer, and she'd blow her top. But DI Blakey had a point; she had to find a way forward and that wouldn't happen without the cooperation of her DI.

"Thanks," Kulkarni said. "I'll take that on board."

"I know you will. You'll figure it out, Anisha. Good luck with it, but remember what I said about Whitehead and co. If his name comes up, or if you're looking at any of his associates, talk to me before you do anything, all right?"

"Of course, sir. It goes without saying."

"All right, Anisha. All the best. Bye."

Blakey ended the call, and Kulkarni set down her phone, realising she'd been hunched over her desk, her shoulders practically up to her ears. She sat back, straightening her spine and rolling her shoulders.

She'd had a setback, but she was still in the game. Kulkarni smiled. *Still in the game.* That was exactly the kind of thing DI Spiller would say. Was she picking up his mannerisms? If so, it was no bad thing. At times like this, a dose of Spiller's down to earth, dogged determination was sorely needed. *It's not over until it's over,* Kulkarni told herself. *Onward and upward.* Solid policework tended to proceed at a snail's pace, but there'd be a break in the case soon. There *had* to be.

CHAPTER 75

D an drove into the Exebrook housing estate, Alan sitting quiet in the passenger seat, both men alone with their thoughts. For his part, Dan was taking in the rows of houses from a different perspective. It was an aspirational kind of place: homes for people who wanted to live in Exeter but couldn't quite afford it. Each house was a step on the ladder, one rung nearer to the home of someone's dreams. There was nothing wrong with that, but where did Naomi sit on that scale? What was her background, and what were her aims in life?

Dan parked his RAV4 outside Naomi's house, the engine cutting out with a stuttering rattle as he turned off the ignition.

"You ought to get that looked at," Alan said. "It sounds like a proverbial bag of spanners."

"Soon," Dan replied. "I'll take it in for a service when I've been paid for this job."

"Do you think it can wait that long?"

"It'll have to." Dan looked up at Naomi's house. "Well, her car is on the driveway, so let's hope she's in."

"I still think we should've called ahead."

"No, that wouldn't have worked." Turning back to Alan, he added, "Listen, whatever I say in there, go with it, okay?"

"I'll do my best, but it would be a lot easier if you told me why we're here."

"You'll see. Come on."

They climbed from the car and strode to Naomi's front door. Naomi answered the door quickly, and though she wore jeans and a t-shirt, just as she had on their previous visit, there was something different about her.

Dan wasn't sure if Naomi was standing a little taller, her posture more upright, or if it was her manner that had changed, but she seemed more confident, defiant even.

Ignoring Dan's greeting, she fixed him with a stare as if willing him to walk away, but Dan held her gaze. He would not be the first to blink.

Oblivious to their staring match, Alan said, "Hello, Naomi. Have you got a minute?"

There was a brief pause before Naomi replied. "All right. I can give you five minutes, but I'm going out soon."

"That's fine," Dan said. "Okay if we come in?"

"Sure." As before, Naomi took them to the small lounge and offered them a seat on the sofa.

"Thanks, but we're happy to stand," Dan said. "We'll try to be brief."

"Whatever." Naomi sat on the sofa and leaned back, her arms spread out to each side. She lifted one leg onto the sofa beside her, crooking her knee, and she tilted her head a little forward, looking up at them through her lashes, a sultry gleam in her eye.

If her open posture was designed to make them uncomfortable it was a partial success. Alan averted his gaze, taking a sudden interest in the curtains, but Dan wasn't going to be taken in. Maintaining eye contact, he said, "Thanks for making time to see us. Actually, I came to offer you an assignment."

A flicker of confusion crossed Naomi's features, the corners of her eyes tightening.

Before she could speak, Dan said, "It's a photography job. I need someone who can handle a camera, someone who can get a good shot even in tricky light conditions."

Naomi's gaze sharpened. "You haven't come to talk about Zadie?"

"Well, it's related to that," Dan replied. "You see, I have a very clear idea of who was harassing her, but I need some evidence to back it up. I want to catch someone in the act, and for that, I'll need some excellent photos. We'd do it ourselves, but we might have to give chase, and we can't do that while we're taking photos. You pointed that out, didn't you, Alan?"

Alan turned back to them with a start. "That's right. It goes without saying."

"It might take a few hours to get the job done," Dan went on, "but I'll pay, of course, whatever your going rate is."

Slowly, Naomi lowered her foot to the floor and sat up straight, her knees together and her hands in her lap. "You know who was stalking Zadie? Was it one of her fans like we all thought?"

"I know the guilty party, but it wasn't a stranger," Dan replied.

"Who was it?"

Dan raised a finger to his lips. "That's confidential. You mustn't try to get it out of me."

"But if I'm going to take photos of them, I'll find out anyway."

"True, but I don't want to say anything yet," Dan said. "There's always a chance I'm wrong. We'll see who turns up at Zadie's house tonight."

"Tonight?" Naomi echoed. "Does it have to be tonight?"

Dan nodded. "I've set things in motion, and the guilty person will be there."

Naomi looked down and to one side, but only for a moment. "I had plans for tonight, but it's nothing that can't be rearranged."

"You'll do it?" Dan asked.

"Maybe. First, I have to know who the subject will be. I have to think about my own safety."

"Oh, that makes things difficult." Dan looked to Alan. "What do you think, Alan? Should we tell her?"

If Alan was bewildered by the question, he hid it well. The twitch in his cheek was so small that Dan was almost certainly the only one who noticed it. After a split-second's indecision, Alan said, "I'll leave that decision to you, Dan. You're the boss."

"Right." Dan sucked air over his teeth, then he nodded to himself. "It ought to be okay. After all, you're going to be one of the team, Naomi." He paused. "I hate to tell you this, but it was Melody."

Naomi's eyebrows shot up, but otherwise she didn't react.

"Melody didn't have a good alibi for the evening when the first note was left," Dan went on. "That story about her hair didn't stand up to scrutiny. She knew Zadie was going out, so she went over and left the note. That was the start of it, and she escalated it from there."

Naomi shook her head. "Melody? I can't believe it. Why would she do something like that?"

"It's all very simple. She's been struggling to make a success of her shop, and she asked Zadie for help. She wanted Zadie to give her a celebrity endorsement on YouTube, but Zadie turned her down flat. To make matters worse, Zadie humiliated Melody, referring to her as Mary, which is the name Melody was born with, the name she's tried very hard to escape from."

"But this is awful," Naomi said. "Are you sure?"

"As much as I can be," Dan replied. "There was some other evidence. Do you remember, I asked you if you smoked? That was because we found some cigarette stubs in the garden. Here, let me show you a photo."

Dan produced his phone and located the images Alan had shared with him. Finding the sharpest shot of the stubs, he held it out to show Naomi.

Naomi leaned forward to see. "Okay, but what does that prove? Melody doesn't usually smoke. The only real smoker I know is Connor."

"Yes, but look what happens when I zoom in." Dan pinched the screen and Naomi looked on, her eyes wide.

"Do you see that dark smear on the cigarette paper?" Dan asked.

"Yes. It's mud, isn't it? It looks like somebody stepped on it to put it out."

"That's what I thought at first, but if you look carefully you can make out a faint tinge of red. It's lipstick."

"So?"

"So I knew Connor hadn't smoked them. All that remained was to follow a logical line of reasoning. Why would someone smoke in the garden? All Zadie's friends knew she'd hate it, but Melody did it anyway. It was a mildly aggressive act, a way of raising a middle finger as it were."

Naomi tutted and made a show of shaking her head in disapproval, but Dan saw the look in her eye. Recognition was a hard response to hide, and he'd just told Naomi something she knew only too well. It was time to put the next part of his plan into action.

Dan pressed his finger against his temple. "I'm sorry, but I'm getting a terrible headache. I get migraines."

"Do you?" Alan started to say, changing his sentence mid-flow to, "Do you need anything?"

"Thanks, but I've got my meds." Taking a small bottle of pills from his pocket, Dan rattled them. "I have to take them straight away. Can I grab a glass of water?"

"Of course." Naomi jumped to her feet, but Dan made it to the door ahead of her.

"It's okay, I can fetch it myself." Dan spotted the kitchen through an open doorway and marched inside. He looked for the fridge, but the appliances were all hidden behind matching wooden doors. Hazarding a guess, he pulled a door open and smiled. *Got it first time.*

But he stood, staring at the shelves in turn, his teeth clenched in bitter disappointment. He'd been so sure of what he'd find, but he'd drawn a blank. There was nothing but food: a tub of spread, another of hummus and a packet of plant-based cheese. The door shelves held a few condiments. He pulled out the salad drawer, revealing a head of celery and a lettuce nestling against a packet of tomatoes. But although he couldn't find the one thing he'd hoped for, there was something on the bottom shelf that really shouldn't be there at all.

"What the hell are you doing?" Naomi had caught up with him. Without waiting for an answer, she wrested the fridge door from Dan's grip and closed it firmly. "Excuse me," she said stiffly. "Could you give me some space, please?"

Dan stood back, and Naomi stepped smartly in front of him, resting her back against the fridge door.

"There's water in the tap," she went on. "I'll fetch you a glass. Why don't you go back to the lounge and sit down? I'll bring the water through to you. Migraines can be horrible, can't they? You need to sit down and rest."

Dan stayed put. He hadn't been dealt the hand he wanted, but he was still holding a few decent cards, and there was only one way to play them. If ever there was a time for a well-executed bluff, this was it.

"I don't need water," Dan stated. "These are just vitamin pills." He showed her the bottle, watching her reaction carefully.

A flash of alarm raced across Naomi's features, but she tried to hide it, wrinkling her nose and tilting her head to one side. "You poor thing. Did you bring the wrong ones. It's easily done."

"I brought them on purpose, Naomi. Can't you guess why?"

"No, I haven't a clue. Are you all right? Migraines can leave you muddled, and you're not making any sense, Dan. You really need to sit down for a bit."

Alan appeared in the kitchen doorway. "What's going on?"

"Dan's having a moment," Naomi said softly. "He seems confused. I think he must've been working too hard. He should go home, but he won't be safe to drive with a migraine. You can take him, can't you, Alan?"

Alan opened his mouth as if to agree, but no words came out. He looked to Dan for help.

"I don't have a migraine," Dan said. "I don't get them."

"Then what...?" Naomi looked at them in turn as if momentarily on the back foot, then her expression hardened. "I don't know what's going on here, but it's time for you to go. Both of you. Now."

Dan smiled. "In a minute. First, I need to ask you something."

Naomi folded her arms. "No. The only thing you need to do is to get out of my house."

Carrying on as if she hadn't spoken, Dan said, "Where's the bottle of water, Naomi?"

Naomi narrowed her eyes, but she didn't reply.

"I was expecting to see it in the fridge," Dan went on. "You gave the game away the other day. When Alan fetched you a glass of water, you asked if he'd taken it from the tap. You were very definite about it. You looked quite worried, but then you'd just had some bad news, so I didn't interpret it correctly. When Alan said he'd used the tap, you perked up. At the time, I thought it was the cold water that brought the colour back to your cheeks, but I was mistaken. You were relieved that Alan hadn't brought you the water from the fridge, the water laced with phentermine."

"What? I don't even know what that is. What are you accusing me of?"

"Oh, come on, Naomi," Dan replied. "Let's not play that game."

Naomi turned to Alan. "You'd better take your friend out of here before I call the police and you both wind up in trouble."

"The police will be here soon enough," Dan said. "As soon as I talk to DI Spiller, he'll send someone to swab you for DNA, and he'll get a match with the cigarette stubs you left in Zadie's garden."

"Is that so?" Naomi demanded. "A minute ago you were sure that was Melody."

"I made that up," Dan replied. "I wanted to see your face, and now I know."

"You know nothing. Are you some kind of fantasist? You seem to be suffering from delusions."

"Ah, you like pop psychology. I should've known." Dan held her attention with his gaze. "When did you get the idea? Was it when you talked to John Callaway?"

"What's John got to do with anything?"

"He made a film called *Wild Yonder*, and when I talked to him about it, he said it was odd that I should mention it. *Odd*, that was the word he used. Why did it seem odd to him, do you think?"

Naomi rolled her eyes. "I have absolutely no idea."

"Here's my explanation," Dan said. "Callaway was surprised because I wasn't the first person who'd brought the subject up recently, even though the film was made a very long time ago and it wasn't exactly noteworthy even at the time. It was a flop, to borrow Mr Callaway's phrase. So who would be talking about it?" Dan clicked his fingers as though the idea had just occurred to him. "Well, it had to be Naomi, didn't it? According to Callaway, the best aspects of the film were the lighting and the colour scheme. Who else would appreciate those things if not a photographer?"

"Okay, I know about John's film," Naomi admitted. "But I don't understand what you're getting at."

"I'm talking about gaslighting, Naomi. Callaway made a film based on the play, but you did it for real. Let me lay it out for you. Where were we?"

"The cigarette stubs we found," Alan replied.

"Ah yes, the missing cigarettes." Dan rubbed his hands together. "The cigarettes belonged to Connor. I thought he'd lost them and Shaun, that's Zadie's decorator, had found them. But Connor said there'd been six cigarettes in the tin when he last saw it, and when Shaun picked it up, there were only three left. We knew someone had taken three cigarettes and smoked them in the garden, but how had they got hold of them in the first place? Simple: they took the tin from Connor. It was a way to hit back at him, stealing the one thing he cares about. Funnily enough, Connor had no idea it had been taken. He thought it was still at home, so who could've stolen his little tin without anyone noticing?"

Dan let his question hang in the air for a moment before

answering it. "We know one person who could get away with it: quiet, timid little Naomi. No one suspected you, did they? Half the time, Zadie and the others act as if you aren't there. We also know that you have a habit of marching from the room when their derision becomes too much to bear. Where do you go when it all gets on top of you?"

"I don't know what you're trying to imply, Dan, but I've had enough," Naomi snapped. "Get out."

"Not just yet," Dan said. "Since you didn't answer my question, I'll make a suggestion. When Zadie and the others get on your nerves, you walk into the garden. You've found a quiet spot with an old bench. You usually sit there until you've calmed down, but on one occasion, you'd stolen Connor's cigarettes and it occurred to you that you may as well use them. You didn't really approve, but it was another way to spite him, wasn't it? You tried a few, but you weren't used to smoking. I doubt whether you even inhaled. You threw the rest away, complete with their tin, choosing the spot where Connor often lit a cigarette before he walked home. If someone found the tin, they'd assume he'd simply dropped it. How am I doing?"

Naomi shook her head, a disparaging frown on her lips. "This is the stupidest thing I've ever heard."

"Is it?" Dan asked. "The silliest thing I've ever heard was when you claimed you'd given those pictures of Zadie to her brother. At the time, you were on the spot, so you did the best you could, trying to deflect our suspicions onto someone else. You told us to keep quiet about the photos, but you knew I'd ask Tobias about them, so you persuaded someone to warn me off. It would never have worked. I'm nothing if not persistent. If anything, it made matters worse. Your accomplice made a mistake when he told me to stay away from Zadie's friends. I suppose he was trying to be clever. If he'd mentioned your name, that would've been a giveaway, but his choice of words backfired; it made me concentrate even harder on Zadie's small circle of friends."

Naomi held out her arms and let them fall to her sides. "What's this now? I'm being accused of having you beaten up, am I? You've lost it, Dan. You've gone too far."

"I didn't say anything about being beaten up," Dan replied. "But then, you already knew about that. And I expect all that business with my fingerprints was your idea. At the time, I couldn't see what my fingers were being pressed on, but it wasn't hard to work out. He used the one thing that's been missing, the one thing that neither I nor the police have been able to find: the only real piece of physical evidence from the night of Zadie's fall."

Naomi furrowed her brow. "What fall? I didn't know Zadie had—"

"You know all about it," Dan interrupted. "You were there."

Naomi turned to Alan, reaching out to him, pleading. "You've got to do something, Alan. I mean, just listen to him. He's raving. You've got to help him. Help *me*, Alan. He's frightening me."

"That's a good try," Alan replied. "I'd give you full marks for effort, but it won't wash. I know Dan, and I know when he's on a roll. You may as well own up."

Naomi stepped closer to Alan, her gaze locked on his. "Alan, I thought I could rely on you. I thought you were the sensible one. I thought you were strong, but you're letting me down. Please, Alan, you have to help me. I have no idea what he's talking about. You must believe me."

"I'm sorry," Alan said, "but I think I know exactly what Dan's referring to. According to Zadie, several things went missing from her room. There were the photos and the model coffin, but they would've been easy to dispose of; they could've been burned, for example. But then there was a water bottle. It was made of stainless steel, double-walled, and it was marked with Zadie's logo. It would've been much harder to get rid of, but why would someone take it in the first place unless it contained valuable evidence? Am I on the right track, Dan?"

"You certainly are," Dan replied. "When Naomi's friend pinned me down, my fingers were pushed onto something cold. It could easily have been that metal water bottle. Assuming the water inside had been laced with a drug, it wouldn't look good if my fingerprints were on the outside."

Alan looked doubtful. "On its own, that wouldn't amount to much. It's no secret you've been in Zadie's house, so you could've touched the bottle at any time."

"Don't you see?" Dan said. "The bottle provides evidence that the water was drugged. Even if it had been emptied out, there'd still be traces of the drug inside, and once my fingerprints were found, I'd have been taken in for questioning. I would've been taken out of the game, my credibility shot to pieces, and that would've suited you very well, Naomi. So you sent someone to deal with me. That wasn't very nice, was it?"

"This is becoming more ridiculous by the second," Naomi protested. "Why on earth would I have put this drug, whatever you call it, in Zadie's bottle? It doesn't make any kind of sense."

"Yes, it does, because you'd already made Zadie frightened," Dan shot back. "Phentermine can leave you disorientated and nervous, especially if you take it at night, and it shouldn't be used by anyone suffering from any kind of anxiety. It must've seemed perfect, because you'd already knocked Zadie off balance. You didn't leave the first note; I know that for a fact. But when you saw the effect that note had on Zadie, how it rattled her, how it knocked her down from her pedestal, you latched on to the idea straight away. The knife was a bit over the top, but it fulfilled its purpose. We were all so busy worrying about the knife, that we didn't think carefully enough about the note.

"I should've paid more attention to the way you'd used words cut from magazines. Your handwriting wouldn't have matched the first note, so you fell back on an idea you'd seen in an old film. It was something of a cliché, but needs must, and after that, you could use whatever notes you'd written on Zadie's typewriter. That was a nice touch, but I'll admit to a bit of guesswork there. If there were any typewritten notes, you must've cleared them away."

Naomi raised a hand. "Stop this, please. You're making a fool of yourself."

"I don't think so," Dan said. "Let's move on to the next phase of your operation. You're a photographer, so you have a flair for the visually dramatic, and you took your scheme to new heights with the coffin and the photos. There was a risk those photos would be linked back to you, but you were clever. The whole idea of the coffin under the bed was so ridiculous, so contrived, no one would believe it. You knew Zadie's history of mental health, and you wanted to capitalise on it. You wanted everyone to believe Zadie had lost her grip on reality, but most importantly, you wanted her to doubt her own sanity. And since she'd drunk from the bottle you'd laced with phentermine, she was already halfway there. It was an extremely cruel and calculating thing to do."

Naomi made to go around Alan, but he sidestepped, blocking the door.

"Let me past," Naomi said.

Alan shook his head. "Sorry, but you should stay here. We'll have to call the police."

"No!" Naomi gestured at Dan, her hand extended in a silent accusation. "He's gone mad, Alan, but you mustn't let him control you like this. I can help you."

"Are these the kind of remarks you were planning to aim at Zadie's friends?" Dan asked, his voice calm. "Poor old Zadie. She's out of control, mad, delusional. She needs help."

Dan saw Naomi's jaw clench, her cheeks tightening as she glared at him. He could almost hear her teeth grinding together. She was close to snapping, but that was fine. He could wait.

"I'll admit, there are a couple of areas I've had to guess at," Dan went on. "I'm not sure how you got into her house, but you could've taken some keys, just like you stole Connor's cigarette tin. The keys to Zadie's house are old and it would've been easy to have them copied. After that, you replaced the originals, knowing you could come and go as you pleased."

"Not quite," Alan said. "Natalya shuts the bolts at night."

"Only on the back door," Dan replied. "Zadie said the police advised her to have a security bolt fitted to the front door, but that was the last we heard of it. That door still has nothing except a very old mortice lock. Zadie loves all things old fashioned, doesn't she, Naomi?"

Naomi's only reply was a scowl.

"Don't be like that," Dan said. "We're not quite done yet. The other thing I don't know for sure is where you got the phentermine, but the police will go through your internet search history, and that will tell a story of its own. The rest was easy to put together.

"You're a good listener, and you tend to sit quietly while the others talk. You soon learned all Zadie's habits, and you knew she kept a bottle of water by her bed. She drank from it just before going to sleep, so the timing was tricky, but she had plenty of bottles, so you could take one, prepare the solution, and switch it later. The timing must've been tricky, but it's a big old house, and Zadie is usually alone at night. You could've moved from room to room without her knowing you were there. Maybe you waited until Zadie was in the bathroom, then you slipped into the bedroom and replaced her bottle with the one you'd prepared. That's where this comes in." Dan gestured to the fridge.

"It's hard to get the dose right, especially in small quantities, and you had no way of knowing how much water was in Zadie's bottle. So you made up a batch, say a litre or more, and you only took what you needed. You left the rest in the fridge in case you needed it later." Dan paused. "The question is, where is it now? Have you tipped it out?"

Naomi's face fell. Her gaze darted first to the fridge and then around the room, taking in every worksurface and shelf. Finally, she looked at Dan, her eyes round.

"You didn't know it was missing," Dan said slowly. "Someone else has taken it, haven't they?"

Naomi shook her head. "No. I don't... There wasn't any bottle."

"Yes, there was," Dan stated. "You referred to it indirectly yesterday when Alan brought you a drink. But it's not here now, so where has it gone? Who's taken it, Naomi?"

"Nobody. There's only me here, and I haven't got any bottled water."

Dan let out an exasperated sigh. "For a start, it's obvious someone else has been here very recently. I know you're a vegan, but I also know a packet of bacon when I see it, and you have one on the bottom shelf of your fridge. You're not going to tell me it's yours, are you?"

"Yes. So what? I lied about being a vegan. Big deal."

"I've a good mind to wave the stuff under your nose," Dan said. "But I won't do that. I've spent enough time around Zadie and her friends to know that they'd never have let you get away with lying about something like that. They'd have sniffed you out in no time, and they'd have ridiculed you at every turn. They'd have enjoyed it, and Zadie certainly wouldn't have stopped them. She might even have joined in. Zadie looked down on you, didn't she, Naomi?"

A spark of anger fired in Naomi's eyes, and Dan pressed home his advantage. Speaking slowly and in a firm tone, Dan said, "Is that why you did it, Naomi? Is that why you harassed and intimidated Zadie, because she behaves as if she's better than you?"

Naomi began murmuring under her breath, and Dan strained to make it out. Her speech flowed in a rapid stream, but it sounded as though she was repeating a phrase over and over again. There was something familiar about the cadence of her words. And then he realised what she was saying.

"Lead us not into temptation," Dan said. "Was that Zadie's crime? Did she lead others into temptation?"

"You know she did," Naomi hissed, her features twisting into a cruel sneer. "She parades around as if she's someone special, telling us all how to live. Oh, we could all be like her if only we tried, if only we wore the right clothes and ate the same food and plastered ourselves in the same makeup. *Be like her?* I'd rather die. She's an empty shell, a jezebel with no values, no moral compass, no sense of the human misery she stirs up. Do you think the kids who follow her can afford those clothes, that make-up? Of course they can't. So what are they left with? Empty promises; the feeling that they're second-rate; the sure and certain knowledge that they're not good enough. It makes me sick, but Zadie laps it up. She revels in it. She grows richer by the day, while her so-called fans lose themselves in an ocean of self-loathing and despair. So what if Zadie was punished? She deserved it. But what did she really suffer? For just a few days she felt the kind of fear the rest of us live with all our lives."

"Naomi, she jumped out the window," Dan pointed out. "Zadie could've died."

"I didn't know she was going to do that; how could I have done?"

"But you were there. You could've called an ambulance."

Naomi gave no sign of having heard him. She stared into the middle distance. "Zadie had to upstage me, didn't she? She had to be the centre of attention, so she spoiled everything." Regaining focus, Naomi's gaze settled on Dan. "I had a mask and everything. I bought it online. It made me look like the Devil himself. I know Halloween is a pagan thing, but it served a greater good." Naomi chuckled distractedly. "I wasn't going to *hurt* her. I wanted Zadie to come out of her room, that's all. She was supposed to catch a glimpse of me, then I was going to run away and disappear into the night. I wore an amazing red dress. It was going to be fantastic. Imagine it. Who would've believed Zadie when she said she'd been visited by the Devil in a designer frock. No one. No one at all."

Her outburst over, Naomi subsided, looking down at the floor with her shoulders slumped, her hands held in front of her stomach, the fingers of one hand plucking at the skin on the back of the other. "It's a shame really," she murmured. "Such a shame. We got on so well in the beginning. The best of friends."

Dan watched the sudden change in her demeanour. Naomi was retreating, adopting the timid expression that had been her defence for a long time. Naomi might feel more secure when she slipped into her customary role, shrouding herself in its warm embrace, but

Dan needed to push Naomi out of her comfort zone once more. There was still one urgent issue he had to resolve.

"Naomi, listen to me," Dan said softly. "I was right about that bottle of water, wasn't I? I know it was here yesterday, because you were worried Alan had used it, but it isn't here now, and you were surprised when I told you it was missing. We both know someone has taken it, and that person is in danger. But you don't want that, Naomi, because the person we're talking about is someone special, maybe someone very special. So who is it, Naomi? And where are they now?"

Naomi looked up. "I told him not to take it. I said, whatever you do, don't touch the mineral water. But he left early, so he must've taken it when he went." Naomi smiled sadly. "He brought me a cup of tea in bed."

"Who did?" Dan asked. "Who took the bottle, Naomi? If that person drinks it, they're going to need help, and I can make that happen. But I can't do anything unless you tell me who to look for. You have to tell me, Naomi. You have to tell me right now. Who took the bottle?"

CHAPTER 76

U sually, Benny didn't think about anything much while he was running. The impact of his shoes against the ground, the swell of his chest on each inhalation, the rush of spent air over his lips when he breathed out, the pumping of his arms: that's all there was. Almost always, the rhythm was enough to occupy him, the monotonous repetition providing some much-needed relief for his mind.

He might've left the army, but it had never quite left him. There were bleak moments of reflection, usually when his mind and body were still, not just at night but in idle moments during the day. Thankfully, Benny knew how to keep the low moods from his door. He'd found one good way to wipe the slate clean, for a while at least. If he worked his muscles hard, pushing up to the pain barrier and beyond, he could break free from the past and be himself.

But today it wasn't working. Today, the memory of that poor woman in the river kept reappearing in his mind. When he'd dragged her lifeless body from the water, the experience had stirred dark memories, summoning them from their shallow graves, and now they wouldn't let him be.

Why was it that the images you most wanted to erase were the hardest to forget?

Benny didn't have the answers, but he had his running shoes on, and that was a start.

The lane climbed as it led up the side of the valley, taking him away from Chagford. Benny shortened his stride but maintained the cadence of his steps, breathing harder. The increased impact made his backpack bounce up and down on his back, the straps chafing his shoulders, but he ignored it. Soon he was surrounded by fields and hedgerows, the sound of birdsong drifting on the air.

This was more like it. Every breath of cool air brought Benny a surge of new energy. His body felt lighter. He was skimming over the ground now, powering up the incline, his gaze fixed on the brow of the hill. Nothing else mattered.

At the top, he jogged to a halt and slipped his backpack from his shoulders. His shirt clung to him where the backpack had been. He was sweating more than usual and that was a bad sign. He'd let his routine slide recently, and that had to change. He needed to get back to peak performance.

Benny took a moment to slow his breathing. His heart was beating hard, and according to his Garmin watch, his heartrate was higher than it ought to be. That was no good.

Breathe, Benny told himself. *Take it easy*. Benny gazed at the clouds, his mind wandering. He'd come straight from Naomi's house, his change of clothes in his backpack, but Mr Callaway would be expecting him to arrive for work before long. For all his charm, the boss could be a stickler. Like that fuss he made about the mud in the car. It had been nothing: a faint trace of dirt. It had taken only a minute to brush it away. Where had Mr Callaway been to get mud on his shoes, anyway?

Out on one of his walks, Benny decided. Mr Callaway didn't like people to know, but he often went for walks on his own, usually up on Dartmoor where no one would see him. He'd walk across the moor, sit for a while and then return home, looking fresh-faced and in a better mood.

That was something people didn't understand about John

Callaway: he was a loner. All his easygoing charm was a front, a way of keeping people at bay. He preferred his own company.

The only friend Callaway had made in Devon was Naomi. Maybe she reminded him of his daughter, or perhaps the boss was a good judge of character. Whatever the reason, the pair of them got on like a house on fire.

Benny recalled the time Callaway and Naomi met. One day after church, Naomi had welcomed them to the congregation. She hadn't realised who Mr Callaway was, and she'd been embarrassed to have made such a silly mistake. But the boss hadn't minded at all, and they'd laughed about it. After that, they'd had quite an animated discussion about one of Mr Callaway's old films. Naomi had known all about it.

Their long conversation hadn't meant much to Benny. Whatever old film they'd talked about, Benny hadn't seen it. His idea of a good film was *The Shawshank Redemption*. He'd said as much to Naomi on their first date, but she hadn't approved. The film was based on a Stephen King novel, and apparently, the man wasn't to be tolerated. Benny hadn't argued. He'd wanted to say that Shawshank was a great film because it made him feel like there was always hope, even for someone like him, but Naomi was smarter than he was, so she was probably right to condemn it.

Benny frowned as a stray thought came to the surface. On that first date, he'd asked if Naomi would like to go to the cinema with him. He'd said she could choose any film she liked, but she'd said no. The cinema wasn't her thing, she'd said. But it was funny how she'd known all about that old film of Callaway's. What was it called? Benny searched his memory. *Wild Yonder*, that was it. *Weird title*, Benny thought. *Probably arty*.

Benny wiped the sweat from his brow, coming back to the here and now. He was thirsty, so he pulled the plastic bottle of mineral water from his backpack and took a good, long drink. That was better.

He took a few deep breaths, or tried to, but there was a familiar fluttering in his chest. *Not this again*. He thought he'd seen the last

MICHAEL CAMPLING

of his palpitations. Working for Callaway wasn't what you'd call demanding, and his heart had been good as gold for a while now. Apart from when he was out on a run or in the gym, he hardly thought about it.

As if to remind him, his heart beat a tattoo against his ribs, and it took Benny back to the day he'd seen the Medical Officer. The mandatory examination had been more than thorough, and the doctor had looked long and hard at the printout from Benny's ECG. Finally, after much muttering with a colleague, the doctor had said there was nothing to worry about. Probably.

That word: *Probably*. It had brought Benny up sharp. The doctor had found an irregularity in Benny's heartbeat, and his report would recommend light duties for Benny pending further investigations. That's what had tipped the balance for Benny: *further investigations*.

Could he have carried on with that hanging over his head and everyone knowing he'd been sidelined? No, he could not. He was out of there. He'd done his time and earned his pension. Why would he stay if he couldn't do it his way?

Benny had another drink. He gulped the cool liquid down, but somehow it wasn't helping. He was still thirsty, still too hot, his heart still thumping. He'd gone too hard at that hill, that was the problem. He'd do some stretches while he recovered.

But when Benny balanced on one leg to stretch his quad, the road tilted beneath him, and he had to put his other foot down fast to keep his balance. *What the hell?* He'd been a commando for God's sake. He could run across a thin girder fifty feet above the ground, carrying a full pack and wearing heavy boots, and he wouldn't think twice about it. But here he was, losing his balance on a stretch of smooth tarmac.

Maybe his age was finally catching up with him. He should've warmed up before he'd set off, and maybe he should've left his backpack in the car. The extra weight wasn't much, but he'd pulled the straps tight and that must've restricted his breathing. He wouldn't make the same mistake twice.

Benny pressed his knuckles against his chest, rubbing at the taut muscles. He took another pull from the water bottle. And another.

His heart was still racing. Benny ran his fingers over his close-cropped hair. His scalp was slick with sweat. He'd need a shower before he got back to work.

He'd been given free run of Mr Callaway's home gym, and it came complete with an en-suite shower. Saunders had questioned whether one employee should be singled out for this special privilege, but Callaway hadn't batted an eyelid. He'd said there was no use in having a bodyguard who was out of shape, so Benny was free to use the facilities whenever he liked, so long as he wasn't needed for his other duties.

Callaway didn't know about Benny's heart, of course. There'd been no need to tell him. Benny kept himself reasonably fit, and since he'd left the army, his heart had never caused a moment's concern. Until now.

Benny stared down the hill. It would be an easy walk back into Chagford, and when he'd caught his breath he could start running again, so long as he was up to it. It wouldn't look good if he was seen in the town, sweating and gasping for air. If Saunders saw him struggling, he'd whisper to Callaway, sowing the seeds of doubt in the boss's mind. That couldn't happen. Benny liked his job, and he'd never find another that suited him so well.

The only fly in the ointment was Saunders. He was always there, making snide remarks, pulling faces behind Callaway's back. He was a snake in the grass, a backstabber, a traitor. In a moment of clarity, Benny saw that Saunders was out to get him. The man had been against him from the start.

Everything had been okay until Saunders had come along. The problem was, the boss didn't see it. He liked Saunders. The boss probably thought it was hilarious to have an upper-class twit doing his admin and running errands like a modern-day Jeeves.

But Benny wasn't taken in. He wasn't impressed by a blazer and a striped tie from some posh school. Benny had a tie of his own, one that proudly bore the crest of his regiment. It was a tie he'd earned by dedicating the best part of his adult life to his comrades. His mummy and daddy hadn't bought it for him; he'd paid for it himself, in sweat, blood and tears.

One of these days he'd make all this plain to Saunders. He'd wipe the smirk off the man's face once and for all. He'd—

The jab of pain seared through Benny's chest, robbing him of his breath, sending a surge of panic rushing through his core.

Benny looked for support and spotted a bench ten metres away. Good. That would do. Clutching his chest, he staggered to the bench and sat down heavily. Christ! What was wrong with him?

A nagging voice told him he shouldn't take Lord's name in vain, but he hadn't been able to help it. He tried to be a good Christian, he really did, but it wasn't easy. There was so much he had to make up for. That was why he'd started going to church in the first place. In the service of his country he'd done things no one should have to do, and now it was his life's work to atone for his sins.

So why in God's name had he strayed from the path, taking himself deeper into the dark? It had been his idea to deal with Corrigan. Naomi said he'd been hassling her, and that was reason enough. He'd taken care of the situation right away. He hadn't been sure about taking the man's fingerprints, but Naomi had sworn they wouldn't use them. It was an insurance policy, she'd said, that was all. Corrigan would know they had his prints, and he'd get the message. Reluctantly, Benny had gone along with it. Corrigan wasn't the type to give in unless he was given a good reason, and the threat of incrimination ought to have done the trick.

Still, the whole thing didn't sit right with Benny. It felt like one of those missions where the officers gave out one objective while keeping the truth—an entirely different goal—close to their chests. In his experience, that state of affairs never ended well.

Why had he done it? He should've been stronger, but Naomi had been so persuasive.

Naomi. He ought to call her. Maybe she'd come and pick him up. He could go back to her place, get himself showered and sorted out. No one else need ever know about his funny turn.

Benny's phone was in his backpack, and it still lay on the ground where he'd left it. He should've picked it up before he'd moved to the bench, but there'd been other things on his mind.

Still, the backpack was only ten metres away, wasn't it? Benny looked for it, but the backpack swam out of focus. He blinked. The damned thing was further away than he'd thought.

Benny made to stand up, but his head spun. He'd never suffered from dizziness before. Never. What the hell was happening to him?

Benny drained the last of the water then let the empty bottle fall from his hand. He felt bad. Benny sunk his head into his heads and leaned forward. His heart lurched and strained, the pressure building in his chest, a wave of pain crushing the breath from his body. This was it. He was going to die, mired in sin, unforgiven and unblessed, fear swamping his mind.

Not like this, he thought. *Not by the side of the road, cringing like a coward*.

But there was nothing he could do. Slowly, his body toppled forward and the ground rushed up to meet him.

A RUSHING SOUND MADE BENNY OPEN HIS EYES. SOMETHING WAS coming toward him. A vehicle. Was it going to hit him? Had he fallen into the road?

An engine roared. Whatever it was, it was coming fast. Benny pressed his hands flat against the road, pushing with all his might, and he lifted his head and shoulders from the ground.

The blue car bore down on him. Closer. Closer.

Benny tried to scramble to his feet, but he was clumsy, his mind fogged by pain, and he couldn't get up. He opened his mouth to speak, to cry out, but his throat was too dry, his lips parched.

He let out a strangled shout, and it worked. The car ground to a halt, its tyres grating on the loose gravel at the road's edge.

The doors opened and three people piled out, rushing to his

side. He felt strong arms grab him by the shoulders and pull him into a sitting position.

Someone blurted words at him: a stream of questions. Benny didn't answer. He was looking at her. She'd come to save him. *Thank God*.

Naomi knelt in front of him, reaching out to stroke his brow. "Oh, Benny," she whispered. "I'm sorry. I'm so sorry. I didn't know… I couldn't…"

A man's voice interrupted. "An ambulance is on its way."

Benny blinked up at the man. It was him. Corrigan. Benny had no idea what to say; he was so muddled, so confused.

"Stay with us," Corrigan said. "Stay awake for me, Benny. Can you do that?"

Benny looked back to Naomi, then he nodded.

"You poor soul," Naomi murmured. "This should never have happened. It's all my fault."

"No." Benny swallowed, licked his lips. "I've done wrong. This is my due. The wages of sin."

Naomi stroked his cheek, tears rolling from her eyes. "No. You didn't deserve this, Benny." Naomi wiped her eyes. "There are some things I have to say while there's still time. The police will be here soon."

"I'll talk to them," Benny said. "I'll tell them what I did. It was my idea to deal with Corrigan." Benny's gaze flicked to Dan. "I shouldn't have done that. It wasn't right."

"Don't worry about that now," Dan replied. "I won't press charges. You'll get off with a caution."

"Benny, the police aren't coming for you," Naomi said. "You're going to be okay."

Benny shook his head. "There's no need to dress it up, sweetheart. I don't care about the cops. It's too late for me. Too late for anything."

"No, you mustn't say that," Naomi insisted. "The ambulance will be here any minute." She hesitated. "But the police will be here too. They're coming for me. I'm sorry, Benny, but I did something wrong, something very wrong."

"You? Never."

"You're so kind, Benny, but it's true. I made a terrible mistake and I'll have to accept the consequences, whatever they may be."

Somehow, Benny summoned a smile. Anything for her. "That's my girl. You're tough."

Naomi held his hand, her grip strong. "I'll pray for you. Every day. And I'll seek guidance. I've been lost for so long, I don't know if I can find a way back, but I'll try." She sniffed back a tear. "Shall we pray together now?"

"Yes," Benny said. "I'd like that. I'd like that very much."

CHAPTER 77

The Wild Boar opened for the evening at half past five, and Dan was waiting on the doorstep. A few minutes later, he settled himself at a corner table and placed his pint of Devonshire Pale Ale on the beermat.

Already, a few more customers had arrived, but Dan barely noticed them. He gazed at his pint of beer, admiring its amber hues for a moment, and then, with a deep sigh, he lifted the glass to his lips and savoured the first sip.

It was a great moment, made even better by the sight of Sam walking toward him, a glass of something clear in her hand.

"Are you celebrating on your own or can anyone join in?" Sam asked.

"Please, join me," Dan replied. "I feel like we've hardly seen each other recently."

"You've been busy and so have I." Sam sat next to him. "Cheers!"

They clinked glasses and took a drink.

"Gin and tonic?" Dan asked.

Sam grinned. "Fizzy water. Got to keep a clear head while I'm working. There's a darts match later and they're a thirsty lot, so I'm taking a break before they all start rolling in. I thought you might like some company."

"I'm always happy to spend time with you. I can think of nothing better."

"Flatterer." Sam regarded him, unimpressed. "Is Alan not joining you tonight?"

"I'm expecting him soon, but I thought I'd pop along early in the hope of getting you to myself for a while."

"So I fell into your carefully prepared trap, did I?"

"People tend to."

"Get away with you." Sam thumped him on the forearm in a way that was only mildly painful.

Repressing the urge to rub his arm, Dan said, "Well, I've solved another case, so I must be doing something right. The culprit has been arrested, the case is over and life is good."

"You definitely got the right person then?"

"Oh yes. It'll all come out eventually, I suppose, but I mustn't say too much before her case comes to court." Dan leaned closer to Sam and lowered his voice. "Between you and me, her name is Naomi Smith. DI Spiller gave me a call earlier, and he was pretty pleased. It seems she's determined to come clean. She's confessed to everything."

"That's a result and no mistake. Well done, Dan. I'm pleased for you, I really am."

Dan smiled. "It took me long enough, and it almost went sideways toward the end."

"It's the result that counts." Sam raised an eyebrow. "Dare I ask if you've been paid for all that work?"

"Not yet, but it shouldn't be too long. I'll send my invoice tomorrow, and if Zadie isn't well enough to deal with it, I'll talk to her brother. He said he'd see me right."

Sam smirked. *"See me right?* Dan Corrigan, you're beginning to sound like a local."

"No, I'm not."

"Oh yes, you are. When you first came here, you'd have said

something like…" Pausing to adopt a haughty expression and an upper-class accent, Sam said, "Oh, I'm quite certain my invoice will be paid in full."

Dan forced a smile, but he toyed with his pint glass, turning it around on its mat. "I was never quite that pompous, was I?"

"You were far too uppity for your own good, but I could see through all that. I knew you were all right." Sam patted him gently on the thigh. "Besides, there's nothing like a posh voice to get a girl's attention. Ask Elizabeth Bennet."

"Right. Just to be clear, in this scenario I'm Mr Darcy, am I?"

"If the breeches fit…"

Dan perked up. "That's all right then. For a second, I thought you were going to tell me I'm the other one: the baddie who made off with Elizabeth's sister."

"George Wickham. Honestly, Dan, didn't they teach you anything at that fancy private school?"

"Sports mainly. And bullying, but that was just the teachers." Dan waited for Sam to laugh at his joke, but her eyes were filled with pity.

"You poor thing," she murmured. "It sounds awful."

"It wasn't so bad, but I didn't go in much for reading flowery novels."

Sam's expression froze. "Jane Austen's books are not *flowery*. That's the sort of thing someone might say if they'd never read any of them. "

"Okay, you've got me bang to rights. I didn't mean to upset you. I never had you down as a—"

"As much of a reader?" Sam interrupted. "Just because I like to sit down with a magazine now and then, it doesn't mean I'm as thick as two short planks."

"No, of course not. I would never think that. I was just going to say, I didn't know you were a fan of Jane Austen. And I was going to say how nice it is that I'm still finding out new things about you. The more I get to know you, the more I…"

"What?"

Beneath the intensity of Sam's gaze, Dan's tongue failed him. "Well, you know…"

"No, I really don't." Sam leaned closer to him. Very close. "What were you going to say, Dan?"

"Just that the more I get to know you, the more I, erm, the more I love you."

Sam's face was a picture of surprise as she mouthed three words, stressing each one for maximum effect: "Oh my God."

"Okay," Dan said. "That wasn't the response I was—"

Sam cut Dan short by planting a kiss on his lips. The background hum of conversation died away. That kiss would be the talk of the village for weeks to come, but Dan didn't mind that in the least. It was a moment of pure, unadulterated happiness and Dan closed his eyes, revelling in every sensation.

Sam broke off and placed her lips close to his ear. Her breath tickled Dan's earlobe as she drew a breath, and Dan braced himself, certain of what she was about to say.

There was a brief moment of delicious suspense, then Sam said, "Oh! Hello."

Sam pulled away from him, and Dan opened his eyes to see Alan standing with a messenger bag hanging from his shoulder and an uncomfortable grin on his lips.

"Sorry," Alan said. "I didn't mean to… that is, I didn't know, erm…"

"It's okay," Sam said with a sigh. "I ought to be getting back to work anyhow." Sam got to her feet, pulling out her chair and offering it to Alan. "What are you having, Alan? pale ale, the same as his nibs?"

"Yes, that would be fine," Alan replied. "But I'll come and get it. I need to pay."

"No, you don't," Dan said. "The drinks are on me tonight. We're celebrating and I've started a tab. You're not to pay for a thing. After all the time you've spent helping me out, it's the least I can do."

"Oh well, I won't argue with that." Alan made himself comfortable, sitting down and sliding his bag onto the table.

"Right, I'll get back to the bar," Sam said. "I'll pop your pint over in a minute, Alan."

"Thank you, Sam. That's very kind."

"It's no trouble." Sam favoured Dan with a warm smile, then she strode back to the bar.

Dan watched her leave, a rueful smile on his lips.

"I'm sorry to play gooseberry," Alan said. "I can make myself scarce if you prefer."

"Don't worry about it. There's a darts match later so Sam's going to be busy. If you weren't here I'd be sitting on my own all night."

"In that case, I've got something to show you." Alan pulled a laptop sleeve from his bag and began unzipping it.

"Honestly, Alan. You're the only person I know who keeps his laptop in a sleeve even when it's inside another bag."

"I'll have you know that this machine is the principal tool of my trade, and it's practically brand new."

"Okay, so why have you brought it to the pub? This is supposed to be a celebration. You can take the night off, can't you?"

"This isn't for me, it's for you." Alan positioned his laptop carefully, his gaze on the screen. "I've been doing some research on Zadie's friends."

"Why? The case is over. We won, or hadn't you noticed?"

"Zadie's case may be over, but we left some loose ends dangling, and there was one thread in particular that I couldn't stop thinking about."

"Oh? Was it to do with Carly and her dubious health products?"

Alan waved the suggestion away. "No, no, that's neither here nor there." Alan paused. "I've been thinking about what happened to Philippa, and it struck me that there's more than one unexplained death in this case."

The sobering effect on Dan was instant. He pushed his drink aside and leaned closer, craning his neck to see the laptop's screen.

"Tell me. What have you found?"

"This is a newspaper report of an inquest. The press don't generally attend inquests, but there was some public interest in this one."

"Why?"

"We'll get to that in a minute. Take a look at the man who died."

Dan scanned the densely packed text. The article was a long one, constrained within the narrow confines of a newspaper column, but he soon found the name. "Stuart O'Neill," Dan read aloud. "I remember the name. He was the drummer from Connor's band; the one who died. They called him Spud. But we've covered that ground, haven't we?"

"Well, that's what we thought."

Alan left a pregnant pause and Dan had to break the silence: "Just now, you mentioned the media interest on purpose; you knew it would get me thinking. Connor's band wasn't famous back then, so that makes me wonder why Stuart's inquest made the papers."

"You've hit the nail on the head, and the answer, in a nutshell, is Connor's father. He was a public figure, so any hint that his son was mixed up with drink and drugs and rock and roll…"

"Was bound to be picked up by the press," Dan said.

"Exactly. Connor's lifestyle must've been a source of great embarrassment for his father. The man wasn't just the head of a merchant bank, he was a knight of the realm: Sir William Griffiths. He was also a close personal friend of Boris Johnson, and reading between the lines, he acted as an unofficial adviser back when Johnson was Mayor of London. Once I started looking, Sir William's name cropped up all over the place. There are photos of him standing beside all kinds of bigwigs, from police chiefs to politicians."

"This is getting interesting."

"It certainly is, but it gets even more intriguing when you look at the coroner's verdict at Stuart's inquest: death by misadventure."

"I've never been totally sure what that means," Dan admitted.

"Connor told us there was an accident. How is misadventure different?"

"Misadventure means that the death was an unintended consequence of an intentional act."

"What was intentional about it? It was tragic, but Stuart made a stupid mistake, and he paid the price. It was pure luck that no one else was seriously hurt."

"On the face of it, I'd agree, but according to more than one newspaper report, the coroner questioned whether Stuart chose to drive of his own free will or if he was persuaded to take the wheel by his friends, even though they must've known he was in no fit state."

"How could they have known?" Dan asked. "Connor said that Stuart was good at hiding his addiction, so everyone else might've thought he was sober enough to drive."

Alan studied Dan for a moment. "Why are you taking Connor's side all of a sudden?"

"I'm not. I'm trying to be objective, and I want to get to the heart of this story. Where are you going with this, Alan? You mentioned two unexplained deaths. Are you trying to link Stuart's accident with what happened to Philippa?"

"You'll see in a minute, and it'll be a damned sight quicker if you stop picking everything I say apart." Alan almost scowled, but his gaze flicked past Dan and his peevish expression melted away. A moment later Sam appeared, bearing a very full pint glass.

"Sorry about the wait," Sam said. "I was helping with the sandwiches for the darts team." She placed Alan's pint in front of him. "If you like, Alan, I can bring you a couple of free sandwiches; we always make too many." Glancing at Dan, she added, "There's nothing vegan, though. It's either cheese and pickle or ham and mustard. Those darts players like what they know, and they know what they like. If I gave them hummus, there'd be a riot."

"We can't have that," Dan replied. "Can we, Alan?"

"No, of course not." Alan smiled at Sam. "Thanks for the offer, but I'm fine. I had dinner before I came out. And thank you for bringing my drink over, that was very good of you. You should have one for yourself, especially since Dan's paying."

"Definitely," Dan said. "Put a G and T on my tab. You can always drink it later when things have quietened down."

"We'll see. Thanks anyway." Sam eyed Alan's laptop. "What are you two scheming?"

"Just following up on a couple of things," Dan said. "Alan was telling me about an inquest."

Alan explained as briefly as he could, and Sam nodded as she listened. When Alan had finished, she said, "So you think that this Connor character lied when he said it was an accident."

"It looks that way, yes," Alan replied. "I haven't shown it to Dan yet, but there was one extremely telling article on the inquest."

Alan tapped the laptop's touchpad and a new page appeared on the screen.

"A different newspaper?" Dan asked.

Alan nodded. "Some of the tabloids picked up the story. This was in *The Sun*. Listen to this headline: No Justice for Drummer's Tragic Death."

Dan leaned closer to the screen and began reading.

'MY BROTHER WAS AN INNOCENT VICTIM,' CLAIMED ALISON O'NEILL, the sister of Stuart O'Neill, a talented young musician known to his friends as Spud. The young man died when the car he was driving skidded out of control and collided with a tree. Spud was the only fatality in an accident that could've been so much worse. The only passenger escaped with cuts and bruises, but Spud was killed outright. He wasn't wearing a seatbelt, and a post-mortem revealed he was three times over the alcohol limit. Even so, his sister claimed the collision wasn't Spud's fault. 'My brother never stood a chance,' she said at the inquest. 'He never touched a drop, but he was easily led.'

The coroner said that this was a case of death by misadventure as he handed the matter over to the Metropolitan Police.

. . .

WHEN HE REACHED THE END OF THE ARTICLE, DAN SAT BACK, STARING at Alan in silence.

"What do you think?" Alan asked.

"I think there's a lot to unpack," Dan began. "To begin with, how come Connor wasn't mentioned by name? That's very suspicious. Secondly, Connor spun us a story about Spud taking pills, but there's no mention of drugs, only alcohol. And last but not least, if Stuart's sister was telling the truth and Spud didn't usually drink, how did he come to be drunk that night? When you put it all together, Connor has some serious explaining to do."

"I totally agree," Alan said. "We should chase this up as soon as we can."

"Maybe," Dan replied. "You've done good work, Alan, but I'm still not seeing the connection with Philippa."

"Well, it's nothing concrete, I grant you, but Connor, he…" Alan grasped at the air as if hoping to catch the words he needed. "He's a downright liar. I don't trust him an inch, and don't forget, he was friends with Philippa."

"That doesn't prove anything," Dan said. "But it's worth talking to Connor again. I suppose we could go and see him tomorrow, but I'd like to know more about that inquest before we go barging in. I wonder how easy it would be to track down Stuart's sister."

Alan smiled. "Funnily enough, I've already spoken to her."

"Tonight? That was quick work."

"I'm good, but I'm not that good," Alan said. "It turns out that I talked to Alison O'Neill a few days ago. I didn't know it at the time, but she married the band's rhythm guitarist, Jeff Dawkins. These days she helps him in the family business, making cigar box guitars."

"What on earth is a cigar box guitar?"

"It's a guitar made from a cigar box, obviously, but that's not important. The key thing is that I have an address and a phone number for their business. It's in a trading estate in Newton Abbot, near Brunel Road. The bad news is that when I called, Mrs Dawkins wouldn't talk about Connor, and as soon as Stuart's name came up, she hung up on me."

"That's okay," Dan said. "We can turn up and see what happens. We could always say we've come to buy one of their weird guitars."

"They sell them in the market," Sam stated. "Newton Abbot. The bloke has a stall with boxes full of old records, and he sells his boxy little guitars. He plays them sometimes. He's very good."

Dan and Alan swivelled to stare at her.

"What does he look like?" Dan asked. "Was he there on his own, or was his wife with him?"

"He's quite nice looking as it goes. He always says hello and gives me a smile, but it's just him on the stall. He doesn't seem to do much business, but he always looks happy."

"That must be Jeff Dawkins," Alan said. "There can't be many people selling that kind of guitar, and he makes them in Newton Abbot."

"It's worth tracking him down." Dan turned to Sam. "When did you last see him?"

"I'm not sure, but he's usually there when the outdoor market's on. That's Wednesdays and Saturdays, so he might be there tomorrow. You can't miss him so long as you're there in time. I'd go in the morning if I were you. It gets quiet in the afternoon and a lot of the traders pack up and go home, especially if it's raining."

"We'll go first thing," Dan said. "Thanks, Sam, you're a star." Looking to Alan, he added, "What do you say? Fancy a jaunt to Newton tomorrow morning?"

Alan grinned as if suppressing laugh.

"What?" Dan demanded.

"Don't you know?" Sam said. "You really are talking like a local. You just called it Newton."

"I don't think so. I said Newton Abbot."

"Oh no, you didn't," Sam insisted. "You're catching on. I knew we'd get you talking proper one day."

"I don't know about that. Listen, are you coming tomorrow or not, Alan?"

"I'll be there," Alan replied, "but only if you admit you just called it Newton instead of Newton Abbot."

"All right, if you say so, I guess I must've done it. When in Rome…" Dan took a drink from his pint and adopted a gruff Devon accent to add, "'Tis only right and proper."

Sam laughed. "What was that supposed to be? We're not all pirates, you know."

"If the three-cornered hat fits," Dan said. "But I think I'd better stick to my own accent. I get in enough trouble as it is, there's no need to go looking for it."

"I'll drink to that." Alan raised his glass. "To trouble, and to not going looking for it." Alan paused for a beat. "Unless it's in the pursuit of justice, of course."

"Quite right," Dan replied. "It goes without saying."

WEDNESDAY

CHAPTER 78

D C Collins stared at the over-bright screen as the CCTV footage played on and on. To his eyes, most of the passengers disembarking from the Chagford to Exeter bus were elderly. Some were in couples, some were on their own, but they all had grey hair and wore coats despite the warm weather. There were a few mums with toddlers in tow, the women dealing with strollers and shopping bags, yet still somehow managing to hold hands with their children as they stepped down to the pavement.

Collins had seen the same piece of footage three times, but as far as he could see, none of the passengers behaved as if they had anything to hide. No one glanced furtively from side to side, no one kept their gaze low. Most of them were smiling, for God's sake, looking forward to a trip into the city: a stroll by the river, tea and cake in a nice little cafe, an hour or two browsing in the shops.

And none of them looked remotely like Jack Devlin, which was a damned shame. Yes, there was that text message from Philippa's phone, sent while Devlin was in custody, but it wasn't enough to put him in the clear. Anyone could've sent that message, and Devlin could be very persuasive. He could've prewritten the message then talked an unwitting accomplice into pressing send.

646

Devlin knew he couldn't have a cast iron alibi, so he'd gone for the next best thing. He'd created evidence that could be used in court to sow the seeds of doubt in the minds of the jurors, and that was all he needed to walk away scot-free.

Collins shut his eyes and pinched the bridge of his nose. *He must've got off the bus at an earlier stop*, he told himself. *It's obvious.* But the same idea had occurred to Collins some time ago, and he'd already searched for CCTV cameras along the bus route. There'd been nothing worth pursuing, and besides, Devlin could've made an excuse and asked the driver to let him off at any point on the journey. The man may never have made it to Exeter at all.

"Think," Collins muttered to himself. "Why did he catch the bus? What was he hoping to achieve?"

"First sign of madness," someone said, and Collins looked up with a start to see DI Spiller standing behind him.

"Sorry, guv, I didn't see you there. I've been through the CCTV and I've got nothing so far. I reckon our suspect got off somewhere else." Collins hesitated. "I was thinking about checking the big stores along the route. He must've got the rope from somewhere, and we've had no luck retrieving DNA from the scene, so he probably had gloves as well. He might even have worn something to cover his clothes."

"Well, well," Spiller said. "You must have second sight, Collins. I had an email from forensics not ten minutes ago. They've found dark blue fibres on the deceased's clothing. Sixty-five percent polyester, thirty-five percent cotton. They say it's from something hardwearing, such as an overall or boiler suit."

"That is interesting." Collins smiled. It wasn't every day you got one step ahead of the boss, and that rarity made the moment all the sweeter. "I'll get right on it."

"Good lad." Spiller nodded, but he showed no sign of walking away.

"Was there something else, guv?"

Spiller pressed his lips together as if in thought. "It occurred to me there's a B&Q along that bus route, and there's a bus stop nearby. Plenty of rope in B&Q, boiler suits too."

"Yeah, of course." Collins tried very hard to hide his disappointment. He wasn't one step ahead, after all, but one step behind.

"I expect you were about to come to the same conclusion," Spiller said. "Fancy a trip out there? With a bit of luck, they'll show us their CCTV right away. We know when the bus left Chagford and when it arrived at its destination. That gives us a pretty tight timeline to work with, and even in B&Q, a person can't wander around forever."

"I'll head out now, but I can take care of it on my own. It won't need two of us."

"I know you're more than capable, Collins, but I'll come along. Two heads are better than one, and I'd like to get this inquiry moving along a bit faster." Spiller lowered his voice to a conspiratorial whisper. "To be honest, I need to get out the office for a bit. If I see one more spreadsheet, I'll go round the twist."

"Fair enough, guv. I'm ready when you are."

"Good stuff. Grab your jacket, Collins. You can drive. Let's go and do some proper police work."

CHAPTER 79

W orking at her desk in Teignmouth's cramped CID office, DS Kulkarni noticed an email from the team examining the VW van she'd found in Exeter. A preliminary report was attached, and Kulkarni opened it, her heart beating a little faster.

But as she read the few short paragraphs, her sense of anticipation dwindled. The team had found plenty of fingerprints and a profusion of trace evidence, including fibres and samples that would likely yield DNA, but there was a huge amount to go through and it would take some time. Reading between the lines, Kulkarni guessed that no thorough analysis would happen until the team knew exactly what they were looking for. As yet they had nothing to compare their samples to, and no suspect to match against any DNA they might retrieve.

Kulkarni still couldn't be sure the body found in the burned-out building on Diamonds Avenue was Ryan Hallett, nor did she know who had lived in the flat where the fire started. But someone had fled the scene, leaving a cache of forged passports behind them, and if they'd taken the van and driven it to Exeter, they might well have left some clue as to their identity.

Typing a quick reply, Kulkarni asked the team to focus on the fingerprints. If they could lift as many prints as possible and perform the usual checks, there was a chance they'd get a hit.

Her reply sent, Kulkarni saw DS Jo Winslow marching toward her.

"I don't know what you said to the DI, but he's singing your praises," Winslow said. "What's your secret?"

"Oh, I may have buttered him up a little," Kulkarni admitted. "And I might've taken a bit of admin off his hands. I'm a dab hand with a spreadsheet. Pivot tables are my party trick."

Winslow grimaced. "I'm not going to even ask what that means, but it worked. You got your wish. We can search Hallett's house."

Kulkarni sat up straight. "When?"

"Now works for me."

"Me too." Kulkarni gathered her things and stood. "Ready when you are."

AT FIRST GLANCE, RYAN HALLETT'S HOME SEEMED MUCH THE SAME AS before, but Kulkarni wasn't about to make any assumptions. The last time, she'd been looking for someone to identify a body, but they hadn't had reasonable grounds to perform a search. This visit was very different.

Hallett may or may not have been the man they'd found in the flat, but he was more than the potential victim of a murder; he was an associate of a group being investigated by Plymouth's Serious Crimes Unit.

Wearing gloves and overshoes, Kulkarni and Winslow worked their way through the front room, opening drawers and cupboards, lifting cushions from the sofa and rugs from the floor.

Kulkarni's keen gaze raked every surface, but there was little to see. There were no old magazines or newspapers, no coats hanging from the hooks in the hallway, and none of the clutter of an ordinary life. Even the waste bins were empty.

It was the same story in the kitchen. Nothing was out of place, and the dishwasher had been emptied. The only sign of recent occupation was a well-stocked fridge, filled with food and cans of beer.

Kulkarni went to the back door and opened it. Beside the door were the usual recycling crates and a wheelie bin; all were empty. That might mean nothing, but a sense of foreboding took root in her mind.

Winslow had moved upstairs, and Kulkarni went to join her. The bathroom was spick and span, and the master bedroom was clutter-free, the bed made and the pillows carefully placed.

"Someone's beaten us to it," Kulkarni stated. "They've cleaned the place from top to bottom."

Winslow nodded slowly. "I haven't seen a single phone charger or a USB lead, have you?"

"No."

"In my house I've got leads and earbuds all over the place," Winslow said. "I've got drawers full of the things and they don't all belong to the kids. I mean, we've all got devices these days, and most people have a charger or two permanently plugged in, don't they?"

"Yes. It would've been nice to find a laptop or a tablet, but there's not much chance of that. All the good stuff will have gone."

"Chin up, Anisha. We're not done yet. There's another bedroom, and you never know."

"Sure."

Summoning a smile, Kulkarni led the way along the landing to the room at the back of the house. The room was small, and in place of a bed was a collection of gym equipment: a weightlifting bench, a freestanding punchbag and an assortment of dumbbells and barbells. Again, there was no clutter, and searching the room thoroughly would almost certainly be a waste of time. Kulkarni made to leave the room, but as she went to close the door something struck her as odd. The doorway was in the corner of the small room, and when the door was fully open it rested against the adjoining wall. But the door wasn't lying flat; there was something stopping it from meeting the wall.

Taking half a step back into the room, Kulkarni closed the door. And she smiled. Whoever had cleaned the house hadn't thought to look at the coat hook on the back of the door, otherwise they would've seen what was hanging there.

The pair of boxing gloves were dark blue with a white Velcro strap, and a single word had been professionally printed on the strap in gold lettering: *RYAN*.

Carefully, Kulkarni plucked one of the gloves from its hook and peered inside. There would be DNA on the glove's lining, but that wasn't all. There, picked out in stark black letters on the white fabric lining was a single word written with a marker pen: *HALLETT*.

"Got him," Kulkarni whispered. Surely the boxer who'd gone to such great lengths to personalise his gloves wouldn't share them with anyone else. With a bit of luck there'd be DNA from only one person inside, and if it matched the victim they'd found in the burnt-out house on Diamonds Avenue, they'd have an identification. Finally, this case was going somewhere.

CHAPTER 80

A fine drizzle hung in the air, but Newton Abbot market was in full swing, the stalls sheltered by striped awnings in bright primary colours.

It wasn't hard for Dan and Alan to find the man they were looking for. If the plastic crates of vinyl records and the display of half a dozen oddly shaped guitars weren't enough, a printed banner proclaimed: *Turkey Bone Jeff - Hand-Crafted Cigar Box Guitars*.

The man standing behind the stall was tall and lean, his blonde hair crowned with a wide brimmed leather hat, and he leaned on his stall with both hands, all the better to watch the world go by, a twinkle in his blue eyes and an expression of benign amusement on his face. Seeing Dan and Alan approach, he straightened up and offered a smile and a nod. "Morning, gents," he called out as soon as Dan and Alan were near enough. "A nice day for a bit of browsing."

Dan returned the man's smile, and despite his best intentions said, "Actually, it's raining."

The man chuckled. "It's what my better half would call a grand soft day, but then, she's Irish so she tends to treat dry days as if they're some kind of miracle. Me, I'm Devon born and bred, so I'll take any kind of weather and be glad of it just the same."

653

"I take it that you're Turkey Bone Jeff," Alan said. "I've heard about your guitars."

The man's eyes lit up. "Then you've come to the right place. If you don't mind me asking, where did you hear about me? Facebook?"

"I came across your website," Alan replied. "I've only just found out about cigar box guitars. They're fascinating."

"That, they are," Jeff said. "They come from a long tradition of folk making their own instruments, but my guitars are something special. Do you play?"

"I used to, but it was a long time ago and my guitar had six strings."

Jeff pulled a face of mock horror. "Oh no, that's three strings too many. But you'll soon learn the error of your ways." He gestured to the display of guitars. "Grab one, have a go. I've a little amp down here, and I'll plug it in for you."

Alan hesitated. "Not right now, thanks."

"Go on," Jeff said. "Have a go. You can just muck about if you like. You'll enjoy it. They're great fun."

"I'm afraid we didn't come here to shop," Dan said. "We wanted to talk to you."

Jeff seemed to deflate. "What about?"

"It's just a chat." Dan produced a business card and handed it to Jeff who eyed it warily. "I'm a private investigator, and I think you have some information that might help to solve a case I'm working on."

"I doubt that very much." Jeff tossed the card onto his stall. "Was it you who rang my wife the other day? She said there was some bloke called Alan."

"That was me," Alan admitted. "I was hoping to speak to you about what happened to your friend, Stuart."

Jeff started to shake his head, so Dan said, "We're not here to rake over the past just for the sake of it. We're looking into that accident because Connor Griffiths was there, and he lied to us about it."

Jeff grunted as if this came as no surprise.

"Something has recently happened to a friend of Connor's," Dan went on. "A woman was killed."

The change in Jeff's expression was dramatic. Deep lines creased his features, and the light in his eyes dimmed. "That's awful."

"It is," Dan said gently. "But there's a chance you can help us to figure out what happened."

"I don't see how. The police must be on it, aren't they?"

"They are, but they're slow. If we can help them out, we will, and you can play a part in that."

"I don't see what I can do. I haven't seen Connor for ages, and that suits me fine. We don't talk. I don't even send him a Christmas card. That life is gone. I've put it behind me."

"I understand," Alan said. "It can be painful to talk about the past, especially when you've lost a friend, but if you could spare us a few minutes of your time, we might be able to draw a line under what happened. If some good can come out of it, that might be some consolation."

"It needn't take long," Dan put in. "Could you close your stall for a few minutes? We can buy you a coffee or a cup of tea."

Jeff didn't react for a moment, but then he nodded. "There's a cafe inside. I can pop in for a tea, but not for long."

"Thank you," Dan replied. "We'd appreciate it."

"Wait here." Jeff gathered a few things into a satchel and slung the strap over his shoulder, then he strolled over to the neighbouring stall. He had a brief conversation with a middle-aged man whose stall was loaded with boxes of secondhand books, both men keeping a watchful gaze on Dan and Alan. Nods were exchanged between the two men, then Jeff marched back. But instead of stopping, he passed Dan and Alan without slowing his pace. "Come on," Jeff called over his shoulder. "You've got five minutes."

Dan and Alan followed in his wake, and Jeff led them through the automatic door and into the market hall.

Close by the door, an area was set out with tables and chairs, and Jeff sank gratefully onto a chair. "Tea with milk and one sugar," he said. "And a bacon roll."

"Oh, I don't—" Dan started to say, but Alan cut him short.

"I'll get these," Alan said. "You sit down and get started."

"Okay. Thanks." Dan sat opposite Jeff who was staring into space and rubbing the fingers of his right hand together nervously. "You used to smoke," Dan said.

Jeff gave a small start. "I gave up years ago. How did you know?"

"It was the way you were rubbing your fingertips as if you were expecting something to be there. Old habits can be hard to shift."

"Tell me about it." Jeff offered a rueful smile. "I don't miss the cigarettes really. No more than ten or twenty times a day. But now and then, I could do with something to take the edge off, you know?" Jeff shook his head in sorrow. "Poor old Spud. It was no way to go. He was far too young. And afterward, it was bad for me, but for my wife… Alison was his sister, I mean, she still *is* his sister. When he died, it broke her heart."

Dan couldn't help but feel for the man. He looked utterly broken, reliving the loss of his friend. Was it right to put him through that? Dan wasn't sure, but Alan arrived bearing three mugs of steaming tea and he set them down on the table, placing one of them in front of Jeff.

"They didn't have oat milk, so I got yours black," Alan said, sliding a mug across the table to Dan. "I hope that's okay."

"It's fine, thanks." Dan took a sip and suppressed his reaction as the strong tea coated his tongue, the tannin setting his teeth on edge. Putting his mug down, Dan offered Jeff a sympathetic smile. "Tell us about Stuart, or should I call him Spud?"

"Spud. It was always Spud." Jeff smiled as if at a fond memory. "It started when he was a little boy. My wife told us all about it. When he was a lad, he had a fondness for baked potatoes; don't ask me why. He'd eat them every day if he could. He'd grown out of it by the time I met him, but the name stuck, and it suited him somehow." Jeff twisted his lips as though chewing his words. "It sounds like a cruel nickname, but it was meant fondly. Spud was a bright lad, but there was something about him. He was big, much bigger than me, and strong with it, but he was a softie, you know? A gentle giant."

"He sounds like a good person to have as a friend," Alan suggested.

"Oh, he was. He'd do anything for anybody. You couldn't meet a nicer bloke."

Jeff looked down and Dan knew there was something more; something Jeff didn't want to say. Choosing his words with care, Dan said, "The world can be tough on gentle people, and I imagine he came across some ruthless types in the music business."

"Yeah, we met some hard-nosed bastards, if you'll pardon my French. But..." Jeff looked up, his gaze sharper now. "But it wasn't the outsiders who made trouble for Spud. It was us, his so-called mates in the band. It was, Spud, fetch us a beer, will you? Spud, can you carry this amp? Spud, do this, Spud, do that. And off he'd go, smiling like a kid in a candy shop, happy to help, happy to fit in. It was all he wanted; to be one of the band. And we took advantage. I can't tell you how much I regret it. I'd take back every word if I could. Every single word."

Dan leaned forward. "Was there any one person in particular who treated him badly?"

Jeff met Dan's gaze. "I know what you're getting at. You want me to say it was Connor, but it's not that simple."

"Perhaps you can make us understand," Alan said. "We'd like to hear your side, if that's okay."

"All right." Jeff paused. "Connor liked to have Spud around, and he'd sometimes tell us off when we made Spud do all the donkey work. But they weren't alike. Connor liked to party, but Spud wasn't into all that. He wasn't interested in drink and drugs; not one bit. He liked the music, and he loved performing but—"

"Hang on a second," Dan interrupted. "Are you saying that Spud didn't drink or take drugs?"

"Yeah. It wasn't his thing."

"Are you sure about that?" Dan asked. "On the night of the crash, you weren't in the car with him, were you?"

"No. Me and Malcolm lived in a different part of town, so we took a bus. We left Connor and Spud with the gear, and yes, I am totally sure about Spud. I don't care what anybody says, the guy *did not* drink. That's why we always trusted him to take the gear. By the end of the night, Spud was the only one who was still sober."

Dan and Alan exchanged a look.

"What?" Jeff demanded. "Are you going to start banging on about the inquest? Because let me tell you, there was something not right there."

"We saw a newspaper article from the time," Alan said. "It said that Alison had spoken out, claiming that Spud didn't drink. But the report was in one of the tabloids and we didn't know how much faith to put in it."

"It was in *The Sun,* and they had it right," Jeff replied. "I remember that reporter. He knew there was a story, but he didn't follow through, and after that, he went quiet. We never saw him again."

"This is all very different to Connor's version of events," Dan said. "He told us a very different story."

"No surprise there. What did he say?"

Dan hesitated. "He said that Spud was an addict, but he was good at hiding it."

The colour rushed to Jeff's cheeks. "The lying little bastard! What the hell did he say that for? It's bad enough that he slithered out of trouble with the cops, but to speak ill of the dead! That's low, even for him."

"What did you mean by that?" Dan asked. "What trouble was Connor in, and how did he slither out of it?"

"That's what I was getting to a minute ago," Jeff replied, his tone growing heated. "Back then, we all thought Connor had been up to something. Maybe he spiked Spud's drinks, maybe he persuaded him to down a few shots. I don't know what happened, but Connor did something. Like I said, they were always together. Spud listened to Connor, doted on him, but it didn't work both ways. To Connor, Spud was like a plaything, a useful guy to have on your side. Connor was always getting into scrapes. He'd drink too much, smoke too much, shout his mouth off to the wrong guys, but one look at Spud was enough to make most folks back off. And if it wasn't, Spud didn't mind banging a couple of heads together.

Spud was gentle to a fault, but he wouldn't stand by and see Connor beaten up. He'd wade in and throw a punch or two. Nothing excessive, but enough to knock some thug off his feet. Then he'd point a finger. 'Stay down,' he'd say, and that would be the end of that. So for Connor to blacken Spud's name like that, it's…" Jeff let out a hiss of frustration. "I've a good mind to find Connor and set him straight."

"We can do that for you," Dan said. "We might even be able to do more than that. But we need the full story, so forgive me, but I'll have to ask again: how did Connor get out of trouble?"

Jeff grimaced. "The same way upper-class people always get out of trouble. Money. After the crash, Connor went running to daddy with his tail between his legs. Next thing we knew, the investigation was dropped. Some fancy lawyer turned up on the scene, and before we knew what was happening, the whole thing went away."

"You don't happen to remember the lawyer's name, do you?" Dan asked.

Jeff shook his head. "I met the guy once, and he wound me around his little finger. The rest of us couldn't afford lawyers. We barely had two pennies to rub together, so when this guy arrived in his three-piece suit and tie, we thought our saviour had come. He told me to keep quiet. I didn't like it, but he talked me around. He said it would be best for the band."

Something changed in Jeff's expression and Dan didn't miss it. There sorrow in the lines on Jeff's face, the kind of semi-permanent sadness that came with years of regret.

Keeping his tone gentle, Dan said, "This lawyer, did he by any chance offer you an inducement to stay quiet?"

Jeff looked away, his throat bobbing as he swallowed hard, and when he turned back, he couldn't look Dan in the eye. "He did. He said he'd pay us off, and to my shame, I caved in. I was pretty shaken up, and I took the money and signed some piece of paper before I really knew what I was doing. And then it was too late. I was stupid, we all were, but what did we know? We were young and we had no idea what we were getting ourselves into."

"We all make mistakes," Alan said. "For what it's worth, I think a lot of people would've done the same in your position."

"I'm not so sure." Jeff took a slurp of tea and pulled a face. "This is cold. I must've been away from the stall for too long." He stood, pushing the chair back so that its legs scraped on the concrete floor. "I hope that helps, but I've got to go."

Dan jumped to his feet and sensed Alan doing the same. "It does help," Dan said quickly. "But before you go, can you please have a think about that lawyer's name. Connor isn't going to tell us, but if you could—"

"I told you, I can't remember!" Frustration animated Jeff's features, but his annoyance quickly faded. "Listen, I'm sorry, guys. None of this is your fault, but I really don't want to drag all this up again."

Jeff took a steadying breath. "I'll tell you what I'll do. I reckon I've still got that piece of paper I signed. It'll be in the attic along with all my old stuff from the band. I'll have a look when I get home, and I'll see if I can find anything with the lawyer's name. If it turns up, I'll let you know." He held out his hand. "You'd better give me another one of those cards."

Dan obliged and Jeff pocketed the card. His gaze on Dan, he said, "I might regret saying this, but if you can find out what Connor did, and you can make him pay for it, I'll go on the record. I'll stand up in court, sign a statement, whatever it takes."

"That's very generous, but it might not come to that," Dan said.

"I'm not sure if the police will reopen Spud's case, but maybe we can find another way to make sure justice is done."

"I hope so." Jeff dropped his gaze for a second, and when he looked up, he seemed even sadder. "You mentioned something about a woman who was killed. That wasn't Connor, was it?"

"We don't know," Dan replied. "But if there's a connection, we'll find it."

"Well, I hope you know what you're doing. If you're going up against Connor and his cronies, they won't give you an easy ride. Connor has deep pockets and no morals whatsoever. He won't go down without a fight."

"It's nothing we can't handle," Dan offered his hand for a shake. "Thank you for talking to us, Jeff. It made a difference."

"That's something, I guess. Sorry to dash off, but I... I've got to go." Jeff briefly shook Dan's hand, then he walked away, hurrying to get back to his stall.

Alan retook his seat, and Dan followed suit, absentmindedly taking a swig of his tea and regretting it.

"The poor man," Alan said. "I hate to think how he's feeling right now, but I'm glad we talked to him."

"Yes, it's a sad story," Dan replied. "But if Jeff comes through for us, and I'd bet anything that he will, the picture will start to come together, and then we'll get to the truth."

Alan looked past Dan. "Ah. Jeff left without his bacon roll, and here it comes."

Dan turned to see a woman striding toward them bearing two plates topped with soft white rolls. She arrived at the table and placed a plate in front of each of them. "Here you go, my lovelies. Two bacon rolls. Enjoy."

They thanked her, Alan much more enthusiastically than Dan, and as soon as she'd marched away Alan pulled both plates closer. "I couldn't resist ordering one for myself, but they didn't have anything for you I'm afraid."

"Never mind. You don't have to eat both. I'll reimburse you."

Alan looked mildly horrified. "I can't let all this food go to waste. I was going to eat one and take the other home, but on second thoughts I'll take them both with me. I have a suspicion that we're heading over to Chagford right away."

"Yes," Dan said. "Those bacon rolls aren't the only things that are going to get wrapped up today. It's time to solve a murder. Let's go."

CHAPTER 81

D C Collins took his place behind DI Spiller as they marched into the Exeter branch of B&Q. The store was quiet, with few customers milling around the aisles of power tools and DIY supplies, and only a couple of the checkouts were staffed, by employees who slumped in their seats, bored at having so little to do.

Spiller stood on the spot, gazing around as if fixing the place in his mind, and Collins stood by him, waiting.

"The customer services counter is over there," Spiller said. "You take the lead on this. If you need me, I'll be right behind you."

"Okay, guv. Thanks." Collins strode up to the counter, sensing Spiller keeping pace with him.

The young woman on duty stood up a little straighter and summoned an encouraging smile. "Good morning, my name is Vicky. How can I help you today?"

Collins had his warrant card ready, and he introduced himself and his boss.

Vicky's eyebrows knitted in concern. "Is everything… I mean, has there been a problem? Nobody mentioned anything."

"There's no problem," Collins said. "But we need to see your recent CCTV recordings. Can we have a word with your manager?"

"Yeah, of course. I'll call him." Vicky pressed one hand to an earpiece while the other worked at something beneath the counter. While she waited for a reply, she chewed on her lower lip, her wary gaze glued on Collins.

"Is he not answering?" Collins asked.

Vicky raised a finger, then half turned away. "Hi, Adrian. It's Vicky. There are two police officers down here, and they need to talk to you. Something about CCTV." A pause and then: "I don't know, they didn't say." She lowered her voice to add, "I think you'd better come right away. Thanks."

When Vicky faced them once more, her smile was back. "The manager will be with you in a moment."

"Thank you, Vicky," Collins said. "We appreciate your help."

"That's all right. It's what I'm here for." Vicky let out a self-conscious laugh. "To help people, I mean. But it's not usually anything so… I mean, it's usually people bringing something back because it doesn't work or because they bought the wrong one by mistake."

"I'm sure you're doing an excellent job," Spiller said. "What's your manager's full name, by the way?"

"Adrian. Adrian Carpenter. Here he comes now."

The policemen watched as a young man in a corporate polo shirt strode toward them. Although dressed like the other employees, there was an assertiveness in his body language; he was the manager and he wanted everyone to know it. As Carpenter introduced himself, making a point of examining both their warrant cards in turn, Collins noticed the man's scrawny beard and youthful complexion. How old was the bloke, anyway? Surely he was too young to be managing a store. Collins banished the thought; there was work to be done.

"So what can I do to help?" Carpenter asked. "You'd like access to our CCTV, is that right?"

"Yes," Collins replied. "We have a specific date and time period we need to see, and we'd like to look at it now."

Carpenter looked uncertain.

A MUST-HAVE MURDER

"It's a matter of urgency," Spiller went on. "It's part of an ongoing murder inquiry."

"Murder? Where?" Carpenter paled. "It wasn't on the premises, was it? That would be—"

Collins raised a hand to interrupt. "It's nothing like that. I can't give you the details, but the crime occurred elsewhere. All we're hoping for is a sighting of our suspect. We have reason to believe he visited your store."

"Oh." Carpenter nodded to himself as though he'd just joined the dots for himself. "In that case, you'd better come through to my office and I'll show you what we have."

"Thank you, sir," Spiller said. "Please, lead way."

Carpenter took them through a heavy door marked *Staff Only*, and along a narrow corridor.

"I've often wondered what goes on behind those doors," Spiller muttered so that only Collins could hear.

"Have you?" Collins replied. "You've been here before?"

"All the time," Spiller said. "There's always one job or another that needs doing. That's the joy of home ownership."

"Not for me. My place is new."

"You'll see, Collins. One day, you'll be a regular in places like this. You'll have a loyalty card."

As if overhearing their last few words, Carpenter turned around, a hopeful expression on his features, but one look at Spiller and Collins seemed to pour cold water on his optimism.

Stopping outside a wooden door with an inset panel of reinforced glass, Carpenter said, "We're in here."

He showed them into a small office and gestured to the two chairs facing his desk. "Please, have a seat. I'll access the camera system and see what we can find."

Collins and Spiller sat facing him, Collins taking out his phone and checking the screen. "We're looking at the Monday of last week. Your recordings do go back that far, don't they?"

"Oh yes. We keep them for a month. Longer if we've caught someone shoplifting." Carpenter smiled expectantly as if

665

anticipating congratulations. When none came, he added, "What time of day do you want to see?"

"Let's start with half past ten," Spiller said. "If you've a camera on the checkouts, that would be best."

"We have several, but wouldn't you rather watch the main entrance?"

Spiller shook his head. "Cameras above a door are generally very visible. They're there as a deterrent, and people expect to see them. Our suspect will have been cautious on the way in, waiting for the right moment and keeping his head down, but by the time he'd got everything he needed, he'll have wanted to get out of here. Chances are, he'll have been in too much of a hurry to notice the cameras above the checkouts."

"Fair enough." Carpenter focused on his computer's screen as his fingers moved the mouse, clicking away in a display of brisk efficiency. He looked up. "Got them."

"Excellent," Spiller said, and both policemen stood at the same time, moving around the desk to flank Adrian Carpenter.

The monitor showed four images, each one covering the checkouts from a different angle. The timestamps in the corner of each image showed 10:30 am. Of the five checkouts visible, only two were staffed, and the cashiers seemed to be sitting idle.

"It's never very busy at that time on a weekday," Carpenter explained. "We get a few customers coming in early, but then it goes quiet."

"Let's play the footage and see what we can see," Spiller said.

"No problem." Carpenter clicked the mouse and the images came to life, one cashier taking out a phone and staring intently at the screen. "She shouldn't be doing that," Carpenter grumbled. "I'll have to have a word with her."

Neither Spiller nor Collins commented; they were too busy watching the screen. At the checkout nearest the door, shadowy figures flitted past on the edge of the camera's field of vision as customers entered the store, but the checkouts were still devoid of customers.

"Can you speed up the playback?" Collins asked.

"Sure." Carpenter obliged and the cashiers appeared to be twitching as their movements were artificially accelerated. "Is that fast enough? I can speed it up more if you like."

"A bit faster would be good," Collins replied. "But be ready to stop it as soon as anyone comes to the checkout."

"Okay. You said *he* earlier. Are you looking for a man?"

"We can't be sure of that," Collins said. "We're looking for someone buying certain items."

"Such as?"

"That's not something we can discuss with you," Spiller stated. "I'm sure you understand."

"Yes, of course. Confidentiality is very important." Carpenter looked up at Spiller. "I suppose, in a case like this—"

"Stop," Collins said. "Quick."

"Oh hell." Carpenter clicked the mouse, freezing the playback. "Sorry about that, I took my eye off it for one second."

"That's okay," Spiller replied, but Collins said nothing. He leaned on the desk, staring at the image of a man standing at the checkout. The man wore a baseball cap, the brim pulled down low to shield his eyes, and he was keeping his head down. His shoulders were hunched inside his denim jacket, and he held a plastic shopping basket close to his body, grasping it with both hands.

"That's Vicky on the till," Carpenter said. "You met her earlier. She's very reliable."

"We'll talk to her later," Collins replied. "Focus on the CCTV. I want you to play it forward slowly. Half speed ought to do it."

Carpenter nodded and there was silence in the room as the action unfolded on the screen, and the man began emptying his shopping onto the counter. The first couple of items were too small for Collins to identify. It looked as though the cashier said something to the customer, and then she lifted her chin as though laughing. That didn't seem promising to Collins. A man who was up to no good wouldn't engage in conversation; he would not want to be remembered. But then a larger bundle appeared in the man's hand, and Collins felt like punching the air. Instead, he kept his cool and said, "That's rope."

"That's correct," Carpenter said. "Polypropylene rope, five metres long. We sell most of our rope by the metre, but that one is pre-cut so it's more convenient."

Collins ignored him. His eyes were on the next package in the unknown customer's hands. It was rectangular and wrapped in clear plastic that caught the light, the reflected glare obscuring what the plastic might contain. But then the cashier moved the package along the counter, and Collins caught a glimpse of dark blue. "Could that be a boiler suit?"

Carpenter hesitated, peering at the screen. "I couldn't say. We have quite a few items of protective clothing, and they all come wrapped. Oh, he's finished, and he's paying with cash by the look of it. We don't see that very often."

Collins ground his teeth together. This was the man they were looking for; he was certain of it. *Look up*, Collins thought. *Even if it's just for a second, look up.*

But the man on the screen did not cooperate. Keeping his head down all the while, the man stowed his goods in a plastic carrier bag and walked away, disappearing from view.

"Check the timestamp," Collins said. "See if we can pick him up as he leaves."

"I'll try." Carpenter ran his tongue over his lips and clicked the mouse, the images on the screen changing. It took him less than a minute to find footage of the man exiting the store, but all it yielded was a view of the man's back as he marched across the car park.

"Jeans and trainers, a denim jacket and a baseball cap," Spiller commented. "He couldn't get more anonymous if he tried."

"I'm sorry it wasn't more useful," Carpenter said. "If it helps, I can retrieve the transactions and tell you what he bought, but it'll take me a while."

"How long?" Spiller asked.

"Twenty minutes or so. If we were talking about yesterday I

could do it right away, but the transactions from last week have been shunted onto another system at head office. It's a bit more fiddly."

Collins nodded. "We'd appreciate it. In the meantime, can you go back to the footage from the till and print off a screenshot?"

"Yes, that's easily done, but it'll only be in black and white."

"That's fine," Collins said. "We want as much of him in the frame as possible."

Carpenter worked quickly, and he looked pleased with himself as he handed Collins the monochrome image. "Is that okay?"

"Perfect," Collins replied. "Now, if you could start looking for those transactions, we'll go and have a word with Vicky."

"Okay," Carpenter said. "I can call and ask Vicky to come up so we can talk privately."

Spiller shook his head. "That won't be necessary. Vicky was nervous enough when we turned up. The last thing we want to do is haul her into the manager's office. We'll talk to her over the counter. Come on, Collins." Spiller made for the door, and Collins followed.

In the corridor, Spiller said, "We're on the right trail, but it's not Jack Devlin. That bloke was too tall for a start, and too broad shouldered."

"So where does that leave us?"

"Following an active line of inquiry," Spiller said. "And that will have to do, for now at any rate."

Back on the shop floor, Vicky watched them approach, her lips drawn tight in apprehension.

With Collins at his side, Spiller wore a friendly smile as he strolled up to the counter. "Hello again, Vicky. If you don't mind, we have a couple of questions for you."

Vicky's hand went to her chest. "Me? What about?"

"Don't worry, you're not in any kind of trouble," Collins said. He handed her the image taken from the CCTV. "This man came in a little over a week ago. It was a Monday."

Vicky squinted at the photo. "I remember. I'm not usually on the till. I was filling in for Sonya. She had a tummy bug."

"You remember the man?" Collins asked.

Vicky screwed up her features. "No, I mean I remember that day, that's all. I don't recognise the man in the photo."

Collins' high hopes vanished, but something wasn't quite right. Collins mentally replayed the scene he'd watched on the footage, and he knew what was bothering him.

"Vicky," Collins began, "when we saw you on the CCTV, you were wearing glasses, weren't you?"

"Oh, I might've been." With a self-conscious smile, Vicky rummaged under the counter and retrieved a pair of green-framed spectacles. Putting them on, she said, "I don't wear them unless I have to. I don't know what I was thinking when I chose these frames. I mean, *green*. Why?"

"They look all right to me," Spiller said. "But, please, take another look at the photo. If it helps, the man's jacket was blue denim and so were his jeans."

"Double denim." Vicky tutted and leaned forward to study the image. "I can't remember much about him off the top of my head, but he rings a bell for some reason. Now, what was it?"

"Any little detail might be useful," Collins said. "What was he buying?"

"Oh, I've no idea. It all goes past in a blur. It could've been tools, or something for decorating. That's what most people come in for."

Collins plastered a patient smile onto his features. "It's important that you don't guess, Vicky. If you don't know what he bought, just say so. It's fine."

"All right. I don't really know what he had in his basket, although come to think of it, I know why he stuck in my mind. You see, we had a little joke. He was buying something age-restricted, and I said I ought to ask for some ID to prove he was old enough. He looked a bit put out, so I told him I was only kidding, and he saw the funny side." Vicky hesitated. "It wasn't like I was chatting him up. I really wasn't, but, you know…"

"You were bored," Spiller suggested.

"A bit," Vicky admitted. "And he was easy to talk to. He was very polite, and in a way, he was kind of good looking. He had a nice smile."

"Could you estimate his age for us?" Collins asked.

"Ooh, I'm not sure, but he didn't dress like his age, if you know what I mean. He could more or less get away with the denim jacket, but all those badges were a bit much."

"What kind of badges?" Spiller said. "Political? Football teams?"

"No. They were those metal pin-on badges. You know, the kind they sell to raise money for charities. We sell them in here sometimes, for cancer research and that sort of thing."

"Enamel pins," Collins suggested. "Did you recognise any of them? Was there one for a particular charity perhaps?"

"No, I don't think his badges were for charity, but I couldn't say what they were. Bands maybe? I think one was in the shape of a guitar."

Gathering his reserves of patience, Collins said, "Was there anything else about him that you can recall? Did he have any identifying features?"

Vicky shook her head slowly. "Not that I can remember."

"How about skin colour?" Spiller asked. "Hair colour? Did he have a beard or moustache?"

"He was white, and I think he had fair hair, but I couldn't see much on account of his cap. He didn't have a beard. He had nice skin, actually. Good teeth too. A nice smile. Confident. But you get that with posh people, don't you?"

"What makes you think he was posh?" Collins asked.

"His voice. The way he spoke. He wasn't like most of the people we get in here. He didn't have an accent. He sounded more like someone from off the telly."

"This is all very helpful Vicky," Spiller began, "but we'll achieve a lot more if you come to the station and help us put an e-fit together. We'll send a car, and we'll square it with Mr Carpenter, okay?"

Vicky nodded nervously. "I suppose so. If it helps…"

"It will," Spiller said. "But before we get to that, what was this man buying that was age-restricted?"

"That's an easy one," Vicky replied. "It was a hawkbill. It's like a knife with a curved blade that folds back into the handle. They're nasty looking things. We can't sell them to anyone under eighteen. We have to be careful."

Collins saw the look in Spiller's eye and knew what they had to do. Seizing the chance to pre-empt the boss, Collins said, "We'd better get back to Mr Carpenter's office. Thanks, Vicky. We'll be in touch."

Spiller added his thanks, then they headed back to the *Staff Only* door, Collins retrieving his phone as he walked.

"You've got the bit between your teeth," Spiller said. "What's on your to-do list?"

"First, we'll get those transactions from Mr Carpenter, then I'll call for a team to collect the CCTV footage. After that I'll arrange for a car to pick Vicky up so we can get a better description of our suspect."

"In the meantime?"

"Back to Chagford? We can ask around, show the screenshot from the CCTV and see if it rings a bell with anyone."

"Absolutely." Spiller tipped him a wink. "You're on fire today, Collins. Positively on fire."

CHAPTER 82

Natalya was taking her first sip of well-deserved coffee when someone rapped on the back door. Natalya sighed. A five-minute break would've been nice. She'd been busy, taking care of Zadie's social media accounts and trying to catch up with the housework, but never mind. The caller would be yet another courier, a delivery of clothes or cosmetics from one company or another. Hardly a day went by without at least one package arriving. *More recycling*, Natalya thought. *What will it be this time, a cardboard box or a plastic bag?* Maybe it would be both.

Natalya crossed the kitchen, setting her cup on the counter as she went, but before she reached the door, it swung open, a man letting himself in. Natalya stopped in her tracks. "Oh, it's you. I wasn't expecting you."

"I know." Tobias Barrington stepped inside and closed the door firmly behind him. "Actually, Natalya, it was you I came to talk to. I wondered if I could beg a few minutes of your time."

"Okay, but I have a lot of work to do, so…"

"This won't take a minute. I've some good news for you. It's about Zadie. Shall we go up to the lounge?"

"I was having a coffee," Natalya said. "There is some left if you'd like a cup."

"And what if I didn't like it, would there still be some coffee left?"

Natalya frowned. "Sorry, I don't understand."

"Never mind, it was just my little joke." Tobias pulled a face. "Lawyers. We argue over every word and reinterpret every question. It's an occupational hazard."

"So would you like a cup of coffee or not?"

Tobias clapped his hands together. "Straight to the point. That's the spirit. You'd make an excellent barrister, though I fancy we'd be on different sides. I can picture you acting for the prosecution, whereas defence is my speciality."

Natalya studied him, waiting.

"Tough crowd," Tobias went on. "Okay, a coffee would be great. If you've no proper milk, I'll take it black. Thanks."

"Fine." Natalya fetched a mug and poured the last of the coffee from the cafetière. She picked up the mug carefully, but when she turned around, Tobias was standing close—too close—and she almost spilled it.

Tobias smiled. "Sorry. Didn't mean to make you jump. I was trying to save you from bringing it to me." He took hold of the mug, wrapping his hand around it, the tips of his fingers brushing her hand.

Natalya clenched her jaw, her stomach tightening, but then Tobias stepped back, lifting his mug as if to say cheers, and her anger dissipated.

"Thank you, Natalya." Tobias took a sip and nodded in approval. "That really is excellent. You can say what you like about my sister, but she buys only the best."

"I buy it from a shop in town. Zadie always has decaffeinated, but I get regular coffee for her guests."

"But you like it too, don't you, eh?" Tobias said. "Nothing like a shot of the old caffeine. Where's yours?"

Natalya pointed past him. "Over there."

"Right." Tobias half turned to see the mug on the counter across the kitchen, then he looked back at her, waiting. He was barring her

674

way, and they both knew it.

"Excuse me." Natalya drew herself up to her full height and took a step forward. "I need to get past."

"By all means." Tobias sidestepped and made a mock bow, extending his free arm.

"Thank you." Natalya marched stiffly to the counter and retrieved her drink. It would be going cold, but she didn't want to take a sip just yet. She needed to keep an eye on Tobias. She'd never entirely trusted him. He was nothing like the lawyers who'd helped her when she'd first come to the UK; they'd been kind and courteous. Tobias, she'd decided some time ago, was a different kind of lawyer. He talked far too much and he used a lot of fancy words, but he never quite meant what he said.

Watching him as he drank his coffee, Natalya said, "You had something to tell me, yes? Something about Zadie."

"Yes. It's great news, actually. She's still not up and about, but they say there's no lasting damage from her head injury. Mentally, she's more or less back to her old self. She's doing so well they're going to let her come home soon. Maybe even tomorrow if all goes according to plan. It depends if they can sort out all the crutches and the physiotherapy and so on."

Natalya smiled. "Ah, this is good news. The best. I've been worried about her."

"I'm sure you have." Tobias tilted his head to one side and looked at her with a gleam in his eye. "You know, when you smile you look so pretty, Natalya. You really ought to do it more often."

Natalya's expression turned to stone. "Mr Barrington, that is not—"

"Please, spare me the lecture," Tobias interrupted. "I know, I know, you're not here as window dressing, and your smile isn't there to make a man happy. I've heard it all a thousand times from my dear sister, but can't a chap give a woman a compliment now and then, dammit? I didn't mean anything by it."

"Is that supposed to be an apology?"

"No, not really." Tobias heaved a sigh. "I hereby withdraw my remark fully, and I sincerely apologise for the outdated terminology I employed. I shall take some time to reflect and to educate myself. Is that better? Is that woke enough for you?"

"It would be okay if you meant it."

Tobias chuckled under his breath. "I've faced some tough characters in court, but you're by far the hardest adversary I've dealt with in a long time. I can see I'll have to put my cards on the table and get to the point."

"Yes please. That would be best."

"Okay." Tobias stepped closer to her, his gaze focussed upward as though his mind was fully occupied with framing his thoughts. "It's like this. Zadie said something to me in the hospital, and it got me thinking. It made me realise there's something we need to discuss."

"Oh? And what is that?"

"You work very closely with Zadie, don't you?"

Natalya nodded, mentally measuring the distance between her and Tobias. She didn't want to be the one to back away, but if Tobias moved even a millimetre nearer she'd have to say something or take evasive action.

"You've always been very loyal to Zadie, haven't you?" Tobias went on. "She appreciates that, and so do I."

"What did Zadie say?" Natalya asked. "You said she told you something in the hospital. What was it?"

"There you go again, straight to the point." Tobias took half a step closer. "Poor old Zadie was feeling a bit emotional when I went to see her this morning. She was talking about coming home, and how she'd missed the house and seeing you, and she said something very interesting. Zadie said she tells you everything."

Natalya pretended to look at something behind Tobias, and when he half turned, she took the opportunity to edge away from him.

Tobias turned his suspicious stare back on Natalya, but before he could speak, Natalya said, "It's not true, what Zadie said. We mainly talk about work. She doesn't tell me *everything*."

"You're being modest. Zadie relies on you, and not just for work. She *trusts* you, and I can understand why. You're a good listener, and I'll bet you have a good memory too."

"This is true."

"I thought as much." Tobias rubbed his chin. "I wonder, did my sister ever happen to mention anything about Connor Griffiths to you?"

Natalya hesitated. An uncomfortable sensation prickled the side of her neck, and her hand went to it. "Like what?"

"I think you know perfectly well what I mean." Tobias lifted a finger in admonishment. "Never try to hide the truth from a barrister, Natalya. I deal with liars all day and every day, and I know the signs."

Natalya bridled. "I am not a liar. Never."

"But that's not quite the same as telling the truth, the whole truth and nothing but the truth, is it? There's such a thing as a sin of omission." Tobias studied her for a second. "Do you understand that expression? A sin of omission. It means leaving something out on purpose. Keeping quiet when it suits you, hiding the truth."

"I know what it means."

"You also know why Connor doesn't drive, don't you? You know about his little accident."

Natalya nodded.

"He blames himself," Tobias went on. "Poor old Connor wasn't driving, but still, he feels dreadful about it."

Despite her best intentions, Natalya's lips curled in disgust, and Tobias didn't miss the change in her expression.

"You *do* know," he stated. "You know what Connor did, so I expect you know what happened next."

Natalya's only reply was a defiant glare.

"Oh dear," Tobias murmured. "That is a shame. A dreadful, terrible shame."

CHAPTER 83

T he Toyota RAV4 juddered as one of its front wheels found a pothole. The car swayed and shuddered as Dan drove on, an ominous creak coming from the suspension, but Dan kept his foot pressed on the accelerator.

In the passenger seat, Alan drew a sharp breath, but he didn't say a word.

They were bowling along a narrow lane that led from Chagford, the road lined by high banks of earth topped with tall hedges. At one time, the treacherous winding byways of Devon might've intimidated Dan, but not anymore. He knew his vehicle's limits, and he scrutinised the lane's width as he drove, ready to stop and reverse into a passing place at a moment's notice.

"Maybe I've got the directions wrong," Alan said. "Connor told us he didn't live far from Zadie's house. If memory serves, he described the walk as a nice little stroll."

"He was being deliberately vague to pull the wool over our eyes," Dan replied. "Connor's a stranger to the truth. We know it took him almost an hour to walk over to Zadie's the other day, but don't worry about it. We'll get there soon."

Dan stopped talking as he braked to take a tight turn, the gearbox emitting a series of alarming clunks as Dan shifted gear and accelerated away. "There's something wrong with the transmission," he explained. "I have to use the clutch twice every time I change gear."

"Ah, the lost art of double declutching. It sounds like the synchromesh has gone. How long has this been going on?"

"Oh, ages. I don't know."

"You've never mentioned it before."

"It was never this bad," Dan replied. "I've learned to live with it, until now."

"Just as well we're almost there. I caught a glimpse of a house on the right. That must be Connor's place; there's nothing else out here. Pull in by that gate, next to the oak."

"Which one? There are trees all over the place."

"You know what an oak tree looks like, Dan. It's right there. Stop!"

Dan applied the brakes and the Toyota ground to a halt in front of a wide wooden gate, a stately oak growing to one side. Beyond the gate, a gravel driveway crossed a rolling expanse of grass and led to a grand house built of pale stone.

"That has to be it," Alan said. "I'll open the gate, but you'll need to back up a bit to make the turn."

Alan hopped out of the car then he swung the gate open while Dan manoeuvred the Toyota into position, the gears whining as he reversed. As soon as Dan had driven through, Alan closed the gate and hurried back to the car.

"You could've left it open," Dan said as Alan retook his seat. "Now we'll have to open it again when we leave."

"That's neither here nor there. You must always leave a gate in the same condition in which you found it."

"Yes, but I can't see any livestock that might escape from Connor's lawn, can you?"

"It's a point of principle," Alan replied. "You know it as well as I do."

Dan knew better than to argue the finer points of the country code with Alan, so he drove on until they reached the house, parking on a broad stretch of gravel, the car facing the front door.

The battered and dust-streaked Toyota looked out of place in front of such an impressive entrance, and as they exited the car, Dan suspected that the engine was already depositing a patch of oil to stain the pristine gravel. One of these days he'd have to trade the Toyota in, but that would have to wait until Zadie or Tobias Barrington paid up.

Looking up at the house, Alan said, "It's a mansion. His family must've been absolutely—"

"Rolling in it?" Dan suggested.

"I was going to say 'loaded', but the effect is the same."

"Indeed. It makes you wonder where all that money came from, especially now we know Sir William was so cosy with the great and the good."

"Do you think the old boy's network came into play?" Alan asked. "Handshakes over brandy in rooms filled with cigar smoke?"

"Would you be surprised if that were the case?"

"No. Not in the least. Shall I ring the bell?"

"Let me." Dan marched to the front door and pressed the polished brass doorbell. Then he did it again, half a dozen more times before holding it down for a few seconds.

"That ought to do it," Alan said. "Assuming he's in."

"He'll be here. Where else could he be? Zadie's still in hospital, and I doubt whether anyone else is tolerant enough to welcome Connor with open arms."

"I think your intuition is about to be proved right. I can hear someone coming."

From beyond the door came the sound of footsteps echoing on a wooden floor. The brass doorhandle turned and Connor appeared in the doorway, a bemused smile on his lips.

"Fancy that," Connor drawled. "An inspector calls."

"Not quite," Dan said. "Can we come in? There's something we need to talk about."

Connor looked as though he'd like to turn them away, but he summoned a humourless grin. "Of course. It's always a delight to talk to you two. Mi casa es su casa."

Connor stood back, opening the door wide and gesturing for them to come in.

Dan and Alan stepped inside, and Connor showed them into a lounge, the room well-lit by tall sash windows. Connor threw himself down onto a worn leather sofa. "Have a seat. Make yourselves at home."

"Thanks, but we'll stand," Dan said.

"Suit yourselves." He gazed up at them, already looking bored. "So what's got you two hot under the collar this time? Has somebody lost their cat or something?"

"It's a good deal more serious than that," Alan said. "Earlier today, we talked to an old friend of yours."

"I doubt it. I haven't got any. Nobody worth talking about anyway."

"This old friend was very keen to talk about you," Dan replied. "It was Jeff. Jeff Dawkins."

Connor snorted. "That deadbeat. What ancient gossip did he come up with? Or did he try to sell you one of his novelty guitars?"

Dan smiled as if he enjoyed Connor's acerbic wit. "We talked about Stuart. Spud. Interestingly, Jeff's recollection was significantly different to yours."

"I can't help that. Poor old Jeff must've got muddled. He was never quite the same after the band split up. The man was a wreck. If you ask me, he had a nervous breakdown and he's never recovered."

"I saw no sign of that," Alan said. "Jeff's memories were clear, and he articulated them perfectly well."

"He must've remembered to take his meds." Connor looked to Dan. "What did you make of poor old Jeff? I expect you saw through his BS. He's nothing but a has-been musician looking for attention, am I right?"

Dan shook his head slowly. "I liked him. More importantly, I believed every word he said."

"Well, well, well." Connor raised a finger and marked off an imaginary stroke in the air. "Score one for Jeff. Time for round two."

"You see this conversation as a conflict?" Dan asked.

"Don't you?"

"No, it's an investigation; the two are very different."

"I'll take your word for it," Connor said. "It seems to me that I'm in the hot seat, so what has Jeff been accusing me of this time? What exactly am I supposed to have done? Did I force cocaine into Spud's nasal cavities?"

"There was no mention of drugs at the inquest," Alan stated. "Only alcohol."

Connor looked unimpressed. "I didn't mean it literally, Alan. The point is, whatever Spud was on, nobody forced him."

"Not directly, perhaps," Dan said. "But you encouraged Spud, didn't you, Connor? You led him astray."

"Ah, now we're hearing from Mrs Dawkins, or as she was then, little Allie O'Neill. I don't know why she blamed me, but I always figured it was the grief talking. She was bitter at losing her brother, but I didn't blame her for that. It was a shame she went public in the way she did. It helped no one." Connor's lips curled into the suggestion of a smirk. "The truth is, Allie always had a crush on me. Unrequited love can do strange things to people."

"There were others who took Alison seriously," Alan pointed out. "The coroner for one. Spud's death was the result of misadventure. It wasn't accidental."

"That was a technicality. They amount to the same thing. My lawyer—"

"Who was your lawyer?" Dan interrupted.

"You'll find out soon enough if you carry on like this," Connor said, a note of warning in his voice. "But trust me, it would be better for you if it didn't come to that. He's like a dog with a bone."

"So am I," Dan replied. "You may as well give me your lawyer's name. I'll find it out anyway. Jeff still has copies of the papers he signed at the time, and he's retrieving the evidence as we speak."

"Is he really, Dan? Is sad old Jeff going to all that effort when there's nothing in it for him?"

"There are more important things than money," Alan said. "Jeff and his wife are looking for a resolution. They want closure."

"Then they'll be disappointed. Spud's death was a horrible accident, but there's no point in trying to foist the blame on me. I'll say it one last time: *it wasn't my fault.* Finding my lawyer will get you nowhere. It's irrelevant."

Dan looked at Connor and cursed himself for being slow. The answer had been staring him in the face, but he'd shied away from it, reluctant to bite the hand that fed him. But he could no longer reconcile himself to that. Keeping his tone level, Dan said, "We both know who your lawyer was, Connor. It was Tobias Barrington."

Connor clamped his lips shut.

"I suppose your father knew him," Dan went on. "Money changed hands, papers were signed, and you walked away scot free. That must've forged a bond between you and Tobias."

"You make it sound like a bromance. There's no *bond* between Tobias and me."

"Oh, but there is," Dan said. "You call him Toby, though he's Tobias to everyone else, and you send for him at the first sign of trouble. It was you who brought Tobias around to Zadie's house the other day, and when I asked you about him, you described Tobias as a steamroller. You said that I wouldn't want to go up against him, but you never explained how you knew that. You deflected my question, and I didn't even notice, but then, you're very good at deflecting, aren't you, Connor?"

"If you say so, but you're barking up the wrong tree. I've got nothing to hide."

"So Tobias *was* your lawyer," Dan said, "and maybe he still is."

Connor sighed. "What if he is? What difference does it make?"

"All the difference in the world." Dan smiled as the pieces fell into place. "You see, this case is all about connections. Tobias connects you to Philippa."

"Nonsense. Philippa was my friend, and that's got nothing to do with Tobias."

"But Tobias was your lawyer, and at one time he was in a relationship with Philippa," Dan insisted. "Tobias helped you out when you were in trouble, paying off witnesses and concealing evidence. That's going to come back to bite both of you, by the way, but here and now, we have to wonder whether Tobias ever told Philippa what you did to poor old Spud."

Connor's face flushed, his cheeks taut with anger. "What *I* did? I did nothing wrong."

"That's not true," Dan stated. "You abused the trust Spud placed in you. He thought you were his friend, but you treated him like an unpaid bodyguard. He meant nothing to you. You toyed with him because it amused you, and your actions led to his death. That makes you culpable. You might've got away with it at the time, but cases can be reopened, and you'll be held to account."

Connor jumped to his feet, pointed an accusing finger at Dan. "You're out of control, you know that? You're living in a dream world. You'd better get out of my house right now, and don't come back. I'll get a restraining order, I'll sue you for defamation, I'll—"

"Why did you kill Philippa?" Dan interrupted. "Was it because she knew what you'd done? Was it simply to keep her quiet, or was there more to it than that? We know she was short of money. She had no income and a big house to maintain, so she had to find some way to support her lifestyle. Renting out a cottage would've helped, but she needed more than that. Did she come to you for money, was that it? Was she blackmailing you?"

Connor glared at Dan, incoherent with rage. "I didn't... that wasn't..." Letting out a growl of repressed anger, Connor blurted, "You have no bloody idea what you're talking about! She was making my life a misery. A misery!"

"Tell me," Dan said. "What did she have over you? Pillow talk between her and Tobias wouldn't get her anywhere; it would be your word against hers."

"Oh, she was a piece of work," Connor sneered. "Toby might've let the cat out of the bag, but she went looking for more. She looked through his papers and took photos of them all. She kept sending me pictures, on and on. There was no getting away from her. I begged her to stop, I pleaded with her, but she wouldn't listen. She wouldn't leave me alone. But I didn't want… I didn't want her dead for Christ's sake. That wasn't meant to happen."

"I've heard enough," Alan said. "I'm calling the police." Alan took out his phone, but Connor sprang at him, lashing out to dash the phone from Alan's hand.

The phone clattered to the floor, and while Alan was still looking stunned Connor grabbed a poker from the fireplace and brandished it, first at Dan and then at Alan.

"No phones!" Connor snapped. "Nobody is calling anyone."

Dan raised his hands in front of him, his empty palms toward Connor. "There's no need for this, Connor. Put that thing down before it's too late."

"Too late? It's already too late." Connor jabbed the poker toward Alan. "You, give me your car keys."

"My car isn't here."

In one stride Connor was behind Alan, the poker across his throat. Connor grasped the metal rod on either side of Alan's neck, pressing the shaft against Alan's flesh.

Dan rushed forward, but Connor yelled, "Stop! One step closer and I'll crush his windpipe."

Dan halted abruptly, his heels almost slipping on the polished wooden floor. "Okay, Connor, calm down. I'll give you my keys if you let Alan go." Dan pulled his keys from his pocket and dangled them from his finger. "You can have them right now. All you have to do is let him go."

"Don't give in to him," Alan said. "I won't be a bargaining chip."

"It's all right, Alan. This is the best solution." Dan held the keys toward Connor. "Come on, Connor. Take them."

Connor tutted in contempt. "Do you really think I'm that stupid? Put them on the table and then back away."

"Okay, but if you don't let Alan go immediately, all bets are off. If you try to take him with you, we will stop you. There are two of us, and we're both in better shape than you. You can't take us both on at the same time."

"Maybe not, but I could still do some damage to your friend and take my chances, couldn't I? You'd look after him before you'd chase after me."

"Is that a risk you're prepared to take?" Dan said. "You might not know this about me, but I'm extremely goal orientated. Yes, Alan is my friend, but I came here to close a case, and that's my one and only priority. Think about it. I've offered you a way out, but if you harm Alan or try to hold on to him, you're not going to leave this room."

Connor tilted his head from side to side as if weighing this up. "Maybe you're right, but that takes us back to square one. Put the keys on the table and back away." Connor's expression hardened. "I'm running out of patience, Dan, and that never ends well."

"Fine." Dan took a step back and laid his keys on the table, but he kept his hand on them. "On the count of three I'll take my hand off the keys. At exactly the same time, you have to let Alan go. If you don't, I'll grab the keys back and put them away. I'm only going to make this offer once. Take this opportunity now or it disappears forever. Do you understand?"

"God, you're a pain in the arse," Connor muttered.

"Yes, but I stick to my word," Dan replied. "You get the keys on the count of three or not at all. What's it to be?"

"All right," Connor said. "One, two…" He hesitated then shouted, "Three!" As the word left his lips he pushed Alan away and lunged for the table, his left arm outstretched while his right still wielded the poker.

There was a brief moment when Connor was looking only at the keys as he snatched them up, but Dan forced himself to stay back. Connor's improvised weapon gave him a longer reach, and he was unpredictable at best. If Dan tried to stop him, there was no telling what Connor might do. Better to let him go.

Connor backed away unsteadily, his gaze flitting between Dan and Alan. "Don't come after me. I'm warning you." Connor waved the poker in the air.

"Just go," Dan said. "Nobody's stopping you."

Connor sent them an evil leer, then he turned and fled. A moment later, they heard the front door slam.

Dan looked Alan up and down. "Are you all right?"

"Fine. I shouldn't have let him get behind me." Alan rubbed at his throat briefly, then he scooped up his phone from the floor. "What are we waiting for? Let's get after him."

"You're sure?"

Alan nodded and Dan jogged from the room, Alan catching him up. They reached the front door together.

"We'll get him at the gate," Dan said. He threw open the front door and they dashed outside. But they needn't have hurried.

Connor sat in the RAV4, the engine running, but he hadn't yet managed to get it moving. He needed to reverse away from the house, but hideous grating sounds were coming from the Toyota's gearbox. Still wrestling with the gear-lever, Connor looked up to see Dan and Alan marching toward him.

"Get back!" Connor yelled, but Dan shook his head slowly and kept walking.

Connor let fly with a string of curses, and by some miracle he got the car into gear. The engine revving hard, the car shot backward, performing a tight turn as Connor wrenched the wheel. The brakes squealed as the RAV4 came to a sudden halt, and metal grated against metal as Connor forced the stubborn gearbox to comply. With a clunk, the first gear engaged, and Connor glared out at them, his teeth bared in a triumphant snarl.

Dan halted, holding out his arm to stop Alan. "Give him some room for a second; he might try to run us down. We'll get him at the gate."

The Toyota leaped forward, its wheels spitting gravel, the engine roaring. The car sped along the driveway, veering from side to side, but as it neared the gate it did not slow down.

"My God," Alan murmured. "He's not going to try and ram it, is he? That gate's solid. I've seen it close-up, and he won't get through it in one piece."

"One way or another, we've got to catch him. Come on."

Dan sprinted after the Toyota, Alan hard on his heels.

The RAV4 gathered speed, bearing down on the wooden gate, Dan and Alan haring after it. *Stop!* Dan thought. *There's still time.*

Dan clenched his jaw, air hissing over his teeth as he pushed himself to run faster, harder.

But the Toyota accelerated, its engine howling in protest. For a split second, the Toyota shimmied as if Connor were fighting for control, and then the car collided with the gate. Wood splintered with an ear-splitting crack, but the gate held fast, and the Toyota's bonnet crumpled. The car's rear wheels briefly left the ground, and then the Toyota crashed down, springs creaking as it bounced on its tortured suspension, the engine dead.

Dan sprinted to the driver's door and yanked it open. The air bag had deployed and Connor was sprawled against it, but then he tried to sit up, his eyes glazed.

"Don't move," Dan said. "You could have a head injury or whiplash or—"

"I'm all right," Connor mumbled, his voice thick. He sat back in his chair, groaning, then he looked up at Dan and added, "I wore my seatbelt." He tried to laugh but it turned into a gasp of pain, and he clutched his chest. "Bloody hell that hurts."

"You've probably cracked a rib or two," Dan said. "Does anything else hurt?"

Alan caught up with them, and he leaned into the car to look Connor over. "Did you lose consciousness? Did you black out?"

"No." Connor fumbled for the seatbelt. "I've got to get out."

Alan placed a firm hand on his shoulder. "No. Stay put until the ambulance arrives."

Connor grimaced but he didn't resist.

"I'll make the call," Alan said. "I'll ask for the police too."

"No, don't talk to the cops," Connor moaned, but Alan ignored him, stepping back and turning away as he took out his phone.

"Please, tell him to stop," Connor said to Dan. "I can make this right. What'll it take?"

Dan stared at Connor in disbelief.

"I'm serious," Connor went on. "I'll pay for a new car, a better one. It's no problem. Nobody got hurt but me. There's no need for the police."

"Forget it," Dan said. "You can't wriggle out of this the way you did with Spud's death. You killed Philippa. You can't walk away from that."

Connor took a slow breath, wincing in pain. With his eyes closed tight, he said, "I didn't kill her, you idiot."

"Come on, Connor. A few minutes ago you practically admitted it."

"No, I didn't." Connor opened his eyes, his gaze growing sharper. "You jumped to the wrong conclusion, but I'm telling you, I didn't kill her."

"So why did you threaten Alan? Why did you run?"

"Because…" Connor leaned his head back against the headrest, staring into space. "Because it's all going to come out. Everyone's going to know about Spud, and I can't take it. I can't go through that again." He sniffed and wiped his nose with the back of his hand. "What happened to Spud was… it was my fault. I as good as killed him. Do you think I don't know that? I live with it every damned day of my miserable bloody life. But I get by, you know? Somehow I manage to drag my sorry arse from day to day, and the one thing that keeps me going, the one thing that stops me from ending it all, is the fact that nobody knows. No one. But then Philippa got hold of the truth, and she was never going to let it go. One way or another, she was going to make me pay."

"What did she want?"

"Money. Not much at first, but then she got a taste for it. She wanted more and more. There was no end to it. But you know what? I didn't care about the money. She could've had every penny as far as I was concerned, but no amount of money was ever going to be enough for her. She wanted to make me the most hated man in the world. She wanted to tell everybody, to drag me through the dirt."

"So you killed her."

"No! It wasn't me. I never wanted Philippa to get hurt, but he —" Connor bit back his words, but he was too late.

"You can't leave it there," Dan said. "I'm not saying I'll believe you, but if you're going to claim innocence, you'll have to tell me who killed Philippa."

Connor clamped his lips shut tight.

"Tell me who did it," Dan insisted. "You have no choice."

Alan turned back to them, his phone still in his hand. It seemed that he'd heard their exchange, and he fixed Connor with a scornful gaze. "The first responders will be here soon, and the police too, so if you know something about Philippa's murder, you'd better come out with it before they get here. If you tell the truth it might go in your favour, but if you withhold evidence, the police will throw the book at you."

"I don't know what happened, not for sure, but I think…" Connor looked down, his voice growing faint as if he was talking only to himself. "I should never have told him. I should've dealt with it myself."

"You told someone that Philippa was blackmailing you, didn't you? Who was it?" Dan asked, although the answer was already forming in his mind. "It was Tobias Barrington, wasn't it?"

Connor looked up sharply, a glint of recognition in his eyes, and that was enough for Dan. Now he knew the truth: Tobias Barrington was a cold-blooded killer.

CHAPTER 84

Natalya saw Tobias Barrington place his mug of coffee on the kitchen table, then he took something from his pocket and worked at it with both hands.

"What are you doing?" Natalya demanded. "What've you got?"

"This? Let's call it a little surprise." Something metallic clicked into place, and Tobias lifted his right hand to show her what he held in his fist.

The knife's blade wasn't long, but it looked strong, its edge cruelly curved like an eagle's beak. She had no doubt it would slice through flesh easily enough.

Natalya braced herself and backed away, bending her knees to lower her centre of gravity.

Tobias held the knife in his right hand, the blade pointed upward as he advanced on her. "Don't make this harder than it needs to be," he murmured. "I won't hurt you unless it becomes necessary, but we're going for a little journey, you and I."

Natalya raised her fists to chest height and squared her shoulders, every sinew taut. "I'm going nowhere. You can't touch me. If you try, I will make you regret it."

Tobias leered at her. "No, you're not going to waste your time and precious energy in a fight you can't win, Natalya. I'm in control here. If you shout or scream, no one will hear you. You're on your own. There's no one to help."

"I don't need anyone. I can take care of myself."

"You could try, but then I'll have to cut your pretty face and that would be such a pity. If I have to use my knife, what will become of that beautiful smile?"

Natalya drew a long, steady breath. This man was big but he was soft, his muscles turned to flab. He bullied with words, but he did not know to fight, he didn't even know how to hold a knife. He was nothing.

She lowered her gaze, concentrating on his hands, on the knife.

"That's better," Tobias said. "I can see you're going to come quietly." With his left hand, he crooked a finger to beckon her.

Her gaze still on the knife, Natalya took half a step closer, then she waited. She needed him closer, needed him to make a move.

Without looking up, she said, "I won't go anywhere with you. I'd rather die. You are a coward. Useless. Pathetic. You are not a man at all. You are—"

Tobias lunged at her, brandishing the blade with one hand while he made a grab for her with the other.

Natalya's reflexes did not let her down. She grabbed his right wrist and turned around, stepping in to his body, placing her feet just right. Tobias crashed into her, but she was ready for that, and she used his momentum against him, pulling him forward, forcing him to stumble over her leg. Tobias went down hard, crashing into the floor, but Natalya held on to his wrist, and she wrenched it upward, twisting it savagely.

Tobias yelped in pain, his fingers opening and the knife falling from his grip, but Natalya did not let go. Tobias was trying to writhe free. He was still a threat, but she hadn't finished with him yet.

Natalya raised her foot and kicked down hard at his shoulder, aiming precisely on the joint, and she felt the bones give way beneath her shoe. Tobias roared in agony, and Natalya dropped his arm, watching the way it flopped to the floor and landed at an unnatural angle. Good. His shoulder was dislocated, and that ought to teach him a lesson.

But Tobias grunted and writhed, trying to roll over, so she'd have to drive her lesson home.

Natalya knelt down beside Tobias, pressing one knee against the man's injured shoulder. Ignoring his cries of pain, she picked up the knife and tossed it up onto the kitchen counter. "I warned you," she said. "I told you I'd make you regret it."

"Please," Tobias whimpered. "I have money. It's yours if you let me go."

Natalya let out a hiss of contempt. "You see? You are a coward." Jumping to her feet, she took a few steps back, then she took out her phone and dialled 999.

While she talked to the calm man on the phone, Natalya kept a watchful eye on Tobias. Groaning and cursing, he shifted himself into a sitting position, and he glared balefully up at her, cradling his arm.

Natalya gestured for him to stay put, and a flash of anger sparked in the man's eyes, but it didn't last long. He could try to get away, but he wouldn't get far in that state, and the reality of his situation seemed to be sinking in. Tobias bowed his head and stared at the floor, lost in a fog of pain and abject self-pity.

Useless, Natalya thought. *Not a man at all*. At least, Tobias was not a good man. The thought of Alan crossed her mind. Where was he now, and what was he doing? She'd call him in a minute; she had a lot to tell him.

And in that moment, her concentration must've wavered, because Tobias was on his feet, facing her, his face contorted in a vicious scowl. He darted half a step closer, baring his teeth, and Natalya brought up the knife, holding it in a reverse grip, the cutting edge facing her opponent.

"Don't be ridiculous," Tobias growled from between clenched teeth. "Put that knife down."

Natalya shook her head.

"You won't use it," Tobias said. "You haven't got the guts."

"Do you think so? Do you think I don't know how to fight?" Natalya looked him in the eye. "Which one of us is hurt?"

"You got lucky."

"No, I have skill. Now be quiet and sit down. The police will be here soon."

"It'll take them half an hour to get here. Do you really think you can hold me off for that long."

"Of course," Natalya began, but before she could say more, Tobias charged at her, his good arm outstretched toward the knife.

Natalya didn't hesitate. She brought the knife up hard and fast, feeling the blade slice through fabric and skin to bite into the muscles beneath.

Tobias staggered to a standstill, staring at the diagonal gash in his jacket's sleeve, the stream of blood already trickling from cuff to dribble over his hand. "Jesus Christ!" he hissed. "You cut me."

"You gave me no choice. If you sit down and hold your arm up, it will not bleed so fast. I can help you."

"No." Tobias shook his head rapidly, his cheeks pale. "No. No. No." Without warning, he made a dash for the door. A second later he was outside.

Natalya ran to the doorway. "Tobias! Stay where you are. You need help."

Taking no heed of her, Tobias half ran, half staggered to his car. He was fumbling with the door handle when a white van pulled slowly into the driveway.

Thank God, Natalya thought. *The police.*

Tobias gave a start, but then his face turned puce and Natalya understood why.

The man stepping down from the van was not a police officer but Shaun, his eyes wide as he took in the scene.

"You!" Tobias shouted. "Get that bloody van out of the way. You're blocking me in. I have to get to the hospital. Now!"

Shaun held up a hand. "You can't drive in that state. You're bleeding. We need an ambulance."

Natalya strode onto the driveway. "Stay away from him, Shaun. He's dangerous. Get in your van and lock the doors, but don't drive away. Leave your van where it is."

"Hang on a minute." Shaun looked from Tobias to Natalya. "Did you do this to him?"

"It was self-defence," Natalya replied. "He was trying to make me go with him. I wouldn't let him."

"He was what?" Shaun stared at Tobias. "Is that right?"

"Of course it isn't. She's lying. She went mad, tried to kill me. We have to get out of here. You have to help me."

Shaun shook his head. "No one is going anywhere. I've got my phone in the van. I'll call for an ambulance and the police. They'll sort this out."

"I already called them," Natalya said. "They're on their way."

"Good." Shaun looked at Tobias and seemed to make his mind up. "You'd better not move, pal. I don't know what the hell's been going on, but to my mind, you looked like you were running away just now, so if Natalya had to fight you off, I reckon you deserved it."

"For God's sake," Tobias muttered, and he stalked toward Shaun. "Get your bloody van out the way, you stupid peasant." Tobias raised his good hand in a fist, his fingers streaked with blood. "If you don't do what I say right now, I will make your life a misery."

Shaun nodded once. "Is that right?"

Natalya didn't see what happened next, but Tobias was suddenly lying on the ground, one hand over his face.

Shaun brushed his hands together, then he looked to Natalya. "Are you all right, miss?"

"Yes, Shaun. I'm fine, thank you." She paused, unsure what to say.

"I only came back to finish one little job. I kept thinking about the stairs, and I was worried someone might put their foot through that broken tread, so I came to fix it. I'd promised to mend it, so it seemed like the least I could do, but…" Shaun shook his head, bewildered. "Are you sure you're all right, miss? I mean, he didn't… *hurt* you, did he?"

"He tried," Natalya said. "Can you keep an eye on him for a minute?"

"No problem." Shaun cradled his right fist in his left hand. "He'll stay down if he knows what's good for him, but I'm a bit worried about all that blood."

"It's not as bad as it looks, but I'll go and find something to stop the bleeding. When I've done that, I'll make you some tea, plenty of sugar."

"Don't worry about me. I'm fine."

"It's no problem," Natalya said. "You've earned it."

CHAPTER 85

D an looked from Connor to Alan. "Tobias killed Philippa," Dan said. "She knew him well, or thought she did, so when he told her to meet him by the river, she went along with it. Philippa thought she was in control, so she let him get close to her."

"You don't know that," Connor said. "Toby wouldn't do something so... he couldn't."

Dan let out a grunt of disbelief. "Are you sure about that? The way he covered up Spud's death was cold and calculating. A man like that is capable of anything. If Philippa told the world what she knew, Tobias would be disbarred. He fixed an inquest and he bribed the witnesses. He'd lose his career and his reputation, he might even face charges. He'd have been ruined, and status is very important to a man like Tobias. It defines him."

Dan paused. "I can't prove it though; not yet. There are still a couple of things I need to know. For a start, when did you tell Tobias that Philippa was blackmailing you?"

"It was—" Connor's voice cracked and he wiped a hand over his eyes. "It was a while ago, just before Zadie started having all that trouble. We went to that damned pub for Melody's birthday, and Philippa was there, watching me all the time, staring at me. It was like she was taunting me. One word from her and all my friends would know what I'd done. The next day, I was tired, strung out, so I did the only thing I could think of. I called Toby and told him I was in trouble."

"That must've been on the Monday," Alan said. "The day before we met Philippa."

"The same day that someone took a bus from Chagford to Exeter," Dan replied. "And after that trip, they came back and took a walk by the river."

Alan's mouth formed a silent O. "That can't be a coincidence."

Connor squinted up at them. "I don't know what you're going on about, but I need to get out of this car. My ribs are killing me."

"Stay right there," Dan said. "Answer a few more questions and I might believe your story, then we'll see what we can do for you, okay?"

Connor cursed under his breath, but he muttered, "All right. Let's get this over with."

"Do you ever take the bus?" Dan asked.

Connor pulled a face. "No. Never. I get a lift or book a taxi. Hell, I'd rather walk than take the bus. Anything's better than being crammed in with all those… *people*."

Dan watched Connor carefully. His display of distaste had been exaggerated, conjured up to conceal a lie. Connor couldn't have known that the bus ticket had been found, so why would he lie? Was it purely from habit, or was there another reason? There was one way to find out.

"Connor, you're a terrible snob," Dan stated.

The look on Connor's face was a picture, surprise and outrage vying for control of his features.

"I'm sorry but it's true," Dan went on. "You don't want to admit it because you think it's beneath you, but I'm willing to bet you take the bus into Exeter fairly regularly. You have to buy your cannabis somewhere, and you don't want to book a taxi in case you're recognised by the driver and someone puts two and two together. On a bus you can mingle with the other passengers, and no one looks twice."

"You're unbearable, do you know that?" Connor said. "A real pain in the arse."

"Yes, but I'm right, aren't I?"

Connor raised a hand and let it flop to his thigh. "All right. I take the bus every couple of weeks. So what?"

"We'll come to that in a minute," Dan said. "Let's focus on Tobias. When you told him you were in trouble, what happened? Take me through it."

"There's not much to tell. I didn't want to give him the whole story over the phone, so I told him I needed help, and he said he'd come over."

"When did he come to see you?" Alan asked.

"The same day. He came straight away."

"Interesting," Dan said. "When you told him you were being blackmailed, what did he say?"

"He said, 'Leave it with me.' Something like that."

"That's all?"

"Well, he told me to keep my mouth shut. Not in so many words, but that's what it amounted to, then he left."

"There must've been more to it than that," Alan said. "Did he ask for money?"

"Nope," Connor replied. "I've told you everything. He was only in the house for a few minutes. Although…" Connor's voice trailed away, but a sudden gleam lit his eyes. "Hang on, there was something else. Just before he left, Tobias asked if he could borrow a pair of trainers."

"Why? Did he give a reason?"

"He said he was going to play squash later on and he'd forgotten his shoes, so I told him to help himself from the cloakroom. He took a pair of basketball shoes. Adidas."

"That's odd," Alan said. "Surely, you don't have the same size feet."

"That's what I said, but he told me that he takes the same size as me: nine."

"Tell that to the police," Dan said. "Tell them the exact model of shoe and the year you bought them, everything."

"What does it matter?" Alan asked. "It's not as if we have a shoe print to compare it to."

"No, but I've got a strong suspicion the police will have found one. Think about it. A man like Tobias Barrington wouldn't play squash in any old trainers. Besides, there isn't a squash court for miles. If he had to travel to play, he probably could've gone home and fetched his shoes, so why borrow a pair?"

"Because he had another purpose for them," Alan suggested. "He wanted to lay a false trail."

"Exactly, and as Tobias knows, the police can access a database of shoe prints."

"Hang on a minute," Connor began. "Are you saying Tobias was framing me? He was setting me up?"

Dan tilted his head in confirmation. "There was a bus ticket too, found at the place Philippa was killed. It could've been planted there, and the police would've eventually found out that you use the same bus service. All the evidence points to you."

"But he wouldn't pretend to be me," Connor protested. "It wouldn't work. He doesn't look anything like me. But…" Connor's voice trailed away, his eyes round.

"What is it?" Dan asked.

"My old denim jacket. I used to wear it on stage, and I could've sworn it was in the cloakroom, but the other day, I noticed it wasn't there. You don't think…?"

"I'm afraid so," Dan said. "With your old jacket and a pair of jeans, his hair hidden under a baseball cap, he might pass for you at a distance, or on CCTV. Those cameras are hardly ever sharp, and he knows the police will be checking them, looking for you. Tobias understands the way the police work, and he laid a false trail for them to follow."

"I'm not sure about this," Alan said. "Tobias wouldn't want the police to look too hard at Connor. Put Connor in an interview room and the truth about Spud might well come out. Tobias doesn't want that to happen."

"No, but who would be sitting at Connor's side in every interview?" Dan asked. "Who would have privileged access to Connor and plenty of time to coach him, to tell him exactly what to say?"

"Tobias," Alan replied. "So he planned to throw Connor under a bus, so to speak, then he would've swooped in to represent him, all the while making sure Connor didn't say too much."

Dan nodded. "While he was at it, Tobias would've convinced Connor to stay silent about Spud. At worst, Connor could've been found guilty of murdering Philippa, but that wouldn't have been a problem for Tobias. As far as he's concerned, Tobias would've won either way."

"That bastard," Connor muttered. "I'm not going to let him get away with this. There's no way I'm going to jail. I'd rather die."

"There is an alternative," Alan said. "If you talk to the police and tell them the truth, you can put the blame where it belongs."

Connor stared at Alan. "I don't know if I can do that."

"You could try," Dan said. "Get yourself a decent lawyer, somebody who has no connection with Tobias whatsoever, and take it from there. If you help the police, I doubt whether they'd come after you for what happened to Spud. There's not much chance of finding any new evidence, so that case is closed."

"Not for me, it isn't." Connor hung his head. "It's over. I can't live like this. It's about time I faced up to what I did. I'll talk to the cops. I'll tell them everything."

Alan patted Connor on the shoulder. "That's good. It's for the best. Think of it as a chance to put things right."

"And you're about to have that opportunity," Dan said. "I can hear a car coming and they're not hanging about." Dan stepped over to the ruined gate and peered into the lane. A black Volvo saloon was speeding toward them, not approaching from Chagford but from the open country beyond. Perhaps it wasn't the police after all, but as the car drew nearer Dan recognised the outlines of the driver and his passenger.

"Is it the first responder?" Alan called out.

"No, it's our old friends," Dan replied. "Spiller and Collins, arriving in the nick of time. Almost."

"They were pretty quick. They must've been near." Alan hesitated. "This is where we hand the case over."

"Yes. Yes, it is." Dan heaved a sigh, not sure whether he was relieved or disappointed. Either way, his part in the case had almost come to a close.

He looked back to Alan, thinking to share the moment, but his friend's eyes were wide in astonishment. Dan followed Alan's gaze and understood. The black Volvo clearly wasn't stopping; it hadn't even slowed. Instead, it swept past the gate and on toward Chagford.

"Strange," Alan said. "They must've got the wrong address."

"Maybe, but somehow, I think not."

Alan's expression brightened. "They're after Tobias."

"They could be." A sliver of ice needled Dan's spine, and he locked eyes with Alan. "If they are, Tobias must be in Chagford."

"Oh hell," Alan said. "What if he's at Zadie's house? Natalya's there."

"I'll go," Dan said. "We can't get Connor out of the car, but I can run. It won't take me long. You'd better stay here and wait for the paramedics."

Connor let out a groan, and Dan turned to see him clambering from the car.

"Go on," Connor said. "If it still works, take the car. I'll stay here. I promise."

Dan searched Connor's expression. "You won't do anything stupid?"

"Define stupid. I might have a large vodka, but that's it." Connor flapped his hands at Dan. "Get a move on. You can't let Tobias hurt anyone else. That can't happen."

Without a word, Dan jumped into the driver's seat and turned the ignition key. The engine stuttered into life, and Dan forced the gear lever into reverse. "Come on," he whispered. "You can do it." He let out the clutch, and with a shuddering squeal of complaint the Toyota backed away from the gate.

Alan dashed forward and unfastened the damaged gate, its hinges groaning as he dragged it open, then he hurried back to the car and climbed in.

Holding his breath, Dan put the Toyota into first gear and started forward. The engine grumbled and whined, a chorus of hollow metallic rattles taking up the tune, but when Dan pressed the accelerator, the car shot forward and they were off.

"You little beauty," Dan murmured. "I knew you wouldn't let me down." He worked his way through the gears, driving as fast as he dared. They'd get to Zadie's house in a matter of minutes. He just had to hope they'd be in time.

CHAPTER 86

A lan clenched and unclenched his fists, his gaze on the road ahead as the Toyota rattled its way into Chagford.

"Nearly there," Dan said. "Take a breath. Try to stay—"

"To stay what?" Alan demanded. "Calm? Are you serious?"

"I was going to say 'focused'. We don't know what we're going to find when we get there, but you should be ready."

Alan didn't reply.

A minute later, Dan parked behind Spiller's Volvo, and Alan jumped out of the car before the engine had stuttered to a halt. Dashing past a white van he found Spiller in conversation with Shaun. Collins was tending to Tobias Barrington who was sitting on the ground, moaning with pain as Collins wrapped a bandage around his blood-streaked arm. Natalya, thank God, was all right. She was standing, as unruffled as ever, carrying a tray with several steaming mugs.

Seeing Alan, she smiled, her eyes bright. "You came. Somehow, I knew you would."

"I should've been here sooner." Alan stood in front of Natalya, gazing into her eyes. "Are you all right?"

"I am fine. Please, don't worry."

"That's easier said than done." Alan glanced at Tobias. "Did you…?"

Natalya nodded. "I had to. He was trying to—"

"There's no need to explain," Alan interrupted. "I'm sure you only did what was necessary."

Alan saw that Dan was talking to Spiller, their heads close together. Fine. They could sort out the details. All Alan cared about was Natalya. Smoothing his shirt with his palms, Alan knew he had to say something to her. When he'd feared that Natalya could've been hurt, it had been as if a cold hand had clutched at his soul. With a sudden jolt of clarity he understood that Natalya meant more to him than he could say. He didn't know how best to put his feelings into words, but he had to try.

"Natalya," he began, but he was cut short by a shout from behind. Alan turned to see Collins sprawled on his back and Tobias Barrington making a clumsy dash for the road, staggering and stumbling as he went. Dan was reacting, ready to give chase, but something snapped in Alan's mind, and he launched himself forward, arms pumping, feet pounding the gravel. There was no way that man was going to get away.

Tobias reached the road and turned left without hesitating, but then Alan was on him. He grabbed Tobias by his unbandaged arm and spun him around, facing him.

"Go on," Alan growled. "Give me a reason."

Tobias was taller than Alan, and more heavily built, but one look at Alan was enough. Tobias paled, his throat bobbing as he swallowed. He looked past Alan, then he closed his eyes, defeated.

Alan stayed stock still, every muscle taut.

Dan appeared at his side. "It's okay, Alan. Let him go. It's over."

Alan shook his head, but Collins was there, his hand on Tobias' arm. "We'll take it from here," Collins said. "He won't get away."

Alan took a breath, then he let go of Tobias and stepped back, watching as Collins pulled the man's arms behind him. Tobias howled in agony, but that did nothing to stop Collins, and Alan heard the handcuffs clicking shut.

"Tobias Barrington, I'm arresting you for actual or intended bodily harm," Collins said. "You do not have to say anything, but it may harm your defence if you do not mention when questioned something that you later rely on in court. Anything you do say may be given in evidence. Do you understand?"

Tobias opened his eyes but he kept his lips shut tight. He said nothing as Collins led him away and bundled him into the Volvo.

"Well, that's a good day's work," Spiller said as he strolled toward Dan and Alan.

"Is that all you're going to charge him with?" Alan demanded. "What about the fact that he was trying to abduct Natalya? What about Philippa's murder?"

"All in good time." Spiller tapped the side of his nose. "Between you and me, there's nothing like springing a further arrest on a suspect during an interview. It tends to focus their minds."

"He did it, you know," Alan insisted. "He killed Philippa and tried to make it look like Connor. He borrowed a pair of Connor's shoes to leave a footprint, and he planted that bus ticket on purpose."

Spiller looked thoughtful. "We'll see what we can find. There'll be trace evidence in his house or his car, maybe even under his nails or on his clothes."

"He'll have been careful," Dan said. "He knows the system."

"And we know our business," Spiller replied. "We'll leave no stone unturned."

"I should damned well hope so," Alan said. "You can't let him slip away. Talk to Connor Griffiths. We left him at his house. He might have broken a rib."

Spiller looked at Alan as though seeing him for the first time. "You have been busy."

"It wasn't us," Dan said. "He took my car and tried to get away. He crashed into a gate."

"I can see I'm going to be busy myself. Why don't you two go inside and take a moment? You've done your part."

Alan nodded. "I need to talk to Natalya and make sure she's all right."

"I don't think you need to worry yourself too much on that score," Spiller replied. "But Ms Rudenko might appreciate the sentiment. She'll be coming into the station before long. We're sending a car."

Spiller said something else, but Alan was no longer listening. He found himself walking away, making straight for where Natalya was waiting. She was exactly where he'd left her, although she'd dispensed with the tray. Alan stood in front of her, wordless for a moment, then they wrapped their arms around each other, and they held each other very tight.

CHAPTER 87

I n the smallest and tattiest interview room in Exeter's police headquarters, DI Spiller turned to DC Collins and said, "You can stop the playback there. I think Mr Barrington has seen enough."

Collins tapped the screen on his tablet, leaving the playback frozen on the image of a denim-clad man at the checkout of B&Q, his features concealed by the peak of his baseball cap.

On the other side of the table, Tobias Barrington stared at Spiller with an air of profound indifference. Sitting beside him, Tobias' lawyer, a barrister named Sarah Minchin, turned her sharp gaze on the screen and said, "Inspector, do you have a question for my client?"

"Oh yes. Who are we looking at, Mr Barrington?"

"I don't know." Tobias leaned slightly forward. "I suppose, it could be… No. I don't think it's him."

Spiller suppressed the urge to break into mocking applause. Tobias Barrington evidently knew how to play a part. All those hours of performing in front of a jury had clearly honed his acting skills almost to perfection. Almost.

There was something about the man's display of nonchalance that didn't stand up to close examination. Tobias was on edge, his nerves frayed as he felt the forces of law and order tightening their grip. All he needed was a nudge in the right direction.

"Mr Barrington," Spiller began, "if you have any idea who this man might be, then it's your duty to tell us, is it not?"

"Yes. Forgive my hesitance, but I wasn't sure. Looking again, I'd have to say that he looks very like a friend of my sister's: a man called Connor Griffiths."

"Goodness me," Spiller said as if in surprise, although he'd been expecting Tobias to say more or less those very words. "Connor Griffiths. Well, well. That is interesting, because we've spoken to Mr Griffiths, and he has an alibi for the time that CCTV was recorded."

"Oh?"

"Yes. A lady from Chagford goes up to his house every Monday to keep the place clean and tidy: a Mrs Nesbitt. It's a big house and it takes quite a while. Mrs Nesbitt bills by the hour, so she keeps an eye on the time when she's at work. She notes everything down on her phone. She's a very careful woman is Mrs Nesbitt."

"Fascinating," Tobias said, "but I don't know why you're telling me. I doubt whether she keeps tabs on her employer."

"No, but Connor Griffiths always makes a coffee for Mrs Nesbitt when she's halfway through, then they sit together and have a chat for a while, so they were together when this footage was captured. I expect you didn't know about Mrs Nesbitt though, did you?"

"No. Why would I?"

"No particular reason. Do you know Mr Griffiths well?"

"Not really," Tobias intoned. "He's an acquaintance."

"That's not true, is it?" Spiller said.

Tobias gazed at him in silence.

"Mr Griffiths was a client of yours, wasn't he?" Spiller went on. "We have paperwork that proves it."

"I don't think so." Tobias pursed his lips as if in thought. "Ah, he did consult with me once, but it was years ago. I'd completely forgotten about it. I've had a lot of clients in my career; I can't say I remember them all."

"Surely, a barrister needs an excellent memory for clients and cases."

"Yes, but I wasn't a barrister back then, and I didn't represent the man in court. He consulted with me, briefly, and that was the end of our arrangement." Tobias paused. "I still maintain that the CCTV you've shown me appears to be a recording of Connor Griffiths. Perhaps he slipped out while his cleaning lady was busy."

"No, he was at home the whole time. It's a nice house. Have you been there recently?"

"No."

Spiller nodded thoughtfully. "He says otherwise. We have a team in there now, looking for trace evidence. It doesn't matter how good his cleaner is, we'll find hairs and fibres and fingerprints, maybe even some DNA. We'll soon be able to prove that you were there. Because you *were* there very recently, weren't you?"

"My client has already answered that question," Ms Minchin stated. "He's here to help, but there's no point in repetition, so I'd ask that you don't waste our time."

"Perish the thought," Spiller said. "Do you play squash, Mr Barrington?"

"From time to time."

"Mr Griffiths claims that you borrowed a pair of his shoes for a game of squash."

"No, that's not true."

"He also says that just after your last visit, a denim jacket belonging to him went missing. He claims you took it."

"Nonsense."

"I'm not so sure." Spiller indicated the CCTV image still frozen on the tablet's screen. "Look at this person's denim jacket. It's a bit tight around the shoulders, isn't it?"

"I wouldn't say that."

"I would." Spiller made a show of studying Tobias. "What size jacket do you take?"

"What's that got to do with anything?"

"It's a simple question."

Ms Minchin caught her client's eye. "You don't have to answer."

"It's all right," Tobias said. "I measure 122 cm around the chest. That's forty-eight inches in old money."

"I thought so," Spiller said. "I'm about the same size, but Mr Griffiths isn't so broad. He tends to wear his clothes on the baggy side though, and that old denim jacket was a couple of sizes too big for him. Still, that was just as well for you or you'd have never got into it. Because that is you, isn't it? You took that jacket from his house while you were borrowing the trainers, or I should say the Adidas basketball boots? You know, the ones you used to leave a shoe print at the scene of a crime, namely the murder of Philippa Darley-Jones."

"Hang on a minute," Tobias blustered. "You can't go around slinging baseless accusations at me like that."

Ms Minchin laid a restraining hand on her client's arm, and his temper subsided.

Spiller waited a beat and then glanced at Collins. "DC Collins, would you mind showing that e-fit to Mr Barrington?"

"No problem, sir." Collins picked up the tablet and tapped the screen a few times before turning it around to show Tobias.

"This e-fit was constructed yesterday," Collins went on. "It was put together with the help of a shop assistant. This is a likeness of the man we saw on the CCTV footage. It's you, isn't it, Mr Barrington?"

Tobias scarcely spared a glance at the screen, but Ms Minchin peered at it closely and looked distinctly uncomfortable.

"No, it isn't me," Tobias stated. "I don't go to B&Q as a rule."

Spiller and Collins exchanged a look. "We didn't say the CCTV was from B&Q," Spiller said. "How could you know that's where it came from? Is there something you want to tell us?"

"I... I saw the logo in the background. I recognised it from their ads in the paper."

Spiller resisted the urge to go back to the footage and check. He was pretty sure the store's logo wasn't visible in the short clip they'd played. Tobias was keeping his head above water, but only by clutching at straws. It wouldn't be long before he'd start to sink in earnest. It was simply a matter of time and the slow drip of questions, one after another, each answer taking Tobias Barrington a little deeper into trouble.

"Take another look at that e-fit," Spiller gently insisted. "Our witness was rather pleased with the way it came out. The process jogged her memory, and she's certain she'd be able to pick out the right person. Would you be willing to take part in an identification procedure, Mr Barrington? It might help us to eliminate you from our enquiries."

"That's something I'd need to discuss with my client," Ms Minchin said. "Shall we take a break while we confer?"

"Later," Spiller replied. "Let's press on. Mr Barrington, you had an intimate relationship with Ms Darley-Jones, didn't you?"

"It was some time ago, but yes."

"How did it end?"

"Amicably enough." Tobias contrived to look hurt. "She broke up with me, but there were no hard feelings. I remained fond of Philippa. I was devastated when I heard what had happened to her."

Spiller tried to ignore the knot of anger drawing tighter in his stomach. Making his voice as neutral as possible, he said, "As you can probably appreciate, since your arrest we've obtained your phone records."

Tobias let out a muted sigh as though bored.

"This is actually quite interesting," Spiller went on. "I don't suppose we'll ever find Philippa's phone, but we have all her records, so we can look at the messages that were sent shortly after her death. We know where they were sent from, and we can see from *your* phone records that you were in the same place at the same time."

"This is going too far," Ms Minchin said. "The location of someone's phone does not prove that they were there, as you well know. I won't have you misleading my client in this way."

"You make a good point," Spiller replied. "Let's go back to the e-fit and the CCTV. The shop assistant remembers selling a hawkbill knife to the person in the footage. She remembers it very clearly, and she's sure she'll recognise the customer again, so we'll go ahead with that identification procedure whether you like it or not."

Ms Minchin looked as though she was about to protest, but Spiller wasn't about to give her the chance.

"I don't need your permission," Spiller went on. "We both know that, so let's press on. We also have records from the B&Q store which show that along with that hawkbill knife, a polypropylene rope was purchased. Fibre analysis proves that this was the same type of rope used in the murder of Philippa Darley-Jones, a woman you've had an intimate relationship with in the past. As well as the rope and the hawkbill knife, a set of overalls were purchased, and again, fibres from exactly this type of garment were found at the scene of Philippa's murder. We later retrieved a hawkbill knife from a property belonging to your sister, Zadie Barrington. The knife has your prints on the handle, and according to Natalya Rudenko, you used the knife to threaten her. Indeed, she says that you attempted to abduct her."

"It was she who assaulted me," Tobias snapped.

Ms Minchin raised a warning finger. "Remember what we discussed."

"Yes, yes, I know, for God's sake." Tobias ran a hand over his hair. "I retract that last remark."

"You're not in a courtroom now," Spiller said. "Anything you say may be given in evidence, as you are aware."

"All right. Get on with it."

Spiller sat back, smiling, making the man wait. When he judged the moment had dragged on long enough, he said, "Earlier, you told us that Connor Griffiths had been a client of yours. You may like to know that Mr Griffiths is being extremely co-operative. He has provided us with a full and frank account of all your dealings with him."

A burst of air escaped from Tobias' lips.

"Something you'd like to add?" Spiller asked. "Something about Mr Griffiths perhaps?"

Tobias screwed up his face, his jaw working as he chewed at the words on the tip of his tongue.

"This is your chance to speak up, Mr Barrington," Spiller said. "We'd be very happy to hear your side of the story. That's what we're here for."

"No. I have no comment. Nothing to say whatsoever." Tobias sent a fleeting sideways glance at his lawyer, the muscles in his cheek twitching. "Except… except Connor Griffiths is a fantasist and drug user. You can't trust a word he says."

"That's for us to determine, but corroboration is a wonderful thing. Thanks in no small part to information received—"

"From whom?" Barrington demanded.

"That will be made clear to you in due course, when it becomes relevant."

Tobias grimaced. "You've been listening to Corrigan. You're not going to take his word against mine, are you? The man's a fool, a jumped-up know-it-all who calls himself a private investigator."

"Mr Barrington, calm yourself," Spiller said. "The point is, we have evidence to support everything Mr Griffiths has told us. We also have a witness who says that you interfered in the inquest of Stuart O'Neill. We're retrieving those records as we speak. Because of Connor's part in that miscarriage of justice, Philippa Darley-Jones was blackmailing him, and we have bank records from both parties to prove it. We also know that you were made aware of this blackmail on the same day you purchased the rope and the knife and the boiler suit. By the end of that week, Philippa Darley-Jones was dead, murdered."

"Wait a moment," Ms Minchin said. "You're making a lot of allegations. I need time to speak with my client."

"And you'll get it, Ms Minchin," Spiller replied. "But please bear with me while I tie it all together. You see, Philippa Darley-Jones could only blackmail Connor Griffiths because she knew the inquest into Stuart O'Neill's death was a miscarriage of justice. And she knew how that state of affairs came about. Philippa knew you'd interfered with the inquest, didn't she, Mr Barrington? She knew you broke the law, and if that fact was made public, it would ruin your career. In short, you had a reason for silencing Philippa Darley-Jones; you had a motive for wanting her dead. And that means there's something I have to say."

Tobias' eyes widened. "No. No you can't. You've got nothing to go on. It's all circumstantial."

"Tobias Barrington," Spiller swept on, "I am further arresting you for the murder of Philippa Darley-Jones. You do not have to say anything, but it may harm your defence if you do not mention when questioned something that you later rely on in court. Anything you do say may be given in evidence. Do you understand?"

"This is ridiculous!" Tobias spluttered. "It's outrageous. It's… it's…"

"Do you understand, yes or no?" Spiller said.

Tobias shook his head.

"For the recording, Mr Barrington is shaking his head," Collins put in. "Perhaps we need to explain the fact that he's under arrest for murder."

"Don't be facetious," Tobias snapped. "Of course I understand, but I'll fight this every step of the way."

Ms Minchin cleared her throat. "Detective Inspector Spiller, I need to confer with my client. Right now."

"Naturally," Spiller said. "But before we terminate this interview, I'd like to make one suggestion if I may. Tobias, you know the score. If we take this to trial, you will lose, and your lack of cooperation will count against you. We can show that you made careful preparations several days before you killed Philippa, and a jury will see that for what it is: premeditation. There's no way you'll be able to claim Philippa's death was an accident, nor can you convince us to charge you with manslaughter. This was a murder, plain and simple. Your best bet is to tell the truth."

"Inspector, it's not for you to advise my client," Ms Minchin said. "This interview is over."

"As you wish."

Spiller gazed at Tobias for a moment. The man's face was pale to the point of being grey, his cheeks flaccid. He was defeated and he knew it. His only way out was to confess and cooperate. He'd almost certainly claim there'd been mitigating circumstances of some kind, but Spiller would be ready. The case against Tobias Barrington had solid foundations, but by the time it came to court, it would be an impenetrable wall of irrefutable evidence. Tobias Barrington was going to jail.

CHAPTER 88

D S Kulkarni hadn't been to Chagford before, but it didn't take her long to find Meadow House. Kulkarni parked in the driveway and climbed out of her car, pausing to look up at the grand house. It was impressive, but its stone walls hadn't been protection enough for the woman who'd lived there. Philippa Darley-Jones had been murdered, but that wasn't why Kulkarni was here.

Kulkarni headed straight for the wooden door that led to the back garden. The door had been propped open, so she made her way through and marched to the idyllic cottage tucked away at the bottom of the garden.

The cottage looked deserted and there was no answer to her knock, so she pushed the door open.

"Mr Devlin?" she called out. "I'm DS Kulkarni, Devon and Cornwall Police."

There was no reply.

"I'm coming in, Mr Devlin," Kulkarni said. "I need to check you're all right."

Inside, the cottage was a mess. There were unwashed dishes on the table and empty beer cans and crisp packets on the floor. The odour of stale sweat and mouldering food hung in the air.

"Mr Devlin?" Kulkarni called again. "Are you all right?"

A faint sound came from the narrow hallway beyond the front room, and Kulkarni strode toward it. In the hallway, a steep staircase led upward, and she climbed it steadily, straining her ears. Again, she heard a faint sound, and this time it sounded like something creaking: floorboards perhaps.

Upstairs there were only two doors. The bathroom door stood open and she glanced inside as she passed. The other door was closed, and that was where the creaking sound was coming from, its slow regular rhythm setting Kulkarni's nerves on edge.

Kulkarni called out again to identify herself, then she pushed the door open.

She stared into the room in silence.

There, sitting on the bed, hugging his knees against his chest, a man rocked back and forth, staring into space.

"Mr Devlin?"

Kulkarni stepped closer. The man glanced at her, then looked away with barely a pause in his relentless motion.

Kulkarni was about to speak when the man murmured, "You're police?"

"Yes. I'm DS Kulkarni. You are Mr Devlin, aren't you?"

The man let out a humourless chuckle. "Not really, but I go by that. When it suits me." He laughed again.

"Mr Devlin, I need you to come with me. We have some questions you need to answer."

"Right, right." Still, he did not look at her.

"Mr Devlin, have you taken anything? Have you used drugs or any medication? Alcohol?"

Finally, Devlin stopped rocking. "No, I haven't had anything, but it sounds like a great idea."

"Mr Devlin, this isn't the time for jokes. I need to talk to you about a very serious matter. A man was found dead in Teignmouth. His name was Ryan Hallett. You have questions to answer, and if you don't come with me willingly, I will arrest you."

"Ryan Hallett," Devlin muttered. "I never knew his surname." He sniffed. "You found the van, I suppose."

"Yes, we have the van Mr Hallett drove and it has your fingerprints all over it."

"I knew I shouldn't have talked to that other cop. Spiller. I was only trying to help, but he had to go and arrest me. They took my prints; of course they did. And that was that. There I was, on the computer, waiting for someone to come along and find me. It's funny, but I'm kind of glad it was your lot. If the others had found me first… if they'd come here…"

Kulkarni kept her voice level. "Who else is trying to find you, Mr Devlin? Can you give me their names?"

Devlin's only response was a grunt of disbelief.

"These people who might be looking for you, are they something to do with the passports we found?"

"That's just part of it. A tiny part. There's more. Much more."

"Mr Devlin, we can talk properly at the police station." Some intuition made Kulkarni add, "You'll be safe there."

Devlin turned his head to look up at her. "Safe?"

Kulkarni nodded slowly, keeping eye contact with him all the while.

"I don't know." Devlin took a breath, and as he exhaled, he let his head slump forward so it rested on his knees. "I don't know, but you… you seem okay. Maybe I can trust you. Maybe."

"Of course you can," Kulkarni said. "My first name is Anisha. Do you mind if I call you Jack?"

"Peter," he replied. "My name's Peter."

"Okay, Peter, let's get you out of here. We'll talk properly when you're safe. How does that sound?"

"It might be all right, but there's something… something I need to know."

"Yes?"

"Witness protection. Is it like you see on the TV? Do you get a new identity, a new life, all that?"

"It can work that way," Kulkarni said, her mind racing. "It depends on the case. Why?"

"What about immunity from prosecution?"

"Again, that depends on the circumstances. It's something we can talk about later, but—"

"Will I get something in writing? If I get something in writing, I'll help. I'll tell you what you want to know. I've thought about it, and it's the only way out."

"I'll see what I can do," Kulkarni replied. "First, we need to have a formal interview, and you should have a lawyer present."

"No. I can't trust anyone. They have people everywhere. Important people. Cops, lawyers, you name it. It's not safe."

"We can find someone for you. In special cases, there are people we can use. We have resources. It depends on the information you have. If it's important—"

"Oh, it's important. I know everything. Dave Whitehead. He's the guy you want, but he's not the top of the food chain. He's nowhere near it. But I know names, faces, dates. They've all come to me for passports, documents for their people. They all used me because I was the best. I knew how to do it right, how to make an identity that stands up."

Kulkarni offered a reassuring smile. "Let's go, Peter." She held out her hand. "Here, let me help you up."

Peter looked at her hand, and then slowly he reached out to take it.

Kulkarni helped Peter to his feet. "Are you okay to walk, Peter?"

"Yeah. I'm a bit woozy, that's all, but I'm okay."

"Right, then let's go. At the station, we'll have a cup of tea or something, maybe a sandwich, okay?"

Peter nodded.

Kulkarni took hold of his upper arm and Peter let himself be led from the room, meek as a lamb.

ONE WEEK LATER

CHAPTER 89

Z adie looked out over the water. Loch Lomond. Its restless waters were so different to the gentle pool she'd enjoyed sitting beside in Devon. But the memory of that place was tarnished now. Tobias had destroyed so much, taken so much from her. It was almost too much to bear, but her loss was nothing compared to the price paid by her friend.

Philippa. Thinking of her name brought a sudden wave of pain, but Zadie had to face it. She had to tackle her grief, one day at a time.

I should've seen something was wrong, Zadie told herself for the thousandth time. *I should've been a better friend.*

Zadie lost herself in thought, watching the wind-rippled water while her emotions ebbed and flowed.

How could she have been so blind? What kind of a person could be so remote, so entirely cut off from the people around them? Looking back, Zadie saw that her circle of friends had not been built on trust or warmth or understanding. She recalled all the arguments, the backbiting, the weasel words and shallow sentiments. Had she fostered that toxic environment? Had she deliberately gathered a group of needy individuals simply to flatter her own ego?

Some people did that, didn't they? They collected strays to fulfil some need within themselves: to feel useful, to shore up their identity. Perhaps that's what she'd done with Naomi. She'd treated Naomi badly, but who could've guessed at the outcome? What had happened to Naomi to leave her so resentful and twisted? What seeds of bitterness had been planted in her heart?

Zadie was avoiding the news and staying away from social media, but she'd had an email from Natalya, so she knew that, like Tobias, Naomi was in police custody. Natalya had also reported that Benny was recovering well. It seemed that John Callaway was a frequent visitor to the Royal Devon and Exeter Hospital, along with a dog called Lucy. Natalya had mentioned something about a viral video, and Zadie hadn't been able to resist the temptation. She'd played the video several times, watching with rapt attention as Benny was brought out into the hospital grounds in a wheelchair, looking pale and drawn until he saw who was waiting for him. His reunion with Lucy was a joy to see: the brave ex-soldier beaming and fussing over the dog while John Callaway, ever the generous movie star, looked on with tears in his eyes.

But Zadie had scolded herself for getting drawn in. This was not her moment; it belonged to somebody else. Watching it online didn't make her personally involved. Why would she waste a moment of her time watching someone far away when there were people close by—real people, each with their own stories, their own needs and desires?

Zadie thought again of Philippa, and when she ran her hands down her face, she was unsurprised to feel tears on her cheeks. She'd wept so often over the last week that she hardly knew when the crying stopped and started. Zadie fetched a crumpled tissue from her pocket, and as she dried her eyes, a pair of birds flew low over the loch and glided to the surface, meeting the water with the smallest of splashes. Zadie watched the birds while they tidied their plumage, their bills busy as they smoothed and straightened their feathers. Preening. The word lodged in Zadie's mind. After all, wasn't that exactly what she'd been doing for years, preening herself?

But the birds preened out of necessity. If they didn't look after for their feathers, they couldn't fly, couldn't keep warm and dry. They cared nothing for how they looked to others.

Zadie sighed. Her old life had seemed so glamorous, but here, sitting by the loch, she could admit that she didn't much like Zadie B. That wasn't okay. From this point on, everything would be different. It had to be.

Zadie needed a new challenge, a new way to be. She'd already made an announcement on her website, a paragraph to tell her followers she was taking time to recover from a traumatic experience. The truth would come out no doubt, and she'd be judged in the court of public opinion, but in the meantime, she'd received countless comments, most of them supportive, and that had helped. Of course, there'd been a few stupid remarks as well. She saw every comment now that Natalya no longer worked for her. It had been sad to say goodbye to Natalya, but there were no hard feelings. She was glad for Natalya, happy to see her moving on.

Working without Natalya was another adjustment she'd have to make, but she'd learn to cope. Zadie had a new life to lead, with fresh adventures and ordeals to experience. She vowed to think only of the here and now, and to pay attention to the people around her.

She'd start by picking herself up and dusting herself down. It wouldn't be easy, but she could do it. She could start again. Not in Devon, but perhaps here in Scotland where the hills and lochs and wild rivers spoke to something in her soul.

And with that thought, Zadie's gaze lifted to the horizon.

CHAPTER 90

Marching back into her old office in Exeter, DS Kulkarni smiled and thanked each of her colleagues as they offered their congratulations. Even Detective Chief Inspector Caroline Montague came out to meet her, and as soon as the DCI appeared, Kulkarni's colleagues suddenly developed a keen interest in their work, heads down and fingers tapping on keyboards.

Standing quietly amid the industrious activity, Montague shook Kulkarni by the hand.

"That was a job well done," Montague said. "I talked to the team from the NCA, and they are very pleased. Very pleased indeed."

"Thank you, ma'am."

The National Crime Agency had taken ownership of Peter Armitage and spirited him away, but everyone in the office knew that something big was about to happen. An ongoing operation in Plymouth was expanding rapidly, officers being called in from across the UK to assist in a series of co-ordinated raids. It looked as though an organised crime group was about to be taken down, and the rumours in CID said that this was all down to the intelligence Peter had provided.

"Solid police work," Montague said. "That's what it's all about."

"Yes, ma'am. DI Spiller says the same thing." Kulkarni scanned the office. "Isn't he here?"

"Ah." Montague lifted her chin. "Haven't you heard? Tim has taken the day off. Between you and me, I'm not sure if he'll be coming back, so you might need to take over some of his work until we can appoint a new DI."

Kulkarni found herself blinking stupidly at the DCI. "He's retiring?"

"Maybe. For the time being, Tim is on compassionate leave, but I think he'll be reluctant to come back."

"Is his wife all right?"

"Yes. As far as I know, Sheila's doing well, but things have been hard on Tim. He was working all hours, but he never knew when he might be needed at home. There's no sense in Tim carrying on until he's burnt out. Better to bow out gracefully."

"Yes, I suppose that's true," Kulkarni said. "Even so, it's a shame. It won't be the same without him."

Montague nodded. "We'll miss him, but we'll carry on. Business as usual. The old guard give way to the new, and it won't be long before you're a DI yourself. You're riding high, Anisha. Make the most of it. Start thinking about promotion."

"Thank you, I will."

"Good." Montague clasped her hands together, surveying the room as if pleased to see so much activity. "I've got a full diary today, so I'll leave you to it. Well done, Anisha. Great work."

Montague strode away leaving Kulkarni alone. Kulkarni peered across the room to Spiller's office, staring at the closed door. Would Tim ever be in there again? She sensed someone watching her and turned to see DC Collins gazing up at her from his desk. They shared a look, and Kulkarni offered a tiny shrug as if to say, 'What can you do?'

Collins spread his palms in reply, his fingers spread wide in a gesture of helplessness.

Kulkarni took her seat and settled herself at her desk. There would be emails waiting for her attention, and a list of tasks that she'd need to prioritise before chipping away at them, one by one.

Who knew what the day might bring? Whatever landed in her lap today, she'd have to tackle it without the benefit of DI Spiller's knowledge and wisdom. True, his absence would create an opportunity for some lucky person. She wasn't ready for promotion herself, but a shakeup in the team might mean a new role for her. Still, there was such a thing as loyalty, and she'd stand up for Spiller any day of the week. This was where he belonged, and that's all there was to it. Take the job away from him, and he'd be unmoored, cast adrift without a paddle. What would become of him then?

He'll be back, Kulkarni decided. *The DCI doesn't know him like we do.*

Tim Spiller wasn't the kind of copper to throw in the towel. He'd be back at his desk in a day or two, cursing at spreadsheets until he could bear them no more, then he'd pop out and persuade Collins to take him along on some case or other.

With that comforting thought, Kulkarni logged on to her computer, opened her first email of the day and began to read.

CHAPTER 91

A lan ran. His feet pounded the earth, his breath coming fast. The forest trail was dry, but there were exposed tree roots under foot and loose rocks to watch out for. Alan took them all in his stride, powering forward.

Ahead, the trail opened onto a clearing and Alan jogged to a halt, turning to look back the way he'd come. And he smiled.

Natalya hadn't been far behind, and now she caught up, puffing out her cheeks, her brow filmed with sweat.

"Thank you for waiting," Natalya said between gasps for air. "But Alan, this… this is horrible."

"I thought so too, at first, but you're doing really well, and if you stick at it, you get used to it."

"Get used to this? No thank you."

"What I mean is, you get better at it. After a while, your heart rate doesn't go through the roof every time you come to a hill."

"Alan, it's not my heart, it's my legs that are aching." Natalya smiled. "There is nothing wrong with my heart. It is full."

"Mine too," Alan said. "Mine too."

EPILOGUE

Dan Corrigan picked his way through the used cars at the third dealership he'd visited in Exeter that day. Since he'd been paid by Zadie, Dan had been poring over cars on the internet and visiting dealers, but he'd had no luck so far.

Dan spotted a Kia Sportage and walked around it slowly, followed at a respectful distance by a cheery-faced salesman who'd introduced himself as Steve.

"Ah, you've spotted our best bargain," Steve said. "Would you like to take it for a spin?"

"I'm not sure," Dan replied. "It's nice but it's not..." he wanted to say, 'It's not me', but that would be far too lame. He thought of Zadie, and the way she'd claimed that objects had power and could call out to a person. *Nonsense*, Dan told himself. *Sentimental nonsense*.

Dan looked at Steve and saw the hope in the man's eyes. He probably had a sales target to hit or a quota to fulfil, but he seemed like a decent enough chap. "Maybe I could try a test drive," Dan started to say, but he was interrupted by a shout from across the lot.

"Dan, over here!"

Sam was waving to him. She'd brought him to Exeter, driving

her Vauxhall Corsa, which she'd kept in much better condition than Dan's old car.

"Excuse me," Dan said to Steve, "I won't be a minute."

Steve smiled. "No problem, sir. Take your time."

Dan trudged over to join Sam, Steve trailing along behind.

"Hurry up, slowcoach," Sam said. "Come and see." Sam set off toward the showroom, but she skirted away from the front door and made for the corner of the building.

"Erm, excuse me," Steve began, but Sam wasn't stopping.

She led Dan down the side of the showroom and stopped in a yard at the back.

"What are we doing?" Dan asked.

Sam extended her arm, gesturing to a row of vehicles.

Catching up with them, Steve said, "I'm sorry, madam, but these cars haven't been prepared for sale. They're vehicles we've taken in part-exchange, but they're not quite up to scratch, if you know what I mean. Now, about that Sportage."

Steve was still speaking, but Dan tuned him out. Smiling at Sam, he said, "Well done, Sam. This is it. It's perfect."

Stopping mid-flow, Steve said, "Pardon?"

Dan pointed. "The blue one. The Toyota RAV4. I'll take it."

"Oh." Steve hoisted his smile back into place. "Well, if you'd like a test drive, I'm sure we can arrange that."

Dan shook his head. "There's no need. I know what it'll be like." He shared a smile with Sam. "Sometimes, you just know when something's right, don't you? And when you're lucky enough for that to happen, you have to go with it. You have to hold on to what's good and make it work, whatever it takes."

"I know exactly what you mean," Sam said. "Steve, this car does come with two keys doesn't it?"

Steve nodded enthusiastically. "Yes, of course. One for each you."

"That's what I was thinking," Sam replied. "It's quite a big step, though, isn't it? Giving someone a key."

"It is," Dan said. "It changes everything, but in a good way, I hope."

Steve's gaze darted back and forth between them as if his mind was working overtime, but he said nothing.

Sam smiled and took Dan's hand. "I'm ready if you are."

"I'm ready," Dan said. "One hundred percent."

Thank you for reading A Must-Have Murder.
I hope that you enjoyed it.

You can get the series prequel free at:
michaelcampling.com/freebooks

AUTHOR NOTES

ARE THE LOCATIONS REAL?

Readers of the series will know by now that Embervale is a fictional village, but I've always imagined it to be in the very real Teign Valley in Devon. This is the area in which I've lived and worked for over twenty-five years, so I hope I do it justice, winding lanes and all.

When other cities, towns and villages are used in the stories, their names aren't changed, but they are somewhat fictionalised. I try to give a flavour of a place, but I have no desire to upset my neighbours. To that end, I happily change street names and neighbourhoods.

In this book, Chagford, Doddiscombsleigh, Teignmouth and Exeter are all real but are presented in a fictionalised way.

Where I use pubs, cafes, restaurants and other businesses, I use fictional names and I try to avoid using a name that can be mistaken for a real business. The one exception to this is when a place is mentioned but isn't used for a scene, e.g. The Nobody's Inn is a real pub, and I felt able to mention it because characters only refer to it in passing.

WHAT ABOUT ALL THAT BEER?

Yes, Dan and Alan are still fond of a pint of ale, and it has become customary in The Devonshire Mysteries to use the names of real ales and breweries. I usually find these brands by searching online, but I sometimes come across a nice beer and think, *Dan would like this* or *Alan would approve*. I particularly like to support Devon's economy by mentioning local producers. Nobody sends me any incentive to mention these beers, but if they feel the urge to do so, I might be persuaded to taste a bottle or two on behalf of Dan and Alan (I'm just saying).

ARE ANY OF THE CHARACTERS BASED ON REAL PEOPLE?

No, I don't do this. For me, a big part of the fun of writing a novel is creating an imaginary scenario and peopling it with a cast of characters. As I get to know the characters, I develop a feel for what they might say and do. This feeling deepens when it comes to the recurring characters such as Dan, Alan, Sam and Jay. I hope readers get a sense that all the main characters are developing and changing over the course of the stories.

To some extent, all the characters are shaped by what life has thrown at them and the way they've responded to various challenges. Again, this is all part of the fun for me. I try to bring the characters to life. Some writers talk about giving characters a flaw or two, but I don't think of my characters in that way. To me, we are all complex, and we all have our difficulties as well as our hopes and dreams. One thing I firmly believe is that we have trouble seeing ourselves as others see us.

This is why Dan and Alan are so lucky to have each other. They may seem like an unlikely pair of friends, but to my mind, it's their differences that make their friendship work; each lends a fresh perspective to the other. They may not know it, and they probably wouldn't admit it, but they need each other.

ARE THE MEDICAL DETAILS REAL?

I always research this kind of thing, but while I try to make the details believable, this isn't a textbook. That said, I received some very useful feedback from early readers of the manuscript, and I was able to significantly improve the medical details. There are times when I get carried away by writing the story, and I was lucky enough to benefit from the knowledge of others.

WHAT ABOUT THE POLICE PROCEDURES?

As with the medical details, I do research police procedures as far as I can, but I try to keep the level of detail fairly light. After all, The Devonshire Mysteries aren't police procedurals. I try to tread the line between the cosy environs of Embervale and the slightly grittier world of Spiller and Kulkarni. That said, I try to avoid a lot of the unrealistic tropes that we see all too often in crime dramas on TV, e.g. the maverick cop who breaks all the rules, or the DI who tramples all over a crime scene while second-guessing the forensic experts.

When it comes to Spiller and his colleagues, I'm more interested in the characters rather than the procedures. Police officers are people, just like you and me. They have lives outside of the job, and they must juggle the demands of their role, trying to remain human while dealing with some dreadful situations.

I've grown fond of Tim Spiller, and I'm currently working on a book in which he has the starring role. More on that below.

WILL THERE BE MORE DEVONSHIRE MYSTERIES?

At the time of writing, all I can say is that it's likely. Many readers have invested a lot of time in Dan and Alan, as have I. Dan is a restless character, and if I don't give him something to do soon, he'll turn up in my writing room and start pacing the floor. Alan will be there too, of course, but he'll sit quietly, regarding me with a smile, but there'll be an expectant gleam in his eye.

The Devonshire Mysteries are close to my heart, but they have been getting longer and more complex, and this book has taken me a long time to write. It is time for some kind of reset, perhaps taking Dan and Alan back to basics.

In the meantime, I'm working on a spin-off book that takes Spiller back to the 90s and the start of his career in CID. This new book is more of a police procedural, and while it is set in Devon, it is different in tone to the Devonshire Mysteries. It's a bit darker and there are no pesky amateur sleuths to cross swords with Spiller. Instead there's a whole new cast of characters, with only Spiller and his wife Sheila from the Devonshire Mysteries. But who knows? I may be tempted to add an Easter egg or two for fans of Embervale to spot.

I have to admit that I'm having fun revisiting the 90s in my imagination. In many ways, it was a simpler time, when we weren't all glued to our mobile phones. I hope people will enjoy the story, and this may be the start of a new series, but we'll have to see how it goes.

WILL YOU TALK TO MY BOOK GROUP?

Let's see what we can do. Please get in touch at:
    michaelcampling.com/contact

ANYTHING ELSE?

If you have other questions you'd like me to answer, please hop over to my website at michaelcampling.com and become a member, then you'll be able to post comments on the site and you'll gain access to members-only content. Membership is free and always will be. It doesn't come with any obligations at all, and it's separate from my newsletter.

SIGNING OFF

Thank you very much for sticking with Dan, Alan and the other Devonians on this epic mystery. This is a long book, and though it took me longer than usual to write, it was a labour of love. I hope it gave you something to really get your teeth into.

There will be more books and stories of one kind or another from me, and the best way to find out about them is via my readers' group, The Awkward Squad, where you can also claim the series prequel, *A Study in Stone*, for free. You'll also get an exclusive, not-for-sale Devonshire Mystery story, *Mystery at the Hall*, plus you'll get access to a specially written serialised Devonshire Mystery, *Death at Blackingstone Rock*.

Here's the place to learn more:
michaelcampling.com/freebooks

I hope to hear from you soon.
Until then, happy reading and take care.

Mikey Campling
November 2023
Teign Valley,
Devon

ACKNOWLEDGMENTS

Thank you to all the fans of Dan and Alan for your patience, your support and your kind words. Your encouragement means a great deal.

I'm especially grateful to everyone who has supported me recently by sending me a mug of tea via Ko-fi.com. To name a few: Lara, Claire, Jill, Bobby, Alonza, Lynn, Rose, John, Doreen, David, Tami, Melinda, Sunshine, DeeAnn, Dave, Nancy, Meredith, Cathy, Tamara, Doyle, Carole, Andria, Gloria and Jules.

Special thanks go to these keen-eyed advance readers: Helen, Kiperly, Jean, Dave, Bev, Doreen, Michael, Rosemary, Jean, Pat, Gary, Pauline, Christopher, Anne, Shelly, Linda, Valerie and Dianne.

The cover was designed by Patrick Knowles. This book was edited by Michael-Israel Jarvis.

ABOUT THE AUTHOR

Michael (Mikey to friends) is a full-time writer living and working on the edge of Dartmoor in Devon. He writes stories with characters you can believe in, and plots you can sink your teeth into. His style is vivid but never flowery; every word packs a punch. His stories are complex, thought- provoking, atmospheric and grounded in real life.

You can start reading his work for free with a complimentary mystery book plus a starter library which you'll receive when you join Michael's readers' group, which is called The Awkward Squad. You'll receive free books and stories, plus a newsletter that's actually worth reading. Learn more and start reading today at: michaelcampling.com/freebooks

facebook.com/authormichaelcampling

x.com/mikeycampling

instagram.com/mikeycampling

amazon.com/Michael-Campling/e/B00EUVA0GE

bookbub.com/authors/michael-campling

ALSO BY MICHAEL CAMPLING

One Link to Rule Them All:

michaelcampling.com/find-my-books

THE DEVONSHIRE MYSTERIES

THE DARKENINGSTONE SERIES:

Printed in Great Britain
by Amazon

41210001R00421